GRIMMS' GOBLINS

LONDON: GEORGE VICKERS, ANGEL COURT, STRAND.

PREFACE.

The idea intended to be carried out in "Grimm's Goblins," was to produce a collection of Fairy Tales and Goblin Lore, combining the best legends of all nations and languages, in such a form as might be confidently admitted by every father of a family into his household library, and illustrated by a new process of Chromoxylography, from designs by the most eminent artists at home and abroad.

There are few (and those few must be very hard indeed to please), who, on taking up the present volume, will not be ready to acknowledge that idea as having been fully carried out. It remains, therefore, only for the Editor, in concluding his task—which, however, is only brought to a conclusion, from a desire not to exceed a moderate price in a work intended for universal circulation—to place before his juvenile readers, in as unambitious language as possible, some brief notes upon Goblin and Fairy Lore, which, without the labour and parade of learning, may place them in possession of the curious knowledge that has been worked out by those who have devoted many years to the subject.

In the first place, then, it is supposed that the different regions of the world have been originally peopled by a general scattering of the people collected in some great central plain of Asia, whence spreading, and extending round to the Northern Sea, and out on the other side to the East, and so over Europe by either side, they took with them—what all nations have preserved in a similar form—the stories and traditions of their forefathers, imparting unto them only such modifications as the circumstances and scenery of the various regions they inhabited naturally suggested.

Hence it is, that for the earliest histories of mankind, and for the earliest pictures of the people of the most remote ages, the learned have had recourse to the study of these legends; and from them, by a careful study, have been able to trace the very habits and thoughts of mankind almost before they had been reduced into society. Thus, the Giants were violent men, powerful and stupid, living by murder and rapine; the Ogres were cannibals; the Fairies were a kind of gentle Providence; the Genii were darker influences of evil-mindedness, representing the "Evil Spirit and all his angels," with other Eastern Fairies and personifications. From the North we have the Trolls or Dwarfs, living in high mountains or solitary uplands, misshapen, stumpy, and humpbacked, inclined to thieving, and carrying away the children of mankind, in place of whom they leave their own misshapen offspring. They have much wealth from mines, and they hate the sound of the church-going bell, so much so, that as the churches and chapels grow up in their vicinity, they retire farther away. Next we have the Nix, or Nixie, little fellows with red caps, like the Bogle of Scotland, not unwilling to help the careful housewife; and then the Elves, who live in trees and groves, and dance in rings, with fair golden hair, and sweet musical voices, and magic harps, and who have a king and a queen. The waters, too, have their spirits, the Merman and the Mermaid; as also have the waterfalls, the Necke, or Nokke, of one of whom, in a Preface to Hans Christian Andersen's Tales, the following pretty legend is narrated:—

Two boys, while playing near a river, saw the Necke rise out of the water and begin to sing, and the burden of the song was still—" And I hope, and I hope that my Redeemer liveth!" And the children said, "What is the use of your singing and playing, Necke? You will never be saved!" The Spirit, at hearing this, wept bitterly, flung aside his harp, and sank below the waters. But when the children repeated what had passed to their father, he told them that they had done wrong in refusing to him all hope, and bade them go back and console him. They found the Necke sitting on the water, wailing most piteously; and they said, "Necke, do not grieve so; our father says, that perhaps your Redeemer liveth also;" and upon this the Spirit again took up his harp, and played a sweet, joyous, exulting strain. In a variation of the legend, a priest says to the Necke, "Sooner shall this dry stick in my hand put forth leaves and flowers, than thou shalt attain salvation." The Necke flung away his harp, and wept, and the priest rode on; but, to his astonishment, he presently discovered that his cane was beginning to bud and blossom, and he went back to tell the glad tidings to the Necke, who, after this, played joyously the whole night through.

Collections of stories, from such various sources as " GRIMM'S GOBLINS " are taken, are rare in the English language, most of them, hitherto, having been compiled from French originals only; and too many of them, if not entirely frivolous, are often vulgar in language, and gross in details, thus rendering them unfit for home purposes and the education of children, by inculcating kindness and goodness in a manner pleasing to the young mind. In " GRIMM'S GOBLINS," everything of such a character has been sedulously excluded, and the Editor trusts, therefore, that " GRIMM'S GOBLINS " will be accepted by all mothers and fathers of families with satisfaction, as one of the most innocent, as well as one of the most entertaining volumes in any language.

In conclusion, the Editor trusts that the public will join with him in appreciating the talent of the artists, especially MR. HABLOT K. BROWNE, some of whose designs in this work will be acknowledged in after years as his masterpieces; the especial skill of MR. EDMUND EVANS, in engraving those designs and printing them in colours (a singular and successful novelty); and finally, the generous ambition of the Proprietors, who placed at his disposal every possible means and advantage for the production of " GRIMM'S GOBLINS " in a manner unequalled, and as yet unrivalled, in literature of its class.

CONTENTS.

CONTENTS.

COLOURED ILLUSTRATIONS,

DESIGNED BY "PHIZ."

GRIMM'S GOBLINS.

THE TAILOR AND THE BLACKSMITH ENTER THE GOBLIN RING.

THE GOBLIN'S GIFTS.

Two young men, one of them a Tailor and the other a Blacksmith, were on their travels together, going from place to place to improve themselves in a knowledge of their trade, and seeking work to support themselves on the road. A merry time they had of it, always hungry, and always working when not walking; and then they used to sing as they stepped along merrily, with light hearts and gay faces,—as who should not, when they can earn their own living, and have enough to eat and drink, and nothing to care for but the thanking God for it? One evening, just as the sun was setting in streaks of gold behind the mountain-tops, they were on their way, and looking out for the spire of the neighbouring village, when they heard, as from a distance, a strain of music, which grew clearer as they approached the spot whence they thought it came. The sound was an extraordinary one, but so charming, that they forgot all their fatigue, and started off at a great pace towards the spot. The moon was already up when they reached the hill-side, on which they saw a crowd of little men and little women dancing in a ring with a joyous air, and holding each other by the hand, and singing all the while after a ravishing fashion! This was the music our travellers had heard. In the middle of the ring stood a very big Old Man, much larger than the others, clothed in a robe of many colours, and wearing a long white beard that descended to his chest. The two companions stood motionless with wonder as they gazed on the dancers; but the Old Man made signs to them to come in, and the little dancers opened their ring to give them entrance. The Blacksmith, who was a bold fellow, stepped in without hesitating; he was a little round in the shoulders, and was saucy and daring, as most hunchbacks are. The Tailor, however, it must be confessed, was rather afraid, and kept a little in the background; but when he saw that all went off so gaily, he plucked up a spirit, and entered the circle of dancers also. No sooner was this done than the ring closed up again, and the little beings took to their singing and dancing again with all their might and main, shouting at the top of their small voices, and leaping and bounding with prodigious jumps. The Old Man did nothing of the kind, but, for his part, he seized hold of a great knife that hung at his girdle, sharpened it on a stone that lay at his feet, and—when he had felt the edge with his finger, and satisfied himself it was sharp enough—he turned towards the side where the two strangers were standing. They were frozen with terror, as you may suppose, and the condition of the poor Tailor was something to feel pity for; but they were not kept long in anxiety, for the Old Man caught hold of the Blacksmith, and, with a twist of his hand, shaved off clean, at one stroke, his hair and his beard! Then he did the same to the Tailor—(oh, the poor Tailor!) When he had finished his job, he slapped them on the shoulder in a friendly manner, as much as to say that they had done well in allowing themselves to be shaved without resistance, and their fear was at an end. Next, he pointed with his finger to a heap of coals that stood just by, and motioned them to fill their pouches. Both of them obeyed, though they could not for the life of them see what good the coals could be to men who had no fire-places; and so they went on their way, looking about for a shelter for the night. Just as they reached the valley, the clock of a neighbouring church sounded midnight; at that moment the song came to an end, the whole rout of dancers disappeared, and there was nothing to be seen on the deserted hill-side, as it shone in the clear light of the moon.

Our two travellers found a little public-house, where they could stretch themselves out to sleep, all dressed as they were, on some clean straw in the stable; but in their weariness they forgot to rid their pockets of the coals, and the unaccustomed burthen they carried about with them woke them up sooner than ordinary. They put their hands to their pockets, and could not

believe their eyes, when they saw that they were full, not of coals, but of lumps of gold! The Tailor began to scratch his head, in his wonder, when, to his still greater surprise, he found that his hair had grown again marvellously, and on looking at the Blacksmith, he saw that his friend's beard had miraculously grown again, as also had his own. Moreover, they had become rich men; only the Blacksmith, who, following the bent of a covetous mind, had well filled both his pockets, was the possessor of double as much wealth as the Tailor.

But the greedy man always longs for more than he has actually got. The Blacksmith proposed to the Tailor to remain where they were for the day, and in the evening to go back again to the Old Man, and gain more treasure. But the Tailor refused, and said: "I have enough, and I am content with it; all I want is to set up shop as a master in my trade, and to marry the charming object of my affections" (this was the way he spoke of the young woman whom he had promised to marry), "and then I shall be a happy man." However, to oblige his friend, he consented to remain another day.

In the evening, the Blacksmith started off, with two sacks on his shoulders, to fetch back a good load of these gold-coals, and took his road towards the hillside, where he found the little party, as on the previous night, dancing and singing in a ring. The Old Man shaved him as before, and made a sign to him to take the coal. He did not hesitate, as you may suppose, to fill his pockets and his sacks with as much as he could stuff into them, and returned, hugging himself with delight, to the village inn, where he went to bed in his clothes as he was, ready to get up again at the earliest possible moment; "for," said he to himself, "when the gold begins to weigh heavy, I shall soon feel it;" and at last he fell asleep, in the pleasant expectation of waking in the morning a rich man.

As soon as he opened his eyes, his first care was to pay a visit to his pockets; but the deeper he dug his hands into them, the blacker they came out with the coal, and nothing but coal. "Well, at any rate," thought he, "I have still got the gold that I gained the other night." He went to take a look at it: alas! this gold, also, had changed back to coal again! He put his black hands up to his forehead, and then felt that his head was all bald and shaved as close as his chin. Even then he did not know the whole of his ill-luck, for presently he saw that the hump that he carried behind him had got another on the top of it!

It was now he felt that he was receiving the punishment of his covetousness, and he began to grieve and groan, so as to wake up the good Tailor, who consoled him, and endeavoured to make the best of his misfortune. "We are companions," said the generous little fellow, "we have had one turn together; stay with me; the wealth I have got will be enough to keep us both well."

He kept his word; but, for all that, the Blacksmith was obliged to wear his two humps all his life, and to hide under a cap the baldness of his too well-shaved head.

THE OLD GRANDFATHER AND HIS LITTLE GRANDCHILD.

ONCE upon a time, there was a poor man, very old, and he had two troubles, deafness, and weakness in his joints. When he was at table, he could hardly hold his spoon, and used to spill the soup over his clothes, and sometimes, even, could not get it to his mouth, or even keep it there. His son's wife, and even his son himself, had taken a great disgust at him; so that, at last, they set him aside, out of their way, in a corner behind a screen, where they gave him his sorry allowance to eat in an old earthen porringer. The old man had often tears in his eyes, as he looked wistfully from his corner at the table; and one day, while his thoughts were thus busied, the basin, which he held with difficulty in his trembling hands, fell from them, and was broken. The young wife overwhelmed the poor old man with reproaches for his carelessness, but he did not dare answer a word; so he only bent his head to her storm of words, and sighed. Then they bought him, for a penny, a wooden basin, in which, hereafter, they gave him his food.

Some days afterwards, his son and daughter-in-law saw their little boy, who was about four years of age, gathering together little pieces of wood.

"What are you making, Peter?" his father asked.

"It is a trough," he replied, "to give papa and mamma their food in, when they are old."

For an instant the husband and wife gazed on one another without speaking; then they began to shed tears, and went and brought back their old father to the table; and ever after that day, until the day of his death, they made him eat and drink with them, and never again spoke harshly to, or slighted, their poor old father.

SNOW-WHITE AND RED-ROSE.

ONCE upon a time, there was an old woman, who was a widow, and lived in a humble little cottage that stood all by itself. This cottage had in front of it a garden, and in that garden were two rose-bushes, one of which bore white roses and the other red roses. Now, the widow had two daughters, who just resembled the two rose-trees; so to one of them she gave the name of Snow-white, and to the other, Red-rose. These two children were the most pious, the most obedient, and the most industrious the world had ever seen, but Snow-white was the more tranquil and gentle in character. Red-rose would run about more willingly in the meadows and over the fields in search of flowers and butterflies; Snow-white would stop at home with her mother, helping her in the house-work, and reading to her when the work was done. The two sisters were so fond of each other, that they held each other by the hand whenever they walked out together; and when Snow-white said, "We will never leave each other," Red-rose would reply, "As long as we live;" while the mother added, "Everything ought to be in common between you."

They often went out into the wood alone, to gather wild fruit, and the different animals looked at them and approached them without fear; the hare would feed from their hands, the roebuck stepped along beside them, the deer frolicked before them, and the birds, perching on the nearest boughs, sang for them their prettiest of songs. Their innocent and happy lives were entirely without fear; nothing that happened was troublesome or disagreeable to them; if night surprised them while in the wood, they would lie down on the moss, close by each other, and sleep until morning came, without their mother feeling any anxiety for their safety.

One time, when they had passed the night in the wood, they saw, just as the morn-breaking awoke them, a beautiful child standing near them, clothed in a robe all white and shining, who regarded them fixedly, with a friendly look, but was lost to their sight in the shadow of the wood, without speaking a word. They perceived soon after, that they had lain down close to the brink of a precipice, down which they must have fallen if they had made only two steps further in the dark. Their mother told them that this boy-child was, doubtless, the guardian angel of good little girls.

Snow-white and Red-rose kept their mother's cabin so tidy that every one admired it. In spring-time, Red-rose had the care of in-doors, and every morning her mother found, on awaking, a nosegay, in which was one flower from each of the two rose-trees. In winter, Snow-white lighted the fire, and hooked the

3

pot on to the hanger, and the pot was of yellow copper, that shone as bright as gold, so well was it rubbed, and scrubbed, and polished. In the evening, when the snow fell, the mother would say, " Snow-white, bolt the door;" and then they would sit down by the fireside, and the mother would put on her spectacles, and read a chapter in the great Bible, while the two little girls listened, and plied their distaffs. Beside them lay a little lamb, and behind them, a dove would be sleeping on its perch, with its head under its wing.

One evening, when they were thus tranquilly assembled, there came a knock at the door. " Red-rose," said her mother, " go and open the door quickly; doubtless it is some traveller knocking, who has lost his way, and seeks a shelter for the night."

Red-rose went and drew the bolt, and waited, expecting to see some poor man enter, when a Bear thrust his great nose within the half-open door! Red-rose took to flight, uttering a loud shriek; the lamb began to bleat, the dove flew all about the chamber, and Snow-white ran to hide herself behind her mother's bed. But the Bear said to them, " Fear nothing; I won't do you any harm; I only ask permission to warm myself a little, for I am half frozen."

" Then come up to the fire, poor Mr. Bear," replied the mother, " but take care you do not burn your furry coat." Then she called out: " Snow-white! Red-rose! come back here; Mr. Bear will not do you any harm, he has none other than good intentions."

Both of them came back immediately, and by degrees the lamb and the turtle-dove also drew near, and forgot their fright.

The girls got the long-handled broom, and brushed the Bear's coat all over for him, and then he stretched himself out full length before the fire, expressing his satisfaction, meanwhile, by divers grunts of comfort. It was not long before they all felt quite at their ease, and even began to play with their unlooked-for guest. They pulled his hairy skin, and mounted on his back, and rolled him on the floor, and gave him little taps with their distaffs, and whenever he grunted, they shouted with laughter. The Bear let them do as they pleased with him, only, when the game was going too far, he would say to them: " Just leave a little life in me; don't quite kill the gentleman that comes a-courting of you."

When they were about to retire to bed, the mother said to him: " Stop here, Sir, and pass the night in front of the fire; you will at least be sheltered from the cold and the inclement weather."

At break of day, the little girls opened the door, and he went forth into the wood, trotting through the snow. After that day, he came again every evening, at the same time, and stretched himself before the fire, while the children played with him just as they pleased. They grew so accustomed to his presence, that they never thought of bolting the door until his arrival.

When spring-time had returned, and all was green outside, the Bear said one morning to Snow-white, " I am going, and I shall not come back again until summer."

" Where are you going, then, dear Mr. Bear?" inquired Snow-white.

" I am going into the wood; it is necessary I should guard my treasures against those mischievous dwarfs. In winter, when the earth is frozen, they are compelled to keep within their dens, without being able to scratch their way out; but just now, while the sun warms the earth, they will be coming out on their plundering excursions. Once let them get hold of anything, and hide it in their dens, and it rarely comes to light again."

Snow-white was very sad at the Bear's departure; when she opened the door, he tore his skin slightly, in passing, against the latch, and she thought she saw something like gold shining under his skin, but could not be quite sure. The Bear departed very quickly, and was soon lost to sight behind the trees.

Some time after this, the mother having sent out her daughters to collect dry wood in the forest, they saw a great tree that had been felled, and descried something near it, moving quickly about here and there in the grass near the trunk, although they could not quite make out what it was. On approaching, they recognized it as being a little Dwarf, with an old and shrivelled visage, and a white beard a full ell long. Now, this beard had been caught in a cleft of the tree, and the Dwarf was jumping about like some young puppy at the end of a string, without being able to extricate himself. He fixed his sparkling eyes upon the two little girls, and cried out to them: " What are you doing, stuck there, instead of coming to help me?"

" Poor little man," inquired Red-rose, " how have you been caught in this trap?"

" Curious fool!" replied the Dwarf; " I wanted to cleave this tree, so as to have small wood, and logs, and lots of shavings for my cooking, as our dishes are small, and the great coals are apt to burn them; we don't cram ourselves with victuals, like your gross and gluttonous breed. I had, then, inserted my wedge in the wood, but the nasty wedge was too slippery; it jumped out just at the moment I least expected it, and the trunk closed in so quickly, that I had not time to draw back my beautiful white beard; meanwhile, it was snapped in, and I have not been able to get it away. There! see how they begin to laugh at me, the spooney, milk-faced wenches! Out upon you, you ugly creatures!"

Now, the children were anxious to extricate him out of his troubles, but found it impossible to disengage his beard, which was held as in a vice. " I will run and fetch some one," said Red-rose.

" Call some one!" exclaimed the Dwarf, in a hoarse voice; " you are already two too many, you useless young scamps!"

" Have a little patience," said Snow-white, " and we will get you out of your trouble."

Then she took out of her pocket a pair of scissors, with which she cut his beard away nearly at the bottom. No sooner was the Dwarf at liberty, than he ran to pick up a bagful of gold, which he had hidden among the roots of the tree, murmuring as he went: " Those vulgar wretches of children! to cut off the end of my magnificent beard! What can possibly recompense me for my loss?" Then he put the bag on his back,

4

SNOW-WHITE RESCUES THE OLD DWARF, BY CUTTING AWAY HIS BEARD.

and went off without even deigning to look upon his deliverers.

Some months after this, the two sisters were out one day, catching a dish of fish for their supper, when they saw something like a large grasshopper, jumping about on the banks of a stream, as if he wanted to throw himself into it. They ran up, and recognized the Dwarf. "What are you doing?" said Red-rose; "why do you want to throw yourself into the water?"

"Well, that's not a bad one!" exclaimed the Dwarf; "throw myself in! As if you did not see how this nasty fish is dragging me in there!"

He had thrown his line, but, unluckily, the wind had twisted his beard in with the hook; and when, some minutes afterwards, a large fish came and swallowed the bait, the strength of this weak little man did not suffice to draw it out of the water; the fish was below, and had the pull, and drew the Dwarf towards itself. He had some trouble to hold on by the reeds and grass on the river bank, the fish still straining upon him, and drawing him towards him, until he was absolutely in danger of being pulled into the water by the fish he had caught. The little girls came up only just in time to hold him back, and they also attempted to disengage his beard, but this was in vain, so entangled was it with the hook. It became necessary to have recourse a second time to the scissors, and to cut off the whole of the end. When the Dwarf saw this, he exclaimed, in a rage: "Is it your habit, you stupid brutes, to disfigure gentlemen in this manner? Was it not bad enough to clip my beard so closely the first time, that you must cut off a good half of it to-day? I no longer dare show myself amongst my brethren. May your feet blister, and your shoes wear out!" Then, taking up a bag of precious stones that had lain hidden in the bushes, he dragged it along after him, without

adding another word, and disappeared quickly behind a stone.

A short time after, the good dame despatched her daughters to town to purchase needles, thread, and ribbons. Their way lay across a plain, over which were scattered great rocks. They perceived here a large bird, which floated in the air, and which, after having a long time hovered above their heads, came down at last, rapidly and with great force, to the earth. At the same time, piercing cries and loud lamentations were heard close by them. They ran up, and saw an eagle, holding in its claws their old acquaintance, the Dwarf, whom it was endeavouring to carry up into the air. The little girls, in the goodness of their heart, held the Dwarf back with all their might and main, and fought so hard and so well against the eagle, that at last he let his prey go, and was glad to make off himself in safety. However, when the Dwarf had got a little over his terror, he cried out with a shrill, sharp, cross voice: "Can't you catch hold of a fellow a little less roughly? You have scratched hold of my new coat in such a manner as to tear it into rags, awkward little boors that you are!" Then he took up a bagful of precious stones, and slipped into a hole among the rocks. The little girls were accustomed to his ingratitude, and did not mind it; so they went on their way to the village, and made their purchases.

On their return, as they were passing over the common, they came on the Dwarf by surprise, and found him counting over a lapful of precious stones from his bag, not supposing any one would be coming that way at such a late hour. The stones shone bright and glittering in the rays of the setting sun, and flashed out such wondrous sparks of light, that the little girls stopped, in mute wonder, to gaze upon them.

"What are you standing there for, gaping like crows, and idling your time away?" he said; and his face, usually grey, grew red with anger.

He was about to continue his abuse, when a fearful growl was heard, and a black Bear came out from a neighbouring thicket. The little Dwarf sprang up in a terrible fright, and was about to take to his heels, but he was not in time to get back to his hole, for the Bear stood just in his way. Hereupon, he took to supplicating, in a piteous manner:

"Dear Mr. Bear! spare, oh, spare me this time, and I will make you a present of all my treasures, all these jewels you now see before you. Grant me my life: what will a noble lord like you gain by killing a poor, miserable wretch like me? I am not enough for a mouthful for your mightiness, you would not so much as feel me between your teeth; besides, I am old and tough. You had much better take those two wicked little girls; they are two nice morsels, as fat as quails; munch them, my dear Sir, and they will do you good."

But the Bear, without hearing him out, gave the nasty little wretch just one pat with his left fore-paw, which stretched him out, quite dead and stiff.

The little girls were running away, but the Bear called out to them: "Snow-white! Red-rose! don't be afraid; wait for me." They recognized his voice, and stopped, and then, as soon as he was close to them,

5

the skin of the Bear fell all at once off from him, and they saw a handsome young man, arrayed in beautiful clothes, embroidered all over with gold.

"I am a Prince," he said to them, "and that wicked Dwarf had changed me into a Bear, after robbing me of my treasures; he had doomed me to run about in the woods, and only his death could release me. At last, however, he has received the well-merited punishment of his many misdeeds."

It was not long before there was a merry and magnificent wedding in that part of the country. The Prince espoused Snow-white, and Red-rose was married to another very handsome young man, the brother of the Prince, who generously shared with them the treasures which the Goblin had amassed in his hole. The good old mother lived for many long years in happy tranquillity near her children's palace; and she planted two rose-trees, one on each side of her window, which she loved to tend, and which bore, every spring, the most lovely white and red roses.

FAITHFUL JOHN.

ONCE upon a time, there was a King, who, being old, and happening to fall ill, took it very much to heart, as old gentlemen do, and made up his mind to die,—which, my dear children, you must always remember, is half-way towards doing so. So, impressed with this notion, he ordered his attendants to summon to his presence his Faithful John, a favourite servant and friend, whom he kept always about his person, as one who loved him for himself, and not for his grandeur, and could, therefore, be relied upon, whatever might betide. He was called Faithful John, because, all through his life, he had been faithful to his master. As soon as he came into the King's bed-room, his Majesty said to him: "My friend, Faithful John, I feel that my end is approaching, and I have no anxiety but the thought of my son, who is yet very young, and will not know how to guide himself. I shall not die happy, unless you give me your promise to watch over him, to instruct him in all he ought to know, and to be to him a second father."

"I promise you," replied John, "that I will never quit him, and that I will serve him faithfully, even though it cost me my life."

"I can now die in peace," said the old King: "after my death, you will take him to see over all the palace, all its chambers, its saloons, its vaults, and the riches they contain; only you must not allow him to enter within the last chamber of the great gallery, where is the portrait of the Princess of the Golden Dome, since, if he once see that picture, he will feel for her an irresistible love, that will be the cause of his incurring the greatest dangers: be it your task to keep him from them."

Faithful John repeated his promise; and the old King calmly settled himself to rest, and laid his head upon his pillow, and breathed his last.

As soon as the old King had been placed in his tomb, John took an opportunity of recounting to his young successor the promise he had made to his father on his death-bed: "I will keep it," he added, "and I will be faithful to you, as I have been to your father, even though it cost me my life."

When the days of mourning were over, John said to the King: "It is time you should know the wealth you inherit; I will take you over the palace of your father."

So he led the young King all over the palace, from the top to the bottom, and showed to him all the riches with which the splendid apartments were filled, omitting only the chamber in which was hung up the dangerous portrait. It had been placed there in such a manner, that, when the door was opened, it struck the eye at once; and it was so admirably painted, that it seemed to live and breathe, and nothing in the world could equal it in beauty and amiable appearance. The young King quickly perceived that Faithful John always passed by this door without opening it, and asked him the reason. "It is," replied the other, "because there is something in that chamber which would make you afraid."

"I have seen all the castle," said the King, "and I wish to know what is here;" and he wanted to force open the door.

Faithful John held him back for awhile, and said to him: "I have promised your father, on his death-bed, not to permit you to enter this chamber; your doing so would result in great misfortunes, for you as well as me."

"The greatest trouble I can have," replied the impetuous young King, "is that of my curiosity not being satisfied. I shall have no rest until my eyes have seen it. I will not go away from here until you have opened the door for me."

Faithful John, perceiving that it was of no avail to refuse longer, went, with a heavy heart, to fetch the key from the great bunch. When the door was opened, he entered first, trying, as he did so, to conceal the portrait with his body; but all was in vain: the King, standing on tip-toe, contrived to look at it over John's shoulders. But when he saw this likeness of a young lady, so beautiful, and so brilliant with gold and precious stones, he fell, without consciousness, on the floor. Faithful John raised him up, and carried him to his bed, murmuring all the while to himself: "The mischief is done! What will now become of us?" Then he gave the King a little wine, to cheer him and restore him.

The first word the young King uttered, when he came to himself, was to ask whose beautiful portrait that was. "It is the portrait of the Princess of the Golden Dome," replied Faithful John.

"So great is my love for her," went on the King, "that if all the leaves of all the trees were tongues, they would not be enough to express it. My life depends on my possessing her hand. You will help me, John, for you are my faithful servant."

Faithful John reflected, for a long time, which was the best way to set about his new duty of bringing the young couple together, for it was no easy matter to come within sight of this Princess. At last, he thought of a way, and said to the King: "Everything about this Princess is of gold,—chairs, plates, dishes, cups, goblets, all furniture of every description. You have five tons of gold in your treasury; it must be placed in the hands of the goldsmiths, to make of it vases and exquisite works in gold, in every kind of fashion and form, as those of birds, wild beasts, and monsters of a thousand shapes. As soon as these are ready, we will set out on the road, with them as our baggage, and in that way we will endeavour to bring about a meeting, and succeed in our mission."

The King speedily summoned all the goldsmiths in his dominions, and they worked night and day until all was ready. When they had freighted a ship for their voyage, Faithful John assumed the dress of a merchant, and the King did the same, that nobody might recognize them. Then they set sail gleefully, and voyaged prosperously, until they reached the city where dwelt the Princess of the Golden Dome.

Faithful John landed by himself, and left the King behind in the ship. "It may be," said he, "that I shall bring back the Princess with me; take care that everything is in order, and that the golden vases are arranged for exhibition, and that the ship is prepared as if for a festival." He then filled his girdle with a number of little trinkets of gold, (for the merchants of Arabia carry money, and precious stones, and small articles of great value, in their sashes,) and went straight to the palace of the King, the father of the Princess of the Golden Dome.

The first person that he saw, on entering the court-yard of the palace, was a young girl, who was drawing water at a fountain with two golden buckets. As she turned round to go, she perceived the stranger, and inquired who he was, and what was his business. "I am a merchant," he answered; and, opening his girdle, he showed her some of the pretty things he had to sell.

"Oh, what beautiful things!" she exclaimed, and, setting down her buckets, applied herself busily to looking over the trinkets one after the other. "The Princess," said she, "must see all these; she will buy them from you, for she dearly loves all kinds of trinkets of gold." Then, taking him by the hand, she led him up into the palace, for she happened to be the Princess's waiting-maid.

The beautiful Princess, herself, was ravished at the sight of the trinkets, and said: "All these are so well executed, that I shall buy them all from you."

But Faithful John answered: "I am only the servant of a rich merchant, and all you behold here is nothing to what my master has with him in his ship; it is there you would see articles in gold, of the most beautiful workmanship, and precious in value."

She wished him to bring them to her in the palace, but he said: "There are too many; there would be no time and no space; your palace would not hold them."

This only the more excited the royal lady's curiosity, so that at last she exclaimed: "Very well; conduct me to this ship; I will go myself, and see these vaunted treasures of your master."

Faithful John led the way, right joyously, to the ship, where the King, when he saw her, found her to be even more lovely than her portrait, and his heart bounded with joy. As soon as she reached the deck, the King offered her his hand; while Faithful John, who remained just behind her, cunningly, in the meanwhile, ordered the captain to weigh anchor on the instant, and spread every sail. The King, who could scarcely conceal his transports of love and delight, had gone down with her into the cabin, and was showing to her, piece by piece, all the exquisite vases and utensils of gold, the cups, the ewers, the basins, the birds, the wild beasts, and the monsters, worked out with the most elegant taste and finish. When he had gone through all, the Princess gracefully expressed her thanks to the pretended merchant, and her admiration of his wares, gave him some very liberal orders, and then prepared to depart for her palace. But when matters had arrived thus far, she perceived that they were out at sea, far away from land, and that the ship was under full sail. "I am betrayed," she exclaimed, in terror, "they are carrying me off! To have fallen into the power of a merchant! I would much rather have died!"

But the King took her hand, and said: "I am no merchant; I am a king, and of as good a family as your own. That I have carried you off by a stratagem, attribute, I beg of you, only to the violence of my love; it is so strong, that when I saw only your portrait for the first time, I fell down, without consciousness, in front of it."

These, and a few other soft words, were a great relief to the Princess; she began to feel more assured and consoled; her heart was touched. The King was a very handsome, amiable, and agreeable young man; so she forgave him this first offence, and consented to marry him.

And so all went on happily; the two royal lovers enjoyed themselves, as lovers only can enjoy themselves, when sailing in a fast-going ship, with favourable breezes, over a sunny sea; sitting all day with their hands locked in each other's, under the shade of the great mainsail, and, in the evening, nestling close together, shoulder to shoulder, against the bulwarks, with the moon and stars shedding their soft light down upon them, and the gentle air sweeping like music through the cordage. They seemed so happy, that all the crew, even, felt a sympathy with them, and all were happy as angels bearing the souls of good men towards Heaven. We must except one man alone, and he was very uncomfortable, for he knew there was a cloud somewhere about in the sky, though it could not be seen at present: this was Faithful John, for he remembered the old King's words.

One day, whilst they were on the open sea, Faithful John was seated in the bows of the ship, looking up to the sky, and thinking of what might happen, when he caught sight of three crows, who came and settled down just near him. Now, it happened that Faithful John understood the language of the birds, and so, when he heard the crows chattering together, he lent an ear to what they were saying,

"So," says the first crow, "he has carried off the Princess of the Golden Dome!"

"Yes," replied the second, "but he won't keep her long."

"How is that?" said the third; "don't you see she is sitting by his side? A nice pair of lovers, truly!"

"What does that matter?" replied the first; "as soon as they land, a roan horse will be brought to the King, which he will endeavour to mount; but, if he does so, the horse will dart up into the sky with him, and he will never be heard of any more."

"But," said the second crow, "is there no means of preventing this?"

"Oh, yes, he has one resource," said the first; "some other person must throw himself upon the horse, snatch a pistol from the holsters, and shoot the horse dead on the spot: that will save the King. But how is any one to know that? And, moreover, whoever should know it and mention it, would be changed into stone from his feet to his knees."

The second crow spoke in his turn: "I know something, even more than this; supposing the horse to be killed, the young King will not even then possess his betrothed. When they are entering the palace together, a magnificent bridal shirt will be presented to him on a salver; it will look as if woven of gold and silver, but is really made of nitre and sulphur; if the King puts it on, it will burn him to the very marrow of his bones."

"Is there not some way for him to avoid this?" asked the third crow.

"Yes, there is one method," replied the second crow; "somebody, with good strong gloves on his hands, must seize hold of the shirt, and throw it into the fire: the shirt once burnt, the King will be saved. But of what avails this? Whoever knew this, and told it, would find himself changed into stone, from his knees to his heart."

The third crow now added his grain to the sack of intelligence: "I know something, even more than this; supposing the shirt burnt, the young King even then will not possess his wife. When they have a ball, on the wedding-night, and the young Queen dances at it—which she will be sure to do—she will faint all of a sudden, and fall down as if dead; and she will really be dead, unless some one raise her up immediately, and suck from her right shoulder three drops of blood, which he must spit out directly. But whoever may happen to know this, and tell it, will be changed into stone, from his head to his feet."

After this conversation, the crows resumed their flight. Faithful John, who had listened attentively, remained some time, sad and silent. To say nothing about what he had heard would be the ruin of the King, but to speak would be destruction to himself. At last he made up his mind: "I will save my master, though it cost me my life."

On their landing, all happened as the three crows had predicted. A magnificent roan horse was presented to the King; "Capital!" said his Majesty, "I will ride him to the palace:" and he was throwing his leg over the saddle, when Faithful John, stepping before him, darted forwards, drew a pistol from the holster, and stretched the horse stiff, stark dead, at his royal master's feet.

Here was a commotion instantly! The other servants of the King, who had no great love for Faithful John, exclaimed that he must be out of his senses, to kill such a noble animal—just as his Majesty was about to mount it, too! But the King bade them hold their peace: "Let him do as he likes; he is my Faithful John, and doubtless has his reasons for what he has just done."

They arrived at the palace, and, in the first saloon they entered, a grand nuptial shirt was placed on a salver, and it looked like a web of gold and silver. The King was about to touch it, but Faithful John pushed him from it, and seizing it with well-gloved hands, cast it into the fire, which consumed it in an instant. The other servants, upon this, resumed their former murmurs; "See!" said they, "look here, how he burns the King's very wedding-shirt!"

But the young King again repeated: "No doubt he has some good reason for it. Let him have his own way; he is my Faithful John."

The wedding was celebrated, and there was a grand ball in the evening, and, as was natural, the young bride commenced dancing. From that moment, Faithful John never took his eyes off from her. All of a sudden, he saw a weakness come over her, and she fell back, in a swoon, like one dead. Dashing towards her instantly, he lifted her up, and bore her through the people to her chamber, where, after laying her down on the bed, he leant over her, and sucked from her right shoulder three drops of blood, which he immediately spat out. At the same instant she breathed again, and came to her senses. But the young King

FAITHFUL JOHN PUTS ON THE YOUNG PRINCES' HEADS.

who had seen all this with amazement, was utterly at a loss to understand the strange conduct of John, and, at last, ended by flying into a passion with him, and throwing the poor fellow into prison.

Next day, Faithful John was condemned to death, and led to the gallows. Just as he was mounting the ladder, he said: "Every man who is about to die has the right of speaking to the people before all is over: have I that right?"

"I grant it to you," said the King.

"Very well; I have been unjustly condemned, and I have never ceased to be faithful." Then he recounted how, while at sea, he had overheard the conversation of the three crows, and how all that he had done had been necessary for the safety of the King.

"O my Faithful John!" exclaimed the King, "pardon me the wrong I have done you; I remit your sentence. Bring him down from the scaffold!"

But it was of no avail; for at the last word he had spoken, Faithful John fell down lifeless—he was turned into stone!

The King and his Queen were sorely distressed. "Alas!" said the King, "that such devotion should have been so recompensed!" He ordered the stone statue to be carried up into his bedroom, and placed near his own bed; and every time he set eyes upon it, he repeated, with tears : "Alas, my Faithful John! would that I could restore you to life at the expense of half my kingdom!"

After some time, the Queen brought into the world two twin sons, whom she reared happily, and who were the joy and delight of their parents. One day, while the Queen was at church, and the two children were at play with their father in his room, his eyes fell on the Statue, and he could not help repeating again, with a sigh: "Alas, my Faithful John! would that I could restore you to life once more!"

But the Statue, carrying on the conversation, said to him : "You have it in your power to do so, if you are willing to devote to me that which you most love."

"Everything that I have in the world," exclaimed the King, "I am ready to sacrifice for your sake."

"Well, then," said the Statue, "for me to recover my existence, it is necessary for you to cut off the heads of your two sons, and smear me all over with their blood."

What a task for a father! The King turned pale on hearing these terrible conditions ; but at the thought of the devotion of the faithful servant who had given his life for him, he drew his diamond-hilted sword from the scabbard, and, with his own hand, struck off the heads of his twin boys at one sweep; then he smeared the stone Statue all over with their blood. At that very instant the Statue became reanimated, and Faithful John appeared, cool and calm, before him. But he said to the King: "Thy devotion to me shall not be unrewarded." Then, taking up the heads of the children, he replaced them on their shoulders, and smeared the wounds with their blood; at the same moment, they came to life again, and set to leaping and playing, as if nothing had happened.

The King's heart was full of joy. As soon as he heard the Queen had come home, he made John and the children hide themselves in a large clothes-press. Immediately she entered, he asked her: "Have you prayed at church?"

"Yes," replied her Majesty, "and I have been constantly thinking of poor Faithful John, so unfortunate for our sakes."

"Dear wife," said he, "we have it in our power to restore him to life, but it would cost us our two dear boys."

The Queen turned pale, and her heart seemed to come to a standstill; nevertheless, she made answer to the King: "We owe to him this sacrifice, because of his devotion."

The King, charmed at seeing they were both of the same feelings and thoughts, went and opened the clothes-press, and made John and the children come out of it. "Heaven be praised," said he, "John is free, and our children are still left to us." Then he recounted to the Queen all that had passed; and thenceforth they all lived happily together, to the very last.

THE QUEEN OF THE BEES.

ONCE upon a time, there was a King, and he had three sons, two of whom went forth, as all King's sons used to do, in search of adventures, and to see the world ; and, shame to say, they fell into such irregularities and dissipation, that they could not venture to go back to their father's house. Their young brother, whom they used to call the Little Niggard, from his being so prudent and careful about his pocket-money, set out in search of them ; but when he had found them, they only mocked at him, for being so simple as to suppose he could take care of himself in that world, wherein both of them, who were so much more clever than him, had quite lost themselves.

As they went along the road together, they came upon an ant's nest, and the two elder brothers wished to turn it over, to amuse themselves with the anxiety of the little ants, and the seeing them run hither and thither, carrying their eggs to some new place of safety ; but the Little Niggard said to them : "Let us leave these poor little creatures in peace ; I could not bear to see them harassed and annoyed."

A little further, they came to a wide-spreading park, in which was a lake, wherein were swimming we don't know how many frogs. The two elder brothers wanted to take a couple out and roast them,—for the people in that part of the world regard the hind legs of frogs as something very nice, when dished up with parsley and bread-crumbs, and fried in a pan with plenty of butter, like fish. But the younger brother stood out against such a proposal, and said: "Leave these poor animals in peace ; I can't bear their being killed."

They went a little further, and saw a tree, in the bottom of which was a hive of bees, so full of honey, that it trickled out and ran down the trunk. The two brothers proposed at once to light a fire at the foot of the tree, and so smoke out the bees, and get at the honey. But the Little Niggard held them back, and said to them : "Now, do let these little creatures remain in peace ; I will not suffer you to burn them out of house and home."

At last, the three brothers arrived at a great mansion, where they could not see any one ; but, on going into the stables, they found them to be full of horses, which, it was easy to see, had been suddenly changed into stone! They knocked loudly at the great gates of the house, but as no one came, they pushed open the huge folding-doors, that swung back upon their hinges, and gave them admission into the spacious hall. From this they wandered—all being silent, and not a person to be seen—through numerous large saloons and long galleries, until they came to a door, which stopped their passage. It was fastened with three locks, and in the middle of it there was a small wicket, through which they could see into an apartment. Here they perceived a little man with grey hair, seated at a table. They called to him once, twice, without his taking any notice ; at the third time, he rose up, opened the door, and came out in front of them ; then, without uttering a word, he led them to a table richly set out, and when they had eaten and

drank, he conducted each of them to a chamber, where they might sleep, alone; but all this without saying a word, and quite calmly and sedately, as if their coming were a matter of course, and they had been expected, and all made ready for them.

Next morning, the little old man came to the bedroom of the eldest of the brothers, and making him a sign to follow him, led him to a stone tablet, on which were written three things that were to be tried, and which had to be brought about, before the castle could be disenchanted.

The first was, to search among the moss in the middle of the wood, for a thousand pearls belonging to the Princess, which had been scattered there; and if the person searching did not find all of them before sunset, without missing so much as one, he would be changed into stone!

The eldest brother spent the whole day in looking after the pearls; but when evening came, he had not found more than a hundred out of them, so he was turned into stone, according as was written on the tablet. Next day, the second brother undertook the adventure; but he succeeded no better than the other, for he found only two hundred pearls, and so he also was changed into a stone.

At last came the turn of Little Niggard. He hunted after the pearls in the moss; but as the task was long and difficult and hopeless, he sat down at last upon a stone, and set to weeping. It was in this condition that the King of the Ants, whose life he had saved, found him, as he happened to come up, marching at the head of an army of five thousand of his subjects;

so his Majesty, pitying his preserver's woful plight, set his army to work, and it was not an instant before the ants, bustling about among the roots of the moss, had ferreted out every single pearl, and piled them all up together into a heap.

The second trial consisted in fishing up the key of the chamber in which the Princess was lying, and this key was at the bottom of the lake in the park. As soon as the young Prince approached, the frogs whom he had saved came to meet him in a great procession; and on learning what was the occasion of his coming, they gave an unanimous plunge, with a wonderful splash, all at once, right down to the bottom of the lake, and presently reappeared, croaking prodigiously loud, as if delighted in bringing up to their benefactor the great key of the Princess's chamber.

But all was not over even then; there was another and a third trial yet remaining, and that was the most difficult of all. For there were three Princesses asleep, and he had to pick out the youngest and the most amiable among the three, only from looking at them while sleeping, without hearing them speak a word, or having seen them before, or known anything about them. What made the task the more puzzling was, that all the three young ladies were exactly alike, and the only thing that could distinguish them was, that, before going to sleep, the eldest had eaten a lump of sugar, while the second had drank a cup of syrup, and the third had taken a spoonful of honey.

Poor young Prince! Even kissing their pretty pouting, rosy lips would not be of any use to him, however pleasant, for they were all sweetened alike. What was to be done?

But the Queen of the Bees, whom he had preserved from fire, came to his aid. She went and hovered over the lips of the three Princesses, and finally rested and folded her wings on the mouth of the one that had eaten the honey; so the Prince recognized her immediately as the youngest, and chanced her being the most amiable, which she was.

Whereupon, the enchantment was broken, and all those who had been changed into stone resumed the human form. The Prince, nicknamed the Niggard, espoused the youngest and most amiable of the Princesses, and became King of the country after the death of the young lady's father. As for his brothers, they married the other sisters, and it is to be hoped that they were better as married men than they were as bachelors.

THE TWO FELLOW-TRAVELLERS.

MOUNTAINS are not in the habit of meeting, but men often come together, and not seldom the good with the bad. A Shoemaker and a Tailor found themselves together, on going their rounds of the country. The Tailor was a jolly little fellow, always gay and good-humoured. He saw the Shoemaker come up alongside him, and, recognizing his trade by the bundle he carried, he began to sing a little ditty:

"Cobbler! cobbler! stoop in your stall,
Bristles, and wax-end, and hammer, and all;
Pierce 'em, and nail 'em, and beat 'em, and——"

"Come, stop there!" said the Cobbler, who did not take it pleasantly, but looked as if he had swallowed vinegar, and could have strangled the Tailor. Happily, the little man spoke to him, and laughed, as he handed his bottle to him for a drink: "Come, my lad, it was only by way of a joke; take a draught, and swallow your anger."

The Cobbler took a long pull at the bottle, and the look of his face grew rather more pleasant. He handed back the bottle to the Tailor, and said: "I have honoured your invitation, having regard both to my present thirst and my future want of drink; are you agreeable to our travelling together?"

"Quite willing," replied the Tailor, "provided we make for some large town, where there is no want of work."

"That's exactly my intention," said the Cobbler; "in these little out-of-the-way places there is nothing to be done; the people walk about barefooted."

So they went on their road together, travelling on foot, like the king's dogs. Both of them had more time to lose than money to spend; for, whatever town they came to, they paid a visit to the master tradesmen in their business; and as the little Tailor was a jolly, good-natured fellow, with rosy cheeks, they gave him work willingly; and often, even, the daughter of his patron would allow him to take a kiss behind the door, to help him on his road. When he rejoined his companion, his purse was always better filled; whilst the Cobbler, perpetually grumbling, pulled a long face as he growled out, "There is no chance but for scamps." But the Tailor only laughed at him, and shared whatever he had with his comrade. As long as he heard the halfpence rattling against each other in his pocket, he would call for the best in the house, and his jokes and his merriment made the glasses ring upon the table; with him, it was light come, light go.

At last, after travelling about for some time, they arrived at a great forest, through which passed the road to the capital of the kingdom in which they were. Here they had to choose between two ways, the one giving a journey of seven days, and the other two days; but they had no knowledge of the difference between one and the other, which was the short one, and which the long one. So they sat down under an oak, and took counsel together, as to which road to take, and how much bread they ought to carry with them. The Cobbler said: "We ought to push the protection as far as possible; I shall take enough for seven days."

"What!" said the Tailor, "drag, on one's back, bread for seven days, like a beast of burthen! No such trouble will I take, be sure, my lad! The money I have got in my pocket is as good in summer as in winter; but when the weather is hot, the bread gets dry and musty. None of your precautions for me! Besides, why should we not fall upon the right

road? Two days' bread—that will be quite enough for us."

Each of them made his own provision, and thus passed the first days of their journey; but when the third came, and they could not see the end of the road, the Tailor, who had consumed all the bread he had brought with him, felt his gaiety begin to ooze away; nevertheless, without losing heart, he put his trust in good luck and the favour of Heaven. In the evening, he went to sleep under a tree, with a hungry belly, and rose up again in the morning, with nothing to satisfy it. So it went on, to the fourth day, when the Cobbler sat down on a fallen tree, as grand as a king on his throne, and ate his dinner; while the poor Tailor had no other resource but to look on while he did so. At last, human nature could put up with this no longer, and he asked his comrade to give him a mouthful of bread; but the other replied, in a jeering tone: "You are always so merry, it is good for you to know what a little trouble is; the birds, that sing too loud in the morning, make a nice supper for the hawk in the evening." In a word, the curmudgeon Cobbler was utterly without pity.

On the morning of the fifth day, the poor Tailor had no longer strength to raise himself from the earth; so great was his exhaustion, that he could hardly utter a word; his cheeks were pale, and his eyes red. The Cobbler said to him: "You shall have a morsel of bread, but on condition that I may scoop out your right eye."

The miserable man, compelled to accept this dreadful bargain to save his life, shed tears from his two eyes for the last time, and offered himself to his executioner, who pierced the poor fellow's right eye with the point of his awl. The Tailor immediately called to mind what his mother had said to him in his childhood, as she whipped him, when she caught him stealing some cakes: "If you eat all you can, you must bear with what you can't help."

When he had eaten the bread that had cost him so dear, he got up on his legs again, and consoled himself for his misfortune with the thought that he could yet see with one eye. But, alas, poor little fellow! on the sixth day his hunger came back again, as strong as ever, and his heart entirely failed him. He fell down at night at the foot of a tree, and, the next morning, weakness prevented him from getting up again. He felt his death approaching, when the cruel Cobbler thus again addressed him: "I will take pity on you, and give you another morsel of bread to keep life in you; but for that I must have the eye you have left."

"What! lose my left eye—my only left eye!" said the poor little man, bitterly weeping over the carelessness which had brought about all these disasters. Then he knelt down, and, after uttering a short prayer, turned round to the cruel Cobbler: "Do your will with me; what cannot be cured must be endured: but remember, that if Heaven does not always punish us in the hour of our crimes, a time will come, when you will have to pay for the evil you have done to me, who have not deserved it at your hands. When I was well off, I shared all I had with you; consider, that in my business, my eyes are my tools; when I have lost them, I cannot work any more, and then I must go beg. But, at least, if I am to be blinded, don't leave me here, where I must die of hunger."

The Cobbler, who had banished all mercy from his heart, took his knife, and scooped out the poor Tailor's left eye; then he gave him a bit of bread, and, stretching out the end of his stick, led him along.

At the setting of the sun, they came to the verge of the forest, and in front of a gibbet which had been erected there by the people of the nearest town. The

Cobbler led his blind companion right up to the foot of the post, where he abandoned him, and continued his road alone. The poor creature fell down in a sleep, so worn was he with fatigue, pain, and hunger, and passed the whole of the night in a deep slumber. At break of day he woke up, and could not make out where he was. Now, there happened to be two poor sinners hanging on the gibbet, with the crows on the top of their heads. One of these men began to speak to the other, and said: "Brother, are you asleep?"

"I have just woke up," replied the other.

"Do you know," went on the first, "that the dew that fell this night upon our gibbet has the property of restoring sight to any blind people who bathe their eyes with it? If they only knew this, how many a poor fellow would come here to recover the sight that he thought he had lost for ever!"

When the Tailor heard this, he whipped out his little handkerchief, rubbed on the grass till it was wet with the dew, and bathed with it the hollows where his eyes used to be. What the hanged man had predicted instantly took place, and two little sparkling and clear-seeing eyes took the place of his old ones. It was not long before the Tailor saw the sun rising above the mountains. In the plain before him a great city was spread out, with magnificent gates and walls, and a hundred steeples surmounted with glittering crosses. Oh! how delighted was he, once more to count the

leaves of the trees, follow with his eyes the flight of the birds, and the circling dances of the gnats in the sunbeams! A king would have felt for his crown, a soldier have drawn his sword, a lover have kissed his mistress; but the little Tailor, he crossed his legs, pulled out a needle, and began to sew up a hole in his breeches. When he found he was master of this, his little heart beat with joy; he threw himself on his knees, and returned thanks to Heaven for its mercy, and said his morning prayers, not forgetting a word for the poor sinners who were hanging on the gibbet, and swinging about in the wind like the weights of a clock. His sorrows were all flown away; he picked up his little bundle, shouldered it merrily, and took to his road again, singing and whistling a hearty tune.

The first being he met was a little brown Colt, that was feeding in the meadow; he seized it by the mane, and was going to mount on it, and have a ride into the town; but the Colt begged him to let him go. "I am too young yet," said he; you are a fine handsome fellow, and not a little tailor, as light as a feather; you would break my back. Let me run about till I am a little older and stronger. A time may come, perhaps, when I may be able to recompense you."

"Go, then," replied the Tailor, "for I can see you are not much of a trotter."

And with this he gave him a switch on the back, and off went the pony, jumping with joy, and darted right across the fields, leaping over all the hedges and ditches in his way. The Tailor laughed to see the little fellow's antics, but the laughing reminded him that he had had nothing to eat since the day before. "My eyes," says he, "have found the sun again, but my stomach has not found anything to eat; the first thing that looks like victuals that I meet, will find its way down my throat."

At this moment he saw a Stork, that was stalking gravely up the meadow. "Stop," said he, "my fine fellow!" as he seized it by the leg; "I am not quite certain whether you are good to eat, but my appetite leaves me no choice; so I must cut off your long neck, and make a roast fowl of you."

"Take care what you are about," said the Stork; "I am a sacred bird, of the highest utility to man, and nobody may do me harm. Spare my life, and perhaps I may reward you for this, some day."

"Too much politeness makes a lean stomach," said the Tailor; "but I don't like to hurt such a civil-spoken gentleman; so make the best of your way off, as quick as you can, you cousin to Old Daddy Long-legs!"

The Stork took to flight, and raised itself calmly, floating in the air, spreading its wings, and letting its long legs hang down.

"What is to come next?" exclaimed the poor Tailor; "my hunger increases, and my stomach grumbles awfully. Whatever falls in my hand this time, is lost to a certainty."

Just at this moment, he caught sight of two Ducks, that were swimming in a pool. "They come just in time," thought he; so, seizing one, he was going to twist its neck. But an old Duck, who lay concealed among the reeds, waddled up to him, with her mouth open, and prayed him, with tears, to spare her little ones: "Think," said she, "of the grief of your own mother, if she saw any one about to give you the death-blow."

"Let your heart be at ease," replied the good little fellow, "I won't touch you;" and he threw back into the water the duckling that he had spirited up.

On turning away from this pool, he saw a large tree, half hollow in the middle, about which were flying a number of wild Bees. "At last I am recompensed," said he; "I shall have a good breakfast of honey." But the Queen of the Bees, coming out of the tree, declared to him, that if he touched her people, or her hive, he would be stung in a thousand places; if, however, on the contrary, he left them at rest, the bees might be able to render him a service, sooner or later.

The Tailor saw very well that he had nothing to gain in this quarter: "Three empty dishes, and nothing in the fourth," said he to himself, "make a bad dinner." He dragged himself along, worn out with hunger, until he reached the town; but, as he did not get in till just as it was striking twelve, dinner was ready in the inns, and all he had to do was to sit down to table. When he had feasted, he went through the town in search of work, and soon found plenty of it on good terms. Being a capital workman, it was not long before he came into general notice, and every one wanted to have a new coat after the cut of the fashionable little Tailor, whose renown increased day by day, until, at last, the King made him Tailor to the Court.

But only to see how things happen in this world! On that very same day, his old comrade, the Cobbler, was named Shoemaker and Cordwainer to their Majesties! Both these royal tradesmen were presented on the same day; and when the Cobbler saw the Tailor with two fine sparkling eyes, his conscience sorely troubled him; he felt himself in great danger, and began to think, that as the Tailor, in his opinion, must always be seeking to revenge himself, it would be wise to spread some snare for him beforehand.

But those who spread snares, very often fall into them themselves. That night, when his work was over, he went secretly to the King's chamber, and said to him: "Sire, your new Tailor is an audacious fellow, and he is boasting all over the town, that he knows where to lay his hand upon that golden crown you have lost for such a long time."

"All right," said the King, "I am very glad to hear of it." So he had the Tailor brought before him next morning, and ordered him to bring back the crown, or quit that city for ever.

"Oh! oh!" said the Tailor to himself, "I am not one of those chaps that promise what they can't perform. Since the King is so out of his senses as to require of me more than a man can do, I shall not wait for any to-morrow, but be off to-day."

So he made up his bundle again; but as he passed out of the gates, he could not help feeling sorry at turning his back upon a town where all had gone so well with him. He passed by the side of the pool, where he had made acquaintance with the ducks. The old Duck, whose little ones he had left unharmed, was

standing on the bank, dressing her feathers with her beak. She recognized him at once, and inquired from him where he was going, and what made him look so sad.

"You'll not be surprised at my looking sad," replied the Tailor, "when you know what has happened to me;" and he told her the whole story.

"Is that all?" said the Duck; "we can soon help you out of that little trouble. The crown has tumbled to the bottom of this pond; we will have it up for you in an instant, so open your pocket-handkerchief to receive it."

Down she went into the water, with her dozen little ones; and, at the end of five minutes, she was back again, swimming in the centre of the crown, which she supported on her wings, while her little ducklings, ranged all round, aided her in carrying it with their beaks. They soon swam up to the brink, and laid the crown down in the handkerchief; and a mighty fine crown it was, we can assure you,—it shone like the sun, in the middle of a ring of sparkling carbuncles. The Tailor, with trembling hands, wrapped it up in his handkerchief, and lost no time in bearing the recovered treasure to the King, who received him with joy, and, in reward, placed a chain of gold round his neck.

This made the little Tailor merrier than ever, and still more a favourite at Court, and fashionable with the gentry and nobility. He invented the Duck paletôt, and everybody wore it. This cut the Cobbler to the heart, for he saw that not only had his blow failed, but that, in missing it, also, he had made the fortune of his intended victim. So, at last, he thought of another expedient, and went and said to the King: "Sire, there is no bearing with that Tailor; he is as proud as ever again, and goes about boasting that he could reproduce the whole of your palace, and all it contains, in wax,—inside, outside, up-stairs, down-stairs, and underneath, furniture, and all the rest."

"Oh! he can, can he, indeed?" said the King; "send for him here. Now, my fine fellow, just go and make a model in wax of the whole of my palace, and all it contains, up-stairs, down-stairs, and underneath, furniture, and all the rest; and just you take notice, if it is not quite perfect, or if you forget so much as a single nail in any one wall, you'll finish your days in one of the subterranean dungeons!"

"Oh! please your Majesty!" said the Tailor, falling on his knees.

"Silence!" said his Majesty, in a voice of thunder, to the Tailor. "Throw the rascal out of the window!" These last words his Majesty addressed to the captain of his guards. The Tailor took the royal hint, and got out of the door before the captain of the guards could fetch his horse to throw him out of the window,—for it happened to be the turn of the Life-guards on duty.

As soon as he reached the street, he ran home, and packed up his bundle again, saying to himself: "This is from bad to worse; I shall not attempt an impossibility." So he left the city a second time, by the same road.

When he arrived at the foot of a hollow tree, where the Queen of the Bees had refused him a breakfast, he sat down in sorrow, stooping his head in his hands, and the tears, trickling from his eyes, fell through his fingers to the ground. The Bees came flying and buzzing all about him, and their Queen, settling on the top of his ear, inquired of him what made him so low, and whether he had got the mulligrubs. "No," said he, "the pain I feel don't affect me there;" and then he recounted to her what the King had demanded of him.

Whereupon, the Bees, after a wonderful buzzing and humming among themselves, finally held a great council, at the end of which, the Queen said to the tailor: "Go home, you kind-hearted little fellow, enjoy yourself for the day, and come here to-morrow with a large damask table-cloth: you will find all will go right."

Remembering what had happened to him before, in the case of the Ducks and Crown, the Tailor placed confidence in what the Bees promised; and he went home, and invited a party of friends to dinner, at which they all enjoyed themselves; and the Tailor sang his merriest songs, to the great spite of the royal Shoemaker, who lived just opposite to him, and who, because he was a bad man himself, and could never be happy, hated all other persons who were so.

But the Bees they spent a busy day, going in and out of the palace through the open windows, rummaging over and examining every detail in the most minute manner; this done, they hastened to regain their hive, in front of which, and under the shade of a broad-spreading tree, they built up a palace in wax with busy promptitude. By eventide all was ready; and when the Tailor arrived next morning, he found a superb edifice awaiting him, white as snow, and exhaling the delicious odour of honey; nor was there a nail wanting in the walls, or a single tile upon the roof.

The Tailor wrapped it up with great care in the table-cloth, and bore it off in triumph to the King. His Majesty gazed upon it with admiration, placed it, as one of the finest works of art, in one of the grandest saloons of his palace, and recompensed the Tailor by the gift of a large mansion.

For all this, the Cobbler did not regard himself as quite beaten; he took heart, and went to the King a third time, to whom he said: "Sire, it has come to the ears of your Majesty's Tailor, that every attempt to dig wells in the court-yard of the palace has been a failure; and he has been heard to boast, that he will bring out there, any day, a fountain of water, as high as a man, and as clear as crystal."

The King, who was never a loser by any of these bargains, sent for the Tailor immediately; and when the little fellow remonstrated against any further orders, told him, in a voice of thunder: "If you don't, to-morrow morning, raise up the fountain you bragged about, as high as a man, and as clear as crystal, your head shall roll on the scaffold to-morrow afternoon, in the court-yard!"

The Tailor did not say a word, but made his way out of the gates of the town, for his life was in danger this time. He journeyed along sadly, the tears rolling down his cheeks, until he was accosted by the Colt, to whom, you will remember, he had given his liberty, who had now grown into a fine brown bay horse.

"Now," says he, "the time is arrived that I can show you my gratitude; I know what is puzzling you, and I am able to help you. All you have got to do is, to get across my back; I can now carry two like you, without feeling it."

The Tailor took courage, and leaped on the horse, who galloped towards the city, and entered the court-yard of the palace. He went three times round it at a gallop, rapid as light, but in the middle of the third course he stopped short. At the same moment they heard a loud crack; a lump of earth was detached, and thrown up like a bomb-shell in front of the palace; then there rose up a jet of water to the height of a man, and as clear as crystal, sparkling and dancing in the rays of the morning sun. When the King saw this, he was very much astonished and pleased, and testified his pleasure by embracing the Tailor in the presence of all the Court.

But the little man was not destined to enjoy a long repose. The King had a great many daughters, each one more beautiful than the other, but no son. The mischievous Cobbler bethought himself of this, and for the fourth time went to the King, and said to him: "This time, at any rate, your Majesty ought to look after your Tailor. He is going about all over the city, telling the people that it all depends on him for your Majesty to have a son and heir."

"That is just what I want," replied the King; "let the Tailor be summoned instantly to our presence, and make my compliments to the Queen, and tell her, her presence is desired immediately. This is a matter I must look into myself."

When the Tailor came, the King did not wait for the Queen, but told him to bring him a son within eight days, and he would give him his eldest daughter in marriage, as a recompense.

"It is a handsome reward, certainly," said the Tailor to himself, "and I should not mind having the Princess Royal to make my gruel and warm my night-cap; but the grapes are sour—the cherries are pretty to look at, but they hang too high, and if I try to climb the tree, the bough will break, and I shall fall to the ground."

So he went home, and sat down on his table, with his legs crossed, to think of what he ought to do.

"No, no! it is impossible!" he exclaimed at last; "I must break the thread; there is no rest here for me!" So he packed up his little bundle again, and started off out of the city.

As he passed by the Duck, and the Bees, and the Colt, he could only shake his head at them, for he knew they had done their best, and could do no more for him.

At last, he came to the meadow, and, passing along it, he caught sight of the Stork, who was walking up and down with wide and rapid strides, like a philosopher, stopping from time to time, to reflect upon things in general, over some good fat frog, which she finished by gobbling.

She came up to the Tailor, to wish him good-day: "What is up now?" said she; "you have got your pack on your back; are you going to leave our city?"

The Tailor related to her the trouble the King had thrown him into, and complained bitterly of his fate.

"Don't make too much of this trouble," replied the Stork; "I'll take the affair in hand for you. Don't you know it is my business to bring the children home?" (which, they say, the storks do, in Germany;) "and I don't see why I should not carry home a little Prince, for once. Go back to your shop, and remain there quietly for nine days, and then go to the King's palace, where you will find me by your side, with a royal baby."

The little Tailor went back to his house, and, at the day appointed he appeared at the palace. In an instant afterwards, a Stork arrived in full flight, and knocked at the window, which the Tailor opened, when the long-legged godmother entered with careful solemnity, and advanced gravely up the marble floor. She held in her beak a boy baby, beautiful as an angel, and he stretched out his little hands to the Queen. The Stork placed the child in her Majesty's lap, and the Queen, in great joyfulness, kissed it, and pressed it to her bosom.

Before quitting the royal presence, the Stork took off her travelling-bag from her shoulder, and presented it to the Queen; it was full of fancy boxes of sweetmeats, of all colours. These were distributed among the little Princesses. The eldest did not have any, for she was too old, but they gave her the handsome little Tailor for a husband. "It is just like gaining a great prize in the lottery," said he; "my mother was right when she said, that, with trust in God and good-luck, a man may always succeed."

As for the Cobbler, he was obliged to make the shoes that the Tailor danced in on his wedding-night; after which, they drove him out of the town, which they forbade his ever re-entering.

In taking the road through the forest, he passed by the front of the gibbet, and, oppressed by the heat, as well as his anger and jealousy, he laid himself down to rest at the foot; but while he was asleep, the crows, who had perched on the heads of the hanging men, flew at him, uttering eager cries, and pecked out both his eyes. He rushed away like a madman, and by this time he must be dead of hunger; for, from that moment, no person ever heard of, or saw him more.

THE GOOSE-GIRL AT THE WELL.

THERE was, once upon a time, a very good old dame, who dwelt, with her flock of geese, in a waste piece of common ground between two hills, where she had a little cottage. This common was surrounded by a large forest, into which this old woman hobbled every morning on crutches. There she was very active, much more so than one could have believed, considering how old she was. She gathered grass for her geese; she gathered, also, all the wild nuts and apples

she could reach, and carried them all home on her back. One would have thought so heavy a burden would have broken it, but she always reached home safe and sound. If any one met her, she greeted him kindly, and would say: "Good morning to you, my dear countryman; what beautiful weather it is! You wonder how I get over the ground, but every one must bear his own burthen." At last, however, people grew afraid of her, and took a by-path, so that they might not meet her; and if a father passed with his children, he would say to them: "Take care of that old woman, she has mischief behind her ears; she is a witch!"

One morning, a very fine lively young gentleman passed through the wood. The sun was lighting up the forest, the birds were merrily singing, and the breeze was gently blowing among the trees; everything looked gay and pleasant. Still he met nobody; suddenly, he perceived the old woman, cutting away at the grass with a sickle. She had already placed a large heap of it in her sack, and by her side stood two

large baskets, filled with nuts, and apples, and wild berries. "Ah, my good woman!" exclaimed the youth, "how are you going to carry all that?"

"I must carry it, my good master," she replied; "but rich people's children do not want to do such things. Will you help me?" she continued, as the youth remained by her; "you have a fine straight back, and strong legs; it will be easy for you. My house is not far from here; it stands on the common, beyond yon hill. How soon your legs could jump there!"

THE OLD FAIRY CHEATS THE YOUNG COUNT INTO CARRYING HER PACK.

The youth took compassion on the old woman, and replied to her: "It is true," said he, "that my father is no peasant, but a rich Count; still, that you may see that poor people are not the only ones who can carry burthens, I will carry yours."

"If you will try it," said the old woman, "I shall be much obliged to you; but there are the baskets with the apples, and nuts, and berries, which you must carry too. Come, it is but an hour's walk which you will have to take, and it will not seem half so long to you."

The youth became a little thoughtful, when he heard of an hour's journey; but now the old woman would

not let him off. She packed the sackful of grass upon his back, and hung the baskets of fruit upon his arms. "There," said she, "how light it is!" "No, it is not at all light," answered the young Count, making a rueful face; "the sack weighs as heavy as if it were full of big stones, and the apples and berries seem like lead; I can scarcely breathe!"

So saying, he would have liked to have put the sack down again, but the old woman would not allow it. "Just see!" cried she, scornfully, "the young lord cannot carry what an old woman has so often borne! You grand people are very ready with your fair words, but when it comes to working, you can be just as ready

No. 3.

with your excuses. Why do you stand shaking there? Come, pick up your legs, for no one will take your sack off again."

Now, so long as the young Count walked on level ground, he got along pretty well; but as soon as he came to the hill, and began to go up, and the stones rolled from under his feet as if they were alive, his strength began to fail him. Big drops of sweat stood upon his brow and ran down his back, first hot, and then cold. "My good woman," he exclaimed, "I can go no further, till I have rested a little."

"There is no resting here," answered the old woman; "when you arrive at our destination, then you can rest; but, now, we must keep on: who knows what good it may do you!"

"You are a shameless old woman!" cried the youth, trying to throw off the sack; but he tried and tried in vain, it stuck as fast to his back as if it had grown there. He turned and twisted himself, but it was of no use—he could not get rid of his sack; and the old woman only laughed at his exertions, and danced round him on her crutches. "Don't put yourself in a passion, young gentleman," she said; "you are getting as red in the face as a turkey-cock. Bear your burden patiently; when we arrive at home, I will give you a good draught to refresh you."

What could he do? He was obliged to bear his fate, and follow after the old woman patiently, who appeared to become more and more active as his burthen grew heavier. All at once, she made a spring with her crutch, and jumped on the top of the sack, where she sat down; and though she was so thin and withered, her weight was greater than the stoutest farm-servant. The youth's knees trembled and shook under him, but if he stopped a moment, the old woman beat him with a strap, and stung his legs with nettles. Under this continual goading, he at last ascended the hill, and arrived at the old woman's cottage, just as he was ready to drop. As soon as the geese saw the old woman, they stretched out their necks, and ran towards her, crying, "Wulle! wulle!" Behind the flock walked a middle-aged woman, with a wand in her hand, who was big and strong, but as ugly as night. "Mother," said she to the old woman, "has anything happened, that you have remained out so long?" "Never fear, my dear daughter," replied the old woman, "nothing evil has come to me, but this kind young Count has carried my sack for me; and, only think! when I was tired, he carried me on his back also! The road has not been very long either, for we came along it very merrily, cracking jokes with one another all the way."

At last, the old woman left off talking, and lifted the sack off the youth's shoulders, and the baskets from his arms, and then, looking at him cheerfully, she said to him: "Sit down on that bench by the door, and rest yourself; you have honestly earned your reward, and it shall not be forgotten." And, turning to the Goose-girl, she continued: "Go into the house, my daughter; it is not proper that you should be alone with this young man; one ought not to pour oil upon the fire, and he might fall in love with you."

The young Count did not know whether to laugh or

to cry. "Such a treasure!" he thought to himself; "why, even if she were thirty years younger, my heart would not be touched!" Meanwhile, the old woman caressed and stroked her geese, as if they were children, and at last went into the house with her daughter. The youth stretched himself on the bench beneath an apple-tree, where the breeze blew softly and gently, while around him was spread a green meadow, covered with primroses, wild thyme, and a thousand other flowers. In the middle of it flowed a clear stream, on which the sun shone, and the white geese kept passing up and down, or paddling in the water. "It is quite lovely here," he said to himself; "but I am so tired, that I cannot keep my eyes open, so I will sleep awhile; but I hope no wind will come and blow away my legs, for they are as tender as tinder!"

After he had slept some time, the old woman came, and shook him till he awoke. "Stand up," said she, "you cannot stop here. Certainly, I did treat you rather shabbily, but it has not cost you your life. Now I will give you your reward; it will be neither money nor property, but something better." With these words, she placed in his hands a small casket, cut out of a single emerald, saying: "Keep it well, and it will bring you good luck." Thereupon, the young Count jumped up, and felt himself quite strong and refreshed; so he thanked the old woman for her present, and set off on his journey, without once lifting his eyes to look at her beautiful daughter; and when he had walked a long way, he heard the loud cackling of geese in the distance.

The poor young Count had to wander three days in the wilderness before he could find his way out, and then he came to a large city, where, because nobody knew him, he was led to the royal palace, where the King and Queen were sitting upon their thrones. There the Count sank on one knee, and, drawing out the emerald casket, laid it at the feet of the Queen. She bade him arise and hand the casket to her; but scarcely had she opened it, and looked at its contents, than she fell into a dead swoon upon the ground. Thereupon, the Count was seized by the King's guards, and would have been led off to prison, had not the Queen, speedily coming to herself, desired him to be set at liberty, for she must speak to him privately, and therefore every one must leave the room.

As soon as the Queen was left alone, she began to weep bitterly, and to say: "How vain is all this honour and grandeur that surrounds me, when every morning I give way to such great sorrow and grief! I once had three daughters, the youngest of whom was so beautiful, that all the world looked upon her as a wonder. She was as white as a snow-flake, with a tint on her cheeks like an apple-blossom; her hair was dazzling and bright, like a sunbeam. When she cried, no tears came, but pearls and precious gems fell from her eyes. When she was fifteen years old, her father, the King, summoned his three daughters to appear before him; when the youngest appeared, the light of her beauty was so great, that it was as if the sun had just risen upon them, and the people gaped with wonder at her great beauty. The King said: 'My daughters, I know not when my last hour will come, and, therefore, to-day I will appoint what each of you are to have at my death. You all three love me, but whoever loves me best shall have the best portion.' They each of them said they loved him best. 'Well,' said the King, ' give me some test, and I shall then be able to judge for myself which of you really loves me best.' 'I,' said the eldest, ' love you like the most delicious thing that is—that is, sugar.' The second said, 'I love you as I love my smartest dress.' But the youngest kept silent. 'And you,' said the King, 'how much do you love me?' 'I don't know,' said she, 'what I can compare my love to.' Her father, at length, pressed her to make some comparison, to which she replied: "The most delicate food is, to me, worthless without salt; therefore, my father, I love you like salt.' When the King heard this, he went into a great passion, and exclaimed: 'If you love me like salt, it is with salt your love shall be rewarded.' Thereupon, he parted his kingdom between the two eldest, and he had a sack of salt bound upon the shoulders of the youngest, and she was led out into the wild forest by two slaves. We all cried and entreated for her," said the Queen, "but nothing would appease the anger of the King. When she left us, her tears never ceased to flow, so that the whole path was strewn with pearls and precious stones, that fell from her eyes.

"The King afterwards greatly repented him of his cruel harshness, and caused the whole forest to be searched for her; but, alas! no one ever saw or heard of her since. When I think she may have been devoured by the wild beasts, I am filled with grief. Often I try to console myself with the hope that she yet lives, concealed in some cavern, or, haply, under the protection of some hospitable person, who has charitably given her shelter. But imagine my feelings, when, on opening your emerald casket, I found a pearl of the same sort that used to drop from my daughter's eyes! You may, perhaps, be able to judge how my heart was torn at the sight of it. But tell me, now, how you became possessed of that pearl."

The young Count then told the Queen, that he had received it from an old woman, living in a wood which seemed to be enchanted, and he thought she was a witch, but of the Queen's daughter he had neither seen nor heard anything. The King and Queen came to the resolution to go and find out the old woman who gave him the pearl, and hoped they might perhaps obtain some news of their child.

The old woman sat at the door of her cottage in the wilderness, spinning at her wheel. It was already dark, and there was but a feeble light from a faggot that burnt upon the hearth. All at once, a noise was heard outside; the geese were coming home from the meadow, making as much noise, and cackling as loud as they could. Soon after, the daughter stepped in, but the old woman scarcely thanked her, and only shook her head. The daughter, taking her wheel, sat down, and spun away as quickly as a young girl. Thus they sat for two hours, without speaking a word to each other. At length, something rattled against the window, and two fiery eyes glared in from the outside; it was an old night-owl, which screeched

thrice, "Hou! hou!" The old woman looked up from her work, and said: "Now is the time, my daughter, for you to go out and do your task."

The daughter got up, and went away over the meadows, deep into the valley beyond. By-and-by, she came to the side of a well, near to which stood three oak-trees; at the same time, the moon shone so brilliantly, that one might have seen to pick up a pin. The girl raised the skin that covered her face, leant over the fountain, and began to bathe herself. When she had done, she dipped the skin in the waters of the spring, and stretched it out on the grass, to bleach and dry in the moonlight. But, oh! how that young girl was changed to look at! You never saw anything like her! Off went the grey tresses, and her golden hair sparkled like the rays of the sun, as she stretched it out like a mantle, and it covered the whole of her fair body. Her eyes glistened, outshining the stars in the bright heaven over her, while her cheeks had the bloom and gently-roseate colour of the apple-blossom.

But, for all this, the pretty girl was sad, and she sat down, and she wept bitterly. One after another, the tears fell from her eyes, and trickled through her long hair down to the ground. There she was, and there she would have remained a long time, if the sound of the crackling of some branches had not reached her ears. Up, like a timid doe, that hears the crack of the sportsman's rifle, she bounded, in wild alarm! Just at that moment, a dark cloud veiled the moon; in an instant the young girl had slipped into her old skin, and disappeared, like a light blown out by the wind.

Trembling like an aspen leaf, she ran towards the house. The old woman was just at the door, and the young girl was about to relate to her what had happened; but the old woman smiled pleasantly, and said, "I know it all, my dear; I know it all." Then she led her to her chamber, and lighted a fresh faggot; but she did not sit down again at her wheel, but took a broom, and began sweeping and dusting the room. "We must have all nice and tidy here," said she to her daughter.

"But, mother," replied the girl, "why begin work at such a late hour? What can you be thinking about?"

"Do you know what o'clock it is?" asked the old woman.

"It is not yet midnight," answered the girl, "but it is already past twelve o'clock."

"Do you not reflect," continued the old woman, "that it is just this day three years that you came to my cottage? Your time is over; we cannot remain any longer together."

The young girl was all in terror, and said: "Ah! good mother, do you wish to drive me from you? Where can I go, who have neither friends or country to give me an asylum? Have I not always done everything you wished? Have you not always been content with everything I have done? Then, mother, oh! mother, do not send me away!"

The old woman was unwilling to tell the girl what was about to happen to her, so she said: "I can't stop here in this place any longer, and when I leave this dwelling, the house, and every room in it, must be in a

19

proper condition; do not hinder me, therefore, in my work. As regards yourself, don't feel any anxiety; you will be sure to find a roof, where you can live, and the wages I will give you, will fully meet your wants and wishes."

"But do tell me what is going to happen," urged the young girl.

"I tell you again, don't trouble me while I am at work, or say another word to me. Go you to your chamber, get out of the skin which covers your body, and put on the silken robe that you wore when you first came into my house; then stop in your room till I call you."

But it is now time that I should tell you what happened to the King and Queen, who were preparing to go in search of the old woman in her solitary cottage. The Count was first of all despatched to the forest alone, and having lost himself in the wilderness, was obliged to wander for two days, before he got into the right road again; in this he travelled till darkness overtook him, and then he climbed a tree, for he feared, in the darkness, he might lose his way again. When the moon shed her light over the country, he saw some one coming over the mountain, and although she had no rod in her hand, he could not doubt but that it was the Goose-girl, whom he had seen before, at home with the old woman. "Oho!" he exclaimed, "here comes one of the witches; and when I have caught her, I'll take very good care the other does not escape me!" But how astonished he was, when, stepping up to the brink of the well, he saw her take off her skin, and wash it, and put it into the moonlight to bleach and dry! and he saw her golden hair unbound, which, enveloping the whole of her beautiful figure, made her appear the most lovely being in the whole world. He scarcely ventured to draw his breath, but stretched out his neck as far as he could from the leaves, and looked at her with fixed and wondering eyes. Unfortunately, he leant too far over, and the bough cracked under his weight; at the same moment a cloud passed over the moon, and at that instant the maiden slipped into her skin again, and disappeared out of sight.

The young Count, however, made haste down from the tree, and followed the girl with hasty strides. He had not gone far before he saw the shadow of two persons wandering across the meadow; they were the King and Queen, who, perceiving from afar the light in the old dame's window, had directed their steps towards it. They were very glad to meet the young Count, and listened with wonder to what he told them about the surprising sight he had seen by the well, which left them little cause for doubting that the beautiful vision in question was their lost daughter. The whole party advanced joyfully, and soon reached the house, round which they found the geese all drawn up in rows, fast asleep, with their heads under their wings, and not one of them stirred. Looking through the window into the sitting-room, they saw the old woman quietly seated at her spinning, with her head bent over it, and her eyes attentively fixed on her work. Everything in the chamber was as neat and tidy as if it were the habitation of the airy sylphs,

20

who never have any dust on their feet, because they always fly about in the sky, and never touch the earth. This was all very well, but they could not see their daughter; so, after considering some moments what was to be done, they took courage at last, and tapped gently at the window.

One would have said the old woman was expecting them, for she rose up, and cried out, in a friendly voice, "You may come in; I know who you are!" On their entering the chamber, the dame said: "You might have saved yourselves this long journey, if you had not, three years ago, unjustly turned out of doors a good, sweet-tempered daughter. However, she has lost nothing by it, for, during the three years, she has been the guardian of my geese, and, during all that time, nothing wicked has come nigh to her, and she has preserved the purity of her heart. As for you, the anxiety in which you have ever since lived, has been your sufficient punishment." Then she stepped up to the chamber door, and said: "My dear child, come forth." The door opened, and the daughter of the King came forth, arrayed in her silken robe, with her golden locks and her brilliant eyes, looking like an angel issuing from the bright portals of the sun. At sight of her father and mother, she ran towards them, threw herself upon their necks, and tenderly pressed them in her arms. What power could have checked the overflowing tears of child and parents thus united? When the young Princess raised her eyes, and saw the young Count standing close to them, her delicate white cheeks became red with blushes, like a moss-rose, and yet she knew not why.

The King said: "Dear child! I have given away my kingdom; what have I in my power to bestow on you?"

"She is in no need of gifts from any one," said the old dame; "I have got, in a box, a store of the tears that she has shed for you, and they are all of them pearls, far more beautiful and precious than those that are found in the sea, and worth more than the whole of your kingdom put together. Moreover, I owe her some wages for taking care of my geese, and I shall pay her by making her a present of this little lodge of mine."

You would not have thought this a very handsome present, to look at the cottage at that moment; but no sooner had the old woman finished uttering these words, than they heard a slight cracking of the walls, and, as they turned round to look at the place where it was, the little lodge had been changed into a superb palace, and a sumptuous banquet was ready served on a royal table, and servants were going in and out, waiting, and busy in their various departments.

There is a good deal more of this story, but the old lady who told it to us had a slight defect in her memory—in fact, she had forgotten the rest. As far as we could make out from the fragments of her memory, the beautiful daughter of the King was married to the handsome young Count, and they lived together in the palace, in the very greatest of happiness, as long as people who are happy, and who have nothing to care for, generally do. Whether the white geese, whose guardian the Princess had been, were, in reality, so many young ladies (we don't mean anything ill-natured to little girls by this allusion), whom the old dame had collected about her,—whether they resumed their human shapes, and their fine silk stockings and pretty little shoes, in place of those ugly goose-pats, and remained in the quality of maids of honour to the young Queen,—we are not quite sure; but we rather think it was so. One thing we know well: the old dame was no wicked sorceress, but a kind fairy, who only desired what was good. Probably, too, it was she who had given the King's daughter, at her birth, the gift of weeping pearls instead of tears,—a privilege which extends to none in our days, or else, how often would poor people become rich!

THE UNGRATEFUL SON.

ONCE upon a time, there was a man, and he was sitting in front of his door, with his wife, eating his dinner, as is customary in some foreign parts. They had before them a roast fowl, just ready for them to regale themselves with, when the man saw his father in the distance, and hid the dish in a great hurry, lest the old man should be hungry, and ask to have some of it; but when the old gentleman came up, he only took a drink of beer, and went on his way.

As soon as his back was turned, the son got up to fetch back the dish, and set it on the table again; but, to his horror, he found the nice roast fowl—browned to a turn, and creaming with froth, as he had left it—

had turned into a great ugly frog, that jumped up in his face, and stuck there, in spite of all his efforts to get rid of it. Whenever anybody tried to take the

ugly beast away, he glared a horrible look at them, as if he would spit his venom in their eyes, and jump upon their persons; and so nobody dared approach him. The end was, that the ungrateful son, who refused his old father a mouthful of his dainty roast fowl, was doomed to feed and nourish this awful frog; for, if he had not done so, it would have devoured his head. So he passed the rest of his days in wandering miserably about the earth, a terror to all, and without the pity of any.

PRINCESS PUSS AND THE MILLER'S BOY.

ONCE upon a time, there was a very old Miller, who had neither wife or child, and so he had no one to leave his mill to, but his apprentices; so, calling them to him one day, he said: "I am old, and shall soon give up my mill; do you all go out, and whichever of you brings me home the best horse, I will give the mill to him, and he shall attend me on my death-bed."

The youngest of the apprentices was a good little lad, but so small, that he was despised by the others, who laughed at the notion of his ever getting the mill, even after them. But they all went out together, and when they had got out of the village, the two brothers said to stupid Hans: "You may as well stay where you are; you'll never find a horse in your lifetime." But Hans would go with them; and, when it became quite dark, they arrived at a hollow, where they all laid down to sleep. The two clever brothers waited till poor Hans was snoring asleep, and then they walked off, and left him by himself. Now, they thought themselves very clever to play this trick, but perhaps they may not fare the better for their unkindness.

By-and-by, when the sun arose and Hans awoke, he peeped all around him, and, finding himself in this deep hollow, cried out, with affright, "O Heavens! where have I got to?" Then he got up, and scrambled out of the hollow into the forest; and, finding himself all alone, he kept on thinking, "Now, what can I do to get a horse?"

While he was thus ruminating, a beautiful little tortoiseshell Cat came up to him, and inquired of him, in a very friendly manner, "Where are you going, Hans?" "Ah! you can help me," said Hans. "Yes, I know very well what you wish," replied the Cat; "you want a fine horse. Come and be my servant for seven years, and I will give you one of the most lovely horses you ever beheld." "Well," thought Hans to himself, "this is a wonderful Cat! but still, I may as well see if all this be true."

So the Cat took him into her enchanted castle, where there were many other cats, who waited upon the lovely tortoiseshell Cat, jumping nimbly up and down the steps, and bustling about in first-rate style. In the evening, when they sat down to table, three cats attended to play music; one played the violoncello, a second the violin, and a third blew the trumpet so loudly, that its cheeks seemed as if they would burst. When they had finished dinner, the table was drawn away, and the Cat said: "Now, Hans, come and dance with me." "No, no," replied he, "I cannot dance with a Cat; I never learnt how." "Then take him to bed!" cried the Cat to its attendants; and they lighted him at once to his sleeping apartment, where one drew off his shoes, another his stockings, while a third blew out the light. The next morning, the servant cats made their appearance again; one drew on his stockings, another buckled his garters, a third fetched his shoes, a fourth washed his face, and a fifth wiped it with her tail. "That was done well and gently," said Hans to the Cat. But all day long Hans had to cut wood for the Cat, and for that purpose he received an axe of silver, and wedges and saws of the same metal, while the mallet was made of copper.

Here Hans remained, doing all the good he could, and making himself useful. Every day he had the best of everything to eat and drink, but he saw nobody but the beautiful tortoiseshell Cat and her attendants. One day, the Cat beckoned him to her, and said to him: "Go, and mow my meadow, and mind you make nice dry hay of the grass;" then she gave him a scythe made of silver, and a whetstone of gold, which she told him to bring back safe. Hans went off, and did exactly what he was told; and when he had well made the hay, he carried it all home, carefully taking back the scythe and whetstone, and then he begged the Cat to give him some reward. "No," said the Cat, "you must first do many useful things for me. See, here are beams of silver, binding-clamps, joists, and all that is necessary, all of silver, and of this you must first build me a small house." Hans built it, and, when it was done, he reminded the Cat he had still no horse, although his seven years had quickly passed away. The Cat asked him if he would like to see her fine stud of horses. "Yes, indeed," said Hans. So she opened the door with her delicate paw, and there stood twelve horses, snorting, and tossing their manes proudly in the air. Hans was pleased enough to see them, but the Cat would not let him look more than a minute, and then she gave him his dinner, and said to him: "Go home; I shall not give you your horse to take with you, but in three days I will come to you, and bring it with me." So Hans walked off, and the attendant cats showed him the way to the mill; but, as they had not given him any new clothes, he was obliged to go home in his old ragged ones, which he had worn all along, until they had grown too short for him, in his seven years' service.

When he arrived at the mill, he found the other two apprentices, and they had both got horses. Hans laughed, when he saw one was blind, and the other was lame. They soon inquired of Hans where his horse was. "Oh," said he, "it will follow me in three days." It was now their turn to laugh, and they cried out: "A wonderful horse it will be, when it does come, no doubt!" Hans then went into the parlour; but the old Miller said he should not sit at his table, all ragged and dirty as he was, for that he should be ashamed of him, if any of their neighbours came in.

So they gave him something to eat and drink out of doors, and, when bed-time came, the two brothers refused to let Hans share their bed, and he, poor fellow! was obliged to creep into the goose-house, and stretch himself upon some dirty hard straw. The next day was the third day, promised by the Cat as that of her arrival; and, as soon as Hans was up, there came a grand carriage, drawn by six horses, whose sleek skins shone, from the beautiful condition they were in. Besides all this, there was a seventh horse, led by a servant, and this horse was for the Miller's boy. Out of this fine carriage stepped a beautiful and dazzling Princess, and who should this be, but the tortoiseshell Cat, that good-natured Hans had so willingly served for seven years! The Princess asked the Miller where her little servant, the Mill-boy, was, and he answered: "We could not think of taking such a dirty, ragged little boy into the mill; so we sent him into the goose-house, where he now lies." The Princess desired him at once to fetch Hans, but, before he could come, the poor fellow had to draw together his smock-frock, in order to cover himself with decency. Then the attendant brought some elegant clothes, and, after washing Hans in rose-water, put them on him, so that no King looked half so handsome and well dressed.

Thereupon, the Princess desired to see the horses the other apprentices had brought home; and, finding one blind and the other lame, she ordered her servant to bring in the horse he had in his keeping, and as soon as the Miller put his eyes on it, he declared his farm-yard had never before contained so fine an animal. "It belongs to your youngest apprentice," said the Princess. "And the mill too," rejoined the Miller; but the Princess said he might keep that, and the horse as well, for himself. With these words, she handed her faithful Hans into the carriage, and then, getting in herself, drove away. They went first to the little house that Hans had built with silver tools, and which had become a noble castle, wherein everything was of gold and silver. There the Princess married him; and he was so very rich, that he never wanted anything all the rest of his life.

JOE THE FISHERMAN, AND HIS WIFE JOAN.

THERE was, once upon a time, a Fisherman and his wife, who lived together, in a little hut near the sea. Every day, the man went out and threw his line, but he might as well have remained at home, for he caught nothing in this blank-looking sea.

One fine morning, as soon as he had thrown his line, it went to the bottom, and when he drew it up, he was delighted to find a fine Barbel hooked to the end of it. The Barbel said to him: "Let me go, I pray you, good Fisherman; I am not a real fish, but an enchanted Prince. What good shall I do you, if you pull me up? I am not nice to eat; put me back into the water, and let me live."

"Ah!" said the man, "you need not make such a fuss; a fish that can speak, I would rather let swim;" and so saying, he put the fish into the water, and as it sank to the bottom, it left a long streak of blood behind it. Then the Fisherman got up, and went home to his wife in the hut.

"Have you caught nothing to-day, husband?" said she. "Oh!" he replied, "I caught a Barbel, who said he was an enchanted Prince, so I threw him into the water again, to swim."

"Did you not wish first?" she inquired. "No," said he. "Ah!" said the wife, "how unlucky is one, always to remain in this nasty, dirty hovel! You might, at least, have wished for a better hut. Go again, and call him; tell him we should like to have a better home, and for certain you will get it."

"Ah!" said he; "but pray tell me how I am to manage that?" "Why," said his wife, "it is easy enough to catch him again, and before you let him swim away, he is sure to give you whatever you ask."

The man was not much pleased, and wished his wife farther, but nevertheless he went down again to the sea. When he came to the water, it was green and yellow, and looked still more blank; he stood by it, and said:

> "Barbel, Barbel, in the sea,
> Hither quickly come to me;
> For my wife, Dame Isabel,
> Wishes what I dare not tell."

Then the fish came swimming up, and said: "What do you want with me?" "Oh!" said the man, "I want to catch you again, for my wife says I ought to have wished before. She won't stay any longer in her miserable hovel; she wants a comfortable cottage."

"Go home again," said the Barbel, "she has it already."

So the Fisherman went home, and there was his wife, no longer in her dirty hovel, but in a clean cottage, before the door of which she was sitting contentedly upon a bench. "Come in, now, and see," she said, with delight; "is not this an improvement?"

So in they went; and in the cottage there was a beautiful parlour, and a noble fireplace, and a chamber, with a soft bed in it; there were, also, a kitchen and a store-room, with nice earthenware, all of the very best, tin-ware and copper vessels, and everything very clean and neat. At the back was a large yard, with hens and chickens; as well as a nice garden, full of apples, and pears, and plums, and all kinds of fruit-trees, as well as vegetables. "See!" said the wife, "is not this charming?" "Yes," said her husband, "so long as it blooms, you will be very well content with it." "We will consider about that," she replied; and they went to bed.

Thus eight to fourteen days passed on, when the wife said: "Husband, after all, this is only a hut, and it is far too narrow for us, and the yard and garden are far too small; the Barbel may very well give us a large house. I should like to live in a large stone palace; go, then, to the Barbel, and ask him to give us a castle."

"Ah, wife!" said he, "the cottage is pretty, and good enough for us, I am sure; why should you wish to have a castle?" "Go along," she replied, "the Barbel will soon give us a trifle like that."

"Nay, wife," he said, "the Barbel gave us the cottage at first; but when I go again, he will perhaps be angry." "Never you mind," said she; "he can do what I wish for, very easily and willingly. Go and try." The husband was vexed at heart, and did not like going, and said to himself, "This is not right." But at last he set off.

When he came to the sea, the water was quite clouded, and deep-blue coloured, and dark, and thick; it looked green no longer, yet it was calm. So he went and said:

> "Barbel, Barbel, in the sea,
> Hither quickly come to me;
> For my wife, Dame Isabel,
> Wishes what I dare not tell."

"Now, then, what do you want?" said the Barbel. "Oh!" said the Fisherman, half frightened, "she wants to live in a great stone castle." "Go home, and see it at your door," replied the Barbel.

The Fisherman went away, and lo! where formerly stood his house, there was a great stone castle! and his wife called to him to come in, and, taking him by the hand, she said: "Now, let us look about us." So they walked about; and in the castle there was a great hall, with marble tables; and there were ever so many servants, who ushered them, through folding-doors, into rooms hung all around with tapestry, and filled with fine golden stools and chairs, with crystal looking-glasses on the walls, all the rooms being fitted up in the same style. Outside the house were large court-yards, with horse and cow-stalls, and carriages, all of the best; and, besides, a beautiful garden, filled with magnificent flowers and fruit-trees, and a meadow, full a mile long, covered with deer, and oxen, and sheep, as many as any reasonable person could wish for. "Is not this pretty?" said the wife. "Ah!" said her husband, "so long as the humour lasts, you will be content with this, and then, I suppose, you will want something else." "We will think about that," said she; and with that they went to bed.

The next morning, the wife got up just as it was day, and looked out over the fine country that lay before her. Her husband did not get up; and there she stood, with her arms a-kimbo, and called out;

"Get up, and come and look here at the window; see! shall I not be Queen over all the land? Go, and say to the Barbel, we choose to be King and Queen."

"Ah, wife!" said he, "why should I wish to be King?" "No," she replied, "you do not wish, so I will be Queen; go, tell the Barbel so."

"Oh! why do you wish this? I cannot say it!"

"Why not? Get you off at once; I *must* be Queen."

The husband set out, quite stupified, but she would have her way; and when he came to the sea, it was quite black-looking, and the water splashed up, and smelt very disagreeably. But he stood still, and repeated:

"Barbel, Barbel, in the sea,
Hither quickly come to me;
For my wife, Dame Isabel,
Wishes what I scarce dare tell."

"What does she want now?" asked the Barbel. "Ah!" said he, "she would be Queen." "Go home; she is so already," replied the fish.

So he departed; and when he came near the palace, he saw it had become much larger, with a great tower, and a gallery in front of it; and before the gate stood a herald, and there were many soldiers, with kettle-drums and trumpets. When he came into the house, he found everything made of the purest marble and gold, with magnificent curtains fringed with gold. Through the hall he went in, and saw the doors where the great Court apartment was; and there sat his wife, upon a high throne of gold and diamonds, having a crown of gold upon her head, and a sceptre of precious stones in her hand; and upon each side stood six pages in a row, each one a head taller than the other.

Then he went up, and said: "Ah, wife! are you Queen now?" "Yes," said she, "now I am Queen!" There he stood, looking, for a long time; at last, he said: "Ah, wife, how do you like being Queen? now we have nothing else to choose." "No, indeed," she replied, "I am very dissatisfied; time and tide do not wait for me; I can bear it no longer. Go, then, to the Barbel. Queen I am; now I must be Pope!"

"Ah, wife! what would you? Pope thou canst not be; the Pope is the head of Christendom—the Barbel cannot make you that." "I *will* be Pope!" replied the wife; and so he was obliged to go, in spite of himself.

When he came to the shore, the sea was running mountains high; the sky was so black, that he was quite terrified, and he began to say:

"Barbel, Barbel, in the sea,
Quickly, quickly come to me;
For my wife, Dame Isabel,
Wishes what I dare not tell."

"What now?" said the Barbel. "She wants to be Pope," said he. "Go home, and find her so," was the reply.

So he went back, and found a great cathedral, as big as St. Paul's, in which she was sitting, upon a high throne, with two rows of candles on each side, some as thick as towers, down to those no bigger than rushlights, and before her footstool were Kings and Queens kneeling. "Wife," said he, "now be contented; since you are Pope, you cannot be anything else." "That I will consider about," she replied, and so they went to bed; but she could not sleep for thinking what she should be next. Very early, she rose, and looked out of the window, and, as she saw the sun rising, she thought to herself: "Why should I not do that?" and so shook her husband, and called out to him: "Go, tell the Barbel I want to make the sun rise." Her husband was so frightened, that he tumbled out of bed; but she would hear nothing, and he was obliged to go.

When he got down to the sea, a tremendous storm was raging, and the ships and boats were tossing about in all directions. Then he shouted out, though he could not hear his own words:

"Barbel, Barbel, in the sea,
Quickly, quickly come to me;
For my wife, Dame Isabel,
Wishes what I dare not tell."

"What would she have now?" said the fish. "Ah!" he replied, "she wants to be Ruler of the Universe!" "Return, and find her back in her hovel," replied the Barbel; and so he did, and there the Fisherman and his wife remained, the rest of their days.

THE SIX COMRADES,

WHO CARRIED THE WORLD BEFORE THEM.

ONCE upon a time, there was a man who was clever in all kinds of craft. They made a Soldier of him, and he served bravely; but, when the war was over, he received his discharge, and a beggarly threepence to carry him home. This did not suit him at all; so he made himself a strong promise, that, if he could only find some comrades to join him, he would settle accounts with the King, by making him hand over all the treasures in his kingdom. Oh! how angry he was, as he took the road towards the forest! There he saw a man, who was taking up, by the roots, six great trees, with no tools but his hands, just as if they were so many blades of grass. So he up and put the question to him: "Are you willing to follow me, and enter into my service?"

"Just the very thing I should like to do," said the other, "but I must go and carry this little faggot to my mother." Then he took one of the trees, and twisted it, like a twig, round the others; jerked the monstrous faggot—as he called this load of timber—to the top of his shoulder, and carried it off; after which he returned to meet his master, who could not help observing: "Here are two of us, I think, that will go through the world!"

They went a little farther, and they came to a Sportsman, who was on his knees, with his gun to his shoulder. The Soldier questioned him: "What are you aiming at, Mr. Sportsman?" to which he replied: "There is a fly, six miles off, settled on the branch of

THE BLOWER DISPERSES THE ARMY OF THE KING.

an oak; I want to send a bullet through his right eye!"

"Oh!" said the Soldier, "come along with me; we are the three fellows to go through the world!"

The Sportsman joined the party, and, after journeying some time, they came to seven windmills, whose sails were turning with the greatest rapidity, although to the right or the left there was not wind enough to stir a leaf. At this wonderful sight, the Soldier said: "I wonder what it is that drives these mills, for there is not the slightest breeze stirring;" and on they went. But when they had gone about two miles farther on, they saw a man perched upon the branch

of a tree, holding one nostril, and blowing out of the other. "My good fellow, what are you driving, up there?"

"Do you not see," said he, "that, two miles from here, there are seven windmills? I am blowing to make those windmills turn their sails."

"Oh!" said he, "come along with me; four such fellows as we are, will be sure to make our way in the world."

So the Blower came down from his tree, and joined the company. A little time after, they came to a man who was standing on one leg only, the fact being, that he had taken off the other, and laid it down beside him. "Here is a fellow," said the Soldier, "who wants to make sure of resting himself."

"I am a Courier," replied the other, "and as I do not want to run too fast, I have taken off one of my legs; when I have got both of them on, I skim over the ground faster than the swallows."

"Oh! you are the man for me!" said the Soldier; "join my troop, for five fellows like us, nothing in the world can stop."

So he went with them; and, a little time after, they met with a man who wore his cap placed right on his ear. The Soldier politely addressed him, and said: "With all due respect, Sir, you will excuse my saying, that you would do better to wear your hat a little more on your head; for, as it is now, it looks just like a fool's cap."

"I know very well what I am about," said the other; "when I wear my cap straight, it makes everything so cold, that the birds freeze in the air, and fall to the ground."

"Oh!" said the Soldier, "if that is the case, you shall come along with me, and we will make up a party of six, that will carry the world before them!"

These six men, all together, entered a city, the King of which had issued a proclamation, that whoever was willing to run a race with his daughter, should have her for a wife if he won it, but should lose his head if he was beaten. The Soldier came forward, and presented himself for a race, but, at the same time, asked if one of his people might be allowed to run in his place. "Certainly," said the King, "but your life and his will be wagered on the result, and if he is beaten, off go both your heads!"

Matters being thus arranged, the Soldier ordered his Courier to screw on his second leg, and instructed him to run without losing time, and neglect nothing that would ensure a victory. It had been settled, that whichever of the runners first brought back a cup of water from a fountain situated at a long distance from the starting-place, should be declared the winner.

The Courier and the King's daughter each received a little jug, and started at the same moment; but the Princess had scarcely taken a few steps, before the man was out of sight, just as if the wind had carried him away. He was quickly at the fountain, filled his pitcher there, and turned back again; but, happening

to feel tired in the middle of the journey, he laid himself down to enjoy a nap, only taking pains to place under his head the skull of a horse, that he found on the ground, so that his hard pillow might not render him too comfortable.

Meanwhile, the Princess, who ran as swiftly as any person could do in their natural state, had reached the fountain, and hastened to return, after she had filled her pitcher. On her way back, she came up with the sleeping Courier. "Good!" said she, joyously, "my enemy is within my power!" and, seizing the cup, she emptied its contents, and ran, with greater speed, on her way. All was now at the point of being lost, had not the Sportsman, by some great good chance, been standing on the castle, looking on with his piercing eyes. "It will never do," said he, "for the Princess to win the race;" so, with one shot of his gun, he cleverly carried away the horse's skull from under the Courier's head, without doing the man any injury. The noise awoke him, and, jumping up, he found his cup empty, and the Princess far ahead of him. This did not, however, damp his courage; he ran back again to the spring, and, filling his cup afresh, returned home ten minutes earlier than the Princess. "Now," said he, "I call this running; before, I did but play at it."

But the King and the Princess were now furious with rage, to think that a miserable common Soldier should carry off the prize; and they consulted together, how they should best get rid of him and his companions. The King, at last, consoling his daughter said: "Do not frighten yourself, my dear child; I have hit upon a plan that cannot fail." Then he called to the Six Travellers, under pretence of regaling them, saying; "In the middle of that room you will find a table, most sumptuously spread; enter, and regale yourselves; eat, drink, and be merry." He then led them into a chamber with an iron floor, iron doors, and the windows all barred with iron, and, as soon as they were inside, he locked and bolted the doors, so that there was no escape. As soon as that was done, he called to his Cook, and commanded him to light a blazing fire beneath, until the iron was red-hot. The Cook soon executed the King's commands, and the Six Companions, who sat at table, began to feel very warm. At first, they thought this arose from the great feast they had made; but, feeling the warmth no longer bearable, and still increasing, they rose to leave the room, and found the doors and windows fastened. They then saw the King was going to play them some wicked trick; "But," cried the man with the little cap, "he shall not succeed, for I will cause such a sharp frost to come upon the fire, that its ardour shall soon be damped, I'll warrant you!" And so saying, he put his cap on straight upon his head, and it became so cold immediately, that all the heat disappeared, and all the dishes froze upon the table. After about two hours, the King, thinking they would all be burnt to a cinder, opened the door, and peeped in himself, to see how they looked. As soon as the door was open, he found them, all six, as fresh and lively as possible, but they begged to come out and warm themselves, as they found the room so very cold, that the dishes were all frozen to the table. Upon seeing this, the King's anger was not to be appeased; he went to the Cook, and angrily demanded of him, why he had not executed his orders. The Cook, however, only pointed to the fire, saying: "There is heat enough there, I should think." The King thought so, too, and saw plainly he should not be able to get rid of his unwelcome guests in that way.

The King now set his wits to work, to hit upon a sure means to free himself from them. So he caused the Master to be summoned, and said: "If you will give up your right to my daughter, I will give you as much gold as you like." "Well, most noble King," replied the man, "only give me just as much gold as my servant here can carry, and you may keep the Princess with all my heart."

The King was delighted; and the Soldier said he would come back and fetch the money in fourteen days. He immediately set to work, and got together all the tailors in the kingdom, and made them all sew him a sack, which took up all the fourteen days before they had finished it. When the sack was ready, the Soldier called the Strong Man (who, by his Herculean strength, had uprooted the trees with his hands); he took the sack upon his shoulders, and made his way on to the palace. "Who," cried the King, "is this powerful young fellow, who carries on his shoulders a woollen sack as big as a house?" and, when he was informed, he shook with fright, for he thought how much of his gold it would swallow up. The King, first of all, caused a ton of gold to be brought, which sixteen ordinarily strong men had great trouble in moving; but the Strong Man, seizing it with one hand, threw it into the sack, exclaiming: "Bring more! bring more! what is the use of these driblets? I shall never get the bottom of the sack filled, at this rate!" Then, by degrees, the King caused all his treasure to be brought, which did not half fill it; still the Strong Man cried: "Bring more! bring more! how can you expect such crumbs as these to fill my sack?" Then they were obliged to bring seven hundred waggons filled with gold, drawn by oxen, from all parts of the kingdom; these the Strong Man stowed into his sack—gold, waggons, and the cattle that had drawn them. Still it was not full; and he promised to take whatever they would bring him to fill his sack. When he had got everything they could find him in the kingdom, he said: "Well, well, I must make an end of this; if one's sack is not quite full, it does not much signify,—besides, one can tie it the easier!" and so saying, he hoisted it upon his shoulders, and walked away, and his companions after him.

The King, seeing one man carrying off all the wealth of his kingdom, was nearly choking with rage; and he ordered his soldiers to mount their horses, and ride after the Travellers, and, at all events, to seize and bring back the Strong Man with the sack. Two regiments, accordingly, rode after them in hot haste, and shouted out to them: "You are our prisoners! lay down your sack, or you will all be dead men within an hour!"

"What is that you are saying?" asked the Blower; "soho! you'll make us prisoners, will you? I think

I'll treat you first to a dance upon nothing!" So saying, he held one nostril, and with the other he blew the whole two regiments far up into the blue sky, so that one regiment flew over the hills on the right, and the other on the left. One old sergeant-major begged hard for mercy; he had seen much service, and had many wounds, and lots of medals and crosses, and therefore the Blower thought he was undeserving such disgrace; so he sent a gentle wind after him, and brought him back without hurting him, and then sent him to the King, to tell him it was quite useless to send men after him, for if he marched out every man in the kingdom, they would be blown away, like the first lot.

When this message reached the King, "Let them go," said he; "the rascals will meet their reward!" So the Six Travellers reached home in safety, with all the wealth of the kingdom, which they divided, and lived upon contentedly ever after.

THE TIME-WASTER.

ONCE upon a time, there was a young girl—oh! such a pretty girl!—but she was a careless and idle lass. When she was obliged to spin, she did it with so little care, that, rather than untie the little knots in her thread, she would break out the flax by whole handfuls, and throw it down by the side of her. Now, she

had a little servant-maid, who was altogether as industrious, and she collected these little bits of flax, arranged them, wove them into a fine thread, and made herself a handsome dress out of them.

There was a young gentleman in their village, and he had asked the idle lass to marry him. The marriage-day was fixed, and, the evening before, the little busy maid was dancing merrily, in her new dress, when the bride began to laugh, and say: "See, how fine she looks in my leavings!" "What is that you say?" said the young gentleman. Then she told him, how her little maid had made that nice new gown she then had on, out of the waste of her spinning.

This set the young gentleman thinking, how much more valuable a helpmate an industrious young woman

27

was likely to make, than a wasteful, careless, flaunting beauty. So he gradually broke away from the idle mistress, and went and paid his addresses to the busy little maid, whom he soon after made his wife, and nobody blamed him.

THE CHILD OF THE GOOD FAIRY TELL-TRUE.

NEAR the entrance of a dense forest, there once dwelt a Woodcutter, with his wife, and an only child, a little girl, three years of age; but they were so very poor, they hardly knew where to find bread to eat from day to day. One morning, the Woodcutter, heart-broken and hungry, went into the wood to work, and, as he stood at work, a most beautiful lady presented herself before him. She wore on her head a splendidly dazzling crown of diamonds and glittering stars. She addressed him, saying: "I am the Good Fairy Tell-true, mother of all good children. You are poor and miserable: bring me your child, and I will take her with me, and will be a mother to her, and provide for all her wants with the greatest care, and take her with me to my Golden Palace in the clouds." The

Woodcutter gladly obeyed, and, calling his child, gave her to the Good Fairy Tell-true, who carefully carried her to her Golden Palace in the clouds. The

little child was extremely happy there; she ate the sweetest cakes, and drank the freshest cream; she wore the softest and most shining dresses, and the Good Fairy's children played with her from morning till night.

When she arrived at the age of fourteen years, the Good Fairy called her to her side, and said: "My dear child, I have a long journey to make, and, during my absence, I shall give into your care the thirteen keys of the doors of my Golden Palace. You may freely open the twelve doors, and survey the marvellous things they contain; but this little key, which opens the door of the thirteenth room, you must not use, for, if you do, great misery and harm will befall you."

The young girl promised faithfully to obey, and, when the Good Fairy had gone, she immediately called her playfellows, and began to visit the rooms in the Fairy's Golden Palace. Each day she opened one, until she had opened all the twelve; and in each of these chambers she saw a beautiful Fairy, surrounded by a brilliant and shining light, so that the child was bewildered with the glory of it: the good little children that accompanied her rejoiced with her.

Now the forbidden door alone remained; an unconquerable desire possessed the maiden, to know what was hidden there, and she said to her companions: "I will not open this door wide; I will open it a little way, and just peep in, to see what it contains." "Nay, do not open the door, and disobey the Good Fairy, or some great mischance will befall you."

The young girl was silent under the reproof of her companions, but still the desire wore into her heart, and she had not the power to resist it; her curiosity so tormented her, that she had no repose. When her good playfellows had one day left her by herself, she thought: "Now I am alone, and can peep in; no one will be the wiser for what I do." So she found the keys, and, taking the right one in her hand, she placed it in the lock, and turned it round. Then the door sprang open, and she beheld three Fairies, sitting on a golden throne, surrounded by a bright and glittering light, in which sparkled millions of diamonds and beauteous gems. The maiden remained some time standing, bewildered by the shining light she beheld, and then, putting forth her hand into the light, she drew it back, and found it covered with gold. When she saw this, great fear seized her, and, shutting the door hastily, she ran away; but her heart beat on so violently, and her fear increased more and more, when she found that the more she washed and rubbed her hand, the brighter it became.

A few days after, the Good Fairy Tell-true returned, and, calling the young girl to her, demanded of her the keys of the doors of the Golden Palace. As she gave them up, the Good Fairy looked in her face, and said, "Hast thou opened the thirteenth door?" and the maiden answered, "No." The Good Fairy laid her hand upon the maiden's heart, and knew, by the violence of its beating, that her command had been disregarded, and that the door had been opened. Then again she asked of the child, "Hast thou opened the thirteenth door?" "No," answered the maiden, for the second time.

Then the Fairy perceived that the child's hand had become golden from touching the light, and she no longer doubted that the maiden was guilty. Then again she said to her: "In truth, hast thou not opened the thirteenth door?" "No," said the maiden, for the third time.

Then the Good Fairy Tell-true said: "Thou hast neither obeyed nor spoken the truth; therefore thou art no longer fit to live among good children, in the Golden Palace in the clouds."

Then a deep sleep came upon the maiden, and she sank down upon the earth, and when she awoke, she found herself in the midst of a great wilderness; then she tried to speak, but could not utter a single word; she arose, and would have run, but was kept from moving by the thick bushes, that held her, whichever way she turned, so that there was no hope of escape. In the midst of the circle in which she was now enclosed stood an old hollow tree, and in this she was obliged to dwell; here she slept at night, and when it rained and snowed, she found shelter within it. Roots and wild berries were her only food, and she gathered all within her reach. In the autumn, she collected the leaves that fell from the trees, and put them into her hollow tree; and when the bitter frost and snow came, she made herself clothes of them, for her own were all dropped into rags, and no longer afforded her any covering; but when the sun shone, she warmed herself in its rays, and she let her long hair fall about her like a mantle. Thus she remained a long time, suffering from all the miseries that want and cold inflict upon the human race.

One day, when the trees had put forth their leaves again, the King of the country was out hunting in the forest, when some game ran past him into the bushes which surrounded the wood; he dismounted, and with his sword cut aside the branches that encircled the old hollow tree, where the animal had taken refuge, and made a path for himself. When he had thus cleared his way, he saw a maiden, marvellously beautiful, who was clothed from head to foot in her own beautiful golden hair, warming herself in the sun. "Child, how came you in this dreary wilderness?" said the King; but the maiden answered not, for she was dumb. Then the King said: "Will you go with me to my palace?" At this, the maiden nodded her head; and the King, taking her in his arms, put her upon his horse, and rode home with her. Then he had her bathed in rose-water, gave her beautiful clothing, and everything she wanted in abundance. Still she could not speak, her lips had been sealed; but her beauty was so great, that the King fell violently in love with her, and married her.

About a year after, the Queen brought a child into the world; and when she was alone on her bed, the Good Fairy Tell-true appeared to her, and said: "Wilt thou confess the truth, that thou didst open the forbidden door? for, if thou wilt, then I will open thy mouth, and give thee again the power of speech; but if thou continuest obstinately in thy sins, then will I take from thee thy new-born babe." Then the power of speech was given to the Queen, and she said: "No, I did not open the forbidden door;" and the Good Fairy took the child in her arms, and disappeared with him.

The next morning, when the child could not be found, the people of the palace grew angry, and said their Queen was an Ogress, and had killed her baby. She heard all they said, but had no power to reply; but the King loved her too tenderly to believe a word they said.

Another year passed, and the Queen brought forth another child, a son. The Good Fairy came to her again, the night after, and said: "If thou wilt now confess to me thou hast opened the forbidden door, I will give thee again the power of speech, and will restore to thee thy child; but if thou obstinately continuest in thy sins, then will I also take from thee thy new-born infant." The Queen answered as before: "No, I have not opened the forbidden door;" and the Good Fairy took the newly-born babe in her arms, and carried it to her Golden Palace in the clouds.

When the morning came, and the courtiers found that the child had again disappeared, a murmur arose among them; they avowed the Queen had slain her babe and eaten it, and the King's counsellors demanded that she should be brought to trial. But the King loved her with so great affection, that he would not believe a word they said, and desired them, upon peril of their lives, not to speak so basely of the Queen again.

In the third year, the Queen gave birth to a little girl; and the Good Fairy came again to her, in the night, and said to her, "Follow me!" and, taking her by the hand, she ascended with her into the clouds, till they arrived at the Golden Palace. Into this the Good Fairy Tell-true led her, and showed her her two beautiful boys, playing with each other in the golden sunlight; and when the Queen-mother rejoiced to see her children, the Good Fairy said to her: "Is thy heart not yet softened? Even now, if thou wilt confess thou hast opened the forbidden door, I will restore to thee thy two lovely children." The Queen replied, for the third time, "No, I did not open the forbidden door;" and, when she had said these words, she sank upon the earth, and her third child was taken from her.

When this got rumoured about, the next day, all the people murmured, and grew exceeding wrath, saying: "Our Queen is in truth an Ogress, and has devoured this babe also." This time, the King could not silence his counsellors. The Queen was brought before a tribunal, and, as she could not answer and defend herself, or give any account of her children, they sentenced her to be tied to a stake, and burned to death.

The wood was collected, she was fastened to the stake, and the flames began to kindle around her, when her heart was softened, and she repented of her great wickedness. "Oh! Good Fairy Tell-true!" thought she, "could I but confess that I opened the door, I should die happy. Oh! Good Fairy!" at length cried she, "I am guilty!"

When her heart was softened, that she spoke the

truth, the rain began to pour in torrents from the clouds, so that the fire was extinguished that surrounded the pile; then a bright cloud surrounded her, and from it stepped the Good Fairy Tell-true, with her two first-born children, one on each side of her, and carrying in her arms her new-born babe. Then the Fairy restored her children to her arms, and the power of speech returned to her again, and she had the full assurance of a happy future; "For," said the Fairy, "whoever will repent their sins, they shall be forgiven."

THE THREE SPINNERS.

THERE was, once upon a time, an idle young lass, who took a dislike to her spinning-wheel. Her mother thought it right to be angry with her about this, but it was of no avail. One day, the good dame lost her patience to such an extent, that she threatened to beat her daughter, and the girl began to cry and make a great noise about it. Just at this time, the Queen of the country happened to be passing by, and, hearing the sobs of the unhappy girl, ordered her carriage to stop, and, descending from it, entered the house, and peremptorily questioned the mother, why she was beating the young woman so hardly, that the cries of her child could be heard even in the street. Now, the worthy dame, though angry with her daughter, had the honour of her family at heart, and could not bear to reveal the laziness of her child; so she said to the Queen: "I could not get the distaff away from her; she insists upon being always and incessantly spinning, and, poor as I am, I cannot afford to keep her in flax."

Whereupon, the Queen replied: "There is nothing I am so fond of as a distaff; the humming of the wheel acts like a charm upon me. Pray give your daughter to me, that I may take her with me to my palace; I can give her flax in any quantity, and she can spin there just as much as she pleases."

Promotion like this was not to be despised; so the mother accepted the Queen's offer with much thankfulness, and her Majesty carried off the young woman with her.

As soon as they had arrived in the palace, the Queen took the little lass into three rooms, that were quite full of the finest flax. "Spin this off for me," said her Majesty, "and when you have done so, I will give you my eldest son for your husband. Never mind your being a poor person; industry like yours, and such a disposition for work, are a dowry worthy an Empress!"

How clever girls are! The young lass never said a word on this occasion; she was not going to throw away the chance of marrying a handsome young Prince, the eldest son of a Queen—not she, indeed! But, nevertheless, in her own mind she felt thoroughly frightened; for if she had gone on working for three hundred years without stopping, and from morning to night, she could never have got to the end of such an enormous mass of tow. As soon as she was left to

herself, she sat down to cry, and so remained for three whole days, without setting her fingers in motion. This was plainly not the way to go on, much less to begin; so, when the Queen came in to visit her on the third day, and see how she was getting on, her Majesty could not help expressing her extreme surprise, at seeing that she had made no progress whatsoever. However, the young lass excused herself, by alleging that she had felt quite overpowered with regret at leaving her mother. The Queen was willing to admit this as a reasonable excuse, but, at the same time, when she took her leave, observed significantly: "Now, my good young woman, it is high time for you to begin your work to-morrow."

When the young girl found herself alone, and utterly unaware of what to do, she went, in her trouble, to look out of the window. Here she saw

three women coming towards her: the first of them had a large flat foot, of enormous dimensions; the second, a hare-lip, the lower one so long that it hung over and covered her chin; and the third, a monstrous, overgrown, long thumb. They planted themselves in front of the window, with their eyes fixed on the chamber, and inquired of the young girl what it was that she was seeking after.

It is not exactly wise and prudent, as we all know, to take strangers too quickly into our confidence; but this poor girl was young, and in trouble, so she was glad to find a listener, and told them at once all her sorrows. The three females instantly offered her their assistance.

"If you will give us your promise," said they to her, "to invite us to your wedding, and address us as your cousins, without being ashamed of us, and ask us to sit down at your table, we will come in and spin your flax, and soon make an end of the job."

"With all my heart!" was the young girl's answer, "so come in, and begin at once."

So she let in these three singular-looking women, and cleared out a place for them in the first chamber, where they quickly set themselves to work. The first drew out the flax and turned the wheel; the second moistened the thread; the third twisted it and turned it on the table with her thumbs, and at each squeeze of the thumb that she gave it, there came down on the ground a skein of the finest thread. Each time the Queen came in to see how the work was going on, the young girl hid the Three Spinners, and showed her Majesty the quantity she had done, which sent the Queen away wondering more and more, every visit. When the first room was emptied, she passed her Spinners on into the second, and then to the third, which they finished up also. Then the three women took their leave, saying to the young girl, "Don't forget about your promise, and you will find all go right."

When the Queen saw how the young girl had completely emptied all the rooms, and had admired the flax all spun, she lost no time in fixing a day for her marriage. The Prince, overjoyed at having so clever and active a wife, fell ardently in love with her, off-hand, and asked her what he could do to oblige her.

"I have three cousins," she replied, "who have been very kind to me, and I should not like to neglect them in my hours of good fortune; will your Royal Highness permit me to invite them to my wedding, and to give them a seat at our own table?"

The Queen and the Prince saw no reason against this very praiseworthy desire of the bride. On the grand day, the three women came, in a magnificent carriage, with numerous attendants; and the bride, as she embraced them, said: "My dear cousins, how very glad I am to see you!"

"Ah!" said the Prince, aside to her, "you have very ugly relations!" Then, addressing her who had the large foot, he said to her, "How did you come by that enormous foot?"

"From using it in turning my spinning-wheel," replied the one who had turned the wheel.

To the second: "How did you get that hanging lip?"

"From using my lips in moistening the thread," replied the woman who had moistened the thread.

And to the third: "Where did you get that very large thumb?"

"From twisting the thread," said she who had twisted the thread.

"Oh!" said the Prince to himself, "is this the reward of industry? My pretty wife shall not spoil

her beauty by over-work, I will take care of that!" So, alarmed at such a prospect, he declared that his bride should never again put her hand or foot to a spinning-wheel, or touch thread with her lips. And so the little lazy puss was cleverly freed from an occupation she so much detested.

I think there is always a moral in Fairy Tales; but myself, and the Lord Chancellor, and Lord Palmerston, have often tried to find out the moral of this Fairy Tale, (for the Three Spinners, you must know, were all of them Fairies, and had been godmothers to the young girl at her birth). We all three puzzled very much about it; and, at last, the Queen, seeing how bewildered we looked, and finding that her Prime Minister and Head Lawyer could hardly attend to her business, inquired what was the matter; and then Her Majesty vouchsafed to tell us the meaning, which was:

"That as soon as ever a young woman is married, it is time she left off working, and gave all her attention to her house, her children, and her husband, whose business it is to get a living for all of them, and to look to his wife to keep his children clean and good, and his house tidy."

FOR WANT OF A NAIL.

A TRADESMAN had once transacted a good day's business at a fair, disposed of all his goods, and filled his purse with gold and silver. He prepared, afterwards, to return, in order to reach home before the evening; so he strapped his portmanteau, with the money in it, upon his horse's back, and rode off. At noon, he baited in a small town, and, as he was about to set out again, the stable-boy, who brought his horse, said to him: "Sir, a nail is wanting in the shoe on the left hind-foot of your animal." "Let it be wanting," replied the Tradesman; "I am in a hurry, and the iron will doubtless last the six leagues I have yet to travel."

Late in the afternoon, he had to dismount again, to give his horse some bread, (for, in some foreign parts, they make the beans and chaff into a loaf, and cut the horse a slice when he is hungry); and at this place, also, the boy came and told him there was a nail wanting in one of the shoes, and asked him whether he should take the horse to a farrier. "No, no; let it be," replied the master; "it will last out the two leagues I have now to travel; I am in haste." So saying, he rode off; but his horse soon began to limp, and from limping it came to stumbling, and presently, from stumbling it fell down, and broke its leg.

Thereupon, the Tradesman had to leave his horse lying in the road, to unbuckle his portmanteau, and to walk home with it upon his shoulders, where he arrived, late at night.

"And all this misfortune," said he to himself, "is owing to the want of a nail! More haste, the less speed!"

31

HEAVEN CARETH FOR THE POOR.

ONCE upon a time, in a city I shall not mention, and a country which you would be none the better pleased if I were to tell you, there were two sisters; one of them with plenty of money, and without children (for people are seldom blessed in all ways), and the other a widow, with five children, and so poor, besides, that she was in want of bread for herself and her family. Under the pressure of this need (for it is a sad thing, and tears a father's or a mother's heart, to see their young ones hungry, and not be able to give them food), the poor widow went in search of her sister, and said to her: "My children are suffering from want,—you are rich; give me a morsel of bread for the poor little things." But the rich woman had a heart of stone, and she answered: "We have got nothing in the house;" and then she dismissed her sister, with stiff politeness.

Now, was not that a cruel woman,—not to say, a wicked, unkind, unnatural sister? But let us see what came of this hard-heartedness. Never be in a hurry, my dear children, to say, the cruel and the wicked get on well, and thrive: wait a while, and look to the end. Everybody is not punished in this world for the wrong they do; but a great many are, for all that, and they make their own punishment, out of their own evil minds.

Some hours after the two sisters had met, it was dinner-time, and home came the rich lady's husband, so gallant, and gay, and smiling, and quite ready to enjoy the good dinner that he knew was always ready for him. He went up to the table, and began to cut off the loaf a piece of bread; but what was his horror, at seeing that, at the first stroke of the knife, drops of blood—real blood—fell from the loaf, just as if he had been slicing at the heart of a fellow-creature! "How

is this, wife?" he asked of the terrified woman, who knew too well, and, in her fright, told him all that had passed between her and her sister. At this the good man was very angry; and, taking up the dish of roast meat from the table, and wrapping up a fresh loaf in a napkin, he went off, in all haste, to relieve the poor distressed widow, and give her hungry children a plentiful meal. I need not say how welcome he was, and how the good-natured fellow enjoyed the eager delight of the young ones, when they caught sight of the nice hot roast leg of mutton, with plenty of gravy! He saw them all well set down to table, and clattering their knives and forks, and chattering with glee, and then went out into the street, to go back to his own house. No sooner had he turned the corner, than he heard a loud shouting, and, lifting up his eyes, saw a dense cloud of smoke darkening the sky, and then a column of flame shooting up through it, and a shower of sparks succeeding. He pushed on, in alarm, and soon perceived that it was his own house that was on fire! In that one short hour, all his wealth—his furniture and plate, and his title-deeds, securities, and bank-notes—all were lost in the devouring flames; nothing was left to him but his evil-minded wife, who ran about wringing her hands, and crying out to all her neighbours: "What will become of us? what shall we do? how shall we live? we shall perish with hunger!"

"Not so, my dear sister," replied the good widow, who ran up to her assistance at the moment; "Heaven feeds the poor."

The woman who had been rich was, in her turn, compelled to have recourse to begging for a subsistence; but no one would take pity on her, who had been so unfeeling for others; and her sister, no longer remembering her hardness of heart, shared with her the alms she herself received.

JACK IN LUCK.

"MASTER," said Jack, one fine morning, "I have served you faithfully for seven years; my time is up; and, if you will be good enough to pay me my wages, I should very much like to go home and see my mother."

His master replied: "What you say is true, Jack; you have been a faithful, honest lad; and as your service has been, so shall be your recompense." Thus saying, he gave Jack a lump of gold as big as his head.

Jack drew his handkerchief out of his pocket, wrapped his golden ingot in it, and, slinging it across his stick, swung it over his shoulders, and began to make his way to his native village, where his parents still resided.

As he went along, carefully putting one foot before the other upon the ground, he came in sight of a man on horseback, who rode along gaily enough, without any trouble to himself, on a brisk, lively-looking animal. "Ah!" said Jack to himself, loud enough to

JACK FINDS A HORSE TOO NOISY, AND WISHES FOR A QUIET COW.

be heard, "what a very fine thing is this riding on horseback! There one sits at one's ease, as comfortably as in a chair, getting to the end of one's journey without knocking one's feet against the stones, or wearing out one's shoes."

The rider, who heard this speech of Jack's, stopped him, and asked him why he walked, if he thought it such a mighty fine thing to ride.

"Well, I am obliged, you see," said Jack; "I have got this lump to carry home; it is gold, to be sure, but then it is very heavy, and hurts my shoulder dreadfully to carry it."

"Well, well," said the man on horseback, "we

No. 5.

might soon settle that; could not we change? I'll give you my horse, and you shall give me your heavy lump of gold.—I see it is a great burthen to you."

"With all my heart!" said Jack, "but I'll tell you fairly, you will soon be tired of your bargain."

The man got off his horse, took the gold, and gladly helped Jack on to the horse; then he gave the reins into his hands, and said: "Now, when you want to go quicker, you must chuckle with your tongue, and cry, 'Gee up! gee up!'"

Jack was as pleased as Punch, when he found himself on the top of a horse, riding along freely and gaily. After a bit, he thought to himself, "It would

33

be as well to go rather quicker;" so he cried, "Gee up! gee up!" as the man had told him. The horse, hearing the "Gee up! gee up!" knew he must make haste, so off he set at a hard trot, and before Jack knew what he was about, he was thrown over head and heels into a ditch which divided the fields from the road. When the horse found out he had thrown his rider into the mire, he would have bolted off, if he had not been stopped by a Countryman, who was coming that way, driving a cow before him.

Jack soon got upon his legs, but he was sadly put out about his tumble. "There is no fun in this," said Jack, "to get upon the back of a beast who cannot stand on his legs, and who, without ceremony, pitches one off, so as nearly to break one's neck. I'll take good care I will never ride on that brute again. Give me a cow, that is the animal I like,—one may walk behind her without any fear; besides, look at the advantage of making sure of milk, butter, and cheese every day. Ah! what would I not give for such a cow!"

"Well," said the Peasant, "such an advantage you may soon enjoy; I will exchange my cow for your horse."

To this Jack agreed, with delight, and gave up the horse, with a thousand thanks; when the Peasant, throwing himself upon it, rode off with as much haste as he could.

Jack now drove off his cow, as steadily as he could, before him, thinking of his lucky exchange, in this manner: "I have a bit of bread, and I can, as often as I please, eat it with butter and cheese; and when I am thirsty, I can milk my cow and have a draught; and what more can I want?"

As soon, then, as he came to an inn, he halted, and ate, with much satisfaction, all the bread he had brought with him for his dinner and supper, and washed it down with a glass of beer, to buy which he spent his two last farthings. When this was over, he drove his cow on again, in the direction of his mother's village. The day, in the meantime, became hotter and hotter, as noontide approached, and just then Jack came to a common, which was an hour's journey across. Here he got into such a state of heat, that his tongue clave to the roof of his mouth, and he thought to himself: "This will never do; I will just milk my cow, and refresh myself." Jack, therefore, tied her to the stump of an old tree, and, having no pail, put his leathern cap below the cow, and began working away, but not one drop of milk could he squeeze out. He had placed himself, too, in a very awkward manner; and at last, the cow perceiving this, and growing impatient, gave him such a kick on the head, that he toppled over on the ground, and for a long time did not know where he was. Fortunately, not many hours after, a Butcher passed by, trundling a young pig along upon a wheelbarrow. "What is the matter here?" exclaimed he, helping up poor Jack; and Jack then told him all that had happened. The Butcher then handed him his flask, and said: "There, take a drink, it will revive you. Your cow is too old a beast to give you any milk; she is worth nothing at the best, but to be turned out to plough, or to fall into the butcher's hands."

"Eh! eh!" said Jack, pulling his hair over his eyes, "who would have thought it? It is very well when one can kill a beast like that at home, and make a profit of the flesh; but, for my part, I can't eat cow-beef, it is too tough for me—besides, it has no flavour. Ah! a young pig like yours, now, is something like; my mouth waters at the thought of the taste of it, to say nothing of the sausages!"

"Well, now," said the Butcher, "I won't mind, just for the love I bear you, making an exchange with you; you shall have my pig, and I will take your cow."

"Heaven bless you for your kindness!" said Jack; and, giving up the cow, he quickly untied the pig from the barrow, and took in his hand the string with which it was tied.

Jack walked on again, reflecting upon his great good-luck, and how everything had turned out just as he wished, and his vexations had all ended to his advantage. Presently, a boy met him, carrying a fine white goose under his arm, and, after they had said "Good day!" to each other, Jack began to boast about his luck, and to tell of the profitable exchanges he had made. The boy related, on his part, how he was carrying the goose to a christening-feast. "Just lift it," said he to Jack, holding it up by its wings; "just feel how heavy it is! Why, it has been up to fatten for these last eight weeks; and whoever bites it when it is cooked, will have to wipe the grease off each side of his mouth, I'll warrant you!"

"Yes," said Jack, weighing it in his hand as he spoke, "it is heavy, truly; but then, my pig's no trifle, I assure you."

While he was thus speaking, the boy kept peering and peeping about, turning his head suspiciously this way and that; and, at last, he asked Jack if he was sure it was all right about the pig; "because," said he, "in the village I have just passed through, there is a great hue and cry about a pig that has been stolen out of the sty of the Mayor himself; and I am afraid, very much afraid, that is the very pig you are now holding by the string. They have sent out people into all parts, to find it. It would be a bad job for you, indeed, if they were to find the pig in your hands. The best thing for you to do is, to hide it in some deep ditch."

Honest Jack was struck all of a heap with fright on hearing this, and cried, "Heaven help me, in this my fresh calamity! You know the neighbourhood better than I do," said he to the boy, "so pray take my pig, and hide it, and let me have your goose."

"That will be a losing game to me," said the boy, "but then I should be sorry to be the cause of your falling into misfortune;" and so saying, he took hold of the string, and drove off Master Piggy as fast as he would go, by a side path; while Jack, relieved of his cares, took the goose up, and putting it under his arm, trudged away home with a light heart.

"If my judgment is worth anything," thought Jack to himself, "I have gained even by this exchange; for, first, there is the prime roast; and then, look what a lot of fat will drop out, so that we shall get goose-broth half the year round; and then, look at the fine white feathers!—when I once get them into my pillow,

34

I shall sleep without rocking! How delighted my poor dear old mother will be!"

As he came to the nearest village to his own home, there stood on the road a Knife-grinder, with his barrow by the hedge-side, whirling his wheel around, and singing:

"Scissors, and razors, and such like, I grind,
While my rags all gaily are flying behind."

Jack stopped, and looked at him for a bit, and then said: "You are merry enough; I suppose it is the thriving trade you carry on makes you so jolly?"

"Yes, indeed," answered the Grinder, "this business has a golden bottom. A true Knife-grinder is a man who finds money in his pocket whenever he puts his hand into it. But, my goodness! what a fine goose you have got! Why, where did you buy that?"

"I did not buy it at all," said Jack, "but I got it in exchange for my pig." "And the pig?" "I exchanged for my cow." "And the cow?" "Well, I exchanged a horse for her." "And the horse?" "Oh! I gave a lump of gold for him, as big as my head." "And the gold?" "Well, that was my wages for seven years' faithful servitude."

"And I see you have known how to benefit yourself by each change," said the Grinder; "could you now only manage to hear the money chinking and rattling in your pockets as you walked along, why, your fortune would be made."

"True," said Jack; "but how can I manage that?"

"Easy enough," said the Grinder; "you must become a Grinder, like me. There is nothing difficult to learn in my trade, and all you will want will be a grindstone; the other necessaries will find themselves. Here is one; it is a little worn, certainly, but then you shall have it cheap; so I will not ask anything more for it than your goose. Is this to your liking?"

"How can you ask me such a question?" said Jack; "why, I shall be the luckiest man in the world—only having to dip my hand in my pocket whenever I want money; I shall have nothing to care for any more!" So saying, he handed over the fat goose, and got in exchange the grindstone.

"Now," said the Grinder, picking up an ordinary big flint stone which lay near, "now, there you have a capital stone, upon which, if you only beat them long enough, you can straighten all your old nails! Take it, and use it carefully."

Jack took up the stone, and walked on with a satisfied heart, his eyes dancing with joy. "I must have been born," said he, "to a heap of luck; everything happens just as I wish, as if I were a Sunday child!" Soon, however, poor Jack, having been on his legs all day, began to feel very tired, and he was plagued, too, with hunger, since he had eaten up all his provisions at one time, in his delight about his cow bargain. At last, he was so tired, he felt quite unable to go a step farther, for the stones were very heavy, and a great hindrance to him, and encumbered him dreadfully. Just at this instant, the thought came into his head, that it would be a very good thing if he had no need to carry the stones any longer; and, at the same moment, he came to a stream. Here he determined to rest, and refresh himself with a drink of the bright water; and, so that the stones might not hurt him in kneeling down, he laid them carefully by the side of him on the bank. This done, he stooped down, to scoop up some water in his hand, and then, by some accident, he pushed one stone a little too far, so that presently they both fell plump into the water. Jack, as soon as he saw them sinking to the bottom, jumped up, and danced for joy, and then kneeled down, and heartily returned thanks, with tears in his eyes, that he should have been able, in so nice a way, and without any act of his own, to get rid of these heavy stones, which were the only things that hindered him from getting to the end of his journey. "I am the luckiest man," said Jack, "under the sun!"

Then, with a light heart, and free from every burthen, he gaily leaped along, singing all the way, until he got to his mother's house.

THE DONKEY, THE TABLE, AND THE STICK.

ONCE upon a time, there was a Tailor, who had three children, and only one Goat, to feed them all with her milk; so, you may guess, the poor Goat stood in need of good hay and fodder, besides being taken out every day to browse at her leisure, and crop the nice herbs and short grass. This was the duty of the Tailor's sons, each in his turn. One day, the eldest took the Goat into the churchyard, where she enjoyed some fine grass, and browsed, and frisked, and leaped at her ease. In the evening, when it was time to go home, the lad asked the Goat, "Have you had enough?" to which she replied:

"I have had quite enough
Of jolly good stuff!
Ma-ma-ma-ma!"

"Then let us go in," said the lad; and he took the rope, and led her into the stable. Just as they were going in, they met the old Tailor. "Now," said he, "has the Goat been well fed?"

"Yes," replied the boy, "she has had enough, and of good stuff."

But the father, wishing to make quite sure, himself, went to the stable, and began to caress his favourite, and said to her: "Riquette, have you had all you wish for?" The Goat replied mischievously:

"To dine in a graveyard is only a farce;
There's plenty of jumping, but little of grass."

"What is this I hear?" cried the Tailor, as he hurried from the stable, and addressed himself to his eldest son: "How could you tell me such a falsehood? You said the Goat had eaten all she wanted, and made a capital dinner; and, after all, I find you left her to starve!" And, in his anger, he took up his sleeve-board, and ran after him, and gave him a good hiding.

Next day, it was the second son's turn to take the

Goat out. He looked out, along the hedge of a garden, a place where there was some capital fresh grass, and this the Goat ate up greedily, to the very last blade. When evening came, and it was time to go within, he put the question to the Goat, as to whether she was satisfied.

> "I've had enough, and plenty;
> Indeed, there's enough for twenty,"

was her reply.

"Well, then, we will go home," said the boy; and he took the beast to the stable, where he fastened her up carefully.

"Well," asked the Tailor, when he saw his second son coming into the room, "has the Goat had her just rights to-day?"

"Oh yes, father; she has had enough and to spare."

But the Tailor, remembering what had happened on the previous evening, bethought himself of the proverb, "It is the master's eye that makes the horse grow fat;" so he determined to go and see to the Goat himself, and inquire of her how she had fared. So he went to the stable; "Riquette," said he, "have you had your fill to-day?"

To which the Goat made answer:

> "Plenty of jumping,
> And little of meat;
> A ditch full of water,
> And nothing to eat!"

"What a wretch!" exclaimed the Tailor, "to allow such a valuable animal to starve!" And, with a sound thrashing with the sleeve-board, he drove his second son out of the door.

The day after, it came to the turn of the third and youngest son; and he, to make things better, sought out a copse, where some delicious wild flowers and tender young leaves afforded a dainty meal for the Goat, who browsed among them, and seemed to enjoy herself very much. When evening came, he inquired of the Goat, before leading her home, whether she had eaten as much as she wanted; to which she replied:

> "Too much, and more than enough,
> Of leaves, and flowers, and dainty stuff."

So he took the Goat in, and fastened her up, and made his report to his father; who, however, having now thoroughly lost confidence, went to the stable, as before, and asked the same question: "Have you had enough to eat, Riquette?" The wicked beast replied:

> "Through the woods, all the day, I did nothing but rush;
> Grass grows in the field, Sir, and not in the bush."

"Only to think of such lying!" exclaimed the Tailor, in a great rage; "one and all cheats and rogues; each as unnatural as the other, and all deceiving their poor old father!" Up he took the very handy sleeve-board again, and plump, plump, it came down on the unlucky shoulders of his unfortunate youngest son, so hard and so fast, that the poor young lad was only too glad to save himself by running out of the house.

Now, at last, there was nobody left in the house but the old Tailor, all alone by himself, and only his Goat in the stable. Next day, the old man cooled down a

little, and went in to the Goat, and patted it, and said: "Now, then, my little kidling, I will take you out to browse, myself." So he took the Goat by the halter, and led her along, by some green hedges, to places where the nice fresh young grass was growing, and to many a corner, such as Goats most do fancy. "This time, at any rate," said he, "you can enjoy yourself to your heart's content." And there he let her stay until the evening; then he asked her: "Have you had enough, my kidling?" And she said:

> "Plenty, plenty;
> Enough for twenty."

"Let us go home, then," said the old Tailor; and he took her to her stable, and fastened her up tightly. Then he went out, but turned back as he reached the door, to repeat his question, "Have you had enough?"

But the Goat took it no better this time than before, and replied to him:

> "It is very fine talking;
> I've had nothing but walking."

When the Tailor heard this, he was quite taken aback, and began to think, that he might have turned his children out of doors most unjustly. "Listen," said he, "you ungrateful creature! It would be too little punishment to turn you out of doors, as well as my poor boys; I intend to mark you in such a manner, that you can never again venture to show yourself among honest tailors!"

And in an instant he had seized his razor, soaped the Goat's head, and shaved it as clean as the back of your hand. Then, as the sleeve-board would have been too great an honour for such a rascal, he took up his goose, and gave the Goat a few thrusts with it on the back, that set her off, flying and kicking with prodigious leaps.

Thus finding himself all alone, in his empty house, the old Tailor was sorely disconsolate. He would have been glad enough to have fetched his three boys back again; but no one knew what had become of them.

The eldest had gone and placed himself as an apprentice with a Cabinet-maker. Being a clever, industrious lad, he applied himself, briskly and carefully, to learning the business, which is that of a superior craftsman; for fitting and joining the various pieces, and polishing and planing the fine woods, is no easy work. When he had reached the age when it was time for him to go the rounds of the trade (which every young workman abroad does, going from town to town, and so learning whatever may be new in his craft), his master made him a present of a little table of ordinary wood, and by no means showy to look at, but which was gifted with one precious property: that whenever any one set it down before him, and said to it, "Table, cover yourself," it covered itself immediately with a handsome white table-cloth and a napkin, a knife and fork, dishes filled with various kinds of meats, as many as there was room for, and a large glass of ruby wine, that would make a man's heart glad. The young fellow thought himself a rich man for the rest of his days, and set to work to travel through the world at his pleasure, without a care

hether the times were good or bad, and whether he
ould find dinner ready or not. Besides, whenever
felt inclined to eat, he had no need to go anywhere,
t would set down his table in a wood, or a field, or
herever he chose, and say to it, "Cover yourself," and
handsome dinner was served to him in a moment.
At last, it came into his head to go back to his
her's house, in the hope that time would have
eased his anger, and that, as the possessor of such
onderful table, he might make sure of a good re-
tion. On his road thither, he went one night to an
, that was full of travellers, who saluted him, and
ed him to make one at their table, as he would other-
e find some difficulty in getting anything to eat.
"No, no!" replied he, "keep your cabbage-soup to
rselves; and, in return for your politeness, I invite
 all to come and take part of my dinner with me."
At this they all laughed, thinking he was a rare
ny fellow; however, he quietly set down his table
the middle of the room, and said to it, like a con-
or, "Cover yourself;" and so it did, with dishes of
at, such as had never been seen to come out of the
chen of that inn, and the very smell of which
eeably tickled the palates of the guests. "Now
n, gentlemen," he exclaimed, "sit down to table."
ing that he really meant it, the guests did not give
 the trouble of farther entreaty, but each man,
fe in hand, performed his duty bravely. What
onished everybody was, that no sooner was a dish
ptied, than another, and a full one, too, took its
ce immediately. The Host, who was in a corner of
 room, saw all that was going on, but did not know
at to think of it; except that he thought, that such
lever cook would be exceedingly useful at his inn.
he young Cabinet-maker and his party spent the
ater part of the night in enjoying themselves; at
, they went to rest, and the young man, when he
down in bed, placed his wonderful table alongside
im. He slept soundly, as do the young and fortu-
e; not so his Host, who was an envious, covetous,
 greedy-hearted man. He remembered that he had
is granary an old table, just like the one the young
n had; so he went on tiptoe, and without his shoes,
ook for it, and brought it down, and put it in the
ce of the other, which he carried off, hugging him-
f at his success in the dirty trick.
ext morning, the young Cabinet-maker, after having
d the night's expenses, took up his table, and went
way, without perceiving that one table had been
n him for another. It was the middle of the day
n he reached his father's house, and tho old Tailor
comed him back right joyfully. "Well, my son,"
 he, "and what have you learnt, all this while?"
The business of a Cabinet-maker, father."
That is a good trade," replied the old man; "but
 much have you brought from your journey?"
Well, father, the best bit of money in my budget,
hat little table."
he Tailor looked at it very knowingly, and turned
 both sides, and then observed: "If that be your
ter-piece, it is nothing very magnificent; why, it
 piece of second-hand furniture, that won't hold
h longer together!"

"Ah! but," replied the son, "it is a magic table;
when I order it to cover itself, it furnishes a capital
dinner, of excellent dishes, I can tell you, and wine
that rejoices one's heart. Go, and ask our relatives
and friends to come and dine with us; that table will
supply enough to satisfy all."

So the Tailor went out; and when he mentioned the
excellent dinner, by first-rate cooks, that he was going
to give, to celebrate his son's return, it was not long
before he had got a good party together, ready to enjoy
themselves with a good dinner, and make merry with
capital wine, in good company. Many came in, shaking
their stomachs, and licking their lips, and as hungry
as hunters; and when they were all assembled, the
son brought out his table, and placed it in the middle
of the room, and said to it, "Cover yourself." But it
didn't! nor did it seem even to hear the order, but
remained just as empty as an ordinary table, when a
poor man orders dinner, without having any money in
his pocket to pay for it. Then the poor young fellow
saw at once that he had been cheated, and stood there,
all ashamed, just like a liar caught in the fact, the jest
of all his relatives, who had all to go back to their
homes, without bit or sup, which, I need not tell you,
was the cause of a great deal of grumbling. His father
said nothing, but looked a great deal, retired quickly
to his shop-board, and took up his needle and thimble.
As for the son, poor fellow! he went and engaged
himself with a Cabinet-maker, and set to hard work
again. Thus much for the eldest son.

Now for the second boy. He had entered into
apprenticeship with a Miller; and, when his time was
out, his master said to him: "As a recompense for your
good conduct, I intend to give you a noble donkey."

"A donkey, Sir!" said the young man; "what on
earth shall I do with a donkey? A donkey wants
grass, and I have not got a house, nor even a garden.
A donkey wants feeding, and so do I; and I had much
rather feed myself than a donkey."

"Ah! you were always a clever fellow," said the
Miller, "and have a good deal to say, that you might
spare yourself the trouble of saying. But never mind;
this is a donkey of a very remarkable breed, and one
that won't put up with either saddle or harness."

"So much the worse for me," said the Miller's
apprentice; "what is the beast good for, then, if one
can neither ride nor drive him? It can't be for his
company, for he is the worst of all singers, and who
can talk to an ass?"

"You might do worse," said the Miller; "but, as I
told you before, this is a noble ass—an extraordinary
ass!"

"All right," said the Tailor's son; "but what is
there wonderful about him?"

"He produces gold!" replied the Miller; "all you
have to do is, to lay down a clean cloth, and make him
step over it, and then, when the donkey steps on the
cloth, all you have to say is, '_Bricklebrit! Bricklebrit!_'
and out comes the gold from his ears."

"Well, that is a wonderful animal, indeed!" said
the young man.

After this, he did not despise the donkey, but cheerfully accepted him as a gift, thanked his master, and

37

set out on his travels over the world. Whenever he wanted money, all he had to do was, to get a clean cloth, and say to his donkey, "*Bricklebrit! Bricklebrit!*" and the good little creature rained out a shower of gold-pieces, without giving him any other trouble than picking them up. So, wherever he went, the best of everything was good enough for him; and as for the price, he liked best what was most dear, for, lucky fellow that he was! his purse was always full.

After travelling about for some time, the thought of home came over his mind, in the midst of all his pleasures and enjoyments. What was all his gold and luxuries to him? He wanted to sit on the old bench under the old cottage porch, and hear his old father sing, and even scold, as he stitched and stitched, hour after hour, on the shop-board in the window. He remembered the village-green, and the old elm, and the geese on the common, and the stream in which he used to float his paper boats, and the mill, whose great arms he had so often watched, swinging round with a surging noise, on the breezy hill-top. In a word, he was homesick, and he wanted to go back, and be quiet, and make his father happy, and enjoy himself among his friends and relations, in the scenes of his boyhood. So he bethought himself, that by this time, surely, his father's anger against him must be appeased, and that he might safely go back to him, and, accompanied as he was by such a treasure of a donkey, might make sure of a good reception.

So off he set, cheerily, on his way to the old house at home; but it happened that, as his road lay by the same way that his elder brother had taken, he put up at the same inn, at which that unhappy lad had been robbed of his magic table.

He was leading his donkey by the bridle, as he came up to the door, and the Host stepped out, in a bustle, to take it, and tie it up; but the young man said to him: "I always tie up my Grizzle myself in his stable, for I like to know, always, where he is."

The Host was a little surprised at such remarkable attention to a mere donkey, and surmised, that a fellow who looked after his donkey himself, was not likely to be a very extensive customer. But when the stranger put his hand in his pocket, and drew forth two gold pieces, and ordered of the best to be served to him immediately, the Host opened his eyes wide, and hurried off to the kitchen and the cellar, to look out something superior for such a noble guest. After dinner, the traveller called for his bill, which the rascally Host did his best to enlarge to the utmost possible amount, and told the young man that it came to just two more gold pieces than he had given him. Instead of objecting to the amount, as the Innkeeper expected, the traveller put his hand in his pocket, to pay him what he asked, but found his pockets empty. The Host looked blank.

"Wait a minute," said the young man, carelessly, "I will go and get some money;" and he went out, taking the table-cloth with him.

The Host understood nothing that the traveller had said, but was curious to see what he was going to do; so he followed him, and, as the young fellow had fastened the stable-door behind him, he peeped through

the window, and saw the stranger stretch out the table-cloth under the donkey, and heard him say "*Bricklebrit! Bricklebrit!*" and then the animal began to let fall gold from his ears, like a very shower of rain.

"Stars and Garters!" cried the Innkeeper, in a very fury of envy and avarice; "all new ducats, too! A treasure like that is a fine bit of luck for his master!"

The young man paid his reckoning, and went to bed; but the Innkeeper slipped into the stable during the night, carried away the donkey that coined money, and put another in its place. Next morning, the young fellow took the donkey, and went on his way again, in the full persuasion that he had with him his magic beast. He reached his father's house at mid-day, just as his elder brother had done before him, and met with an equally warm reception at his father's hands.

"What became of you, my son, after leaving me?" inquired the old man.

"I am a Miller, my dear father," he replied.

"What have you brought back with you?"

"Only a donkey."

"We have quite enough of that breed here at home, already," said the father; "you had better have brought us a nice goat."

"But," replied the son, "this is not a beast, such as others are; this is a magical donkey. I have but to say, '*Bricklebrit!*' and at once he lets fall gold ducats, enough to fill a table-cloth. Go, and ask our relations to come here; I should like to make them all wealthy men at one stroke."

"That is just the style of thing I like," said the Tailor; "I need not tire myself with stitching any more."

And away went the old fellow, with a light heart, to invite his relations to come together, each of them to have a sum of money presented to him. Didn't they come at once? and curiously enough, and anxiously they looked on, as the young Miller spread a clean white cloth on the floor, and brought his donkey on the middle of it. "Now," said he, with pomposity looking round on his relatives, "attention!—'*Bricklebrit!*'"

But this donkey understood nothing whatsoever about magic; and what he did let drop, did not at all resemble pieces of money. The poor fellow saw that he had been robbed, pulled a long face, and apologised to his relations, who went back to their homes, quite as much beggars as they had come. His father took to his needle and scissors again, perforce; and, as for himself, he got a place as servant at a mill.

The third brother had entered an apprenticeship with a Turner; and, as the trade is a hard one to learn, stopped with him some time longer than his brothers had done with their masters. They wrote to him, and told him the misfortunes that had befallen them, and how the Innkeeper had stolen the magic gifts of which they had been the possessors.

When the young Turner had finished his apprenticeship, and the time for his departure had arrived, his master, in rewarding his good conduct, gave him a bag, in which was a large stick.

"The bag I can understand," said the youth; "I can carry that over my shoulders. But what is

ood of this stick? it will only fatigue me with its
eight."

"I am going to tell you its use," replied his master;
if any one ill-uses you, all you have to do, is to say,
Stick! stick! come out of the bag!' and in an
nstant the stick will leap on to their shoulders, and
elabour them so vigorously, that they won't be able
o move for eight hours afterwards; and the game
ill go on, until you say, 'Stick! stick! jump into
our bag!'"

The young fellow thanked his master, and went
aily on his way, with the bag on his shoulders. If
ny one came too close, and wanted to molest him, all
e did was to say, "Stick! stick! come out of your
ag!" and the cudgel went to work at once in dusting
he jackets of those gentlemen, without giving them
ime to take them off, and so quickly and smartly, that
o one passing by could tell where it came from.

One evening, he arrived at the inn, where his bro-
hers had been so wickedly robbed. Here he laid down
is haversack upon the table before him, and began to
alk of the many wonderful things he had seen in his
ravels over the world. "Yes," said he, "there are
ome who have found tables that cover themselves
ith dishes and meat, without any cooks; and asses,
lso, that spit out gold; and many other fine things
s well. But what are all these, that these people
ave seen, and also that I have seen myself?
othing!—I say positively, nothing, in comparison
ith the treasure that I carry in my bag!"

Hereupon, the Host, who was always listening to
hat the travellers talked about, pricked up his ears,
nd said to himself: "What can there possibly be in
he bag? No doubt, it is full of precious stones; I
hould like to add them to the store I have already in
he donkey and the table,—all good things go by
hrees."

When it was time to go to bed, the young man
tretched himself along a bench, and put his bag
nder his head, by way of a pillow. When the Inn-
eeper believed him to be fast asleep, he drew near to
im stealthily, and gave a gentle pull at the bag, to
ry if he could draw it away, and put another in its
lace. But the traveller watched him for some time,
s a cat does a mouse, before she pounces upon it; and
ust at the moment when the villain gave a stronger
ull than before, cried out, "Stick! stick! come out
f your bag!" and instantly out jumped the stick on
o the scoundrel's shoulders, and hammered away at
im, until there was not a whole thread left in his
oat. The unhappy wretch bawled out for quarter,
ity, pardon! but, the more he yelled, the more the
udgel drubbed his shoulders, and so heartily, that at
ast he fell down exhausted on the ground.

Then the Turner said to him: "Now, my fine
ellow, you have caught it this time! All good things,
ou know, go by threes; and if you don't at once
estore to me the donkey and the table that you stole
rom my brothers, why, we will just begin this same
ance over again."

"Oh, no! pray, don't!" cried the Host, in a feeble
oice; "I will give back all; only make that wicked
ttle imp go back into his bag!"

"It would only be doing justice to give you another
dose," said the young fellow; "but I pardon you, if
you perform your promise." Then he added, "Stick!
stick! go back to your bag!" And the stick did so,
and left the Innkeeper to rub his bruised bones in
peace.

Next day, the Turner arrived at his father's house,
with the magic table and the gold donkey. The
Tailor was delighted to see him, and asked what trade
he had learnt.

"My dear father," he replied, "I have become a
Turner."

"A good business," said the father; "and pray
what have you brought home from your travels?"

"A fine specimen, my dear father; a stick, in a bag."

"A cudgel!" exclaimed the father; "that was worth
the trouble, certainly, when you can cut as many as
you want, in any wood!"

"But not such an one as mine, dear father. When
I say, 'Stick! stick! come out of your bag!' it leaps
out on those who want to hurt me, and sprinkles them
with a shower of hard thumps, until they are glad to
ask for mercy. With this cudgel, may it please you,
I have recovered the donkey and the table, of which
that thief over there had robbed my brothers. Let us
send for them here; and go you, and invite all our
relations; I intend to give them a treat, and fill their
pockets."

The Tailor went to look up his relations, but with
no very great confidence in the result, after his recent
mortifying disappointments. The Turner laid down a
cloth on the floor of the room, and led upon it the
donkey; then he invited his brother to pronounce the
magic words. The Miller said, "Bricklebrit! Bricklebrit!" and the gold-pieces began to fall down as thick
as hail, nor did the shower cease until every one had
got as much money as they could possibly carry—(you
would have liked to have been there, I think, my
young readers!) Then the Turner brought out the
table, and said to his brother the Cabinet-maker, "Now
is your turn, my boy!" Scarcely had he uttered the
words, "Table, cover yourself!" than a rare dinner was
served, with the richest sauces and finest wines. So
there was such a feasting as the oldest man among
them had never seen before in that house; and all the
company stuck to the table, and kept up the merry
feast until night.

Then the Tailor carefully locked up in a drawer his
needle, thimble, yard-measure, sleeve-board, and goose,
and lived in peace and happiness, with his three sons.

"Is that all?" you ask; "what became of the
Goat, that had been the cause of the Tailor turning
his three sons out of doors?"

I am just going to tell you. As she had always
been very proud of her hairy face, she ran off to conceal herself in a Fox's earth, until her beard should be
grown again. When the Fox came home at night to
supper, and popped his head into his hole, he saw two
large round eyes, that shone like burning coals. Fear
seized him; he drew back his head, and ran off at
once. As he was hurrying along, he ran against a
Bear, who, seeing he was in great terror, said to him:

"Hallo, friend Reynard! whither away now? What gives you that scared look? there are no hounds out at this time o' night."

"Oh!" answered the Fox, "there is, at the bottom of my hole, a terrific monster, who stared at me with fiery eyes!"

"We'll soon drive the gentleman out," said the Bear, and he went and looked down to the bottom of the Fox's hole; but, as soon as he saw those terrible eyes, fear got the better of him also, and, to avoid disputes with the monster, he thought it best to shuffle off as quickly as possible.

On his way, a Bee met him; and the lady, observing that he did not seem quite sure of his skin, said to him: "Eh, Godpapa! you wear a very woful look; where is all your old fun gone to?"

"It is all very fine talking," replied the Bear; "but at the bottom of the Fox's hole is a monster of terrible aspect, and we can't get him out."

The Bee made answer: "Really, I feel quite pity for you, Godpapa. I am only a weak little creature, whom you disdain to look at in your road; but, nevertheless, I am of opinion that I can be of use in this instance."

So she flew off to the Fox's earth, placed herself on the shaven head of the Goat, and stung her so sharply, that she could not help crying out, "Ma-ma!" and then rushed into the wood, like one frantic. From that time to this, nobody has ever known what became of her,—except that, just about that period, the Bear invited the Fox to a supper, which they both of them seemed to relish uncommonly.

IF THE STARS WERE TO FALL!

LOOK up in the heavens, on a bright starlight summer night: don't the stars look like so many golden guineas? and how full our pockets would be, and how many pretty things we should be able to buy, if, only, the stars were to fall!

Once upon a time, there was a little girl, whose father and mother were both dead. So poor, so very poor, was this little one, that she had neither roof to cover her, nor bed to lie down upon; neither had she any clothes but those she had on her little body, and but a morsel of bread, that some kind soul had given her out of charity. But, for all this, she was good and pious.

Now, you must not forget to think, my dears, that if you—who are tenderly nursed, and delicately cared for, and warmly clothed, and fed with the best of food, and plenty of it, and whom every one tries to please and amuse—find it so hard to be good children, and to do your duty to your good fathers and kind mothers, without murmuring, and to pray thankfully to God, without wishing for anything more than you have got;—if you, my dears, find this not quite so easy, think, oh! think, what must it be to a poor, cold, starving child, without home, or parents, or friends, to be always good, and pious, and thankful to God!

Consider her temptations, how many and how great, and yours, how small, and how carefully you are shielded from them. So, now you can understand how much I mean, when I tell you, that this poor, forlorn, desolate, starving, cold little girl was good and pious.

Thus abandoned, as she was, by all the world, she set out on her life-journey, trusting in the care and kindness of God. On her road, she met with a poor man, who said to her: "Alas! I am sorely hungry; give me a little bit to eat." She held forth to him her

morsel of bread—the whole of it—and said to him: "Heaven has come to your aid." Then she went on her way again.

A little farther on, just at a turning in the road, she saw a young child sitting by the wayside, weeping. "What is the matter, my little man?" she kindly inquired, in the hope of soothing his little troubles. "Oh! I have lost my cap! oh, my head is so cold! oh, give me something to put on it!" She took off her little cap at once, and gave it to him. A little farther, she met with another child, who was frozen with cold, for want of a jacket, and she gave it her own. Lastly, another child begged her petticoat of her, and she gave away that also.

It was now night, and she was drawing nigh to a wood, in which it was her intention to sleep. Just as she was entering a copse, another child asked her for her chemise. The pious child considered for a moment, and then said to herself: "It is quite dark night, no one will see me; I can easily give her my chemise." And then she gave away that, too.

So that, at last, she possessed nothing in the world whatsoever. But, at that very moment, the stars in the heaven above began to fall, and, on reaching the ground, were changed into bright shining guineas; and though she had taken off her chemise, and given it away, she found herself, nevertheless, arrayed in the finest linen. Then she gathered up the guineas,—there was a rare heap of them, surely!—and so was made rich for all the rest of her life.

"WILT THOU HAVE THIS MAN FOR THY WEDDED HUSBAND?"

THE MAN IN THE BEARSKIN.

THERE was, once upon a time, a very fine young fellow, who determined to seek his fortune as a Soldier, and he became so brave and courageous, that he was always in the front ranks in the heat of the battle. As long as there was any fighting going on, all went well enough; but when peace was proclaimed, he received his discharge, and the Captain told him he was free to go where he liked. His parents, meanwhile, had died; and as he had no longer any home to go to, he paid a visit to his brothers, and asked them to give him a home until war should again break out. His brothers, however, were hard-hearted, and said, "What could we do with you? for we could make nothing of you; you are fit for nothing, and therefore you must provide for yourself, and manage your own matters." The poor Soldier possessed nothing but his gun, so, putting it upon his shoulders, he started off, to take his chance.

By-and-by, he came to a large common, on which he saw nothing but some trees, growing in a circle;

so he sat himself down under them, sorrowfully considering his unhappy fate. "I have no money," thought he, "I have learned no trade but soldiering; and now, since peace is concluded, I am of no use to anybody. Well, I can see plainly enough I shall have to starve." All at once, he heard a rustling noise, and, turning round, saw a Stranger standing before him, dressed in a green coat, who looked very stately, but he had a very ugly cloven foot. "I know very well what you want," said he to the Soldier; "it is money, gold, and other possessions; you shall have as much as you can spend, but, that I may know first that I do not throw away my money foolishly upon you, I must be convinced you are not a coward."

"That is impossible," replied the other; "a Soldier, and a coward! You can put me to any proof you choose."

"Well, then," replied the Stranger, "look behind you."

The Soldier turned, and saw a monstrous Bear, which growled at him, and looked very ferocious. "Oho!" cried he, "my boy, I'll tickle your nose a bit for you, so that you shall not be able to grumble at me much longer!" and, raising his musket, he shot the Bear in the forehead, so that he tumbled all in a heap upon the ground, and never moved a limb afterwards.

"Well," said the Stranger, "it is pretty plain you do not lack courage; but there is still one condition you must fulfil."

The Soldier, knowing who addressed him by the cloven foot, replied, "If it does not interfere with my future happiness, I shall willingly do your bidding."

"That is your own look out," said the Stranger; "for the next seven years you must not wash yourself, nor comb your hair or beard, neither must you cut your nails, nor say your prayers. Then I will give you this coat and cloak, which you must wear during all these seven years; and if you die within that time, you are mine, but if you live, you are rich and free all your life long."

The Soldier reflected for awhile on his many pressing wants, and, remembering how often he had braved death, he at length consented to the conditions, and ventured to accept the offer. Thereupon, this wicked Old Cloven-hoof pulled off his green coat, and handed it to the Soldier, and said, "If you at any time want money, search in the pocket of your coat, when you have it on, and you will always find your hand full of it." Then he also pulled off the skin of the Bear, and said, "That shall be your cloak and your bed; you must always sleep on it, and not dare to lie in any other bed, and on this account you shall be called Bearskin." Immediately Old Cloven-hoof disappeared.

The Soldier, directly he had put his coat on, dipped his hands into his pockets, to make sure of the reality of his bargain. Then he hung the bearskin round his shoulders, and went about the world, chuckling to himself at his good fortune, and buying whatever money could buy, that pleased his fancy. For the first year, his appearance was not so very remarkable, but in the second, he began indeed to look an ugly monster. His hair covered nearly the whole of his face, his

beard looked like a piece of dirty old blanket, his nails were like claws, and his countenance was so covered with dirt, that one might have sown mustard-and-cress upon it, if one had but the seed! Whoever looked upon him, ran away; but, because he gave the poor gold coin wherever he went, they all prayed that he might not die during the seven years; and, because he always paid very liberally, he never wanted for a night's lodging. In the fourth year, however, he came to an inn where the landlord would not take him in, and refused even to let him sleep in the stables, lest the horses should be frightened, and become unmanageable. However, when the landlord saw the gold ducats which Bearskin pulled out of his pocket every time he put his hand in, he yielded the point, and gave him a place in one of the outbuildings, but not before he had made him promise not to show himself, for fear the inn should get a bad name.

While Bearskin sat by himself in the evening, wishing from the bottom of his heart that the seven years were over, he heard a loud groan come from the corner. Now, the Soldier was a kind-hearted man, so he opened the door, and saw an old man weeping violently, and wringing his hands. Bearskin advanced towards him, but the old man jumped up, and tried to run away; but when he recognized a human voice, he let himself be persuaded, by the kind and soothing words of the Soldier, to disclose to him the cause of his great distress. His daughters, he said, would have to starve, for all his property had dwindled away by degrees; and, as he had now no money to pay the landlord, he should be put into prison.

"If that is all that is the matter with you," replied Bearskin, "I can soon mend that; I have plenty of money." And causing the landlord to be called, he paid him the old man's reckoning, and put a purse of gold, besides, into the old gentleman's pocket. The latter, when he saw himself thus speedily released from his troubles, knew not how to thank the Soldier sufficiently, so he said to him: "Come along with me; my daughters are all wonders of beauty, you shall choose one of them for a wife. When they hear all you have done for me, they will not refuse you. You certainly are a strange man to look at, but they will soon set all that to rights." Bearskin was very pleased at this speech, and he went home with the old man.

As soon as the eldest daughter caught sight of his countenance, she was so terrified, that she shrieked out with the fright, and ran away. The second stopped, and looked at him from head to foot; but at last she said to him, "How can I take a husband who is so much more like a bear than a man? The grizzly bear who came to see us once, and gave himself out as a man, would have pleased me far better, for he did wear a hussar hat, and had white gloves on, besides."

But the youngest daughter said: "Dear father, this must be a good man, who has assisted you so willingly out of your troubles; if you have promised him a bride for the service, you know your promise must be kept."

It was a pity the man's face was covered with dirt and hair, or she would have seen how glad at heart hese words made him. Bearskin then took a ring off his finger, and broke it in two; then he gave one half to the youngest daughter, and kept the other half for himself. On her half he wrote his name, and on his he wrote hers; then he begged her to preserve hers carefully, saying: "For three years longer I must wander about; if I come back again then, we will celebrate our wedding; but if I do not, you are free, for I shall be dead. But pray to God that he may preserve my life." He then bade her adieu, and took his leave.

When he was gone, the poor bride clothed herself in black, and whenever she thought of her bridegroom, she burst into tears. Her sisters, when they saw her grief, thought it fine fun, and mocked her, bidding her to "Pay great attention to his beautiful, delicate claws, when he shakes your hand," said the eldest; while the second said, "Take care! bears are fond of sweets; and if you please him, he will eat you up, perhaps, for a sugar-plum." "You must," continued the eldest, "always do as he pleases, otherwise, he will treat you to a growl with his pretty gentle voice." Then the second sister again congratulated her, saying, "At all events, we shall have a merry wedding of it; for bears are famed throughout the world for their good dancing."

The bride kept silence, and let her sisters say what they liked, without being angry with them, remaining constant to her vow.

As for Bearskin, he was wandering all over the world, doing good wherever he could, and always relieving the wants and necessities of all in sickness and trouble; so that he never left without a heartfelt prayer that his life might be long.

In the course of time, the last day of the seven years had arrived, and Bearskin went again to the heath, and sat himself down beneath the circle of trees. In a very short time, a mighty wind arose, and whistled among the trees, and Bearskin, looking up, again saw Old Cloven-hoof standing before him, with vexation and disappointment in every look and gesture. He threw the Soldier down his old coat, and demanded of him again his rich green coat and cloak. "You are a little too fast," said Bearskin; "wait awhile, old fellow; you must wash and clean me, first!" Then Old Cloven-hoof, whether he liked it or no, had to go to the spring and bring water, and well wash the Soldier, comb and dress his hair, and put his nails in order. When all this was done, Bearskin looked again like the brave Soldier that he was, and, to say the truth, was much handsomer than before.

As soon as Old Cloven-hoof was out of sight, he felt relieved of a great weight from his heart, as he knew he could not torment him any more; so, going into the nearest town, he bought a magnificent velvet coat, and got into a carriage drawn by four thoroughbred white horses, and in this princely style he went to the house of his weeping bride. No one knew him; the old father took him for some officer of state, and introduced him into the room where his three beautiful daughters sat. The two eldest compelled him to sit between them, while they helped him to wine, and

loaded his plate with every delicacy within their reach, declaring he was the handsomest and most noble gentleman they had ever beheld. But the bride sat opposite to him, in her black dress, with downcast eyes, not even venturing to address a single word to him. At length, the father asked the Soldier, if it would be agreeable to him to marry one of his daughters. The two eldest, upon hearing this, ran immediately to their chamber, to dress themselves in their gayest dresses, each one heaping upon herself all the ornaments she thought would add to her beauty, and each one feeling quite sure that she should be selected as the happy bride of this noble courtier.

Meanwhile, the Soldier was left alone with his affianced bride; and, taking the half of the golden ring from his pocket, threw it to the bottom of a glass of wine, which he poured out and offered her. When she saw the half of the ring at the bottom of the glass, her heart beat violently. She seized the other half, that hung round her neck suspended by a ribbon, and putting the two halves together, found they joined exactly. Then the Soldier, looking upon her lovingly, said: "I am your bridegroom, whom you first knew as Bearskin; but, through a merciful Providence, have regained my human form once more, and am purified from my faults."

Then he took her in his arms, and embraced her closely. Just at this moment, her two sisters entered, in full dress; but when they saw that this handsome young man belonged to their sister, and that he was the Man in the Bearskin, they took to their heels and ran off, ready to burst with rage and spitefulness; the eldest went and drowned herself in a well, and the second hung herself on a tree in the garden.

In the evening, there was a knock at the door, and when the betrothed went to open it, she saw Old Cloven-hoof, in his green coat, who said to her, "It is all right; I lost one soul, but I have gained the others."

THE JEW IN THE BRAMBLE-BUSH.

A RICH man had once a Servant, who was honest, and who always served his master faithfully. He was the first to get up to his work in the morning, and the last to leave off and go to bed at night; and, besides, whenever there was one job more difficult than another to be done, which nobody else would undertake, this Servant always undertook to do it, and performed his task to perfection. Above all this, he never complained, but was contented with everything, and happy under all circumstances. When his first year of service had come to an end, his master paid him no wages, for he thought to himself, "He cannot leave without his money, and thus I shall, by this clever trick, keep my good servant, and save to myself the money he has earned; he is sure to remain quietly in my service." The Servant said not a word, but went on with his work as faithfully the second year as he had done the first; yet, at the end of the second year, he received no wages. Still he showed no unwillingness, never complaining, and working on as before. At the expiration of the third year, the master, with much sly consideration, put his hand in his pocket, but drew it out again without anything in it. So the Servant said: "I have been a good and faithful servant to you for three years, and now I should like to go and see the world a bit; pay me, good Master, therefore, what you think I deserve."

"Yes, yes, my honest fellow," said the avaricious old man, "you have served me with never-ceasing industry, and, therefore, you shall be generously rewarded." With these words, he slipped his hand into his pocket, and, with a grand and patronizing air, pulled out three farthings! These he gave to the Servant, saying, "There you have a farthing for every year; think yourself indeed fortunate, for it is a more liberal reward than you would get from most masters."

The young man knew very little of money, took up his earnings, and thought himself the happiest man in the kingdom. "Why need I trouble myself with so much hard work?" said he; "my pockets are well filled." So off he went, skipping about upon the road from one side to the other, jumping and laughing, and as full of glee as he could hold.

He went on his way, over hill and valley, singing in the joy of his heart; and presently he came near to some bushes, when out stepped a little man, saying, "Where are you going, you merry dog? The world's cares don't trouble you much—that's a sure thing, from what I can see."

"Why should I be sorrowful?" said the young man; "have not I my pockets full of the three years' wages I have earned? and what more can I wish for? Hark! how they jingle!"

"Yes, indeed, they make noise enough. How much is your treasure?" asked the Dwarf.

"How much?" said the young man; "why, it is three farthings, paid in good coin, and well reckoned."

"Well," said the Dwarf, "give me your three farthings. I am poor and destitute, and too old to work; you are young and strong, and can get your bread whenever you like to work for it."

The Servant had a kind, compassionate heart, so he took pity upon the poor old Dwarf, and handed him the three farthings, saying, "Take them, for the love of God, and I shall never miss them."

Thereupon, the little old man said: "Your heart is compassionate and generous, therefore I will grant you three wishes, one for each farthing, and each wish shall be fulfilled."

"Ah! ah!" said the Servant; "I see you deal in magic! Well, if it is to be so, first, I wish for a gun which shall bring down all I aim at; secondly, I wish for a fiddle which will oblige everybody to dance who hears it; and thirdly, I wish that whenever I make a request to any person in the world, it shall be out of their power to refuse it."

"All this shall be yours," said the Dwarf; and thrusting his hand into the middle of a thicket of bushes, he put them on either side, and there, in the middle, lay the violin and gun, all in readiness for

him,—one would have thought they had been ordered a month before.

Both of these he gave to the Servant, saying, "Whatever you ask, no one in the world will have the power to deny you your request;" and with that he vanished.

"Am I not a happy fellow?" said the Servant; "I have every desire of my heart gratified." And he walked merrily onwards, singing away, till at last he met with a Jew, having a long beard like a he-goat. He stood still, listening to the song of a bird who was perched upon the highest branch of a tree. "This," said the Jew, "is one of the wonders of the world, that so small a bird should have so powerful a voice! How I wish I could catch him! I would that I could but strew some salt on his tail, and then he would be mine."

"If that is all you want," quoth the Servant, "the bird shall soon be at your feet;" and, aiming with his gun, and pulling the trigger, down came the bird into the middle of a bramble-bush, that grew at the bottom of the tree.

"Go now, you rascal," said he to the Jew, "and fetch out your bird!"

The Jew advanced on all-fours into the bramble-bush, and crawled into the middle of it, and stuck so fast among the thorns that he could not rid himself of them. The good Servant, seeing the Jew in this hobble, felt very rogueishly inclined; so he took up

his fiddle, and began to play. At the same moment, the Jew got upon his legs, and began to jump and dance; and the longer the violin played, the better and faster danced the Jew. But the thorns tore to tatters the rags of the Jew, pulled out his beard, and pricked and scratched his body all over. "Good master," cried the Jew, "you play very well, but your fiddling is wasted on me; I do not like music, and I do not want to dance." But the Servant did not take the slightest notice of him, but went on grinning and fiddling, while the Jew danced faster and more furiously than before, until all his rags were torn from his body, and hanging upon the bushes.

"You have fleeced people enough," said the Servant; "and now the thorns will give you a turn, just to see how you like it."

"Oh! miserable me!" cried the Jew; "I will give

44

you whatever you ask, good master, if you will but cease your playing,—you shall have a purse full of gold."

"Well, as you are so considerate and generous," said the Servant, "I will stop my merry fiddle; but, before we part, you must allow me to compliment you on your excellent dancing; it is really quite perfection." So saying, he took the money, and went on his way.

The Jew looked after him at parting, and when he had got out of sight, then he cried out as loud as he could, and abused him with all his might: "You miserable musician! you pot-house player! wait, if I do but catch you alone, I'll make you run till your feet are bare; you smallest change out of a penny! you detestable bundle of nothing!" and much more he added, that readily suggested itself to his wicked imagination. As soon as he had got his breath again, and arranged his dress the best way he could, he ran into the town to the Justice. "My Lord Judge," said he, "I have a sorry tale to tell you: see how I have been beaten and robbed by a rascally man, and that, too, on the King's highway! The very stones on the ground might pity my miserable condition; my clothes in rags, my body all torn and bleeding,—even my poor money and purse the fellow dared to take from me! Oh, woe! woe! oh, my good gold ducats, each one better than the other! and now I am overcome with poverty and misery. For the love of Heaven, let the guilty wretch be put in prison!"

"Was it a Soldier," cried the Judge, "who thus cut you on your body with a sabre?"

"It was no sword," said the Jew, "the ragamuffin had; but he carried a gun on his shoulder, and a violin slung round his neck. Let him be quickly followed; the evil wretch will easily be known."

So the Judge sent his people out after the guilty one, and they soon came up to the Servant, whom they drove slowly home before them, and they then searched him, and found upon him the purse of gold. As soon as he was brought before the Judge, he said: "I never touched the Jew; I never took his gold from him; he gave it me willingly, of his own accord, because he had had enough of my fiddling, and could no longer endure it."

"Heaven defend us!" cried the Jew; "he tells lies as fast as flies swarm to a honey-pot."

The Judge would not listen to his defence; "For," said he, "no Jew in his senses would give away his good gold for such a trifle." Thereupon, he sentenced this good Servant to be hanged by the neck, because the robbery had been committed on the King's highway.

When he was being led to the scaffold, the Jew fell to abusing him again, saying, "You fiddler to dogs! you hog of a musician! now you shall dance upon nothing, as your just reward!" But the Servant walked on quietly with the Hangman to the gallows; but when upon the last step of the ladder, he turned round, and said, "Grant me but one request before I die."

"Well," said the Judge, "I don't mind doing that; but have a care you don't ask for your life, for you are a dead man, as sure as a gun."

"Rest yourself easy," said the Servant; "I shall not ask for my life; I only request that I may be allowed to play one tune on my favourite fiddle before I die."

Upon hearing this, the old Jew howled aloud with fright. "In the name of all that's good," said he, "do not permit it!" But the Judge said, "I cannot see why we should not grant him this one last wish; it is the last gratification he will enjoy on earth; as it is nearly all over with him, he shall have this last favour granted." (The truth is, he could not deny it, if he would.)

The Jew roared out, in agony, "Tie me, tie me! bind me tight!" The good Servant took his violin, and began to screw up, and, at the first bend of the bow, the Judge, the Clerk, and the Hangman began to go through their steps, and the man who was going to bind the Jew let fall the rope. At the second scrape, all put themselves into position, and raised a leg to begin the dance, the Hangman letting fall the rope, and setting the Servant free. At the third scrape, the Judge, and the Jew, and the Hangman, being first performers, began to dance; and as he continued to play, all joined in the dance, and even the people who had gathered in the market-place, out of curiosity, began to dance—fat and lean, young and old, on they whirled together. The dogs, likewise, as they came by, got upon their hind legs, and began curling their tails and capering about. The longer the fiddle was played, the higher the dancers vaulted into the air, and the more furious became the dance, till at last they all toppled down one upon the other, shrieking terribly. At length, the Judge cried out, quite out of breath, "Stop fiddling, I pray, and I'll give you your life!"

The good Servant had compassion, and, dismounting the ladder, he hung his fiddle round his neck again. Then he stepped up to the Jew, who lay puffing and panting, and almost at his last gasp, and said: "You rascal! now tell me whence you got that money?" "Oh me! I stole it! I stole it!" cried the Jew, "but you honestly earned it."

Upon hearing this, the Judge caused the Jew to be hanged upon the gallows as a thief; while the good Servant went on his way rejoicing, at finding kindness and honesty rewarded.

THE NEEDLE, THE SPINDLE, AND THE SHUTTLE;

AND HOW THEY BROUGHT THE WOOER HOME.

ONCE upon a time, there was a young girl, who had lost her parents in her infancy. Her Godmother took her to live with her, in a humble cottage at the farther end of the village, where they lived on the produce of their Needle, Shuttle, and Spindle. Here, under the kind care of the old woman, Jeannette learned to work, and was brought up in the fear and love of God.

Now, my dear children, I dare say some of you think it must be a very hard thing to have to earn your own living by work; but you are quite mistaken. Labour is not a curse, but a blessing, and none are so truly miserable as the idle and the unemployed. If you want to judge of this truly, only look at the laborious ease of those who have to live without work; what pains they take to give themselves something to do, which they call pleasure! How they are always travelling about, and calling from house to house, to help one another out of their nothing-to-do-ishness! And how they toil after something to stir up their minds and bodies, with never-ending care, until they declare, at last, that they are worn out and tired to death! Now, those who have to work have no feelings of this kind; labour is their duty and their pleasure; and wages, and honest, hearty enjoyment, good appetites, merry minds, and shining faces, their reward.

When the young girl had reached the fifteenth year of her age, her Godmother fell ill, and, calling her to her bedside, said to her: "My dear child, I feel my end approaching; my cottage, and all that is in it, I leave to you,—it will serve you as a shelter from the wind and rain. I give you, also, my Shuttle, my Spindle, and my Needle, which will serve to keep you in food." Then, laying her hand on the young girl's head, she blessed her, saying, as she did so, "Never forget your prayers; keep God always in your heart, and happiness will be sure to reach you at last, however long delayed." Then she closed her eyes in death; and the poor young girl followed her to the grave, and rendered the last duties with many tears.

After that, she dwelt quite alone, modest and retired, yet sweet and pretty, like a violet under a hedge, bravely working at her spinning, weaving, and sewing; and the blessing of the old woman seemed to follow her in all things. One would have said that her supply of flax was inexhaustible, and that no sooner had she woven a piece of linen, or made a shirt, than a purchaser presented himself for it, who paid her for it generously; so that, in this fashion, not only had she enough to supply all her wants, but could afford to give something to the poor.

Now, it happened about the same time, that the son of the King of that country set out on his travels all over his father's kingdom, in search of a wife. Princes, in these Fairy Lands, are not, like our English Princes, compelled to marry their cousins or foreign relations; and so this Prince had no restriction on his choice of the partner of his happiness and future throne, except that he might not choose a poor girl for his wife, and had made up his mind not to have a rich one. So he said to himself, that he would take that lass, if he could find her, who should be, at one and the same time, the richest and the poorest.

On arriving at the village, where dwelt our young maiden, he requested, after his usual fashion, the first person he met to direct him to the abode of the poorest and richest young woman in that neighbourhood. The Peasant, without any hesitation, pointed out the latter; "and as to the first," said he, "that must be the young girl who dwells in the lonely hut, right at the farther end of the village."

As the Prince passed by, the rich young woman of the village was sitting at her door, in all the gorgeous

46

array of full dress; she rose up, and came forward to meet so elegantly dressed and handsome a young man, riding such a fine horse, with a grand courtesy; but he only gave one look at her, and kept on his way, without saying a word, until he arrived at the hut of our poor young girl. Now, she was not seated by the door, but close within her chamber.

The Prince stopped his horse, and looked at the little hovel with some compassion,—it was so poor and so lonely, so mean, yet so neat withal; and the garden was trim, and the windows were all clean and tidy, and everywhere there were signs of a cheerful, industrious, contented disposition, willing to make the best of everything. So he got off his white horse, and laid the silver-mounted bridle on the neck of the beautiful steed, as he went to take a peep into the apartment, which was just lighted up by a golden ray from the setting sun. She was seated at her wheel, and spinning away as if she liked it, and had her heart in her work. The Prince stood for a moment, enraptured at the fair vision before him. On her side, too, she gave a furtive glance at the Prince, who kept his eyes fixed on her; but she instantly became all rosy with blushes, and, lowering her eyes to the ground, went on with her spinning,—though I could not undertake to say that all her threads, that moment, were quite even and regular. Thus she continued, spinning away, until the Prince had gone. When she saw him no longer, she ran to open the window, saying to herself, as if in excuse, "How warm it is, to-day!" and then she followed the handsome young gentleman with her eyes, until she could no longer perceive the white plume in his hat. Then she heaved a gentle sigh, and sat down again by her wheel, and began to spin once more.

But there are some thoughts that won't be got rid of, try all we can; and, somehow or other, that white plume, and that handsome face, and that beautiful white horse, kept before her gaze, whichever way she turned her eyes, At last, there came to her memory some lines of a little song that she had often had to repeat to her old Godmother, and she sang as follows:—

"Hasten, Spindle, and don't delay,
Run, and show my love the way."

What do you think happened? The Spindle leaped that very moment from her hands, and rushed out of the cottage door. She followed it, in mute astonishment, with her eyes, and saw it running and dancing across the fields, and trailing along behind it a bright thread of gold. Having no longer a Spindle, she took up her Shuttle, and applied herself to weaving.

The Spindle continued its course, and, just as its thread was at the end, it came up with the Prince. "What do I see?" he exclaimed; "surely this Spindle has a wish to lead me to some adventure." So he turned his horse round, and followed the golden thread at a gallop.

The young girl still kept on at her work, singing, as she did so—

"Hurry, Shuttle, bring for me
My betrothed one to my knee."

The Shuttle directly slipped out of her hands, and darted quickly towards the door; but as soon as it had got over the sill, it began busily weaving the handsomest carpet you ever set eyes upon. The two sides were all flowering with garlands of roses and lilies, and in the centre a green vine sprang upwards from a golden bed; hares and rabbits leaped and played among the foliage; stags and does pushed their heads through them; and on their branches perched birds of a thousand colours, who did everything but sing. The Shuttle kept on running, and the work advanced marvellously. But the poor young lass, having now lost both her Spindle and her Shuttle, was obliged to have recourse to her Needle, for she could not afford to sit idle; nevertheless, all the while she merrily sang—

> "Needle, dear, he's coming here,
> Take care all things neat appear."

At the word, the nimble Needle lightly sprang out of her fingers, and began to dart about all over the room, as rapid as lightning. It was just as if a number of invisible sprites had all set to work together; the tables and the settles were covered with green tapestry; the sofas were dressed in velvet, and the walls with silk damask.

Scarcely had the Needle pierced its last hole, than the young girl caught sight of the white plume in the Prince's hat, as he passed by her window, in following the golden thread. He quickly entered within the cottage, passing over the beautiful carpet into the apartment, where he saw the young girl standing, as if half alarmed, and still arrayed in her poor garments, but brilliant, nevertheless, even in the midst of such sudden luxury, like the wild rose of the eglantine in a hedge.

"You are exactly what one may call at once the poorest and the richest of your sex!" exclaimed the Prince; "come, will you be my wife?" She held out her hand to him, without answering; and he, as in duty bound, took that for a consent, and impressed a kiss upon it; then, taking her up behind him on

his beautiful white horse, caparisoned with gold, he conveyed her to his father's court, where their nuptials were celebrated amidst great rejoicings.

The Needle, the Shuttle, and the Spindle, were preserved, ever after, in the royal treasury, as the most valuable of curiosities.

THE THREE GOLDEN HAIRS

OF THE

DARK KING OF THE BLACK MOUNTAINS.

ONCE upon a time, a poor woman brought a male child into the world, who had a caul on his head when he was born, and on that account it was predicted of him, that in his fourteenth year he should marry the King's daughter.

While all this was going on, the King, by chance, passed through the village, without being recognized by any one; and, seeing the good folks standing about in groups, eagerly discussing some important matter, demanded of them, what news there was in the village? Whereupon, they replied, that there was one just born into the world with a caul, of whom it was said, that everything he took in hand he should succeed with; and it was also predicted of him, that when he should arrive at the age of fourteen years, he should espouse the King's daughter.

The King, who had a cruel and wicked heart, was very angry when he heard this foretold of the babe. He went in search of the parents of the newly-born child, and, having found them, entered their cottage, and said to them, in a most kind and friendly manner: "You are poor, and cannot afford to keep your child as you would wish; give it to me—I much desire it—and I will see that all its wants are well provided for." But the kind-hearted parents refused to give up the child, and the mother shed many bitter tears at even the thought of it. The stranger then, putting his hand into his pocket, pulled out a handful of golden guineas, which he offered them, still persuading them to give him up the child. "If," said he, "he is born with a caul, everything that happens to him must be for the best." So at last they took the gold, and reluctantly consented to deliver up their babe to the care of the stranger.

The King put the helpless nursling into a box, and, mounting his horse, rode with his burthen until he came to the bank of a deep and rapid river, into which he immediately threw it. "Well," said he, "at all events, I have delivered my daughter from a gallant she would not very much have cared for." Now, it so happened, that the box in which the babe lay did not sink to the bottom of the river, but floated on it like a little boat, without so much as letting in one single drop of water. It made its way safely to leeward, until it arrived within two leagues of the capital, when it was stopped by the lock of a mill that stood beside the stream. The Miller's boy, who had the good fortune to perceive it, quickly put in his boat-hook, and drew it ashore, fully expecting, when he looked at it, to find a great prize; but judge his surprise, when he saw it was only a pretty little boy, as fresh as the morning, and as lively and bright a babe as was ever brought into the world. He determined upon carrying it home to the mill; so away he went, and when the Miller and his wife saw it, and heard the truth, great indeed was their astonishment; and, as they had no children of their own, they heartily thanked God for the little stranger, and the good wife, taking it in her bosom, determined to bring it up as her own child. She treated him with the greatest kindness, giving him the best of everything she could procure, and he grew up a handsome and promising lad, endowed with great strength, and every good and virtuous quality.

One day, it so happened, that the King, surprised by a storm, sought shelter in the mill, and, seeing there the poor driftaway, asked the Miller, if that fine, noble-looking young man was his son. "No, Sire," he replied; "he is a foundling, who was drifted hither by the stream into our mill-lock; some wretch had placed it in a box to perish, had not our mill-boy, seeing him, saved him from so sad a fate."

The King very soon saw how his evil intentions had been frustrated by the good-hearted folks, and that this lad was no other than the little luck-child he had cast into the stream. Determined still to avert the omen, he said to the Miller, "Could not your adopted son carry a letter from me to her Majesty the Queen? He shall be most amply repaid for his trouble, for I will give him two golden pieces."

"Your Majesty's commands shall be obeyed," said the Miller; and, turning to the young man, he desired him, with all despatch, to hold himself in readiness. The King then wrote a letter to the Queen, signing it with his sign-manual, in which he commanded that, on the receipt of it, she should immediately cause the messenger to be seized, and put to a violent death, taking care that his body should be buried the moment he had ceased to live; and to mind his commands were fulfilled to the tittle, before he, the King, returned home.

The lad took the letter, and, being prepared for the journey, went merrily on his way, as long as daylight lasted; but at nightfall, he lost his road in the dark, and wandered into a dense forest. At last, glimmering through the darkness, he perceived in the distance a faint light, and directing his steps towards it, at length arrived at a small house, which he entered, and found an old woman seated by a good fire. She expressed great surprise upon seeing the young man, and asked him whence he came, and where he was going to.

"I come from the mill," said he, "and I carry a letter to the Queen; and, having lost my way in this dark forest, I pray you give me a bed, that I may rest till morning, for I am so tired, I cannot proceed a step farther."

"Unfortunate youth!" she cried; "your end approaches. You have fallen into a den of thieves; and if they find you here, they will quickly put an end to your life."

"Well," said the young man, "I thank God I am no coward; and as for going on my journey, that is impossible, for I am so tired I cannot go a step farther."

48

So saying, he threw himself upon a settle which was beside the fire, and was quickly in a sound sleep. The thieves entered a few moments after this, and, seeing him sleeping upon their settle, they angrily demanded how it was a stranger had dared to rest his bones under their roof, threatening to put him to death instantly for his temerity. "Ah! spare him," said the old woman; "he is but a poor lad, who has lost his way in the wood; I took him in out of compassion. He carries a letter to the Queen."

The robbers seized the letter, and, having read it, found therein that the Queen was enjoined to put the messenger to death instantly upon his arrival.

In spite of the hardness of their hearts, they did not much like the idea of putting so brave a youth to death, in cold blood; and so, being touched with pity for him, they determined to frustrate the wishes of the King. The Captain of the band first tore up the letter, and then writing another in its place, returned it to the belt of the sleeper, from whence he had taken it. In this he desired the Queen to celebrate, immediately upon his arrival, the marriage of the bearer of the letter with his daughter the Princess Royal. This being done, the robbers let the lad sleep soundly until morning broke; and when he was fully awake, and as lively as a bird, they showed him the right road for his journey.

He soon arrived at the palace, and the Queen, having read the letter, immediately set about obeying the commands contained therein. Calling her officers of state around her, she desired them to prepare, with all splendour, for the celebration of the marriage of the Princess Royal with the stranger who was born to such good luck. Everything being arranged, the marriage was solemnized, and he became the happy

THE DARK KING'S LANDLADY PLUCKS THE THREE GOLDEN HAIRS.

husband of the Princess Royal; and, as she was very beautiful and very amiable, he was but too delighted to remain and live with her.

Some time after this, the King returned again to his palace, and found, to his dismay, that the prediction had been verified, and that the lad who was born with a caul was indeed espoused to his daughter. Whereupon, he angrily demanded how this had been brought about; "For," said he, "the instructions in my letter had a very different purport." The Queen said she had obeyed his orders, and showing him the letter, bade him read for himself. He hastily seized it, and, on perusing it, at once saw that his own had been changed

for the one he held in his hand. He then demanded of the young man what had become of the letter he had confided to his care, and why he had dared to exchange it for another. "I know nothing of the matter," replied he; "if it is not the same, they must have changed it in the night, while I slept, in the robber's house in the forest."

The King, foaming with rage, and gnashing his teeth, said: "Such an excuse is of no use to me; you will not get off so easily. Whoever pretends to my daughter's hand, must go into the very heart of the Black Mountains, and bring me three golden hairs from the head of the Dark King." The King, in the treachery of his heart, knew it was almost impossible for him to return again from such an errand.

The young man replied: "I will fetch your Majesty the three golden hairs, for the Evil One himself would not frighten me." Thereupon, he politely bowed to the King, and went upon his way.

As he journeyed, he came to a city, and the sentinel at the gate demanded of him, what was his condition, and what he knew.

"Everything," replied he.

"Then," said the sentinel, "you can do us a great service. Tell us why the fountain in our market-place, that always used to give us wine, is dried up, and will not even supply us with water?"

"Wait," said the young man, "and, on my return, I will answer your question."

A little farther on, he came to another town. The sentinel at the gate demanded of him his condition, and what he knew.

"Everything," replied he.

Then the sentinel let him pass, saying: "You can do us a great service, if you tell us why the large tree that stands in the middle of our town, that always bore golden apples, does not now bear even leaves."

"Wait," said he, "and I will tell you on my return."

Then he went a little farther on, and he came to a wide river, over which he wished to pass, when the ferryman demanded of him his condition, and what he knew.

"Everything," replied he.

"I am glad to hear it," said the ferryman, "for you will be able to tell me if I am always to remain here at my post, as ferryman, without ever being relieved by any one."

"Wait," said he, "and I will tell you when I return."

When the youth had arrived at the other side of the water, he soon came to the opening that led to the heart of the mountain, where the wicked Dark King dwelt. It was all dark, and smelt most horribly of sulphur. The Evil King was not at home at the time, and there was no one there but his Landlady, who sat in an easy chair before a large fire. "What do you want?" said she, in a mild and gentle voice.

"I must have," said he, "three golden hairs from the head of the King of these regions, without which I shall never obtain my wife."

"That," said she, "is no small request. If the King should see you when he returns, you will pass an uncomfortable quarter of an hour, I can tell you. Notwithstanding this," said she, "I have taken a great fancy to you, and will give you every help that is in my power."

Then the good dame changed him into an Ant, saying: "Now do you creep among the folds of my dress, and there you may hide in safety, and lie snug enough."

"Many thanks," quoth the Ant; "well, here I am, and everything goes well, but still there are three things I want to know, before I return: one is, Why a fountain in the great city, that used always to supply wine, does not now even supply water? the second is, Why a tree, that used to bear golden apples, does not

now even bear leaves? and the third is, If the ferry-man at the river will be always obliged to remain at his post, without ever being able to get any one to relieve him?"

"Well," said the dame, "they are all three difficult questions; but do you lie very close, where you are—keep quite still, and listen attentively to the answers the Dark King will give me, each time I pluck from his head a golden hair."

When the night came, the Evil King returned to his underground home, in the centre of the Black Mountains; but he had not been in long, before he began snuffing the air, and turning his fiery eyes in every direction, saying to his Landlady, "What a remarkable smell there is! What have you here?" he angrily demanded; "I am certain I smell human flesh." He then got up, and ferreted all round the room, and in every hole and corner, his eyes flashing with fresh fury every moment, for he made a practice of devouring all his subjects who came within his grasp; but, fortunately, did not succeed in finding his prey.

The Landlady now began to grow very angry with the Dark King, and sought to quarrel with him. "I have just swept my room," said she, "and put it in nice order; and now here you are, with your whims and fancies, turning it all topsy-turvey. You are always smelling human flesh! Can't you sit down contentedly, and eat your supper?"

In this manner she quieted the wicked Dark King; and, having eaten his supper, he felt tired and sleepy, and he rested his head in the lap of his Landlady, and told her she must smooth and clean his hair for him; but he had been there but a very little time before he was fast asleep, and the earth shook with his loud snoring.

The old woman took advantage of this opportunity, and, seizing one of the golden hairs, pulled it out, and put it on one side. "Hold!" roared the Black King; "what are you after, there?"

"I had fallen asleep," cried she, "and having a bad dream, I caught you by the hair, in my fright, and pulled it."

"What have you dreamed?" demanded he.

"I dreamed," said she, "that the fountain in the market-place, that used to give forth wine, was dried up, and that now they could not even obtain water. Whatever could be the cause of such a calamity?"

"Ah!" said the Dark King; "I suppose you would like to know. Well, then, there is a toad upon the stone over the mouth of the fountain; if some one would but kill that, then the wine would again begin to flow."

The Landlady, having obtained this answer, cunningly began to smooth and clean his hair again, and off he fell to sleep, snoring so loud, that he shook every window. Then she seized another golden hair, and plucked it out. "Hold, there!" cried the Dark King, in a towering passion; "what are you doing? I'll teach you to be more careful."

"Oh, pray do not disturb yourself," she cried; "it is only a dream that troubles me."

"What are you dreaming about, now?" he asked.

"Why," said she, "I dreamed that in the middle of a town there stood a tree, which had always brought forth golden apples, but that now it did not bear even leaves."

"Ah!" said the Evil King, "you would like to know that, too, I suppose. Well, there is a mouse that is constantly gnawing away the roots of the tree; some one must kill it, and then the golden apples will grow again upon the tree; but if he remains alive, ever gnawing at the roots, the tree will decay until it dies entirely away. And now," said he, "don't bother me with your dreams any more, but let me sleep; for if you go dreaming again, you will get a good cuff on the head."

The Landlady appeased his anger as well as she could, and, smoothing his hair again, he was soon sleeping and snoring as before. Then she seized the third golden hair, and pulled that out also. "What," he asked, with eager curiosity, "dreaming again?"

"I dreamed," she timidly replied, "that the ferryman at the river made loud complaints at having always to be at the river-side, to take people across in his boat, without ever having any one to take his place."

"Ho! the fool!" replied the Dark King; "he has nothing to do but to place the oar in the hand of the first person who crosses, and he will be obliged to become ferryman in his turn, and carry over the passengers."

When the Landlady had succeeded in pulling the three golden hairs from the Dark King's head, and had cunningly drawn from him the answers to the three questions, she left him to rest quietly, and he slept on until the morning came.

When the Dark King had washed and dressed himself, and left his sulphur palace, the good woman took the Ant out from the folds of her dress, and restored him to his human form. "See," said she to him, "here are the three much-desired golden hairs; but are you quite sure you heard the answers to the questions I asked?"

"Every word of them," he replied; "and trust me for not forgetting them."

"Well," returned the good woman, "you have got rid of all your troubles; and so now you may return by the way you came, and be happy with your wife."

He gratefully thanked the kind lady, who had so good-naturedly given him her aid, and joyfully quitted the Dark King's sulphureous dominions, full of joy at having so happily obtained his end.

When he arrived at the ferry, before giving the promised answer, he got himself conveyed to the other side of the river, and then he gave to the ferryman the advice given by the Dark King. "The first person," said he to the man in the boat, "who comes to cross the river, you have nothing to do but to place the oar in his hand, and he will henceforth be obliged to become ferryman in his turn."

As he journeyed on a little farther, he came again to the barren tree. The sentinel was there, awaiting his answer. "Kill," said he, "the mouse that gnaws the roots, and the golden apples will grow again." The sentinel, delighted with the answer, in order to

show his gratitude to the young man, ordered two asses to be laden with gold, which he presented to him.

At length, he came to the city where the fountain was dried up, and he said to the sentinel: "Upon a stone in the fountain there is a toad, who dries up the source of the fountain; search for it and kill it, and immediately the wine will begin to flow again in abundance. The sentinel thanked him most heartily, and he likewise gave him two asses laden with gold.

At last, the young man who was born with the lucky caul arrived at his wife's palace, and she was rejoiced in her heart at seeing him return; and he told her how lucky he had been, and related to her how all had happened to him on his journey. Then he took the three golden hairs of the Dark King, and laid them before the King whose daughter he had married, who, when he saw the asses laden with gold, and all the wealth the youth had brought back, was fully satisfied, and very delighted. "You have," said he, "fulfilled all the conditions of your marriage, and my daughter is your wife; may you be happy. But tell me, my dear son-in-law, how it is that you, who went away from here so poor that you had not a penny in your pocket, should return carrying such enormous treasures?"

"I found them," said he, "at the other side of a river I had to cross, in the sand upon the bank of it."

"Can I get any more?" quickly demanded the King, for he was an old miser in his heart.

"Oh, yes," said the son-in-law, "as much as you please; you will find a boat, and ferryman. Speak to the man, and ask him to take you over the water; and when you get to the other side, you can fill your sacks at your leisure."

The greedy old King directly prepared for his journey; and when he arrived at the bank of the river, he asked the ferryman to take him to the other side. The ferryman bade him enter his boat, and, putting the oar in the King's hand, leaped out as quickly as he could. The King was now obliged to be ferryman, as a punishment for his sins.

"And I wonder if he still remains there?"

To be sure he does, for no person has yet been found who would take the oar out of his hand.

THE BOLD LITTLE TAILOR.

ONE bright summer's morning, there sat in a window, upon a table, a little Tailor, carolling away as blithe as a bird, and stitching as fast as his fingers would let him, and all the while he seemed to think it fun, and not work. Presently, up came a countrywoman with her cans, calling out, "Fresh cream for sale! Fresh cream for sale!" This word "cream" sounded very agreeably refreshing to the ears of the little man, and, putting his mite of a head out of the window, he said, "Here, my pretty girl, come in here, and you will not long want a purchaser."

She went up the steps, tottering under the weight of her heavy cans, into the shop of the little Tailor, and began to unpack all her pots of cream, that the little Tailor might choose for himself, and make sure they were all fresh and good. "Well," said he, "this is indeed good cream!" dipping his finger, to taste it, into one pot after the other; he then finished by ordering the countrywoman to make him a pennyworth, and be sure to give good measure. The woman did as he wished, although she grumbled very much at having so much trouble for so little gain.

"Heaven," exclaimed the Tailor, "will surely give me health and fresh vigour!" and, taking the loaf in his hand, he cut a thick slice, and spread the cream upon it as thickly as he could. "That will taste by no means badly," said he; "but suppose, before I eat it, I sit down and finish this waistcoat; it will not take me long." He put the bread and cream upon the table beside him, while he worked away joyfully, making longer stitches every moment. Meanwhile, the fresh cream was so tempting, that the flies that covered the wall came swarming upon it, devouring it off as fast as they could. "Who invited you here?" said the Tailor, driving them away in no very gentle manner; "begone, I tell you!"

But the flies, who did not understand English, came back again in double numbers. This time, they came buzzing around his head and face, and one settled upon his nose; so that he got in such a passion, that he seized a strip of cloth, and laid it about him as heavily as he could, having little regard for the lives of his tormentors. When this was done, he set to work to count the dead. "There are no less than seven, I declare," cried he, "lying dead, with their legs outstretched!" and, astonished at his own valour, he said to himself, "All the town shall know of this!" In his enthusiasm, he took a piece of cloth, and, cutting a band from it, he stitched it round, and then worked on it, in large letters, "SEVEN AT ONE BLOW!"

"The town shall know it, indeed; aye, and not only the town, but every city and town—all the world shall know it!" and his heart fluttered with joy, just like the tail of a little lambkin. He put on his girdle, and resolved to travel through the wide world with it, for his shop seemed much too small to hold a man who could accomplish such a valiant deed. Before he set out, however, he looked all about his house, to see if there was anything that might be of use to him in his travels, but he found only an old cheese, which he put in his pocket; and then turning to go out, he espied a bird before the door, caught in a trap; this he also took, and put into his pocket with the cheese. He then started directly on his travels; and, as he was lithe and active, he could travel a good way without being fatigued.

On he journeyed, till he came to a very high mountain, on the top of which was seated, at his ease, an enormous Giant, who looked about him very complacently, upon everything that met his gaze. The Bold Little Tailor went straight up to him, however, saying, "How do you do, comrade, this fine morning? In faith, you sit there like a king, with the whole world stretched at your feet? As for me, I am on

52

my travels in search of adventures. Have you a mind to come along with me?"

The Giant turned up his nose disdainfully at the little Tailor, exclaiming, "You contemptible vagabond! you ninth part of a man!"

"How can that be?" said the Dwarf; and, unbuttoning his coat, he showed the embroidered girdle to the Giant: "here you can read what sort of a fellow I am."

The Giant read, "Seven at one blow!" and, thinking that they must be seven men that he had killed at one blow, he immediately felt some little respect for his bravery. Therefore, to prove the truth, the Giant took up a stone, and squeezed it so hard that water came out of it. "There, my fine fellow," said he, "do that after me, if you wish to prove your vaunted strength."

"If that is the hardest test you'll put me to," said the Tailor, "it is soon done—it is but sport to me!" and, thrusting his hand into his pocket, he cunningly brought out the cheese, and squeezed it till the whey ran out, and said, "I think I beat you there."

The Giant did not know what to say, for he could not understand how a little Dwarf could have the power to accomplish such a feat. He then took up another stone, and threw it so high into the air, that it was quite lost sight of to the eye, saying, "Now, do that if you can, you little mannikin!"

"I allow it was well done," said the Tailor; "but, after all, your stone will be sure to fall down again to the ground, some time or other; but I will throw one up that shall not come down again;" and then, dipping into his pocket, he drew out the bird, and

rew it into the air. The bird, joyous at being
stored to liberty, flew straight up, and then using
s wings to the best advantage, flew far away, and
d not return again. "What do you think of that,
l boy, for a fling?" asked the Tailor.

"Certainly that was very well done; you throw
mously," said the Giant; "but I should like to see
you are as clever at carrying a weight as you are
throwing a distance." He then led the Tailor into
e forest, to an enormous oak that had fallen to the
und. "Now," said he, "if you are as strong as you
y, just help me to carry this tree out of the forest."
"Most willingly," replied the little man; "do you
e the trunk on your shoulders, and leave me the
ughs and branches—they are the heaviest; it will
fine sport for me."

The Giant took the trunk; but the knowing little
ilor, who was behind, where he could not be seen,
mped into the branches, where he quietly installed
mself; and as they went along, he sang gaily to
mself the little air—

"There were three Tailors riding along,"

if it were mere child's play to carry big trees.
e Giant, staggering under the weight of his burden,
uld not move another step farther, and cried, "Do
h hear? I must let the tree fall!" The Tailor,
inging lightly down, seized the tree in both his
ms, as if he had carried it all the while. "You
ve not," said he, "much strength to boast of; a
an of your size ought to carry this tree as I would a
ther."

They continued on their way, and, at last, they
me to a cherry-tree, that was laden with ripe
erries. The Giant caught hold of the top of the
e, where all the best and ripest fruit hung, and,
nding it down, he put it into the Dwarf's hand,
ding him to eat the cherries. But the little Tailor
d not strength to hold it; and directly the Giant
go his hold, up sprang the branch again into
e air, carrying cherries, Tailor, and all, tossing
e Tailor down, however, on the other side of the
e, without any injury to his bones. The Giant
d, "How comes this about? have you not got
ength enough to hold a twig like this?"

"You can't suppose my strength failed me,"
swered he; "what could that be to one who has
lled seven at one blow? I sprang over the tree
cause there are a lot of huntsmen shooting in that
icket, and I like to be out of harm's way. Spring
er after me, if you can."

The Giant tried his best, but he found it was no
e; and as he could not clear the tree, he only got
mself entangled in the branches for his trouble; so
at in this, too, the Tailor got the advantage of him.
After all this, the Giant, not knowing what to make
it, said: "Since you are such a valiant little man,
me home with me to my cave, and stop the night
th us." The Tailor consented; and when he arrived
the cavern, there sat, before a great fire, two other
ants, who each had a roast sheep in his hands,
nich he was eating with great relish. The little
ilor sat himself down, thinking, "This is a sight

worth coming out into the world to see; what a
fortunate thing it was I made up my mind to leave
my paltry workshop!" Then the Giant showed him
a bed, where he might lie down and sleep the night
through; the bed, however, was too big for such a
little man as he, and so he slipped out of it, and rolled
himself up in a corner to sleep. At midnight, the
Giant, thinking his visitor was in a sound sleep, seized
a heavy bar of iron, and striking a tremendous blow
right in the middle of the bed, sent the bed right
through; the Giant, making sure he had done for the
little Tailor's clever tricks, was well pleased at having
killed him with one blow. At the break of day the
Giants got up, and went out into the forest, having
forgotten all about the little Tailor; when, presently,
up he walked before them, singing gaily, with the
greatest possible degree of effrontery. The Giants did
not know what to make of this, and, thinking that he
would certainly kill them all, they were seized with a
panic, and taking to their heels, ran away as fast
as they would carry them. Then the little Tailor
journeyed on, following his nose; and after wandering a long time, arrived at the garden of a royal
palace, when, finding himself very tired, he laid down
upon the grass to rest, and soon fell into a profound
sleep. While he lay there, the people passing to and
fro gathered round him, and read on his belt, "Seven
at one blow!" "Ah!" said they, "what does this
thunderbolt of war here, in time of peace? He must,
indeed, be some powerful hero." So they went and
told the King, showing him, that should war break
out, this wonderful man would be of too much service
to him to allow him to slip through his fingers, and
recommended him to attach the stranger to his royal
person, at all hazard and at any price. The King
listened to their counsel, and sent one of his aide-de-
camps to the little man, to enlist him into his service,
so soon as he should have opened his eyes and
stretched his limbs a bit. The messenger politely
waited until the Tailor thought fit to awake, and then,
in a most courteous manner, delivered his message to
him.

"Ah! ah!" said the little man, drawing himself up
to his full height, and speaking as pompously as he
could; "that is the very business I came here upon,
and it was my intention to enter the King's service.
Introduce me at once to his Majesty." So they led
the little Tailor, with all due honour and ceremony,
into the King's august presence, who appointed a
handsome suite of apartments in the royal palace for
him to reside in.

But all the military men of renown in the kingdom
became jealous of this pigmy fighting-man, and wished
him a thousand miles away: "For," said they, "we
shall be shorn of all our glory, if we go to war; and
if we seek a quarrel with him, he will fall upon us,
and kill seven of us with one blow; not one of us will
be left alive." In the heat of their rage at being thus
slighted, they went in a body before the King, and
tendered a resignation of their commissions, if he
would be graciously pleased to accept them, telling
him, they were not prepared to keep company with
a man who killed seven at one blow. The King was

very much distressed when he heard their determination, for he did not at all relish the idea of losing these, his most loyal subjects and bravest warriors, for the sake of one, and wished he had never seen the Tailor, and would willingly now have been quit of him, if he had known but the way. But he dared not dismiss him, fearing the Tailor might kill him and all his fighting-men, and then place himself upon the throne in his stead.

The King, after being some time in deep thought, hit upon an expedient; when, sending for the little man, he made him an offer that no hero of any renown could fail to accept. "There is," said he, "in a forest near to our royal city, a cavern, in which dwell two Giants, who are always committing all sorts of depredations and violence, by murder, robbery, and fire, and no one dares for their lives to offer them any resistance, or approach their stronghold. If you will vanquish these terrible Giants, and put them to death, I will reward you with the hand of my only daughter in marriage, and will give you for her dower the half of my kingdom." He then put an escort of one hundred horsemen at his service, to assist him at any moment he might need their aid.

The Tailor declared his willingness to march out against the Giants, and engage them in mortal combat, but disdained the aid of the escort of one hundred horsemen, saying, "He who has killed seven at one blow, need not fear to attack two adversaries at one time."

The bold Tailor marched on his way, followed by the hundred knights, until he came to the border of the forest, when, turning to his brave army, he addressed them, saying, "I would rather meet these two Giants alone; do you stay here until I return." Then off he rushed into the forest, cautiously peering about him, and had not gone far when he perceived the two Giants fast asleep under the shade of a large tree, and snoring so loud that they shook the leaves from the branches above their heads. The little Tailor filled both his pockets with stones, and clambered up the tree without loss of time; he then slid gently along one of the branches that immediately overhung the sleepers, and let fall one stone after another quickly upon the stomach of one of them. The Giant was a long time before this sport disturbed him; but at last he awoke, and, giving his companion a hearty shove, said, "What do you mean by knocking me about?"

"You are dreaming," answered the other; "I never so much as touched you."

With this they both composed themselves to sleep again, and presently the Tailor threw a stone upon the other Giant, who exclaimed: "I'll teach you to give over that fun. Keep your blows for some one who will take them, and don't be knocking me."

"I never touched you," said the first Giant; "you did but dream it."

They quarrelled for a long time, and were both in a very ill-temper at being thus disturbed, but at last, being very tired, they fell off to sleep again. Then the Tailor commenced his game again, and choosing the biggest stone he had, he threw it with all his force,

54

plump upon the stomach of the first Giant. "That's too bad!" cried he; and, jumping up like a madman, he fell upon his comrade, who soon gave him the change for his money. The combat went on so fast and furious, that they uprooted the largest trees near them, and knocked one another about with these weapons; and the affair did not cease until they were both laid dead upon the grass.

Then the little Tailor came down blithely from his perch, and said, "It is a happy thing for me they did not pull up the tree on which I was so comfortably seated, otherwise, I must have leaped like a squirrel into the next; but I have done my business very cleverly." Then he valiantly drew his sword, and, approaching the Giants, he gave to each of them two of the fiercest cuts he could deal them across the throat, and then he went back triumphantly to the hundred armed men, saying, "That job is done; I have put a finishing stroke to those gentry; it was rather warm work, as they violently resisted, and even uprooted the large trees to hurl at me; but of what avail was their warfare against a man like me, who can kill seven at one blow!"

"Have you escaped unhurt? are you not wounded?" inquired the soldiers.

"Not I; a very likely matter! You see, they have not even rumpled a hair of my head."

The soldiers would not believe him, until, upon entering the wood, they really found the Giants slain and weltering in their blood, with the trees torn up and lying all around them.

The little Tailor then presented himself before the King, and claimed his promised reward; but he (being unlike most Kings) did not keep his word, and began much to regret the promise he had made, and sought again for a means whereby he might get rid of this hero. "Before," said he," you receive my daughter as your wife, and the half of my kingdom, you must perform some other deed of daring. My forests are rendered dangerous by a rampant Unicorn, who wanders about them, destroying everything, and spreading desolation wherever he appears. You must first kill him."

"A Unicorn to kill! that's rare sport! It shall be done in a trice; it is nothing, after the Giants. 'Seven at one blow!'—that's my motto."

Then he took with him a rope and an axe, and desired those who accompanied him to await him on the outskirts of the forest. He had not long to wait; the Unicorn soon made his appearance, and as soon as he saw the Tailor he made a rush at him, to pin him to the ground with his horn. "Softly, softly, my friend," said the Tailor, "that's not so easily done;" and he waited quietly until the animal was about to make his final spring, and then he leaped behind the trunk of a large tree; the Unicorn, rushing against the tree with all the force he was master of, struck his horn so firmly into it, that it was impossible for him to draw it out again, and in this position he was easily taken prisoner. "I have caged my bird," said the bold Tailor; and coming from his hiding-place, he first bound the rope round the animal's neck, and then with his axe he cleverly cut the horn out of the tree, and when all this was finished, he led the Unicorn into the presence of the King.

But the King could not, even then, make up his mind to keep his promise, and he still imposed a third condition, which was, that before the wedding-day he should destroy a wild Boar, who did much damage in his woods, and to the surrounding country. The King's huntsmen were ordered to take the beast by sheer force and numbers. The little Tailor assured the King he had been used to hunt wild Boars all his life, and that nothing had a greater charm for him than hunting this animal. He then made his way to the wood, where he left the huntsmen outside, to their great satisfaction, for this same Boar had so often hunted them, that they had no farther liking for the sport. As soon, however, as the wild Boar caught sight of the Tailor, he began to froth at the mouth, showing his enormous tusks to the Tailor, in token of his readiness to fight, and tried to throw him on the ground; but our hero made a flying leap through the open window of a little chapel that stood near, and out again through another one on the other side, in a moment. The brute made an entrance after him, but the Tailor skipped round, and shutting the door upon the now raging beast, he was easily trapped, for he was much too heavy and maddened with rage to find his way through the window. After this exploit, he called the huntsmen, and showed them the prisoner with their own eyes; he then presented it to the King, who was obliged this time, in spite of himself, to keep his promise, and give the Tailor his daughter to wife, with the half of his kingdom for his fortune. It would have grieved him still more to the heart, had he known his future son-in-law was no great and noble warrior, but only a mean little knight of the thimble. So the wedding was celebrated with much magnificence, but very little rejoicing; and thus was a King made out of a Tailor.

Some little time afterwards, as the young Queen lay beside her husband, she heard him talking in his dreams, saying: "Work away, you boy, and finish that waistcoat, and stitch up the seams of those trowsers, or I'll lay the yard-measure well about your ears!" She heard quite enough to understand that the young man she had espoused was only a miserable shopman; and she supplicated her father, in the morning, to deliver her from the husband he had given her, who had no noble blood in his veins, and was, in truth, nothing but a miserable Tailor.

The King consoled her by saying: "When the night comes, leave your chamber door open; my servants shall remain without, and when he is fast asleep, they shall enter and bind him with chains, and bear him to a ship that lies ready to carry him to a distant land."

The young Queen delightedly consented to this arrangement; but his equerry had overheard all their conversation, and, as he had a great liking for the young Prince, discovered to him the whole of the plot.

"I will put all that straight," said he, "I'll put a bolt on the door."

When night came, they went to rest as usual, and when the Queen thought he slept, she got up and opened the door, and then went and laid herself down again by his side. But the little man, who only feigned sleep, exclaimed in a loud voice, "Be quick, you boy, and finish that waistcoat, and stitch up the seams of those trowsers, or you will soon get the yard-measure about your ears! I have killed seven at one blow; I have slain two Giants; I have hunted a Unicorn, and taken a wild Boar captive: shall I, then, be afraid of a handful of men who stand without my chamber door?" When they overheard these words, they fled for their lives, and never afterwards could they induce any one in the kingdom to take part against him; so the Tailor remained a King for the rest of his life.

THE LUCK OF THE THREE HEIRS.

A FATHER summoned his three sons before him, and gave them each a gift: to the first a Cock, to the second a Scythe, and to the third a Cat.

"I am an old man, now," said he to them; "my death is drawing nigh, and I wish to take care of your future prospects before that time. Silver and gold I have none to leave you, and I dare say what I have given to you to-day will not appear of any great value to you; but all depends upon the manner in which you use them. Let each of you look out for some country, in which what you have is yet unknown, and your fortunes will be made."

On the death of his father, the eldest of the sons set forth with his Cock; but everywhere he went to, the Cock was already a well-known bird; in every town he saw the bold bird figuring away on the tops of all the steeples, turning round with every wind; in the country he heard its crowing unceasingly; and nobody ever showed so much surprise, on seeing his fowl, as to give him a chance of supposing that he was on the high-road to fortune.

At last, good-luck brought him to an island, where nobody knew what a Cock was, and where they were, consequently, greatly embarrassed in dividing their time. They could tell very well when it was morning or evening; but at night those who did not go to sleep could not tell what time it was. "See," said the eldest son to them, "this brilliant bird; he has a crown of rubies on his head, and wears spurs at his heels, like a knight. He calls out three times every night at a certain hour, the last being when the sun is about to show himself; when he shouts in mid-day, it denotes that the weather is about to change."

This discourse greatly excited the admiration of the inhabitants of the island in question, as well as their curiosity. Next night, there was not a man, woman, or child asleep throughout the country, and every one listened with the greatest attention, as the Cock announced, in succession, two o'clock, four o'clock, six o'clock in the morning. They inquired anxiously whether this beautiful bird was for sale, and how much its proprietor wanted for it.

"I must have as much gold as a donkey can carry," was his answer; and they all exclaimed, that such a price was a mere trifle for an animal so wonderful and clever, and lost no time in paying him down the price.

When they saw their eldest brother come back a rich man, the two younger ones were filled with astonishment; so the second took heart, and resolved to take his departure also, and see if his Scythe would fetch anything. But everywhere, as he passed along, he met with peasants provided with scythes quite as good as his own. At last, by great good-luck, he landed from a ship on an island, where no one knew what a scythe was. When the barley was ripe in this country, they used to fire the cannon from the city walls, and cut it all down at one volley. But this did not always do the work in a regular manner; sometimes the cannon-balls struck off the ears instead of the stalks, so that much of the grain was lost; and, more than all, about market-day the noise was insupportable. When our young friend set to work, and mowed down in their presence all their barley, so quickly and so quietly, they all regarded him with gaping mouths and staring eyes. They gave him whatever price he chose to ask for so wonderful a mowing machine; so he brought away a horse-load of gold.

This set the third brother all agog to try his luck with his Cat. Like his two elder brothers, he found no desirable opportunity for investments in cats so long as he was on *terra firma;* for every one had got cats, and the trouble was, not to get them, but to get rid of them, so that in some places they drowned the whole litter of kittens as soon as they were born. At last, however, he went voyaging on shipboard, and came to an island where, as good fortune would have it, no Cat had ever been seen, but, by way of amends, the mice thrived and grew so fast, and so impudent, that they danced about on the tables and chairs, in the very presence of the master of the house. Every one felt the annoyance of this pest; the King himself was not safe in his own palace; the squeaking of mice was heard in every corner, and they spared nothing that they could get at with their teeth.

This was the very place for a Cat! No sooner was she introduced, than she purred, and put up her tail, and jumped out of her owner's arms, and whisked briskly round the grand audience saloon, scattering

the mice in scampering crowds before her. She cleared this and the royal saloon; and then the Courtiers, headed by the Lord Chief Justice of the kingdom, crowded in before his Majesty, to petition that such an invaluable animal might be at once secured for the State. Whereupon, the King, without any chaffering, paid a he-mule's load of gold; so that the third brother returned to his native land even richer than his two elders.

THE INDUSTRIOUS GOBLINS.

IT so chanced, many years ago, that a Shoemaker became so impoverished in his circumstances, that he had only money left to buy leather to make a single pair of shoes. On the overnight he cut out the leather, thinking he would get up early in the morning and do his work; so, having said his prayers, he laid himself down to sleep. In the morning he rose, and went to sit himself down to work, when, to his surprise and delight, he found the shoes, already finished, upon the table. You may easily judge how puzzled he was to imagine who could possibly have given him a helping hand; he turned the shoes over and over, to see if they were properly made and fitted, but not one single stitch was wrong; they were, in fact, a very masterpiece of shoemaking.

The Shoemaker put these beautiful shoes in his window, and very soon after a customer came in, who was so delighted with them, that he offered to pay for them just double the price that the Shoemaker thought to ask; so he took the money, and, thanking his lucky stars, he went out, and this time he had money enough to buy leather to make two pairs of shoes. He took the leather home, and gleefully sat himself down and cut them out overnight, that he might work away at them in the morning. When he awoke from his slumbers, he prepared for his work, when, upon opening his shutters to let the daylight in, there stood the shoes ready finished upon the board, as perfect as they could be. Neither were customers wanted, for two soon came in, who bought the shoes at so good a price, that he was enabled to go to the leather-sellers, and buy enough wherewith to make four pairs of shoes. These he cut out and laid ready, and, in the morning, there they were, finished; and so it went on day after day, that whatever he cut out was finished by the following morning, until, at last, his whole time was occupied in buying leather, and cutting out shoes, which were always sure to be ready for him the next day; so that in a very short time he not only regained his former position as a Shoemaker, but became a very opulent tradesman.

One night, just before Christmas, the Shoemaker's wife, who had grown so curious she could not contain herself, said to her husband, "My dear, suppose we remain awake to-night, that we may see who it can be who thus kindly helps us with our work?" The Shoemaker consented, and they left a candle

THE INDUSTRIOUS GOBLINS CARRY ON THE COBBLER'S BUSINESS.

burning, and then they concealed themselves behind a chest, where they used to keep their clothes, and so arranged themselves as to be secure from observation.

As soon as midnight had struck, the door opened, and in walked two pretty little Dwarfs, who had not a vestige of clothing to keep them from the cold, and down they sat to work, and plied the bristles and twine so merrily, and hammered away with such hearty good-will, that the Shoemaker could not take his eyes off them, until, at last, the swiftness of their movements quite bewildered him. The shoes were all done in a trice, and placed in pairs upon the board;

No. 8.

and then these good little men skipped lightly from their work, and vanished out of the room.

The next morning, the wife said to the husband: "Did you ever hear of such a thing in your life, as these good little folks coming to assist poor people in their distress? How I wish we could recompense them for the great trouble they have taken for us, and the kindness they have shown to us. I think they must be very cold, though, without anything to cover their pretty little bodies. I think I will make them some clothes to cover them—a shirt, and coat, waistcoat, and trowsers, and I will also knit them a pair of nice warm stockings each, and do you set yourself to work, and make two of the very smallest and neatest pairs of shoes you can possibly put together."

All these the good folks got ready, as a grateful offering to these little industrious Goblins; and then, instead of the usual work, they laid these gifts upon the shop-board, and hid themselves to await the result.

Exactly as the clock struck twelve, in came these wonderful little workmen, who, seeing the beautiful little clothes, so warm and comfortable, instead of the work, took them up, and put them on in delighted haste, singing—

> "Happy little Dwarfs are we,
> Well dressed, and comely now to see;
> No longer Shoemakers we'll be."

Then they commenced jumping over stools and chairs, and at last they jumped out at the door, and never came to work again. But from that day, everything the Shoemaker did, prospered; and he or his wife never wanted money again so long as they lived.

THE FROG'S BRIDE.

BEFORE you or I were born, I have heard them say, it was only to wish and to have; and it was in these good olden times that there lived a King, who had many beautiful daughters, but the youngest was so very lovely, that it was a treat even for the sun himself to come out and shine upon her.

Near this King's castle there was a dark gloomy forest, where the evil people dwelt, and in the midst stood an old lime-tree, beneath whose branches danced the waters of a fountain. One day, as the weather was very hot, the King's youngest daughter ran off into the forest, and sat herself down by the cool fountain, and, to amuse herself in this solitude, she began tossing a golden ball into the air, and catching it again. This was her favourite amusement; but it happened that the King's daughter missed catching the ball, and it rolled upon the grass to the edge of the fountain, into which it fell. The King's daughter looked after it as long as she could see it, but it had disappeared under the water, and she could not see to the bottom. Then she began to lament for the loss of her golden ball, and cried aloud. Then a voice called out, "Why do you weep, oh! beautiful daughter of the King? Your tears would melt a stone to pity."

She looked to the spot from whence the voice came, and saw a Frog stretching his flat ugly head out of the water. "Was it you that spoke, you ugly old water-paddler?" said she; "was it you? I am crying for my golden ball, that has rolled into the water."

"Oh! pray don't cry, dear Princess," said the Frog; "I can fetch your ball up again. But what will you give me, if I do?"

"Why, what would you like, dear Frog?" she asked; "will you have my dresses, or my fine pearls and jewels, or the grand golden crown I wear?"

The Frog replied, looking lovingly up in her face,

"It is not your dresses or your jewels, or the golden crown which you wear, that I want; but I want your love, and to be your companion and playfellow, and to sit at your table, and to eat from your little golden plate, and drink out of your cup, and sleep in your nice little bed. If you will promise me all these, then I will dive down into the deep water, and fetch you your pretty golden plaything up again."

"Oh! I'll promise you all that," said she; "only get me my ball up again." But she thought to herself, "What a silly old chattering Frog that is! I shall let him remain in the water, with the friends he is fit to mix with; he cannot suppose he is fit for good society."

But the Frog, relying on her promise, put his head under the water, and dived away till he got to the bottom. Then he took the ball in his large mouth, and was soon again upon the surface of the water, when, by a jerk of his head, he threw the ball up, and the Princess helped him out with it. The King's daughter seized it with joy, and ran off as fast as her legs would carry her.

"Stop! stop! dear Princess," cried the Frog; "you are going without me; pray wait a minute, and take me with you. I cannot run as fast as you can." But the young Princess turned a deaf ear to the poor Frog's croaking, and getting to her father's palace as fast as she could, she very soon forgot the Frog who had been so kind a friend to her in her distress. So he was obliged to jump back again into the fountain.

The next day, when the King's daughter was sitting at the dinner-table with him and his courtiers, all in full state, and was eating out of her own little golden plate, there was a great noise in the courtyard, and the Princess, fancying she heard a slight croaking, listened, and then she heard "splish-splash, splish-splash," on the marble hall, and "splosh-splash," up the marble steps, till it came to the door of the state dining-room, when it stopped, and there was a strange knocking at the door, and a hoarse voice cried, "Oh! loveliest daughter of the King, open the door, I pray you!" So she arose and opened the door, wondering who it was who called her; but when she caught sight of the Frog, she slammed the door very vehemently, and sat down again at the table. But the King, seeing his daughter turn very pale and tremble violently, asked her if there was a giant at the door to fetch her away.

"Oh, no, Papa," she answered; "it is only a great ugly Frog."

"A Frog," replied the King; "what can he want with you?"

"Oh, my dear father, when I was sitting yesterday playing by the fountain, my golden ball fell into the water, and because I cried so much, the Frog fetched it out for me."

"Is that all that happened?" said the King; "tell me all the truth."

"Indeed," said she, trembling, "he insisted upon my promising that he should be my companion, and as I thought he could not come out of the water, I consented; and now the ugly thing has jumped out, and wants to come in here."

Just at that moment there was another knock, and a voice said—

"Open the door, King's daughter, I pray,
And by thy side for me make way;
Hast thou forgotten thy promises, made
At the fountain so clear, 'neath the lime-tree's shade?"

Then the King said: "What you have promised, that you must perform. Go, and let him in." So the King's daughter was obliged to go and let him in, and the Frog hopped in after her, right up to her chair; and as soon as she had sat herself down, the Frog cried, "Now take me up;" but at this she hesitated, until the King, growing angry, said, "Take him up directly." Then she knew she must obey, and helped the Frog on to the chair, where he was no sooner seated, than, wiping the water from his hands and face with a table-napkin, he said to her, "Now push your plate near me, and we will eat together." She did so, but everybody could see it was from fear of the King, and not willingly. The Frog seemed to relish his dinner very much, eating of everything but the salads, as he always had plenty of watercresses in the fountain. He took wine out of the Princess's glass, but she was nearly choking all the time she tried to eat, till at last the Frog, returning thanks for a good dinner, said, "My dear Princess, I have now satisfied my hunger and thirst, and I feel very tired and sleepy; take me in your arms, and carry me up-stairs to your chamber, and make the bed ready, that we may sleep together!"

Then, when the King's daughter heard this, she repented terribly of her promise, and began to cry, for she was afraid of the cold Frog—despite of his bright skin, she dared not touch him; besides which, he actually wanted to sleep in her beautiful nice clean bed!

When the King saw her cry, he became very angry, and said, "He who helped you when you were in trouble, shall not now be despised by you;" and he insisted upon her helping the Frog. So she took up the Frog in her two fingers, and, holding him at arm's length, she carried him into her bedroom, and put him down in a corner. But as she lay in her bed, he crept up to it, and said, "I am so very tired, that I shall sleep soundly; so take me up, or I will tell the King your father."

Upon hearing these words, the King's daughter could not contain herself for passion; so, catching the Frog in her hand, she dashed him with all her might against the wall, saying, "Perhaps you will be quiet now, you ugly beast!"

But, as he fell, he was changed from a Frog into a very handsome young Prince, with the most beautiful eyes in the world, who became her constant companion, and to whom, with her father's consent, she was soon after married. Then he told her how he had been changed from a Prince to a Frog by a wicked Witch, who doomed him to remain in the fountain until the King's daughter came and took him out, as no one else in the world had the power to do it; and he proposed that on the morrow he should go to visit his own kingdom.

The next morning, as soon as the Princess had put on her dress, there drove up to the door a carriage drawn by eight white prancing steeds, with the whitest of ostrich feathers in their heads, and the brightest of golden bits in their mouths; and the reins, and the bridle, too, were all of gold; and behind the carriage there stood the Faithful Henry, the servant of the young Prince, with a golden stick in his hand. Now the carriage was ready to carry them to the country of the young Prince, and the bride and bridegroom were ready seated, when Faithful Henry placed himself behind; and the Prince and Princess having bade a last adieu to the King, the horses started off at full speed. They had not proceeded far, when there was a loud crack heard; but the Prince, not wishing to alarm his bride, took no notice, and they travelled on, when presently another loud crack was heard; this time the Princess started likewise, and they both thought some part of the carriage had broken with a tremendous crack. Still they kept on, till at last another crack greatly alarmed the Prince, and, putting his head out of the window, he inquired of Faithful Henry if any part of the carriage had given way, and what that loud cracking noise meant. "Ah! my Prince," said Faithful Henry, "it is not the carriage that is broken, but the cracking of the three iron bands I had bound round my heart to keep it from bursting, when it was in such grief that you, my master, were changed into a Frog." Then they travelled on gaily to their journey's end, the heart of the Trusty Henry being free and happy.

HOP-O'-MY-THUMB.

A POOR labourer was sitting, one evening, in his chimney-corner, while his wife was spinning away opposite to him. He sat, moodily thinking, some time, and looking in the fire; at last, he lifted up his head, and said: "What a sad thing it is for us, that we have not any children! how silent is our hearth and home, while every one else is so gay and cheerful!"

"Yes," replied his wife, with a sigh; "if we had only one, and he no bigger than my thumb, I should be content, and we would both love him with all our hearts."

Meanwhile, what they were hoping for was taking place; and, at the end of seven months, she brought into the world an infant, well formed in all its limbs, but no bigger nor higher than her thumb. "Oh!" said she, "see here! I have got just what I asked for; but, little as he is, he is none the less our dear child."

So, because of his size, they christened him Hop-o'-my-Thumb; and though they brought him up with every care, and gave him the very best kind of food, he did not grow an inch, but remained just the same size as he was when born. For all this, he showed no want of spirit; his eyes sparkled with intelligence; and he showed on every occasion an address and activity that, however small his person, gave evidence of his ability to carry out whatever he undertook.

His father was getting ready, one day, when he was going to cut down some trees in a neighbouring forest, and said to himself, "I much wish I had got some one with me, to drive the cart."

"Father," said Hop-o'-my-Thumb, "I will go with you, and drive it—don't trouble yourself about that; I will take care that the cart is there in good time."

The good-man began to laugh: "That can't be," said he; "you are a clever little chap, certainly, but you are too little to lead a horse by the bridle."

"That's not the point, father; if mother will harness the horse, I will get up in his ear, and tell him which way to go."

"All right," said the father, "we'll make a trial of that plan."

So the good-dame put the horse in the cart, and seated Tom Thumb comfortably in the horse's ear, where the little man called out to Dobbin the road it ought to take—"Gee! woa!" and the rest of it—so cleverly, that Dobbin stepped along just as if a real carter had been driving him, and the cart was brought to the wood-side by the best and nearest road.

While the cart was turning the corner of a hedge, and the little fellow was shouting to the horse, two strangers were on the road. "Hallo!" said one to the other, "what have we here? Here is a cart going along, and one hears the voice of the carter, but sees no one!"

"There is something not quite clear about all this," said the other; "we must follow the cart, and see where it will stop."

The cart went on, until it came to a place in the forest where the trees were just felled. When Hop-o'-my-Thumb saw his father, he called out to him, "See here, father, how well I have driven the cart! and now help me to get down."

The father, taking hold of the bridle with one hand, took his son out of the horse's ear with the other, and set him down on the ground, where the little fellow sat down merrily on a shaving.

When the two strangers first caught sight of Tom Thumb, they hardly knew what to think, they were so much astonished. One of them took the other aside, and said: "This funny little chap would make our fortune, if we could get hold of him, and show him for a shilling throughout the country. We had better buy him at once." So they went up to the father, and said to him: "Sell us this little dwarf; we will promise you to take good care of him."

"No," replied the honest fellow, "no; he is my child, and all the gold in the world would not purchase him."

But Hop-o'-my-Thumb, who, during this conversation, had climbed up among the folds of his father's blouse, mounted on to his shoulder, and whispered in his ear, "Father, let these gentlemen have me; I will be sure to come back soon." So his father handed him over to the two men, for a round sum of money. "But where shall we put you?" said they to him.

"Oh! put me on the brim of your hat; I can walk about there, and enjoy a fine view of the country; leave it to me to take care I don't tumble off."

They did as he wished; and when Hop-o'-my-Thumb

had taken leave of his father—who did not half like his going off in that manner, and began to think what he should say to the boy's mother for coming home without him—the men started off, with the child under their care, and kept on the road until evening. But Hop-o'-my-Thumb began to think that the joke, or rather himself, had been carried quite far enough for that day, at any rate; so he called out, "Stop, stop! I want to get down!"

"Remain where you are, on my hat, my little man," said the one who carried him; "I don't mind what you do there; I am used to the birds."

"No, no," said Hop-o'-my-Thumb; "let me down, let me down, quick!"

The man took him off his hat, and set him on the ground, in a field by the road-side; he ran for an instant amongst the clods of earth, and then suddenly plunged into a field-mouse's nest, that he had been looking after for that purpose.

"Good-night, gentlemen; you must go without me," he cried out to them, with a laugh. They tried to catch him again, by poking their sticks into the mouse's nest, but it was all labour in vain; Hop-o'-my-Thumb ensconced himself still farther up the nest, and night having by this time come on, they were compelled to go home, in a great rage, empty-handed.

As soon as they were out of sight, Hop-o'-my-Thumb came out of his hole. He feared to risk walking at night in the open field, for a leg is soon broken. Luckily, he met with the empty shell of a snail. "Heaven be praised!" said he; I can pass the night in safety, down here;" and he nestled quickly down in it.

Just as he was dropping off to sleep, he heard two men, who were passing by, say one to another, "How shall we set about robbing the old rector of his gold and silver?"

"I can tell you!" cried out Hop-o'-my-Thumb to them.

"Who is that?" exclaimed one of the terrified thieves; "I am sure I heard some one speak."

They halted to listen; and Hop-o'-my-Thumb cried out again, "Take me with you, and I will help you."

"Where are you, then?"

"Look on the ground, where my voice comes from."

The thieves found him at last. "You little extract of a man! how do you think of being useful to us?"

"Look here," he replied, "I will slip in between the bars of the Rector's window, and pass out to you everything you want."

"Very well; so be it," said they; "we will put you to the proof."

As soon as they had arrived at the Rectory, Hop-o'-my-Thumb slipped between the bars, and glided into the chamber; then he set to crying out, as loud as he could, "Do you want all that is here?"

The thieves, in great alarm, said to him, "Speak lower; you will raise the whole house."

But Hop-o'-my-Thumb kept going on, as if he had not heard them, and shouted out again, "What is it you want? do you want all that is here?" A servant, who was sleeping in a room on the other side, heard his voice, sat up in her bed, and listened. The thieves had beaten a retreat, but at length took courage again, and thinking that the funny little fellow only wanted to amuse himself with their fears, returned under the window, and said to him, in a low voice, "No more of this fun; pass us out anything you can lay your hands upon." Whereupon, Hop-o'-my-Thumb began to shout again, as loud as he could, "I am going to give you all; hold out your hands."

This time the servant-girl heard plainly enough; she jumped out of bed, and ran to the door, which the thieves perceiving, fled as if the Evil One had been at their heels. When the girl came back, Hop-o'-my-Thumb, without her seeing him, hastened to hide himself in a truss of hay. The servant, after rummaging in every corner without discovering anything, went to bed again, fully convinced that she had been dreaming.

As for Hop-o'-my-Thumb, he got up into the hay, and made himself a snug bed in it. He reckoned upon lying there until daybreak, and then going back to his parents; but he had one or two farther trials to go through yet—so much of evil is there in this world. Up rose the maid-servant, with the early dawn, to give the cattle their fodder. Her first visit was to the hay-loft, and, unluckily, the first truss she came to was poor Hop-o'-my-Thumb's bedroom! Off this she took up an armful of hay, with Hop-o'-my-Thumb snugly asleep within it. Sound enough he slept, you may be sure; for he saw nothing, and only woke when in the mouth of a Cow, who had taken him up with a pull of hay. At first, he thought he had fallen into a fulling-mill, but he soon made out where he really was. With all his attention engaged in avoiding being crunched between the Cow's teeth, he ended by sliding down her throat and into her paunch. His lodging seemed to him rather confined without a window, and he could see neither sun nor candle. He did not at all like his residence, nor was his stay rendered the more agreeable, by the fact, that fresh quantities of

hay kept continually coming down to him, so that the space grew still narrower and narrower. At last, in his terror, he shouted out, as loud as he could, "No more hay! no more hay! I don't want any more hay!"

Now, it happened that, just at this moment, the servant-maid was busy milking the Cow; the voice which she heard, without seeing any one, and which she recognized as that which had awakened her in the night, terrified her to such a degree, that she fell down off the stool, scattering the milk to the right and left. She ran off in all haste, to find her master, and exclaimed to him, "Oh, good gracious! oh, Mr. Rector! here is a Cow that speaks like a man!"

"You are out of your senses, child," replied the Rector; but, nevertheless, he went himself into the stable, to make sure of what was going on there.

Scarcely had he set his foot within, than Hop-o'-my-Thumb cried out, "No more hay! I don't want any more hay!" Fear seized the worthy Rector, in his turn, and imagining the Cow to be possessed, he said she must be killed. So they knocked the poor Cow on the head, and the paunch, in which poor Hop-o'my-Thumb was still a prisoner, was thrown on the dung-hill.

The little fellow had a great deal of trouble to get out of this, and was just on the point of passing his head outside, when a new trouble assailed him. A famished Wolf rushed upon the paunch of the Cow, and swallowed it at one gulp. Hop-o'-my-Thumb, for all that, did not lose courage. He did the right thing directly; for, since he could not do what he wanted to do, he set to work to think what was next best to be done. "Perhaps," thought he, "I may be able to do something with this Wolf." Then he called to him out of his belly, in which he was shut up, "My dear friend, Mr. Wolf, I can point out to you where you can get a capital dinner, after this excellent breakfast of yours."

"And where may that be?" said the Wolf.

"In such-and-such a house; you have but to slip in by the drain that runs under the kitchen, and you will find there pots of butter, and bladders of lard, and cakes, and sauces, that you can't help relishing." Then he described to him, with sufficient exactness, his father's house.

The Wolf did not want to be told twice, but wriggled his way into the kitchen, and had a good tuck-out at the expense of the larder. But after he had dined to his heart's content, and wanted to creep out, he found himself so blown out with such a nourishing repast, that he could not manage to squeeze out by the same drain as he had come in by. Hop-o'-my-Thumb, who had reckoned upon this, now began to make a terrible noise inside the Wolf's body, by leaping and shouting with all his might and main. This made the Wolf uncomfortable in more senses than one. "Will you keep quiet?" said he; "do you want to wake up all the family?"

"That is good, surely!" replied the little man; "you have had a capital dinner, and now it is my turn to amuse myself." Then he set to shouting as loud as he could.

At last, he succeeded in rousing his parents, who

ran to the door, and looked into the kitchen through the keyhole. When they caught sight of the Wolf there, they armed themselves, the man with a hatchet, the woman with a scythe. "Stay you behind," said the man to his wife, as they entered the chamber; "I am going to hit him with my hatchet; if I don't kill him at the first blow, do you rip up his stomach."

Hop-o'-my-Thumb, who heard all this, and recognized his father's voice, began to think that plan might not suit his present lodging, so he called out, "Father! father!"

"Oh, you traitor!" growled the Wolf.

"It's I, dear father, your own Hop-o'-my-Thumb; I am in the Wolf's belly."

The Wolf snapped at him, but only bit himself, and howled with the pain.

"Thank Heaven!" said the father, "our dear child is restored to us." Then he directed his wife to lay aside the scythe, for fear of hurting their son; and, lifting up his hatchet, with one sure blow, the Wolf lay stretched out dead. Then he took a knife and a pair of scissors, and opened the Wolf's belly, where he found poor little Hop-o'-my-Thumb, in a very dirty and dilapidated and half-digested condition.

"Ah!" said he; "what trouble we have been in about you!"

"Yes, father, I have been running about the world a good deal, and at last, as you see, have happily come to light again."

"Where have you been, then?"

"Ah, father, I have been in a Mouse's hole, in the paunch of a Cow, and the belly of a Wolf; and now, at last, I am stopping with you."

"And we will never sell you again, for all the gold in the world," said his parents, as they embraced him warmly, and pressed him to their hearts.

Then they gave him something to eat, and put him on some fresh clothes, for those he wore were quite spoiled by his travels; and there we will leave him, snug and warm, for the present: but I shall have a great deal more to tell you about this same little gentleman afterwards.

DON'T BUY MONEY TOO DEAR.

ONCE upon a time, there was a poor woman, and because she felt very much the grievance of her poverty, she had a very strong wish to possess some money, if only once, by some accident or miracle (for in that way only could it come to her); for she had a notion, that if she once could get any money, all her sorrows and her troubles would be at an end.

After a very long time of patience, the accident, or the miracle, happened at last; for, one day, the poor woman heard that, on the slope of a certain hill, there grew a miraculous weed, which, if any one collecting the other grasses had the good fortune to pluck, the mountain would open, and the gatherer of the weed, holding it in his hand, would find the entrance to a large cave open to him. Within this cave he would see

Seven Old Men, sitting round a table, counting out money, from the stores of which, lying all about, they would allow any one possessed of the miraculous weed to take away as much as they could carry.

From the moment the poor woman heard this story, she made her most important business, during the whole of that summer, the fetching fresh grass from that hill-side for her cow, in the hope of plucking amongst the grass the miraculous weed.

At last, she did so. One day, she had been toiling till the evening in plucking handfuls of grass, and had pressed it down into a basket, which she was carrying heavily upon her head, holding her little daughter by the hand; when, on a sudden, she saw a huge rock turn noiselessly, as if it were a door upon well-oiled hinges, right in front of her, and on peeping within, she saw Seven grave-looking, grey-bearded Old Men, sitting round a table, counting money, with piles of gold and silver all about and around them.

The poor woman, seeing her opportunity, entered the cave, emptied out the grass from her basket, and filled it with gold. Then she put it on her head again, and was about to go forth, when one of the Old Men said, "Woman, forget not the best thing."

But, intent on her gold and long-looked-for happiness, she heeded him not, and went on her way. Scarcely had she reached the mouth of the cave, than the entrance rolled into its place, sharp behind her, with a roll like thunder. She turned to look back, and missed her little daughter! The unhappy child, who had lingered behind, playing with the gold, had been shut in!

Then the mother's grief and agony were such as no one could bear to see; her insupportable grief could not be endured; and at last she flew, despairing, to consult a Clergyman, in the hope that, as no earthly medicine could avail to soothe her distress, some aid from Heaven might be found to alleviate it. When the good old Curate learnt what had happened, he told her that there was no help for her, but to wait seven years, when a change might occur, and she would find her daughter again. When that period of time had elapsed, he said, she was to go again to the hill-side, at the same hour in which she had lost her child, and there she was to wait for what might happen. The mistake she had committed was, he told her, in quite emptying her basket for the sake of putting as much gold as she could into it; because, when she threw away the grass, she had thrown away the miracle-weed also.

On hearing this, the poor woman remembered the Old Man's words, and saw, to her sorrow, how much she had erred in valuing gold as the greatest of blessings. What was that gain of gold now, when compared with the loss of her beautiful golden-haired child? Then she began to think over things, and soon convinced herself that there were in life many blessings, the loss of which no gold can repay,—as the love of friends, a good name, the loss of a father, a mother, or a child, banishment from one's native land, the loss of one's good conscience, fame, and honour; give gold for these, and on which side does the loss really lie? in comparison with these, how much does gold become reduced in value! She had a long seven years to think over all this; and to her credit be it said, that, during all that time, she would not touch, nor even so much as look at, the hated gold she had brought from the Old Men's Cave.

At last came the day, at the expiration of the seven years, on which she might venture to entertain a hope of seeing her lost child once more. The woman hastened to the hill-side, near to the rock that shut in her daughter from her longing gaze; and, behold! as she came nearer and nearer to the spot, her straining eyes could distinguish, first a dark spot, then a form, then—yes, yes! it was!—her heart's treasure, her dear young daughter, lying, in a gentle sleep, outside the rock,—just seven years older, but as fresh, and as blooming, and as beautiful, as when she lost her. She raised the child tenderly in her arms, and gently kissed her, to awaken her without alarming her, and then led her, with a thousand kisses and embraces, on the road towards their home, saying to herself, "Oh! if all the gold I have left there should be gone when I get back, I shall still be as happy as if I had found all the treasures in the world!"

But the gold was still there, and she enjoyed the advantages of wealth, with a better knowledge of its true value. So she made the best possible use of it, in the proper education of her daughter; and the well-trained young maiden became, in herself, a great and more valuable treasure.

OLD MOTHER GOOSE.

THERE once lived, in a pretty little rose-covered cottage, an old widow-woman and her two daughters. The eldest, who was her step-daughter, was very beautiful and obliging, and very industrious, while her own child was altogether as lazy and ugly. She, however, behaved most kindly to the ugly one, and the other had to do all the hard and dirty work, and drudge away from morning till night, without giving any satisfaction. This poor maiden, when she had done all her housework, was not allowed to sit quietly down and rest herself, but was forced out into the highway, where she was obliged to sit and spin so hard, that the blood ran from her fingers. Once it happened that her hands were so tired with spinning, and her spindle so covered with blood, that she was obliged to go to the well, and kneeling down beside it, she tried to wash it clean again, but, unhappily, she let it fall down the well into the water. She was very sorry, and ran crying to her step-mother, to tell her her misfortune; but she was angry with her, and behaved very cruelly to her, saying, "Since you have let your spindle fall down the well, you must yourself go and fetch it up again."

So the poor maiden went mournfully along to the well, wondering how she should get it up again; and not knowing what to do, in her great distress, she jumped down the well to fetch the spindle out. She

became so frightened when she found herself going down, that she lost all consciousness; and when she revived again, she found herself in a beautiful meadow, with the sun shining, and all kinds of bright and sweet-smelling flowers blooming around her. So she got up, and finding she had not broken any of her bones by the fall, she walked along in the fresh air, enjoying herself, till, at length, she came to a baker's, where the oven was full of bread, which cried out, "Draw me out, draw me out, or I shall be burnt! I have been baked quite long enough." So she sought for the baker's peel, and having found it, she drew out all the loaves one after the other. Then she walked on again, until she came to an apple-tree, whose fruit hung in very thick clusters, and it cried out, "Shake us, shake us; we apples are all ripe!" So she shook the tree, and all the apples came showering down upon her; and when there were none left upon the tree, she gathered them all together in a heap, and travelled on.

At last, she came to a cottage, and an old woman was peeping out of it, who had such very ugly large teeth, that the maiden was terrified, and ran away. The old woman, however, called after her, and bade her come back, saying, "What are you afraid of, my child? Stop with me; if you will put all things in order in my house, and keep everything neat and clean, then everything will go well with you; but you must take very great care that you make my bed well, and shake it heartily, so that the feathers fly well, for then," said she, "it snows on the earth, and makes the ground ready to bring forth in the summer-time. They call me 'Old Mother Goose.'" As the old woman spoke so kindly, the girl took heart, and consented to become her servant. She was very contented with everything she got; she did her work well, and kept the house tidy, not forgetting every morning to shake the bed most industriously, so that the feathers flew down like flakes of snow; therefore, her life was a very happy one, and there were no cross words, because she did her duty. She had baked and roast meat every day of her life.

She remained with the old woman for a long time; but all at once she began to grow thin and pine away, and got very sad, and did not know what was the matter with herself. At last, she found she was homesick, and thought she should like to see her mother and sister; for she was kind-hearted, and although her life at home was very unhappy, and she fared a thousand times worse at home, still she could not forget them, and longed to see them. So she told her mistress, "I wish to go home, and if it does not go so well with me there as here, I must return."

The mistress replied, "I could see you wanted to go home; and since you have been such a good and obedient servant, I will take you up again myself." So saying, she took her by the hand, and led her before a great door, which she undid; and when the maiden was just beneath it, a great shower of gold fell, and a great deal stuck about her, so that she was covered with gold from head to foot. "That is the reward for your industry," said the old woman; then she gave her the spindle that had fallen down the well. Then she bade the maiden adieu, and closed the door, when she found herself upon the earth, not very far from her mother's dwelling; and as she came in at the gate, the Cock sat upon the house-top, and called—

"Cock-a-doodle-doo!
Our golden maid's come home again!"

Then she softly opened the door, and went into her mother's house, who was glad to see her daughter, all shining with gold, and so she received her kindly.

The maiden told her mother everything that had happened to her; and when her mother heard how easily she had gained all these great riches, she determined that her ugly daughter should try her luck. So her mother insisted upon her going out, also, to sit by the well and spin; but the ugly daughter did not like it, and showed a great many airs about it, but at last her mother drove her out. So, in order that her spindle might be covered with blood, as she was too lazy to spin, she took a thorn and pricked her finger, and then threw her spindle into the well, and jumped in after it; but she came with a very hard bump into the meadow, where her sister had gently fallen. When she arrived at the baker's, the Bread called out, "Draw me out, draw me out, or I shall be burnt! I have been baked long enough already." But she answered very ill-naturedly, "Then you must burn; do you think I shall dirty my hands with that rough peel?" So she left the loaves to burn, and went on her way, until she came to the Apple-tree, which called out, "Shake me, shake me! my apples are all ripe, and will spoil." She replied: "A very pretty thing to ask me to do! No, indeed; I'll not stay to have my head knocked by your falling upon it;" and so she continued her journey, till she came to the cottage where Old Mother Goose lived. She was not afraid of her ugly teeth, because she had heard her sister say how kind she was; and so she engaged herself to her.

The first day, she really set to work in earnest, keeping the house clean and tidy, and shaking the bed tremendously, for she thought of the gold she should get. On the second day, she did not get half through her work, but idled about in the garden, and lazed the day away. Then, the third day, she would not do anything, and was too lazy to get up in time to get the milk in the morning; she did not shake the beds, either, as she ought, and the feathers did not fly, so that there would be no snow in the winter.

Then the old woman got very tired of seeing her house going to rack and ruin, through her servant's neglect, and she dismissed her from her service. At this the lazy puss was well pleased, "For," thought she, "now I must prepare for the golden shower. I will put on a wide petticoat, that I may catch it all." Her mistress then led her to the door, as she had done her sister; but when she was beneath it, instead of gold, a tubful of pitch was poured upon her. "There!" said Old Mother Goose; "that is the reward for your services, Miss Lazybones!" and she shut the door in her face. Then she made her way home to her mother's house, all covered with pitch; and when the

Cock on the house-top saw her coming in at the gate, he cried—

"Cock-a-doodle-doo!
Our dirty maid's come home again!"

But as she was too lazy to wash the pitch off her while it was fresh, it stuck to her as long as she lived.

THE MILLER AND THE WATER-SPRITE.

ONCE upon a time, there was a Miller, and he and his wife had lived many years happily together, with money to lend and to spend, for their prosperity went on increasing year by year. But misfortune, says the proverb, comes creeping in by night; and their good fortune began to grow less and less, just as fast as it had grown up, until the Miller, at last, could scarcely call his own the mill out of which he was earning his subsistence. Sad at heart was the poor fellow, and many a long night used he to lie and toss about in his bed, instead of sleeping sound after his work. One morning, after a sleepless night of care, he rose with the first streak of daylight, and went out to get a little fresh air, in the hope that the brightness of the morning might sooth his wearied soul. As he came along by the mill-dam, it glistened in the first rays of the sun, and seemed to wake up from its night's quiet sleep. He heard a slight rippling sound of the waters, and turning quickly round, saw a beautiful woman raising herself gently out of the water. Her long hair, which she loosened over her shoulders with her delicate hands, fell down on either side, and covered her shining white body. The Miller saw at once that it was the Water-Sprite of the Lake, and he scarcely knew, in his fright, whether to stop or take to flight. But the fair Water-Sprite spoke to him in a soft silvery voice, and addressed him by name, and inquired why he was so downhearted. Until this, the Miller had kept silence; but when he heard her speak so graciously, he took courage, and told her how, having lived for so long a time in wealth and honour, he was at present so poor that he did not know what to do.

"Set your heart at rest," replied the Water-Sprite; "I will make you richer and happier than ever you have been; only you must promise to give me whatever is next born in your house."

"That will be a puppy or a kitten, doubtless," said the Miller to himself, in a low voice. So he made the promise she asked.

The Water-Sprite plunged down back again beneath the waters, and he returned consoled to his mill; where he had hardly arrived, and was about to turn into the keeping-room, when the servant met him at the door, and exclaimed, that she had to wish him joy, for his wife was just brought to bed of a fine boy! The Miller stood as if struck with a thunderbolt, for he saw at once how the malicious Water-Sprite had

THE WATER-SPRITE LURES THE YOUNG KEEPER INTO THE LAKE.

known what was going on, and had played a trick upon him. On his entering his wife's room, he could not assume sufficient cheerfulness to deceive her; and seeing him with his head bowed down, when near her bed, she asked him, "How is this, dear? are you not rejoiced at the coming of our dear boy?"

At first, he would have concealed from her what he had promised; but the sight of the baby overpowered him, and he burst into tears, and told her what had happened. "Of what use," said he, "will be wealth and prosperity to me, if I must lose my child?"

But what was to be done? None of the relations,

who came together to congratulate them, could suggest any remedy.

However that might be, from that day, good-luck came back to the Miller's house. Whatever he undertook, prospered; his coffers and his chests seemed to fill of themselves, and the money seemed to turn over in his desk at night; so that, at the end of no long period, the Miller was as rich as he had been before. But wealth brought him no repose of mind, and however he might enjoy himself, he did so without tranquillity; the fatal promise he had made to the Water-Sprite was ever gnawing at his heart. Every time he passed by the lake, he dreaded seeing her come up to the surface, and claim her debt. He would not let the child go near the water. "Take care," he used to say to the boy; "if ever you touch it, a hand will come out and catch hold of you, and drag you down to the bottom."

But as years and years rolled on, one after the other, and the Water-Sprite never made her appearance again, the Miller began to feel a little more comfortable.

When the boy grew up to a young man, they placed him with a Gamekeeper. He was a fine lad, and honest, and hard-working; so that, when he had gone through a year or two's practice, he made a capital Keeper himself; and a nobleman, whose estate was near the village, took him into his own service. Here the Keeper soon fell in love with a pretty girl; and his master, on learning this, gave him a small cottage, and otherwise made matters comfortable for their marriage.

One day, the Keeper was in full chase of a deer. The animal came out from the forest into the plain, and he went after it, and at last got a shot at it, and brought it down. Eager after his sport, the young man did not perceive how near he was to the dangerous pond; and when he had killed and cut up the deer, sportsman's fashion, he went and washed his blood-stained hands in its waters. But scarcely had he plunged them into it, than the Water-Sprite came up from the bottom, and entwined him, with a smile, in her humid arms, and drew him down so quickly, that the wave closed over him as it went rippling along.

When evening came on without the Keeper's return home, his wife, who stood watching at the door, went within in great trouble. Then she went forth to look after him; and as he had often related to her how he was under obligation to be on his guard against the allurements of the Water-Sprite of the mill-pond, and how he dared not risk himself within the vicinity of its waters, she had some suspicion of what had happened. She ran to the pond, and, seeing the game he had killed lying on its banks, she had no longer any doubt of his unlucky fate. Lamenting and wringing her hands, she called, in vain, on her loved one; and ran from one side to the other, and called him again, and reproached the Water-Sprite in unmeasured language; but still to all there was no reply. The face of the water remained smooth as a mirror, and seemed to smile at her distress, the moon's half-full face looking up at her from its surface without motion.

The poor wife would not quit the side of the mill-pond; unceasingly she kept on walking up and down, on one side or the other, sometimes in sad silence, with smothered sobs; sometimes with low moanings, and now and then loudly shrieking. Poor creature! her strength was at last exhausted, and she sank down upon the ground, and fell into a deep slumber. But her mind was too full for quiet sleep, and she was soon in a dream. She seemed to be in great trouble, going up, up, between two massive rocks; while the thorns and nettles on the rugged overgrown way pricked her feet, and the rain beat on her face, and the wind blew her long hair about in wild dis-

order. But the top of the mountain once reached, all things wore a totally different appearance. There the sky was blue, the air warm; the earth sloped downwards with a gentle descent, and in the middle was a cottage in a verdant meadow enamelled with bright flowers. To this she made her way, with a feeling of light-heartedness, and went up to the door and opened it. Inside was seated an old Dame, with long white hair, who looked as if she belonged to the old, old time, and was dressed in very old-fashioned garments. This old Dame raised her eyes, and was just opening her mouth to address her, when the Keeper's wife awoke.

She had slept so long, that the day was already just about to dawn. Her dream strongly impressed her, and she made up her mind to follow its guidance. There was just such a mountain, and just such a rugged path a few miles off, and she had never been up to the top of it.

Hither, therefore, she hastened, and climbed up the arduous steep, after much pain and labour; she found all just as it appeared to her in her dream at night.

The old Dame received her graciously, and pointed out a seat, which she invited her to take. "Doubtless," said she, in a kindly manner, "some misfortune has befallen you, or you would hardly visit my lonely, out-of-the-way cabin." Then the unhappy wife up and told her tale, with many tears.

"Oh! be comforted, my dear," said the good-natured old Dame; "I will come to your aid. You see this golden comb: take it, and wait until the moon is full; then go down to the mill-pond, and sit on the bank, and pass the comb through your long black hair. When you have done this, lay the golden comb down at the brink of the pond, and wait and see what will happen then."

Home went the wife, hopeful, and more calmed in spirit. But how long the days, and how weary did the hours seem to her, before the moon came to the full; then she betook herself to the mill-pond, and sat herself down on the bank, and passed the comb of gold through her hair so long and so black; and when she had done, she took her seat right at the edge of the pond. It was not long before the pond began to bubble up from the bottom, and a wave rose and rolled towards the brink, and carried away the golden comb in its backward motion. Hardly was there time for the comb to have reached the bottom, than the surface of the water divided into two parts, and the head of the Keeper rose upon the top. He spoke not a word, but looked upon his wife with a sad and sorrowful regard. At the very same instant, a second wave came bustling forward with a sullen sound, and covered the Keeper's head out of sight. All having disappeared, the treacherous pond became smooth and tranquil as before, and the face of the full moon shone calmly and unwavering on its bright surface.

The unhappy wife went back still more wretched and despairing; but she felt comforted when, that same night, in another dream, she saw the cabin of the old Dame again.

Next morning, as soon as she woke, she was up, and on her way—poor creature!—to the good Fairy, to whom she told her pitiful tale.

The old Dame gave her, this time, a golden flute, and said to her: "Wait until another full moon, and then take this flute; place yourself on the brink of the pond, play some little air on this instrument, and when you have done, lay it down on the gravel by the edge, and you will see what will come of it."

The Keeper's wife did all this exactly as the old Dame had told her. Scarcely had she laid the flute at the edge of the pond, when the water began to bubble up from the bottom, like a boiling pot; a wave rose and advanced towards the edge, whence it drew in the golden flute as it flowed back again; nor was it long before the water opened from within, and not only the head of the Keeper, but he himself rose right out of the pond, even as far as the half of his body. With eyes beaming with regretful love and tenderness, he stretched forth his arms towards her, but a second wave, once more, came dashing forward with a roaring, angry sound, and covered him all over, and overwhelmed him within its watery grasp, and drew him down with it to the bottom! "Oh!" exclaimed his wretched wife, at this dreadful spectacle; "alas! alas! what avails it thus to see my beloved one, only to lose him again immediately!"

Sorrow once more took possession of her bosom; but she was led by a dream again, for the third time, to the dwelling of the old woman. She went there, and the Fairy gave her a golden spinning-wheel, and spoke words of comfort to her, and said: "Now, wait for another full moon, my dear; then take your spinning-wheel, and place yourself at the edge of the pond, and spin until you have filled your bobbins; and when you have done this, lay the spinning-wheel down by the water-side, and you will see what will then happen."

The Keeper's wife followed these instructions to the letter. As soon as the full moon showed itself, she carried the golden spinning-wheel to the water's brink, and spun away diligently until all her tow was exhausted, and the thread quite filled the bobbins. Scarcely was the wheel laid down upon the edge, when the bottom of the pond bubbled up more violently than ever; a strong wave came hastening forward, and carried off the wheel with it. Immediately, the head and the whole body of the Keeper showed them-

selves on the surface. Quickly he leaped out to the edge, seized his wife by the hand, and took to flight. But scarcely had they gone a few paces, than the whole pond rose up, entire, with a horrible boiling and bubbling, and spread itself with irresistible violence all over the plain. Already the two fugitives saw nothing but death before their eyes, when the wife, in her agony, called the old Dame to her aid; in an instant they were changed, the one into a toad, the other into a frog. The eager flood following upon them, came up quickly, caught them, and rolled all over them, but it could not drown them; however, it separated them, and carried them away in different directions, far from each other.

When the waters retired, and they once more could put their feet on dry land, they resumed their human forms. But neither of the two had any knowledge of what had become of the other, and they found themselves among the people of a far distant country, who had no knowledge of their native land, from which high mountains and deep valleys separated them. To gain their living, both of them were obliged to look after sheep, and for many years they led their flocks along the woods and fields, weighed down with sorrow and regret for each other's loss.

One day, just as the sweet spring-time was beginning to awaken the flowers from the earth's bosom, it so happened, that both of them came forth with their flocks, and chance so willed it, that they led them along until they met. Upon the sheltered slope of a distant mountain, the husband saw a flock, and directed his own sheep towards the same side. They arrived in the valley, both at the same moment; but they did not recognize each other, although they were both pleased at no longer being alone. From that time they led their flocks every day to pasture side by side; and though they never spoke to one another, yet still a feeling of consolation pervaded their minds.

One evening, as the full moon was shining in the heavens, and the sheep were reposing all about them, the Shepherd took his flute out from his wallet, and played a charming, though sad, air. He remarked, when he concluded, that the Shepherdess was weeping bitterly. "Why those tears, Shepherdess?" he inquired.

"Ah!" replied she, "it was just such a bright full moon, when I last played that same air on the flute, and when the head of my beloved one appeared to me above the surface of the water."

He gazed earnestly upon her; it was just as if a veil had fallen from before his eyes. He recognized his lost and loved one; and as he turned his eyes upon her, while the moon shone bright upon his face, she recognized him also, in her turn. They sprang into each other's arms, embraced, and were happy beyond all farther want or care.

THE PRINCE IN THE IRON SAFE.

IN ancient times, the son of a powerful King, who had offended an old Witch, was enchanted by her, and she shut him up in a great Iron Safe, which she placed in a wood, and made him live there. Years and years passed on, but nobody could be found who had the power to release him; until, one day, the daughter of a neighbouring King, who had lost herself in the wood, and could not find her way home, came at last, after nine days' weary wandering, to the place where the Iron Safe stood. As she got near to it, she heard a voice say, "Where do you come from? and where are you going to?"

She replied, "I have lost the way to my father's kingdom, and I am unable to find my home, and shall surely perish with cold and hunger."

"Oh! if that is all, I will help you, and that quickly," said the voice from the Iron Safe; "but you must consent to do what I desire. I am the son of a far more powerful King than your father, and am willing to marry you."

The Princess shrugged up her shoulders at this suggestion; "For," said she, "what can I do with an Iron Safe?" but, nevertheless, as she could do nothing better, and was longing to get home, she consented to what he wished. Then the Prince told her that she must go to her father's palace, and fetch a knife, and then return and make a hole in the Safe; then he gave her such exact directions as to her road, that she could not fail to reach it, and in two hours she was at home by her father's fire-side. There was great rejoicing in the house when the Princess returned; the old King affectionately embraced her, calling her his dear child, and did not know when to cease his caresses; but she was sore troubled, and said, "Ah! my father, strange things have happened to me since I left your roof; I never should have returned to it, or have been able to get out of that deep wild wood, had it not been for the kindness of an Iron Safe, to which I have given my word to return and become its wife."

When the old King heard this, he became terribly alarmed, and fell into a swoon, for he dearly loved his only daughter. When he revived, and was able to talk again, they resolved between themselves, that the Miller's daughter, who was an exceedingly pretty girl, should go instead of the Princess; so they led her into the forest, and, giving her a knife, told her to scrape a hole in the Iron Safe. So she went on scraping and scraping, hour after hour, all through the day and night, but not the smallest hole could she make. When day was about to break, a voice from within the Safe exclaimed, "It seems to me like daylight breaking."

"Yes," replied the girl, "it seems so to me, too; and, if I am not mistaken, I hear the clacking of my father's mill."

"Oh, then, my pretty lass, you are the Miller's daughter, are you? Well, then, the best thing for you to do, is to hasten home again, and send the Princess to me."

The girl, therefore, did as he bid her, went back to the King, and told him the Iron Safe did not want her, but her mistress, the Princess. This news sorely distressed the King, and the Princess began weeping and bewailing her hard fate. The King tried to console her, by saying he would send his Swineherd's daughter in her stead. Now this girl was more beautiful than the Miller's daughter, and the King offered her a piece of gold, if she would go instead of their beloved Princess. Thereupon, this girl also went away, and scraped away with as little success as the former. When morning arrived, a voice from the Iron Safe exclaimed, "It seems to me like daylight."

"Yes," said the girl, "it is so; for I hear the sound of my father's horn."

"Soho!" said the voice; "you are, then, the Swineherd's daughter? The wisest thing for you to do, is to get quickly back to the Princess, and tell her there is no help for it—all must be as I have said; and therefore, if she does not come herself to me, the whole kingdom shall fall into decay, and crumble away, so that not one stone shall remain upon another to tell where it stood."

As soon as the Princess heard this, she fell to crying, but this was of no use, for she was bound to keep her promise. So, with a heavy heart she bade her father adieu, and taking with her a knife, made her way to the Iron Safe in the forest. As soon as she reached it, she began scraping away with all her might, and before two hours had elapsed, had succeeded in making a small hole in it; then, putting her eye close to it, she peeped in, and what should she behold on the inside, but a most charming Prince, whose handsome dress all glittered with gold and most valuable precious stones! She immediately fell violently in love with him; and she then began scraping away with all her might, and very soon had made a hole large enough for her beloved Prince to get out. "For ever now you are mine, and I am thine," he said, as he stepped upon the earth; "you are my bride—I am your husband, because you have saved me."

Then he wished at once to take her home with him to his father's kingdom, but the Princess did not think this quite proper, without going first to her father, and bidding him good-bye; so she begged the Prince to allow her to do so. The Prince agreed to this, if she would promise not to speak more than three words to her father, and immediately return. Thereupon, the now happy Princess went back to her father; but, alas for female human nature! she spoke many more than three words; and the consequence was, the Iron Safe entirely disappeared, and was carried far away, over many icy mountains and snowy valleys, but without the Prince, who was fortunately saved by the powerful efforts and kind intentions of the Princess; he was now free to roam, being no longer consigned to his dreadful prison-house.

As soon as the Princess could tear herself from her father's presence, she, with many regrets and a sorrowful heart, again bade him adieu. Then she took what gold from his coffers she thought absolutely necessary, and made her way back to the wood. She

68

sought for the Iron Safe, but could not find it, though she looked for her lost love nine long days and nights, without intermission. At last, her hunger became so great, and her body so enfeebled, that she thought her end was near, and that she must surely perish of hunger, as she knew not how to help herself. When the cold night came, she put forth all her remaining strength, and climbed up into a little tree, so that she might be free from the wild beasts, who were sure to seek their prey at dark. To her great joy, she saw a little glimmering light in the distance. "Ah!" she exclaimed, "there, at last, I may find shelter;" and quickly getting down, she made all possible haste towards the light. As she was a good and pious Princess, she said a little prayer, trusting that she might be brought safely through her difficulties. Soon she came to a little hut, around which there was much deep grass growing, and before the door stood a pile of logs of wood. "However came you here?" thought she to herself; and so she stooped down and peeped through the window, when she saw a family of very fat little Toads seated round a table laden with hot savoury meats, and good red wine, and plates and dishes made of gold and silver, such as she had seen at her father's palace. She took courage, and knocked, and immediately a Toad politely said—

"Little Toad, with leg so long,
Eye so bright, and back so strong,
The lattice door pray open wide,
And see who 'tis that stands outside."

As soon as these words were spoken, a little fat Toad came leaping up, and opened the door, and the tired Princess walked in. They all bade her welcome, and begged her to be seated and rest awhile; and then they asked her where she came from, and where she was going? She told her kind friends, the Toads, all her troubles, and how she had been, through delight at seeing her kind old father, induced to speak more than three words, and the heavy calamity that had followed the breaking of the promise she made the Prince; and now she was about to seek over hill and dale for him, until she should once more behold him. When she had made an end of telling the kind Toads her tale, the old Toad, in a tone of compassion, cried out—

"Little Toad, with wrinkled skin,
Pray fetch for me a basket in;
Then fill it high with dainties rare,
And give it to this Princess fair."

So the little Toad went and brought the basket in to the old one, and she caused the finest wine and the nicest food at her command to be placed before the Princess. After she had refreshed herself with the delicacies set before her, and rested awhile, she showed her to a beautiful bed, white as snow, and of the softest down, with hangings of pale blue silk and velvet, spotted with silver, in which, having said her prayers, she slept soundly.

As early as the sun arose, the young Princess, anxious to pursue her search after her beloved Prince, left her bed, and, having dressed herself, she wished the old Toad a good morning, who, as a parting gift,

presented her with three very large needles, which she took from her pocket, to take with her, saying they would be of use to her, since she would have to pass over a mountain of glass, three sharp swords, and a big lake, before she would regain her lover. The old Toad gave her, also, a plough-wheel and three nuts; and with these this kind old Toad started her afresh upon her road.

Presently, she came to a very steep mountain of glass, which was so very smooth, she was not able to get any foothold; and so she bethought herself of the large needles, and placing them in the mountain, she stepped her foot so that it rested against them, and so at last succeeded in making her way to the top. When she had arrived there, she put the needles in a secure place; and soon she came to the three swords, over which she rolled easily, by means of her plough-wheel. She then journeyed on afresh, and soon came to a wide lake, over which she swam, and then she beheld before her a fine old castle. Into this castle she made up her mind to enter; and meeting with a man crossing the courtyard, she offered herself as a servant, telling him she was a poor girl, who had once rescued a young Prince from an Iron Safe which stood in a forest.

After some delay, she was hired as a scullery-maid, at very low wages, and soon found out that the Prince had an intention to marry another lady, because he imagined his former lady-love was long since dead and gone. One evening, when she had done her work, and was very tired, she thought she would refresh herself by washing and making herself neat and tidy. When this was done, she sat down and reflected upon her hard fate, when she suddenly bethought herself of the three nuts the old Toad had given her, and drawing one out of her pocket, she cracked it. Instead of finding a kernel, there was a magnificent dress!

When the young Bride heard this, she insisted upon having this royal dress, as it was not fit for a servant-maid. But the Princess would not listen to the offer made to her, and indignantly refused to sell it; but, being sorely pressed, she at length consented, upon the condition that she should be allowed to pass the night in the chamber of the Prince. This request was at length acquiesced in; the Bride being so very anxious to possess the dress, that she went and told her sweetheart the silly servant-girl wanted to pass the night in his room. "So be it," said he; "if you are contented, so am I." Then she handed to him a glass of wine, in which she had put a sleeping potion. In consequence, he slept so soundly, that the young Princess could not awaken him, although she cried the whole night, repeating to him, "I saved you out of the wild forest, and rescued you from an Iron Safe; I have sought you, and travelled over a mountain of glass, and over three drawn swords, and across a wide lake; and now I have found you, will you not —oh! will you not—listen to one word I have to say to you?" The Prince's servants, however, who were sleeping in an ante-chamber, heard the wailing, and told his Royal Highness of it in the morning.

The next evening, the Princess, after she had

FAIRY BOOKS FOR BOYS AND GIRLS.

finished her hard work, was glad to dress herself in clean and decent clothes again; and then she sat herself down, and putting her hand in her pocket, pulled out another nut, and having cracked it, found in it a dress surpassing in beauty the one she had already given up to the new Bride; who, the moment she set her eyes upon it, declared that, cost her what it might, she had made up her mind to possess that also. The Princess would on no account part with her dress, except on the same condition as she had yielded up the other to the Bride's entreaties; and the Prince gave his permission for her to occupy the place she had done the night previously. The Bride, however, being of a somewhat jealous temper, would not let the opportunity pass her of handing the Prince a glass of wine in which was a sleeping draught, so that he slept so soundly, that the Princess made her plaint to him in vain, and in vain reminded him of all she had suffered for his sake, and all she had done for him. The servants, however, again heard the crying of the unhappy Princess, and told it the next morning to the Prince.

On the third evening, the poor despairing Princess broke her third nut, and found in it a dress more exquisite than the rest, spangled all over with beautiful golden stars. This the Bride eagerly demanded, and the poor maid was obliged, most unwillingly, to submit, but upon the same conditions as before, as she positively refused to give up the privilege of sleeping in the Prince's room. This time, however, the Prince would not take the wine from the hand of his Bride, and, filling a glass for himself, drank it without the sleeping potion. Therefore, when the Princess began to cry, and exclaim, "I saved you out of an Iron Safe in a wild forest, and have travelled over a glass mountain and through many difficulties to find you, and now you will not listen to me,"—on her saying these words, the Prince leaped out of bed, and, folding the Princess in his arms, exclaimed, "I am thine, and thou art mine!" Then he ordered a carriage to be got in readiness, and under cover of the night they travelled away, as fast as they could go, not forgetting to take away all the Bride's clothes, that she might not follow them. When they came to the lake, they found a boat, and quickly rowed over to the other side; then they crossed the swords by the aid of the plough-wheel, and the glass mountain by the use of the big needles, when they soon arrived at the little hut where the kind Toads resided, which they no sooner entered, than it changed into a most magnificent castle. At the same moment, all the Toads were disenchanted, and stood before them in all the pride and dignity of manly beauty, heightened as it was by the splendour of their dresses,—for they were the sons of the King of the country.

The wedding ceremony was at once performed, and the Prince and the Princess remained in the castle, as it was much more grand than her father's. However, the old King grieved so much at his beloved daughter's continued absence from him, that they went to live with him, and united the government of the two kingdoms in one; and so, for many years afterwards, they were jointly ruled in peace and prosperity.

70

THE THREE BROTHERS.

A CERTAIN man had three sons, and had nothing to give them—that is to say, he had no fortune to leave them; but he had a fine house, in which he lived, and which either of his three sons would have been proud to inherit; but he was at his wit's end how to manage to act fairly to all, and not disoblige any. To be sure, there was one plan open to him, which was, to sell the house, and divide the money amongst them; but the difficulty could not be resolved this way, for the house was the dwelling of his ancestors, and could not legally be sold out of the family. At last, he called his sons together, and said: "Go out in the world, each of you, and try your best; make yourselves masters of some trade or calling; and when you come back, he who shows himself cleverest shall have the house as his inheritance."

This proposal was agreeable to all: the eldest determined to be a Farrier, the second a Barber, and the third a Fencing-master. They separated, after an agreement to meet again at their father's house on a settled day. Each of them apprenticed himself to an excellent master, who taught him his business from the very beginning. The Farrier got the appointment of shoeing the King's horses, and made certain, from this, that the heritage would come to him. The Barber shaved the most noble chins, and so he, too, made sure of having the house. As for the Fencing-master's apprentice, he got more than one touch with the foil; but he kept his tongue between his teeth, and would not let himself be downhearted. "For," thought he, "if I show fear, the house will never fall to my lot."

When the appointed time arrived, they came back, all three, to their father's house. But their great difficulty was, to find an occasion for displaying their respective talents. While they were settling how best to proceed, they saw a hare running across the plain. "By Jove!" said the Barber, "this comes as handy as March in Easter!" So, catching up his shaving-dish and soap, he got up a lather while the animal was approaching; then, running towards him, he soaped its face while it was still in full career, and shaved off its moustache without stopping its course, without cutting it in the least degree, or even disturbing the fur on the rest of its body. "Well, this is clever, indeed!" said the Father; "if your brothers don't do something better, the house will belong to you."

An instant after, a travelling carriage, drawn by four horses at a gallop, darted down the road before them. "Now, Father," said the Farrier, "you shall see what I can do." Then he ran after the carriage, took off all the four shoes of one of the horses, while at full gallop, and put on him four fresh ones. "You are, indeed, a real clever fellow," said the Father, "and quite equal to your brother; in truth, I shall be puzzled to decide between the pair of you."

But the third brother said: "Let me, also, have my turn, Father." Now, as it was beginning to rain, he drew his sword, and shook it in various directions above his head, in such a manner as not to allow one drop of rain to fall upon his cap. The rain increased, and at last fell just as if buckets full of water were being thrown from the sky; he parried every drop, however, with his sword, and remained in the rain to the end, as little wetted by its falling as if he had been under cover in his bedroom. When the Father saw this, he could not conceal his astonishment. "You have won it, my boy," said he; "the house is yours."

The two other brothers were also full of admiration at such a clever exploit, and approved of their father's decision. Then, as they were all three very fond of each other, as good brothers ought to be, they all remained together in the same house, and each carried on his respective business, by which they gained a great deal of money, and lived happily together until an advanced age. At length, one of them having died, the two others took his death so much to heart, that they fell ill themselves, and died also; whereupon, because of their general cleverness and their mutual affection, their neighbours and friends had them buried all three in the same grave, and raised a tomb over their remains, with this escutcheon—

BROTHER AND SISTER.

ONCE upon a time, there was a Brother and Sister, who evinced the greatest affection for each other, and they were never happy when they were parted. In early life they had the misfortune to lose their own Mother, who was no sooner dead than their Father married again; and their Stepmother was very unkind to them, and did not even like their Father to fondle and kiss them; indeed, she was always doing and wishing them all the harm in her power. One day, it happened that they were playing and enjoying themselves with other children in the meadow, gathering the bright flowers that grew before the house; and in the middle of this field there was a pond, which ran past one side of the house; round this these merry children used to run, joining hands, and singing—

"Eneke, Beneke, set me free,
  And I will give my Bird to thee;
  The Bird shall bring some hay so sweet,
  And that the Cow shall have to eat;
  The Cow will give milk for the Baker's flour,
  And we'll have a pudding in half an hour;
  The Cat shall have of the pudding a slice,
  And for that she'll catch me the Queen of the Mice;
  Then I'll chop her up quick into sausage meat,
  And I'll call you all in, and give you a treat."

While they sang, they ran round and round, and upon whom the word "treat" fell, they had to run away,

and the others must pursue and catch them. The old Stepmother stood at her window, biting her nails with vexation, to see the children so happy. She did not watch them from the window long, before she began wishing them all kinds of evil; and as she understood wicked witches' arts, she wished both the children might lose their natural shape, and the one be turned into a Lamb, and the other into a Fish. Immediately after she had uttered this wish, the Brother leaped into the pond, and began swimming about in the form of a Fish; while the pretty little Sister became covered with fleece, and trotted to and fro in the shape of a Lamb, very sorrowful and unhappy, and she could not eat or touch a single blade of grass; while the little Fish swam as close as he could to the edge of the pond, but could only look lovingly up in her face, without being able to say a single word to console her.

Thus days and weeks passed on, till, at length, some foreign visitors of distinction came to stay a few days at the castle. "This will be a rare opportunity," thought the old Stepmother, "to rid myself of these tiresome children." So she called the Cook, and desired him to fetch the Lamb out of the meadow, and kill and cook it, for there was nothing else in the house for her noble guests. The Cook did as he was told, and having led the Lamb into the kitchen, he tied its feet, that it might suffer patiently; then, in order that he might kill the poor animal quickly, he took his long knife to the grindstone, to make it very sharp; and while he was doing this, a little Fish swam up the gutter to the sink, and looked imploringly at him. Now, this Fish was the Brother, who, having seen the Cook take away his dear Lamb, suspected how matters stood, and so swam from the pond to the house. Directly the Lamb saw him, she cried—

"See the Cook, with cruel knife,
  Seeks to take my tender life!
  Quickly give me, then, some aid,
  Before the last fell blow is made."

The Fish answered, as plainly as his grief would let him—

"Ah! my Sister, gentle Lamb,
  Swimming in the deep I am,
  And much I fear, with all my art,
  I can never take thy part."

When the Cook heard the Lamb and the Fish conversing in this sorrowful manner, he was frightened, and let the knife fall from his hand, for he knew it could not be a natural animal who had spoken thus, but that they had been bewitched by the wicked woman in the house. So he comforted the Lamb, saying, "Be still, and I will not kill you;" and then he made haste and fetched another Lamb, and dressed it for the guests. Then he led the Lamb gently away to a good honest countrywoman, and told her all he had seen and heard. Now, it so happened, this woman was the children's Nurse, and had brought them up in their Mother's lifetime. Conjecturing what had really happened, she took the Lamb and the Fish to the house of a wise woman, who said a blessing over them, and they were thereby restored to their natural shapes. The loving Brother and Sister went deep into the forest, where they built for themselves a pretty little cottage, which she kept clean and tidy, while he grew corn for their bread in their garden; and thus they lived happily and contentedly, though alone.

THE GIANT SUCKLING.

THERE was once a Peasant, and he had a son who was no bigger than his father's thumb, and he would not grow at all, and for many years his height did not increase so much as a hair's breadth. One day, when his Father was going out into the fields to work, the little one said to him, "Father, I should like to go out with you."

"Go out with me!" said the Father; "stop you here, lad; you will only put me out up there, and more than that, I might lose you."

But the little fellow began to cry, and at last, for peace sake, (fathers and mothers do a great deal on that account, both with their children and each other,) his Father clapped the bantling into his pocket, and carried him off with him. When they got to the place of work, he sat him down on the edge of a furrow just opened. While they were there, a great Giant made his appearance, coming over from the other side of the mountains. "Do you see that?" said the Father, who wished to frighten the child, so as to render him more obedient; "he is coming to take you!"

But the Giant, who heard this, came up to the furrow in two strides, took up the little Dwarf, and carried him off without saying a word. Struck dumb with terror, the Father had not time even to utter a cry. He thought his boy was lost, and that he should never set eyes on him more.

The Giant took him home with him, and had him suckled, and nurtured him himself so well, that the little Dwarfling took, all at once, to thriving and growing, and became big and strong, after the manner of the Giants. When two years had elapsed, the Giant went with the boy into a wood, and by way of trying him, said, "Cut yourself a switch."

The boy was already so strong, that he tore up a young tree by the roots. Nevertheless, the Giant thought there was some farther progress to be made yet; and taking him home with him, he fed him well for another two years, by which time his strength had so increased, that he could tear up an old tree by the roots. But this was not enough to satisfy the Giant, so he had him suckled for another two years; at the end of which, he went with the boy into the wood, and said to him, "Cut yourself a stick of a reasonable size."

Whereupon, the lad tore from the earth the largest oak in the forest, which made terrible groanings on the occasion; but such an effort seemed only sport to him.

"That will do," said the Giant; "your education is finished." So he took him back again to the plot of land whence he had carried him off.

His father was busy at work, when the young Giant came up, and said to him: "Well, Father, your son, as you see, has become a man."

The terrified Peasant exclaimed: "No, you are not my son; I don't want anything to do with you. Be off!"

"Yes, I am your son; allow me to work in your place. I can plough quite as well and better than you."

"No, no; you are not my son, and you do not know how to plough. Go—go away!" But as he was afraid of the Colossus, he let go of his plough, and

kept away at some distance. Then the young man, seizing the handles with one hand, leant upon them with such force, that the share dug down deep into the earth. The Peasant could not help crying out, "If you really wish to plough, there is no need to dig so heavily forward; that will make a bad furrow."

Then the young man unyoked the horses, and yoked himself to the plough, saying to his father, "Go to the house, and tell my mother to make ready a plentiful dinner for me, while I plough this bit of land for you."

The Peasant, on his return home, carried the message to his wife. As for the young man, he ploughed the whole field, which was a good four acres, all by himself; and then he harrowed it, drawing two harrows at a time. When he had done, he went up to the wood, tore up two oaks by the roots, which he put on his shoulder, and suspending by the one the two

72

THE GIANT CARRIES OFF THE PEASANT'S LITTLE SON.

harrows, and by the other the two horses, he carried them home to his parents as easily as if they had been a truss of straw. Just as he was entering the yard, his mother, not recognizing him, exclaimed, "Who is this frightful Giant?"

"That is our son, my dear," said the Peasant.

"No," said she, "not so; our son is no more. We never had such a great fellow; he, poor boy, was altogether as small." Then, addressing him again, "Be off!" she cried; "we don't want to have anything to do with you."

The young man did not say a word—the right way with a woman when she scolds, and always respectful to a mother—but he put his horses into their stable, and gave them some hay and oats, and did all that was requisite for their comfort. Then, when he had done, he came back to the room, and sitting down on a bench, "Mother," said he, "I am hungry; is dinner ready?"

"Yes," replied she, placing before him two large dishes of meat and vegetables, quite full, enough to have fed her and her husband for a whole week.

The young man quickly devoured all this, and then asked if she had got any more.

"No; that is all we have."

"It was just enough to give me an appetite. I must have something else."

No. 10.

She did not dare to resist, and placed on the fire a great kettle filled with the lard which was kept for cooking purposes.

"That's just welcome," said he; "here's a mouthful of something to eat." Then he swallowed it all at one gulp; but his hunger was not, even then, satisfied. Then he said to his father, "I plainly see that you have not at home enough to keep me; so get for me, only, a bar of iron, sufficiently strong not to break over my knee, and I will go travel over the world."

The Peasant was delighted. He harnessed his two horses to his cart, and brought back from the smithy a bar of iron so large and so thick, that it was all the horses could do to carry it. The young fellow took hold of it, and—ratch! he broke it across his knee like a twig, and threw the pieces on either side. His father harnessed four horses, and brought back another bar of iron, that they could scarcely drag. But his son broke it over his knee, for all that, saying, "This won't do at all; go and get me a stronger one." At last, his father took eight horses, and brought one that they could hardly convey. When the son took it in his hand, he broke off a small piece at the end, and said to his father, "I see plainly that you can't get me a bar of iron such as I want; I will go away from your house."

Those who travel round the country, in the lands about which we are writing, must belong to some trade, or else they are liable to be locked up as vagrants; so our young Giant bethought himself that he would go about everywhere as a Blacksmith's assistant; and when he arrived at a village, where there was a covetous fellow—a Blacksmith, who never gave anything to anybody, and wished to keep everything for himself—he presented himself at his forge, and asked for work. Delighted at seeing such a vigorous young fellow, and reckoning what a capital stroke of the hammer such a workman could give, he hired him, off hand at once, as a profitable assistant.

"What wages do you require?" he asked.

"None," replied the lad; "only, every fortnight, when you pay the others, I bargain for the right of giving you two blows with my fist, and that you shall bind yourself to receive them."

"Strange wages!" thought the greedy Blacksmith; "but a cheap workman;" so he made no objection. Next day, it was the new assistant's duty to give the first blow with the hammer; and when the master had brought out the bar red-hot from the fire, and placed it on the anvil, the young stranger struck it such a blow, that the iron was crushed and split into pieces, and the anvil was driven so deep into the earth, that the united labour of the whole smithy could not pull it out again.

The Blacksmith flew into a great rage, and said to him, "You won't suit my business; you strike too hard. How much do you want of me for this one only blow that you have struck?"

"All I want is, to give you one gentle tap—that's all;" and he gave him a kick that sent him vaulting over four hay-stacks. Then he picked out the largest iron bar he could find in the forge, and, taking it in his hand for a walking-stick, went on his way.

74

He travelled on a little farther, and he came to a farm, where he asked the Farmer if he was in want of a Head-man.

"Yes," replied the Farmer; "you have come just at the right time, for I do happen to be in want of just such a man. But what wages do you require, my fine fellow?"

He replied, that he did not look for any wages, except the right of giving the Farmer, every year, three blows, which the Farmer must pledge himself to receive.

"A capital bargain!" thought the Farmer; for he, also, was an avaricious fellow.

Next day, it was the business of the morning to fetch timber from the forest. The other labourers were up with the early dawn, but our young man lay still snug asleep, rolled up in his blankets. One of the men called out to him, "Get up, lad; it is full time. We are going to the wood, and you must come with us."

"Be off with you, as quickly as you please," he sharply replied; "I shall be there and back as soon as any of you."

The other labourers went to look for the Farmer, and told him what a queer sort of a Head-man he had put over them—how he was lying snoring in bed, and would not go with them to the wood. "Go and wake him again," said the Farmer; "tell him to put the horses to."

But the Head-man only replied, "Go along, go your ways; I shall be back as soon as any of you."

He remained in bed two hours longer; at the end of which time he got up, went and picked two bushels of peas, boiled them into a good soup, and made a tolerable breakfast. When he had finished, he harnessed the horses, and drove off with his cart to the wood.

To arrive at the forest, where they were felling the trees, it was necessary to pass through a narrow lane; up this he drove his cart, and then halting his horses, he went back, and hedged the road across with a barricade of trees and shrubs, so closely that there was no means left for passing.

When he came to the forest, the other labourers were on the return, with their carts laden. He said to them, "Go on, go on as you please; I shall be at the house before you." Then, without pushing on any farther, he contented himself with plucking up by the roots two enormous trees, which he flung on to his cart, and took the road homewards. As soon as he arrived in front of the barricade that he had put up, the others were all stopping there, not being able to pass. "Well," said he, "now you see that if you had stopped with me this morning, you might have had an hour's more sleep, and not have been the later in reaching home to-night."

Then, as his horses could not go any farther forward, he took them out, put them on the top of the cart, and himself taking the yoke in his hand, drew them all along together, as easily as a handful of feathers. On reaching the other side, "You see," said he to the others, "I get along faster than you;" and went on his way, without attending to their calls for his aid. When he arrived in the courtyard, he took one of the trees in his hand, and showing it to the Farmer, said, "Is not that a jolly faggot?" and the Farmer could not help saying to his wife, "That is a capital servant; if he gets up later than the others, at any rate he comes home before them."

He remained in this Farmer's service for one year. When the term had expired, and the other labourers were receiving their wages, he asked to be paid his also. But the Farmer, terrified at the prospect of the blows he had to receive, begged very earnestly to be let off, declaring to him that he would much rather become the servant himself, and make the young Giant the farmer in his place.

"No," replied the young Giant, laughing; "I have no wish to be a farmer or a master. The servant snores at night, and sings at his work in the day; while the master lies awake at night, and cares all day. I am a Head-man, and I wish to remain such; but our bargain must be carried out."

The Farmer offered to give him everything he chose to ask, but in vain; his reply was still the same— "No." So the Farmer, seeing nothing was to be got by prayers, claimed a respite of a fortnight, in the hope of finding some hole to creep through; to this the other consented.

Then the Farmer assembled all his people, and asked their advice how to act. After turning the matter over for a long time, and a great deal of shaking of heads and whispering in corners, they came to the conclusion that this young Giant was a very dangerous fellow indeed; that with such a head-labourer on a farm, no man could be sure of his life; and that he was just such a person as would kill a man with as little regard as a fly. They were therefore of opinion, that he should be made to go down into a well, under pretext of cleaning it, and when once down, that certain mill-stones, which were lying just by, should be cast upon his head, so as to kill him on the spot.

This counsel was agreeable to the Farmer's inclination, and the Head-labourer got ready to go down into the well. When he was at the bottom, they cast down the enormous mill-stones, and they made sure his head was crushed; but he hallooed up from below: "Drive away those hens up there! they are scratching in the gravel, and knocking the sand into my eyes."

You should have seen the Farmer's face! "Chut! chut!" he went, as if he were driving away the fowls. Again, too, he was something to look at, when his Head-labourer, having finished the job, came up again, and said, "Look at my fine necklace!" He had got one of the largest of the mill-stones slung round his neck!

The Head-labourer again required his wages, but the Farmer asked him again for a fortnight's time, to consider what was to be done. His people, this time, advised him to send the young fellow to grind his wheat in a certain Enchanted Mill, during the night; no person having been known to come out of it alive in the morning. This advice pleased the Farmer, and he commanded his Head-labourer, on the instant, to carry eight sacks of barley to the mill, and grind them during the night, as he wanted them all directly. The

young man put two sacks of barley in his right pocket, two in his left pocket, and four in his wallet, two behind and two before; and laden in this fashion, he betook himself to the Enchanted Mill. The Miller there told him that he might grind his barley very readily in the day-time, but not in the night; for those who had risked the doing so, had all been found dead the next morning.

"I am not the man to die in that fashion," said the young man, with a grin; "go you to bed, and sleep on your long ears."

Then he went boldly into the mill, and ground his barley, singing all the while, as if nothing had happened:—

THE SONG OF THE FOX.

The Fox went out, one moonshiny night,
He stood on his hind legs bolt upright,
Crying, "Something for supper I must have this night,
Before that I lie down, O!"

Chorus (which the young Giant sang himself, only much louder than the rest of the song)—
Down, O! down, O!
Something for supper I must have to-night,
Before that I lie down, O!

Soon a farmhouse he drew near;
The ducks and geese they did appear:
"One of you fowls shall grease my beard,
Before that I lie down, O!"
Down, O! down, O! &c.

He seized the old grey Goose by the neck,
And she gibbled, and she gobbled, and she fell upon her back,
Which made the old Goose go "Quack, quack, quack!"
And her legs hung dangling down, O!
Down, O! down, O! &c.

Old Mother Widdle-waddle jump'd out of bed,
She threw up the window, and popp'd out her head,
Crying, "John! John! John! the grey Goose is gone,
And the Fox has run up the town, O!"
Town, O! town, O! &c.

Cousin John rode up the hill,
And blew his horn both loud and shrill;
The Fox he was at the bottom of the hill,
When the hounds came rattling down, O!
Down, O! down, O! &c.

When he got to the bottom of the glen,
There sat his little ones, nine or ten;
He and his wife they ate the flesh,
And the little ones pick'd the bones, O!
Bones, O! bones, O! &c.

Towards eleven o'clock at night, he came down from the mill, went into the Miller's counting-house, and sat himself down on a bench. But things did not go on so quietly there as they had up in the mill; the door opened of itself, and he saw a large table come in, without any one carrying it. Upon this table were laid all sorts of delicate dishes, and bottles filled with choice wines. "Come, come," said he, "this is a handsome reception; these are the sort of Goblins I like!"

Presently, a set of chairs drew up to the table, without any person appearing; and there was a rattling of knives and forks, and a moving of the dishes, and a carving of the meat, and a pushing about of the

75

sauces, and a filling of glasses, just as if a grand banquet was going on; but all the while there was not a single guest to be seen.

At last, however, the young Giant caught sight of some fingers, and nothing more, filling the plates and skirmishing about among the knives and forks.

"A great-many hands, and only one stomach," said the young Giant, laughing at his own rough joke; "at any rate, I shall give mine a treat!" So he sat down, and made a famous supper.

When he had ended his meal, and the invisible beings had equally finished theirs, he distinctly heard them give a puff, and the candles were all put out together; and then, in the darkness, he received on his cheek something like a blow.

"If they do that again," said he, "I shall try my hand at the same game." Scarcely had he uttered these words than he got another, and returned it as quickly; and so they kept on all night, giving and returning blows, until daylight came, when all was silent. The Miller came in, and was astonished at finding him still alive. "I have had a good feast," said the young Giant to him, "and I have had some hard knocks; but I gave them as good as they brought."

Joyful was the Miller that morning, to think his mill was so well rid of his Goblin customers; and he wanted to make the Giant a handsome present in money, to show his gratitude. But the young fellow would have none of it; "I want no money," said he, "I have more than enough already."

Then he took his sacks of flour upon his back, and returned to the farm, and declared to the Farmer that his service was ended, and that he would have his wages. The Farmer was struck with terror; he could not rest any longer, but walked up and down his chamber, the drops of heat running off his brow, from extreme fright. He felt all over in a flame, and threw up the window, as he wanted to get some fresh air to cool him; but before he could play any more of his tricks, his Head-labourer gave him a blow that sent him through the window flying right up into the sky, where he kept mounting up and up, until nearly all the breath was blown out of his body. Then the Head-labourer turned to the Farmer's wife, and said: "Every one in his turn; the next thump belongs to you."

"No, no!" she screamed, "no one strikes a woman!" Then she opened the window, for she, also, was in a terrible heat from fright; but the whack she got, though dealt with a gentler hand, sent her up spinning in the air even higher than her husband, as she was so much lighter, and her spreading petticoats made her fly up like a shuttlecock. Her husband cried out to her, as she passed him in the clouds, "Come along with me; keep with me, Dolly!" but she replied, "Do you come along with me; I can't go along here as I like." And so they kept on floating about in the air, blown and buffeted about by the circling winds, without the power of coming together; and, as far as I can judge, there they are skimming about still.

As for the Young Giant, he took up his bar of iron again, and went on his way.

THE HARE AND THE HEDGEHOG.

THIS story, children, may appear to you untrue, and yet it is quite true; for my grandfather, whenever he told it me, never failed to add: "It must be true, for if it was not, I should not tell it." Here is the story, exactly as it happened.

It was on a summer morn, just about harvest-time, when the buckwheat is in flower; the sun shone in the heavens, the morning breeze swept over the cornfields, the larks were singing in the air, the bees buzzing about the flowers, and folks were going to the village fair in their Sunday clothes, and everybody felt glad, not excepting the Hedgehog. Now the Hedgehog was standing at his front door; he had his arms folded, and was singing his little ditty, no better or worse than a hedgehog does sing it on a fine summer morn. While he was humming away, he hit on the daring notion, while his wife was washing and dressing the children, of going a little way out, and seeing how his crop of turnips was getting on: they were close to his house, and he was in the habit of eating them, he and his family, so he naturally looked on them as his own property. No sooner said than done; the Hedgehog shut the front door after him, and started off. He had scarce got away from home, though, and was just skirting a little hedge which bordered the field in which his turnips grew, when he met Master Hare, who had gone out with the similar intention of inspecting his cabbages. When the Hedgehog saw the Hare, he cordially wished him "Good morrow!" but the Hare, who was a high and mighty gentleman in his way, and, in the bargain, of a very haughty temper, did not return the Hedgehog's bow, but said, in the most impertinent manner in the world, "How comes it that you are running about the fields on such a fine morning?"

"ı am taking a walk," said the Hedgehog.

"Taking a walk!" the Hare answered, with a laugh; "I fancy you would want another sort of legs to do that."

This answer displeased the Hedgehog extremely, for he was never angry, save when an allusion was made to his legs, which were naturally bandy. "You fancy, perhaps," he said to the Hare, "that your legs are better than mine?"

"I flatter myself they are."

"I should like to try that," the Hedgehog went on;

"I do not mind wagering that, if we were to have a race, I should beat you."

"With your bandy legs? You are jesting!" said the Hare; "but, however, I am willing, if you are anxious about it. What shall we bet?"

"A sovereign and a bottle of wine," said Hedgehog.

"Done!" cried the Hare; "and we can have it out at once."

"No; there is no such hurry," said the Hedgehog; "I have not eaten anything yet this morning; I shall go home first, and have a snack, and in half an hour I shall be on the ground."

The Hare agreed to this, and the Hedgehog went off; on the road he said to himself, "The Hare trusts in his long legs, but I will play him a trick; he is very bounceable, but he is only a donkey, and will have to pay for it." On reaching his home, the Hedgehog, therefore, said to his wife, "Make haste and put your bonnet on; you must go into the country with me."

"What's the matter?" asked his wife.

"I have made a bet with Master Hare, that I can run faster than he, and I want your help."

"Goodness gracious, husband!" said poor Mrs. Hedgehog; "are you in your senses, or have you lost your wits? How can you think of such a thing?"

"Silence, ma'am!" the Hedgehog replied, sternly; "that is my business. Don't interfere in what concerns men. Go and get ready, and we will be off."

What could Mrs. Hedgehog do? She was obliged to obey, whether she liked it or not.

As they were walking along together, the Hedgehog said to his wife, "Pay attention to what I am going to say to you. We are going to race on that large piece of ground you see over there; the Hare runs in one furrow, and we in the other, and we shall start down there. All you have got to do is, to hide yourself in the furrow, and when the Hare comes up to you, pop out, and cry 'Here I am!'"

While talking thus, they reached the spot, and the Hedgehog showed his wife the place where she was to stop, and then went up the field. When he reached the other end, he found the Hare there, who said to him, "You really mean racing?"

"Of course I do," replied the Hedgehog.

"Be off, then!"

And each took his place in a furrow. The Hare cried, "One, two, three!" and started off like a whirlwind. The Hedgehog went about three yards, then popped down, and kept quiet.

When the Hare, with his enormous leaps, reached the end of the field, Mrs. Hedgehog cried out to him, "Here I am!" The Hare was greatly astonished, for he really fancied it was the Hedgehog himself, his wife being so much like him.

The Hare said to himself, "There's something queer about this;" then he cried, "Let us try again!" and he ran off at such a pace that his ears floated on the breeze. Mrs. Hedgehog did not stir; but when the Hare reached the other end of the field again, the husband squeaked, "Here I am!" The Hare, half mad with spite, said, "Another try!"

"I don't mind," the Hedgehog replied; "I am ready to go on as long as you like."

The Hare ran in this way seventy-three times in succession, and the Hedgehog held out to the last. Each time the Hare reached either end of the field, the Hedgehog or his wife cried, "Here I am!"

The Hare could not finish the seventy-fourth heat; he rolled on the ground in the middle of the field, the blood poured from his neck, and he expired on the spot. The Hedgehog took the sovereign and bottle of wine he had won; he called Mrs. H. out of the furrow, and they both went off in good spirits; and, if they are not dead, are living still.

The moral of this story is, in the first place, that no one, however important he may fancy himself, may laugh at the expense of the smallest creature, even if it be only a hedgehog: and, secondly, if you think of taking a wife, you must choose her from your own condition of life, and like yourself. If, then, you are a hedgehog, be careful she is one, too, and so on through all classes.

THE TOMB.

A RICH Farmer was standing one day at his door, regarding his fields and orchards; the plain was covered with his crops, and his trees were laden with fruit. The wheat of the previous years so encumbered his granaries, that the beams gave way under the foot. His stables were full of fatting oxen, of plump cows, and horses glistening with health. He entered his room, and turned his eyes on the strong box in which he kept his money. But while absorbed in the contemplation of his wealth, he fancied he heard a secret voice saying to him, "With all that gold, have you rendered those who surround you happy? have you thought on the wretchedness of the poor? have you shared your loaf with the hungry? were you satisfied with what you already possessed, or did you crave for more?"

His heart did not hesitate to answer, "I have ever been harsh and inexorable; I never did anything for my relatives or friends; I never thought of God, but solely of increasing my riches. Had I possessed the world, I should yet not have had enough." This thought terrified him, and his knees trembled so that he was compelled to sit down. At this moment, some one rapped at his door. It was one of his neighbours, a poor man, burthened with children whom he could not support. "I know very well," he thought, "that my neighbour is even harder than he is rich; he will doubtless repulse me; but my children ask for bread, and I must try."

He said to the rich man, "You do not like giving, as I am well aware; but I apply to you in my despair, just as a drowning man catches at any branch. My children are hungry; lend me four measures of wheat."

A beam of pity for the first time melted the ice round this avaricious heart. "I will not lend you four measures," he said, "but give you eight, on one condition."

"What is it?" the poor man asked.

"That you pass the first three nights after my death in watching over my Tomb."

The poor man did not much like the transaction, but, in his present need, he would have consented to anything. He therefore promised, and took away the wheat to his house.

It seemed as if the Farmer had foreseen the future; for, three days later, he died suddenly, and no one regretted him. When he was buried, the poor man remembered his promise; he would have gladly got off it, but he said to himself, "That man was generous to me—he supported my children with his bread; besides, I pledged my word, and am bound to keep it."

At nightfall he went to the cemetery, and stationed himself near the Tomb. All was tranquil; the moon lit up the grave-stones, and now and then an owl flew past uttering mournful yells. At sunrise he returned home, having incurred no danger, and on the second night it was the same.

On the coming of the third day, he felt a secret apprehension, as if something more were about to happen. On entering the churchyard, he saw under the wall a man of about forty years of age, with a scarred face and quick piercing eyes, and who was wrapped up in an old cloak, under which only a pair of big riding-boots were visible. "What are you seeking here?" the Peasant shouted to him; "are you not afraid of being in the churchyard?"

"I am seeking for nothing," the other answered; "but what should I be afraid of? I am an old discharged Soldier, and came to pass the night here, because I have no other shelter."

"Very good," the Peasant said; "as you are not afraid, come and help me to watch this Tomb."

"Right willingly," the Soldier made answer, "for mounting guard is my trade. We will remain together, and share the good or evil fortune that may befall us."

They both sat down on the Tomb. All remained quiet till midnight; at that moment, a shrill whistle was heard in the air, and the two watchmen saw before them the Enemy of Man in person.

"Be off with you, you scoundrels!" he shouted to them; "this dead man belongs to me; I have come to fetch him, and if you do not decamp at once, I will wring your necks."

"My lord with the red feather," the Soldier answered, boldly, "you are not my Captain. I have no orders to take from you, and you will not frighten me. Go your way; we remain here."

The Stranger thought he could buy over these two poor scamps with money; so, assuming a more friendly tone, he asked them familiarly if they would not consent to retire for a purse of gold.

"That's what I call sense," the Soldier replied; "but a purse of gold will not be enough for us; we will not quit the spot till you give us as many sovereigns as will fill one of my boots."

"I have not so much about me," said the other; "but I will go and fetch it. In the town close by dwells an Usurer, a particular friend of mine, who will gladly advance me the amount."

When he had gone, the Soldier pulled off his left boot, saying, "We will come the old soldier with him; give me your knife, my fine fellow." He cut off the sole of his boot, and reared the upper-leather against a neighbouring tombstone in the tall grass. "All's right!" he then said; "the black sweep can return whenever he pleases."

They had not long to wait: the Old Gentleman came back with a little bag of gold in his hand.

"Pour it in," the Soldier said, lifting the boot a little; "but you have not enough there." He emptied the bag, but the gold fell to the ground, and the boot remained empty. "You old goose!" the Soldier said to him; "that is not enough—I told you so. Go back, and fetch more."

He went off, shaking his head, and returned at the expiration of an hour with a much larger bag under his arm. "That looks better," said the Soldier; "but I don't fancy you will fill the boot yet."

The gold fell in with a clinking sound, but the boot remained empty. The Stranger satisfied himself of the fact with sparkling eyes. "What impudent sized calves you must have!" he said, with an angry grin.

"Do you fancy I've got a cloven hoof like your's?" the Soldier replied. "When did you begin to grow so mean? Go and fetch more bags, or else there will be no dealing between us."

The Evil One went off once again. This time he remained away longer; and when he at length returned, he bent beneath the weight of an enormous sack he carried on his shoulder. But, although he emptied it into the boot, it grew no more full than before. He grew furious, and was about to tear the boot from the Soldier's hand, when the first sunbeam illumined the heavens; at the same moment he disappeared with a yell. The poor soul was saved.

The Peasant proposed to divide the gold, but the Soldier said to him, "Give my share to the poor; I will go to your house, and we will live on the rest peaceably together."

THE BEAR AND THE BIRD.

ONE day, the Bear and the Wolf were taking a walk together in the woods. The Bear heard a bird singing; "Brother Wolf," he asked, "who is that fine singer?"

"It is the King of the Birds," replied the Wolf, making fun of his comrade, "and we must pay our respects to it."

It happened to be a Wren.

"If that is the case," said the Bear, "his Majesty must have a palace: just show it to me."

"That is not so easy as you fancy," the Wolf answered; "we must wait till the Queen has returned."

At this moment Jenny Wren arrived, both she and her husband holding in their beaks worms to feed their young. The Bear would have willingly followed them, but the Wolf caught him by the cuff, saying, "No; wait till they come out again." They merely marked the spot where the nest was, and then went their way.

But the Bear did not forget that he had not yet seen the King's palace; so he soon came back again. The parents were absent, but he ventured a glance, and saw five or six little ones lying in the nest. "Is that the palace?" he shouted; "it is a poor hole! and as for you, you are no King's sons, but paltry little creatures."

The little Wrens were very angry on hearing this, and cried, on their side, "No, Bear, we are not what you say; our parents are noble, and you shall pay dearly for this insult."

At this threat, the Bear and the Wolf, struck with terror, took refuge in their lairs; but the little Wrens continued to cry and make a disturbance. They told their parents, when they brought them food, "The Bear has been here to insult us; we will not leave this place, or eat a morsel, until you have restored our honour."

"Be at rest," their father said, "it shall be done;" and flying with Jenny to the Bear's hole, he cried to him, "Old Growler, why did you insult my children? I will serve you out for it, as I am about to declare war to the knife!"

When war was declared, the Bear summoned to his aid the army of Quadrupeds—the ox, the cow, the donkey, the stag, the roe, and all their relations. For his part, the Wren assembled every living thing that flies—not only the Birds, large and small, but also the winged insects, such as the flies, gnats, bees, and hornets.

When the day of battle drew near, the Wren sent out spies, to know who was the General of the enemy's army. The Gnat was the smartest of all; he flew to that part of the wood where the enemy was assembled, and hid himself under the leaf of a tree near which the council of war was held. The Bear summoned the Fox, and said to him: "Gossip, you are the most crafty of all animals, so you shall be our General."

"Good," said the Fox; "but what signal shall we agree on?"

No one spoke. "Very well, then," he went on; "I have a fine long brush, tufted like a red plume; so long as I hold it erect, all is going well, and you will advance; but if I lower it, it will be the signal for a general bolt."

The Gnat, who had listened attentively, went back, and told all, word for word, to the Wren.

At daybreak, the Quadrupeds rushed to the battle-field, galloping so fiercely that the earth trembled. The Wren appeared in the air with his army, which buzzed, croaked, and flew about, so as to make any looker-on giddy; and a furious engagement began. But the Wren sent off the Hornet, with orders to perch himself on the Fox's brush, and sting it with all his might. At the first prick, the Fox could not refrain from taking a leap, though still holding his brush in the air; at the second, he was forced to lower it for a moment; but at the third, he could stand it no longer, but tucked his tail between his legs, while uttering piercing cries. The Quadrupeds, on seeing this, fancied that all was lost, and began flying each to his den; and thus the Birds gained the victory.

The Wrens flew back straight to their nest, and said: "We are victors, children; eat and drink in gladness."

"No," the children said; "the Bear must first come and apologize, and declare that he recognizes our noble birth."

The Wren thereupon flew to the Bear's den, and said: "Old Growler, you will come and apologize before my children's nest, and declare to them that you believe them nobly born; if not, look out for your ribs!"

The terrified Bear crawled up, and made the apologies demanded. Then the little Wrens felt fully satisfied, and spent a jolly evening.

THE WANDERING MINSTRELS.

A MAN had a Donkey, which had served him faithfully for many years, but whose strength was now exhausted, so that it became with every day less fitted for hard work. The Master thought about killing it, for the sake of its hide; but the Donkey, perceiving that the wind blew from an ugly quarter, bolted along the road to London. "There," he said, "I will join a Rifle Volunteer Band; there are plenty to choose from."

After he had been walking some distance, he met on the road a Dog, panting as if he had come a long journey. "What makes you snap like that, old fellow?" he asked him.

"Ah!" the Dog answered, "because I am old, grow weaker every day, and can no longer go hunting, my master wanted to kill me; then I ran away, but what shall I do to gain a living?"

"Well," said the Donkey, "I am going to London, to offer my services as bugler. Suppose you come with me, and also enter the band; I will play the bugle, and you can shake the cymbals."

The Dog accepted, and they journeyed along together. A short distance farther on, they found a Cat lying in the road, and with a face as sad as three days' rain. "Who's trodden on your corns, old Whiskerandos?" the Donkey asked him.

"A fellow can't feel good-tempered, when not safe of his life," the Cat answered; "because I am growing old, my teeth are worn out, and I prefer lying before the fire to running after mice, my mistress wished to drown me, so I ran away in time; but what am I to do now?"

"Come with us to London; you are a good hand at music, so you can join a band, as we mean to do."

The Cat thought the advice so good, that he set off with them. Our vagabonds soon passed a courtyard, on the door of which a Cock was perched, crowing lustily.

"You pierce our very marrow!" the Donkey said; "why are you making that atrocious noise?"

"I was announcing fine weather," said the Cock; "but as there will be company to dinner here to-morrow, my mistress has no pity on me; she has told the cook to make broth of me, and I shall have my throat cut this very night; so I am making use of my lungs, so long as they are left me."

"Good!" said the Donkey; "you had better come with us to London, Redcomb; you have a powerful voice, and will prove an honour to our band."

The Cock accepted the proposal, and all four started together. They could not reach London, however, the same day, and at nightfall they reached a wood, where they proposed stopping. The Donkey and the Dog posted themselves under a large tree, up which the Cat and the Cock climbed—the latter, indeed, going right to the top, where he should feel safe, he said. Before going to sleep, as he looked around, he fancied he saw a little light some distance off, and announced the fact to his comrades, that there was a house handy.

"If that is the case," said the Donkey, "we'll be off at once in that direction, for I can't say much for our present lodging."

"Indeed," the Dog added, "I should not refuse a few bones with some meat hanging to them."

They therefore proceeded in the direction of the light; they soon perceived it glistening through the trees, and as they drew nearer still, they saw it was a noble mansion. The Donkey, as the tallest, approached the window where the light was, and looked in.

"What do you see there, Greyhead?" the Cock asked him.

"What do I see?" said the Donkey; "a table covered with meat and drink, and a parcel of Burglars seated round it, and enjoying themselves."

"That would be just the thing for us," the Cock remarked.

"That it would," the Donkey went on; "I wish we were only there!"

They began thinking of the mode to expel the Burglars, and at length determined on showing themselves. The Donkey first stood up with his feet on the sill of the window; the Dog mounted his back; the Cat clambered on the Dog; and, lastly, the Cock perched himself on the Cat's head. This done, they began their performance simultaneously: the Donkey brayed, the Dog barked, the Cat miawled, and the Cock crowed; then they rushed through the window into the room, breaking the glass to shivers. The Thieves, on hearing this terrible din, started up, not doubting but that the police were on them, and escaped into the wood. Then the four comrades sat down to table, disposed of what was left, and ate as if they had been fasting for a month.

When the Four Musicians had finished, they extinguished the lights, and looked for a place to rest in, each according to his nature and convenience. The Donkey lay down on the straw; the Dog behind the

door; the Cat in the fireplace near the hot ashes, and the Cock perched on a rafter; and as they were fatigued by their long journey, they soon fell asleep. Soon after midnight, when the Burglars saw that there was no light in the house, and all appeared quiet, the leader of the gang said, "We ought not to have let ourselves be startled so easily;" and ordered one of his men to go and see how matters looked in the house. The man sent found all quiet; he entered the kitchen, and prepared to light a candle; he therefore took up a match, and as the Cat's sparkling eyes seemed to him two live coals, he put the match to them. But the Cat did not understand jests of this nature, so he sprang in the fellow's face, and scratched him terribly. Struck with a tremendous fear, the man ran to the door, in the hope of escaping; but the Dog lying close by, sprang at him, and took a piece out of his leg. As he passed through the yard, the Donkey let fly with his hind-legs; while the Cock, aroused by the disturbance, and wide awake, crowed from his rafter, "*Kikeriki!*"

The Robber ran at full speed to his leader, and said, "In that house there is a gruesome witch, who blew at me, and scratched my face with her long nails; in front of the door there is a man armed with a knife, who pricked my leg; in the yard lurks a black monster, who dealt me a tremendous blow; and on the roof sits the judge, who shouted in a stern voice, 'Bring that villain before me!' Hence, I was not long in making my escape."

Since that time, the Burglars have not attempted to enter the house again; and the Four Wandering Minstrels felt so comfortable in it, that they never thought of leaving it.

THE OGRE BIDS THE SOLDIER STAND BACK FROM THE TOMB. (*See page* 78.)

THE PRINCESS'S RIDDLE.

By some chance, there once lived a Princess, who was very proud, and who thought herself handsomer and grander than any other in the world. It was her custom to propose to all her lovers, when they came courting, a riddle; and if the unfortunate wight could not propound it to her Haughtiness, she treated him with scorn and ridicule, and spurned him from her presence. As a matter of course, all the people in the realm made such strange conduct on the part of the Princess a matter of conversation; and many a gossip was had, and many a guess made at her probable

intentions. Some said she had a lover abroad, and that it was to gain time from her father, who pressed her to marry at once, trusting in the interval that elapsed her beloved one would return. Others said, and truly, that she had promised to marry whoever was lucky or clever enough to guess her riddle. Just as this rumour was in everybody's mouth, there came into the town, where the Princess dwelt, three Tailors, companions travelling together; the two elder of them made sure they should be successful without doubt, as they were not only handsome, fine-looking fellows, but they could set the finest stitches in the world. The third Tailor was a little, lazy good-for-nought, who never did anything for himself or anybody else; and as to work, the only stitch he knew was gobble-stitch; yet he, likewise, thought he should be sure to be successful, as it was little to do, to gain a Princess for a wife; besides, he knew he was a good hand at guessing riddles. The two others tried all in their power to persuade him to stop at home; but he was obstinate, and would not listen to a word. He said he had made up his mind, and go he would; thereupon he marched off, as grand as a lord who owned all around him.

The three Tailors presented themselves in due form before the Princess, and told her they were come to solve her riddle; they said, they were the only proper people to do so, as their understanding was so fine, they could thread a needle with it!

"Then," said the Princess, "I have a hair upon my head of two colours; tell me which are they?"

"Soon guessed," said the first man; "any child might see they must be black and white, like pepper and salt cloth."

"You are wrong, my man," said the Princess. "Now, second man, you have a try."

"Black and white!" said he; "ridiculous! Why, it is brown and red, to be sure—just like my father's holiday coat."

"Wrong once more!" exclaimed the Princess, with glee. "Now try, third man; I can see you will be sure to guess rightly."

The little Tailor put his best foot forward, as bold as brass, and said, "The Princess has a gold and silver thread upon her head; and those, I am sure, are the two colours."

No sooner had the little Tailor uttered these words, than the Princess became as pale as death, and falling to the ground, swooned with fright; for the little Tailor had rightly guessed her riddle, of which she thought nobody in the whole world could have the least perception. As soon as she recovered herself, she cunningly devised a plan, which she thought would release her from her promise; so she said to the Tailor, "That is not all you will have to do to get me for your wife, indeed! for below, in the stables, there lies a grisly Bear, and you must pass the night with him; and if I find you alive when I come in the morning, then will I surely marry you."

The little Tailor, nothing daunted, consented, merrily exclaiming, "Faint heart never won fair lady!" But the Princess gladdened her heart with the thought that she should get rid of him easily, as the grisly Bear had never yet spared any one who had come near enough to shake hands with him. When the night arrived, the little Tailor went very unconcernedly to the stables; but no sooner did the grisly Bear hear his footsteps approaching, than he made ready to spring upon the Tailor. "Gently—softly, my fine gentleman," said he; "can't you see I have come to teach you manners?" So he took some nuts out of his pocket, and very leisurely began cracking them, and eating the kernels with great relish.

The Bear, seeing how good they seemed, thought he should like to have some, too. "Do not eat them all yourself," said the Bear; "I, too, like the good things of this world."

"With all my heart," said the Tailor; and he put his hand in his pocket, and, pulling out a handful, politely handed them to the grisly Bear; these were not nuts, but pebbles.

The Bear put them into his mouth, and made all sorts of grimaces, in vain attempts to crack them; but try as he would, it was all in vain. "Why, what a blockhead I am!" cried he to himself; "I cannot even crack a few nuts! Will you be good enough to crack a few for me?" said he to the Tailor.

"With all my heart," he replied; "but with such a fine large mouth as you have got, 'tis hard to think you cannot crack a small nut." So saying, he cunningly changed the pebble for a nut, and having quickly cracked some, he handed them to the Bear.

"They are very nice," said the Bear; "I must try once more." So he began munching and chumping, but all, as you may well suppose, to no good; for the hard pebbles were stronger than his teeth, and all his efforts were to no purpose.

The Tailor, seeing the Bear was getting tired with his vain efforts, and that his temper was a little bit ruffled, thought it advisable to divert his attention a little; so he pulled a violin out of his coat pocket, and began playing a tune upon it. As soon as the grisly Bear heard the music, he began to lift up first one paw and then the other, until he started off, in spite of himself, in regular jig fashion; and a merry dance he had of it, before he had done, I can tell you. When he stopped, he asked the Tailor whether the art of fiddling was soon learned.

"It is as easy as kiss my hand!" said the Tailor; "only just put your left hand upon the strings, and with the right you flourish your bow, and away merrily it goes in a twinkling!"

"Oh, indeed! if it is as easy as you say, I may as well learn fiddling at once; it will be such a rare accomplishment to dance to my own music. I shall never then want amusement." The vain grisly Bear thought how he should be admired among his fellow Bears, when he reached home again, and anticipated with delight the pleasure he should have in dancing with all the lady Bears of his acquaintance, who would be sure to choose so clever and accomplished a partner. So, turning to the Tailor, he asked him to give him some instructions.

"All right!" said the Tailor; "I will do that most willingly; but first of all, I must look at your claws. Dear me!" he exclaimed, "how frightfully long! you will never be able to play with expression; you can only twang the strings with such nails as these; you must just allow me to trim them up a bit for you." By good chance, there was a vice in the room; and the Bear did as the Tailor desired him, and laid his paws upon it, when the Tailor immediately, with a good strong twist, screwed them up as tight as he possibly could. The Bear, racked with pain, now began to dance without music; but the Tailor said, "Now wait there a bit, while I fetch the scissors." Then, leaving the Bear groaning and moaning, he laid himself down at the farthest end of the stables, on a truss of clean straw, and was very soon fast asleep.

All this time the Princess was at home, thinking to herself how fortunate she had been to get rid of the Tailor so very easily; as, when she heard the Bear growling, she thought it was with satisfaction at his prey. In the morning she arose, and having dressed herself, went down to the stables, according to her promise, just to see the poor Tailor, and assure herself that the grisly Bear had got rid of him for her. But when she looked in at the window, there was the Tailor, washed and dressed, as spruce as he could make himself, and as lively as a kitten, awaiting, with much satisfaction to himself, the arrival of the Princess.

She was terribly alarmed at the thought of being really married to a Tailor, after she had caused so many noble gentlemen to be devoured by the Bear; but there was no breaking away from her promise, as, this time, she had pledged her word to the marriage before all the people.

Then the King, her father, ordered a carriage to be brought; and they got into it, and off they drove to church to be married. Just as they had started, the two other Tailors, jealous of their brother's good fortune, hastened into the stables, and released the Bear, who immediately ran off growling after the carriage that contained the bridal party. The Princess heard the Bear growling with rage and groaning with pain, and cried out to the Tailor, "Oh dear me! here is the grisly Bear coming to tear you away; and I am sure he will kill me, too!"

"Be easy," said he; and up he got in a minute, and placing his head on the bottom of the carriage, he put his feet and legs out of window, making them into the form of a vice. "Do you see this vice?" he exclaimed; "if you come near me, you shall have another taste of it."

The Bear looked at him a minute, and then, seeing something like the shape of a vice, he turned tail, and rushed back as fast as his heels would carry him. Then the Tailor went on to church with the Princess, and there he made her his wife.

After their marriage, as the Tailor was well pleased with his style of living, and there was nothing to find fault with or grumble at, they managed to live very happily together the rest of their lives; and they may be living yet, as I have never seen their death in any of the newspapers.

THE HOUSEMAID AND THE GOBLINS.

How quickly time passes in pleasant places! How long the holidays are in coming; and, oh! how fast they seem to go! and yet, after all, when we come to think of it, the longest quarter of an hour that ever was, never exceeded fifteen minutes, though a thousand years, sometimes, may pass away as a single night!

Once upon a time, there was a girl, humbly born, who lived in a gentleman's family as Housemaid, and was so active, and tidy, and ready at her business, as well as civil and obliging, that every one in the house liked her and respected her. It was a sight to see her sweep the house down, she was so quick without bustle, and so tidy without primness. Not that you often saw her about her work, for the dust used to disappear as if by magic, and all the rubbish and waste found its way outside the door almost without its being observed. People said the Fairies must have done her work for her, as she was always so quick and so clean, and yet got through three times the work of the noisy, bustling ones. I don't know how this was, but somehow or other, early one fine spring morning, when she happened to be sweeping the children's schoolroom, and had just flourished her broom into a favourite corner, bringing forth a doll's arm, the leg of a horse (wooden), the ivory top of a whistle, the handle of a humming-top, a boot-lace, the two middle pages of a spelling-book, the crust of a half slice of bread-and-butter, a baby's coral, a drumstick, a bit of string, three marbles, a brass medal, and a little sock; when, just at her feet, she saw a letter, which, on picking up, she found was directed to herself, and unopened. Having been well brought up, little Peggy the Housemaid was able to read writing, and soon opened her letter. Judge her surprise, when she found it was an invitation!—actually an invitation to a christening—a christening of a Goblin child! But what was more, the Goblin parents, who wrote very politely and very friendly indeed, said they were most anxious that she should not only come to the christening-party of their dear infant BOBBLE-BABBLE-BILLY-GO-RUMPEL-STILTZSKIN (that was to be the young gentleman's name, for he was heir to old Mr. Rumpel-stiltzskin's gold mine), but should also stand godmother to that beloved and beautiful Goblin baby.

At first, little Peggy could hardly make up her mind how to act—for it is not every one, you know, that likes to visit uncommon people; besides that, the being a godmother is a very serious task, and, more than all, the standing godmother to a Goblin baby! But, at last, she thought that, as it might be dangerous to refuse, and as no particular harm could come to her by going, she would accept the invitation.

Three Goblins came to fetch her in a very neat little covered cart, just such an one as the laundress brings home the clothes in from the washing; and away they went, until they came to Primrose Hill, right into which they drove, the ground opening before them, and closing behind, into a great vaulted road, like a railway tunnel, only quite light; and they stopped at a beautiful little house, with a bright green little door, and a polished little brass knocker. There was a little porter at the door, and a little maid to take their cloaks, and offer them a cup of tea; and little carriages by hundreds, with little horses, and little coachmen, and little footmen, driving up fast to the little door, and knocking loud little sharp rat-tat-tats; and then the little porter threw open the doors, and down the carriage steps came the little ladies, with little silk stockings, and little shoes, and large—oh! such large petticoats, and little bouquets, and little flowers in their hair; and little young gentlemen to hand them out, with little flat hats under their little arms, and with eye-glasses, and little gold watches, and little chains hanging out of their little waistcoat pockets. These little gentlemen, Peggy could see, made pretty little speeches to the pretty little ladies, which made the little ladies give little laughs and little smiles at the little gentlemen. It was plain that there was a large and fashionable party of the little people; and Peggy felt very much pleased at being invited, for every one paid her the greatest attention, as if she had been a Princess-Goblin herself, instead of plain Peggy the Housemaid, of Bayswater.

Their enjoyment was great, although everything was so little; and the splendour and magnificence everywhere seen was something to wonder at. The lying-in lady was on a couch of polished black ebony, exquisitely carved and incrusted, wherever space could be found, with pearls. The coverlet was embroidered in gold, and the cradle of the baby was of ivory. The baptismal font was made of massive gold.

After the ceremony had taken place, Peggy was desirous of going home at once, as she feared her mistress might want her, although she had got leave for a holiday. The Goblins, however, begged her so earnestly to prolong her visit during her three days' holiday, that she could not refuse, especially as she wished to nurse her little, her very little godson; and so she remained for that period, which was spent in parties, and balls, and every kind of pleasure; for the Goblins, one and all, seemed as if they could never make too much of her, or prove to her sufficiently how much they liked her, and how obliged they all were by her visit to their house. That, my dears, is the way to make people happy when they come to see you!

At the end of the three days, as she positively would not stop any longer, they filled her pockets with golden sovereigns, and took her back just to the outside of Primrose Hill. At first, she thought the place looked rather strange, and that she did not remember the houses, for she thought it was all fields about there, but then she thought she might be on the other side of the hill; and she was the more persuaded of this, by seeing the out-of-the-way fashion in which the people were dressed. So she went on, until she came to the road, where she got into an omnibus, of a singular shape, as she then thought, and was carried to Bayswater. When she arrived at her mistress's house, she let herself in by the area gate; and not seeing the Cook in the kitchen, as she went through, but only a strange middle-aged woman, waiting for her, as she thought, she ran up stairs, laid aside her bonnet and shawl, and then, taking her broom in her hand, set to work at her ordinary housework. She opened the door of her mistress's bedroom, and was going in, when, to her surprise, she saw a lady she did not know seated at her mistress's toilet-table, who, on her entering, asked her what she wanted, and who she was.

"I am Peggy the Housemaid," she replied.

"Peggy the Housemaid!" said the lady, staring as if half frightened; "what Peggy? what Housemaid?"

"I thought this was mistress's room," said Peggy.

"So it is," replied the lady; "who do you think I am?"

"I don't know," replied Peggy.

"I am the mistress here, at any rate," said the lady, getting up to ring the bell; "so leave the room."

The bewildered Peggy was about to obey, when the door opened, and in came a servant-maid, that Peggy did not know, and had never seen before.

"What does this young woman want here?" asked the lady.

"I don't know, ma'am," said the maid, looking hard at Peggy, and half frightened at her broom; "I don't know her; I never saw her before."

"Why, I am Peggy the Housemaid," said the poor little girl, almost ready to cry.

"And pray who is Peggy the Housemaid? and whose Housemaid is Peggy?"

"Mrs. Marsh's Housemaid, I am," said Peggy, boldly.

"Why, Mrs. Marsh has left this house for two years past!" and then both the lady and the servant began to be frightened and to scream.

Up came a stout gentleman, and a thin footman, and a squabby page, and a nursery-maid with a baby, and the elderly woman that Peggy had seen in the kitchen—all looking like people belonging to the house, but, among them all, not one face that Peggy could recognize. The poor girl was struck dumb with fear and amazement. Where was her dear mistress? where her darling children? where Mrs. Fritters the cook, and Joe Dumpling the page, and Mr. Brusher the footman, and Philadelphia the parlour-maid? Not one of them in sight or hearing; and still the lady and maid kept on their screaming, and could not be pacified.

At last came out the fact—oh, those mischievous Goblins!—it was not three days, nor three years, that poor Peggy had stopped in the Goblins' cavern under Primrose Hill, but seven whole years!

Pray read this over to your nursery-maids, my dear little friends; and tell them, when they go out for a holiday, to think of the story of our poor little Peggy, and remember how quickly time flies away, when we are spending it pleasantly.

THE MAGIC SOUP-KITCHEN.

AT the time my story begins, it was very cold weather; the snow was on the ground, and the bittter winter had driven a poor family into a miserable shed for shelter from the blast. The eldest little girl of the widowed mother was a very pious little girl; so the child thought, if she went out into the forest, God would, perhaps, direct her steps to some place where she might find some wood, to make a fire and warm her mother. She had not gone very far, when she met an old woman, who was a good Fairy, though the child did not know it. The old woman, who knew beforehand what great trouble the girl was in, presented her with a Pot, which possessed the wonderful power of boiling, with nice sweet soup in it, the moment you said to it—

> "Pot, Pot, boil away,
> That I may have some soup, to stay
> The hunger that gnaws me day by day;"

and when they were satisfied with the soup they had eaten, they must say—

> "Stop, Pot, stop! we've had a rare treat,
> For we've had as much as we can eat."

The little girl took the Pot home to her mother; and now poverty and misery vanished, for they only had to ask the Pot for a dinner whenever they liked, and they were sure to get it. One day, however, the little girl had gone to carry some soup to a sick neighbour, who was very poor; and the mother, finding it dinner-time, put on the Pot, remembering the words she had to say to it. Then they all sat down, and ate as much as they wished for; but when the woman wanted to take off the Pot, she had forgotten what they had to say to it, and so the Pot went on boiling and boiling over, until at last the place was full of soup. Then she went out, and called in her neighbours to bring all their pots and pans, and to eat as much as they could; still it made little progress in stopping the overflowing of the Pot, for it now flowed over in a stream, and rolled out of the door into the street. Then they got together all the animals and pigs, to eat as much as they could. The pigs, who were very greedy, ate until they burst, and still it was of little use, for the Pot flowed over as fast as ever, until the streets were full, and the houses were full; and it seemed now as if it would overflow the whole world, since, although there was the greatest necessity for stopping the Pot, no one knew how to do so. At last, when only one very small cottage was left unfilled with soup, the little girl returned, and at once put an end, by the magical words, to the Pot's boiling; but, from that day to this, whoever wants to go through this village, must eat his way through soup!

THE RABBIT'S WIFE.

LITTLE Mary's mother had a garden, and it was filled with cabbages; but the place was infested with rabbits. One day, the mother saw a large black-and-white Rabbit munching away at her finest savoys, and she said to her daughter, "Go, Mary, and drive that great saucy Rabbit out of the garden."

Out ran Mary; but as she was very kindhearted, she did not try to frighten the Rabbit, who was a very fine fellow, but only said, "Now, you little Rabbit, pray do not eat all our cabbages."

"Pretty Mary," said the Rabbit, "pray don't be unkind; I come here to look at you, and not to eat your mother's cabbages. I want you to sit upon my pretty tail, and to let me carry you on it to my furry house."

Of course Mary would not do this; but for three days the Rabbit persisted in coming, and each time he came, Mary's mother sent her out to drive him away; and every time he said to her, "Come and sit upon my fine tail, and ride home upon it to my warm nest."

But at last little Mary, as too often happens, was over-persuaded, by the Rabbit's persisting, to do what she had made up her mind not to do; and when he asked her again, she did sit herself down upon his handsome tail, and he carried her off to his hut under the warm sunshiny bank, in the warren by the woodside. When they got there, he said to her, "Welcome home, my dear; and now cook me those green lettuces and some bran, and I will go and invite the guests to our wedding."

So he went out, and poor Mary was very frightened at being left all alone. Then the wedding guests came in, all Rabbits, except the Crow—who attended as the Clergyman to marry the bride and the bridegroom—and the Fox, who was to act as the Clerk.

"Now then, my dear," said the black-and-white Rabbit to little Mary, "get up and dance, and look a little more lively, for all our wedding guests are very merry and pleased. Are you not pleased?"

"No," said Mary, and began to cry.

Away went the bridegroom, rather out of temper. Presently he came back, and said, "Come, my dear, is supper ready? our wedding guests are hungry."

"No," said Mary, sobbing more and more, and the Rabbit took himself off, even more displeased; but presently he came back again, and said, "Now, my dear, you must come; the wedding guests are all waiting for you."

"No," said the bride again, pouting; but as soon as the bridegroom turned away, she got up, and made up a little doll, and gave it red lips, and stuffed it with bran, and placed it on the stool where she had been sitting; and then she ran away as fast as her little legs could carry her, and went home to her mother.

Once more the black-and-white Rabbit came to the seat, and said, "Get up! get up!" and finding his bride did not move, or take any notice of him, or answer even "No," as before, he went up to the doll, and gave it a knock on the side of the head, and it tumbled down on one side to the ground. "Oh dear! oh dear!" he squeaked; "I have killed my bride!" and then he was so frightened, that he ran away, and never came near that side of the country any more; and so little Mary escaped the consequences of making a very bad match, and I hope it will act as a warning to other young ladies, not to go off with the first young gentleman that asks them.

THE ROGUES' HOLIDAY.

ONE fine morning, the Cock in the farm-yard, having enjoyed a good crow, and gone up to the top of his dunghill, looked over the palings, and seeing the road clear, turned to Dame Partlet, his wife, and said: "My dear, it is a beautiful day, and this is the nutting season; we ought to go up to the woodside, where the Squirrel has gathered them all together for a hoard."

"A capital notion!" answered Dame Partlet; "let us be off at once; a day's pleasure will do us both good."

So they went off together to the woodside, where they remained until the evening set in. Then, whether it arose from vanity, or from their crops being too full of nuts, nothing would suit them but that they must ride home in a carriage! No walking upon claws for them, indeed!—that was much too common for such a high-minded Cock and Hen; so the Cock was obliged to make up a neat little carriage out of walnutshells. When it was ready, Dame Partlet stepped up proudly, one foot before the other, into the inside; and then, shaking down her feathers, said to her husband: "My dear, you had better harness yourself into the shafts."

"Odds bobberies and tenpenny nails!" said the Cock, ruffling up his comb, just as an angry alderman would pull out his shirt-frill. "Pray what do you take me for, my fine Dame? It would be far better for me to go back on foot than in harness, like a horse. No, that is not in our bargain, my love; I prefer playing coachman, and sitting on the box; but as for dragging the carriage myself, that is a part I can't undertake."

While they were thus disputing, a Duck came waddling up, and quacked out, "Halloa! thieves! thieves! who has given you leave to come here, under my walnut-trees? Look to yourselves; I will settle your business for you!"

So the Duck rushed at the Cock with open beak; but that gentleman happened to be of Irish extraction —he liked a quarrel, rather than not, and was always ready for a fight. So he gave the Duck a ready answer, and a sharp pecking, that soon brought the poor fowl to her senses; so that at last she begged his pardon, and consented to be harnessed to the chariot, as a punishment for the attack. Then the Cock proudly mounted the coach-box, took the reins in his left claw, shook his tail-feathers well under him, gave a loud crow; and away they went at a rattling pace.

They had hardly gone over half their journey, when they came upon two travellers, who were journeying along on foot. These were a Needle and a Pin. They were both very hot, and in a great perspiration, and seemed quite tired.

"Stop! stop!" they exclaimed immediately; and on the Cock pulling up politely, to inquire what it was they wanted, they told him, that as it was already dark, and the road was muddy, and they had been detained taking a glass of beer together at the sign of the Cross-legged Tailor, they should esteem it a particular favour if he would give them a place in his carriage. The Cock, observing that they were both

remarkably lean in the body, and would take up very little room, consented to give them a lift, on condition that they did not tread upon anybody's toes.

It was getting quite late at night, when they arrived at an inn, where, as they were not inclined to risk a night on the road, and the Duck was getting fatigued, they resolved to take up their quarters. At first, the Host raised difficulties; his house was already full, and these fresh comers did not seem altogether first-class people; but at last, yielding to their very fine words, and a promise they made of leaving for him the egg which Dame Partlet was shortly about to lay, and also the Duck's, which laid one every day, he agreed to receive them for the night. They ordered a capital supper, and spent the evening in carousing and making merry, and quacking and crowing, and singing noisy songs.

Next morning, just before daybreak, while all the world was still asleep, the Cock woke up his wife, and pecking the egg with his beak, they both made a good breakfast off it, and then threw the shells in the chimney. Next, they went and took by the head the Needle, who was still sleeping, and stuck him, point upwards, in the cushion of the Landlord's arm-chair, and did the same with the Pin in his towel. This done, they made the best of their way out of the window. Here they found the Duck, who had lain down of her own accord in the open air. She rose up as she heard them pass by, and waddling down to a stream that ran at the end of the garden-wall, she floated along it much more quickly than she had travelled post-haste the night before.

Two hours afterwards, the Landlord got out of bed, and after washing his face, took up his towel to dry it; but the Pin scratched his countenance, and made a great red scar across it from ear to ear. He threw down the towel in a great rage, and scolded his wife for her carelessness; to which the good Dame, popping out her head from under the bedclothes, replied by telling him he must have got out of bed the wrong way that morning. Down he went grumbling into the kitchen, and stepped to the fire to light his pipe; but as soon as he puffed at the embers, to get up something of a blaze, the remnant of the eggshells jumped out in his eyes.

"Everything conspires together against me this morning!" said he, as he threw himself down into his

arm-chair, for comfort's sake. But didn't he jump up quickly! and how he hallooed! for the Needle had stuck right into him—and that not in his head. This last accident crowned his anger. His suspicions fell, all at once, on the travellers whom he had taken into his house the night before; and, in fact, when he went to look for them, he found they had all decamped. Then he swore lustily that, for the future, he would never harbour any more such wandering vagabonds, who put one to great expenses, which they never pay, and for every kindness shown, play off some wicked trick or other upon you.

As for what became of the party: they all met with their deserts within a very short period. The Hen was broiled for breakfast that very morning; the Duck was stuffed with chesnuts and roasted the same evening. His master carried the Cock to a fight, where he was cruelly beaten, and lost an eye, and had his leg broken. The Pin died in a gutter; and as for the Needle, he fell into company with a tipsy little Tailor of very bad character, who kept him incessantly working, and gave him no wages; until, at last, he grew rusty and worthless, when he was sold as old iron, and cut up into points for a Sewing-Machine,—which I need not tell you, my little dears, is a kind of treadmill for naughty Needles, whence they are never liberated, until they are ground into dust.

THE GOBLIN CHANGELING.

One day, the Goblins, in playing off their mischievous pranks, took a woman's baby out of its cradle, and left there, in its place, one of their own little monsters, with a great head and two staring eyes,—one of those craving little creatures, that are always wailing and crying, and will always be hankering for something, and never stop eating and sucking. Tired out of all patience, and worn down with fatigue, the poor mother went to ask her neighbour's advice, as to what she ought to do.

"Bring the little monster into the kitchen," said the good Dame, "lay him on the hearth, light a fire close to him"—(you must remember, this was in a cottage, where they only burn wood, and have no fire-grates); "then you must take two egg-shells, and set water to boil in them, and that will make the little monster laugh; and if he once laughs—the mischievous little rascal!—he will be obliged to go away and leave you."

The poor woman thanked her good neighbour for her kind advice, and quickly returning to her own cottage, resolved to follow it without delay. So she took the little monster out of his cradle, and brought him down, all squalling as he was, and made him up a nice little bed in the front of the kitchen fireplace, where she laid him down softly and comfortably (for she was very goodnatured), in spite of all his squealing, and squeaking, and kicking. Then she lighted a fire close beside his bed, so that he could not help seeing it, and, with a very grave face, she took two egg-shells, and filled them with water, and set them down on the fire to boil, just as if they had been two heavy cauldrons.

When he saw this, the little monster began chirping with mischievous glee; and at last, to her great terror (for it is not a pleasant thing to hear a baby speak before he has cut his teeth), he cried out—

"For forty years I've lived, i'fegs!
And ne'er seen water boil'd in shells of eggs!"

and then he laughed as if his sides would crack. Whereupon, a crowd of Goblins came tumbling in, carrying with them the poor woman's baby, which they laid down gently in the corner; and then all set to work, and, grinning, kicked the little man, like a football, up the chimney, up which they also disappeared themselves, and never came back again.

THE ENCHANTED STAG.

A loving little Brother and Sister, once had the misfortune, in early life, to lose their own darling Mother, and their Father brought home, soon after her death, a wicked Stepmother, who had no love in her heart for these poor children, whom she constantly ill-used.

One day, the little Brother took his Sister by the hand, and, kissing her, said, "Since our dear mother's death, we seem no longer to have a home here; we are rendered truly miserable by the kicks and blows we receive; and, besides, we are often so hungry, we know not what to do with ourselves; at the best, we get nothing but dry crusts of bread and hard cheese, while even the little dog, sometimes, gets a dainty morsel of meat for his dinner. Come, let us wander forth together, and seek some more hospitable shelter."

So they went forth, and wandered through the woods and meadows all the day long. In the evening it came on to rain, and the Sister said, "See you, dear Brother, Heaven weeps at our misfortunes!" Presently they walked deep into a forest, where, being thoroughly tired out with grief and hunger, they laid themselves down in a hollow tree, and were soon fast asleep in each other's arms.

When they awoke the next morning, the sun was already high in the heavens, and its powerful beams made the tree so hot, that they did not know what to do with themselves. "Sister," said he, "I am so thirsty with the heat; I wish I knew where there was a nice brook, I would go and quench my thirst."

"Listen, then," said the girl, "and I think you will hear one running."

He rose up, and putting his arm round his little Sister's waist, they walked in the direction from whence the sound came.

Now, you must know that this Stepmother was a Witch, and, therefore, well knew the children's thoughts, and had watched their going away. Then sneaking after them, like a snake in the grass, as is the habit of witches, she enchanted all the springs in the forest.

A brook now came trippingly over the pebbles to their very feet, and the Brother stooped down to drink, when the Sister's quick ear caught the words the brook spoke as it ran—

"Whoever drinks one drop from me,
He to a Tiger changed will be!"

"I pray you, dear Brother, drink not, or you will be changed into a cruel Tiger, and will tear me to pieces, and devour me!"

So the Brother overcame his great desire to drink, to please his Sister, and they travelled on until they came to another brook. As they neared this next one, the Sister began to cry, saying, "Dear Brother, do not drink, I pray you; listen to the brook's babbling, and you will hear what it says "—

"To quench your thirst at me don't try,
Or a fierce Wolf full length you'll lie."

When he heard this, he said, "Well, I will not drink this time; but, say what you please, at the next I must drink, if I die for it."

So saying, they went on until they came to a beautiful grassy spot, neatly cut and rolled, with a bright sparkling brook running through it; then the Brother's thirst knew no bounds; but the Sister heard the stream say—

"The waters that so gently wash this lawn,
Will quickly change you to a timid Fawn."

Then she fell upon her Brother's neck, and entreated him not to drink; "For," said she, "you will be afraid of me, and will run away from me."

But the Brother had already stooped down, and drank; and at the very first drop of water he tasted, his shape became that of a Fawn.

At first, the little girl shed many tears of grief over her dear changed Brother; but, at last, the little maiden, embracing the Fawn, said, "Be quiet, dear little Fawn, and I will never leave you or forsake you."

Then she untied her little golden garter, and she fastened it with loving hands round his neck; then she stripped some rushes, and when they were white, she wove a girdle of them with pretty flower-buds in between; and fastening one end to the golden collar, by the other end she led him by her side, and they travelled on deeper and deeper into the forest.

After a long journey, they came to a pretty little hut, with some wild roses growing over it, and blue-bells and cowslips in the grass around it. Then the little maiden looked in, and saw it was all nice and neat, with a little chair and table, but nobody in it. Then said she to herself, "How quiet and pleasant it would be to live here with my dear Brother, where he would be safe, and I could attend to his wants." So she led him in, and then went and brought him soft moss and dried leaves to make him a couch to sleep upon. Every morning, she went out and gathered dried roots and berries and nuts for herself, while for the Fawn she brought the freshest herbs and youngest grass she could find; and the Fawn, thankful for her loving kindness, played happily around her all the day long. When night came, she said her prayers, and then lay her little head upon the Fawn's back, on which soft and warm pillow she always slept soundly until daybreak. Had the Fawn but regained his natural shape, what a merry Brother and Sister they would have been!

Time wore on, and they still lived in this forest. One day, however, the King of those parts had a great hunting-party, and they all met in this very forest to hunt. The horns blew sweetly among the trees, the dogs impatiently barked and whined, and the huntsmen hallooed so lustily, that the little Fawn became eager to join the hunt, and could not restrain himself. "Dear Sister," said he, "I must indeed join the hunters, or I shall die of sorrow;" and he likewise begged his Sister so earnestly, that she consented to let him go.

"Come back again to me in the evening," she said; "I must shut the door against those dreadful wild hunters, and I shall not open it again until I hear your voice bidding me do so. You must say—

"Sister dear, who sits within,
Open the door that I may skip in."

As soon as she had said this, off he bounded into the fresh breeze, right glad and merry to get his freedom once again.

Just as he had fully stretched his legs, the King himself caught sight of him, and seeing what a beautiful animal he was, determined upon pursuing him; but although he used every effort, he could in no way catch him; the Fawn cleverly avoided the hunters, and just as the King had made sure of him, he nimbly sprang over the bushes, and was lost to sight again.

It was now nearly dark; so, running up to the door of the little hut, he repeated the words his Sister had desired. The door was instantly opened by the anxiously-watching girl, to whom he related the pleasant run he had had, and then lay down upon his soft bed, and slept all night.

THE ENCHANTED FAWN ARRIVES AT HIS SISTER'S HUT, FOLLOWED BY THE KING.

When morning broke, the sportsmen were at the hunt again; and as soon as the Fawn heard them, he said, "Sister dear, pray open the door; I must go to the hunt."

"Go your ways," said she; "but mind you return safely in the evening, and repeat the same words as before."

When the King again saw this beautiful animal, with his golden collar, he was determined to take him, and followed him up close; but he was too nimble and brisk for them. All the day long they were trying in vain to come up to him, until towards night, when the huntsmen made a circle round him, and one wounded

him very slightly on the foot behind, so that he could not run quite so swiftly. Then one of them slipped after him to the little hut, and heard him repeat the words to his little Sister, and saw that the door was immediately opened, and shut again after him. Whereupon, the huntsman, filled with surprise and wonder, went and told the King all he had seen and heard.

The Sister, however, was terribly frightened, and grieved much in her heart, when she saw her dear Fawn was wounded. So she washed and bathed the wound, and made a nice dressing of fresh medical herbs for the healing of the foot; then said, "Now, dear Fawn, lie you down and sleep, that your wound may get well."

In the morning, it was so much better for his Sister's kind treatment, that it scarcely troubled him at all. Then he heard the Tan-ta-ra outside; he said, "I cannot restrain myself; I pray you, kind Sister, let me go, and none shall come up with me again, I will promise you."

The Sister wept bitterly, saying, "Brother mine, you are the only one I have to love in this wide world, and if you go, soon they will kill you, and I shall be left alone, unloved, uncared for; I must say nay—I cannot, dare not, give my consent."

"Then I must die here of vexation, if you say me nay; if you do not let me go, I feel I must jump out of my skin when I hear the horns."

Then she lifted the latch, with tearful eyes and a heavy heart; and in a moment he was free, bounding away, with the huntsmen at his heels.

The King desired his men to keep close beside him until night came, when he arrived at the door of the hut, and having knocked, repeated the words gaily to the Sister. When the door was opened, the King himself stepped in, and saw, to his astonishment, a maiden, more beautiful than any he had in his whole kingdom.

Then the Sister was seized with a great fright, when she saw, instead of her Fawn, a noble gentleman step in, with a golden crown upon his head. But the King smiled lovingly upon her, and taking her by the hand, he gently pressed it, saying, "Dearest maiden, will you come with me to my great castle on the hills, and remain with me, as my dearly loved and cherished wife?"

"Oh, certainly; with all my heart!" replied the maiden—for it was decidedly love at first sight on both sides—"only, you must let me take my Fawn with me, or I shall not be happy. I never will forsake him."

The King said, "Take him with you, and he shall never leave you, nor shall he want for anything."

In the meantime, the Fawn had come in, quite well and happy; so she took her little girdle, and tied it to his collar, and led him out of the hut.

Then the King lifted the pretty maiden upon his horse, and rode swiftly home to his own castle, where the marriage was honourably celebrated with much show and magnificence. Now she had become Queen, she enjoyed her life exceedingly with the King her husband, who very seldom left her side; while her dear Fawn was well attended to, and played all day long in the castle garden, underneath her casement window, where she could watch his merry gambols.

The good-for-nothing old witch of a Stepmother, who had been so cruel to the dear children, and who hoped they had long ago been devoured by wild beasts, or that the dogs had hunted the Fawn to death, no sooner heard how happy and prosperous they had become, than her wicked heart was inflamed by jealousy, and she had no peace day or night, for thinking how she could work their misery and downfall. Her own daughter, who had been born to her after the children had left home, was one of the ugliest girls that ever came into the world; she had but one eye,

for which she was continually reproached. She said, "To think of that pert hussy becoming a Queen! that luck should have been mine."

"Be quiet, now," said the Witch-mother; "be content with your station; we shall see what happens when the right time comes. I shall be at hand, I'll warrant you."

One day, the King went out hunting, and it so happened that, during his absence, the Queen brought into the world a most beautiful little boy. The wicked old Witch was as good as her word; true enough, there she was, to work mischief. She got into the Queen's bedroom, where she was lying, in the form of a Head-nurse. "Will it please your Majesty to go to the bath I have provided for you; it will restore your health and vigour, and you will quickly be well again; it is quite ready—you had better be carried to it while it is warm." Then the daughter, who was near at hand, helped her to carry the sick Queen into the bath, and having placed her there, left the room, and shut the door; but first these wicked women had made up an immense fire in the stove, which must inevitably suffocate the poor young Queen.

When all this was done, the old Witch dressed up her ugly daughter in the Queen's clothes, and putting the Queen's cap upon her head, she laid her in the bed in her place. She gave her, too, the form and appearance of the Queen as much as she could, only she had not the power to put another eye in her head, so she laid her upon the side where there was no eye, and covered the bedclothes close around her.

When all this was done, the King came from the hunt, and was overjoyed to hear a son and Prince had been born to him, and could not restrain himself from going to his wife's bedside, to see for himself how she was getting on, and to give her an affectionate and consoling embrace. When he would have gone to his wife, the old Witch-nurse called out, "For your life do not undraw the curtains! the smallest ray of light will kill the Queen; she must be kept quite quiet." So the King left the room without discovering the wicked cheat that had been played upon him.

When the dead of the night came, the real Nurse, who was watching the Royal Infant's cradle, and wide awake, saw the door open, and the real Queen glide gently in. She took the sleeping babe in her arms, and tenderly caressing and rocking it, shook up its little bed and pillow, then putting it back again, covered it warmly over. Nor was the Fawn forgotten, for, going to the corner where it lay, she tenderly stroked its back, and then, with silent step, left the room again.

In the morning, the Nurse, not knowing what to make of this, asked the guards if any one had passed them into the castle in the night.

"Nay," they replied; "our watch has been well kept, and we have seen nobody."

For many nights the true Queen came constantly, and never spoke a word, but always nursed her child, and petted her Fawn. When some time had passed away, the Queen began to speak, and said—

"Farewell, Sweet Babe, and you, my much-loved Fawn;
Twice more I'll say farewell before the morn."

The startled Nurse made no reply, but went straight to the King, and told him all that had happened.

Then the King was seized with a great dread, and exclaimed, "May Heaven avert any calamity to my much-loved wife! What can this mean? This night I will myself keep watch by the child."

So he went into the nursery, and—as the Nurse had told him—about midnight, the Queen glided in, and said—

"Farewell, Sweet Babe, and you, my much-loved Fawn;
Once more I'll say farewell before the morn."

And she nursed the child, and then disappeared as she had done before.

The King dared not speak, but he watched the next night also; and the Queen, again appearing, said—

"Farewell, Sweet Babe, and you, my much-loved Fawn;
No more farewell I'll say before the morn."

At these words the King could no longer contain himself; but he sprang up, and catching the Queen in his arms, he said, "You, and you only, are my own, my much-loved wife!"

"Yes," she exclaimed, "I am your dear wife!" and at this moment her life was mercifully restored to her, and she was as charmingly beautiful again as she ever had been.

Then the King, infuriated with rage, when he found out the wicked treacherous trick played upon him by the Witch and her daughter, had them both tried for their lives. The sentence passed upon the daughter was, that she should be devoured by wild beasts, and the Witch-mother was to be tied to a stake, and be miserably burned to death.

As soon as she was reduced to ashes, the little Fawn was unbewitched, and took his natural form, and a fine handsome young man he had grown. He now lived with his Sister all the rest of his life, and the King made him master of the Royal Buckhounds, and he spent his time merrily in hunting.

THE DWARF OF THE MOUNTAIN.

IN a lovely secluded spot, by a swift-flowing stream, there once dwelt a Miller. He was proud of the beauty of his only daughter, and justly so, for no damsel could show a prettier face or a more graceful figure. Now, it so happened that this Miller had, one day, to go before the King; and in order to make his Majesty think he was a rich man, and a person of some consequence, the Miller told him he had a daughter at home who knew how to spin straw into gold!

"Gold is not a thing to be despised," said the King; and, moreover, he was even more fond of it than most people. So he thought to himself, "If I could but learn this art, it would suit me exactly,—nothing could be better." Then he turned to the Miller, and said, in an off-hand manner, as if he did not care much about the matter, "By-the-bye, Mr. Miller, you may as well bring this daughter of yours with you to-morrow, and then I can judge for myself whether you speak the truth or not."

"Good!" said the Miller; "I will do as you desire."

Now the Miller wondered how he should get out of the hobble he had got into; but he left all to chance. The next morning, he took the maiden to the palace; as soon as the King saw her, he led her into a room which was filled to the top with straw; then he gave her a spinning-wheel and a reel, and said: "Now, my pretty little dear, spin away as fast as you can, and get all this straw spun into gold before the morning. If you do not, a sad fate awaits you—you must surely die." With these words, he shut-to the room door, and left the maiden, all alone, to deplore her sad fate.

Then she sat for some time as one bewildered, wondering how she could possibly avert the dreadful sentence. As for spinning the straw into gold, she had never even heard tell of such a thing; how then could she save her life? In the midst of all this tormenting perplexity, she began to weep bitterly. Soon after, the door slowly creaked upon its hinges, and first the head and then the body of a Little Man entered the room. "My dear child, said he, "why are you spoiling your sweet face by crying? Come, tell me your troubles, and depend upon it I will help you, if I can."

"Oh, kind Sir!" said she, "I must spin this straw into gold before the morning, and I know no more how to set about it than the Man in the moon."

"Well," said the Little Man, "what will you give me if I do it for you?"—thinking perhaps he should get a kiss from the pretty girl, for he was a kind-hearted, loving fellow.

"I'll give you my beautiful necklace," said she.

The Dwarf accepted it; and down he sat in front of the wheel, away it flew round and round, until it made her dizzy to look at it. Presently one bobbin was quite full; then he set up another, and another, until all the straw was gone, and all the bobbins were full of glittering gold. When this was done, the Little Man wished her good morning, and left her happy enough, at finding how he had so cleverly saved her life.

As soon as ever the sun was up, the King, who had grown anxiously impatient to know the truth, entered the room, and, to his great astonishment, beheld the heaps of gold that filled it. Instead of feeling thankful and satisfied with all that gold, the greedy King thought he would have more. He turned to the maiden, saying, "You have worked well, but you must work faster yet before I shall be content." Then he led her to another room, much larger than the one she had been in before, and said, "If you value your life, spin all this before the sun rises." The maiden was in terrible trouble; she could not spin the straw, although she had seen the good Dwarf do it easily enough. She was just despairing, when in came the Little Man, and said, "What will you give me, if I do it for you?"

"Well," she answered, "I will give you this brilliant ring off my finger."

So he drew off the ring, and then went merrily to work again; and very soon all the straw was glistening gold. She was about to thank him very much, for her heart was filled with gratitude, when the Little Man slipped quietly away.

91

In the morning, the King came again, and was very pleased to see his vast stores of wealth all around him; but yet he was not satisfied, and wanted more. The King took the maiden by the hand, and led her into a very large room, twice as big as any she had seen before; this, also, was full of straw, like the other two. The King said, "If you spin this into gold before the morning, I will make you my wife;" for he thought, "Search the world through, and I shall not find a richer wife than this; for the more gold I require, the more work I can make her do."

Then he shut the door close; and when the girl was left alone, the Dwarf came in for the third time, and said, "Now, deary, what will you give me, if I finish this work also for you?"

"Alas!" she cried, "I have nothing left to give you!"

"Then promise me your first-born child, if ever you should become Queen."

"That I may safely promise," said she; for she never for a moment thought the King would keep his word. So, not knowing how to get on by herself, or to help herself out of this trouble, she consented, though not very willingly.

Directly she had pledged her word, the Dwarf, pleased enough, began his spinning; and so eager was he to conclude the bargain, that he had no sooner begun than it was all finished.

When the morning broke, the King entered as usual, and found all finished, just as he wished it should be; and having been much smitten by the maiden's beauty, he had a great desire the wedding should be celebrated directly. So he had his handsomest carriage, with his finest horses, brought to the gates, and the King and the Miller's daughter drove to the church, and were married.

She found everthing so comfortable and so much to her liking when she was married, that she never troubled herself about anything, not even about her promise to the Dwarf. Time rolled on; and one day she gave birth to a very lovely little baby. Nothing could exceed her joy; she nestled her helpless little one in her bosom, and shed tears of gladness over it; she petted it, and caressed it, and thought that now she could never again know sorrow.

You must know, that the little Dwarf was one of the kindest-hearted men in the world; but having been twice married, and not having any children to love and cherish of his own, he waited anxiously for the time when the Queen should become a mother. Just as the Queen was falling to sleep, the door opened stealthily, and the Dwarf entered.

"What do you want?" cried the Queen, rousing herself up.

"Has your Majesty forgotten your promise?" demanded he.

Then the Queen was in a great fright, and shook like an aspen leaf. "Oh! leave me my darling babe!" she exclaimed; "anything else I possess shall be yours, but in pity leave me my tender babe!"

The Dwarf was well-nigh crying, himself, when he saw how her heart was grieved; but he had set his mind upon something human he might love, and who

would love him in return. He could not give up the child; however, he gave the Queen one chance, saying, "I will come again to you in three days' time; and if, during that interval, you can find out my name, then the child shall be yours."

All the night through she kept awake, thinking of all the out-of-the-way names she had ever heard; and in the morning she had a list of the names of all known persons throughout the kingdom; and when the Little Man arrived, she began guessing, "Abednego, Esarhaddon, Ahashuerus;" but at every name she mentioned, he replied, "That is not my name."

The second day, the Queen sent again among her people for all curious and odd names; and when the Dwarf presented himself again before her, she said, "It is Crooked-legs, Hump-back, Squint-eye."

"No," said he to each; "that is not my name."

Then the Queen had only one other day left in which to guess this wonderful name; and she was wild with emotion, when she found she could not guess it.

The third day, the messengers went out again, and returned without having found any new names; but one of them told the Queen that, as he passed the wildest, darkest mountain in those parts, where even the rabbits and hares are afraid to burrow near, "There," said he, "I saw a very odd little man, dancing about on one leg before the door of a hut, where a fire was brightly burning. The old man sang aloud, and as he sang, I listened to these words—

'To-day I will brew, and then I will bake
A sweet cake for the babe I am going to take;
For much it will puzzle the brains of the Queen,
To know Rumpelstiltskin's the name I mean.'"

When the Queen heard this, she felt sure all was right; for who else could this little man be? As soon as she had composed herself, the Dwarf walked in, carrying a nice soft blanket to wrap the baby in, warm and snug, so that it might not catch cold. This time, his face was beaming with smiles; he thought the desire of his whole life was about to be accomplished. He said, "Your Majesty, no doubt, will guess this time."

"I hope so," she replied, in a tone rather too confident to let the Dwarf feel easy. So she looked at him a moment, and said, "It is Rumpeltumple."

"That is not my name," he answered, eagerly.

"Well, it is Stiltskin."

"No, your Majesty;" and while she was getting ready her third answer, he was opening the blanket, and placing it so as to receive the treasured child.

"Well," said the Queen, "it must be RUMPELSTILTSKIN!"

"Some Witch has told you; hang the witches! drown them all!" Then he howled with disappointment, and stamped about the room so hard, that he set his foot right through the flooring, so that he could not draw it out again. Then he took hold of his leg, and pulled it so hard that it came off, in his efforts to release himself; and at last he went off, rending the air with his painful lamentations; and the Queen, who pitied him very much, was allowed to remain without any more visits from the Mountain Dwarf.

THE SPIDER'S MISFORTUNE.

ONCE upon a time, there dwelt together, in the same house, a Spider and a Flea; they agreed very well together, they ate off the same dishes, cooked their food at the same fire, and brewed their beer in the same egg-shell,—very good beer they made, too.

One day, when the Spider was brewing and stirring the hot liquor well about, she unhappily fell into the copper. Thereupon, the Flea began to scream and hop about. "What are you screaming at?" asked the Door.

"Because poor little Spider has scalded herself in the beer-tub," replied she.

Then the Door began to creak, as if it were in pain; and the Broom, which stood in the corner, asked, "What are you creaking for, Door?"

"Because," the Door replied,

"The little Spider's scalded herself in the beer,
And the little Flea weeps with fear."

So the Broom exerted itself, and began to sweep away industriously; and presently a little Cart came by, and asked the Broom why she swept.

"May I not sweep?" replied the Broom;

"The little Spider's scalded herself in the beer,
And the little Flea weeps with fear;
The little Door creaks on its hinges with pain."

Thereupon, the little Cart said, "Then I will run away;" and began to run very fast, past a Heap of Ashes, which cried out, "Why do you run, little Cart?"

"Because," replied the Cart,

"The little Spider's scalded herself in the beer,
And the little Flea weeps with fear;
The little Door creaks on its hinges in pain,
And the little Broom sweeps the house in vain."

"Then," said the Ashes, "I must burn furiously."

Now, near the Ashes there grew a little Tree, which asked, "Little Heap, why do you burn?"

"Because," said the Heap,

"The little Spider's scalded herself in the beer,
And the little Flea weeps with fear;
The little Door creaks on its hinges with pain,
And the little Broom sweeps the house in vain;
The little Cart runs on in haste."

Then the Tree cried, "I will shake myself;" and went on shaking, until not a leaf was left upon it. A little Girl, passing by with her water-pitcher, saw the Tree trembling and shaking, and said, "What is the matter with you, Tree? why do you shake yourself?"

"Why may I not, when

The little Spider's scalded herself in the beer,
And the little Flea weeps with fear;
The little Door creaks on its hinges in pain,
And the little Broom sweeps the house in vain;
The little Cart runs on in haste,
And the Ashes burn themselves to waste?"

"Oh! if that is the case," said the Maiden, "then I will break my pitcher;" and she threw it down, and broke it. Then the Streamlet, from which she drew the water, asked, "Why do you break your pitcher my little dear?"

"Why should I not?" she replied—

"For the little Spider's scalded herself in the beer,
And the little Flea weeps with fear;
The little Door creaks on its hinges in pain,
And the little Broom sweeps the house in vain;
The little Cart runs on in haste,
And the Ashes burn themselves to waste;
The little leaves fall from the Tree,
But the Streamlet runs on till it reaches the Sea."

"Ah, well," said the Streamlet, "then it is time I began to flow;" and it flowed and flowed along in a broad stream, which kept getting bigger and bigger, until, at last, it swallowed up the little Girl, the little Tree, the Ashes, the little Cart, the little Broom, the little Door, the little Flea, and, last of all, the little Spider. Then it flowed on, until it was broad enough and strong enough to reach the Sea.

HOW THE CAT MARRIED THE MOUSE,

AND WHAT CAME OF IT.

STRANGE things happen now and then, and singular people come together. Once upon a time, a Cat went into partnership with a Mouse. It was a female Mouse, to be sure, so that, after all, the strength and the cunning were on the right side. They lived in the same corner of a stable, and kept house very comfortably together.

One day, after dinner, as they were basking in the sunshine, the Mouse lying close hid under the sill of the stable-door, the Cat blinked his eyes, and said, "My dear Mrs. Mouse, this is very pleasant, but it won't go on for ever. This sunshine will not last above another three months, and then come the frost and the snow. We must lay in some store for the winter, or we shall come off badly. I had better go out and see about it; for you, my dear Mrs. Mouse, must not venture anywhere, for fear of an accident."

The cunning old fellow meant by this, that he should like to have the handling of Mrs. Mouse's money, for she always kept a small sum by her. She handed it all over to him, as innocent as a dove, and he went out with it. After two or three days, during the whole of which time poor Mrs. Mouse was in a great flutter about him, lest her poor dear old Tom had been caught in a trap by some of the wicked gardeners thereabouts, Tommy came back, as bold as a lion, and as impudent as a monkey, but looking very much as if he had been sitting up very late. He told the little lady some roundabout cock-and-bull story, concerning the dearness of provisions, and commercial distress, and how bad things were in the City; and then he showed her a large brass Kettle, full of beautiful Fat, that he had bought at a tallow-melter's; and this, he said, had cost all the money, and would amply suffice to keep them handsomely in soups, sauces, meat, and gravy, through the winter months. Mrs. Mouse, who was

93

altogether innocent of money matters, and hardly knew the difference in price between a leg of mutton and a shin of beef, was quite delighted with Mr. Tom's cleverness, and satisfied both with his bargain and his return.

But the next question was, now that they were so rich, what was to be done with their wealth? Where were they to put the Pot? Not in the stable, certainly, for the hens would scratch it out, and the dogs would soon lick it clean. At last, the Cat bethought himself of the organ-loft in the village church, just under the organ; "For no one," said he, "thinks of robbing a church." So they put it there, snugly hid away, and resolved not to touch it until they really wanted it.

But although they did not eat it at once, it gave them great pleasure and comfort to think of it, and know they had it for when they wanted it; for all prudent and saving people, you must know, have more than enjoyment of their money. This feeling made Mrs. Mouse quite happy; but, somehow or other, Tommy went on thinking about the Pot, until his memory began to gloat over the Fat, and he licked his chops in imagination, and got quite dry in the throat, and parched in the tongue, for the want of a little greasing in those parts. At last, he could not bear it any longer; so he pretended, one morning, to have just received a letter by post, and said to Mrs. Mouse, "Dear me! what a nuisance! Here I am obliged to go out to a christening! My aunt, Mrs. Reginald De Grimalkin, writes to ask me to be godfather to her six-and-thirtieth son, a charming kitten, grey, with black marks— the true squirrel breed. I really don't see how I can refuse."

"Certainly not, Tom; go, by all means; and if you see any nice cakes, slip one in your pocket for me; and don't forget to drink my health in a half-glass of your Aunt's best port wine. By-the-bye, dear, you will want a guinea to give the nurse."

And so the poor deluded little creature pulled out her purse from the pocket of her grey pelisse, and slipped it into Tom's claw, who grinned as if he had been one of his Cheshire ancestry, and walked off, purring with delight; for it was all a fib on his part— he had not got any Aunt, and nobody had invited him to stand godfather.

No! He went right off to the church, ran up the tower, climbed into the belfry window, sneaked into the organ-loft, crept under the organ, and there sat himself down to look at the Pot of nice Fat. But he did not look long; his whiskers and moustaches curled their ends towards it, and his nose stretched out that way, and his tongue pushed itself out, and his mouth opened, and at last his head dragged his body up to it, and down he pushed himself on to the top, and began licking the edges all round, bit by bit, until he got into the middle. "Why, there's all the top off!" he exclaimed; and he ran off, feeling quite ashamed of his own greediness, but, nevertheless, much comforted in his stomach. He could not go home at once, as a christening is a long operation, and the party after it generally sit late; so he wandered about on the tops of the houses, made a few calls on some of his lady

friends; and having altogether spent a very pleasant evening, and enjoyed himself, returned home.

"You are a little late, Tom," said Mrs. Mouse, as Tom scratched at the stable-door. "I hope you have had a pleasant day."

"Oh! a charming day!" replied Tom, stroking his whiskers, as he thought of the delicious Fat.

"What name did you give the young kitten?" inquired Mrs. Mouse.

"Top Off," replied Tom, as glibly as you please, remembering just then how nicely he had topped off the Fat in the great brass Kettle.

"Well, that is a strange name, indeed!" remarked Mrs. Mouse, quite innocently. "I suppose it is some family surname?"

"Yes," said Tom; "my great-grandfather's uncle came from Russia."

"Oh, indeed!" said Mrs. Mouse, very much impressed with the greatness of her Tom's relations.

It was only a few days afterwards, that Tom began to feel the same wicked liquorishness after the Fat in the brass Pot. He could not get the taste out of his mouth, anyhow. He caught birds and crunched them, and rats, but found them coarse food; and he saw some of Mrs. Mouse's relatives home, very politely, two or three evenings, and ate them up just before they arrived at their own door-steps; but after all, nothing would do; there was not enough fat—not sufficient sauce and gravy—about them.

"My dear girl," said he, one morning, to Mrs. Mouse—he always called her his dear girl when he wanted to diddle her—"My dear girl," says he, whisking his tail round his front paws, in a most engaging and elegant manner, "I really must get you to live without me for another day."

"Oh, Tom!" said Mrs. Mouse, coaxingly, yet inquiringly.

"Yes, my dear Mrs. Mouse; I am asked again to stand godfather——"

"Not Mrs. Reginald de Grimalkin again, surely," exclaimed Mrs. Mouse, with a little scream, and a slight emphasis on the ly (as I have marked it); "that can't be!"

"No, Mrs. Mouse, no!" replied Tom, twirling his moustache; "Augustus Von Tibby, my great-grand-aunt's thirty-fourth cousin, wishes me to do him the honour of being godfather to his youngster, a charming bold little kitten, he informs me, who has a black head with a white ring round his throat, just as regular and white as the Curate's neck-tie. How am I to refuse?"

Mrs. Mouse could have told him how he might refuse, but she thought it would be ill-natured; so she consented to his going, and off he did go, in high feather, full scamper, not to Captain Augustus Von Tibby's residence, but straight to the organ-loft, and under the organ, and on, with a jump and a whisk of his tail, to the rim of the great brass Pot full of nice Fat.

It was something to see him lick it round in great circles, one after another, the Fat melting and running out of his jaws, as he gulped it in! At last, he felt he could not go any farther; his skin began to swell as if it would crack, and he ceased from eating, because he could not eat any more. Then the greedy fellow lay down by the side of the great brass Pot to recover his breath, and as he looked at the diminished quantity of Fat, exclaimed, "Why, good gracious! I have already eaten it half out!"

After a refreshing sleep, and a cool walk in the moonlight, he went home, for he felt too bilious and dull to pay visits.

"Ah, Tommy," said Mrs. Mouse, smiling, as he entered, "you are a good boy this time, indeed! Why, it's only just seven o'clock."

"I did not stop tea," said Tom; "there was to be a concert, and I hate squalling, as you know, especially those fashionable Italian bravura songs, that go rattling away for an hour, all up among the higher notes."

"But what name did you give the kitten?" inquired Mrs. Mouse.

"Oh!—ah!—yes!—surely," said Tom, trying to think of some kittenish name; but not one would come into his head. At last he bethought himself; "HALF OUT," said he—"We called him 'HALF OUT.'"

"HALF OUT!" squeaked Mrs. Mouse. "What do you mean, Tom, by 'HALF OUT?' 'TOP OFF' before, and 'HALF OUT' now! Really, Tom, these names have such a curious sound as to make one suspicious."

"Quite as good names as 'Cheese-nibbler,' and 'Crumb-stealer,' Mrs. Mouse, and those are the best names to be found in your family, I am thinking," retorted Tom, savagely.

Mrs. Mouse was silent. It is not every lady that is so, when her husband speaks sharply to her; but Mrs. Mouse was a discreet person, and remembered that Cats have claws.

Two days afterwards, Tom came shuffling down stairs in his slippers to breakfast, and told her, in an off-hand manner, that he was going out again that day to another christening.

"Indeed!" remarked Mrs. Mouse, as sarcastically as a well-bred lady can venture to speak.

"Yes," he went on, "Mr. and Mrs. Beauchamp Megrim have a beautiful brindled kitten christened to-day. It is a genuine tortoiseshell Tom."

"Oh! pray go, pray go!" said Mrs. Mouse; "the dear elegant creature! Why, such a thing does not occur once in a hundred years!"

So off he went, with flying colours; and he sat down and finished the Pot clean out, and came home that night, full of Fat, and tired with gormandising.

"Well, my dear," said the Mouse, as he returned; "how is the charming infant, and what have you named it?"

"Oh, it is 'ALL OUT,' it is 'ALL OUT!'" cried Tom, thinking of the Pot of Fat.

"ALL OUT! ALL OUT! what do you mean by 'ALL OUT?' 'TOP OFF,' 'HALF OUT,' and 'ALL OUT!'—who ever heard of such names? There is not one of them in the calendar!"

"I dare say not," said Tom; and he rolled himself up to sleep.

However, there was no more awkward questioning about names, for the Cat was not asked out to any

more christenings; but as the winter came on, and provisions of the ordinary character began to run short, Mrs. Mouse bethought herself of their comfortable store.

One morning, she came down to breakfast with her grey pelisse and bonnet on, and laying down her gloves, as she sat down to pour out Tom's coffee—

"I am going to the church this morning," said she.

"Going to church!" cried Tom, struck all of a heap, with the pangs of conscience gnawing in his inside, yet pretending not to understand her—"going to church, my dear girl!" (oh! the rascal!) "What for? It is not Sunday."

"I am going for the Fat in the Kettle, Tom," said Mrs. Mouse. "We want something warm and nourishing for dinner to-day."

"But the snow," said Tommy, "is very deep. Let me go instead of you."

The rascal wanted to sneak off.

"We will go together, my dear," said Mrs. Mouse; "the Kettle is too heavy for one to carry, unless we do it at twice."

"I have done my half already," thought Tom.

However, there was no help; Fate and Fat stared Tom in the face. Go he must; and so they went together. When they arrived at the organ-loft, there was the Pot in its right place; but where was the Fat?

Gone like the summer flowers!

"Now I see it!" cried Mrs. Mouse; "a nice partner you are, Mr. Tommy—a trusty friend—a faithful spouse! Oh! oh! oh! oh! oh! oh! oh! oh!"

"Don't take on so," said Tom, feeling very foolish, and beginning to grow angry; "I can't bear it!"

"A fine godfather, truly, and a fine family——"

"Don't abuse my family," growled Tom, glad to find an excuse for quarrelling.

"A nice lot!—Tibby and Grimalkin! I have heard of Cats that eat their kittens; perhaps you come of that Russian family, and have swallowed your godchildren. But I forgot—the Russians are all famous for liking fat—"

"Will you stop your tongue?" said the Cat, lashing his tail.

"First, there was your 'TOP OFF'—Prince TOP OFF, of course! How is your Imperial Highness?"—and here Mrs. Mouse made a mock curtsey. "Then there's your 'HALF OUT'—Captain HALF OUT, of course! Oh, brave soldier! Then there's——"

"Silence!" yelled the Cat, "or I'll eat you!"

But poor Mrs. Mouse could not hold her tongue, and "ALL OUT" would slip off it with a hiss.

Scarcely was the word out of her jaws, when the ruthless Cat made a spring at her, snatched at her across the loins, broke her back, threw her over, scrunched her bones, and swallowed her!

You will see this sort of thing going on in the world every day.

———

THE WHALE, THE SEAL, AND THE PORPOISES.

In the very old, old times, there dwelt on the coast of Greenland a very poor woman, who had been twice a wife, and twice a widow. Her family consisted of four sons; the elder, by her first husband, was of a kind and generous nature; he loved his brothers with the warmest affection, and would at all times sacrifice his own pleasures to their wishes and happiness, and was always trying to supply their wants. His brothers, on the contrary, from some evil-born aversion, returned all his kindness with detestation. This spirit of hatred grieved the elder brother, who was too well-intentioned to retaliate upon them, but trusted to time and continued kindness, to turn their hearts in love and peace towards him. In this he was sadly mistaken; for with their growth their hatred grew, and they became not only a torment to his heart, but a great hindrance to him in his worldly avocations, for whatever good he did, they were sure to undo. His snares were unset, his nets were destroyed; and, turn where he would, he saw the effects of their ruthless united power.

Now, this elder brother was a mighty Sorcerer, but of this his brothers had no knowledge. He could at any time have severely punished their wickedness, but he still hoped by love to soften their hearts. At last, when all his efforts had failed, he consulted a familiar spirit, another great Sorcerer, hoping they might fall upon some expedient that would teach the three brothers a lesson, and subdue their hearts without injuring their persons. Then the Sorcerer caused a large Seal to appear upon the shore; and the three brothers, fearing lest the elder one should obtain this great prize, ran with hot haste, and together struck their harpoons into the animal.

No sooner had the harpoons struck the Seal, than the brothers found themselves dragged into the water after them; they had no power to disengage their hands from the staff. Then they spoke with hurried confusion to each other, and shouted out for their brother to come to their assistance, but he was nowhere to be seen. Then the Seal, whom the Sorcerer had created for the purpose of carrying out his own ends, began to move on the waters, at first slowly, and then with rapid motions, dragging them from reach of the shore, just as their mother arrived on it, and, with many tears and loud outcries, called vainly upon them to return.

Days and nights passed, and still these starving miserable men were dragged on through the water; it was as much as they could do to keep themselves alive. At length, the elder of the three, who was well-nigh exhausted, said to his companions, "This harm has come upon us because we have so cruelly persecuted our loving brother. Oh! if he were only here, that we might speak our sorrow to him, and ask his forgiveness before we die."

"True," replied the others, "that is the only thing that torments our consciences."

No sooner had this good feeling taken possession of

their hearts, than the Seal changed his course towards the south, and quickly arrived at a small island, that looked green and pleasant. When he was quite close, the brothers, to their great satisfaction, found they could release themselves from their harpoons, and so they landed in safety upon the island.

Now a new anxiety awaited them: they were hungry, and yet were obliged to conceal themselves, having little doubt they were in an enemy's country. While they were hidden, they saw a very small boat approach them, pulled by a man of most diminutive stature. When he came to the spot opposite to where they were crouching among the bushes, he anchored his boat by a big stone attached to a long line, and then leaped over the side of the boat down into the deep water, without perceiving them. After being absent some time, he rose again to the surface, bearing with him a large fish; this he did many times, always waiting each time to look in the bottom of the boat, and count his fish.

The three brothers were now so tormented with hunger at the sight of these fish, that they said, "Why should we die of starvation, while food is within our grasp?" The younger then offered to swim to the boat while the little man was away, and steal enough fish for their immediate wants. This plan succeeded, and he returned to his brothers well pleased; but the little Fisherman had no sooner returned with another fish, than he missed the one they had stolen. He immediately took a willow wand, and stretched it out towards the horizon; the wand travelled until it pointed to the place where they lay concealed.

He now pulled up his anchor, and quickly reached the shore, and immediately discovered the three brothers. Although small, he possessed superhuman strength; he very soon bound them hand and foot, and threw them into the boat, then he pulled back again from whence he had come. Having rounded a distant point, they came upon a village, in which the people were all as small as their captor; their houses, their boats, their implements, and utensils, being all in proportion to themselves.

The three brothers were then taken out, and cast, bound as they were, into an outbuilding, whilst the inhabitants were in full council to decide upon their fate. While they were thus engaged, an immense flock of birds, having quills like porcupines, instead of feathers, hovered over the inhabitants, shooting their quills upon them with such deadly effect, that in a very short space of time, in spite of the little people's valorous defence, there was not one left with any seeming life in them; they lay covered with the piercing darts of their aërial persecutors. When all resistance ceased, the birds went off as they came, leaving the dead to bury themselves.

Now, it was through the kind sympathy of their elder brother, the Sorcerer, that this flying troop had been sent to their assistance, because, by his magic power, he read with gladness the softening of their hearts.

The three unhappy brothers beheld with wondering eyes the passing conflict, and at last, by unheard-of exertion, one of them contrived to free himself from

THE LITTLE PEOPLE ENGAGE THE WHALE TO CARRY THE THREE BROTHERS HOME.

his fetters. He then set his two Brothers free from their bonds, and the three proceeded together to the battle-field, where they began to pull the quills from the apparently lifeless bodies. No sooner had they done this, than the little people all instantly recovered their consciousness. When they were quite restored to health again, they were anxious to show their gratitude to their deliverers, and offered to grant them whatever they desired.

"Well," said the Brothers, "the greatest return you can possibly make us, will be to send us home to our native place."

Whereupon, the little folks held a council among

themselves, and decided that these Brothers justly deserved what they demanded at their hands; but in what manner could they possibly convey them? The decision was made known to the Brothers, but neither could they devise any plan to reach home, as they had no boat to carry them.

The Elder Brother all this time was an unseen listener to what was going on. He caused, at that moment, a great Whale to come in sight, who was also a brother Sorcerer.

No sooner had the inhabitants caught sight of the Whale, than they hailed this as a lucky chance to take the wanderers back again. Then the little folks brought food for them, and placed them upon the Whale's back, well knowing that all Whales, at that season of the year, made straight for the shores they were anxious to visit.

However, when they had gone about half way, the Whale got very tired of remaining upon the surface of the water, and he knew he dared not dive into the deep with this cargo on his back. He thought himself a great fool for the trouble he was taking, and at last he hit upon a plan that he deemed himself justified in adopting.

"I can," said he, "very easily turn these lads into Porpoises, and then they can swim by my side, and I shall not have the labour of carrying them." This plan he put into execution, and the three Brothers took the shape of Porpoises, and went swimming by his side through the water.

Now, although the Whale is endowed with greater power than any other animal, yet no magic could again turn these Porpoises into men; thus they remained, swimming about, so long as they lived; and hence arose the great enmity which has always existed between Seals and Porpoises, they being the first cause of the latter's great misfortune.

After the departure of the three Brothers with the Seal, the Mother, in great agony of mind, had remained wringing her hands upon the shore, and rending the air with her lamentations; nor could any entreaty prevail upon her to return home again.

One day, the Whale happened to pass, and taking pity upon her great distress, turned her into a stone; and there she remains to this day.

TIMOTHY NEVER-SHAKE.

THERE was once an old man, and he had two sons; one, George, who was quick and ready to learn and to do anything; the other, Timothy, who was so dunderheaded that he could not be brought to learn anything, and so stupid that you would have thought he was really a donkey, only his ears were not long enough.

This grieved his old father very much; the more so, when he heard people make their remarks upon it, and say, "We wonder how long this Timothy Never-shake will hang about at home, and be a burden to his poor old father!"

Now, young Timothy had got the nickname of Never-shake for the following reason:—as he never went anywhere, or did anything, his elder brother, George, was always sent out; but sometimes, when his father wanted him to go into the village late in the evening, as the way lay across the churchyard and the path was a dismal one, he did not like to go, and used to say, "Please, father, don't ask me to go, for it does make me shake so!" In fact, if the truth must be told, Master George, for all his cleverness, was a bit of a coward; for when the tales told by the fireside on a winter's evening used to grow very interesting, he would often stop the story-teller, and

say, "Pray don't go on, for it makes me tremble and shake so!" Now, it happened that young Timothy heard this; and he used to say, with his unmeaning face and staring eyes, "Make him quake and shake! I wonder what at? I wish I could shake!" So they named him "Timothy Never-shake."

One day, Timothy's father called him out of the corner by the fireside, and said, "Timothy, my lad, it is time you learned some trade, so as to get your living. You must work; you see how your brother works, and I work, and everybody works."

"Well, father," replied Timothy, brushing up his forelock, "I will learn to shake."

"Learn to shake!" exclaimed his father; "what can the boy mean? You'll never get your living by that, lad, though you'll learn to shiver and shake, I doubt not, soon enough."

But his elder brother, George, laughed when he heard of it, and thought to himself, what a rare simpleton Timothy was!

Just at this moment, the Sexton of the parish came in from the churchyard close by, and seeing his neighbour vexed, asked the cause. The old man told his troubles, and the silly answer that Timothy had given him.

"Oh!" said the Sexton, "mine is the trade to make him shiver and shake! Send him to me; I warrant he will not be long in learning!"

The father was glad of the offer, for a beginning is a start on the road always. So Timothy was handed over to the Sexton, who took him with him to the church tower, to help him ring the Bells.

"Ding-dong!" went the Great Bells; and Timothy liked the fun very well for two days, until he was called out of bed at midnight, to toll the Passing Bell for some poor creature that had just died in the village.

"Now then, my fine Mr. Never-shake," thought the Sexton to himself, "you shall soon know what it is to shiver and shake!" and he got up and went out as well.

Timothy walked on through the churchyard,—up the moonlit path among the gravestones, and into the deep shade under the aged yew-trees, and right down into the darkness of the overhanging porch, steadily and unmoved went Timothy; he feared nothing, for he knew nothing, and thought of nothing; and, in truth, there was nothing to fear.

But when he had mounted the tower stair, and wound himself up into the belfry, and was about to lay his hand upon the rope,—just as he turned round, he saw a figure in white!

"Who's there?" said the boy; but the figure never moved nor spoke. "Answer," said the boy, "if you are an honest man, or be off at once. You have no business here at this time o' night."

But the Sexton, who had put on the Parson's surplice, in the hope of frightening the lad, answered never a word, and did not stir.

"Speak!" went on the boy, getting angry; "speak, and say who you are, and what you want, and why you are here, or else I'll throw you down stairs."

"Well, come," thought the Sexton, "that's not bad

for a young one; he don't want for courage, certainly. But still he made no reply. Then the boy called out to him for the third time; and no answer being given, he sprung suddenly upon the sham ghost, and pitched him down the stairs, close to which the Sexton was standing, who rolled down the steps, and then laid groaning in a corner. Whereupon, the boy went back quietly, and tolled the bell in his usual deliberate fashion; which duty fulfilled, he returned home to the Sexton's house, went up to bed, and there slept soundly. The Sexton not coming home, his wife began to feel alarmed, after the village public-house had been closed for an hour; so she woke Timothy, and inquired if he had seen her husband, who had gone out just before him, intending to visit the belfry.

"Not I," said the boy; "Master never came near the place while I was there; but there was a fellow all dressed in white, whom I thought to be no good, as he would not tell his name, or say what he wanted, or how he came there, so I reckoned him to be a thief, and pitched him headlong down stairs. He could not be Master—if he was, I am sorry for him; but at any rate, he is not lost if he was so, for you will be sure to find him where I left him groaning in a corner, at the bottom of the belfry stairs."

Away ran the wife in a terrible alarm, and found her husband, with one of his ribs broken. So she raised him up, and conveyed him home; and then down she went to Timothy's father, to beg him to take Master Never-shake away. "Your boy has brought bad-luck into our house. He has upset me, thrown my husband down, and broken his bones. Pray take him home, away from us."

Then the old man was greatly alarmed, and went after Timothy directly. "Miserable boy!" cried he, "will you bring me nothing but sorrow? What wretched tricks have you been at now?"

"Father," said the lad, "I am innocent of any wrong. Why did he stand there like an evildoer? I warned him off three times."

"You are an unlucky varlet," said the father. "Go away out of my sight and knowledge; you will bring me into my grave, and have given me the gout already. Go away; I don't want to see you any more."

"Father," said Timothy, submissively, "to-morrow morning I will begin life, and go out and learn what shivering means, so that I may have one trade, at any rate, that will keep me."

"Learn whatever you please, you great simpleton," replied his father; "I don't care what you do. There is a bag with fifty crowns in it—begin the world with that; but don't say I am your father, nor say you came from here, for you are no credit to any of us."

"Yes, father, I will do just as you tell me; and I only wish it was something more that you gave me to do," was Timothy's dutiful reply.

When the day broke, the young lad packed up the crowns, threw his knapsack on his shoulder, and went out of the cottage on to the high road.

As he went on, he kept muttering, "I wish I could learn to shiver and shake, as other people do; it is all because I didn't do so last night that I have to turn out this morning."

He had not gone far along the road, when a man came up, and overhearing him thus talking to himself, just as they were passing a place where the town gallows stood, said, "Look you there, now! There are seven men, thieves and murderers, hanging up there. If you only sit down under them, and wait till the midnight hour, I will warrant you will shake and shiver enough before cock-crow."

"Just the very thing I want," said Timothy Never-shake; "I will follow your advice, and if it turns out right, come to me in the morning, and I will give you fifty crowns."

Then the lad went and sat down under the gallows, and waited for night; but as it was long in coming, and he felt cold, he lighted a fire. Then, while he was sitting by it, he saw the bodies of the thieves and murderers swinging in the wind, and he thought to himself, "If I find it so cold here, how very cold you must be up there!" So he climbed up, and cut the bodies down, and sat them round the fire with him—a horrible companionship!—but he thought nothing about it. Then he poked the fire, and as they did not seem to enjoy it, he brought them closer and closer, until their clothes caught fire. This made him angry with them for being so careless, and he threatened to hang them up again; and as they did not seem to mind, he carried his threat into effect, and then laid himself quietly down by the fire, and went to sleep soundly.

He was awakened by the man, who came for his fifty dollars, according to promise. "I suppose," said he, "you know what shivering and shaking means now?"

"Not at all," replied Timothy; "those chaps there were sulky, and would not speak a word."

Then he told the man what he had done; and the man was so frightened tha he ran away, saying that he had never met with such a strange fellow before.

Timothy also went his way, wondering what this wonderful shivering and shaking could possibly be, that he seemed as if he never was to know it. A Waggoner, jogging along the road, overheard him talking about it to himself, and said, "Who are you, my lad?"

"I don't know," replied Timothy.

"What do you here?"

"I can't say."

"Who is your father?"

"I dare not tell."

"What are you grumbling about?"

"I want to learn to shiver and shake."

The Waggoner laughed heartily at the young simpleton, and told him to come along with him, and he would show him a little of the world as they went on, where he would find plenty of cause and opportunity for shivering and shaking. So on they trudged together, and about evening reached an inn, a large straggling place, where the Waggoner was in the habit of putting up his horses for the night.

"That's a nice young lad you have with you," said the Host to the Waggoner.

"Yes," replied the jolly Waggoner, "he is a good sort; but he wants one thing."

"What's that?" asked the Landlady.

"Oh! I wish I could be made to shiver and shake!" said Timothy.

"That's no difficulty in these parts," said the Landlord; "you can soon have an opportunity."

"Don't be cruel, Benjamin," interposed the Landlady; "you know how many people have lost their lives by going to that Castle; surely you can't wish this nice young man, with such soft blue eyes, to risk his neck and limbs in any such silly adventure. No good can come of it; so hold your tongue about it."

But Timothy was all alive directly, and told them that he did not care how difficult the trial was; that he had left home for that very purpose; that all he wanted was to shiver and shake; that he should never be happy—never feel himself a man—until he did so; and finally, that he was determined to go.

And he persevered, until the Host told him, that on a wood-crowned height, a short distance off, there stood an Enchanted Castle, where any one who was bold and brave, and strong enough to watch there three nights, would doubtless learn to shiver and shake to his heart's full content before that time was over. Moreover, he acquainted the youth that the King of that country was greatly annoyed about that Enchanted Castle, and that he had publicly promised to give his daughter, the Princess Ramagusta, a young lady of exquisite beauty, and of a charming temper, to whosoever should venture to sleep three nights in the Castle, and succeed in clearing it of the Ghosts, Goblins, Sorcerers, Magicians, Demons, Witches, Giants, and Ogres, that now infested it. Nor was this all; for the Host told him, that he had good reason for saying, that within the vaults of the Castle was stored an immense amount of gold and silver, and ancient plate, and precious stones, all of them under the guard of a band of Evil Spirits; and that whoso succeeded in sleeping the three nights in the Castle, and disenchanting it of the Ogres, and Demons, and Goblins, and Evil Spirits, would be rewarded with a sum that would make him free of care and happy all his life, and turn any poor man's son into a rich lord with a golden inheritance.

"First-rate!" exclaimed Timothy; "that's the way I should like to get my living; I will be off there at once."

"Softly, softly, my nice young fellow," said the Hostess; "my husband ought to have told you, that many have already gone forth to sleep the three nights in this Enchanted Castle, but not one has ever been known to come out of it again."

"At any rate," said Timothy, "I shall learn to shiver and shake there."

"That you will, my brave lad, I warrant you," said the Host.

"Wait for the waggon, until the morning," said the jolly Waggoner; "we shall be going into the City of Blobjott, where the King resides; I have got a barrel of Allsopp's Pale Ale for him; and while I am delivering it, we can talk the matter over with his Majesty."

The next morning, the youth was introduced to the King by the Waggoner, and Timothy spoke out like a man, and said: "An' it please your Majesty, I wish
100

to be permitted to keep watch for three nights in the Enchanted Castle on the wood-crowned height of Cephalopodia."

The courtiers stood aghast at such temerity; but the King took a long look at Timothy Never-shake through both his hands, and being pleased with his general appearance and countenance, he said: "Certainly, young man, certainly; you know the risk and the reward, of course?"

"I have that happiness," said the young man, blushing—a fact which was immediately reported to the Princess Ramagusta, who ran down, with her hair in papers, to catch a peep of the young pretender to her hand.

"Young man," resumed the King,—who was a monarch of majestic appearance, with stout legs, a portly stomach, and broad shoulders, but rather a squeaky voice,—"Young man, you are at liberty to ask for three things, which you may take with you; but they must not be alive. What shall we have the pleasure of giving you?"

Then Timothy thought for a minute, and replied, "I wish for a knife, a lathe, and a cutting-board."

"A strange wish!" observed the monarch; "but you shall have them."

These articles he was permitted to carry by daylight into the Enchanted Castle; and in the evening he took up his quarters there, having first lighted a bright fire in one of the pleasantest bedrooms he could select. He placed his knife and his cutting-board by the fireside, and then sat down on his lathe in front of it.

Presently he began to rub his head, and say, "I don't like this—it is growing too comfortable; it does not seem as if I should learn to shiver and shake in such pleasant quarters." Then he gave the fire a spiteful poke, and just as the great clock in the courtyard of the Enchanted Castle struck the hour of midnight, "Mi-ou! mi-ou!" shrieked suddenly a voice in a corner; "mi-ou! I am so cold!"

"The more fool you, then." said Timothy. "for sitting so far away from the fire. Why don't you come here and warm yourself?"

As he was uttering these words, two monstrous Black Cats, with fierce fiery, wild-looking eyes, sprang forward towards him with an immense leap, and flopped themselves down, one on each side of the fire. At first, they growled and spat, and looked savage at him and each other; but as he did not seem to mind it, and they gradually grew warmer, they began to purr and sheathe their claws; and presently one of them said, "Comrade, would you mind a hand at cards?"

"With all the pleasure in life," replied Timothy; "but I must first have a look at your claws."

So they stretched out their paws, and he said, "Ah! it is just as I thought; this won't do at all—your nails are too long to play fair; wait a while, I must shorten them first."

So saying, he caught hold of them sharply by the back of their necks, and put them on his board, and screwed their feet down. "I don't like your game, since I have seen your hands, gentlemen," said e, "so I must take my leave of you." Then he killed them instantly, and threw them into the moat that was under the window. He now thought to be quiet, and sit by his fire; but presently out rushed from every corner of the room Black Cats and Black Dogs in crowds; and they yelped, and barked, and squealed, and miawled all round him, so that he could not get anywhere to hide himself. They howled, and they spluttered, and they jumped on his fire and scattered it about the room. He looked on for some time, but as he did not want his fire put out on such a cold night, he thought it was time to interfere; so he picked up his knife, and cried out, "Get out, you rascally crew!" and drove them away, after chopping a great number, and hacking and wounding some, and killing others, which he threw into the moat, to keep company with their King and Queen. This done, he swept his fire together again, and blew up the sparks, and warmed himself once more thoroughly and comfortably, until his eyes began to feel heavy and drowsy, and he wanted to go to sleep.

Looking round for some accommodation for this purpose, he saw a large four-post Bedstead, of antique fashion, with carved headboard, footboard, and massive hangings, in the corner. Into this he turned, with his clothes on, fearing it might be damp. He laid down, said his prayers, pulled the great counterpane over him, and composed himself for a snooze. But he found himself mistaken; for no sooner had he closed his eyes, than the bed began to move about the room of its own accord, and soon swept out into the corridor, flirting its draperies about it, and set forth travelling all round the Castle.

"Just so!" said Timothy Never-shake, "only, we will have it done a little better still." Upon hearing this, away went the Bedstead at a rapid pace, galloping off just as if six blood-horses were pulling at it, up steps, and down stairs, and along corridors, and through galleries, and across great halls, and into saloons and drawing-rooms, and all over the kitchens and butteries, and into the cellars, and up again to the great gates of the Castle, like a mad thing. There it overset, all at once, turning bottom upwards, with its tester on the ground and its castors in the air, and Timothy at the top instead of the bottom, with the bed, pillows, bolster, and mattresses all lying in a heap on him like a mountain. Up he got, half smothered with the weight, the dust, and the feathers; and kicking the pillows and bolsters up into the air, "He may travel that likes!" said he, and betook himself once more to his fire, laid himself down beside it, and slept soundly till long after daybreak.

When the King came, Timothy was still fast asleep, and the King thought he was dead, and said, mournfully, that he regretted to see the finest young men in his kingdom thus carried off one after the other, and that he must withdraw the promise of his daughter's hand, that tempted them to their death, and let the Enchanted Castle remain as it was, in the hands of the Demons and Goblins.

Just at this moment, the youth opened his eyes, sprang to his feet as gay as a lark, and as smiling as a sweep on May-day, and—if the truth must be told—

almost as black, what with the dust, and the fighting, and the rolling about during the previous night.

"I am not dead yet," said Timothy.

"I am glad, and I am astonished!" said the King; "but how did you fare?"

Timothy told him, and the King laughed heartily at the whimsicality of the adventures, and Timothy's comical treatment of the Cats. "Well, well," said his Majesty, "one night has passed, and the other two may be got over as successfully. But come, let us to breakfast; my daughter is desirous of seeing you."

On their way to the palace, Timothy was accosted by the Host of the inn, who told him he never thought to see him alive again, and asked whether that night had not taught him a good lesson in shivering and shaking.

"Not at all, not at all," said Timothy Never-shake; "it is of no use my trying to learn to shake and shiver. Oh! if any one—man, woman, or child, Ghost, Goblin, or Demon—would but teach me how! They should have my fifty crowns cheerfully, and I would give them a good berth in my intended father-in-law's palace."

Full of this thought, he went up to spend his second night in the Enchanted Castle, where, having lighted his fire again in the same room, he sat down by its cheerful blaze, still crooning over his old song as he looked into it—"I wish I could shiver and shake!"

The Castle clock struck midnight, and there was heard, as if from some far away distant apartment, the ringing of a bell; then from the corridor came the sound of the rattling of a chain, first indistinct, then gentle, then more clear, then rattling and loud, as if approaching. But, for all this, Timothy Never-shake never trembled; the fact was, he was not at all frightened, as most people would have been, for he had never known what alarm or terror was.

After these noises came a loud outcry, and then a pause; and presently, with a tremendous clap and noise, the upper half of the body of a man fell down the chimney!

"Halloa!" cried Timothy, "what is a-coming now? What! Only half a man, to answer all that ringing and shouting? Surely servants in this Castle are lazy or scarce."

Upon this, there was a loud laugh, and then more roaring, and howling, and yellings, and then, flop! down the chimney came the lower half of a man.

"Two halves make a whole," remarked Timothy, quietly; "and as I am to have company, I may as well poke the fire first."

While he was doing this, and before he could look round, having risen from his seat, the two halves of the body had joined themselves together, and an ugly-looking fellow was seated in his place.

"That won't do," said Timothy; "it is not in the bargain; that lathe is mine;" and he just shunted the Ugly Customer off.

The Ugly Man tried to push Timothy from the bench, but Timothy pushed again; and after a sharp pushing-match, Timothy got the best of it, and shoved the Ugly Customer into the fire. Presently, down the chimney came tumbling nine more Ugly Men, every one with a human thigh-bone in his hand. Then up jumped the first Ugly Man, and out of his pocket he pulled two human skulls, and the other nine men set up each the thigh-bone he carried in his hand, and they all set to playing a game of skittles, making use of the two skulls as balls.

"Not a bad game that!" coolly remarked Timothy Never-shake, "although, I must say, I don't quite admire your playthings. I should not mind throwing a ball or two myself; have you any objection, gentlemen?"

"Have you got any money?" asked the leader of the party.

"Quite enough and to spare," replied Timothy Never-shake, rattling his bag with the fifty crowns in it.

"Then play in," said the leader.

"All right," went on Timothy; "but your balls are not quite round, and I like to have things quite right." So he took the skulls, and turned them in his lathe.

"Now they will roll well," said he; and they all set to playing with great spirit, and—to their credit it must be said—quite fairly. So Timothy enjoyed himself very much at the game, although he lost a few crowns, for his Ugly Customers were capital players.

Presently a cock crowed, and they all disappeared. So Timothy laid himself down, and after waiting awhile, in expectation of another gallop, as on the previous night, which, however, did not happen, he composed himself to sleep, and never woke until late in the morning, when the King came to him for news.

"No news but ninepins!" said Timothy; "I played all night at skittles, and lost a couple of crown-pieces."

"What! have you not trembled or shivered this night?" inquired the King, anxiously.

"Certainly not," replied Timothy Never-shake; "I only wish I had; I only wish I could! Oh! how I wish somebody would make me!"

So they marched down to the palace to breakfast, the band of the King's Royal Horse Guards, Green, preceding them in their state uniforms, with their golden kettledrums. As they entered the courtyard, the Princess came to her window in a pretty new morning cap, with her hair in long ringlets, as if she had just jumped out of bed to have a peep, and always slept with her hair curled. Timothy felt very much flattered and pleased when the pretty Princess smiled upon him; but, for all that, he did not tremble or shake, as young lovers are said to do sometimes; nevertheless, a smile from so charming a lady gave him courage to go through his third lesson, and made him eagerly look forward to the possible adventures of the coming night, which was to close his trials.

At last came the expected evening; and Timothy strolled up to the Enchanted Castle by moonlight, the Princess walking part of the way with him, accompanied by her Royal father, and a numerous party of attendant courtiers. Timothy shook hands with the King at parting, and I won't say that he didn't give the Princess a sly kiss in return for a tender squeeze of the hand—but I can hardly venture to speak positively as to the circumstance, as it was not mentioned in the *Court Circular*.

It struck eleven as Timothy entered the great hall of the Enchanted Castle, and proceeded upwards, lighted by the moonlight that fell upon the floor of the galleries through the tracery of the windows, to his usual bedroom. This time he found his fire ready lighted, and all things in order, as if he were an expected guest. So down he sat on his bench opposite the fireplace, and, stretching his legs as he warmed his hands, thought over what had happened on the previous night, which, from his entire occupation during the day, in gossiping with the fair Princess, and laughing with the ladies of the court, had almost escaped his memory. This brought him back to his one old thought, "Oh! how I wish I could shiver and shake!" and he was just saying so, when bang! went the turret bell, and the hour of midnight struck solemnly.

While the sound was yet reverberating along the passages, the door of Timothy's apartment was slowly opened, and he could see the long array of a funeral, black feathers, and scarves, and mutes, coming up the corridor. The black herald, bearing the high corpse-feathers, first entered; then the coffin, borne by six very tall men, and then the mourners, many of whose faces, as the moon shone bright and white upon them, he could distinctly recognize as those of some of his own relations.

"What's going on now?" said he; "surely this is another funeral of my Cousin Jack, who died and was buried six weeks ago." Then he saw through the mockery, and beckoning with his finger, called out to the coffin, "Come, Cousin Jack, come here to me!"

The pall-bearers halted, and the procession stopped, and the six tall men laid down the coffin on the ground, and Timothy went and lifted up the lid, and there lay what looked like a dead man's body within; and when he put his hand on the face, the cheeks felt quite stone cold!

"Stop awhile," said Timothy; "poor fellow! he is quite cold; I will soon warm him." Then he lifted out the body, and sat it on his knees before the fire, and rubbed it and chafed it; but for all that it was not any warmer. Then Timothy called to mind what he had read in the "Rules of the Royal Humane Society," as to the restoration to life of persons apparently drowned; and he got into bed, and took the body with him. After a little while, the body got warmer and warmer by degrees, and the blood seemed to circulate in its veins, and it began first to breathe and then to move. "See, Cousin Jack," said Timothy, exultingly, "have I not warmed you, as I said I would?"

"Yes," replied the body, leaping to its feet; "yes! you have warmed me to life again, and now—now I will strangle you!"

"Oh! is that what you call gratitude?" replied Timothy Never-shake, giving the body a knock on the head; "you may as well go back to your coffin again, for you certainly are not fit to live."

So he took up the body, and threw it into the coffin, and shut the lid fast down upon it.

"Now then, move on with your mummery," said he to the Chief Undertaker, "and don't let me catch you here again!"

Then the six tall men walked in again, wiping their mouths, as if they had gone out for a little refreshment, and been unexpectedly summoned back in a hurry; and they took the coffin up again on their shoulders, and just as they reached the door the whole procession, mourners, feathers, coffin, and all, vanished into the air, and nothing was heard but the whizzing of the wind amongst a few withered leaves that were blown about in a corner of the spacious apartment.

"Oh dear! oh dear!" exclaimed Timothy, when he saw it was all over; "whenever shall I be able to shiver and shake?"

"I'll shiver and shake you! you impious young rascal!" said a voice of thunder close to his ear.

Timothy turned round in a hurry, at such a large voice and big words, and he saw a very Old Man, with a face all wrinkled, and a long white beard. He was a much taller man than all the others, and than any Timothy had ever seen before, and his eyes were like glittering steel, cold, grey, and cruel; his aspect was horrible, and he roared out, as he stretched a bony hand, like a huge claw, towards Timothy: "Now, you wretch—now you shall learn to shiver and shake, or you shall die! I will kill—kill—kill—kill—kill you!"

"Once is enough to ask a lady to dance," said Timothy, "and twice to marry you; but why you should kill me so many times, without my own consent, I don't exactly see. So keep your hands off, old gentleman; I don't want to die yet, and I don't think it is you that will make me do it."

"I will seize you," said the ugly Old Man, advancing.

"Perhaps not," replied Timothy; "don't you see, I am stronger than you?"

"That has to be proved," said the Stranger; "if you really are stronger than me, and I can't hold you——"

"What then?" asked Timothy.

"Why then," said the Old Man, "I will let you go."

"I thought as much!" remarked Timothy; "it is a way they have all got in these parts."

"But we must try first," said the Old Man, sternly. So he led the way, and Timothy followed him through the darkness, lighted, as far as he could make out, only by some luminous exhalation proceeding from the body of the ugly Old Villain himself, until they had passed down a long way into the vaults under the Castle, where, at the end of a passage, they finally reached a smith's forge.

Here the Old Man took up an axe, and striking at the anvil, cut it through with one blow, right down to the ground.

"There is nothing wonderful in that," said Timothy; "I can do it better;" and he went to another anvil, close up to which the Old Man—who now regarded the daring lad with much apparent curiosity—came and stood, his white beard hanging down so low as almost to overshadow the anvil.

"Now for it!" cried Timothy, as he swung the axe round and split the anvil at the blow, wedging the Old Man's beard down into it at the same time.

"Now I have got you, old chap!" said he; "now death's come upon you!" and he took up an iron bar from the smithy, and beat the Old Fellow till he groaned again, and yelled, and shouted to him to let him go, and he would tell him where all the money was, and make him a rich man for life.

Now, as Timothy did not like the idea of beating an old man about the head with an iron bar more than was absolutely necessary, he was glad to have a reasonable excuse for leaving off; so he threw up the axe, and loosened the Old Man's beard, and set him free. The Old Fellow kept his word, and led Timothy, without delay, back into the lower part of the Enchanted Castle, and then into a cellar, where he pointed out to him a stone, under which were three huge chests of gold and jewels.

"One for the poor," said the Old Man, in a solemn voice.

"Of course," said Timothy.

"One for the King."

"Long life to his Majesty!" said Timothy.

"And one for yourself."

"Thank'ee," said Timothy; "but now, Old Gentleman——"

Just then a cock crowed, and the Old Man vanished, and with him the light; and Timothy found himself alone in the dark cellar, underground, without knowing the way he had come, or how he should get out. That was the time to tremble and shake!

But Timothy Never-shake did neither the one nor the other. He only groped his way, first out of the cellar, and then along one passage, and then by another, until he caught a distant glimpse of the light of day, towards which he hastened, and so found his way up into the hall, and thence to his own chamber, where he fell asleep on the bench by the fire, and never woke until the shrill fanfara of the trumpets of the Royal Horse Guards, Green, as they tramped into the courtyard of the Enchanted Castle, escorting the King, aroused him. Loud and vaunting rang their notes, as if exulting over the discomfited Demons, when the trumpeters saw Timothy Never-shake show himself, all alive and well, at the window.

"My dear boy! my dear boy!" said the King, exultingly, "how have you fared? Have you learned to shiver last night?"

"No, indeed, your Majesty, I have not; I wish I could; I wish I knew what it was. My dead Cousin Jack came here last night, on purpose to teach me, I suppose, but his kindness was of no avail; and a good Old Gentleman, with a very long beard, also was thoughtful enough to give me a lesson; but it all ended in his showing me a lot of gold and jewels in some great trunks; for shivering and shaking seems to me as far off as ever, and I shall remain Timothy Never-shake all my life. Oh dear! oh dear!"

Well, they went down into the cellar before they went to breakfast, and brought out the gold and jewels, and carried the huge trunks in procession to the palace; and then they sent word to the Archbishop of Canterbury, and they fetched the Lord Chancellor, and they married his Royal and Serene Highness Prince Timothy, Reigning Grand Duke of Never-shake and Count of the Enchanted Castle, to the Princess Ramagusta, eldest daughter and co-heiress

103

of John the One Thousandth and Third, King of Blobjott.

Nothing seemed wanting to the happiness of this Royal and Serene young pair, except that one unsatisfied desire would every now and then rise paramount in the bosom of the Royal Timothy. "Shall I ever shiver? Oh! if I could but shake!" he would say, in his dreams; and, at last, the Princess Ramagusta, happening to be awake with the toothache—some months previous to the birth of their first child—heard him say this.

Then, like a good wife as she was, she determined to do her best to please him; and she slipped out of bed, and went to the brook that flowed through the garden, and drew up a pail of water all full of little tittlebats; and she laid aside the bedclothes off the Prince quite quietly, and then poured the cold water over his naked legs, while the little fishes all swam about, and dabbed their tails against him, and slipped all about and over him.

This disturbed the drowsy slumbers of his Royal and Serene Highness, and first he drew up one leg, and then he drew up the other; but the water was cold, and the fishes still kept blobbing and bobbling against him, and at last he quite woke, and exclaimed, "Bless me! what is it makes me shiver and shake so?" And then he became conscious, and knew what shivering meant, and kissed his pretty Princess, and was a happy man for ever afterwards.

The moral of this story is, my dear readers, that the man who has never trembled at anything all his life before, may make sure of doing so if he take a wife.

KING WOLF AND KING LOCUST.

THERE once reigned two very powerful Kings, whose territories adjoined each other. Now, these Monarchs, although they were obliged to behave with extreme courtesy and politeness to each other when they met, hated each other secretly in their hearts, and were always seeking means whereby each might, in some way, do some injury either to the person or property of the other. Thus, they both resolved that they would by stratagem remove the boundary marks of the other's kingdom, or otherwise devastate the country on either side, and spread desolation and ruin.

At last, they hit upon the expedient of transforming themselves into the shape of some animal capable of doing great damage; and with that wicked thought in their hearts, the one quickly changed himself into a Wolf, and the other into a Locust.

"I will devour all my enemy's flocks and herds," said the Wolf; "I will tear his soldiers from their horses; and if I come near his children, I will eat them."

The Locust contented himself with the happy prospect of devouring all the young and tender crops, thus in time leaving the country to famine, and when the inhabitants were thinned in numbers by its cruel

ravages, to march against them, and, by the aid his trusty sword and gallant soldiers, to subject kingdom to his own sway.

The Wolf and the Locust both set out, bent on th wicked designs, and worked away with a good w The Locust left fields barren and profitless, that day before were cheering to look upon, and e morning the farmers stood aghast to see the fear progress of their unknown enemy. Had matt proceeded long in this manner, there would not h been a single green blade in the whole kingdo Meantime, the Wolf had not been idle; the lambs calves were all found dead, and their bodies mangl while the cows and horses were lacerated, and dyi on all sides of their wounds. Nor did the inhabita of this ill-fated country escape, for if a child did go out of its mother's house, it was sure to be stroyed.

When this had gone on for some days, it so chance that the Wolf and the Locust met; and, after ma salutations and much converse, the Wolf began boast of his extraordinary powers of destruction, of the great ravages it was in his power to make.

"I," said the Locust, "am not far behind you the mischief I can do; I can eat up the bread of nation in a single night, so that its people shall, want of food, become as children in my hands."

"You talk well," said the Wolf, "but I am inclin to think you are given to boasting; for how can small an animal as you do so much damage. As me, all the world knows I am a person to be dreade and could do more harm in a single night than y could in a year."

The Locust did not like being looked down up and replied, "If you but knew my power, you wou tremble at it."

The Wolf laughed in his sleeve at this; "Fo thought he, "am I not a King?"

The Locust, who was very proud, exclaimed, "I take the human form at will, and then even you wou fly before my power!"

"Did I wish it, I could become a King," said t Wolf; and so they continued to cavil, until it w decided that they should each appear in human for to satisfy the other.

Then they disputed which of the two should ma the change first. The Wolf wished to change firs for, after the little hint he had received from Locust, he thought that should he really be able to as he had said, he might slay him as an enemy mankind.

At last the Wolf gained the day, and in a few m ments he stood before the terrified Locust as direst enemy, the King of the adjoining territory.

"Now," said the Wolf, "I have performed my p now do you do the same."

The Locust was so astonished at seeing who it w that stood before him, that his presence of mind fo moment deserted him, and the change was effected a bungling and careless manner.

No sooner did the outline of the Locust form fa and the half-defined shape of his opponent appe than the truth flashed across the Wolf's mind, a

THE WOLF GOES OUT TO WATCH HIS THREE WIVES.

with deadly force and concentrated hate, he rushed upon the Locust and killed him.

The Wolf rejoiced exceedingly at this great victory, and determined upon travelling through the Locust's country in his Wolf form. One day, when he was leisurely sauntering by the side of a river, his attention became riveted upon three lovely Maidens, who were following their customary avocation of damming the river to catch the fish in their leaps, as it was their only means of subsistence. The Wolf's heart was at once touched with the beauty of these lovely girls, and he determined to carry them to his kingdom, and make them his wives.

When night came, he returned to the river, and broke all their dams, and set the fish free; so that when the girls came in the morning, they saw, with much grief and many loud lamentations, the terrible mischief that had befallen them. Then they set to work, and repaired the mischief that had been done; but all was useless, for each morning, when they returned to take the reward of their labours, there was nothing but hunger staring them in the face.

One morning, when the poor girls were seeking some means to avoid the recurrence of such fatal results, the Wolf appeared before them, and in the most ardent manner declared the tenderest attachment for them;

and entreated them to become his wives, promising to make them Queens, and provide them with unheard-of luxuries. Now, these three Maidens happened to be the daughters of that very King Locust whom the Wolf had murdered. The death of their father in some unknown foray—for his body had not been found—had rendered the kingdom desolate, and reduced them to poverty; as the armies of the Wolf had invaded the undefended provinces, and ravaged and laid waste the whole country. Hence is was, that though they knew not who the Wolf was, or that he had murdered their father, yet they rejected with scorn and loathing the offers made by an odious and beastly-looking stranger, of such savage aspect.

"Refuse me," said the Wolf, "and you must perish with hunger; accept me, and you will become the richest, as you are the most beautiful, of mortals."

The poor girls resisted his appeals until they were almost famished, and then unwillingly consented.

The Wolf conducted them to his own dominions, where they became his wives; but their misery was complete—they hated the advances of their gaunt, ungainly husband. Then he thought to dazzle them with his greatness as a sovereign and his fame as a warrior, and appeared before them, to their great surprise, as the King of the country adjacent to the dominions of their beloved father, King Locust—a King whom they had been taught to hate and detest as a wicked and ruffianly monarch, without justice or mercy. So the King Wolf took nothing by this change and exhibition of himself. But when, in addition to this, he, not knowing whose daughters he was addressing, boasted to them of his having conquered the Locust King, and told, with self-satisfied glee at his own cunning, the crafty manner in which he had overcome and murdered their much-loved father, the aversion and horror of the young girls increased against him until they became hatred.

The Wolf, unknowing what he had done, lavished the most costly presents upon them, entertained them with the sweetest music, and fed them on the greatest dainties, intending, when he had gained their love, to appear to them in his proper form. Time, however, had saddened them: they sighed for the light-hearted, happy days when they used to wander forth in quest of their day's food, and, having obtained it, returned to enjoy it with happy thankfulness. Whenever they could avoid the presence of their Wolf husband, they used to wander by the river's side, and pass their time in consoling each other that they were not separated in this fearful calamity. At other times, they would cry aloud, in the anguish of their hearts, and rend the air with their unrepressed grief.

The Wolf, finding all his efforts to gain upon their love futile, suddenly conceived an overmastering jealousy, and determined upon watching their every movement, lest some more favoured lover should be the cause of his ill success.

One day, they for awhile avoided his vigilance, and had gone to their favourite spot to lament over and console each other.

The Wolf, as soon as he missed his three Queens, set off in search of them, and found them on the river's

106

bank. Jealousy took possession of his soul, and his eyes were blinded to the truth. He saw, in his heated and angered imagination, his wives awaiting the coming of some more favoured lover, and immediately transformed two of them into pillars of stone bearing their form, and the third he made into a yawning cavern.

Then he changed himself into a rock on the opposite shore, that he might ever after watch their every look and movement.

THE FINGER AND THE RING.

ONCE upon a time, there was a rich Miller, who had an only daughter, whom he loved far better than all his riches, and was very anxious she should marry well; but of all his neighbours, there was not one he thought well enough to do in the world to be her lover.

About the time this handsome daughter was old enough to be sought in marriage, there came a Stranger into the town, who could show as much gold as the richest of them. He was well made, and well dressed, and he boasted of his riches, and declared he had come for no other purpose than to find a pretty wife.

The Miller, hearing this, thought he must get a peep at this fine fellow, and see if he looked like a fit match for his dainty Gertrude. Next market-day, he stopped at the inn where the Stranger was, and soon got into conversation with him. The manners of the young fellow pleased him, and he determined to take him home with him, and let matters go on in their due course.

The Stranger fell violently in love with the Maiden, and the father, not knowing anything to his disadvantage, promised him her hand. The Maiden, however, did not like this suitor; she had not the love for him in her heart that would justify her becoming his wife; neither had she any confidence in him, for as often as she looked upon him, and every time he approached her, her heart sank within her, as with some inward dread.

Once, when they were sitting alone, he said: "You are my affianced bride, and yet you never come to see me."

"I have never yet heard where you live," said she; "how could I come?"

"I dwell deep in the shades of the forest," said he; "and you must promise to come and pay me a visit next Sunday."

"Indeed, I cannot," she replied; "I should lose my way."

"Oh! we will soon get over that difficulty; I will strew the path with ashes, and you cannot fail to find me," he said.

After much coaxing, she unwillingly consented; but yet she felt she could not trust her Bridegroom.

When Sunday came, the Maiden prepared to set out, but was very anxious, and felt a growing knowledge of some coming evil in her heart: so she filled her pockets with peas and beans, and strewed them along the side of the path, that they might guide her back home again. When she had got to the thickest and gloomiest part of the forest, she came to a solitary house, that looked so dark and desolate, that she quite repented having ventured alone. She went in, but the house appeared empty, and a mysterious silence reigned throughout. At last, a voice said—

"Return, fair Maid! venture not here to roam:
This is no Bridegroom's, but a Murderer's home!"

The Maiden looked round, and saw it was a bird in a cage who sang these words. Once more it uttered them—

"Return, fair Maid! venture not here to roam;
This is no Bridegroom's, but a Murderer's home!"

Then the Maiden went running all over the house from one room to another, trying to understand what all this meant, until at last she had visited every place but the cellar; this she next explored, and there sat a withered Old Woman, shaking her head.

"Can you tell me," asked the Maiden, "whether my Bridegroom lives here?"

"Married!" said the Old Woman; "when do you think to be married? You are in a Murderer's den, and Death is the only Bridegroom you will find here!"

The poor girl was ready to sink with fear.

"Do you see," said the Old Woman, "this large seething cauldron? Should they catch hold of you, they will kill you without mercy, and cook you and eat you, for nothing comes amiss to their cannibal appetites. If I do not take compassion upon you, and help you, there is at once an end of your life."

Thereupon, the Old Woman led her behind a great cask that stood at the farthest end of the cellar, saying, "Keep as quiet as a mouse; one single movement will betray you into the Murderer's hands. At night, when the Robbers are asleep, I will, if possible, escape with you; such has long been the desire of my heart."

She had scarcely done speaking, when the murderous band returned, dragging with them a lovely young damsel, whose shrieks and cries they utterly disregarded. They made her drink some wine—three glasses, one red, one white, and one yellow; then she immediately fell down in a deep swoon.

Meanwhile, poor Gertrude, hidden behind the cask, beheld her Lover at the head of the band, and shuddered and trembled from head to foot to see what a fate would have been hers.

Presently, one of the Ruffians perceived a gold ring on the little finger of the poor girl's hand. As it would not come off easily, he took a hatchet and chopped away the finger, which flew so far with the blow, that it fell behind the cask right into the lap of the trembling Bride. The Robber took a light to hunt after it.

"Have you looked behind the cask?" asked another.

"Oh, do come and eat your supper!" said the Old Woman, frightened out of her wits; "the finger will keep till morning—it cannot run away."

"The Old Woman is right," said the Robbers; and desisting from their search, they began to eat with an appetite and relish sickening to look upon. Then they shouted for wine, which the Old Woman poured them out in brimming goblets, not forgetting to administer an ample sleeping-draught to each of the cruel Ruffians.

In a very short time they all laid themselves down upon the floor, and were stretched in a deep sleep. As soon as the Maiden heard them snore, and saw the convulsive heaving of their bodies, she ventured from her hiding-place behind the cask, and stepped gently over the sleeping Ruffians who lay side by side.

The Old Woman was as good as her word, and helped the Miller's daughter to get out of the Murderer's den. They both started along the road, and found the ashes had been blown away by the wind; but the peas and beans that Gertrude had scattered by the wayside had sprouted up, and served to guide them to the mill, which they reached by sunrise, when the daughter related her adventures to her distressed father, the Miller, who was very thankful his child had escaped so dreadful a death.

The day for the solemnization of the marriage arrived, and the Miller assembled a great party of guests from far and near, to celebrate the event with all due honour. After dinner, each of the guests was called upon to tell a story, and the Bride sat listening. Presently, the Bridegroom said: "Have you nothing to say, Sweetheart? cannot you find something to tell?"

"Oh, yes," she answered; "I will tell you a dream of mine: I thought I had wandered deep in the forest until I came to a house, where there was no one within, only a little bird hung on the wall, who sang—

'Return, fair Maid! venture not here to roam;
This is no Bridegroom's, but a Murderer's home!'

It sang this twice."

Here the Bridegroom joined in—"My treasure! So dreamed I."

"Then I ran from room to room, but they were all alike desolate. So I went down into the cellar, and there sat an old withered woman, shaking her head. I asked her, 'Does my Bridegroom dwell in this house?' 'Alas, dear child!' said she, 'your Lover does indeed live here; but he is a Murderer and a Cannibal, and he will kill you and eat you!' Then I thought she hid me behind a cask; and presently a band of murderous Robbers came in, dragging with them a beautiful maiden, whom they forced to drink three glasses of wine, one red, one white, and one yellow. When she had drunk the last, her heartstrings snapped asunder."

"My treasure! So dreamed I," said the Bridegroom.

"Then one of the Robbers saw a gold ring on her finger; and because he could not draw it off easily, he took a hatchet, and chopped off the finger, which flew into my lap behind the cask; and—there it is, with the ring on! Did you dream that?" Saying this, she threw it down before him, in the presence of all the guests.

The Robber, who had become paler and paler during the narration, now jumped suddenly up, and would have rushed from the house, but was held by the guests, who delivered him over to the custody of the gaoler, to be taken before the judges.

Very soon afterwards, he and the whole of his murderous band were condemned and executed for the wicked deeds they had committed; and the pretty daughter of the Miller was married to the Parson of the parish, and lived happily for many years afterwards.

THE GOLDEN GOOSE.

THERE was once a man, who had three sons, the youngest of whom was named Sawney, and on that account he was laughed at and pointed after by all the lads in the village, and, indeed, held in derision by everybody.

The eldest son was a Woodcutter; and it was his mother's custom to prepare some food early, that he might carry it with him. One morning, when he was about to start to hew wood in the forest, his mother gave him a meat pie and a bottle of wine to take with him.

No sooner had he entered the forest than he was accosted by a Little Grey Man, who appeared very tired and careworn.

The Grey Man bade him good morning, and said: "For pity's sake, my good lad, give me a mouthful of your pie and a sup of your wine, for I am dying of hunger and thirst."

The youth, however, was over-prudent. He said: "If I give you my pie and wine, what shall I have left for myself? No; move on with you, and look for work; don't hang about here, begging your bread." So he left the man as he found him, and went on his way.

He soon reached the spot where he had to fell some trees, and set to work with a right good will; but he had not worked long before he made a false stroke—he missed his aim, and the axe buried itself so deeply in his arm that he was obliged to get home the best way he could, and have his wound bound up and attended to by his mother.

Now, this unlucky stroke was caused by the Little Grey Man.

The next day, the second son went to hew wood in the forest, and he likewise received from his mother a pie and a bottle of wine.

The same Little Man met him also, when he had entered the forest, and begged hard for food to allay his hunger and thirst. He rudely repulsed the Little Man, and replied, "Pack off with you! your eating won't fill my stomach. I have no more than I want for myself." Then he left the Little Old Man, and went on his way to his work.

He soon reaped the reward of his conduct; for he had only struck two blows, when the axe hit his leg with tremendous force, and obliged him to betake himself homewards, limping and groaning, to his mother.

The two elder lads being thus laid up, Sawney begged his father to let him go into the woods and hew; but the old man would not listen to the request. "No, no," said he; "your brothers, who are clever workmen, have cut themselves terribly; and I am sure you will meet with the same fate, as you know nothing of handling an axe." But Sawney entreated his father so earnestly, that at last, to be rid of him, he said: "Well, get you gone; but, mark me, you will pay dearly for your experience."

His mother had only some bread and hard cheese to give him, and a bottle of sour wine.

As he entered the forest, the same Little Grey Man accosted him, and asked: "Give me some of your dinner; just a little bit of bread and cheese, and a drop out of your bottle, for I am both hungry and thirsty."

Sawney answered: "I wish my fare was better, for your sake; but if you have a mind for any of it, let us sit down and eat together."

So they sat down; and as soon as Sawney had opened his wallet, lo and behold! his bread and cheese was turned into a pie, and the sour stuff into good sound wine. They ate and drank to their heart's content. When they were both satisfied, the Little Man said: "Because you have thus given me of your meat, in the unselfish kindness of your heart, I will make everything lucky you undertake. There stands an old tree; hew it down, and you will find your reward."

Sawney went to work, and the tree was soon cut down; and there, sitting among the roots, the astonished lad found a fine fat Goose, with feathers of the purest gold.

He seized the bird with eager joy, and carried it with him to an inn, where he intended to pass the night. The Landlord had three daughters, who could not take their eyes off the Goose—so great a wonder they had never before seen. They could not repress their covetousness, and determined in their own minds, at all events, to possess themselves of a feather.

The eldest girl, who was quick at most things, thought she would watch, and she should be sure to find an opportunity to get one. Her eyes followed Sawney every time he moved, and the moment he had gone out at the door, she caught hold of one of the wings; but when she seized a feather, her finger and thumb stuck there, and she could not move. Soon after, the second sister came, thinking she could pluck out a feather; but no sooner had she touched her sister than she was bound so fast to her that she was not able to stir. At last, the third sister must needs go to try her fortune. Now the two sisters cried out to her, "Keep away! you'll rue the hour you come near us!" but she did not see any reason why she should, and made a spring, and soon touched her sister. She, too, was then made fast; and in this unpleasant fashion, all linked unwillingly to each other, the three covetous sisters had to pass the whole of the night with the Goose.

The next morning, Sawney took his Goose under his arm, and walked off, never so much as troubling himself to look at the three girls, who were obliged to hang on behind him. As he travelled at a pretty good pace, they were kept on the trot all the while, now on this side, now on that, just as it suited his fancy to shift the Goose.

In the middle of a common, they were met by the Parson of the parish, who, gazing with much wonder at the procession, cried out, "What bold-faced hussies you are, to run after the young man in that manner! Shame upon you! Why are you prancing over the fields in that disgraceful way? Pray leave off, and go home to your mother!" So saying, he laid his hand on the youngest, to take her by force; but no sooner had he touched her, than he also stuck fast, and was obliged to follow in the unwilling train.

Soon after this, the Clerk came up, and saw with surprise his master, the Parson, following the footsteps of the three girls. The sight shocked him very much, and he said, "Halloa, Master! where are you going so quickly? Have you forgotten there is to be a grand christening to-day?" Then he ran up to the reverend gentleman, and tried to pluck him away by the gown. But the Clerk stuck fast himself, and they were all five obliged to go on, tramp! tramp! after each other.

At last, they met two Countrymen, returning from their day's work, with their hatchets in their hands. The Parson called out to them, and entreated them to come and release him and the Clerk from their ludicrous position. The good-natured fellows made the attempt, when they were fast stuck on to the Clerk; and so now they were, all seven, in a line, dancing after Sawney and the Golden Goose.

By-and-bye they came to a city, where there dwelt a King who had a daughter so melancholy and moping, that no one in the whole kingdom had ever been able to make her laugh; so that her father, in despair of seeing her cured, had published a decree, that whoever could cause her to laugh should have her for his wife.

Now, when Sawney heard this, he thought he would have a try for a royal wife and a good dower. So he went, with his Goose and all his train, before the Princess; who had no sooner set eyes upon them all on the jog-trot after Sawney, holding on to the Goose, than she began to laugh so immoderately that they thought she was never going to leave off. Sawney, thereupon, demanded her for his wife, according to the King's decree. But this bright youth did not much please the Monarch for a son-in-law; and, after some consideration, his Majesty said he must also bring him a man who could drink a cellarful of wine.

Sawney thought of the Little Grey Man and his promise. "Ah!" said he, "I shall get help from that quarter." Then he went to the forest again, and at the very spot where he had felled the tree he saw a man sitting, looking very miserable, with a woe-begone, haggard face. Sawney asked him why he looked so wretched. "Can I help you," said he, "in any way?"

The man replied, "My thirst is so intolerable, I cannot quench it. Cold water is a liquor I cannot endure, and a cask of wine I very soon see the bottom of; for what is the use of so small a drop as that to a thirsty soul?"

"I can help you!" shouted Sawney, delighted enough to have found the man he wanted. "Come with me, and you shall have your fill, I'll warrant you."

Then Sawney led the man into the King's cellar, where he drank long and deep, until his very veins stood out swollen as big as cart-ropes; and before the day was out, he had emptied every barrel in the King's cellar.

Sawney now made certain of his bride, and demanded her of the King; but his Majesty did not like to part with her to such a clodhopper as Sawney;

besides, his name was unbearable, and he was as ugly as he could be. Therefore, the King made another condition, that whoever had his daughter must eat through a whole mountain of food.

"I'm off to the Little Grey Man again," thought Sawney; and he quickly made his way to the spot where he had before been, and there sat a man on the same tree-stump, binding his body round with a broad leathern girdle, making horrible faces, and crying, "I have eaten a whole oven-full of rolls; but what is the use of so small a mouthful to so large an appetite? My stomach is so empty, that if I do not strap it together, I must die of hunger!"

Sawney capered with delight, saying, "Come with me; I will give you as much bread as you can eat, and meat to boot, or I am much mistaken." Then he took this hungry chap to where the King had collected all the flour in the whole kingdom, and had caused a mountain of bread to be baked with it. The hungry man began to eat, and in an incredibly short space of time the mountain of bread had disappeared.

But the King, who acted anything but fairly, when Sawney demanded his bride this time, made all sorts of excuses, and said he must first bring him a ship that would travel by land and by sea.

Sawney, a little downcast, went again to the forest, and there sat the Little Grey Man to whom he had given the bread and cheese and beer. Then he asked Sawney what he wanted, and why he looked so down in the mouth. When he heard the reason, he said, "I will give you a vessel that can travel by sea and land, because you were good-natured, and gave me to eat and to drink."

As soon as the King saw the ship, he could find no other excuse to postpone the wedding, and so it was at once celebrated; and after the King's death Sawney inherited the kingdom, and they reared a happy and prosperous family of Prince Sawneys, most of whom married into the Royal Families of Germany; and their descendants are to be met with in almost every Court of Europe.

HOW THE WOLF CAME TO BE DROWNED.

IN those strange old days, when the beasts of the field used to talk and keep house, there lived a respectable female Goat, whose husband, who was a Civil Engineer, had died from an accident while building a bridge over the Taffy, and had left her a widow, with seven small Kids of various ages.

Now, the Goat was an industrious mother, not at all inclined to ask friends to do for her what she could do for herself; so she earned a living for herself and her children, by going out every day to sell her milk— a circumstance that compelled her to leave her young Kids very much by themselves in the morning and evening.

One morning, when she had to go some distance, she called her little ones together before leaving the house, and said: "My dear children, be careful how you open the door to-day, for I hear that the Wolf is prowling about, and if he can only get his nose within the door, he will gobble you all up."

"Oh! we know the nasty old fellow," said the eldest Miss Goat, "and we can keep him out."

"Don't be too sure of that, Ethelinda," said the Widow Goat; "this cruel monster assumes all sorts of disguises; but he can't hide his rough voice and his black feet, so look for them, and pray take care, or else—

> He will beat you, beat you, beat you,
> He will beat you all to pap;
> And he'll eat you, eat you, eat you,
> Gobble you! gobble you! Snap! snap! snap!"

Then the old lady gave an affectionate bleat, and trotted off on her road, very much eased in mind by the intelligence and courage her young children exhibited in the face of danger.

She had not been gone long—indeed, she could hardly have turned the corner—when tap! tap! came a knock at the door of the hut, and a voice, disguised, but still rough, called to them, "Now, my little darlings, here's Mother come back! Open the door, quick; I have brought a cake for each of you."

"Oh! make haste and open the door, Linda!" exclaimed the youngest Kid of the seven, jumping off her legs with delight at the mention of cake.

"Not so fast, Kathleen," replied the eldest; "don't you hear how rough the voice is? That is not our Mother's tongue—that's a Wolf's. Go away, Sir! your voice is too gruff: we know you are a grim gruffin!"

And then all the little Kids set up a laugh, and the Wolf slunk away, with his tail between his legs, sulky and discomfited.

But he had made up his mind to a Kid for dinner, and was resolved not to be disappointed; so as soon as he reached the town, he turned into the first Apothecary's shop, and said to the young gentleman at the counter, "I have got a sad cold and hoarseness, and how I shall speak this evening at the Meeting of the Society for the Prevention of Cruelty to Animals, I cannot imagine. Can you give me anything that will soften my voice?"

The young Doctor gave him Horehound, and Everton Toffee, and Dr. Locock's Wafers, and no end of Pectoral Balsam, and a pailful of Syrup of Squills, and a bushel of Patent Pills, and a sack of Lozenges—all of which the Wolf patiently swallowed and paid for, but still he was no better; while his voice, if anything, became rougher, from the extreme uncomfortableness and sickness he felt at having so many pills and balsams in his inside. At last, he got very cross, and grinned so savagely, and growled so fiercely, that the Doctor's boy became frightened; and when the Wolf asked for something more, he took up a lump of chalk and gave it him, and said that was certain to make a perfect cure.

The Wolf looked at the great lump of chalk somewhat ruefully, and asked whether he was to swallow it all.

"Yes," at once replied the Doctor's boy, "after you have walked about half a mile; and mind you take it on an empty stomach."

116

"What about the Pills, and the Balsam, and the Lozenges, and the Toffee, and the Horehound?" inquired the Wolf.

"Oh! reckon them as nothing," said the Doctor's boy.

"I wish I could," observed the Wolf, writhing with pain.

Then he started off on his way back to the Widow Goat's hut, which was about two miles off, so that he had both eaten his chalk and increased his appetite by the time he arrived there.

He knocked loudly this time, and said in a softened voice—made much milder by so many medicines, to say nothing of the great lump of chalk—"Here I am, loves! open the door; I am very tired, and have brought home your new frocks."

"New frocks!" said little Billy, one of the male Kids; "Mother promised me a pair of shoes;" and he peeped up just over the window-sill. "Oh! look, Linda! look at his black paws!" exclaimed Billy, all alive in a minute, as he caught sight of the Wolf's feet, that he had placed upon the window-sill. "This is the Wolf! the Wolf! not our Mother! Keep him out; do, Linda, keep him out!" and the Kid shrieked with alarm. So the Wolf could perceive he was detected, and took himself off once more.

"Those children are too clever to live," said he to himself, licking his chops, as he entered a Baker's shop. "I have scalded my fore-paws, Mr. Doughey," said he; "I must trouble you for a pennyworth of flour, just to powder them with."

Having thus got his feet well whitened, he hastened for the third time to the hut, and knocked, and called upon the Kids to open. But they insisted on seeing his feet, that they might see if they were white, as their Mother's were. So he put them up, and the poor little Kids thought that, as they were quite white, they must be all right; and they opened the door, and in walked THE WOLF!

There was a scream, you may be sure! and then a general scuttling off anywhere to hide themselves—under the table, into the bed, up in the cupboard, into the kitchen, into the oven, under the wash-tub, and in the clock-case.

But the Wolf followed them all, with greedy eyes, and foaming jaws, and eager tongue, and sharp teeth. Nor was he long before he had ferreted out and swallowed them all up, one after the other, snap! snap! snap!—all except the youngest Kid, that was hid in the clock-case, and which he did not find. The fact is, that what with gorging, and gobbling, and his long walks backward and forward, the Wolf was quite tired, as well as full. So he dragged himself lazily out of the hut, and laid himself down in a green field just nigh; where, under the shade of a wide-spreading beech-tree, he soon fell fast asleep, caring little, like most unprincipled scoundrels, what misery and mischief he had brought about, so long as his own evil desires were gratified, and his own ends served.

Oh! the poor Mother Goat! When she came home soon afterwards, what a pitiful sight met her afflicted gaze! The door of the hut was wide open, but no merry voices saluted her return—no quick-pattering little feet rushed forth to welcome her. The bench, the stools, the table, were all overset; the wash-tub (a new one) smashed to pieces; the bed all disordered, and the sheets and pillows torn off and lying on the floor; the children nowhere to be seen! The truth quickly flashed across her mind, and she called in agony on them by name, one after the other. Still no reply—no Linda, no Billy. At last, when she came to the name of the youngest Kid, a little bleat answered her out of the clock-case, "Here I am, Mother! oh, the Wolf!"

Then the poor little Kid told her all the terrible story,—how the Wolf got in, how they all screamed and ran away, and how the cruel monster had gobbled up at a mouthful, one after another, all his brothers and sisters.

At last, the forlorn Mother Goat and her poor little Kid went forth from the miserable hut together. But the sunshine with its brightness, and the merry wind playing among the flowers, only made them feel the more unhappy. All the joy and happiness of nature went on the same, though that happy home was so desolate—those hearts broken and bleeding! Thus they strolled along, sobbing and sighing, whither they knew not, until chance directed their wandering footsteps to the place where, stretched at full length, lay the gaunt Wolf, sleeping the sleep of innocence and of a full stomach, and snoring so loud and strong, that the very boughs of the tree above him cracked and quivered with the noise.

The Widow Goat advanced toward the cruel beast, with fierce intent to avenge her murdered offspring; but as she sternly gazed on her prostrate foe, she perceived a creeping and stirring motion in the skin of the Wolf's belly.

A sudden hope was roused in her breast. Could it be possible? Might her children yet be living? Swallowed whole by the ferocious monster, might they have gone down his throat uninjured, and be still alive and well. as well as whole? O, delicious hope! Not a moment was to be lost. She ran home to her hut, brought back her scissors, her needle and thread, and in a moment whipped the point of her scissors into the monster's stomach, and cut open his hairy skin, sharply yet gently.

At the first slit, little Billy popped his head out; at the second, out came Ethelinda; then followed the other four—six in all—not one of them injured in the slightest degree, for the greedy monster had not waited to bite them, but swallowed each of them whole, at one gulp, in his haste! O joy! O wonder! The Kids began to skip and bleat and play round their mother. But she bade them be quiet, and not wake the Wolf, who still lay fast asleep: so quietly and comfortably had the clever old Goat used her scissors.

Then they all ran off as she directed, and each came back with a large round boulder stone from the brook, which she slipped quietly into the Wolf's stomach, to fill up the space lately occupied by her Kids, and then, still quietly and steadily, but with great haste, she sewed up his huge stomach again, while he was still fast asleep.

I need not tell you, she took care to get herself and children safe out of his sight and of all chance of meeting him when he awoke, which he did soon after. He rose up, and stretched himself, and found his stomach feel very hard and heavy. "Dear me!" said he to himself, "I am afraid my dinner has disagreed with me. Perhaps it is the Everton Toffee?—or the Pectoral Pills?—or the Syrup of Squills?—or the Lozenges?—or the Chalk? That is what makes me so dry; I feel as thirsty as a lime-burner."

So he started off at a trot for the brook-side; and as he went the stones walloped and wabbled, and rattled against his sides and each other. So he sang out—

> "Be quiet, be quiet!
> Oh! spare my poor bones!
> You merry little Kids
> Must be changed into stones."

As soon as he reached the edge of the brook, he stooped hastily over the brink to take a great drink; but the stones in his stomach all rolled forward directly, and overbalanced him with their weight, and he fell in, and sank under the water; for they pulled him down so that he could not scramble out again, or even get his nose out to breathe; and that is how it happened that the Wolf was drowned.

THE FERRYMAN AND THE FAIRY.

Ogg the Son of Beal had been born in a boat, and lived at a ferry on the river Humber. His living was a scanty one, for few were at that time the inhabitants of the now flourishing city of Hull, and still fewer the travellers that crossed from Yorkshire into Lincolnshire. even although then, as now. it was the easier and shorter way to London—if London was then the leading city of England.

One evening, after having been out all day on the river, which was swollen. fierce, and angry with the wintry floods, Ogg came into his cottage on the bank, cold and shivering, and sat down supperless by his scanty fire of sputtering logs, to think over his hard fate. and ruminate on the poor chances he had of a dinner for the morrow.

Just at that moment a tap came to the door, and a humble voice inquired if the Ferryman were within, or over on the other side of the river.

"Can't you see my boat tied up there under the alders?" replied Ogg the Son of Beal, somewhat impatiently; "I have not had the luck of a single cast-over the whole of the day."

Then he looked at the woman. and saw she did not seem likely to be much of a customer, as she sat moaning and sighing on the brink of the river, with a child in her arms. She was dressed all in rags, too, and had the worn and withered look of poverty, long and vainly struggled against. and scanty food.

"I want to be rowed over the river," she said, faintly.

"My fare is a halfpenny." said Ogg the Son of Beal. half doubtful of his customer.

Now, a halfpenny of that period, you must know, was equal to a half-crown of these days—that is, a halfpenny then would buy as much as a half-crown now-a-days.

"I have not got it," said the poor woman, wringing her hands and drawing her baby more closely to her breast, as the soughing of the wind came sullenly down the river.

"I can't help that," replied Ogg the Son of Beal; "the night is growing dark, the wind blows stormily, the floods are coming down. It will not be safe to cross the river, even if you had the money, and I cannot go without; so you must tarry till the morning."

"Alas! I have no shelter."

"You shall have shelter here," said the kind-hearted Ferryman, throwing open his half door, over which he had been leaning to converse with the poor woman. "Tarry then, I pray you; so shalt thou be wise, and not foolish."

But the woman was wilful, and would not remain, and so she went on still to mourn and crave.

Then Ogg the Son of Beal—who, for all his roughness, was a soft-hearted bachelor—could no longer endure the plaint of the woman and the wailing of the child. So he stepped forth, and he said to her, "I will ferry thee across; it is enough—thy heart needs it."

And he ferried her across the raging waters. And it came to pass, when she stepped ashore on the other side, that her rags were turned into robes of flowing white, and her face became bright with exceeding beauty, and there was a glory round it, so that she shed a light on the water, like the moon in its brightness.

Then she turned to Ogg the Son of Beal, and said: "I am a Fairy, but this was my hour of need, for all Fairies have some hours when their power deserts them, and they are exposed to need and danger like ordinary mortals. I will reward thee, Ogg. Say, what desirest thou?—wealth, honour, arms? wilt thou be a King?"

"No," said Ogg the Son of Beal; "I don't want to be anybody but a Ferryman. It is pleasant to sit in the boat upon the stream, and right merry to hear the news and tales of my passengers. No; I don't want to change."

Whereupon, the Fairy said: "Blessed art thou, Ogg the Son of Beal, in thy contentment; and blessed shalt thou be, for that thou didst not question and wrangle with the heart's need, but wast smitten with pity, and didst straightway relieve the same."

"Thank'ee, ma'am," said the sturdy Boatman; "much obliged for your good word; but, bless you, my lady! we poor folks never think we are doing such great things when we are helping each other. It comes to us natural-like and hearty! It would be hard if a ferryman was to stickle for a fare with a poor woman and child that craved for a cast-over on a night like this. But I must be going back, my lady, for it looks very dirty to the northward."

"Stop, Ferryman, and hear my good gift," said the Fairy: "from henceforth, whoso steps into thy boat shall be in no peril from the storm; and whenever it

112

puts forth to the rescue, it shall save the lives both of men and beasts."

Under this blessing of the good Fairy, the kind-hearted Ogg lived, thrived, and drove a prosperous trade; and when the floods came, many were saved by reason of the blessing on that boat.

At last, it befel that, in the fulness of years, Ogg the Son of Beal died; and behold, in the parting of his soul, the boat loosed itself from its moorings, and was floated with the ebbing tide in great swiftness to the ocean, and was seen no more. Yet it was witnessed in the floods of after time, that, at the coming on of evening, Ogg the Son of Beal was always seen with his boat upon the wide-spreading waters, and the Good Fairy sat in the bows, shedding a light around as of the moon in its brightness, so that those who were rowing in the gathering darkness, endeavouring to escape the floods, took heart at the sight, and pulled away with fresh courage.

THE DRAGON AND HIS GRAND-MOTHER.

ONCE upon a time, there was a mighty war being carried on in a far country, and the King of it had a great many Soldiers at his command, all fighting under his orders; but he paid them so badly that they could not get any food to eat, and had scarcely strength enough left to fight. Now, these Soldiers did not mind the fighting, but they could not bear the hunger that was constantly gnawing their stomachs; so three of them agreed together that upon the first opportunity they would run away.

One of them asked the others if they did not think that was a foolhardy plan of ridding them of their troubles. "You know," he said, "if they catch us, we shall swing on the gallows-tree, without judge or jury."

"You see that great corn-field in the distance," said another; "we will hide ourselves there, and we shall be safe enough. The army dare not for their lives seek us among the standing corn; and besides, they are under marching orders for to-morrow morning."

It happened, however, unluckily for this calculation, that the army did not move from their quarters, but remained in their old encampment.

The three Soldiers did not know what to do now, for they were obliged to remain two days and two nights in the corn, and then they were so starving hungry they were near to death; while, had they gone back, their fate was inevitable—death was certain.

"Of what use has been our desertion to us?" said they; "then we had little—now we have nothing, and must die of hunger!"

While this conversation was going on, a great Dragon came flying over the ground, darkening the earth by the shadow of his wings. He alighted near the spot where they were, and said, "It is not like Soldiers to sneak in the grass. Why don't you face

THE DRAGON PROPOUNDS HIS RIDDLE TO THE THREE SOLDIERS.

the enemy? I have a great many men fighting in my service, but woe be to those who desert my cause."

"We deserted," said they, "because our pay was so small and we were badly fed; and now we have no choice left, but to die here of hunger or return to be hanged on the gallows."

"Serve me," said the Dragon. "You shall neither complain of the pay nor the food. I will carry you through the midst of the army, so that no one shall see you."

"There is no choice but to run when one's driven," replied they, "and so we must accept your proposal."

No. 15.

The Dragon was glad to have enlisted these three able Soldiers into his service. He caught them up right quickly in his claws, and flew away with them, high over the heads of their comrades. Presently he set them down where they would be safe from pursuit. Then the Dragon presented each Soldier with a whip, and said: "If you crack these whips well, money will shower about you in abundance; you will always have as much as you require; you can buy houses and lands, horses and carriages, and live as grand a life as the first lords in the land; but at the end of seven years you will be my Soldiers, and must fight for me so long as you live. No desertion then, mind." With these words, he handed them a book, in which they signed the articles of their agreement. "Even then," said he, "I will give you one chance of your freedom, if you can expound a riddle I shall propose to you." Then he bade them good-day, and flew away.

"This is something like a master," said they; "a long holiday and plenty of pleasure to begin with." Then they cracked their whips to their hearts' content, and the gold came tumbling about them, with which they bought smart clothes and everything fine they could fancy. They travelled about in their own coaches, or bestrode their own horses at their pleasure. In fact, they lived in the greatest splendour, eating and drinking the nicest delicacies, to their hearts' content. To their credit, however, be it said, that no bad or wicked action could ever be brought against them, although their wealth seemed to place everything at their command.

As the end of the seven years approached, two out of the three Soldiers began to feel very miserable and low-spirited at the thought of giving up all this luxurious living, and all this pleasant ease and comfort, to go and fight the Dragon's battles. But the third said, gaily, "Cheer up, old boys; I am a match for this easy-going new master of ours; I'll guess his riddle, I promise you."

Then they journeyed onwards to the fields, where they sat down and made very long faces. Presently, an Old Woman came along. "Why do you look so miserable?" said she.

"What is that to you?" they replied, rudely. "Alas!" said they, "alas! you cannot help us."

"How do you know I can't?" said she. "I can tell you, if you are wise, you'll let me into your confidence."

Then they told her how they had entered into the service of a certain great Dragon nearly seven years ago, and that he had given them a long holiday, with as much money as they liked to spend; but now the time was approaching when they must fight under his banner, and give up their life of ease and pleasure, unless they could guess a riddle he was going to ask them.

"If you really wish to be helped, one of you must go into the forest, where he will find a huge rock overthrown, and used as a hut to dwell in; into this he must creep, and help awaits him."

The two dispirited Soldiers laughed at the notion of getting over their troubles in this way, and declared they would not go a step towards the forest; but the merry one said, "I'm off, then!" and started away. He was soon in the forest, where he reached the overturned rock and the hut, just as it had been described to him.

In this place, there sat an Old Woman crooning over the fire, and rocking herself to and fro, muttering a low chaunt between her teeth. This Old Woman was the Dragon's Grandmother.

When the Soldier entered, she said: "Where do you come from? and what do you want?"

He told her everything, just as it had come about, in such a pleasant manner that she took a great liking to him, and said she would assist him. Then she

raised a large heavy stone, that formed the entrance to the cellar, and said: "You must conceal yourself in this cellar, but mind you keep awake, and listen to all the conversation that passes this evening. Sit still, for your life, and keep very quiet; and when my Grandson the Dragon returns, I will ask him about this puzzling riddle; but you must be sure to keep in mind the answers he makes."

"All right," said the young Soldier; and down he went into the cellar.

About twelve o'clock, the Dragon flew into his Grandmother's hut. He flapped his wings wearily, tucked his forked tail under him, sat down, rubbed his ears, untwisted his fiery tongue, and demanded something to eat. His Grandmother busily laid the table with plenty of food and drink, which he ate and drank with a relish astonishing to ordinary appetites. Then she said: "What success have you had to-day? Have you had many volunteers—many to take your bounty money?"

"Things did not go over well to-day," said he; "still, I shall have three Soldiers safe enough, who gladly received the bounty."

"Ah!" said she, "I suppose, as usual, you have set them something impossible to do. What may it be?"

"They cannot escape me, as you well know; they are mine safe enough. I have given them a riddle to guess, that never was guessed yet," said he, joyfully.

"I feel curious to hear this riddle," said the Grandmother.

"You shall," said the Grandson: "In the Great North Sea lies a dead cat—that stands for their roast meat; the rib of a whale shall be their silver spoon; an old hollow horse's hoof shall be their wine-glass."

As soon as the Dragon had let his Grandmother into his secret, he went to bed; and as soon as he was laid fast asleep, the Old Woman raised the stone, and let the Soldier out.

"Have you listened well?" said she.

"Oh yes, thank you," he answered; "the boot is on the right leg—I can help myself now."

Then she assisted him to slip out, secretly, at the window, and by a new road he reached his companions as quickly as he could. He related to them how the crafty Old Granny had wormed the riddle out of the Dragon, and told them the solution of it. Then the two other Soldiers resumed their whips, and began whipping away as much money for themselves as they should want, so that it lay in heaps all around them.

A few days afterwards, the seven years were at an end, and the Dragon paid them a visit, with his big book under his arm. He opened it, and pointed to their signatures.

"Now, my lads, I hope you are in good order; you shall come to my dominions, and there you shall have a feast. Tell me, now, what roast meat will be prepared for you, and you shall keep your whips, and go where you please."

"In the Great North Sea there lies a dead cat, and that shall be our roast meat," said the first Soldier.

The Dragon looked very hot and angry at this answer; he stammered and stuttered, and asked the second man what should be his spoon.

"The rib of a whale shall be the silver spoon," replied he.

The Dragon now grew hotter and more angry than before, and began to grumble very much. Then he said to the third, "Perhaps you, Sir, can tell me what your wine-glass will be?"

"An old horse's hoof!" he exclaimed, in an exulting manner.

That very moment the Dragon flew away, making so loud an outcry, that the Soldiers trembled in their shoes; but their joy soon overcame their fright. They had entirely rid themselves of their fierce master, and were at liberty to do as they pleased. So they set to work, and whipped money until they had no power to whip another sixpence. Then they lived together happily upon it, as long as they were upon the earth.

THE LOVING SISTER AND HER TWELVE BROTHERS.

THERE was once a King and Queen on the throne of the Fortunate Islands; and lucky it was for them that they were a King and a Queen, for they had twelve children, all of them boys. Their Mother got on very well with them; but they plagued the poor King out of his life, totally upset his dignity, spent his treasures, and played tricks upon his courtiers and ministers of state.

He bore it for some years; but at last, finding the conduct of the younkers intolerable, he said one day to his wife, "There's that young Benjamin taken before the magistrates for robbing the Lord Chancellor's orchard."

"What a shame of the Lord Chancellor!" was the Royal Mother's reply.

"I tell you what, my dear," said his Majesty, "I can't put up with this any longer. If our thirteenth child, whom you are about to bring into the world, should happen to be the girl we have so long desired to have, I will smother our twelve boys at once, so that she may inherit our throne, and become very wealthy as the sole possessor of all our treasures. No fears, madam; I am resolved!"

When the King spoke in this tone, the Queen knew was of no use replying. So she did as her Royal husband told her, and ordered twelve coffins to be made, and nicely padded with shavings, with a pillow in each, all ready. These twelve coffins were brought to the palace in the Royal Stationery Van, so as not to be seen; and when they were all safely deposited in a room in one of the great turrets, the King locked the door and carried the key to the Queen, charging her to keep these preparations secret.

But the Queen was a woman, and could not keep a secret; besides, she was a mother, and loved her boys, troublesome as they were. So she sat crying, hour after hour, in her bedchamber window, until her son Benjamin, who being the youngest was generally with her, could not but notice his mother's grief, careless as he was, and inquired lovingly, "Mother, dear Mother, what is it that so troubles you?"

At first she replied that she could not tell him,—it was some state secret about the Lords of the Admiralty. But when she heard him say that he would go and speak to his eleven elder brothers, who would at once kick all the Lords of the Admiralty in sacred places for making their mother cry, she became alarmed, and, at last, was overpersuaded to take the key out of her secret pocket, and show him the twelve coffins stuffed with shavings, with a pillow in each of them, all ready for himself and his eleven brothers, in case his mother should give birth to a Princess.

Prince Benjamin, as you may suppose, was rather surprised at hearing the benevolent intentions of his Royal Male Parent; but when he saw how afflicted his poor mother was, and how she wept and wrung her hands, he said, "Do you be comforted, my dear Mother; I dare say we have all been very bad boys, and deserved it; but as we are old enough to help ourselves, the best plan will be to take the chance while it is left to us, and go away."

Then it was settled between the Queen and the Twelve Royal Princes that they should go off into a neighbouring wood, and that one of them should climb up into a high tree and keep watch, looking towards the tower of the Royal Castle.

"If I have a little girl," said her Majesty, "I will have a red flag hoisted, and you must flee for your lives. But if a white flag be hoisted, that is a sign of a baby boy and brother. Then come back, all together, as quickly as you can, and gladden your poor mother's heart with the sight of all her dear children in safety."

Then all the Princes came to pay her a visit in her bedchamber, and she gave them her blessing, and a pound of nice plum-cake each, and a large basin of caudle that the Royal Nurse made for them on the sly; for the old woman was herself very fond of the twelve rackety boys, and had done her best to spoil them all in their childish days.

Then the Twelve Brothers went into the forest, and they took it by turns for one of them to go up into a high tree, and keep a look-out towards the tower. Thus eleven days passed in anxious expectation, and they saw nothing from their lofty watch-post but the green sea of waving foliage underneath them, and the old brown towers of the castle in the grey distance. At last, it came to Benjamin's turn, and he was lucky enough to see the long-expected flag raised on the tower. But it was a red one, and announced the dismal news of their death-doom!

At this, a secret feeling of rage and indignation at the injustice done them seized upon the Twelve Royal Youths. "What!" said they, "shall we twelve suffer death for one infant girl-child? Nay, it were unworthy manhood! We will not bear it. Let us all swear vengeance on the hated sex. Wherever we meet a young maiden, we will immolate her to our just wrath?" This they did swear, in an awful manner; and then, in place of going to the castle to die, they went deeper into the forest, where, in the gloomiest of its recesses, they found an enchanted glade, and a charmed hut in which they could live unseen; for the whole of that part of the wood was impervious to the steps of ordinary mortals.

As Benjamin was the youngest and the weakest, upon him devolved the domestic duties of the establishment. He cleaned the house, and got the dinner ready, whilst his brothers went forth into the forest, and shot the wild birds, the pigeons, the hares, and the fawns. In this agreeable manner ten years soon elapsed.

We must now go back to the castle, where we may be quite sure the Queen did not lead the King a very pleasant life, for the loss of her twelve boys. But the little tiny daughter, whose birth had been the cause of so much family sorrow, grew up, meanwhile, a gay and lovely child, winning all hearts, for she was good as she was beautiful, and so sweet-tempered, that the Fairies, who had been her godmothers, had given her a golden star to wear constantly on her brow, in token of the perpetual sunshine in her heart.

Now, it happened one day that there was a great wash at the castle, owing to a general tidying-up previous to the Royal Family going to the sea-side for the summer. The little Princess, who was strolling about by herself—for all the servants were busily occupied, and the King, as he always did on such occasions, had found some business that summoned him away for the day—suddenly came upon the lawn in the little back garden, where the clothes were hung up to dry. To her great surprise, she saw twelve boys' shirts hanging up all of a row—a sight which struck her as being so curious, that she immediately ran to the Queen, and said, "My dear Mamma, whose are those twelve shirts hanging up on the lawn in the back garden?"

"My dear," replied the Queen, "you should not ask such questions. Little girls should not know shirts when they see them. They are your father's, of course."

"Oh no, Mamma, that can't be; they are much too small for Papa, and they have got nice little frills."

Then the Queen kissed her little daughter, and began to shed tears, and replied to the child's farther questioning, with a heavy heart, "Those twelve pretty shirts belong to your Twelve Brothers."

"Brothers!" exclaimed the little girl, joy dancing in her eyes. "Brothers! I never knew I had any! How I should like to have some! How is it I have never heard of them before? Where are they? Oh, take me to them at once, dear Mother!" Then her little bosom heaved with the new love that filled it, and her emotion showed itself in tears.

"Where are they?" replied the desolate mother; "who can tell? They wandered away into the wide, wide world. But come with me, and you shall see a sad and sorry sight, and I will tell you the doleful story of their departure, and its cause."

Then she led the little Maiden by the hand to the Great Turret, and unlocked the door, and showed her the twelve coffins with blue cloth and silver nails.

"Dead! Are they then all dead!" exclaimed the young Princess. "Oh, Mother! why have I only known that I had brothers, but to mourn their loss?"

"They are not dead; they went away when you were born, to avoid being killed by your father, out of his too great love and preference for you, you being a girl."

Then she showed her the shavings and the pillows inside the coffins, and told her how everything had happened. Then they both wept. At last, the young Maiden rose, and wiping away her tears, smiled brightly upon her mother, and said, "Weep not, dear Mother; good shall yet come of this. I will go forth into the wide, wide world, and seek my brothers." Then she took the twelve little shirts with her, and walked straight out of the great castle gates into the forest. She wandered along all day, and just as the shades of evening fell, came in front of the charmed house in the enchanted glade, where her Brothers had found refuge. Being rather tired, she was pleased at seeing such an elegant cottage, and walked up to the porch, intending to enter and request lodgings for the night. But before she could do this, a young man stepped forward to meet her; and although she could perceive from his countenance the astonishment he felt at her sudden appearance, her great beauty, her royal robes, and the golden star she wore on her forehead, nevertheless he addressed her in a decided tone, and said: "Whence come you, young Maiden, alone in these deep recesses of our impenetrable forest? What has brought you hither? Whither are you going?"

"I am the daughter of the King of these dominions," replied the fair Princess; "and I have left my father's palace in search of my Twelve Brothers, and I will go as far as the heaven is blue until I find them."

"Surely you are a loving sister, gentle Princess," said Benjamin; "pray take a seat. But what has your Royal Highness got in that bundle?"

"The twelve little shirts belonging to my brothers," said the charming little Princess, unrolling them.

"Why, they are only just washed, and only just dry!" said Benjamin.

"Yes," said the Princess; "I took them off the line myself, and started away immediately, only waiting to see the twelve little coffins with the blue cloth and silver nails, with the shavings inside and the pillows. That was the first I had ever heard of my poor dear lost brothers." Then she began to cry.

"Not lost," said Benjamin, embracing her; "not lost, for I am one of them, and you will soon see the other eleven. I am Benjamin, your youngest brother!"

Then she cried for joy, and he cried for joy, and they kissed each other, and sat happy, side by side. But on a sudden, Benjamin jumped up in great alarm, and rushed to the door, and drew the bar across.

"What is the matter, dear Brother?" said the little Maiden.

"Alas!" he said, "we are all under a terrible compact. Our indignation at our father's injustice made us all swear an oath together, on the day you were born, that every maiden that fell in our way should suffer death, because we were obliged to fly from our father's palace, to avoid suffering death ourselves, on account of a maiden."

"Nay then, surely," replied the Maiden, raising her eyes to heaven, "I will willingly die, if by my death my dear Brothers can be restored to their former state."

"Thou art indeed a loving Sister," said Benjamin; "but thou shalt not die."

Then he turned over the brewing-tub, and told his Sister to get under it, which she did; when night came, and they heard their Brothers singing "Tra-la-la!" in the distance, as they returned from hunting.

Dinner was ready and smoking on the table; and as they sat eating it and enjoying themselves, they asked Benjamin, "What is the news?"

"Oh!" replied Benjamin, "don't you know? haven't you heard?"

"No," replied they.

"Indeed!" said he; "people who stop at home sometimes find out more than those who go wandering about all day."

This excited their curiosity very much, especially as they could perceive from his manner that something out of the common way had come to his knowledge.

"Let's have it at once, Benjamin," they all cried.

"Not until you promise me first that you will not kill the first maiden you see."

"Never mind the girl; let's have the news."

"Will you promise, then?"

"Oh yes!" said they, all together; "we will pardon her for your sake. Now then, the news!"

"Our Sister is here!" said Benjamin, as he turned over the tub, and from beneath rose up the beautiful young Maiden, in her Royal robes, with the golden star on her brow, and a countenance radiant with joy and affection.

"Hail to our gentle Sister!" said they all, rising up from their seats, "and welcome—thrice welcome!"

Then they fell upon her neck, and kissed her, and loved her with all their hearts.

Ah! those were merry days that she spent with them in their woodland cottage, staying at home to do the housekeeping with Benjamin, and helping the little fellow in his work, whilst the eleven stalwart Brothers went forth into the forest hunting and shooting, bringing home deer and birds and hares, which their Sister cooked for dinner. There was no want of wood for the fire there, and Benjamin worked in a nice garden for the vegetables, whilst the Princess saw to the pots on the fire, and made the gravies, sauces, and soups, and took care that the dinner was always ready when the Brothers came home. Then she would sit and spin by the fireside in the long evenings, and prattle prettily, and sing songs to them, most of them about love, and very gentle, except when her Twelve Brothers made them noisy and jolly, by repeating the last two lines in full chorus, and adding their "Tra-la-la!" as a merry burthen. Never was a cottage kept in such beautiful order; and instead of letting her Brothers sleep on dry leaves, as they had done before, she made cases, which she stuffed with the feathers of the birds they had shot, and covered them with beautiful white and clean sheets of linen of her own spinning. The Brothers were delighted with their Sister, and she rejoiced in the new and agreeable duties of looking after and attending to them, and thus the family lived, happy and united.

Ah, my dear little readers! those of you who have brothers and sisters can hardly imagine the feeling of those who are without them. One must have something to love that is like one's self; and after one's mother and father, what and who is there that is really so much one's self as one's own brother and sister?

Now, in the garden of this cottage, where Benjamin, as I have told you, was in the habit of working in the cultivation of vegetables for the family, there were a great number of very pretty flowers; in these his gentle Sister took great delight. Amongst them was an African Marigold, on one stem of which grew twelve golden flowers. One day—it was a summer afternoon—when the Brothers had all dined early, and had made a most excellent meal, and regarding it as a kind of holiday, that day happening to be the once much-dreaded birthday of their Princess Sister, they all rose together to drink the health of their Loving Sister, and flourished their wine-cups, and sang their "Tra-la-la!" Then the Princess went from the table into the garden, and—with the intention of giving each of her Brothers a flower, all of the same colour, size, and beauty—she plucked the stem of the African Marigold, and broke off the twelve flowers.

But, oh! dismal fate! no sooner had she broken off the flowers than, one by one, her Twelve Brothers were changed into Twelve Black Crows, and away they flew off into the forest. That very same moment the cottage collapsed like a house built of cards, and the garden ran off wild into bushes and brambles. The poor Maiden stood alone in the wild forest; and as she gazed round in her desolation, hardly able to comprehend her misery in its fulness, she saw an Old Woman standing near her.

Then the Old Woman said: "Why didst thou pluck those twelve flowers, my child? Thou hast ruined thy Twelve Brothers, and changed them into Crows."

"Oh! what can I do to save them?" asked the Maiden, weeping piteously.

"I only know of one plan," said the Old Woman, "but that is impossible for you to carry out—no woman can ever do it; you would have to be silent for seven whole years."

"That is easy enough," said the young Princess.

"Try it," said the Old Woman, "and see how you like it;" and then she vanished.

The Princess began to consider how best to insure the preservation of this perpetual silence; and at last she determined that it would be wisest to live in the wood, and also, to avoid accidental meetings with people, by sitting all day up in a tree, and only coming down at night to sleep.

This was the life of a bird, and the Princess enjoyed it much, sitting among the leafy boughs, and spinning in the sunshine. This went on for five years, and all the while, through the guardianship of the kind Fairies, her godmothers, there was no change in the weather, no winter, or fog, or snow, or rain, but always pleasant breezes, and warm bright days. The apples on the trees were always ripe or ripening; the filberts always full and brown; and the currants and gooseberries on the bushes dried themselves into sweetmeats and preserves, to give variety to her diet.

117

The Royal robes she wore all this while were none the worse for her wearing them; they were as clean and neat, and unspotted, and untumbled, and untorn, as if they had been just taken out of the wardrobe in her Mother's Palace, and had never come in contact with trunks of trees and thorny branches, in her climbing up and down to her nest of leaves and bed of moss.

But, somehow or other, as it always happens, there came a handsome young King to hunt in the forest, and he had a large deerhound, which had a very fine nose, and so the wise dog at once ran to the tree up in which the Princess was sitting. It was of no use calling the dog away; so the King, who knew how clever the hound was, followed the sound of his barking and baying, to discover what it could be that so strongly excited the brute's attention. He saw the animal leaping round the tree, and endeavouring to spring and bound up the trunk. Then the King rode up, and saw the lovely Princess, with the golden star upon her brow. He tried to engage her in conversation, but she only shook her head and smiled; looking so bewitching as she did so, that the handsome young King, having all the conversation to himself, was so enchanted with her grace and beauty, that he asked her, off hand, if she would become his bride. "If anything will make a woman speak," thought the King to himself, "that will." But the fair Princess did not speak a word, but she looked him up and down with a pleased expression, and then put out her hand, and slightly nodded her head. Then the King mounted the tree briskly, folded her Royal robes around her, brought her down gently, placed her on his horse, and carried her home, proudly, to his Royal Palace.

I need not tell you that the Queen Dowager, the courtiers, and the ministers of state of his kingdom, were rather surprised at such an extraordinary marriage act, especially as the Royal bride, though she laughed very heartily and often, never spoke a word, not even to say "I will," in the marriage ceremony.

The Queen Mother for two whole years incessantly nagged and worried her Royal Son about the young beggar-woman, as she called her, that he had brought home from the forest to his Royal bed; and she invented so many falsehoods, and said so many wicked things about this poor innocent young Queen, that at last her husband believed some of them, from hearing them so constantly repeated. So he called his council together, and ordered them to proceed to the trial of his Queen for witchcraft.

They were not long in finding her guilty and sentencing her to death. A great pile of wood was built up round a stake in the Palace courtyard; to this the poor young Queen, in spite of her many tears, her imploring eyes, and beseeching looks, was fastened, and fire was set to it. The poor young Queen knew very well that if she were allowed to live only a few minutes longer, the seven years would have expired, and her Brothers be restored to their former shapes; but she could not control the cruel haste of the myrmidons of the Queen Dowager's hatred, jealousy, and revenge. The dry bushes crackled with the quick-rising blaze, and the white smoke of the fresh-burning wood circled in mazy eddies all around her, and the roar of the multitude was ringing in her ears, when suddenly a clock struck one. Then came a hurrying whirlwind, that blew away the smoke, scattered all the faggots, and dashed the burning embers in the faces of the cruel executioners and the high officers, who had crowded close round the pyre, to gloat upon the dying agonies of their lovely victim.

She was safe—saved! but not so the cruel Queen Dowager, whose robes of state, donned for what she thought a festive occasion, were set on fire by the blazing faggots confusedly thrown about, so that she was dreadfully scorched and burnt all over her body, as well as trodden under foot and her limbs broken by the mob of terrified spectators, in the alarm and horror of their first rush in attempting to escape from the fire that was so widely scattered amongst them. The King rushed down from the Palace, and seized his innocent young Queen in his arms. Whilst he was doing this, a loud whirring was heard in the air, and Twelve Crows flew, swiftly rushing, to the spot; as they touched the ground, they each resumed the royal and manly form of a Prince—the Twelve Brothers, whom the Loving Sister had thus rescued from enchantment by a painful silence of seven years' duration, and at the imminent risk of her own life.

They speedily untied her from the stake, and then, drawing their swords, stood around her like guardian angels; not forgetting, however, to threaten condign punishment on the King, whose weak and foolish listening to slanderous councils had brought such peril on their innocent Sister.

But when she spoke to the King in her own charming voice, and also told to her Brothers the whole story as it had happened, they forgave the King, who was rejoiced to find her innocent; and, after paying a visit to their own father and mother, who received them with great joy, they returned to their Sister's Palace, with whom they lived in great happiness and brotherly love, to the very end of their days.

THE TAILOR'S BRIDE.

It is generally reported of Tailors, that they are but the ninth part of men, and cannot arrive at any very high position in the world; but I see no reason why a Tailor should not travel as far, or be as brave, as any other man. The only thing that is necessary is, that he should go to the right place, and have good fortune attending him.

A very clever and nimble young Tailor went out once upon his travels, and the first thing he did was to journey towards a deep forest, in which, because he did not know his way, he lost himself. Night came on apace, and he had no choice but to make a bed and spend the night in this dreary solitude. He might easily have rested well enough, tired as he was, upon the soft moss; but then the wild beasts haunted his imagination, and they were not desirable bedfellows. So at last he resolved to look out for a tree, where he might safely pass the night.

He picked out a tall oak, and climbed to the top of its wide-spreading branches, being well pleased that he had brought his goose with him, as its weight kept the wind that whistled among the trees from blowing him away. After he had been shivering and shaking some time in the boughs, he saw glimmering through the darkness a small light. "I am all right now," said the Tailor, "for wherever that light is, there must assuredly be some sort of a habitation; and I should not mind exchanging the boughs of a tree for a bed, even if it were a rough one." So he descended cautiously, and made the best of his way towards the light.

Presently he came to a little hut, made of clay and straw. Here he knocked boldly, and the door opened immediately to him of itself; and he saw just inside a little old grey-headed Man, dressed in a frock of many colours, which was all in rags.

"I should like to know who you are, and what you want?" said the Old Man, roughly.

"Oh," replied the Tailor, "I am only a poor man; having lost my way in the forest, I am benighted, and having no shelter, I humbly entreat you to let me remain in your hut until daylight comes."

"Get out with you!" cried the Old Man, peevishly; "I will have no idle, roving vagabonds about me. Go where they will be better pleased to see you!" And so saying, he tried to push the young man out.

The Tailor, being very much afraid of the dark forest, was impelled by his fears to entreat most earnestly; so he caught hold of the Old Man's coat, and would not be said nay to, until at last, tired of refusing, he yielded, and having admitted him into his hut, put something to eat before him, and then told him he might lie down and sleep upon a bed that stood in the corner of the room.

It was not necessary to coax the Tailor to sleep; he soon proved by his snoring he could do that well enough, if he could do nothing else. He slept on until morning came, and even then had no inclination to rouse himself, but a loud noise suddenly awoke him. Terrible piercing shrieks and cries rang through the cottage. The Tailor courageously jumped up, and hastily dressing himself, went forth.

No sooner was he outside the door, than he saw close to him a dreadful-looking Beast engaged in hot contest with a pretty little Goat. They were goring each other with their horns, and fighting in the most savage and frantic manner. The very earth trembled under their repeated attacks, and the air resounded with the noise of their bellowing and cries. For some time the chances of victory or defeat were equal, until the Goat gained an advantage over its enemy, by thrusting its horns into his side with such a home push that the ponderous animal was brought to the ground with a fearful howl, after which his business was soon settled by a few more vigorous strokes on the part of the Goat.

The Tailor was still standing by, lost in astonishment, when the fight was concluded; but no sooner did the Goat catch sight of him, than it rushed upon him, and caught him on its horns. Away it bolted with him, through hill and dale, land and water, field and forest. He had the good luck, somehow, of being able to scramble upon the Goat's back, and held on firmly by its horns, and then resigned himself to his fate, which came sooner than he looked for it, for the Goat stopped before a ridge of rocks, and then let the Tailor gently down to the ground.

He lay in an exhausted state for some time, and when he recovered at last, the Goat was standing by him, and showed signs of pleasure at his revival. Then it made a spring at the rock, and thrust its horns with such force against what seemed to be a door in it, that the force of the blow split it open. No sooner was this done, than flames of fire came belching forth, and then the dense smoke rolled in such volumes, that the Goat was entirely hidden from the Tailor, who was at his wit's end to know where to turn or how to act.

While he stood quaking and trembling, considering what to do for the best, a Voice came from the rock, which said, "No harm will happen to you; step in hither, and fear not."

The Tailor hesitated awhile; but having no power over himself, he did as the Voice commanded him, and passing through the iron door, found himself in an immense hall, formed of bright and shining marble in square blocks, on each of which characters were written which he vainly tried to decipher. He looked upon all these things with the deepest astonishment, and was about to make his way out again, when the Voice said, "Step upon the stone which lies in the middle of the hall, and there await your fate."

The Tailor knew no fear now, and was quickly upon the stone pointed out to him. No sooner had he placed himself there, than the stone began to sink slowly, deeper and deeper. Presently it remained steady, and the Tailor, looking about him, saw another large chamber, like the first in size and form, but it contained more in it to excite his wonder and attention. In the walls were niches, in which were large vessels of pure glass, filled with coloured subtle essences, some in gases and others in a liquid form. On the floor of this second hall there stood two large glass cases, and he at once determined to see what they contained. One, to his astonishment, held a handsome building, similar to a castle, with all its necessary outhouses and farm-buildings, stables and gardens attached, and surrounded by every article requisite for comfort or necessity. Everything was very small, but the workmanship was incomparable, and executed with the most cunning ingenuity. The Tailor could not take his eyes away from this wonderful curiosity, until the Voice cried, "Enough! the other case demands attention!" On turning and looking at the other case, great was his wonder when he perceived in it a beautiful Maiden, lying fast asleep, and shrouded from head to foot with the streaming masses of her own yellow hair! Her eyes were closed fast, but there was a living colour in her cheeks, and the rising and falling motion of a ribbon on her breast left no doubt that she lived and breathed. The Tailor's heart beat violently as he gazed, when all at once she opened her eyes, and giving a joyful cry, closed them again. When her eyes met the Tailor's, she exclaimed, "My liberty approaches. Quick, kind Sir, quick! help me out of my miserable prison; push back the bolts of my glass case, and I am free!"

119

The Tailor tremblingly obeyed. As soon as he had raised the glass lid, the Maiden stepped out, and quickly wrapped herself in a cloak which she fetched from the corner of the hall. Then she sat herself down upon a stone, and calling the young Tailor to her, gave him a very friendly kiss, and then said, "My long-expected deliverer, you have been led hither to-day to put an end to my sorrows. On the same day that they end, your good fortune begins. You are to be my beloved husband, the chosen by fate; you will spend your life in undisturbed peace, and will inherit all my earthly wealth. Sit down, I pray you, and hear the story of my misfortunes.

"I am the daughter of a rich Count. My parents died when I was quite a baby, and delivered me, as a last bequest, to the care of my elder Brother, by whom I was to be well educated. We loved each other with the most tender affection, and we were both of one mind in everything we did and said. We could not bear the idea of being separated from each other, and therefore we both agreed to remain single and live together all our lives. We always had a very large circle of friends staying in our house with us, to whom we behaved with the greatest hospitality. It so happened, that one evening a Stranger rode into our castle gates, saying he had lost his way, and could not reach the next town, and he begged he might have shelter for the night. He was received with the greatest courtesy, and refreshments were laid before him. When he had sufficiently regaled himself, he amused us for the rest of the evening by his pleasant and cheerful conversation, and related to us his various adventures. My Brother took so great a fancy to him, that he pressed him to remain with us a couple of days, to which he gave his consent with some seeming reluctance. Late at night the Stranger was shown to his sleeping apartment, and I hastened to my bedroom, and being very weary, was soon asleep upon my beautiful soft bed of down.

"I could scarcely have forgotten myself, when the most deliciously soft strains of music came floating on the air. I was at a loss to know from whence they proceeded, and I tried to move, that I might call my servant, who slept in an adjoining room. To my utter astonishment, it seemed as if I had been riveted to the bed, and all power of speech or utterance had left me; I was unable to speak a single word. Meanwhile, I saw by the light of my silver lamp, that was always burning, the Stranger step into my room, through doors I thought to be fast closed. He approached me, saying, 'By the aid of my enchantments I have caused this soft music to surround you, and I stand here at all risks, to offer you my heart and hand.'

"My indignation knew no bounds at his unwarrantable conduct, and I did not deign to give any answer to such an impertinent proposition. After waiting motionless some time, apparently for my favourable decision, and not receiving any, he declared, with the most passionate vehemence, that he would take most signal vengeance upon me, and punish my haughtiness He then quitted my room. I passed the rest of the night, as you may suppose, in a restless anxiety, and could not sleep at all until the morning,

120

when I fell into a gentle doze. When I awoke I arose, and, dressing myself, proceeded to my Brother's room to tell him of the insult I had received, when, to my astonishment, I heard that he had ridden out at daybreak with the Stranger to hunt. This foreboded no good to me; I dressed myself quickly, ordered my favourite palfrey to be saddled, and attended by only one servant, rode at full speed into the forest. On our way the servant let his horse fall, and his knees were broken, so that it was impossible for him to follow me; but I continued to gallop on without any hindrance, and in a few minutes I saw the Stranger coming towards me, leading a Goat by a string. 'Where is my Brother?' I eagerly demanded; 'and where did you obtain that Goat?' from whose large eyes tears were streaming fast. Instead of answering me, he began to laugh loudly; thereupon, I became in a violent passion, and slipping an arrow in my bow, aimed it at the monster; but the arrow bounded from his breast without doing him any harm, and pierced the heart of my favourite horse. I was thrown to the ground, and the Stranger murmured some words over me, which rendered me insensible. When I recovered my senses, I found myself in this subterranean chamber. The Stranger appeared once more, and told me he had changed my Brother into a Black Goat, had shut up our castle in a glass case, with all its buildings surrounding it, and another case contained my servants, changed into gases, contained in coloured glass bottles. 'Are you willing now,' said he, 'to fulfil my wishes? if so, I will quickly put everything back again into its original form and natural shape.' I treated his proposals with the same silent contempt as before, and he withdrew, leaving me lying in my glass prison house, where I presently fell into a deep sleep. The consoling visions came across my mind, of a youth gentle and loving, who delivered me from the power of the Magician; and when I opened my eyes just now, and saw you, I knew that my dreams were fulfilled. Kindly help me now," she said, smiling sweetly upon him; "help me to complete what I then dreamed. Carefully take this glass case, which contains my castle, and place it upon this stone."

As soon as it was placed upon the spot indicated by the Maiden, the stone began to rise, carrying them both up with it; it made its way through the floor of the upper room, and from thence quickly into the open air. Here the Maiden lifted the lid of the case, and it was marvellous to see how soon the castle, and farm buildings, and stables, all became their original size.

Then the Maiden and Tailor returned into the cave again, and put the bottles filled with the gases upon the stone; and when it rose with them, and they were opened, the gases passed out; but no sooner had they come into contact with the air, than the forms of men and women appeared, whom the Maiden recognized as her attendants and servants.

Then the Maiden turned her head towards the forest, and, to her unspeakable delight, she saw her dearly beloved Brother, in his own natural form, coming towards her. So the Maiden, in the joy of her heart, gave her hand in marriage to the Tailor that very same day, and made him a Prince.

FORTUNATUS, HAVING SLAIN A BEAR, IS ACCOSTED BY A BEAUTIFUL LADY.

THE NEVER-FAILING PURSE AND THE WISHING CAP.

IN the city of Famagosta, in the island of Cyprus, there lived a gentleman possessed of great riches. His name was Theodorus. He married the most beautiful lady in Cyprus, and she was as rich as himself; she was called Gratiana. They thought themselves, to be sure, extremely happy in being able to keep the finest house and gardens imaginable, and in entertaining their friends, not only with the most delicate repasts, but diversions of every kind. Among the rest, they rode out on stately horses covered with the richest housings; they had pleasure-boats painted with the finest colours, to take them on the water when the weather was not too hot; and had all sorts of musical instruments besides.

No. 16

121

In addition to all this, the Lady Gratiana brought her husband a fine little son; so that one would think nothing could have prevented Theodorus and the Lady Gratiana from being the happiest and most contented persons in all the world.

This, however, was not long the case. The Lady Gratiana, it is true, was as contented as could be; but Theodorus, when he had enjoyed all these gratifications for some time, grew tired of them. Not even the smiles of the pretty little Fortunatus—for he was christened by that name—could prevent him from thinking he should find more pleasure in going into company with the gayest gentlemen of Famagosta.

Theodorus, accordingly, made acquaintance with some young noblemen of the Court, with whom he sat up all night, drinking and playing cards, and in a few years spent with them his whole fortune; so that he was obliged to send away his servants, and at last had no longer the means of providing his family with even a loaf of bread.

He was now very sorry for what he had done, but it was too late; and there was no remedy for his foolish conduct, but to work at some trade to support his wife and child.

For all this, the Lady Gratiana did not say affronting things to him, but continued to love her husband as before; saying, "Dear Theodorus, I do not, it it true, know how to work at any trade; but, if I cannot help you in getting money, I will help you to save it; for I will clean the house, and make the bread, and wash our clothes, all with my own hands; and though they have not been used to such hard work, they will soon be able to bear it, if you will but love your Gratiana and your Fortunatus."

So Theodorus set to work; and the Lady Gratiana, who had always been accustomed to ring her bell for everything she wanted, now scoured the kettles and washed the clothes with her own hands.

They went on in this manner for several years, till Fortunatus was sixteen years of age. One day, when they were all seated at dinner, Theodorus fixed his eyes very sorrowfully on his son, and sighed deeply. "What ails you, my father?" said Fortunatus. "Ah! my boy," says Theodorus, "I have reason enough to be sorrowful, when I think of the noble fortune I have squandered, and that my folly will be the means of obliging you to labour, as I do, for subsistence."

"Father," replied Fortunatus, "never grieve about it. I have often thought that it is time I should do something for myself; and though I have not been brought up to any trade, yet I trust I can find how to gain a subsistence in some way or other."

When Fortunatus had finished his dinner, he took his hat and wandered to the sea-side, determined to employ himself in thinking of what steps he could pursue, so as to be no longer a burthen to his father and mother.

It happened that just as he had reached the sea-shore, the Earl of Flanders, who had been to Jerusalem, and on his return home had touched at Cyprus, was getting on board his ship with all his retinue to set sail for Flanders. Fortunatus instantly thought

of offering himself to be his page. The Earl, seeing he was a very smart-looking lad, and hearing the quick replies he made to the questions he asked him, was very willing to engage him; so without farther ceremony he went on board.

On their way, the ship touched at Venice, where Fortunatus had an opportunity of seeing many new and surprising things, which both helped to raise his desire of travelling and to improve his understanding.

Soon after they arrived in Flanders, and had not been long on shore before the Earl, his master, was married to the daughter of the Duke of Cleves; and the ceremony was accompanied by all sorts of public rejoicings, tilts, tournaments, and entertainments, which lasted several days. Among the rest, the Earl's Lady gave two jewels as prizes to be tilted for, each of the value of one hundred crowns.

One of these was won by Fortunatus, and the other by Timothy, an attendant on the Duke of Burgundy, who afterwards challenged Fortunatus to run another tilt with him, so that he that should win should have both the jewels. Accordingly, they tilted; and at the fourth course, Fortunatus hoisted Timothy a full spear's length from his horse, and thus won both the jewels, which pleased the Earl and Countess so much, that they praised Fortunatus, and held him in greater esteem than ever.

Upon this occasion, also, Fortunatus received many rich presents from the nobility who were present; but the high favour he enjoyed made his fellow-servants jealous; and one among them, whose name was Robert, who had always pretended a great friendship for Fortunatus, made him believe that, notwithstanding all the Earl's kindness, he in secret envied Fortunatus his great skill at tournaments and tilting, assuring him that he had heard the Earl give private orders to one of his servants to find some means of killing him next day, while they should all be out a-hunting.

Fortunatus thanked the treacherous Robert for what he thought a great kindness, and next day, at daybreak, he took the swiftest horse in the Earl's stables, and left his dominions.

The Earl, hearing that Fortunatus had suddenly withdrawn himself, was much surprised, and questioned all his servants respecting what they knew of the affair; but they all denied knowing anything about it, or for what reasons he had left them; to which the Earl replied, that he was a lad for whom he had a great esteem; that some of them must have offered him an affront; and that, whenever he found it out, he would not fail to punish it severely.

In the meantime, Fortunatus, being out of the Earl's dominions, stopped at an inn for some refreshment. Here he began to consider what he was worth; and, having taken out all his fine clothes and jewels to look at, he could not help putting them on, and looking at himself in the glass, admiring vastly what a fine smart fellow he looked like. Then taking out his purse, he counted the money that had been given him by the lords and ladies at the tournament.

Finding that, in all, he was worth five hundred crowns, he bought a horse, taking care to send back

FORTUNATUS DEFEATS TIMOTHY AT THE TOURNAMENT.

that which he had taken from his master's stables. He then set off for Calais, crossed the Channel, landed safely at Dover, and proceeded to London, where he soon introduced himself into genteel company, and had once the honour to dance with the daughter of a Duke at the Lady Mayoress's ball. But this sort of life, as may well be supposed, soon exhausted his little stock of money.

When Fortunatus found himself penniless, he began to think of returning to France, and soon after embarked in a ship bound to Picardy. Here he landed; but finding no means of employing himself, he set off for Brittany, when, happening to cross a wood, he lost his way, and was obliged to stay in it all night.

The next morning, he was but little better off than before, for he could find no path; so he wandered about from one part of the wood to another, till at length, on the evening of the second day, he happened to meet with a spring, at which he drank very heartily, but still he had nothing to eat, and was ready to die of hunger.

When night again came on, hearing the growling of wild beasts, he climbed up a high tree for safety. No sooner had he seated himself in it, before a Lion walked fiercely up to the spring to drink. This frightened him exceedingly. The Lion being gone, a Bear came to drink also; and as the moon shone very bright, he looked up and saw Fortunatus, and immediately began to climb up the tree to get at him.

Fortunatus, however, drew his sword, and sat quietly till the Bear was come within arm's length, and then pierced him with it in the body several times, which made the Bear so very furious, that, making a great effort to get to Fortunatus, the bough broke, and down he fell, and lay sprawling and making a hideous yell on the ground.

Fortunatus, looking round on all sides, and seeing no more wild beasts near, thought this would be an excellent opportunity to get rid of the Bear at once; so down he comes, and kills him at a single blow. Being almost famished for want of food, he stooped down and was going to suck the blood of the Bear, when, once more looking round, to see if any wild beast was coming, what was his astonishment at beholding a beautiful Lady standing by his side, with a bandage over her eyes, leaning upon a wheel, and looking as if she intended to speak!

The Lady did not make him wait long before she pronounced the following words: "Know, young man, that my name is Fortune; I have the power to bestow on mortals wisdom, strength, riches, health, beauty, and long life. One of these I am willing to bestow on thee; choose for thyself which it shall be."

Fortunatus was not a moment before he answered: "Gracious Lady, I prefer to have riches in such abundance that I may never again know what it is to be so very hungry as I now find myself."

The Lady then presented him with a purse, telling him that, in whatever country he might happen to be, he had only to put his hand into the purse as often as he pleased, and he would be sure to find in it ten pieces of gold; that the purse should never fail of producing the like sum as long as it remained in the possession of him and his children; but that when he and his children should be dead, then the purse should lose this extraordinary quality.

Fortunatus could scarce contain himself for joy, and began to thank the Lady very eagerly; but she told him he had better think of making the best of his way out of the wood, and accordingly directed him which path to take, and then bade him farewell.

He walked by the light of the moon, as fast as his weak condition would allow of, till he came near an inn; before he went in, however, he thought it would be prudent to see if the Lady Fortune had been as good as her word; so he put his hand in his purse, and to his great joy counted ten pieces of gold.

Having nothing to fear, Fortunatus walked boldly into the inn, and called for the best supper they could get ready in a minute; "For," says he, "I must wait till to-morrow before I am very nice; with my present appetite anything will do."

Fortunatus very soon satisfied his hunger, and called for every sort of wine the house afforded; and after supper began to think what sort of life he should now lead; "For," says he, "I shall now have money enough for everything I can desire."

He slept that night on the very best bed in the house; and the next day ordered the most sumptuous provisions of every kind. If he rang his bell, all the waiters tried who should run fastest to inquire what he pleased to want; and the Landlord himself, hearing what a princely guest was come to his house, took care to be standing at the door to bow to him when he should be passing out.

Fortunatus inquired of the Landlord if any fine horses could be got in the neighbourhood; also, if he knew of some smart-looking clever men-servants who wanted places. The Landlord, fortunately, was able to get him provided with both to his great liking.

Being thus furnished with everything he wanted, he set out on the handsomest horse that was ever seen, attended by two servants, for the nearest town, where he bought some magnificent suits of clothes, and put his two servants in liveries laced with gold, and then proceeded to Paris.

Here he took the finest house that was to be got, and lived in great splendour. He entertained the nobility, and gave the finest balls to all the most beautiful ladies of the Court. He went to all public places of entertainment, and the first lords in the country constantly invited him to their houses.

He had lived in this manner for about a year, when he began to think of returning to Famagosta, to visit his parents, whom he had left in a very poor condition. "But," says Fortunatus, "as I am young and inexperienced, I should like to meet with some person of more knowledge than I have, who would make my journey both useful and pleasing to me."

He had not long wished this, before he fell into company with a venerable old gentleman, called Loch Fitty, who, he found, was a native of Scotland, and had left a wife and ten children, a great many years ago, in hopes to better his fortune; but was now, owing to different accidents, poorer than ever, and had not money enough even to take him back to his family.

Loch Fitty, finding how much Fortunatus desired to obtain knowledge, related to him many of the strange adventures he had met with; and gave him an account of all the kingdoms he had been in, as well as of the customs, dress, and manners of the inhabitants.

Says Fortunatus to himself, "This is the very man I stand in need of." So, without farther ceremony, he made him a very advantageous proposal, which the old gentleman accepted, on condition that he should be first permitted to go and visit his family.

Fortunatus assured him he had not the least objection; "and," added he, "as I am a little tired of being always in the midst of such noisy pleasures as one finds at Paris, I will, with your leave, go with you to Scotland and see your wife and children."

They set out the very next day, and arrived at the house of Loch Fitty; Fortunatus not having once, in all the way, desired to change his kind companion for the splendid entertainments he had quitted.

Loch Fitty embraced his wife and children, five of whom were daughters, and the most beautiful creatures he had ever beheld. When they had taken some refreshment, his wife said to him, "Ah! dear Lord Loch Fitty, how happy I am to see you once again! Now I trust we shall enjoy each other's company for the rest of our lives! What signifies that we are poor? We will be content, if you will but promise you will not again think of leaving us to get wealth, only because we have a title."

Fortunatus listened with great surprise. "What!" said he, "are you a Lord? Then you shall be a rich Lord, too; and that you may not think you owe me any obligation for the fortune I shall give you, I will put it in your power to make me, on the contrary, much your debtor. Bestow on me your youngest daughter, called Cassandra; and let us have the pleasure of your company as far as Famagosta; and take your whole family with you, that you may have pleasant company on your way back, when you have rested in that place from your fatigue."

Lord Loch Fitty shed some tears of joy, to think he should at last see his family restored to all the honours it had once enjoyed; and, after accepting Fortunatus as a husband for his daughter Cassandra, he related to him the misfortunes that obliged him to live in poverty at Paris, and call himself by the plain name of Loch Fitty.

When Lord Loch Fitty had ended his story, they agreed that the Lady Cassandra should the very next morning be asked to accept the hand of Fortunatus; and that, should she consent, they would embark in a few days for Famagosta.

The next morning, the proposal was made in form, as was agreed on, and Fortunatus had the pleasure of hearing from the lips of the beautiful Cassandra, that the very first time she cast her eyes on him, she thought him the most handsome and accomplished gentleman in all the world.

Everything was soon ready for their departure. Fortunatus, Lord Loch Fitty, his Lady, and their ten children, embarked in a large commodious ship; they had prosperous winds, and landed happily in the port of Famagosta. They spent a few days in the necessary preparations, and the marriage was then celebrated with all the magnificence and rejoicings imaginable.

As Fortunatus found that his parents were both dead, he begged Lord Loch Fitty would be kind enough to stay and keep him and his lady company; so they lived all together in the finest house that was to be got in the city of Famagosta, and gave the most splendid entertainments.

By the end of the first year, the Lady Cassandra had a little son, who was christened Ampedo; and the year following, another, who was christened Andolocia.

For twelve years Fortunatus lived the happiest life imaginable with his wife and children and his wife's relations; and each of her sisters having received a fortune from the bountiful purse of Fortunatus, they soon married to great advantage. But by this time his taste for travelling returned; and he thought, as he was now so much older and wiser than when he was at Paris, he should not want a companion, for Lord Loch Fitty was at this time too old to bear fatigue.

After obtaining, with great difficulty, the consent of the Lady Cassandra, who, at last, insisted on his staying only two years, he got everything ready for his departure; and taking his lady into one of his private rooms, showed her three chests of gold, one of which he desired she would keep for herself, and take charge of the other two for their sons, in case any accident should befal him. He then led her back to the apartment where the whole family were sitting; and after tenderly embracing them all one by one, he set sail with a fair wind for Alexandria.

Fortunatus being told, on his arrival in this place, that it was customary to make a handsome present to the Sultan, sent him a piece of plate that cost five thousand ducats. The Sultan was so extremely pleased, that he ordered a hundred casks of spices to be presented to Fortunatus in return; these Fortunatus sent immediately to the Lady Cassandra, with the tenderest letters imaginable, by the very ship that brought him, which was then going back to Famagosta.

Fortunatus took an early opportunity of telling the Sultan he wished to travel through his dominions by land; so the Sultan immediately ordered him such passports and letters of recommendation as he might stand in need of to the neighbouring Princes. He then purchased a camel, hired proper attendants, and set off on his travels.

He went through Turkey, Persia, and from thence to Carthage; he next proceeded to the country of Prester John, who rides upon a white elephant, and has Kings to wait on him.

Fortunatus made him some rich presents, and went on to Calcutta; and returning, took Jerusalem in his way, and so back to Alexandria, where he had the good fortune to find the same ship which had brought him, and to learn of the captain that his wife and family were all in perfect health.

The first thing he did was to pay a visit to his old friend the Sultan, to whom he again made a handsome present, and was invited to dine at his Palace.

After the repast, the Sultan said: "It must be vastly amusing, Fortunatus, to hear an account of the different places you have seen; pray favour me with a history of your travels."

Fortunatus did as he was desired; and pleased the Sultan extremely, by relating the many curious adventures he had met with, particularly the manner of his acquaintance with the Lord Loch Fitty, and the desire of that nobleman to maintain the honours of his ancestors.

When he had finished, the Sultan expressed himself much delighted with what he had heard, and added, that he had in his possession a greater curiosity than anything Fortunatus had told him of; and immediately leading him into a room nearly filled with jewels, he opened a large closet, and taking out a cap, told Fortunatus it was of greater value than all the rest.

Fortunatus imagined the Sultan was jesting, and told him he had seen many a better cap than that.

"Ah!" said the Sultan, "that is because you do not know its value. Whoever puts this cap on his head, and wishes himself in any part of the world, is instantly conveyed thither."

"Indeed!" says Fortunatus; "and pray is the man living who made it?"

"That I know nothing about," said the Sultan.

"Really one would scarcely have believed it," says Fortunatus. "Pray, Sir, is it very heavy?"

"Not at all," replied the Sultan; "you may feel it."

Fortunatus took up the cap, put it on his head, and could not help wishing himself on board the ship that was going back to Famagosta. In less than a moment he was carried through the winds on board of her, just as she was ready to set sail; and there being a brisk gale, they were out of sight in less than half an hour.

The ship arrived in safety at Famagosta after a happy passage, and Fortunatus had the satisfaction to find his wife and children well; but Lord Loch Fitty and his Lady had died of old age, and were buried side by side.

Fortunatus now began to take great pleasure in educating his two boys; and accustomed them to all sorts of manly exercises, such as wrestling, tilts, and tournaments. Now and then he recollected the wonderful cap he had in his possession, and at such times would wish he could just take a peep at what was passing in different countries; when, though his wish never failed to be acomplished, yet, as he always contented himself with only staying an hour or two, the Lady Cassandra never missed him, and had no farther uneasiness about his love of travelling.

At last, Fortunatus began to get old, and the Lady Cassandra fell sick and died. The loss of her caused him so much grief, that soon after he fell sick; and believing he had not long to live, he called his two sons to his bedside, and told them the secret of the purse and cap, which he desired they would on no account disclose to any one. "Follow my example," says Fortunatus; "I have had the purse these forty years, and no living creature knew from what source I obtained my riches."

He then recommended them to make use of the purse between them, and to live together in harmony; and embracing them, died soon after.

Fortunatus was buried in great pomp by the side of the Lady Cassandra, in his own chapel, and was for a long time mourned by the people of Famagosta.

It was not long after the death of Fortunatus, when Andolocia came to his brother Ampedo, who, being the eldest, had the purse in his possession, and begged he would let him have it for a certain time, as he wished to set out on his travels for distant countries; to this Ampedo would by no means consent, and they came to high words concerning it. At length, however, Ampedo consented to let his brother have the purse for six years, and accordingly, after filling all his coffers, he gave it into his hands; with this agreement, however, that he was afterwards to keep it for as long a time himself.

As Andolocia possessed exactly his father's temper, in his love of travelling to distant countries, he was overjoyed to think he had obtained the purse, and immediately began his preparations for setting out. The first place he visited was Paris.

In this place there was a famous wrestler, called Strongfist, who had never yet been thrown by any man. Andolocia sent him a challenge, which Strongfist willingly accepted, and a day was appointed for the combat; in the meanwhile, the news reached all the inhabitants of Paris, who accordingly resolved to be witnesses of the scene.

The combatants met at the time and place appointed, and fell to with great spirit; but it was soon seen

ANDOLOCIA OVERTHROWS STRONGFIST, THE FAMOUS WRESTLER.

that Strongfist was not half so skilful as Andolocia, who, after a few blows, made him cry out he could fight no longer.

No sooner, however, was Strongfist recovered of the blows he had received, than, enraged to think he had been conquered by a stranger, and lost his reputation, he sent Andolocia another challenge; and they accordingly met as before.

But Strongfist gained nothing by this second attempt, for Andolocia made him once more cry out he was satisfied; so that the air resounded with the acclamations bestowed on Andolocia, while Strongfist was so maimed that he could never after engage in wrestling.

After staying some time longer in Paris, where he was loaded with every mark of distinction, the news of his great skill reached England, and he was invited by the King to the Court of London; for, being just at that time going to war with the King of Scotland, he wished to have Andolocia's advice how to conduct his army.

Andolocia accepted the proposal with joy; for it was the King of Scotland's father who had deprived his grandfather, the Lord Loch Fitty, of all his fortune, and caused him to leave his Lady and his home, and live in a mean condition in Paris.

He lost no time in preparing for the journey, and reached London in safety, where he was received with marks of the greatest kindness by the King and the whole Court; and Andolocia informing his Majesty of the ill-will he owed the King of Scotland, on the late King's account, it was immediately agreed on that he should head an army of the choicest troops in the English dominions, and march against him.

They accordingly set out for Scotland, had a furious battle with the King, and defeated him and his whole army; and, returning to London, Andolocia was loaded with the highest honours at the Court of the King of England.

Andolocia took a magnificent house in the finest square in London, and frequently entertained the King and all his nobles, whom he treated in so sumptuous a manner, that the King could not help wondering how a private gentleman could possibly have so much wealth.

One day, Andolocia being at Court, he happened to see the King's daughter, Agrippina, with whom he fell violently in love, and made her such costly presents as surprised the King more than before, so that he could not help telling the Queen he could not imagine how he came by such a fortune.

The Queen immediately set herself to work to find out the secret; and, accordingly, she told her daughter Agrippina, when she should be alone with him, to find it out, if possible.

Soon after, Andolocia, being seated by the Princess, told her how very beautiful he thought her, and how much he wished for the honour of having her for his wife. The Princess thought this a very good opportunity for finding out the secret; so she answered, that she liked him very well, but supposed he could not possibly have sufficient fortune to maintain the daughter of a King.

Upon this, Andolocia pulled out his purse, and threw ten pieces of gold at a time into her lap; and at length told her how it came into his father's possession, and every particular concerning it.

The Princess Agrippina hastened to tell the Queen all she had heard, who pretending the greatest fondness for Andolocia, took him into her closet, and presented him with a glass of the richest cordial, into which she had put a drug that soon threw him into a sound sleep, when, putting her hand into his pocket, she took his purse, and had him immediately conveyed to his own house, fast asleep.

The Queen then gave the purse to the young Princess, saying, as it was for her sake she had taken it, it was but right that it should be in her possession.

When Andolocia waked, and missed his purse, he was almost frantic; when he had run about the house for a long time, not knowing what to do, he at last thought of what had happened to him at the Palace, whither he immediately went, and asked to speak with the Queen, and was told she could not be seen. He then inquired for the Princess, and obtained the same answer. All this convinced Andolocia that the Queen had taken his purse, and did not intend to return it. The first thing he did was to borrow a hundred crowns of his steward, by means of which he got to Famagosta as fast as he could, and with great difficulty prevailed on his brother to spare him the cap for a short time, that he might transport himself in a moment wherever he pleased.

Having obtained it, he put it on, and instantly wished himself in Princess Agrippina's chamber, whom he intended to consult about getting back his purse from the Queen.

But no astonishment could be greater than his, when, looking at the Princess, he saw his purse fastened to her girdle. Andolocia, perceiving this, desired of the Princess to restore it, which she refusing, he clasped her in his arms, and wished himself in an orchard full of fruit-trees in the neighbourhood of Constantinople.

His wish was instantly accomplished, and they found themselves sitting under a large fig-tree; when the Princess, seeing what fine figs were on it, entreated him to get her one to eat. Andolocia, who loved Agrippina very much, notwithstanding she had used him so unkindly, immediately threw his cap upon the ground, and began to climb the tree.

The Princess, quite ignorant of the virtue in the cap, being greatly fatigued with the scorching of the sun, put it on her head, and happening at the same moment to be wishing she was in her cold bath at the Palace of her father, she was immediately taken up into the air, and was out of sight in a minute.

When Andolocia looked round, and saw that both the Princess and his cap were gone, he knew not, so great was his vexation, what step to take; but after walking about some time, finding himself thirsty, he began to eat some apples, when two large horns sprang directly out of his forehead.

He now ran like a madman about the orchard, and his cries were heard by an aged Hermit, who came up to him and inquired what was the matter. When Andolocia had related the manner in which the accident had happened, the Hermit assured him that if he would eat some apples from another tree he would soon find his horns disappear.

Andolocia lost no time in doing as he was desired, and the horns accordingly disappeared. Having first filled his pockets with some of both sorts of these extraordinary apples, he set out on foot for the palace of Princess Agrippina's father, where he stood at the gate disguised as a poor man who had the finest apples to sell that ever were seen in England.

The Princess, as she passed out, observed the apples, and seeing that they were as fine as those she had seen in the orchard near Constantinople, began to buy them with great eagerness, and turned back again to the Palace to eat them.

Immediately two great horns sprang from her forehead; upon which the Princess screamed so loud as to alarm every one in the Palace, and the King, among the rest, came in to her assistance.

Seeing what had happened, he called in all the physicians, to obtain a cure, if possible; but not one was found who understood her case.

At length, Andolocia, disguising himself as a physician, with a great false nose, went to the Palace and offered his services, which were willingly accepted.

Upon being shown into her room, he perceived his cap lying disregarded on a chair; so pretending he must speak with his patient in private, he sent the nurse out of the room, and in the meanwhile found an opportunity to put the cap into his pocket.

Andolocia then produced some of the apples that were a cure for the horns occasioned by those he had sold her, and having cut them very small, he desired her to eat them immediately, when the horns from that moment began to grow less.

The Princess was so delighted at this, that she thought she could not too hansomely reward her physician; so taking out her purse, he snatched it from her, clapped on his cap, and wished himself at Famagosta, whither he was immediately conveyed. But as he was in love with the Princess, he took care not to give her enough of the apples to remove the horns entirely, that no other gentleman might fall in love with her.

Having related his adventures to his brother Ampedo, the latter said he had no inclination to have either the cap or purse, since they brought their possessor into so much danger, and would give them wholly to Andolocia, provided he consented to pay him a handsome allowance as long as he lived.

Thus Andolocia kept the purse and cap to himself; but though he had such immense treasures, and besides, the power of conveying himself wherever he pleased in a moment, he was not quite happy.

Being convinced, however, that nothing was wanting to make him so but Agrippina, he first set about building a magnificent Palace, taking care every now and then to put on his cap and wish himself at the Court of London, where he sometimes had the good fortune to see the Princess as she took an airing in her carriage, and found means to know if the horns still remained on her head as before.

When the Palace was finished, Andolocia equipped himself with all the splendour imaginable; and taking with him some of the handsomest gentlemen of Famagosta, who looked like great lords, and in addition the most costly jewels that were to be got, as presents for the Princess, he set out for England, to demand her formally in marriage.

The King of England received him very courteously; the Queen, supposing it impossible that any Prince would offer to marry a Princess with horns on her head, and perceiving there was no other way of getting the purse, gave her consent also; and the Princess Agrippina, who had always wished to bestow on him her hand, said she really loved the Prince, but that she would never bring so great a misfortune on him as to be his wife while she had horns on her head.

"Dear Princess Agrippina," replied Andolocia, "then all our wishes will be gratified, for I have the power to make them disappear immediately."

Saying this, he left the room, and returned in a few

minutes with some of the apples he had given her once before, and which he had taken care to be provided with; when, presenting them to the Princess, he asked her if she did not remember the physician with the great nose, who some time before had made her horns grow less.

The Princess fell to eating the apples presented her by Andolocia, and the horns immediately disappeared. She embraced Andolocia with tenderness; they were married that very day, and shortly after were conducted in the greatest pomp to the Palace built for her reception at Famagosta, where they lived a long and a happy life.

Andolocia kept his cap and purse in a cabinet set apart for that purpose; and for fear of further accidents, he never suffered the key of it to be touched by any one but himself.

THE DEATH OF THE COCK.

ONCE upon a time, a Cock and Hen got married, and lived together very happily; the Hen loved her husband very tenderly, and the Cock took her to live in a nut-grove; and they agreed that whenever they found a nut they should divide it. Now, the Cock once found a beautiful tempting kernel, and he thought how he should like to eat it all,—" I can," said he, " soon find another for my dear Hen." So he made a gobble at it; but the nut was too big for him to swallow, and it stuck in his throat, so that he lay suffocating for want of breath. Then the Hen came up, and he said, " Water, water! quick, quick!"

So the Hen, seeing her dear husband was being stifled, ran as fast as she could to the Brook, saying, " Brook, you must give me some water; my husband lies in the nut-grove, and is nearly killed, through swallowing too large a kernel."

" Run," said the Brook, " first to the Bride, and get me some red silk."

So off ran the poor distracted Hen, and said, " Good Bride, give me some red silk; the Brook wants it before she will give me water to take to my husband, who lies choking in the nut-grove, through having swallowed the whole of a kernel."

The Bride said, " First go fetch me my garland that hangs upon yonder willow."

So the Hen ran and fetched the garland, which she took to the Bride, who gave her the red silk, which she took to the Brook, who gave her the water, with which she ran in haste to the Cock.

But, alas! in the Hen's long absence, he, poor fellow, had died, and lay stretched in the grove where they had spent so many happy days together. The Hen fainted at the sight, and when she came to, she went into a violent fit of hysterics, and shrieked so loud, that all her friends and neighbours came to see what was the matter. Then they all mourned and grieved for the Cock, and six Mice built him a little coach, that he might go respectably to the grave; and as soon as it was ready they harnessed themselves to it, while the Hen followed as chief mourner.

On the road, they met the Fox. " How is this?" said he; " where are you going?"

Then the Hen replied, " Going to bury my dear husband."

" May I go, too?" said the Fox.

" Yes," she said; " place yourself quite behind, for my horses will not allow any one to precede the carriage."

The Fox went behind, and so did the Wolf, the Bear, and the Goat, and many of the beasts of the forest. The funeral procession had not moved far, when they came to a stream.

" How shall we get over here?" said the Hen.

" I will lay myself across," said a Swan, " and you can pass over me."

But as soon as the six Mice attempted to cross, the bridge broke, and they all tumbled into the stream, and were drowned.

Then there was need of another bridge, and a large Coal came up, and said, " See how big and strong I am. I shall land you all well enough." So the Coal set himself in the water, but he had forgotten he could not swim, so he sank to the bottom, and was lost.

Then a Stone set herself firmly in the mud, and taking pity upon the poor Hen, said, " Step your foot firmly on me, ma'am, and I will help you over."

So the Hen drew the waggon over to the other side, and landed the dead body safely. But then the coach had to go back for the rest, but this was much too heavy a load, and they all sank in the water, to rise no more.

Now the poor widowed Hen was left alone to bury her dead husband. So she dug him a grave, and buried him decently, throwing a large heap of mould over him. Then she mourned over him so long, that she fell exhausted on her husband's grave, and died also; and all the birds came to her funeral.

THE GIANT MAIDENS.

ONCE upon a time, in the good old days, there lived a King, who was so generous, that he was everywhere known as the Bountiful King. Such was the peace and plenty of his reign, that gold used to lie about the country as plentiful as meal, and you might see on the highways golden bracelets and armlets that had fallen from men's arms, and remained untouched from year's end to year's end. The fields required no ploughing or sowing, but bore plenteous harvests of their own accord; there was a fowl in every pot, and a maiden-love for every bachelor.

Now this Bountiful King had been a great conqueror in his time; but he had only gone to war to rid his country of the Giants that used to oppress the poor peasants; and having defeated and slain them all, he hung up his armour in his palace halls, and lived a quiet and comfortable life.

It happened that the last Giant whom the Bountiful King had subdued had two daughters, and that the King, taking pity upon the two little girls—who were

E EVANS Sc

THE GIANT MAIDENS GRINDING OUT FIRE AND WAR!

not at that time above seven-and-twenty feet in height —had brought them home, and employed them as handmaidens in his hall. Their business was to grind at the Quern, or Handmill; for at that time of the world, all bread used in the house was made from flour ground in a handmill, under the master or mistress's inspection; and even Kings and Queens would, in those good days, have been ashamed not to look carefully after the affairs of their own household. The Bountiful King, though generous, was just, and, being a widower, used to look pretty sharp after his servant-maids, especially these two young Giantesses, Frenja and Menja.

But the Handmill, or Quern, at which they had been turning, was one of some importance to the happiness and prosperity of the Bountiful King's realm, for out of it he used to grind Peace and Gold. No wonder he kept them briskly working it; indeed, he would not allow them any longer rest from their grinding than the song of the cuckoo lasted, or, as a special favour, as long as they could sing a song themselves.

The Quern was a magic one, and though the Bountiful King did not know it, could grind out anything that the grinder chose, if he happened to know the right word of command. Hitherto, as long as the Bountiful King had used its power, it had ground

No. 17

nothing but Gold and Peace; but at last came a day when the two Giant Maidens were grinding together, and they sang a song, and asked for rest and pity in plaintive strains, but the Bountiful King would not let them stop. Then they turned to the Quern, whose name was Grotti, and they twisted the handle round fast and furious; and there came upon their angry memories snatches of old rhymes sung to them by Witch-nurses in their Giant babyhood; and they yelled forth songs of their slaughtered father, and screamed ditties of battle and bloodshed; and Frenja shouted—

"GROTTI!"

and Menja cried—

"GRITTI!"

and they ground more furiously; and before the astounded King could interfere, or his appalled courtiers rush to stop them, they ground out FIRE and WAR!

That night, in Dragon-shaped galleys, came over the sea Mysing the Sea-Rover and his Norsemen; and they landed, and burned the Palace of the Bountiful King, and slew him and all his men; and they carried off Grotti the Quern, and with it the Giant Maidens, Frenja and Menja.

Loud sang the valiant Sea-Rovers as they sailed away, their path over the waters lighted by the burning Palace of the Bountiful King. Then said the stout-hearted Mysing, as he stood by the helm, arrayed in glittering silver armour, holding the bright-flashing sword of Destiny bare in his redright hand—

"Grind me some salt, ye Giant Maidens!"

And they took with their hands Grotti, the Magic Quern, and they ground him salt; and they ground, and they ground, and they ground on patiently until midnight, when Frenja asked, "Hast thou not salt enough, O Mysing?"

But the Sea-Rover shook his head and frowned, and told her to grind on, for he was going to the cod banks of Newfoundland.

So they ground on, and the hold of the ship was filled with salt, and the Giant Maidens grew weary as the sun began to rise; and Menja spoke: "Hast thou not salt enough, O Mysing?"

But the Sea-Rover frowned angrily, and bade her still grind on.

Then sang Frenja the wild song of her childhood, as her dark hair floated in the winds, and her eyes flashed fire; and Menja took up the impassioned strain. Then howled the wind, and then uprose the sea, and the Dragon-headed galley flew over the waters.

Then Menja said—

"GROTTI!"

Then Frenja said—

"GRITTI!"

And round flew the handle of the Quern until it smoked again, and louder sang the Giant Maidens, and wilder grew their song, and fiercer rose the tempest, and shriller blew the wind, and the sails shrieked in the cleats and earings, and the masts of the Dragon galley creaked, and the lightnings flashed upon the silver armour of Mysing the Sea-Rover, as he stood undaunted at the helm.

"Grind! grind!" he cried.

130

And the Giant Maidens ground, and the salt poured from the Quern until it filled the ship and sank it; and down went Mysing, and Menja and Frenja, and Grotti, and all the crew!

And there, at the bottom of the deep Ocean, still are the Giant Maidens grinding, and still ever pours forth the salt from the Magic Quern; and THAT'S WHY THE SEA IS SALT!

LAZY HARRY'S HOME.

"WHAT'S to be done to-day to amuse our Royal selves?" said the King of the Goblin Elves, as he sat over his slow-burning charcoal fire, in a deep cavern in the Hartz Mountains: "things are very dull; there's no opposition in the Elfin Parliament, both parties being seemingly agreed in spending all the money they can. There is no war, and our opposite neighbour seems resolved to keep on shaking hands with us, and making fine speeches, in spite of all we do to show we are afraid he should come over and rob and murder us. What's to be done to-day for a little excitement? Even our Queen is in a good temper, and there is not even the chance of a breeze in the family. We are inclined for mischief—does any one know of any? Where can we go?"

"An' it so please your Majesty," said Nimbletooth, the youngest of the King's Goblin Courtiers, "I think I know where we may pick up some fun. Let us go and pay a morning visit to Lazy Harry's Home, and take the family by surprise."

"Agreed," said the King. "Forward!"

"Home! Home! Sweet, sweet Home! There's no place like Home!" and certainly there were few places that could be like Lazy Harry's Home. It was a comfortable farmer's house once on a time, but Harry was a lazy farmer, and Mrs. Harry was a lazy housewife, and their daughter Unathrifty was a slattern; so you can judge for yourself what sort of a Home was Lazy Harry's.

Just as the party of Goblins reached the door, Lazy Harry was saying to his wife, "My dear, I don't find fault with a nightcap in the teapot, because that might have happened in straining off the leaves, and is a sign of careful attention; but how did my shaving-brush get into this beefsteak pie?"

"Don't be so inquisitive, Harry," replied the wife; "wait until Unathrifty comes down to dinner."

"She never does that until it is three parts over," said Lazy Harry.

"To be sure not, my dear," replied his wife; "because you are always too lazy to call her."

"Call her yourself," was the surly reply of the husband.

"I will fetch her down," said Nimbletooth to the King of the Goblins.

Then the cunning rogue swelled himself up until he was the height of a full-grown young man, and puffed himself out to comely proportions, and made a new suit of clothes for himself out of some dock-leaves growing by the door, choosing a row of daisies for his buttons; and then he knocked at the door, and entered into the house in the appearance of a rich young Farmer in the neighbourhood, whom Lazy Harry and his wife very much wished to have as a son-in-law, and their daughter Unathrifty would have had no objection to as a husband.

The sudden entrance of the handsome and wealthy young Farmer, to all appearance in the character of a suitor, threw Lazy Harry's Home into great confusion. Nothing was ready, and no one fit to be seen. All was unswept, and every one unwashed and uncombed; the table-cloth dirty, the dishes greasy, the knives and forks rusty, with the handles half off; the glasses cracked, the table crazy, and the very legs of the chairs unsteady. In fact, the household was almost like that of a beggar; but appearances must be kept up before this smart young fellow, from whose visit to see Unathrifty at home so much was expected. Yes, appearances must be kept up—but how?

Now, it happened that Lazy Harry had for some months past gone about the farm with the sleeve of his coat torn; but this very day it so occurred that he had got a new arm in his coat. Oh! lucky chance! now was the time for him to show off.

"Pray take a chair, Sir," said he to the Goblin Farmer—the King of the Goblins and the rest of the mischievous sprites watching with merry eyes from the various corners of the chimney, in which they had hid themselves—"Pray take a seat, Sir," said Lazy Harry; "but, bless me! what a terrible dust there is in the house!"

So he bustled and busied himself, rubbing and wiping all the settles, stools, chairs, and tables, with his new sleeve, cunningly keeping up the other behind his back all the while.

Mrs. Lazy Harry, for her part, had only got on one shoe. "Dear me," she said, "how untidy everything is here!" and she went about, sidling and slipping out this one foot only, tapping and pushing it against the furniture to put it in order.

"Where is your daughter, Sir?" inquired the pretended young Farmer. "I hope she is not ill, that she keeps her room."

This the wicked Goblin spoke in a tone of pretended anxiety, as if he admired the young Miss Lazy, and had come a-courting her, and was disappointed at not seeing her.

Then they both called out to Unathrifty to come down. But the daughter had got a new cap—the only clean thing about her—and she was not half dressed; but wanting to see her sweetheart, all she could do was to put her head in at the door, and there she kept nodding, first on one side, then on the other, and said sharply to her mother, "How can I be everywhere at once?"

This was too much for the King of the Goblins, who contrived that just then there came a strong wind, which blew down the door, and showed Miss Unathrifty behind it, all in her dirty petticoat, with a fine new cap on her head.

Then the Goblin Farmer gave a loud laugh, and all the Goblins vanished up the chimney together, leaving the family at Lazy Harry's Home utterly disconcerted.

THE BLUE BIRD.

THERE was once a King, potent both by his dominions and treasures; but losing by death a much-loved wife, he became inconsolable. He shut himself up for eight days together in a little cabinet, where he bruised his head against the walls, so greatly was he afflicted, until his servants, being afraid lest he should kill himself, conveyed mats between the walls and the hangings, to prevent him doing himself any mischief. All his subjects resolved to wait upon him, and try the most proper consolations to assuage his grief. Some prepared grave and serious discourses; others, pleasing and delightful stories; and others, quaint and merry tales. But all this made no impression upon his mind, for he gave little or no attention to what they said. At length, a woman presented herself before him, so muffled up in black crapes, veils, and mantles, and weeping and sobbing so bitterly and so loud, that the King was strangely surprised at it. She told him she came not to lessen his sorrows, but rather to increase them, as nothing could be more justly lamented than the loss of a good wife; that, for her part, having lost the best of husbands, she was resolved to weep for him as long as she had any eyes; and thereupon redoubling her lamentations, the King, in imitation of her, did the like.

He received her more kindly than any other person, and told her a thousand stories of his wife's good qualities; the woman, too, enlarged upon the virtues of her deceased husband; and thus they talked over their stock of sorrow, till it was quite spent, and neither had any more to say, nor one tear to shed. Now, when the artful widow saw the King's supplies of grief were all exhausted, she withdrew her veils a little, and the afflicted King refreshed his sight with looking upon the countenance of his companion in despair, who rolled two fine blue eyes, arched with beautiful black eyebrows, and showed also an agreeable countenance. The King viewed her wistfully, and by degrees talked less of his wife, and by-and-bye said no more of her. But the widow continuing to say she would never leave off weeping for her husband, the King desired her not to perpetuate her grief; and, to conclude, all the world was astonished to see them in a few days married together, and the doleful sable changed into green and rose-colour.

Now, this King had only one daughter by his first wife, who was looked upon as the eighth wonder of the world, and, because of her youth, beauty, and blooming complexion, was called Florina. She was never seen to wear rich apparel, rather choosing plain vestments, fastened with a few diamonds, and many flowers, which had an admirable effect when they were placed in her beautiful tresses. She was fifteen years of age when the King married again.

The new Queen sent for her own daughter, who had been bred up with her godmother, the Fairy Soussio; but, for all that, she was neither better in disposition nor more beautiful. Yet, though Soussio's endeavours in her education had failed, she nevertheless loved her dearly. She was called Truitonne, because her face was speckled like the back of a trout; her black hair was so coarse that nobody could touch it, and her tawny skin was quite disgusting. The Queen, too, loved her even to a degree of folly, and talked of nothing but her charming Truitonne. And because Florina had all manner of advantages over her, the Queen grew quite impatient of her, and sought, by every means in her power, to make the King displeased with her. There was not a day passed but the Queen and Truitonne did some injury to Florina; but the Princess, being of a mild and sensible disposition, endeavoured to set herself above these mean artifices of narrow-souled malice.

The King one day said to the Queen, that Florina and Truitonne were old enough to be married, and that he would endeavour to bestow one of them upon the first Prince that came to the Court.

"I expect," replied the Queen, "that my daughter shall be first considered; and, as she is older than yours, and infinitely more amiable, there can be no doubt about it."

The King, who loved peace and quietness, said she was in the right, and that it should be just as she wished.

Some time after, news was brought that The Charming King was coming. Never had any Prince transcended him in gallantry and magnificence, nor was there anything in his mind or person but what was perfectly answerable to his name. When the Queen heard the news, she set all her embroiderers, milliners, and other tire-women at work, to make clothes for Truitonne; she also begged the King not to let Florina have anything new; and having bribed her women, she caused all her apparel, jewels, and ornaments of every kind, to be stolen the very day The Charming King arrived, so that when Florina went to dress herself, she could not find so much as a ribbon. She was at no loss to imagine who had done her this good office; so she sent to the shops for more silk, but the mercers sent her word the Queen had forbidden them to sell her any. So she was forced to content herself with an ordinary gown, which made her so ashamed, that she placed herself in a corner of the room when The Charming King appeared.

The Queen received him with all the ceremony imaginable; she presented him her daughter, more glittering than the sun, yet more conspicuously deformed in those splendid trappings than usually she seemed to be. The King turned away his eyes, and would not even look upon her; though the Queen flattered herself that she pleased him exceedingly, only that he was afraid of being engaged too suddenly; so she continued to place her in his way. But instead of courting Truitonne, he asked whether there were not yet another Princess, called Florina.

"Yes," said Truitonne, pointing to her with her finger; "there she is, hiding herself in a corner, because she truly thinks she is not dressed fine enough to show herself."

Florina blushed, and looked so lovely, that The Charming King, in raptures at the sight of her, immediately rose and made her a profound reverence. "Madam," said he, "you are too well adorned by your incomparable beauty, to have occasion for any foreign garments."

"Sir," replied she, "I am not accustomed to be addressed in this manner, and you would have done me a favour not to have taken notice of me."

"It would have been impossible," cried The Charming King, "that so wonderful a Princess should have been in any place where admiration and respect could have eyes for any other object."

"Oh, Sir," said the Queen, in a passion, "I come not hither to hear all this extravagance. Believe me, Sir, Florina is coquette enough already. She has no occasion to be thus gallantly addressed."

The Charming King immediately perceived the motives which made the Queen talk in this manner; but as neither his rank nor inclination inclined him to put any constraint upon himself, he continued to show his admiration of Florina, and discoursed with her nearly three hours.

The Queen, in rage and despair, and Truitonne, no less inconsolable, to see the Princess preferred before her, made loud complaints to the King, and forced him to consent, that while The Charming King stayed, Florina should be confined in a tower, where nobody could see her. Accordingly, as she was entering her apartment, four men in masks seized and carried her to the top of the tower, where they left her in solitude and darkness, and overwhelmed with sorrow; for she well knew she was used thus only to prevent her being seen by The Charming King, for whom she had already conceived an affection, and would gladly have married him.

The Charming King was ignorant of the violence done to the Princess, and waited with impatience to see her again; he talked of her to those whom the King had sent to wait upon him, but they had orders from the Queen to speak all the ill they could imagine of her. They told him she was a coquette, vain, inconstant, and ill-tempered; that she tormented her friends and servants, and was so covetous, that she rather chose to appear like a poor shepherdess, than lay out the money which her father allowed her to buy rich habits.

The Charming King gave a hearing to all this, but was so provoked that he could hardly contain his anger. "No," said he to himself, "it is impossible that Heaven can have placed so bad a mind in a form so wonderfully beautiful. She was, indeed, not properly dressed when I saw her; but her blushes on that account plainly proved she was not accustomed to it. What! can she be ill-natured, with that enchanting air of modesty and sweetness? No; I rather believe it is the Queen who thus defames her, in order to recommend her own daughter, Truitonne, who is too deformed and disagreeable for any one to have a personal regard for her."

While he was thus reasoning with himself, the courtiers who surrounded him divined by his countenance that they had not pleased him by speaking ill of Florina. But there was one among them more adroit and cunning than the others, who, changing his tone and his language, on purpose to sound the Prince's sentiments, began to speak highly in praise the Princess. Upon which, The Charming King, starting like a man suddenly wakened out of a profound sleep, joined the conversation, joy diffused itself over his countenance, and he appeared quite another man. O Love! how difficult is it to conceal thee! When a man is in love, everything betrays the sentiments of his heart.

The Queen, impatient to know The Charming King's sentiments, sent for her confidants, and put questions to them; but their answers only confirmed her fears that he was in love with Florina.

In the meantime, in what a condition was the poor Princess! She lay all night upon the bare ground of that dismal dungeon into which the four men in masks had carried her. "I should have had less reason to complain," said she, "had they confined me here before I had seen this amiable King; for now the idea of his perfections, which is so deeply implanted in my mind, only serves to augment my sufferings. I doubt not but the Queen thus cruelly exerts her tyranny over me, to prevent my ever seeing him again. Alas! that little beauty which Heaven has bestowed, how dear will it cost me! how fatal will it be to my repose!" Saying this, she wept so bitterly, that even her enemies, had they been witnesses of her afflictions, must have pitied her.

Thus passed away that night; and the Queen, who was desirous to engage The Charming King, by all the demonstrations she could possibly give him of her regard, sent him garments made after the fashion of the country, of inimitable richness and magnificence, together with the Order of the Knights of Love, which she had obliged the King to institute upon the day of their nuptials. The ensign of this Order was a heart of gold enamelled with flame colour, encompassed with several arrows, and pierced through with one, with this device, "One, only, wounds me." The Queen had caused a ruby, as big as an ostrich's egg, to be cut into the shape of a heart; every arrow was an entire diamond as long as your finger; and the chain which held the heart was made of pearls, the least of which weighed a pound. In short, the like was never seen since the world was a world.

The Charming King was so surprised at the sight of it, that for some time he could not speak a word. At the same time, they also presented him a book, the leaves of which were of vellum embellished with admirable miniatures, the cover of gold set with precious stones. In this book, in the most tender and polite style, were curiously written the statutes of the Order of Love. The Charming King was told, that the Princess whom he had seen requested him to be her knight, and had sent him that present.

"How!" cried he, "does the fair Princess Florina think upon me in such a generous and obliging manner!"

"No, Sir," said the messengers, "you mistake the name; we come from the amiable Truitonne."

"Is it Truitonne that would have me be her knight?" said the King, with a cold and serious air; "I am sorry I cannot accept the honour. A sovereign is not so much master of himself as to undertake all engagements that are offered him. I know the duties of a knight, and what I undertake I would fulfil. I had rather not receive the favour she offers me, than render myself unworthy of it."

Saying this, he immediately replaced the heart, the chain, and the book, in the same manner they were brought, and sent all back again to the Queen, who, together with her daughter, were ready to burst with rage at the contempt with which The Charming King had received so particular a favour.

So soon as he could go to wait upon the King and Queen, he repaired to the Court, in hopes to see Florina there; he looked round him every way, and when anybody entered the apartment, immediately turned his head towards the door, in visible anxiety. The malicious Queen easily perceived what passed in his mind; but seeming to take no notice of it, she talked to him of nothing but parties of pleasure, to all which he constantly gave wrong answers; and at length asked her in downright terms where the Princess Florina was.

"Sir," said she, with the fierceness of a tigress, "the King her father has forbid her to stir out of her chamber, till my daughter is married."

"And what reason," replied The Charming King, "is there for keeping this amiable lady prisoner?"

"I know not," answered the Queen; "or if I did, I should not make you acquainted with it."

The King was highly incensed at this reply; he looked upon Truitonne with an eye of contempt, imagining that it was for the sake of that lump of deformity that he was deprived of the pleasure of seeing the Princess, and quitted the Queen in a surly haste, not enduring the sight of persons who were the cause of his anguish.

When he was returned to his apartment, he told a young Prince who accompanied him, and for whom he had a very great regard, that he would give the world to gain one of the Princess's women, whereby he might have a moment's conversation with her. The Prince soon found ladies who engaged to gain him what he wished; and one of them assured him that Florina should be at a little window that looked into the garden, where they might converse together, provided he was cautious to prevent their being discovered; "For," added she, "the King and Queen are so severe, that they would put me to death, were they to know that I favoured The Charming King's passion." The Prince, overjoyed to have brought the affair to such perfection, promised her whatever she desired, and flew to acquaint The Charming King with the hour of rendezvous. But the treacherous confidant went and informed the Queen of all that had passed between the Prince and her. The Queen immediately resolved to send her own daughter to the window; for which purpose she gave her such proper instructions, that Truitonne failed in nothing, though she was naturally a great fool.

The night was so dark, that The Charming King could never have perceived the trick put upon him, even had he been less prepossessed than he was; so that he approached the window with inexpressible transports of joy, and said everything to Truitonne that he would have said to Florina, to convince her of his regard for her. Truitonne, to carry on the deceit, told him she was the most unfortunate person in the world to have so cruel a stepmother; but that she must be contented to suffer until her daughter was married. The Charming King assured her, that if she would accept him for a husband, it would give him the highest pleasure to share with her both his crown and his heart. Saying this, he pulled his ring from his finger, and put it upon Truitonne's, adding, it was an eternal pledge of his faith, and that she need only to make her escape as soon as she could. Truitonne answered his importunities as well as she could; and the King did not leave her till she had promised to meet him the next day at the same place.

The Queen being informed of the good success of this interview, assured herself of a happy conclusion. In short, the day being fixed, The Charming King came in a flying chaise, drawn by winged frogs, of which an Enchanter, a friend of his, had made him a present. The night was very dark; Truitonne came out softly through a little door, and the King, who waited for her, receiving her in his arms, renewed his vows of eternal fidelity; and, as he was not disposed to fly far in his chaise before they were married, he asked where she would have the ceremony performed. She answered, that her godmother, a celebrated Fairy, named Soussio, lived not far off, and that if he thought fit, she would go to her castle. Though the King knew not the way, he had only to tell his frogs to carry him thither, for they were acquainted with the whole world, and in a short time brought the King and Truitonne to Soussio's residence.

The Castle was so brightly illuminated, that The Charming King would soon have discovered his error, if Truitonne had not been very careful to keep her veil over her face. She asked for her godmother, spoke to her apart, told her how she had deceived The Charming King, and begged of her to appease him.

"Alas, child!" said the Fairy, "this will not be easy to do; he loves Florina too well; and I am but too certain he will soon destroy all our hopes."

All this while The Charming King stayed in a room, the walls of which were of diamonds, so clear and transparent that he saw through them Soussio and Truitonne consulting together. He thought himself in a dream. "How," said he, "have I been betrayed? Have the Demons brought this enemy of our repose hither? Comes she to disturb our nuptials? But where is my dear Florina, that she appears not? Surely I brought her along with me, for nobody took her from me by the way."

Thus a thousand different imaginations distracted his senses. But it was still worse; Soussio and Truitonne entered the room together, and Soussio, with an imperious tone, said, "Charming King, here is the Princess to whom you have plighted your faith. She is my goddaughter, and I desire you would marry her immediately."

"Who, I?" cried The Charming King, "I marry that monster! Surely, you must think I am very easy to persuade, or you would not make me such a proposal. No, no, I never made her any promise; and if she says the contrary, she——"

"Hold!" cried Soussio, interrupting him, "and be not so remiss in the respect you owe."

"I respect you," replied The Charming King, "as much as a Fairy ought to be respected, provided you restore me my Princess."

"Why, am not I your Princess, perjured Prince?" cried Truitonne, showing him his ring. "To whom didst thou give this jewel for a pledge of thy faith? To whom didst thou vow and protest at the little window, if it was not to me?"

"How!" replied he, "I have been cheated and deceived, then! No, no, I will not be your dupe, however. Come, my pretty frogs, let us be gone; I will not stay a minute longer here."

"Hold!" cried Soussio, "that is not in your power, unless I consent." With that she touched him, and his feet became fastened to the floor.

"Though you turn me into stone," said The Charming King, "though you flay me alive, Florina only shall have my heart; I will be hers, and only hers; this is my resolution, and you may use your power as you please."

Soussio employed gentle persuasions, menaces, promises, prayers; and Truitonne wept, cried, sighed, sobbed—sometimes was enraged, and then became calm again; during all which, the King said not a word, but, looking upon both with an air of indignation and contempt, he gave no answer to anything they said.

Twenty days and twenty nights passed in this manner, during which time they never ceased talking, nor ever eat, drank, slept, or sat down the whole time. At length, Soussio, being quite tired, said to the King, "Well, I see you are resolved not to hear reason; and therefore choose you, either to undergo seven years' penance for breaking your plighted faith, or else to marry my goddaughter."

The King, who had hitherto kept a profound silence, cried out of a sudden, "Do with me what you please, so I am but delivered from this ugly beast!"

"No more a beast than yourself," cried Truitonne, in a passion. "You are a pretty gentleman, indeed, with your croaking equipage, to come into my country to abuse me, and break your word! If you had a grain of honour in you, you would behave in a different manner."

"Oh, these are killing reproaches, indeed!" replied the King, laughing; "who would not be glad of such a lovely person for a wife?"

"'Tis very well," cried Soussio, in a rage, "and therefore you shall not have her. You may fly out of the window, if you please, for you shall be a Blue Bird for seven years to come."

The shape of the King's body instantly began to change; his arms were covered with feathers, and transformed into wings; his legs and feet became black and slender, with little claws instead of toes; his body lessened to the size of a dove, adorned with fine smooth feathers of a bright sky blue; his eyes grew round, quick, and sparkling, like two stars; his nose was changed to an ivory beak; and from his head rose up a white tuft, in the form of a crown. He sang to admiration, and had the use of speech also.

this condition, he fetched a deep sigh, to see himf so metamorphosed, and, spreading his wings, flew m Soussio's fatal Palace.

Thus overwhelmed with melancholy, he hopped m bough to bough, and made choice only of those es which were consecrated either to love or sadness, metimes upon myrtles, sometimes upon cypress; he g none but mournful airs, wherein he deplored his n and his Florina's misfortune. "Where," said he, ave her malicious enemies concealed her? What become of the fair victim? Where shall I find her ? Does the barbarous Queen yet suffer her to athe? Where shall I seek her? Am I condemned waste away seven whole years without her? Pers in this time they will marry her, and I shall for r lose the hope which keeps me alive." These ious thoughts afflicted the poor Blue Bird to such a ree, that he wished himself dead.

On the other side, the Fairy Soussio sent Truitonne k to the Queen, who laboured under great impace to know how the nuptials were concluded. But en she saw her daughter, and had received from a full relation of what had happened, she fell into iolent rage, the dire effects of which fell all upon poor Florina. "I'll make her dearly repent," said "her having pleased The Charming King."

Saying this, she immediately ascended the tower h Truitonne, whom she had dressed in her richest its. Truitonne wore a crown of diamonds upon head, and three daughters of the greatest Lords in kingdom bore up the train of her Royal mantle. e had also upon her finger The Charming Prince's , which Florina had observed upon his finger when y discoursed together. And this, together with itonne's pompous dress, surprised her extremely. Here is my daughter come," said the Queen, "to g you her nuptial presents; The Charming King married her, and loves her to distraction; never, eed, were any pair better satisfied."

Immediately they spread before the Princess several ffs of gold and silver, precious stones, laces, ribbons, in large baskets of filigree-work in gold; and as y delivered these presents, Truitonne took care to ke The Charming King's ring sparkle with its atest lustre; so that Florina, no longer questioning truth of her misfortune, with an air of the utmost ef and despair desired them to take the fatal prets from her sight; saying she should never desire wear anything but black for the future, but that should rather wish to have a speedy death. Saythis, she fell into a swoon; and the cruel Queen, rjoyed at the success of her deceit, would not suffer one to help her, but left her alone in that derable condition, and went with a malicious tale to King, that his daughter was so transported with derness, that nothing could equal her extravagances, that it behoved him to take care how he let her out of the tower. To which the King answered, t she might do what she pleased; and that he uld always be satisfied with whatever she did. When the Princess came to herself, and considered barbarously she was used by her unworthy stepther, and that all hopes of ever marrying The

Charming King were entirely vanished, her grief became so violent, that she wept all night; and in this condition went to the window, where she vented her sorrows in tender and moving lamentations till day began to approach, and then, shutting the window, she renewed her sorrows.

The night following she opened the window, and vented the deepest sighs and sobs, shed a torrent of tears, and when day appeared concealed herself in her chamber as before. In the meantime, The Charming King—or to speak more properly, the Charming Blue Bird—ceased not to hover about the Palace, believing that his beloved Princess must be shut up in it; and if she made such sad complaints, his were no less deplorable. He got as close to the windows as he could, that he might look into the chambers; but his fears lest Truitonne should perceive him, and imagine it was he, hindered him from doing what he would. "It is as much as my life is worth," said he to himself; "for if these wicked Princesses should discover where I am, they would certainly be revenged upon me. I must either keep at a distance, or expose myself to imminent dangers." These reasons obliged the Blue Bird to be very cautious; and he seldom sang but in the night time.

Opposite the window where Florina placed herself, there grew a cypress tree of a prodigious height, in which the Blue Bird came and perched; but had scarce settled on it, when he heard the complaints of somebody in deep distress.

"And must I long be a sufferer?" said she; "and will death always refuse to come to my relief? They who fear it, meet it but too soon; I desire it, but it cruelly flies me. Ah, barbarous, inexorable Queen! how have I offended you, that thus you detain me in this horrid captivity? Have you not other means enough to afflict me? You need only make me a witness of your unworthy daughter's happiness with The Charming King."

The Blue Bird lost not a tittle of this complaint; he was strangely surprised at it, and waited impatiently for day, that he might have a sight of the afflicted lady; but before he could see her, she had shut the window and was retired.

The inquisitive Bird failed not to return the next night; the moon shone clear, and he saw a lady at the window of the tower, who renewed her lamentations.

"Fortune," said she, "thou that once didst flatter me with the hopes of a kingdom, thou that madest me the joy of my father, what have I done, that thou shouldst plunge me thus into an abyss of sorrow and affliction? Must I, at an age so tender as mine, begin to feel the violent effects of thy inconstancy? Oh, barbarous Fortune! relent, relent, if it be possible; I request no other favour from thee, but a period to my misfortunes."

The Blue Bird attentively listened to all this; and the more he listened, the more he was convinced it was his lovely Princess who made these complaints. "Adorable Florina," said he, "the wonder of our days! why would you so soon cut the thread of your own life? Your misfortunes are not without remedy."

135

"Oh! who's that speaks," cried she, "such words of consolation to a grieved soul?"

"An unfortunate King," replied the Bird, "who loves you, and will never love any other."

"A King that loves me!" added she; "what artifice is this my persecuting enemy is now contriving to ensnare me with? But what will she get by it? If she seeks to discover my thoughts, I am ready to confess to her."

"No, Princess, no!" replied the Blue Bird; "the lover that speaks to you is not capable of treachery." And so saying, he flew to the window. Florina, at first, was afraid of a Bird so extraordinary, that spoke with as much wit as if he had been a man, though with the voice of a nightingale; but the beauty of his feathers, and what he spake, dissipated her fears.

"Am I permitted to see you once again, dear Princess?" cried the Bird; "can I taste a happiness so perfect, and not die for joy? But, alas! how is this joy disturbed by your captivity, and the condition to which the wicked Soussio has reduced me for seven years!"

"And who are you, my Charming Bird?" replied the Princess, caressing and stroking him.

"You have repeated my name," added the King, "and yet you feign as if you did not know me."

"How!" said the Princess; "is it possible that the greatest King in the world—The Charming King—should be that little Bird which I hold in my hand?"

"Alas! fair Florina, 'tis too true," replied the Bird; "and if there be anything that can give me comfort, it is that I endure this punishment rather than renounce my passion for you."

"For me!" said Florina; "oh, seek not to deceive me! I know, I know too well, that you are married to Truitonne. I saw your ring upon her finger; I saw her quite brilliant with the lustre of those diamonds which you gave her. She came to insult me in my sad imprisonment, with a sumptuous crown upon her head, and a Royal mantle, which you had given her."

"Did you behold Truitonne in such an equipage?" said the King; "did the mother and the daughter dare to say those jewels came from me? O Heavens! is it possible for me to hear such horrid falsehoods, yet not be able to show my revenge? Know, then, they contrived to deceive me by counterfeiting your person, and engaged me to carry off the deformed Truitonne instead of you; but as soon as I perceived my error, I abandoned her, and rather chose to be a Blue Bird for seven years together, than fail in my fidelity to fair Florina."

The pleasure which Florina took to hear her royal lover talk in this manner was so great, that she no longer remembered the misery of her imprisonment. She omitted nothing that wit could invent to comfort him for the misfortune of his transformation, and to convince him that she would do as much for him as he had done for her. But by this time day appeared, and the greatest part of the officers about the Court were stirring, so that they were forced to part, though with the greatest unwillingness, after having promised thus to entertain each other every night.

They were so overjoyed that they had found each

136

other, that it is hardly in the power of words to express it. Nevertheless, Florina was in great trouble every day for the Blue Bird. "Who shall secure him," said she, "from the busy fowlers, or from the claws of some half-famished vulture or eagle, who will make no more of devouring him than if he were a common bird? O Heavens! what would become of me, if once these light and delicate feathers, driven by the wind, should reach my window, the unhappy messengers of the disaster which I fear!"

This very thought would not suffer the Princess to close her eyes; for when people truly love, illusions seem to be real truths, and what we would have thought impossible at another time, appears to be easy then; so that she spent the day in tears, till the hour was come that called her to the window.

The Charming Bird, hid in the hollow tree, had spent the day in thinking upon his lovely Princess. "How happy," said he, "am I, that I have found her; how engaging, how endearing is she! how deeply sensible am I of her goodness!" And then reflecting upon the tedious hours of his penance, that hindered him from marrying, he relapsed into his melancholy, looking upon every minute to be no less than the tedious delay of a thousand years. Nevertheless, he resolved to show Florina all the gallantry in his power, he flew to the capital city of his kingdom, went directly to his Palace, and getting into his cabinet through a hole in the glass that was broken, took from thence a pair of diamond pendants, so perfect and so beautiful as not to be paralleled in all the world, and brought them to Florina, desiring her to wear them for his sake.

"I would consent," said she, "were you to see me in the day; but since we can only talk together in the dark, it will be to no purpose."

The Blue Bird promised to watch his opportunity so well, that he would come to the tower at whatever hour she pleased. She then put on her pendants, and they passed the night in sweet conversation, as they had done the former.

The next day, the Blue Bird flew again to his kingdom, went to his Palace, and entering his cabinet, brought away the richest bracelets that ever were seen; they were made of one entire emerald, cut into focets, and hollowed through the middle for the hand and arm to pass.

"Think you," said the Princess, "that my sentiments for you have any need of being improved by presents? Alas! you are but ill acquainted with them."

"No, Madam," replied the Blue Bird, "I do not imagine the trifles which I offer you are necessary for the preservation of your tenderness; but I should injure my own affection did I neglect any opportunity of demonstrating my desire to serve you; and when I am absent from your sight, these trifles will recall me to your remembrance."

Florina hereupon said a thousand obliging things to him, which he answered by a thousand others.

When day appeared, the Blue Bird returned to his hollow tree, where he lived upon the fruits and berries of the neighbouring groves. There sometimes he warbled his melodious notes so charming to the ear

THE CHARMING KING CARRIES OFF THE UGLY PRINCESS, BY MISTAKE FOR THE FAIR FLORINA, IN HIS CAR DRAWN BY WINGED FROGS.

of all that passed that way, that they stood still to hearken, more astonished when they looked about and could not see from whence the melody could come; which made them conclude that the groves were frequented by spirits. This opinion became so generally believed, that nobody durst frequent the wood, and a thousand fabulous stories were spread abroad of strange things seen there; so that the general terror caused the particular safety of the Blue Bird.

Not a day passed but he made some present to Florina; sometimes a necklace of pearl, sometimes jewels the most brilliant and curiously set; diamond clasps, bodkins, posies of diamonds in imitation of all the colours of flowers, delightful books, medals. In a word, she abounded in treasures, but never adorned herself with them but in the night, to please The Charming King; in the day-time, having no other place to put them, she hid them carefully under her straw.

Two years thus slipped away, during which Florina never complained of her captivity. And, indeed, what reason had she to complain? She had the satisfaction every night to converse with him she loved, nor was there ever more agreeable discourse between two lovers.

In the meanwhile, the malicious Queen, who so barbarously detained her in prison, used many fruitless endeavours to marry Truitonne; she sent ambassadors to propose her to all the Princes whose names she did but know; but when they arrived, and proposed Truitonne, they were immediately dismissed. "But," said they, "if you had come to offer the Princess Florina, you would have been joyfully received. As for Truitonne, she may live a vestal, for nobody will disturb her."

These answers transported the mother and daughter with implacable fury against the innocent Princess whom they persecuted. "How," said they, "notwithstanding her close imprisonment, shall this arrogant still conspire against us? She must certainly hold correspondence in foreign countries; she is at least a state criminal, and must be treated as such; therefore let us find means to convict her."

They broke up their council so late, that it was after midnight when they resolved to go to the tower to examine her. She was then at the window with the Blue Bird, adorned with all her jewels, and her lovely hair dressed with that care and exactness which is not usual with persons in affliction; her chamber and her bed were strewed with flowers, and certain Spanish perfumes, which she had just burnt, spread a fragrant odour round the room. The Queen, listening at the door, heard a duet sung, for Florina had a heavenly voice; she cried out, "We are betrayed, my dear Truitonne, we are betrayed!" and opening the door in a hasty fury, how was Florina amazed at the sight of her! She immediately opened the little casement to let her Royal Bird escape, being more concerned for his preservation than her own, but he had not power to fly away; his piercing eyes perceived the danger to which the Princess was exposed; he saw the Queen and Truitonne, and how great was his affliction not to be in a condition to defend her! They accosted her like furies that were ready to devour her.

"We know your intrigues and combinations against the state," cried the Queen; "think you that your rank shall save you from deserved punishment?"

"With whom do I conspire, I beseech you, Madam?" replied the Princess. "Have not you been my guardian these two years? Have I seen any other persons than those you sent me?"

Whilst she was speaking, the Queen and her daughter surveyed her with astonishment; for her beauty and extraordinary dress quite dazzled their eyes.

"And where, I pray you, Madam, did you get these glittering jewels, which excel the sun in splendour? Will you make us believe, too, that there are mines in this tower?"

"I found them here," replied the Princess; "that is all I can tell you about them."

The Queen looked wistfully upon her, to penetrate, if possible, the bottom of her heart.

"No, mistress, no, we are not your dupes: you hope to make us believe this; but, Princess, we are acquainted with what you do from morning till night. All these jewels are given you with a design to make you sell your father's kingdom."

"I am in a very fit condition to deliver it," answered Florina, with a disdainful smile; "a poor unfortunate Princess, that has lain for these two years languishing in captivity, is able to do much in a conspiracy of this nature!"

"For whose sake, then," replied the Queen, "is your chamber so scented with rich perfumes, and your person so magnificently dressed, that in the midst of the Court you would not have appeared so splendid?"

"Oh!" said the Princess, "you allow me leisure enough; 'tis no wonder, then, that I should amuse myself sometimes in dressing, for I spend so many hours in bewailing my misfortunes, that these few moments may not be envied me."

"Come, come," said the Queen, "let us see whether this pretty innocent has not some treaty on foot with the enemy."

She sought all about, and coming to the straw, caused it to be removed, and found under it such an amazing quantity of diamonds, pearls, rubies, emeralds, and topazes, that she could not conceive how it was possible they could come there. She resolved to drop papers in a certain part of the room, the contents of which might serve for an accusation against the Princess, and when she thought herself unobserved, she accordingly hid some in the chimney; but, luckily, the Blue Bird was perched on the top of it, whose eyes were more piercing than those of a lynx, and who heard all that passed. He immediately cried out, "Florina, beware! your enemy is laying snares for your ruin!"

This unexpected voice so amazed the Queen, that she dared not proceed in her purpose.

"You see, Madam," said the Princess, "that even the Spirits that fly in the air are favourable to me."

"I believe," cried the Queen, in a violent rage, "that the Demons themselves assist you; but in despite of all your magical artifices, your father knows how to do himself justice."

"I wish, indeed," cried Florina, "I had nothing else to fear but my father's anger."

The Queen left her, not a little troubled at what she had seen and heard. She held a council to consult what was to be done with the Princess. They told her, that if any Fairy or Enchanter took her into their protection, the true way to provoke them would be to load her with new afflictions; and that it would be best to attempt a discovery of her intrigue. The Queen approved this advice, and sent a young maid to lie in her chamber, with proper instructions, and to say, that she was sent to serve her. But the scheme was too gross to succeed; the Princess looked upon the maid as a spy, and thought a greater misfortune could not have befallen her: "What," said she, "must I no longer converse with my Charming Blue Bird, that is so dear to me? His company made my misfortunes easy, and soothed his afflictions. What will become of him? What will, indeed, become of me ?" These considerations drew from her a flood of tears.

She durst not now appear at the little window, though she heard the Blue Bird flutter about it; she had a longing desire to open it, but she was afraid of endangering his life. Thus she spent a whole month, which made the Blue Bird almost desperate. What complaints did he not make? He was quite in despair, and almost grieved himself to death.

At length, the Princess's spy, who had watched day and night for a whole month together, was so overcome with drowsiness, that she fell into a profound sleep, which Florina perceiving, opened the window, and sang—

"Gentle Blue Bird, fly to me,
And bless me with thy company."

The Blue Bird understood her meaning so well, that he came directly to the window. What joy was there, to see each other again! what tenderness, and what protestations of fidelity were renewed a thousand times over! The Princess not being able to refrain from tears, the Bird sympathized with her, and endeavoured to comfort her the best he could. At length, the hour of separation being come, before the jailor waked, they bid each other adieu in the most moving manner.

The next night, the spy slept as before, and the Princess, not negligent, opened the window, and sang the same little verse again.

The Bird appeared, and the night was spent without hurry or noise, to the great satisfaction of both; and they flattered themselves that their sentinel would take so much pleasure in sleeping, that she would do the same every night. The third night passed without the least disturbance; but the following night, the sleeper having heard a noise, listened without appearing to be awake. At length, she looked about her as well as she could, and by the light of the moon she saw the most beautiful Bird in the world, which talked to the Princess, and caressed her with his ivory bill and little feet. In a word, she heard a great part of their conversation, whereat she was greatly astonished.

The day appeared, and they took their leaves with an ominous foreboding of their approaching misfortune; they bid adieu with more than ordinary affliction. The Princess threw herself upon the bed, all bathed in tears, and the Royal Bird returned to his hollow tree. Her jailor ran to the Queen, and gave her an exact account of all that she had seen and heard. The Queen sent for Truitonne and her confidants, and having consulted with them a long time, they concluded that the Blue Bird must be The Charming King.

"What an affront is this, my dear Truitonne!" cried the Queen; "this insolent Princess, whom I thought in such affliction, enjoys in full repose the pleasing conversation of our ungrateful Prince. But I will be revenged in so bloody a manner, as shall make it the discourse of the world." Truitonne besought her not to lose a minute; and as she thought herself more concerned in the affair than the Queen, she was ready to die for joy at the thoughts of the sufferings preparing for the lover and his mistress.

The Queen sent back her spy to the tower, with strict command not to show the least suspicion or curiosity, but to seem more sleepy than before. She went early to bed, snored aloud, and the poor deceived Princess, opening the window, sang as usual.

But she called him all night in vain, for no Blue Bird appeared. The wicked Queen had caused the cypress tree to be stuck with swords, knives, and daggers, so that when he came flying into it, these murderous weapons cut his feet, and falling from thence upon others, they cut his wings; so that at last, being wounded all over, he made shift to get to his hollow tree, to which you might trace him by his blood.

Why were you not there, fair Florina, to succour the Royal Bird? But, alas! you would have died had you been witness of his deplorable condition. Yet, believing she was accessary to his disaster, he refused to take any care of his life. "Ah! barbarous Princess," cried he, with a desponding voice, "is it thus thou repayest the most sincere and tender passion that ever harboured in a lover's breast? If thou didst desire my death, why didst thou not demand it of me thyself? I would have rejoiced to receive it from thy hand! I came to thee with so much love and confidence; suffered, too, for thy sake, and suffered without complaining; and for this thou hast sacrificed me to the most cruel of women! She was our common enemy, but thou hast made thy peace with her at the expense of my blood. 'Tis thou, Florina—'tis thou that hast stabbed me; thou hast borrowed Truitonne's hand, and directed it to my heart!" These dismal ideas so overpowered him, that he resolved to die.

But the Enchanter, his friend, who had seen the Winged Frogs return home again with the chariot, but without the King, was so troubled to know what was become of him, that he went eight times round the world in search of him, but in vain. He was making the ninth tour, when he passed through the wood where he was, and, according to the rules which he had prescribed to himself, he sounded his horn, and cried out five times with a loud voice, "Charming King, where are you?" The King knew the voice of his best friend, and immediately cried, "Come hither to this tree, and behold the unfortunate Prince whom you seek, weltering in his blood." The Enchanter looked about him on every side in great surprise, but could see nothing.

"I am become a Blue Bird," said the King, with a feeble and languishing voice. At these words, the Enchanter found him without much trouble, in his little nest. Any other person would have been more astonished than he was; but being versed in all the arts of necromancy, it cost him only a few words to stop the King's bleeding; and by the help of certain herbs which he found in the wood, over which he pronounced two or three powerful charms, he cured the King as effectually as if he had never been wounded.

After this, the Enchanter desired the King to let him know by what accident he became a Bird, and who had wounded him so cruelly. The King satisfied his curiosity, and told him farther, that it was Florina who had revealed the mystery of the secret visits which he had paid her; and that to make her peace with the Queen, she had suffered the cypress tree to be stuck with knives, daggers, and swords, by which he had been

139

almost cut to pieces; exclaiming, at the same time, against the Princess's infidelity, and wishing he had been so happy as to have died before he discovered her treacherous heart. The Enchanter was enraged against her and the whole sex, and advised the King to forget her. "How terrible would your misfortunes be," said the Enchanter, "should you continue to love this ungrateful woman! After what she has done to you, what is there you have not to fear from her?" But the Blue Bird could not comply with his advice; he still loved Florina too dearly.

The Royal Bird desired his friend to carry him home to his house, and put him in a cage, where he might be secure from the claws of a cat, and all other enemies.

"But," said the Enchanter, "will you linger out five years longer in this deplorable condition, so prejudicial to your affairs, and so unsuitable to your dignity? For, in short, your enemies give out that you are dead, and are preparing to seize upon your throne, and I am afraid you will lose your kingdom before you can recover your form."

"Is it not possible," said he, "for me to return to my Palace, and govern my kingdom, as I was wont to do?"

"Oh!" cried the Enchanter, "the case is quite different. They who will obey a man, will not obey a Parrot; and they who feared you when you were a King, surrounded with pomp and grandeur, will pluck your feathers from your back, when they see you are only a little Bird."

"Alas! how great is human weakness!" cried the King, "that a gaudy outside, though it is nothing in comparison with merit and virtue, should yet become so necessary as not to be dispensed with! Well, then," continued he, "let us be philosophers, and despise what is not in our power to obtain; our condition will not be the worst of all others."

"Hold!" said the Necromancer, "I am not so soon discouraged. I have hopes of being able to discover some expedient."

In the meantime, Florina, the disconsolate Florina, grown desperate at no longer seeing the King, watched day and night at the window, incessantly singing and repeating the usual words.

The presence of her spy no longer laid her under a restraint, for her despair was such that she cared not what she did. "What is become of you, Charming King?" cried she; "have our common enemies made you feel the cruel effects of their rage? Are you fallen a sacrifice to their inexorable fury? O Heavens! art thou then dead, and must I never see thee more? Or, tired with my misfortunes, hast thou abandoned me to the severity of my fate?" Tears and the most bitter lamentations accompanied these sorrowful complainings. She became quite dejected, ill, and altered in her countenance, so that she could scarcely support herself, being persuaded some fatal accident had befallen The Charming King.

The Queen and Truitonne triumphed: revenge gave them greater pleasure than the offence had given them pain; and this, because the King had refused to marry a monster, whom he had a thousand reasons to hate.

But now the father of Florina, who was grown old, fell sick, and died, and his death brought a change in the fortune of the Queen and Truitonne, who were looked upon as favourites who had abused their power; and the people ran with violence to the Palace, demanding Florina, and acknowledging her for their Sovereign. The Queen Dowager at first thought to carry things with a high hand, and appearing in a balcony, began to threaten the people; but the insurrection becoming general, they broke open the doors of her apartment, plundered it, and stoned her to death. Truitonne, who narrowly escaped their fury, fled to her godmother, the Fairy Soussio.

The grandees of the kingdom assembled immediately, and went to the tower where the Princess lay sick. She was ignorant of her father's death, and the punishment of her mortal enemy; so that when she heard so much noise, she was in hopes they were come to put her to death, for life was become hateful to her, since the loss of her Blue Bird. But her subjects, throwing themselves at her feet, soon gave her to understand the change of her fortune; yet it made no alteration in her countenance or behaviour. However, they carried her to her Palace, and there crowned her. The infinite care that was taken of her health, and her own eager desire to go in search of her Blue Bird, extremely contributed to her recovery, and soon gave her strength to appoint a council that might take care of her kingdom in her absence; which done, she took a vast treasure of jewels, and one night privately departed by herself, no one knowing whither she went.

In the meantime, the Enchanter who managed The Charming King's affairs, not having sufficient power to destroy what Soussio had done, resolved to go to her, and propose an accommodation, whereby she should restore the King to his natural shape. He took his Winged Frogs, and flew to the Fairy's Castle, who was at that instant talking with Truitonne. Now, you must know, that between a Necromancer and a Fairy there is very little difference. They had been acquainted five or six hundred years, and during that period had been friends and enemies a thousand times. She received him very courteously, and asked him his business. "Is there anything that I can serve you in?" said she.

"Yes," said the Necromancer, "it is in your power to grant me all I desire; and it is for one of my best friends, a King that you have rendered miserable."

"Oh, oh! I understand you," cried Soussio; "I am sorry for it, but there is no favour to be expected in his behalf, unless he marry my goddaughter; here she is, fair and handsome, as you see. Let your friend consider what he should do."

The Necromancer had a mind to say no more, he thought her so ugly; however, he resolved not to leave her till he had done something, because the King had run a thousand risks since his confinement in the cage: for the nail broke, the cage fell down, and his feathered Majesty suffered greatly by the fall; the cat, also, being in the chamber, gave him a scratch with her paw, that had like to have blinded one of his eyes. Another time they forgot to give him water, so that he was within a drop of being choked. Another time, a little unlucky monkey, having broken his chain, caught him by the feathers, through the bars of the cage, and showed him no more mercy than he would a jay or a magpie. But the worst of all was, that his next heirs were just going to seize upon his kingdom, giving out every day new stories of his death, to confirm their title. At last, the Enchanter agreed with Soussio, that she should bring Truitonne to The Charming King's Palace; that she should remain there for some months, in which time the King might be persuaded to marry her; and that she should restore him to his former shape, upon condition that he should be a Blue Bird again if he refused the match.

The Fairy dressed Truitonne most pompously in gold and silver, and taking her behind her upon a Dragon's back, they proceeded to The Charming King's dominions, who had already arrived there with his friend the Enchanter. Soussio, with three strokes of her wand, made the King resume his former shape, and appear as amiable as ever. But he paid dear for the change, as the very thought of marrying Truitonne made him tremble. The Enchanter used the best arguments he could to persuade him, but they made no impression upon him; and he was less employed in the management of public affairs, than in seeking which way to prolong the time which Soussio had allowed him to marry Truitonne.

In the meantime, Queen Florina, disguised like a country girl, in a straw hat, with a bag of linen on her shoulder, began her journey, sometimes on foot, sometimes on horseback, sometimes by sea, sometimes by land, making all the haste she possibly could. But not knowing her way, she was in continual fear, lest she should go one way while her Charming King was going the other. Having one day stopped by the side of a fountain, that washed an infinite number of smooth pebbles as it murmured along, she had a desire to wash her feet. She sat down upon the green turf, and put her feet into the water. At that instant, there appeared a little Old Woman, stooping with age, and leaning upon a great crutch, who making a stop, "What are you doing there, my pretty maid," said she, "thus alone?"

"My good Mother," replied the Queen, "I have, nevertheless, too much company, for I am followed by regret, sorrow, and misfortune." Saying these words, a flood of tears burst from her eyes.

"How! so young, and weep!" said the Good Woman. "Come, come, my child, do not afflict yourself; tell me the cause of your sorrow sincerely, and perhaps I may relieve you."

The Queen gave the Old Woman a full account of everything,—how the Fairy Soussio had dealt with The Charming King, and finally, how she herself was going in quest of the Blue Bird.

The Old Woman, having stroked her arms and her face, all on a sudden appeared handsome, young, and richly habited, and looking upon the Queen with a gracious smile, "Incomparable Florina," said she, "the King whom you seek is now no more a bird; my sister Soussio has restored him to his former shape; he is in his kingdom. Do not afflict yourself; you shall

arrive there, too, and shall succeed in your design. Take these four eggs; break them in your pressing necessities, and you will find in them all you want in your distresses." Saying these words, she vanished.

This unexpected accident afforded not a little consolation to the fair Florina. She put her eggs in her bag, and travelled towards The Charming Prince's kingdom.

After she had travelled eight days and nights without stopping, she arrived at the foot of a prodigious high mountain, all of ivory, and so steep that she could not set her feet upon it. She made a thousand attempts, but in vain, for her feet always slipped; so that at length, quite tired, and despairing to overcome so insurmountable an obstacle, she sat down with the resolution to die upon the spot; but recollecting the eggs which the Fairy had given her, she took out one, and holding it in her hand, "Now," said she, "let us see whether this Fairy was in jest or earnest, when she promised me the assistance I should want."

She had no sooner broken it, but there came out several small golden cramps, which she fastened to her hands and feet, and by the help of them ascended the ivory mountain without any trouble. But when she arrived at the top, she had a new difficulty to descend into the valley, which was one entire looking-glass, two leagues broad, and six in length, and there were above sixty thousand women admiring themselves in it with extreme pleasure, for in this glass every one beheld herself as she wished to be. Red hair appeared white, and brown hair seemed black; the old looked young, the young continued so; in a word, all defects were so well concealed in this mirror, that women came from all parts of the world to view themselves in it. And you would have died with laughter, to behold the grimaces and ridiculous distortions of the greatest part of these coquettes. Nor were the men less numerous, or less pleased, who looked in this glass; for it made some appear with fine heads of hair, and others taller and better shaped, with a martial and majestic mien; the women, whom they laughed at, were not less merry with them. This mountain was called by a thousand different names. No one had ever got to the top of it; so when they saw Florina there, the women screamed out, saying, "No doubt she is able to walk upon our looking-glass, and will break it to pieces as soon as she sets her feet upon it." Saying this, they made a noise ten times louder and more frightful than before.

The Queen knew not what to do, finding the descent exceedingly dangerous; and therefore she broke another egg, out of which there came two pigeons and a chariot, growing immediately big enough to contain her. She placed herself in it, and the pigeons descended gently with her to the bottom of the valley. When she was down, "My pretty little friends," said she, "if you will carry me where The Charming King keeps his court, you will oblige one who will not be ungrateful." The obliging and obedient pigeons never stopped, night nor day, till they arrived at the gates of the city, where Florina alighted, and gave to each a sweet and tender kiss, more inestimable than a crown.

141

How did her heart beat when she entered the city! She daubed her face that she might not be known, and inquired of several that she met where she might see the King: this set many people a-laughing. "See the King!" said they; "why, what wouldst thou have with the King? Go, wash thy face; thy eyes are not clear enough to see such a monarch." The Queen made no reply, but went forward, and asked others whom she met, where she might place herself to see the King. "You may see him to-morrow," said they, "for he will then go to the temple with the Princess Truitonne, whom he has at length consented to marry."

"Heavens!" cried Florina, "what do I hear! Truitonne—the detested Truitonne—on the point of marriage with the King!" She was ready to sink into the earth, and had not strength to speak or walk any more: but at length got under a porch, and seating herself upon the stones, covered with her hair and her straw hat. "Unfortunate that I am," said she; "am I come here to augment the triumph of my rival, and be a witness of her satisfaction? It was for her sake, then, that the Blue Bird ceased seeing me! It was for that little monster that he committed the most cruel of all infidelities: while I, overwhelmed with grief, and restless day and night, disquieted myself with a thousand cares for the preservation of his life! But the traitor had changed his affections, and, minding me no more than if he had never seen me, left me to consume with grief and anguish for his long absence, without in the least regretting mine."

When we are greatly afflicted, we seldom have any appetite: the Queen therefore sought a lodging, and went to her repose without any supper. She arose at break of day, and went to the temple, where she was thrust back a thousand times by the guards and soldiers, before she could get in; but at last, being entered, she beheld two thrones, one for the King, the other for Truitonne, who was already looked upon as Queen. What a killing sight was this for a person so tender and delicate as Florina! She drew near her rival's throne, and stood leaning against a pillar.

The King appeared first, handsomer and more amiable than ever; Truitonne followed him, magnificently arrayed, but so ugly that she was even frightful: and casting a squinting look upon the Queen, "Who art thou," said she, knitting her brows, "that thus presumest to come so near my incomparable person and my throne of gold?"

"I am called Souillon," replied the Queen, "and am come a great way off to sell you certain rarities." Saying this, she took out of her bag the emerald and the bracelets, which The Charming King had given her.

"Ho, ho!" said Truitonne, "these are very pretty things; must I give thee sixpence for them?"

"Show them to those who understand them," said the Queen, "and then we will agree about the price."

Truitonne, who had as much tenderness for the King as such a fool was capable of, being overjoyed at having an opportunity to speak to him, went to his throne and showed him the bracelets, desiring his opinion what they were worth.

142

The King no sooner saw the jewels, but he called to mind the bracelets he had presented to Florina, turned pale, sighed, and was a long time before he could answer. But at last, fearing lest his disorder should be perceived, he made an effort, and replied, "These bracelets, I believe, are worth as much as my kingdom; I thought there had been but one pair in the world, but these are the same with mine."

Truitonne returned to her throne, where she sat with far less grace than an oyster in the shell. She asked the Queen how much she would have, at a word, for her bracelets.

"You will not find it easy, Madam, to pay me what they are worth," said Florina; "but if you will procure me one night's lodging in the Cabinet of Echoes, which is in the King's Palace, I will give you my emeralds."

"Very willingly, Souillon," replied Truitonne, laughing and showing her teeth, which were longer than the tusks of a boar.

The King never informed himself from whence the bracelets came, not so much out of any indifference for her who presented them (though her appearance did not excite curiosity) as from an invincible abhorrence of Truitonne. Now, it is necessary to know, that while he was a Blue Bird he had told the Princess, that under his apartment there was a cabinet called the Cabinet of Echoes, which was so ingeniously contrived, that whatever was but whispered there, the King could hear it as he lay in his chamber; and as Florina was resolved to upbraid him with his infidelity, she could not imagine a better means.

She was shown into this cabinet by Truitonne's order, where she began her complaints and lamentations. "The misfortune which I apprehended is but too certain, cruel Blue Bird," said she; "thou hast forgotten me, and lovest my detested rival. The bracelets which I received from thy disloyal hand could not recall me to thy remembrance, so far am I from thy thoughts." Sighs then interrupted her speech; but when she had power to speak, she renewed her sorrows till break of day. But the groom of the chamber, having heard her sighs and lamentations, acquainted Truitonne with it, who, sending for her, asked her the meaning of it. The Queen replied, that she slept soundly, but frequently dreamed and talked aloud in her sleep. But the King, by a strange fatality, had not heard her, for ever since he had been in love with Florina he could never sleep, so that when he went to his repose he was obliged to take opium.

The Queen passed part of that day in great disquiet. "If he heard me," said she, "can there be more cruel indifference? If he did not hear me, what shall I do to make him? She had no more rarities that were extraordinary, for all diamonds are brilliant, and she wanted something which might flatter the vanity of Truitonne. Her recourse was therefore to her eggs, of which she had no sooner broken the third than there came forth a little coach of polished steel curiously embellished, and inlaid with gold. It was drawn by six green mice, driven by a rat in a rose-coloured livery, and the postilion, who was also of the rat-family, wore a livery of rose-colour and white

There were in the coach four puppets, merrier, more witty and diverting, than any you see at the German Fair; they played a thousand surprising tricks, especially two little gipsies, who in a hornpipe or a minuet would have contended with any of our most celebrated performers.

The Queen was ravished with this new masterpiece of necromantic art, but she said not a word till the evening, which was the time that Truitonne walked abroad to take the air; and she then placed herself in one of the walks, and set her little mice a-galloping with the coach, the rats, and the puppets. This novelty so astonished Truitonne, that she screamed out two or three times, seeing the Queen, "Souillon! Souillon! will you take fivepence for your coach and all that belongs to it?"

"Ask the men of learning, and the doctors of the kingdom, what such a wonder as this may be worth," said Florina, "and I will agree to their valuation."

Truitonne, who was impatient in everything, replied, "Well, not to be troubled any longer with thy nasty company, tell me thy lowest price."

"Well, then," said the Queen, "let me pass one night more in the Cabinet of Echoes, that is all I demand."

"Pr'ythee go, poor fool," cried Truitonne, "thou art very much in love, I find, with the Cabinet of Echoes." Then turning about to her women, "Is not this a great fool," cried she, "to part with these great curiosities for nothing?"

Night being come, Florina said everything she could imagine most tender and moving, but with no better success than before, because the King always took his opium. The pages concluded among themselves that certainly the girl was crazed; "For what," said they, "can she talk about all night as she does? And yet," said they, "there is wit and passion in what she utters." The Queen impatiently waited for day, that she might see what effect her complaints had produced. "What!" said she, "is this barbarian become deaf to my cries? Will he not hear his dear Florina? Oh! what a weakness is it in me still to love him! and how well do I deserve these marks of his contempt!" But these reflections were in vain, for it was not in her power to forget her love for The Charming King.

She had now only one egg left, in which all her hopes consisted. She broke it, and out came a pasty, containing six birds well larded and baked, and they sang wonderfully fine, told fortunes, and were as well skilled in physic as Dr. O'Connor himself. The Queen was charmed with this admirable acquisition, and went with her talking pasty into Truitonne's antechamber.

While she was waiting to see Truitonne pass by, one of the King's pages accosted her, saying, "Mrs. Souillon, did not my master take opium every night to make him sleep, you would certainly disturb him, you make such a noise every night in the Cabinet of Echoes."

By this Florina understood the reason why she was not heard; and putting her hand in her bag, "I am so little afraid of disturbing the King's repose," said she, "that if you will not let him have opium to-night, all these pearls and diamonds shall be yours." The page

could not resist so great a temptation, and promised her what she desired.

Presently after, Truitonne appeared, and spied the Queen with her pasty, who feigned as if she was going to eat it. "How now, Souillon," said she, "what are you doing there?"

"Madam," replied Florina, "I am eating astrologers, musicians, and physicians." Immediately all the birds fell a-singing more harmoniously than syrens; and after that they cried, "Give us a white piece, and we will tell you your fortune." Presently a drake, who seemed to be the superior among them, cried out, "Quack, quack, quack! I am a physician, and cure all diseases, and all follies, except that of love." Truitonne, more surprised than ever she was in her life at these wonders, declared it was an excellent pasty, and she would have it.

"Here, here, Souillon, what must I give thee?"

"The usual price," replied the Queen, "another night's lodging in the Cabinet of Echoes."

"Here," cried Truitonne, generously (for the acquisition of the pasty had put her in a good humour), "thou shalt have this guinea to boot."

Florina, better pleased than she had yet been, because she was in hopes the King would hear her, retired, giving her many thanks. As soon as night came, she repaired to the Cabinet, between hope and fear of the page's keeping his word, and giving the King, instead of his opium, something else which might keep him awake. When she thought that sleep had locked up everybody's ears and eyes, she renewed her usual complaints. "To what perils and dangers," said she, "have I exposed myself, to find thee out, while thou cruelly fliest me, and art going to marry Truitonne! What have I done, hardhearted Prince, that thou shouldest thus forget thy oaths? Recall to mind thy change of form, my kindness, and our tender conversations." And she repeated them almost all over, with a memory which proved that nothing was more dear to her than the remembrance of them.

The King slept not a wink, and thus distinctly heard Florina's voice and all her words, although he could not conceive from whence they came. But his heart, being touched with tenderness, so sensibly recalled to his mind the idea of his incomparable Princess, and the cruel disaster which had parted them, that he began to complain in his turn: "Aye, Princess," said he, "too cruel to a lover that adored you! was it possible that you could sacrifice me to our common enemies?"

Florina heard what he said, and failed not to answer him, giving him to understand, that if he would condescend to converse with Souillon, she might perhaps satisfy him in regard to many things of which he was yet ignorant. Upon these words, the King with impatience called one of his gentlemen, and asked him if he could find Souillon, and bring her to him. The page replied, that nothing was so easy, because she lay that night in the Cabinet of Echoes.

The King could not tell what to think. How could he imagine that so great a Queen as Florina should be disguised in the habit of Souillon? and on the contrary, how could he conceive that Souillon should have the Queen's voice, or know her secrets, unless it were

143

she herself? In this uncertainty he arose, dressed himself in haste, and descended through a private passage into the Cabinet of Echoes, the key of which the Queen had taken away; but the King had a key which opened all the doors of the Palace.

He found her in a thin white taffeta robe, which she wore under her disguises. Her hair flowed in loose ringlets over her shoulders, and she was lying upon a couch, with a lamp at some distance, that cast only a faint light. The King hastily entered, and his love transporting him above his resentment, as soon as he saw her he fell at her feet, bathed her hands with his tears, and was ready to die of joy, grief, and a thousand different passions by which he was at that instant agitated.

Nor was the Queen in less disorder; her heart beat so that she could hardly breathe; she cast a wistful look upon the King, without being able to speak a word; and when she was able to speak, she had not power to upbraid him. The pleasure of seeing him again made her forget the causes of complaint which, as she thought, she justly had against him. At last their misunderstandings were cleared up, they were reconciled, their tenderness was renewed, and all that now disturbed them was the Fairy Soussio.

At this instant, the Enchanter, who was the King's friend, arrived with a famous Fairy, the very same who had given Florina the four eggs. After the first compliments, the Enchanter and the Fairy declared, that their power being united in favour of the King and his Queen, Soussio could not hurt them, and therefore their marriage need not be delayed.

The joy of these two young lovers may be easily conceived. So soon as it was day the whole Palace rang with it, and the whole Court was overjoyed to see Florina. The news soon reached Truitonne's ears, and she flew to the King; but how was she surprised when she saw her beautiful rival! and she was just going to open her foul mouth to load her with reproachful language, when the Enchanter and the Fairy appeared, and immediately transformed her into a Sow, that, so, she might retain at least some part of her shape and nature. In this condition she trotted away grunting and nuzzling with her snout into the outer court, where she was the laughter and derision of the lacqueys and footboys.

The Charming King and Queen Florina, thus delivered from so odious a person, were now wholly intent upon the accomplishment of their nuptials, which were solemnized with equal gallantry and magnificence. And it is easy to judge of their felicity, by the tediousness and severity of their previous sufferings and misfortunes.

THE WITCH OF THE WOOD.

THERE lived, once upon a time, on the borders of a great forest, in what is now the kingdom of Prussia, a humble, hard-working Peasant and his wife. They had dwelt and worked together, and loved each other, for twelve years, when, in one fatal autumn season,

144

there came a bad harvest, and the father fell ill, and the mother lost heart in nursing him; and when he got well, and was able to go to work again, she fell ill and died of that fatal marsh fever and ague which always hangs about the neighbourhood of a rich uncultivated soil, left to grow waste and wild in wood and forest.

She left the poor man alone in the world, with the additional care of two children; one a girl, Grethel, very fair, white-haired, rosy and pretty; the other, Hansel, a bold, chubby, dark-eyed, black-haired, quick and lively boy. The children were young, and the father not old; so, principally, as he thought, to have his children taken care of, the good man took unto himself a second wife. But however pleasant a second wife may make herself to her first husband, a stepmother is seldom or ever so agreeably inclined towards the first wife's children, the more especially when she finds herself likely to have children of her own. Now, this was just as it happened in the worthy Peasant's house; the children were a perpetual eyesore and standing obstacle in the wife's way; so at last she resolved to take them both into the wood and lose them.

Very early the next morning, their Stepmother came into their room, and pulled them out of bed, bidding them follow her. She gave them a very, very small piece of bread each, which they carried with them.

The Stepmother led them deeper into the wood than they had ever been before, and then, making an immense fire, she said to them, "Sit down here and rest; and when you feel tired, you can sleep for a little time, and I will come and fetch you."

When noon came, Grethel shared her bread with Hansel, who had eaten his on the road; then they both went off to sleep. It was soon dark, but no one came to see after these poor children. When they awoke, Hansel comforted Grethel, saying, "Wait until the moon comes to our assistance, and then we can easily find our way home."

The moon shone, and up they got; but, alas! not a trace of the way homewards could they discover. Hansel kept telling Grethel they would very soon find their way; but they did not, and wandered about all night, and all the next day, without discovering any path out of the wood. The poor little creatures grew very hungry, as they had nothing to eat but the wild berries they found on the bushes. At last, they got so tired they could not move another step, and were obliged to lie down under a tree, and go to sleep.

It was now three days since they had been left by their cruel parents, and yet they were wandering deeper and deeper into the wood. Poor Hansel's heart gave way, for he saw that if help did not come, they must die of hunger and want. As soon as it was noon, they caught sight of a most beautiful Bird, as white as snow, sitting up in a bough, and singing so sweetly that they could not help listening to the beautiful music it made. However, it soon left off, and spreading its lovely wings, flew away. The children followed it until it settled upon the top of a cottage; and when they got quite close, they saw that the cottage was made of sweetbread and cakes, and the window-

THE TWO CHILDREN ARRIVE AT THE COTTAGE MADE OF CAKES.

panes of clear sugar, while all round the cottage hung cocoa-nuts filled with beautiful fresh milk.

"Oh!" said Hansel, "how fortunate we are! Let us go in here, and have a rare feast. I will eat a piece of the roof, and you can break a large piece out of the window-pane;" and the children capered with joy at the thought. So Hansel reached up, and broke a nice piece off the roof, just to see how it tasted, while Grethel began to nibble away at the window.

Then a sweet gentle voice said from within, "Rap-a-tap, rap-a-tap! who knocks at my door?" and the children answered, "The wind, the wind that blows from heaven."

So they went on eating without any interruption. Hansel liked the roof amazingly, and so he took off a very large piece; while Grethel broke a great corner bit out of the window, and sat down to eat it very happily and contentedly.

Just then the door opened, and the children started, when they saw a very Old Woman hobble out, resting upon crutches. Hansel and Grethel were dreadfully frightened, and let what they were eating fall to the ground; but the Old Woman said very kindly to them "Ah! you dear pretty children, what has brought you here? Come in, and stop with me, and I will give you everything you want, and take great care of you."

No. 19.

So saying, she took them by the hand, and led them into her little cottage. A most inviting meal of milk and pancakes, with all kinds of sweetmeats, and apples and nuts, was spread upon the table. There was nice warm water to wash them, and a large fire to comfort them, and two very beautiful little white beds, as soft as down, for them to go to sleep upon. You may be sure they were very pleased at being so well treated.

Now, although this Old Woman had behaved very kindly to these poor children when they arrived, she was in reality a wicked Old Witch, who waylaid children, and had made the sweet-cake house to entice the innocent young things in; but as soon as they were nice and fat, she killed them, and cooked them, and ate them up, making a great feast over their poor little bodies.

Witches have red eyes, and can only see a very short distance; but then, like wild beasts, they can scent out their prey a very long way, so that this wicked Old Woman always knew when any children were coming near her dwelling.

So, as Hansel and Grethel were walking along, the old wretch said to herself, "Here come two nice children; they shall not get out of my clutches. I'll snap them up as soon as they are fit to eat and just to my liking."

Early the next morning, before these little children were awake, the Old Witch went into their room, and looked at them greedily as they laid in bed asleep, with their rosy-red cheeks, and their little chubby arms; then she mumbled to herself, "Oh! here will be a bite, and there a rich mouthful." So she stretched out her bony hand, and seized Hansel very roughly, and put him into a lattice coop, that had a door and latch, and shut him up in it to get fat. Although he screamed as loudly as he could for help, no one came to him to help him. Then turning to Grethel, she called out to her, "Get up, you lazy hussy, do, and fetch some water, that I may cook something to make your Brother fat, for I am longing to eat him; and he must stay in that stall, shut up, till he is ready for me."

Poor Grethel! a heart of stone would have pitied her; but she was obliged to get the water, and cook for her Brother; and when he was well fed, she got nothing for herself but a crab's claw to pick, which was not very satisfying.

Every morning, the Old Woman used to go to Hansel's cage, and say, "Stretch out your little finger, that I may see if you are fat and fit for eating."

Hansel used to put out an old bone for her to cut at; and she, with her old blind eyes, did not find it out, but kept saying, "How tough and lean he is! I wonder he doesn't get fatter with such rich soup."

When four weeks had passed, and Hansel's finger apparently got no fatter, the Old Witch exclaimed, "Get some water hot: I'll wait no longer; fat or lean, I'll cook and eat him!"

Oh! how the little gentle loving Sister grieved when she was forced to fetch the water; the tears rolled down her cheeks, but it was of no use, she was obliged to do as she was bid. "It would have been better to

have been eaten by lions in the forest—then we should have died together; but, oh! I cannot bear to see my Brother killed."

"Hold your noise, you stupid blockhead!" roared out the Old Witch. "All your crying is of no use to you; it will only put me in a passion with you, and, then, see how you'll fare."

Early in the morning, Grethel was obliged to go out and fill the big copper pot, and make up a fire.

"Now," said the Old Woman, "we will bake first, at all events. I have already set my bread, and heated my oven."

Then she pushed poor little Grethel up to the hot oven, where the flames were burning fiercely; then she said, "Creep in there, and see if that is hot enough for my bread." But it was her intention, as soon as Grethel got in, to shut to the door, and so bake her, that she might have baked meat as well as boiled.

Grethel saw what she wanted to do in her heart, and said to her, "I am willing to do so, if I knew how, but I never baked any bread before. How shall I get in?"

"Oh, that is easy enough," said the Witch; "just step aside, you stupid goose; the opening is wide enough, I am sure. Why, I could get in myself." And so saying, she got up, and just put her head into the opening of the oven. Whereupon, Grethel summoned up a desperate courage, gave her a good push, and in the Old Witch tumbled, right into the oven! Grethel shut the door and fastened it, and left the Old Woman to howl and bake, just as the Witch had let many a little child do before.

Then she ran to Hansel, and opening the door, let him out, saying, "Oh, dear Brother, we are saved! the wicked Witch is dead!" So he sprang like a bird out of his cage, and fell upon his Sister's neck, and kissed her; and they wept with delight, to think they were safe.

They had nothing to fear now; so they rummaged the Witch's house all over, and found there, in various cupboards and cabinets, caskets of pearls, and precious stones in every corner.

"These are better than pebbles," said Hansel, as he filled his pockets with the treasures.

"And I, too," said Grethel, "will take some home." So she filled her pinafore full.

Then Hansel said, "Now we must be off, and find our way out of the enchanted forest." But when they had walked for two hours, they came to a large piece of water, into which Hansel threw a stone, and found it was very deep.

"What shall we do now?" said they; "we cannot get across here, try as we will."

"I see no bridge across," said Hansel, disappointed at this new difficulty.

"No," answered Grethel, "nor yet a boat. How unfortunate! But yonder comes a pretty Duck; I will get her to help us over." And as the Duck came towards them, they sang—

"Two little children, here we stand,
Who know not how to reach the land;
Then, pretty Duck, your aid pray give,
And we will thank you while we live."

Then the Duck shook her feathers, and said, "Get upon my back, and I will carry you over."

"But Grethel said, "We are too heavy for you, and shall hurt you, if you take more than one at a time."

Then the kind bird carried over Grethel first, and then Hansel, and thus they both arrived in safety and very happy on the other side of the water.

Then the Duck told them which path to take, as she knew her way in the forest; and they very soon came to a part with which they were acquainted, and every step they knew better and better, until they quickly arrived at their Father's door.

Then they burst into the house, and leaped upon their Father's neck. He had not had one happy hour since he had lost the children in the forest. Meantime, his wife was dead, and the children had no enemy to fear. Grethel opened her pinafore, and let all the pearls and glittering precious stones roll down upon the floor; and Hansel, with a shining face, pulled out his treasures from his pocket. Then said the Father, "We have riches enough now to last as long as we live." Thus their sorrows were ended, and now they live on in happiness.

And now my tale is ended. See! there runs a mouse! Catch her, catch her, and make a pretty little cap with her fur!

THE MUSICAL ASS.

"What a sad-thing it is," cried a Queen one day to the King her husband, "that we have no children! Loving each other as we do, it is a sad denial to us. I would never repine, could I have but one child, even if he were as ugly as an Ass."

"Perhaps," replied the King, "our wishes may some day be granted us; we are both young yet, and know not what is in store for us."

"Alas!" she answered, "I fear our life is but as a barren field, where nothing will grow!"

Now, it so happened, that not very long after this conversation, the Queen's wishes and prayers were granted her, and a little child was born; but when the nurses took it, they exclaimed, "Ah me! what a fright! it has the shape of a little Ass, and not of a Prince of noble blood."

Deep was the Queen's anguish of mind when she heard this. She lay there groaning and crying out that she would rather be without a child than have such a horrid little monster. "Away with him!" she cried; "take him to the sea, and drown him, he is only fit for food for the fishes."

The King, however, said, "No! Heaven has given this little child to us, and we must be thankful for it; he is my son and heir, and shall sit upon my throne at my death, and wear my golden crown."

So the little Ass was brought up well, and carefully educated, while his ears grew to a good size, and were long and well formed. Now, he was a very pleasant, good-tempered, frolicsome animal, and used to jump and gambol about like a kitten; above all, he had an absorbing passion for music, so much so, that he went to the most celebrated musician of the day, and offered him a large sum of money if he would instruct him in that soul-inspiring art.

"Truly, my Lord Prince," replied he, "I should be most happy to teach you the use of the lute; but I fear it would be most difficult for you to learn, as your fingers do not appear to me to be so delicate as they should be to draw forth the dulcet sounds you so much admire. How could you touch the strings?"

The Ass would not listen to one word of all this, but applied himself so industriously and perseveringly to the attainment of the art, that in a very little time he could play as well as his master.

One day, the Ass had a mind to saunter in his father's grounds, and spend the time in rolling on the grass, and talking to his single attendant. Presently he came to a running brook, bright and clear, and looking into it, he saw his own image reflected like an Ass. This sight made him unhappy and miserable; so he wandered far away from his home and all its grandeur, having with him only his trusty friend.

They travelled to and fro many a weary month, until at last they came to a kingdom where reigned a very old King, who had one very beautiful and interesting daughter.

"Here we will stay," cried the Ass-Prince; and, knocking at the Palace door, said, "Open your gates; a visitor of importance stands without, who waits for entrance."

The door was not opened; and so the Ass sat down on the door-steps, and began playing his lute (which he always carried with him), in the most delightful manner, with his two fore feet, charming all who heard him by his great taste and execution.

When the Guard saw and heard all this, he made the best of his way to the King, and exclaimed, "May it please your Majesty, here is a young Ass who is sitting on the door-step, and playing the lute like a first-rate musician!"

"Let him appear before our Royal presence," said the King.

Then he was ushered into the King's hall, amidst the grins of the attendants, who were astonished to see such a long-eared lute-player.

"Sit down there," said they, "with the slaves, at the lower end of the hall."

"No!" he exclaimed; "I shall not debase myself by so doing. I am no common animal, but a distinguished Ass."

"Oh! if that is the case," they replied, "pray take your standing among the soldiers."

"No; I will sit by the King himself," said he.

"Well, be it so," answered the King, good-humouredly; "since you desire it, come hither."

By-and-bye, his Majesty said, "How does my daughter please you?"

The Ass turned his head towards her, and nodding, said, "Oh! very much; she is indeed more beautiful than I have ever seen anybody before."

"Well, then, you shall sit by her," said his Majesty.

"That is as it should be," said the Ass, and he showed all sorts of polite attention and respect to the Princess; he ate with her, and drank wine, selecting

147

for her the greatest dainties at the table, for he was very well-bred, and, of course, knew how to behave himself at the table of a King.

At this Court he stayed many months, until at last he began to consider, "Of what use is all this to me? I may as well hasten home to my father's kingdom." So he went to his Royal Host, and told him his wishes.

"Why, what is the matter, my dear friend?" said the King. "Has my doctor been giving you nasty physic, or have you swallowed all the vinegar out of the cruets, that you look so sour this morning?"

"No," said the Ass, shaking his head.

"Do you need treasures or jewels?"

"No," he replied, looking melancholy.

"Will you have half my kingdom?"

"Ah! no, no, no!"

"I wish I knew what would content you. Will you have my beautiful daughter for your wife?"

"Oh!" replied the overjoyed Ass-Prince, "that I will! It is all my heart desires; it is the very thing I crave!"

So a large and magnificent wedding was celebrated. At night, when the bride and bridegroom were about to retire to their sleeping apartment, the King had a great wish to know if the Ass-Prince would retain his own form or not, so he desired one of his servants to conceal himself in the room. By-and-bye, when they were safely in their apartment, the Ass, thinking they were quite alone, threw off his Ass's skin, and stood before his bride a very handsome and well-formed young man.

"Now you see," said he, "I am not unworthy of you."

Then she ran up to him, in a transport of delight to see the good change, and caressed him, and embraced him, and loved him dearly all the rest of her life.

As soon as morning came, he arose and put on his skin, so that no one could for a moment think he was anything but an Ass.

Soon the old King came in, and when he saw the Ass, he exclaimed, "Ah! what, up already!" and then turning to his daughter, he said to her, "Alas! my daughter, I am afraid you sadly grieve, because you have only an Ass for your husband."

"Oh no, dear father; I love him as passionately as if he were the handsomest man alive, and will fondly cherish him as long as he lives."

The King went away rather astonished at what he heard; but the Servant followed him, and told him all that had happened.

"How can that be?" said the King.

"Then, to-night, may it please your Majesty to watch yourself," said the Servant, "and you will see with your own eyes the truth of what I have said; but I would advise you to steal the skin, and burn it, and then your handsome son-in-law must appear as he really is."

"Good," said the King; "I will do as you say."

The next night, when everybody slept, the King stole quietly into the chamber where the Ass-Prince lay, and saw by the moonbeams he was a very comely and proper young man, and no Ass. Upon the floor lay the skin, as he had thrown it down when he un-

148

dressed himself. The King caught up the skin, and hastening away with it, caused a great fire to be lighted, into which he threw the skin, and watched it as it was burnt up to ashes.

At daybreak the young Prince awoke, and hunted about for his Ass-skin, but could nowhere find it. Then he cried out in heart-breaking lamentations, "Alas! alas! I am irreparably ruined! I must make my escape from my beloved wife. What shall I do?"

But as he was leaving his room, he encountered the King, who said, "Where are you going, my son, so early in the morning? What is your intention? Remain here. You are too handsome a husband to be parted with readily. I will give you now the government of half my kingdom, and at my death you shall have the other half."

Then the whole household rejoiced, and the King put half his kingdom under the Prince's care, and at his death, soon afterwards, the young King was called upon to take the management of the entire kingdom; and in about a year and a half afterwards his own father died, and he was called upon to rule over his kingdom likewise. And so he was King of both countries, and they both prospered; and he and his Queen lived happy and contented the rest of their days.

The moral of this pretty story, my little dears, is, that many an ass may be a fine musician, and many a great man may be an ass.

THE PRINCESS ROSE.

ONCE upon a time, there was a King and a Queen in a country where all was so good and so beautiful, that everyone therein lived happily, and nothing ever went wrong. Yet, with all this, since perfect felicity cannot be hoped for anywhere, the inhabitants of even this delightful country had occasional intervals of weariness and melancholy. Whether it was, that the very weight of their riches fatigued them, there was always a something wanting to their thorough enjoyment; yet not one of the wise men among them could divine the reason why.

Now, the King and the Queen of this wonderful country, whose Palace was built of diamonds and rubies, who had servants with wings that they might be the better waited upon, who were arrayed in robes of gold and silver tissue, and who, to crown this, had all the most exquisite things in the world at their choice,—this King and this Queen, we say, were without any child; and children, we know, are the bright stars of life. Their want of children, then, was a great source of grief to the Royal pair.

The Queen, however, having a friend who was a Fairy with a Palace in the clouds, prevailed upon her to sympathize with her chagrin; and requested her to use her magic power, that a pretty little baby girl might be added to the Royal family. The Fairy kindly replied, that the Queen's wish should be gratified.

So it happened, that some days after, when the Queen was walking among the flowers in her garden, she observed something gently moving under a bush charmingly perfumed roses, and on going near, perceived, lying on a bed of soft moss, the prettiest little girl that ever was seen, fair as a lily, with cheeks like a blush-rose, and beautiful blue eyes. She hastened to take up the infant, and caress it warmly;

THE QUEEN OF HAPPY-LAND FINDS A FAIRY CHILD.

indeed, so great was her joy, that she could not help shedding tears, while from the very bottom of her heart she rendered thanks to the good Fairy for the happiness thus bestowed upon her. At that moment, a cloud came sailing from the sky, and the Fairy stepped down from it, smiling and radiant with a light, soft yet sparkling, as the dawn of day; then, addressing the Queen, she spoke as follows:—"Fair Queen, I have given you what you asked of me; that gift is the most precious of all treasures; it is yours to guard it with your utmost care. You must watch over it, as well as tenderly nurse it. The spirit of this little one I place in your hands, to develope it for good. It is your duty to commit that sacred office to no other person; for a mother who knows not how to fulfil a trust so precious is greatly to be blamed, and stores up for herself, in the future, the bitterest remorse. The mother's care is to a child what the sun is to the flower; it developes and cherishes its life. The same prudence which would prevent you entrusting your jewel-casket to the care of servants, should, in a greater degree, prohibit your confiding to such persons a treasure so great as I give you in this infant. I am willing to take upon myself the office of her godmother, and now I bestow upon her the name

of Rose, in remembrance of the charming rose-tree which served her for a cradle. Be thou, fair Queen, a good mother to this babe, and, in return, she will be a good daughter to thee!" The Fairy then remounted her cloud-chariot, and vanished in the far-off sky.

No sooner was she out of sight, than the Queen set off running towards the Palace, to show this pretty little girl to the King her husband. All the Court were called in to look at it. A lovely white she-goat was brought in to suckle it and a cradle of gold, lined with soft-wadded silk, for it to lie upon, with lace curtains as fine as the finest cobweb, to shade it while sleeping. All the Fairies came together to the Palace, and vied with each other in the most charming presents. The little girl never uttered a wish that was not satisfied on the instant; and so things went on, until she had reached the age of ten years, without having shed a tear, or felt even the slightest vexation.

The King and the Queen were the happiest parents in the world; yet, after all, a serious thought would sometimes cross their minds, at seeing their daughter apparently indifferent to all their wealth, and the many pleasures provided for her. She was happy; nevertheless, she occasionally wore an air of sadness, and seemed to feel a languor, a vague desire of something, a wish that could neither be explained nor distinctly stated. In a word, in this happy country, where sorrow was unknown, the Princess Rose was seen, all at once, to become languishing and ill. Now, in such a country, as might be expected, there were no doctors, for no complaint had ever been heard of there. What was to be done? The Queen had again recourse to her friend the Fairy, who came as quickly as possible to her summons; but even the Fairy could not understand the case of the young Princess.

As no one could tell to what cause the wretchedness which hung over the Princess was to be attributed, the Fairy said to the Queen: "At some distance from here there are countries where physicians abound; and, possibly, in them there may be similar maladies to that which afflicts our dear child. I will take her with me in my cloud-chariot, and we will go and consult one of their celebrated doctors."

The Queen, who had never left the little Princess since her birth, was much troubled at parting with her, even for a few hours. However, at last, she consented, especially as the journey could not be a very long one; for those who travel on the clouds go very fast indeed.

The Fairy and the Princess Rose traversed a great space before they descended to the earth. The place they landed upon bore very little resemblance to that they had recently quitted. Here were poor people, without food to eat or clothes to wear, dwelling in wretched huts built, for the most part, of mud, and thatched with straw; swarming with dirty children, puny, and half famished. It is true there were plenty of palaces as well, and rich people and princes, and great lords; but these scarcely troubled themselves about their unfortunate fellow-citizens, the poor receiving from them neither care nor succour.

Before the Princess and the Fairy could arrive at the house of the celebrated physician whom they

149

knew the Prince very well, for he had often before seen him walking about the fields; but what did the Prince want with his sister? So Tuvni did not stir.

"Go and fetch her, my lad!" said Goldstick-in-waiting.

"Go and fetch her, Sir!" shouted the Groom of the Stole.

"What for?" inquired Tuvni, who loved his sister too well to allow any harm to come near her; "what for, your Royal Highness?"

This was a question the Prince did not exactly expect; but, taken at the minute, he replied at once (as other people have been known to do to other people's brothers, in reply to similar inquiries), "What for? Why, to marry her, to be sure."

"A bargain," said Tuvni; "and these two gentlemen for you, and Pepperpot for me, shall be our witnesses."

"Agreed," said the Prince. "Goldstick! give him your hand upon it."

The Lord-in-waiting did not seem best pleased at placing his white jewelled fingers in the coarse, brown, horny palm of the hardworking shepherd-boy, but held it out with a slight grimace; nor did the Prince mend matters by telling his Groom of the Stole, at Tuvni's request, to take care of the lad's sheep, while he went on the Royal errand.

"Shall I leave you the dog?" inquired Tuvni.

"Not for worlds!" replied the Lord-in-waiting, his teeth chattering with horror, at the prospect of being left alone on a common for two or three days, perhaps, with such a savage-looking animal.

"Come along, Pepperpot," said Tuvni; and started off on his road to fetch his sister to be married to the Prince.

As soon as he reached his parents' house, he let the

TUVNI CONSENTS TO TAKE SELMA'S DOG, FANFAN, IN THE BOAT.

old people know the great news, and had not much trouble in obtaining their consent; so he said to his sister, "You must come along with me to the castle, for the Prince intends to marry you."

Now, Selma, his sister, whose face was as fresh as morning cowslips, and her complexion as fair as the first cream, did not seem so wonderstruck as he expected, at hearing the Prince wanted to marry her, nor so ready to go as he thought she would be, at the first invitation.

"I wish boys would learn to mind their own business," was her answer to Tuvni's grand tidings; "I don't want to leave home, and I shall not go to the castle; and I don't want to marry the Prince."

This answer sadly puzzled poor Tuvni, who would have known what to do with her, if she had been an obstinate sheep. Since, as we have said, he did not know what to do, he did nothing but scratch his head, and stand waiting for her.

"No," went on the pretty Selma, "I will not leave

152

this dwelling, until all the stones that surround it are ground to powder."

Tuvni, though he was no talker, was a great doer; so he took her at her word, picked up all the stones, broke them and crushed them, and ground them into powder. It was a long job and very hard work, as you may well suppose.

As soon as he had finished, "Now, then, Selma," said he, "come along."

"No," replied the young girl, "I can't think of going and leaving my work half done. Look at all those hanks of flax"—(for the scene of our story is laid, you must know, in Finland, where all the peasant girls collect and dress the flax, that afterwards comes over here and is made into linen)—"I shall not quit this cottage until every one of them has been spun!"

Tuvni felt much vexed at this, for he knew the Prince was waiting; and he began to think how very awkward the Groom of the Stole would be in tending

THE PRINCE OF THE SEA CUTS THE SILVER CHAIN, AND RELEASES THE LOVELY LADY.

the sheep, and how very silly the poor sheep would think him.

But this time Selma went to work herself with a will; the wheel went briskly humming round, and the distaff fairly span in her fingers. The work throve well; hank after hank of the flax was reeled off; and at last the great heap that had so frightened Tuvni sank to nothing. "Now, then, are you coming, sister?" said her brother to Selma.

"No; I will never quit this house for the Royal Castle, to be married, until the threshold of the door shall be worn out by the rubbing of my gown as I go over it."

No. 20.

"That will be a long time, indeed!" said Tuvni; but the cunning fellow knew, by the way she said this, that she only wished to be cheated; so he broke the stone without her seeing him, and then told her her gown had worn it out. What we wish to happen, we are not slow to believe; and as there was a fine young Prince on one side of the door, and only an old father and mother on the other, she shed a few tears, embraced them, bid them good-bye, and got ready to set out with her brother Tuvni.

But as she was going to be married, she thought it right to take her best clothes with her (and we believe there are few young ladies of her age who would not be of the same opinion) ; so she went to the great wooden chest by the side of her bed, and took out her best gown, and her boddice, and her petticoat, and her cloak, and followed Tuvni along the road.

Now, before they could reach the Castle of the King, it was necessary for them to cross the sea ;, we don't mean the wide ocean, but one of those inlets up which the sea runs a long way into the country, which are called *fiords* or friths, and by crossing over which in a boat, many, many miles of distance are saved, in going from place to place.

On getting down to the shore, they found their little dog Fanfan, a very clever and cunning fellow, with pretty long broad ears, and a feathery tail, had ran down before them. He begged so hard to go with them, nestled his head down in the sand at their feet, looked up in their faces, rolled on his back, wagged his tail so delightedly, and whined so piteously, that Selma, who could not help fancying there was something remarkable in the conduct of the animal, had not the heart to send him back; so, at her request, Tuvni, who was in too great a hurry to be off to care much about anything, agreed to let Fanfan go with them in the boat.

You have all of you heard of Grace Darling, and her bravery in starting out through the storm, and of her dexterity in managing a boat. She saved the lives of the passengers from a wrecked ship; and we dare say many of you have said—our little girl readers, we are now addressing—"Ah! we would have done the same, had we been Grace Darling, and seen the wrecked passengers crying for help; we would have risked our lives to save theirs, only how could we have done so, for we could not row the boat?" But in countries where the farm houses are by the sea-side, and in islands where there are no roads, but water between them, all the women can row, and steer, and manage boats, the same as the men. So when Selma got into the boat that was to carry her over the *fiord* to the Castle of the King, where she was to marry the Prince, she went forward and took up an oar, and calmly sat down to pull one of them, while her brother Tuvni pulled the other. And so they went along merrily, these two young people, the good-natured brother and the pretty gentle sister, singing a song to the time of the measured stroke of their oars, as they glided over the deep blue waters of the northern sea, that sparkled fresh and bright at each dip of the blades. And merry, why not? for they were good and innocent, and happy surely, for they loved each other dearly, and everybody else well, and one of them was on the way to be married.

But there is no sky without a cloud! At the first halt they made, at the foot of a promontory, they saw standing on the shore an ugly Old Woman. whom Selma recognized as Senjata, one of the wicked Witches who at that time abounded in the country.

"Ah, my dear children, I am so glad to see you! I was beginning to be very much afraid I should have to walk all the way round to the Castle, where I am bound to go to-day, to pay my taxes. I am so thankful you have come; you will take me with you, won't you, my pretty dears?"

"Shall we take her in, Selma?" asked Tuvni, who, from being always out in the fields all day, and too sleepy to talk or listen when he came home at night, knew very little of his neighbours or their characters. "Poor old lady, she seems quite tired ; let her get into our boat."

"No!" replied Selma ; " let us avoid keeping company with bad people."

At the next halt, they found Senjata there beforehand, waiting for them. She addressed them again with a similar request, more strongly urged. Tuvni, who was soft-hearted by nature, began to hesitate. But his sister, who was firm though gentle, said again, "Don't take her with us ; let us avoid the ill-disposed."

At the third halting-place, the confiding Tuvni allowed himself to be softened by the supplications of the perfidious Senjata.

His sister said to him, "You will see what will come of it. Now may Heaven protect us !"

Grinning malignantly at Selma, but with an awkward curtsey of much politeness to Tuvni, the Witch Senjata took her seat in the boat between the brother and the sister, and began to show her gratitude at once by throwing a spell over the boat, by which they both were made deaf.

"My dear sister," said Tuvni, " get up and set your dress to rights ; we shall soon be at the King's Castle. There, where you see the white cliffs and the sandy beach yonder, that is where we are to land."

But Selma could not hear him. "What does he say?" she inquired of the Witch.

"Your dear brother," replied the wicked Senjata, " says you are to stop rowing and throw your dog into the water."

Then the poor girl wept and was sore grieved, for little Fanfan was the dearest thing she had in the world ; but at last she threw him overboard. "When my brother says it, I must do it ; but Heaven knows how it hurts me to throw you over, little Fanfan," she said.

Selma ceased rowing, but remained motionless in the boat. Senjata seized the oar.

A moment after, Tuvni said to Selma, "Stand up; you will see the Castle immediately."

"What does he say?" inquired Selma.

"He says you must take off your clothes and throw yourself headlong in the waves."

The young girl, without a word, resigned herself to this cruel order ; for she could only fancy that her brother had brought her out in the boat with that abominable old woman, solely for the purpose of killing her. She took off her gown, her robe, her petticoat, boddice, and cap, but she still kept in the boat.

"Here we are, close to the Castle," said Tuvni, whose back was all this while turned to them ; " get ready, my dear sister, to jump ashore."

Selma again inquired of that dreadful Old Woman what it was her brother was saying ; and the wicked Witch replied, "He declares that he must either tear out your eyes, or break your arms, or throw you into the sea."

"I prefer throwing myself into the sea," murmured the young girl, sadly, as she cast herself into the water.

Tuvni, horror-struck, would have dashed in after her, to save her; but Senjata prevented him, and went on rowing, and the unfortunate Selma disappeared under the stream.

"Alas! what shall I do?" exclaimed her brother. "How dare I show myself before the Prince, without the bride I promised him."

"Don't alarm yourself about that," replied the Witch, trying to look amiable and pretty, and pulling the ugliest face in the world. "See how like I look to Selma. Present me to the King as your sister, and you will be richly rewarded."

The feeble-minded Tuvni, not knowing what to resolve, accepted this proposal.

On the shore stood the Prince, awaiting with impatience the arrival of the beautiful Selma. When he saw Senjata—who, in spite of all the best clothes of Selma, which she had awkwardly put on, could not hide her natural ugliness—he shuddered. "Is that person, there, your sister?" said he, turning angrily and wildly upon poor Tuvni.

"Yes," replied Tuvni, drooping his head, and wishing himself, at the same time, a hundred miles off, or under the waters of the *fiord*, fifty fathoms down, by the side of his dear Selma.

"Very well," went on the Prince; "I am not a man to go from my word; I will marry your sister, for it is no fault of hers that she is not handsome. But you, my lad, shall be punished for having taken me in with your portrait of her."

But when they came to the Palace, and the King saw the loathsome-looking bride, with a long nose,

THE PRINCE ASTONISHED AT SEEING HIS UGLY BRIDE.

and a mouth like a snout, and hair like a furze-bush, he was almost scared. But there was the wedding all ready, and all the brewing and baking done, and a great feast spread, and a host of hungry guests, and all the great personages invited to the wedding; and so the King could not help himself, but was forced to take her for better or worse.

He ordered his servants to cast the young Herdsman down to the bottom of a deep ditch full of serpents; which was accordingly done. Next day, when they came to look into the ditch, the men employed perceived Tuvni to be entirely uninjured, for the snakes refused to bite the good young man.

"This is something strange," said they to each other; "but perhaps the snakes are not hungry, or it is one of their fast days, or it may be the last criminal thrown down, who was a very bad one indeed, disagreed with them. Let us wait and see what to-morrow brings forth."

The first Thursday evening after this ugly wedding, as the Prince's Kitchen-maid, having finished her work, was going to bed in the Palace kitchen, where she slept, there came in a Lovely Lady, who in the prettiest possible manner begged the young woman to lend her a brush. When she got this, she began to brush her beautiful long hair, which was wet and tangled with sea-weed; and as the hair became dry, and she brushed and brushed it until it shone, down dropped gold. A little dog came in after her, and to him she said, "Run out, little Fanfan, run out and see whether the morning dawns." These words the Lovely Lady spoke to the pretty dog thrice, and at the third time the dog ran out, and when he came back, told her day was breaking.

"Then," said she, "I must go;" but as she went she sang—

"There you are, you Ugly Bride,
  Warm and snug by the Prince's left side,
  While I under waters cold am sleeping,
  And over my brother the snakes are creeping.
      Who would not weep!"

Next morning, the wondering Kitchen-maid ran

open-mouthed to meet the Cook, and told her all she had seen and heard. The news filled the Palace, and soon reached the Prince's ears. His Royal Highness summoned his Council of State on the occasion, and learning from some of the wise old men that the Lovely Lady would be bound, if a Spirit, to appear again on the following Thursday evening in the same place, he determined to keep watch on that night himself. So as soon as it was dark on that night, down the Prince went into the kitchen and sat up all night with the Kitchen-maid. But it was of no use, for of course his ugly Witch Bride had heard the story of the Lovely Lady in the kitchen as well as himself; so all his endeavours to keep awake were fruitless, for she sang and chaunted till his eyes shut themselves, and when the Lovely Lady came in again, the Prince was fast asleep and snoring. Then the Lovely Lady, when she saw him so overpowered, wrung her hands and wept; and then she borrowed a brush, as before, and brushed her hair dry, until it shone and the gold fell from it. She also sent out little Fanfan three times, as before, and sang the same song as she went away.

In the morning, when the Prince awoke, his anger was dreadful; but who was to blame but himself? So he summoned another Council of State, and was advised to await and watch another Thursday night. But this time he employed two men to hold him, one under each arm, and they were to jog him and keep him awake. But his Ugly Bride began to sing again and chaunt, and the poor Prince's eyes soon winked, and his head hung down, and he fell fast asleep. Then in came the Lovely Lady, as before, and borrowed the brush, and brushed her golden tresses till the gold fell, and sent out her little dog Fanfan three times, and when the dawn broke, began to go forth from the Palace kitchen, singing as she went—

"There you lie, you Ugly Bride,
Warm and snug by my Prince's left side,
While I under waters cold am sleeping,
And over my brother the snakes are creeping.
Who would not weep!"

"Now I come back never more," she said, and went towards the door; and though the two men pulled hard at the Prince, and pinched him, and shouted in his ears, they could only wake him just in time to see the Lovely Lady disappear on the sea-shore, as if into the waves.

But the little dog Fanfan remained on the shore, running about disconsolately, and him the Prince took up in his arms and carried back into the Palace, and didn't he bark at the Ugly Bride when he got there!

We must now change the scene from land, with its green hills and bright skies, to the depths of the sea and its coral caves and treasures. All the while what we have just told was happening at the King's Castle, another royal personage, the King of the Sea, charmed with the beauty of Selma, when she fell into his arms, bore her to his realm, where he had a Palace of Crystal constructed for her, in which she might walk about without wetting her feet, and admire all the wonders of the world of waters. The King's son asked her to marry him, made her presents of necklaces of pearls and bracelets of coral, and all the treasures of the many ships sunk in the waves. But Selma, who had heard

from a sea-snake the frightful situation of her brother, had no thought for any one but him, and when alone, sat down to embroider a necktie of gold and silver. Then she supplicated the King of the Sea to permit her to go up to the surface of the waters for the purpose of sending this cravat on to the Prince, and so moving his pity on behalf of Tuvni.

The King told her he would consent to her doing so, but only on condition that she should be fastened to his Palace of Crystal by a chain of silver.

Near the shore, on that spot, dwelt a kind and intelligent Widow, whose house abutted on some stairs, which descended into the sea. At midnight, the Palace of Crystal rose up above the waves in a direction towards this point. It was encircled by a legion of fishes and Water Nymphs, who danced and sang about it. As soon as she placed her foot on the stairs, Selma perceived a little dog that was looking for its mistress, and running incessantly from the shore to a boat, and from a boat to the shore.

"Fanfan, my pretty Fanfan," said the young girl to him—for she recognized immediately her faithful little dog—"go, open the Castle door very gently; don't wake the servants or the cat; slip up into the chamber of the Prince, and place this elegant necktie upon his pillow, so that he may take pity upon my poor brother." The intelligent Fanfan carried out his mistress's orders punctually; and then came back leaping and dancing to rejoin her.

"Be here to-morrow at midnight," said Selma to him; "I shall want you again." After these words, she re-entered her Palace of Crystal, and slowly went down in it back again to the bottom of the sea.

Next morning, when the Prince awoke and saw the cravat lying on his pillow, he exclaimed, "Who can have done this charming embroidery?"

"I did it," responded the roguish Senjata, with a smirk of affected benevolence that made her look three times as ugly; "I have been working at it all night, while you have been asleep."

The Prince did not say a word; in the first place, because he was too much of a gentleman to contradict a lady; and, in the second place, as for contradicting his wife, that handsome and elegant person had already signified to him her determination, not only to have her rights, but also to have everything her own way. He did not believe, nevertheless, that this female was able to execute any such beautiful work, and if at all, certainly not in one night; especially when he knew for a certainty, from the straining of one of his ears, that she had been snoring loudly by his side for three parts of the night at least. He made inquiries whether any one had been seen to enter the Castle; but the servants answered there had not. He then inquired about the young Herdsman, and in what condition he was at that time. The report from the Royal Executioner to the Home Secretary was placed before him, and it said that he was safe and sound as before.

"I can't understand this at all," said the Prince.

Perplexed at what had been seen in the kitchen, the singular conduct and appearance of the strange woman to whom he was married, and the remarkable preservation of the young Herdsman, he determined consult The Widow who lived on the sea-shore, the rumour of whose sagacity had reached his ears.

"Listen," said he to this Widow; "I caused a man to be thrown into a ditch full of vipers. In the usual course of things, they would have devoured their prey in a few hours, but this man they only look at, and don't bite. I cannot unriddle this prodigy."

"For what cause was it that you had that man thrown into the ditch of vipers?"

"Because he cheated me; because he told me he had a sister of extraordinary beauty, and his sister is hideous. Oh!——" And here the Prince was almost taken ill at the thought of his bride.

"You are under an error," replied the Widow; "the young man's sister is at the bottom of the water; it is she who sent you an embroidered cravat; while the woman you have taken as your bride is the malignant Witch Senjata."

The Prince jumped up horror-struck, rushed from the house, ran up into the top room of his Castle, where he shut himself in, and remained for the whole day absorbed in turning over these matters in his mind, and thinking what was to be done.

Meanwhile, Selma was at work, making a shirt of the finest cambric. As soon as she had got it done and nicely ironed, she asked leave from the King of the Sea to go up again to the surface of the waves, and there found her faithful little dog Fanfan, waiting for her on the very last step of the stairs.

"Fanfan," said she to him, "my pretty Fanfan, open the door of the Castle very gently; don't wake the servants or the cat; slip up into the Prince's bedroom, and place this shirt on his pillow, so that he may take pity on my poor brother." The alert Fanfan did what he was ordered, and just as well as at first.

Next morning, when he awoke, the Prince exclaimed, "Who is it has worked for me this beautiful shirt?"

"I," answered the undaunted Senjata, moving towards him to put her arm round his royal neck, and looking as if she expected a grateful kiss; "I have been at work all night, while you were asleep."

The Prince was going to let drop out of his lips a very short and not very polite word, but he gulped it down in time; however, we are permitted by the Court Newsman to mention, that it was a word by which his Royal Highness intended to impart the information of his not placing entire faith in what it had pleased his Royal Bride to say to him.

And we are ourselves inclined to be of the same opinion; else why, in place of an agreeble chat with her Royal Highness over his cup of coffee at breakfast, did he mount a milk-white steed, light a cigar, and, unattended by any of his Court, with a wide-awake on his head in place of his crown, a comforter round his throat instead of the Order of the Bath, and a pilot-coat in place of the Royal robes,—why, we say, did he go off at once in the same morning to the house of the Wise Widow by the sea-side, to consult her about the fresh surprises that had befallen him; first, in the shape of a new cambric shirt, with handsomely embroidered front; and secondly, that again he had heard that morning from the Chief Commissioner of Police, who had placed several detectives on

watch during the whole night to prevent deception, that the young Herdsman was a great deal better than could be expected, and quite as well as the day before?

"I tell you," said The Wise Woman to the Prince, "that it is not that vile Senjata, who has worked you that beautiful cambric shirt. It is the lovely Selma, who is now at the bottom of the sea, and who has come up as far as this house, in her Palace of Crystal, dressed in a robe of gold and silver."

"Will she come back again?" the Prince inquired.

"Yes, she will come back again yet once more. After that, she must be wedded to the Son of the King of the Seas. If you wish to carry her off from this pretender, you must have a long chain of iron made, and a strong, sharp-cutting sickle. As soon as she puts her foot on the shore, cut with the sickle the chain that fastens her to the Palace, and carry her off with your own chain. By the magic of the King of the Seas, she will assume numerous shapes to get away from you; but be firm, and you will keep her."

Midnight arrived: the moon shone brightly on the glistening waters, but the stairs of the pier were in dark shadow. All was silent on sea and land; when, suddenly, a thousand ripples were seen sparkling up in the water, as the pointed pinnacles of the Palace of Crystal rose above the surface, while the Sea Nymphs floated around, singing their softly-murmured songs, and the fish in bright shoals dashed and flashed about, and the soft breeze united to blend all in a charming chorus. Forth from the Crystal Palace, over a bridge of crystal, which fell from it down to the water's edge, glistening like large diamonds in the moonlight, stepped the charming Selma, calm in gentle beauty as the stars of heaven, and clothed from head to foot in robes of gold and silver tissue. As she advanced, the water plashing from her white feet like a tide of silver, the chain which attached her to the Palace of Crystal, as she had promised the King of the Seas, might be seen shining brighty in the moonbeams. She carried in her dainty hand a superb waistcoat that she had stitched for the Prince.

"Fanfan," said she, "my pretty Fanfan, open the door of the Castle very gently——"

But at this instant the Prince, who had kept himself close hidden under the bridge, rushed out at her, threw his own chain round her, and cut with his sickle the links of that which bound her. She wanted to fly; she changed herself into a squirrel—into a bird —into a beetle. All to no purpose. The Prince was firm, as The Wise Widow had warned him, and did not trouble himself about any of these transformations; so at last the beautiful Selma, all panting and blushing, was obliged to surrender herself.

"Alas!" she exclaimed, "alas! that frightful Senjata will cut my throat!"

"Don't fear anything of the kind," replied the Prince, with the air of one used to command. "Do you stay, I pray you, until to-morrow, here, with the Good Widow. To-morrow Senjata shall have ceased to live; to-morrow your brother shall be freed!"

This was a tolerably strong promise on the part of the Prince, considering, in the first place, that the lady to be got out of the way so speedily was his wife, and secondly, that she was herself a Witch. But what is impossible to True Love?

As soon as he had partaken of supper with the fair Selma and The Good Widow, and made sure that the beautiful Bride of the Sea (though such no longer) was snugly sleeping in a warm bedroom, under a strong roof, on solid ground, for the rest of the night, in place of a cold Crystal Palace at the bottom of the sea,—he bade farewell to The Wise Widow, and mounting his horse, returned to his Palace in an excellent good humour, whistling and singing, and smoking his cigar as he rode along.

On entering the Castle, he inquired whether her Royal Highness had retired to rest; and on receiving news to that effect—which seemed rather to add to his feelings of satisfaction—he ordered his servants to dig a hole three feet deep in the bath-room, which, at the proper time, was filled with melted pitch, and covered over with a handsome carpet.

In the morning, Senjata rose and walked along majestically into the bath-room to take her bath, scolding her Maids of Honour very soundly as she went. She had just ordered them, in her pride, not to walk so close to her, "as she was not fond of contact with common people," when she put her foot on the carpet, and fell into the hole full of burning pitch, where she was suffocated.

The marriage of the Prince and the beautiful Selma was celebrated with great pomp. On coming to the throne, his Majesty named his brother-in-law, Tuvni (who had been several years at school in the meanwhile), Prime Minister; and as for the pretty Fanfan, he was carried to the wedding in a golden carriage, and appointed Master of the Bones to the Royal Dog Kennel, for the rest of his days, with two deputy assistants to do his business, his only labour being, to lie on a crimson cushion at his mistress's feet on State occasions, and receive a handsome salary, which was paid weekly for his better accommodation.

THE SINGING BONE.

In a certain country, many years ago, the fields of the peasantry were laid waste and desolate by the ravages of a Wild Boar. He killed the cattle, and not unfrequently tore to pieces the unfortunate inhabitants. Now, the King of that country was sorely troubled at this dreadful plague, and offered a very large reward to any person who should be bold enough to attack and fortunate enough to kill the monster; but this powerful brute was so strong and so big, that no one had the courage to venture into the forest within whose precincts it raged. At last, the King sent out his heralds to proclaim to the people that whoever should take or kill this mortal foe, should become the husband of his only daughter.

Two Brothers, at last, declared their intention to undertake this adventure. The eldest of them was bold and brave from pride, the younger from innocence of heart. They thought the best method of attacking the brute would be to enter the forest at opposite sides; so the elder started on the adventure in the evening, and the younger on the following morning. When the youngest had gone a short distance, a little Dwarf accosted him, with a black spear in his hand, saying, "Take this spear; attack the Boar boldly with it; he cannot do you any harm, for your heart is innocent and good."

"I heartily thank you," replied the Youth, accepting the spear gratefully. Armed with this weapon, he walked on full of courage. In a short space, he saw the Wild Boar rushing on to him with all its force; but he held the spear right in front of him, so that the savage animal, in its blind rage, flew on it with such headlong rashness that its heart was pierced quite through. Then he slung the beast over his shoulder, and prepared to go home to show the King what good success he had attained, and to claim the Princess as his wife.

But matters fell out differently; for just as he came out on the other side of the wood, there was a house of entertainment on the outskirts, where people met to make merry and dance and sing, one with the other. Here sat his Elder Brother among a number of guests, singing aloud, and drinking deep to keep his courage up, never dreaming that while he was enjoying himself, his Brother had already gained the laurels. When, therefore, he saw his Brother coming out of the forest, stooping under the weight of this monstrous Boar, his ill-natured, envious heart would not let him rest. So he called to his Brother, "How tired you look, my dear Brother! Come in here and refresh yourself; here is plenty of good wine to be had for the drinking."

"Thank you," replied the Young Man, as he stepped in, never thinking of harm. Then he told the story of the good-natured little Dwarf, who had so kindly given him the spear with which he had killed the Boar.

The Elder Brother kept him there in conversation until the evening, when they departed in company with each other. The night was very dark, and they had to cross a bridge over a stream, when the wicked Elder Brother gave the other a knock on the head, from behind, which killed him at once. Then he buried him in the sand; and taking the Boar, carried it before the King, where he falsely related how he had slain it, and so received the Princess in marriage, as a reward for his valour. He then wickedly reported that the Boar had torn the body of his Younger Brother to pieces; and as he did not come back, everybody believed the treacherous falsehood he told.

But as all wicked doings are sure to come to light some day or other, so was the knowledge of this black deed brought home to this wicked man; for some time after, as a Countryman was driving his herd of cattle across the bridge, he saw something lying at the bottom of the brook, in the sand, as white as snow. "It is a Bone, and will make me a good mouth-piece," said he. So he stooped down and secured it; then taking out his knife, cut it to the shape of a mouth-piece for his horn. But no sooner had he blown through it than, to his astonishment, it began to sing of itself—

"My Brother killed me with one blow,
Then under the sand he laid me low;
The Boar *I* stabbed through the heart with a spear;
But *he* falsely wedded my Princess dear."

"My heart! what a wonderful Bone!" exclaimed the Herdsman; "why, it sings of itself! Oh! I must certainly take this and show it to the King."

It was no sooner before the King than it began the song again, of its own accord; but while all around wondered, the wise King perfectly understood it. So he caused the sand to be dug up under the bridge, and then all the Younger Brother's bones came to light.

The Elder Brother was so alarmed when the crime was thus brought home to him, that he could not deny the deed; and his punishment was, that he should be sewed up in a sack and drowned.

Then the whitened bones of the Good Brother were collected together, and decently buried in the nearest churchyard.

A GREATER ROGUE THAN HIS MASTER.

CERTAIN man, called John, was once very desirous of having his Son brought up to some profitable calling; and as he had no great notion of his own ability, he thought he would go to the Parson, and ask his opinion concerning him. Just as he entered, the Clerk was standing near, and he cried out, "The Rogue, the Rogue!" At these words, the peasant went away, taking this for his answer; and when he met his Son he said, rubbing his hands with glee, "The Parson says you must be a Rogue, so I must get some one to teach you your business very cleverly, and mind you learn it well."

So they set out, asking every one upon the road if he were a Rogue, until at last they reached a forest, and found a little hut, with an Old Woman sitting in. "Good Dame," said John, "pray can you tell me of anybody in these parts who can teach Roguery?"

"Yes," answered she, "my good man is a perfect master of the art."

Then John talked a long time to the Man, to try and find out if he was well learned in his profession. The Rogue said, "Your son will be taught by a first-rate master. Return in four years, and then, if you know him, I will not ask any reward or payment in return; but if you do not, I shall demand a sack of dollars."

John went home, well pleased at having found a master for his Son who would train him well in Roguery and Witchcraft. Four years passed quickly by, and then the Father set out to see his Son. He began to wonder in his own mind whether he should know him. On the road, he met with a Man who said, "Why are you looking so miserable this morning? Have you lost anything?"

"Oh dear!" answered John, "four years ago I left my dear Son here to learn Roguery, and the Master said if I knew him when I returned I should have nothing to pay, but if I did not know him I must give

him a sackful of money; and since I cannot anywhere recognize my son, I am troubled to know where I can get the money from."

"Oh! if that's all," said the Man, "you take a basket of bread with you, and set it down in the Rogue's house, and out will come a little Bird from a hollow tree; that will be your Son."

John went and did just as he was told, and out flew a little Bird to peck at the bread. "Halloa! my Son, are you here?" cried John.

The Son was pleased to hear his Father's voice, and said, "Now we will go home, Father."

But the Rogue-Master called out, "I am cheated of my dues by some greater Rogue; some Witch has told you."

So the Father and Son made the best of their way on the road home; and all at once the Son said, "Father, I will change myself into a fine Greyhound, and then you can make a lot of money by me."

Presently, a Grand Duke, who was riding in his carriage, called from the window and said, "You have a fine dog there, Master; will you sell him to me?"

"Yes," answered John.

"How much money do you require for him?" said the Grand Duke.

"Thirty dollars," was the reply.

"Too large a sum a great deal," said the Grand Duke; "but on account of his beautiful shape and sleek skin, I will give it you." Then the money was paid to John, and the Dog put inside the carriage; but when they had ridden on a mile or two, the Greyhound took advantage of the window being let down for air, and with one springing bound leapt from the carriage, and quickly rejoined his Father.

After this adventure, they thought it wisest to go home again; and the following day, as there was a fair held in the market-place in the neighbouring village, they directed their footsteps to it. On the road, the Son said, "Father, I will change myself into a Horse, and then you can sell me. But mind now what I tell you; you must be sure to unfasten my bridle, then I can change myself again into a man."

The Father rode this fine Horse into the market, and the Rogue-Master, who chanced to be there, bought him for a hundred dollars; but the possession of the money so fully occupied John's thoughts, that he forgot to undo the bridle.

The Rogue rode the Horse home, and put him into the stable; and when the Maid brought the corn, the Horse whispered in her ear, "Untie my bridle, untie my bridle."

She immediately untied the bridle, exclaiming, "Can you speak?" The Horse thereupon turned himself into a Sparrow, and flew away out of the stable, with the Rogue-Master at his tail, changed into another Bird.

Then they flew till they were close upon one another. The Rogue changed himself into Water, and the other into a Fish; but finding he could not catch him so, the Rogue changed himself into a Cock, when the other instantly became a Fox, and bit his Master's head off, so that he died; and I have heard no more of him from that day until this.

159

THE SENSIBLE SPARROW.

A NEWLY-MARRIED Sparrow had the good fortune to hatch four young ones of one brood, in the very early spring, and as she had very little time upon her hands, she was obliged to make her bed in a vacant Swallow's nest. But just as these pretty darlings—of whom she was very proud—were fledged, some naughty, wicked boys discovered the nest, and pushed the young ones out; happily, however, for them, a slight breeze was blowing at the time, and bore them up, so that they did not fall and break their tender wings. Now, the Mother Bird was in great distress and trouble, because her dear little ones had gone into the world before she had time to give them any good advice, or to teach them how to behave, like well-bred, decent birds, of good parentage.

About the end of summer, a great number of Sparrows chanced to meet in a cornfield, and among others, the Father Bird happily saw his own dear young ones. "Ah! my darling children," he said to them, "what pleasure I feel in meeting you once more! I have had great trouble about you ever since we were parted, because you had to face the world without a parents' advice; but now I have had the joy of finding you, you must listen to what I say, for young and handsome Birds like you must needs meet with great dangers in the world." Thereupon, he asked his eldest young one where he had been through the summer, and how he had provided for his wants.

"Well," replied the little cock Bird, "I have been in a garden, eating worms and caterpillars, until the tempting cherries were ripe."

"Ah! my dear son, that garden work is very pleasant, and nothing is more delicate than bill-grubbing, but then the danger is very great; you must always be sure to keep your eyes wide open—keep a good look-out, I pray—for there are a set of inhuman people who come into the gardens with long poles in their hands, that look like sticks, but are hollow, and have holes at the top, and if they come within reach of you, they will blow you to pieces with their hot breath."

"Yes, my dear Father," replied the young Bird; "but where I have lived, we take care of ourselves; we put a green leaf, with flax on it, over the hole."

"Why, where have you seen that?" said the Father.

"Oh! in a merchant's garden," was the reply.

"I do not understand their ways," said the Parent; "but merchants, I hear, have cunning crafty ways, and belong to the world's children. Truly, you have seen a great deal; but be not too confiding, make a good use of all you learn."

Then he asked the second young one where he had been. "Oh!" said he, "I reside at Court!"

"At Court," he replied; "why, what business can Sparrows have at Court? they do not belong to such places as that," said the Father. "At Court, I have heard, there is much gold and velvet, silk, and shining armour, and such birds as hawks, and falcons, and owls live there. Take my advice, and do you keep to barn-doors and stables, where they store the oats, and thrash out the corn, and you will be sure to find plenty of good food, that will make you grow fat and strong."

"That is all very true, Father; but if the lazy boys weave the straw into meshes instead of working, there is many a one of us may chance to get hanged."

"Where did you ever gain such dreadful knowledge as that?" asked the Father.

"At Court, among the stable-boys."

"Ah! my son, stable-boys are bad boys! If you have been at Court with all the fine lords and ladies, and yet have brought all your feathers away, why then I think you must be a clever Bird, and learnt how to behave yourself very cleverly in the world; but pray beware; I feel very anxious, as I know that beasts of prey will often kill the cleverest dogs. And where have you got your living?" he inquired of the third young one.

"On the highways and by-ways; I have turned over tubs and ropes, and so have chanced on many a good picking of corn and barley seed."

"Fine eating, indeed," said the Father; "but look out to see that no one stoops down to pick up a stone to throw at you; for if so, it is time for you to start."

"Very true," said the young Bird; "but suppose you meet with people who carry little pebbles in their bosoms or pockets, before stone walls?"

"What wonders you travellers see!" said the Parent, "where did you see that?"

"Among the miners, dear Father," he replied, "for when they travel, they carry about with them stones secretly, which they throw at people."

"Oh! miners—curious people they! If you have been as far as that, you must, indeed, have seen and experienced a great deal." Then the fond Parent turned to the youngest, and said, "And you, my dear little Cackanestle, where have you been? You were always the weakest and most delicate. Do stay at home with your mother, for there are so many wicked rough birds to peck at poor Sparrows, that I wish you would be content to eat the flies and spiders that swarm around our dwelling."

"Ah! my dear Father, he who finds his own living without any injury to others, fares well, and need fear no hawk, owl, eagle, or falcon shall do him harm, for at all times he desires his food from the Giver of all good, who feeds all the forest birds, even the young ravens. He listens to their cries, and without Him will not even a Sparrow falls to the ground."

"Why, where did you learn all this?" cried the old Bird, in astonishment.

"When the breeze first took us all away," he answered, "I was carried into a Church, where I got my food by eating the spiders and flies from off the windows; and there I heard a sermon preached by a man who never kills birds; and the Father of all Sparrows nourished me through the summer, and kept me from all misfortune and fierce birds."

"True, my son, you have been well taught," said the old Bird; "fly back to the Church, and take such food as is there provided for you. And, above all, forget not to chirp to the Great Creator daily, like the ravens; and thus, were the whole world full of knavish cruel birds, you need fear no evil, but pass your days happily, possessed of a quiet conscience, clear from sin, and looking humbly to Heaven for your daily food."

"UP STARTS THE BLACK PUDDING, AND STICKS FAST TO THE POOR WIFE'S NOSE!"

THE THREE WISHES.

THERE was once an honest Man, not very rich, but his Wife was very pretty, and he was very fond of her. They were sitting by the fire, one winter's evening, talking of the happiness of their neighbours, who were richer than themselves; and the Wife happened to say, "If it were in my power to have what I wish, I should soon be happier than all of them."

No. 21

"So should I, too," added her Husband; "but I am afraid that the tax-gatherers and the road-surveyors have driven all the Fairies out of our parish. I am sure, if we had Fairies now, one of them would grant me what I want to ask."

At that instant, they saw a very Beautiful Lady in their room, who addressed herself to them, and said,

"I am a Fairy, and I promise to grant to you the three first things you shall wish for. But take care; when you have had your three wishes, I will not grant you another."

The Fairy, smiling, disappeared, leaving the Man and his Wife bewildered and greatly perplexed. Each looked at the other: at last, the Wife was the first to speak—an occurrence by no means unusual, although generally she was the last as well. "For my own part," said she, "if it is left to my choice, I know very well what I shall wish for. I am easily contented. I am not wishing yet; but if I had my desire, I know nothing that can be so pleasant as to be handsome, rich, and a person of good quality."

"Silly woman!" replied her Husband; "supposing you were all these, might you not, also, be sick and fretful at the same time, as well as die young? It will be wiser to wish for health, cheerfulness, and long life."

"What is the good of long life with poverty?" said the Wife; "have we not had almost enough of it already? Your wishes would only prolong our misery. The Fairy need not have been so sparing; she might as well have given us a dozen wishes, for I am sure there are at least a dozen things that I can think of, that I want."

"You are right, my dear," said the Husband; "and as we have so many things to choose from, let us take our time to make up our minds; let us think over, through the night, what are the three things we should best like, and then wish."

"To be sure," said the Wife; "I'll think all night about them. Meanwhile, let us stir the fire together, for it is very cold."

At the same time, the Wife took up the tongs, and, without thinking on it, said, "Here's a nice fire! I wish we had a yard of black-pudding for our supper; we could dress it easily." She had hardly uttered these words, when down came tumbling through the chimney a yard of black-pudding.

"Plague on your greediness, with your black-pudding!" said the Husband. "Here's a fine wish indeed! Now we have only two left. For my part, I am so vexed, that I wish the black-pudding fast to the tip of your nose."

The Man soon perceived that he was sillier than his Wife, for, at this second wish, up starts the black-pudding, and sticks so fast to the tip of the poor Wife's nose, that there were no means to take it off.

"Wretch that I am!" cried she; "you are a wicked man for wishing the pudding fast to my nose."

"My dear," answered the Husband, "I vow I did not think of it. But what shall we do? I am about wishing for vast riches, and propose to make a golden case to hide the pudding."

"Not at all," answered the Wife, "for I should kill myself were I to live with this pudding dangling at my nose. Be persuaded, we have still a wish to make; leave it to me, or I shall instantly throw myself out of the window."

With this, she ran and opened the window; but the Husband, who loved his Wife, called out, "Hold, my dear, I give you leave to wish for what you will."

"Well," said the Wife, "my wish is, that this pudding may drop off."

"At that instant, the pudding dropped off; and the Wife, who did not want wit, said to her Husband, "The Fairy has been laughing at us; she was in the right. Possibly we should have been more unhappy with riches than we are at present. Believe me, my dear, let us wish for nothing, and take things as it shall please Heaven to send them. In the meantime, let us sup upon our pudding, since that's all that remains to us of our wishes."

The Husband thought his Wife judged rightly, so they supped merrily; nor did they ever again give themselves farther trouble about the things which they had designed to wish for.

———————

THE WONDERFUL TRUMPET.

IN days long ago, there lived a King named Dinube, whose power extended over all the provinces of Bothnia. He was the father of three daughters, of whom he was extremely fond. The first was called Helen, the second Diva, and the third Sophia. Being anxious to learn the destiny of his three girls, the King convoked an assembly of fortune-tellers, who came together in large numbers from all parts of his empire; and, after going through all the various rites of their sorcery, announced that, for the next twenty years, it would be desirable to keep the Princesses very carefully shut up, if it were wished not to expose them to a very great danger.

King Dinube, a sovereign much accustomed to have his own way, for he had been some years a widower, ordered these young Princesses to be placed at once under guard of some faithful servants within the walls of his Palace: and he caused to be constructed in his garden a spacious building entirely of glass, in which they could play and walk about in perfect safety. Thus they grew up, and became very beautiful. But, the more they grew, the stronger they felt awakening within them a desire to breathe the fresh air. The constraint they were under made them sad; and, by degrees, it became the general remark, that they were growing pale. At last, the kind old King, troubled at their evident suffering, said to himself, "My darling daughters are no longer children. The youngest of them is now fifteen years of age. It is useless to keep them in captivity any longer." That day, therefore, he gave them leave to go out; but not all at once, without having them accompanied by numbers of his officers, and what is more, by the warden of his Castle, named Koljoumi, a man of unequalled stature and strength.

The young ladies started off through the gates of the Palace, with childish glee. The sight of the fields, the hills, the rivers, threw them into ecstacies. In their lively eagerness, they took it into their heads to climb a cliff, covered with lovely green moss and spotted with flowers, when, all of a sudden, the rock opened, and swallowed them up! The giant Koljoumi threw himself on the rock, broke it with a blow from his powerful fist, and was about to seize the Princesses, when a sword of fire sprang forth and struck him, and he fell dead.

The officers returned to the Palace, and announced the dreadful tidings to King Dinube—a task by no means enviable, from the strong nature of his emotions. Great was the desolation of the Royal household, and great the mourning. The poor father, after ordering the execution of all the officers who had gone out with his daughters, and not brought them back again, was so overpowered by his feelings, that he fell into a gloomy sadness, and, thenceforth, all the world was indifferent to him.

Now, His Majesty had at his Court three men who pretended to a knowledge of all the mysteries in the world. These very wise and knowing persons were called the HEIMDALLER, or LEARNED HUMBUGS. They offered the King to go in search of his daughters; and His Majesty gave them permission to take with them as many of his servants as they thought they wanted. Now, amongst many noble and brave young gentlemen who were most anxious to share in this expedition, was a young Page of the Court, named Gulpho; but the Heimdaller declined his company, and departed in the full conviction that nothing could prevent the successful result of their enterprize. After wandering about, however, for a long time, on every coast, without discerning anything, and when the provisions for their voyage were almost exhausted, they came back to Hisisburg, for so the King's Castle was called. When, some days after, they were about to start on an expedition, Gulpho again asked their permission to accompany them; but the Heimdaller treated him as a presumptuous boy.

Poor Gulpho went off very sad, to walk in the forest, and as a means of getting rid of his vexation, betook

GULPHO CUNNINGLY CLIPS THE OLD GENIUS' FINGERS IN THE OAK.

himself to trying the strength of his arms, by striking his hatchet into the trunk of a large oak.

Suddenly, he saw appear near him an old man of colossal stature, who watched his proceedings with an air of raillery, and said to him, "Poor boy! is this the way you pretend to strike down these huge trees? Give me your axe, and I will show you the way to use such a tool."

Gulpho saw directly that this Old Man must be one of the Genii of the forest; but he could not tell whether he was the bad Genius Ahtolisnen, or the good Genius Pellerwoin. He reflected for a moment as to how he ought to act, then drove his hatchet with all his might into the trunk of the oak, and pretended he was not able to draw it out again.

"Kind old gentleman," said he, "will you oblige me by putting your hands in this cleft, so as to enlarge it, that I may be able to withdraw my axe from it?"

The Genius confidently did as he was asked, and at the same instant the dexterous Gulpho drew out his axe. The fingers of the Old Man were caught in the cleft of the oak. He tried vainly to release them, and begged the young Esquire to come to his assistance.

Gulpho replied to him quietly, "You will not recover the use of your hands, until you point out to me the place where the three young Princesses, the daughters of my King, are shut up."

"If that be the case," answered the Genius, "I will tell you."

"Take a bull by the horns, and a man at his word," added the saucy Page.

Then the Genius went on to say, "The Princesses are hidden in the hollows of the rocks of King Kammo. The youngest of them is down a hundred feet deep, in the chamber of iron, with a crown of iron upon her head, and a ring of iron on her finger. The second is a hundred feet lower, in the chamber of silver, with a crown of silver on her head, and a ring

163

of silver on her finger. The third is in the chamber of gold, with a crown of gold upon her head, and a ring of gold upon her finger."

"I am much obliged to you for the information," went on Gulpho; "but the question is, how am I to get the Princesses out of all these places?"

"Oh!" answered the Old Man, "that will not be at all a hard task. I will give you the means to do so, if you will take my hands out of this fix, as sure as I am the Genius Pellerwoin."

The young Page, made happy by hearing the Old Man was the good Genius Pellerwoin, set him loose immediately, by driving his axe once more into the oak.

Hereupon, Pellerwoin gave him a Rope a hundred fathoms in length, a Sword, a Vial of Magic Water, and a Trumpet, with these words: "With this cord you must go down into the caves of the rock, and as soon as the full moon shall shine on the mountain, sound this Trumpet, and I will be quickly near you."

The young Page went back, full of hope, to Hisisburg, where he awaited the return of the Heimdaller. But these wise and knowing gentlemen had not discovered any more this time, although they had plenty to tell of the strange things they had seen in the far-off countries they had travelled over, and the dangers of all kinds they had confronted. All these stories, however, brought no consolation to the poor old King, who never ceased weeping for his three pretty daughters, and had now lost all hope of setting his eyes upon them again.

Now, perceiving his Royal Master to be in such deep distress, Gulpho, who was a brave lad and a loyal subject, felt greatly grieved; so stepping forward respectfully in front of the King's throne, he bowed with great humility, and asked the royal permission to undertake, in his turn, a search after the Princesses; telling His Majesty that he had some very good

notions on the subject, with the addition, that he required no assistance from the Heimdaller, who might stop at home. The King replied to him, in a sad tone, "I make no doubt of your prowess, my good young man, but only of your success, since the cleverest men in my empire have been checkmated in the same enterprize. But go, since such is your desire."

On the first day of the full moon, the courageous Page set forth on his way, taking with him all the Genius had given him for that purpose. No sooner had he reached the forest, than he sounded the Trumpet, and Pellerwoin appeared.

"Are you quite ready?" said he.

"Quite," replied Gulpho, with an undaunted air.

"All right! follow me," said the Genius.

Now, it happened that the Heimdaller, struck with the tone of confidence in which Gulpho had announced his design to the King, set a spy upon him, and followed him thither to rob him of it.

Pellerwoin stopped in front of a mass of rocks, and pointing out to the young Page a deep crevice, "It is here," said he, "you must go down, but I will accompany you."

"Very well," replied Gulpho.

And the two went down. At the depth of a hundred feet, they were stopped by a door of iron.

"Draw your sword," said the Genius, "and strike upon the door."

Gulpho obeyed, and the door fell to pieces.

Whereupon, they entered the chamber of iron, in which the Princess Helen was seated, with the crown of iron and the ring of iron. A frightful Kobolde (that is to say, one of those earth-demons that are so terrible to miners and all who work underground), with a horn on his head, and an eye in the middle of his forehead, was guarding her.

"Ho! ho!" he cried, "I smell the flesh of a man!"

GULPHO BURNS OUT THE WICKED KOBOLDE'S EYE WITH A RED-HOT POKER.

"Make yourself easy," replied Helen; "it is only a Crow flying over the top of the mountain, holding in its beak a morsel of meat."

Now, as the Kobolde was old, and his eyesight very weak, he had not seen the entrance of the Page, and so believed what the Princess told him. But there was a large fire burning on the hearth, and near it an iron stake, which the Kobolde used as a poker. Gulpho caught up this poker, made it red-hot, and plunged it into the eye of the wicked Warden, whose head he next cut off.

"Extremely well done," said the Genius; "at present the Princess is delivered; leave her Crown here, break her Ring in two, and take care of the half of it."

Next, they both went down, with Helen, a hundred feet deeper, until they came to a door of silver, which Gulpho broke to pieces in the same way as the first. He set at liberty in like wise the second Princess, then the third, breaking each of their Rings, as the Genius had recommended him, and taking care of the halves. The three sisters embraced each other with inexpressible joy; but the kind Pellerwoin hastened to make them go out of the cave where they had been so long held captive.

But the Heimdaller were waiting at the entrance of the crevice, and as soon as they saw the Princesses appear, they cut the cord by which Gulpho was suspended, and the unhappy young gentleman fell senseless to the bottom of the abyss.

The good Pellerwoin fled in terror.

Then these perfidious, these barbarous Heimdaller, drew near to the three sisters, and forced from them a promise, under a solemn and terrible oath, to declare to their father, that they, the Heimdaller, were their deliverers. After which, they conducted them to the Castle.

The King was the happiest man in all the world, nor could he tell how sufficiently to show his gratitude to the Heimdaller.

Poor Gulpho's name was never mentioned. The Princesses, alone, gave a thought to their murdered preserver; but they could not violate their oaths.

Meanwhile, this is what came to pass. After remaining in a fainting fit, Gulpho raised himself up, felt all his limbs over, and found, to his great joy, that in so terrible a fall he had not broken any bones. All he felt from it was an extreme weakness. Suddenly he called to mind the Vial of Magic Water that Pellerwoin had given him, and found it uninjured. He drank a portion of it, and at once revived. Next came the difficulty of getting out of this abyss, where no human aid could be looked for. As he wandered from one side to the other to find some exit, he put his hand by chance on the Trumpet, and, for amusement, sounded a few notes. At the moment, the good Genius appeared to him.

"What makes you so dull?" said he.

"I have reason to be sad," answered the Page; "I have saved the Princesses, and here I am, without any means of getting out, at the bottom of this abyss."

"I think I see a Crow up there, skimming about," replied Pellerwoin; "perhaps he may be able to carry you out of the cavern."

"It is quite possible," replied Gulpho; "I have grown so thin!"

The Genius called the Crow down to them; the Page placed himself across its wings, and a few moments afterwards was out of the abyss, in which he had thought he was going to perish. But though for the present escaped from so great a danger, what was he to do next? To go back to the Palace was not wise, as he would be sure to run against the Heimdaller there; and where else could he betake himself? for he was an orphan, and had not a friend in the whole world.

GULPHO SURPRISES HIS BLACKSMITH MASTER WITH A SILVER CROWN.

"Forward's the word," said he; "we must go on, anyhow, and leave the rest to God."

So he turned his steps towards the residence of the King; but the nearer he approached, the more his heart misgave him, and he thought he would look about him for a while first, and watch how things were going on. He entered himself, therefore, at a Blacksmith's, as an apprentice, by way of filling up his time.

Now, it happened one day, that his master, who was a clever workman, was sent for to Hisisburg. The young Princess desired a Crown of Iron, such as she used to wear when in prison; and the Blacksmith, who had never seen a Crown of such a kind, was much puzzled how to make one like it. Nevertheless, he went to work at it, for such were the King's orders. After a patient trial, he succeeded in making a capital Crown; but it was not at all what Helen wanted; and he returned home, much vexed at his ill success.

When Gulpho learnt the cause of his master's vexation. "Perhaps," said he to him, "I may be able to make this Crown." And that evening, as soon as the Blacksmith went to sleep, he sounded his Trumpet. Pellerwoin came quickly.

"What do you wish for now?" asked the Genius.

"A Crown of Iron, such as the Princess Helen used to wear when in the rock."

"Thou shalt have it."

The Genius went and fetched the one they had left behind in the subterranean cavern. Gulpho placed it on a bench. His master, on awaking, stared at it with joyful surprise. "Ah!" said he to his apprentice. "I know not how you have become such a skilful workman; but since you have made this beautiful article, you ought to be the bearer of it yourself to the Princess."

"No," answered Gulpho; "it is not becoming for the apprentice to play the part of the master. Go you to the Palace with this Crown, and say, if you wish it, that it is the work of your pupil."

The Blacksmith went to the Castle. The Princess was delighted; and the King recompensed the ingenious artizan with great generosity.

The next day, Helen's second sister wanted a Crown of Silver made. A second time the Blacksmith was sent for to the Palace, tried a second time to execute the order, and a second time failed; and once more Gulpho, in the morning, handed over to him the precious diadem.

"Oh!" exclaimed the eldest of the Princesses, when she saw the man arrive with his treasure, "this pupil of yours is assuredly a man of marvellous talent. If he can make me a Crown of Gold like that I used to wear in my rocky prison, he shall be my husband, and have the half of my kingdom."

"Now, then, to work!" exclaimed the Blacksmith, as he re-entered his workshop. "Go to your anvil, and take up your hammer, and make a Crown of Gold, my lad; and thou shalt be a King's son-in-law." As he said these words, he set himself to watch Gulpho for the purpose of seeing by what mysterious art he would accomplish the task. But the young Page, who guessed his intention, waited for the hour when his master could no longer withstand his drowsiness, and as soon as he saw him in a deep sleep, summoned Pellerwoin, and made him bring the Crown of Gold.

Next day, the Blacksmith, seeing this splendid work sparkling in his forge, said to Gulpho, "This time I will not take thy place. It is thou who art the master, beyond all compare; as for me, I am not worthy to be thy apprentice. Go, then, thyself to the Castle."

"So be it," replied Gulpho.

He took the Crown, and set out on his way. But at some distance from the forge he sounded his Trumpet, and prayed Pellerwoin to procure him a handsome carriage.

This was done as soon as said. A superb equipage came out from the forest, drawn by four prancing grey horses, caparisoned in red housings, mounted with silver.

Gulpho got into the carriage, and drove towards the Castle. The Heimdaller were waiting in the passage,

166

resolved to slay and rob of the Crown that strange apprentice whom the Princess had promised to marry. But when they saw this handsome young gentleman in his royal carriage, they did not recognize the apprentice, but bowed respectfully to him, as some royal visitor or ambassador.

Gulpho entered the court-yard of the Palace, was shown to the King's apartments, and presented his crown. When the Princess, who was reading some papers to her father, cast her eyes upon the Page, she uttered a scream of joy, while all the courtiers crowded round to pay their compliments to the fortunate artizan.

Then Gulpho, taking from a purse which he kept in his bosom one half of the Ring of Iron, advanced towards Helen, and said to her, "Is not this a portion of your Ring?" The two halves of this circle, when brought together, fitted exactly. He presented, in like manner, two halves of the Ring of Silver and the Ring of Gold to the other two sisters. Finally, the Princesses unanimously declared that he was the man who had set them free, and the Princess Sophia married him. Their nuptials were celebrated by fêtes of extraordinary grandeur.

THE PRINCESS SOPHIA RECEIVES THE CROWN OF GOLD, AND IS MARRIED TO GULPHO THE PAGE.

The Heimdaller were punished, as they deserved; and the King, in commemoration of these events, caused the three crowns to be emblazoned on his escutcheon, where, to this day, they continue to form the armorial bearings of that country.

THE TRUE MAIDEN.

YEARS and years gone by, there lived a real Old Witch, and very ugly and wicked indeed she was. Now, this Old Witch-woman had two Daughters—one as ugly and dark as night, and very wicked, and the other as bright and fair as day, who was very good. The Old Witch loved the ugly one, who was her own Daughter, and like herself, and hated the beautiful girl, who was her Step-daughter, and very like her own mother.

One day, a kind aunt of the Step-daughter's gave her a pretty new dress, of a very beautiful pattern; and it so pleased the other one, that she desired to have it, above everything else in the world, and was so jealous and covetous about it, that she went to her mother, and said, have the dress she must and would.

"Be quiet, my dear child, and you shall have it," the Mother replied. "Your sister deserves to die for opposing your wishes; and to-night, when she is asleep, I will come and cut her head off; but mind, now, that you lie next the wall, and push her quite close to the edge of the bed."

Fortunately for the poor Maiden, she was behind the curtains in the room, and overheard all the Old Witch said, or it would have fared very badly with her; but all day long she was afraid to go out of doors, and when night came, she was obliged to go to bed in the very place she had heard them talking about; but, happily for her, she waited until the other sister was asleep, and then contrived to creep under the bed.

Presently, the Old Witch sneaked into the bed-room, with a sharp axe in her right hand, and going to the bed-side, felt with her left for the head nearest to her; then she lifted her axe, and with one blow she chopped off the head—of her own ugly Daughter.

As soon as she had gone away, the Girl got up, and went to the house of her sweetheart's mother, when she knocked at the door, and called Roland, which was her sweetheart's name.

"Dearest Roland, protect me from my cruel Step-mother!" she cried; "she would have killed me this night, but in the dark she has cut off the head of her own Daughter instead. What shall I do? If daylight appears before we get beyond her reach, I am for ever lost; her anger will know no bounds, when she discovers what she has done with her own hand."

"Take my advice," said Roland; "first secure her Magic Wand, or of what avail will your running away be? She will be sure to catch us—we cannot help ourselves."

So the Maiden stole away the Wand; and taking up the head, she let three Drops of Blood fall upon the ground—one by the bed-side, one by the kitchen fire-place, and one upon the door-step; and then away she hurried with her lover, as fast as they could travel.

When the morning came, and the Old Witch had finished dressing herself, she called to her Daughter, and would have given her the dress, but no one answered to her call. Then she said, "Can't you speak? where are you?"

"Here! upon the door-step," replied one Drop of Blood.

The Old Woman went out, but could not see anybody; so she said again "Where are you?"

"Here! here! in the kitchen, warming myself before the fire," answered the second Drop of Blood.

She went into the kitchen, but seeing no one, she cried again, "Where are you?"

"Ah! here I am, sleeping in the bed," said the third Drop of Blood.

So the Old Woman went into the bed-room, and what a dreadful sight met her there!—her own child lying dead, killed by her own wicked hand! The Old Woman went into a terrible passion, and flew out of window, and there she saw, in the far-off distance, her Step-daughter hurrying away with Roland. "You may as well come back!" she shouted; "your legs won't help you, for I'll be after you in a trice; were you twice as far, I'd pretty soon be at your heels."

Then she drew on her travelling shoes, that took such long steps, that at every step she travelled as fast as the young couple could in an hour. By this means she very soon came up with the runaways.

The Maiden looked back, and saw the Witch coming, and knew it was time for her to act; so she touched Roland with her Step-mother's Magic Wand, and turned him into a Lake; and then she changed herself into a Duck, and swam upon its waters.

When the Old Witch arrived at the Lake, she cunningly threw in some bread-crumbs, to entice the Duck, and tried every means in her power to induce the Duck to come to her; but it was of no use, and she waited until dark, and then took her way home again, without being able to hurt the Duck in any manner whatsoever.

She had no sooner gone, than the young Girl took her own natural form again, and restored Roland likewise; then on they journeyed, as swiftly as they could, all through the night, until morning came. Then the Maiden changed herself into a beautiful Rose, and Roland became a Fiddler.

Very soon the Witch came up. "What a lovely Rose!" she said; "allow me to pick it, good Fiddler; how sweet it smells!"

"Oh, yes; you may pick it, if you please, and I'll play you a merry tune in the meanwhile."

Up the bank she climbed in great haste to seize the flower, and as soon as she was in the hedge he began to play a tune, and the Old Witch was forced to dance to it, whether she liked it or not, for it was a bewitching air that he played. On he went, scraping and flourishing his bow along the strings of the fiddle, and having no mercy upon her, until, after an hour or two, she fell down dead with fatigue, and torn to pieces by the briars in the bramble-hedge.

Then, when Roland saw they had no more to fear from her, he said to the Maiden, "Now, my dear, I will go home to my mother's, and make ready for our wedding. We shall be so very happy."

"Very well," said she. "But as I am to be so long here, I will change myself into a Red Stone, and wait until you come and fetch me."

Roland went away, intending to return very soon

for her. But, alas! when he got into the city, he met another pretty Damsel, who enticed him, and he took so great a fancy for her, that he forgot all about his True Love, who was so anxiously waiting for him, and pining to death at being thus neglected by her dear betrothed, Roland. At last, in despair of ever seeing him again, she changed herself into a very lovely Flower, thinking, perhaps some one would take a liking to her, and gather her, and take her home with him.

Very soon after, a Shepherd, who was tending his flock, chanced to see this Enchanted Flower, and being surprised at its rarity and beauty, he broke it from its stem, carried it home in his bosom, and put it carefully by in his chest.

Never was there so great a change in a house as there was in the Shepherd's from that day. When he awoke in the morning, his breakfast-table was laid, his porridge made, his hearth swept and cleaned, and his fire burning merrily; and again at dinner, when he came from the fields, there was always a good meal awaiting him. It puzzled him sorely to find out who could have rendered him all these services, for he could never catch a glimpse of anybody moving about, and there was no cupboard or corner anywhere to conceal even a cat.

He was highly delighted at the manner in which everything was conducted, but was so perplexed in his own mind about it, that he determined upon going to a Wise Woman, to ask her to give him some clue to this great mystery. The Woman said, "There is some witchery in all this. Listen very attentively to-morrow morning, and try if you can hear any noise anywhere; and if you do, and can but catch a look as if anything moved, throw a clean white napkin over the place immediately, and the spell will be broken, and you will see what will come of it."

The Shepherd, full of expectation, watched eagerly next morning, and just as day peeped, he saw his chest open, and the Flower come out of it. He sprang up instantly, and threw a white napkin over it. The spell was broken, and a most beautiful Maiden stood before him. In answer to his inquiries, she acknowledged that she was the Handmaid who had arranged all his household affairs for him, and had put everything in order. He thought himself a most fortunate man, and proposed that he should marry the Maiden; but she told him the whole of her pitiful tale, and said no, for she must still continue true to her dear Roland, who always had her heart. However, she promised the Shepherd she would remain with him, and look after his cottage and keep it in proper order.

The time had now arrived for Roland's wedding, which was celebrated according to the old custom, and proclaimed with trumpets all the country round, so that every maiden might assemble where the wedding was held, and sing songs in honour of the newly-wedded pair.

Alas, poor girl! when she heard this, she nearly swooned with agitation; her heart beat convulsively, until tears came to her relief; and she would not have gone to the wedding at all, had not some young people near insisted upon her going with them.

When it came to her turn to sing, she trembled with emotion, and stepped modestly back to the farthest end of the room, and then she began; but no sooner had the first words fallen from her lips, than Roland jumped up, exclaiming, "I know that voice; that is the voice of my Beloved, my own True Bride! no other will I have!" All his old love rushed back, and again took possession of his heart, so that he could not let her go.

And now the wedding of the True Maiden and her dear Roland was celebrated with much magnificence; and their sorrows and their troubles being all over, they had nothing left them to do but enjoy themselves all the rest of their lives.

THE WEDDING OF WIDOW FOX.

In one of the rich meadows that skirt a forest in Bohemia, snug and warm under a hedge, a certain Fox had his dwelling. He was a wealthy and well-to-do Fox, and a very clever Fox besides; so clever, indeed, that so far from ever having lost his brush in a trap, he was actually the possessor of nine noble tails. But, clever as he was, his Wife was cleverer still, as he thought; so poor Mr. Fox led a miserable life through his jealousy. At last, he determined to put an end to his doubts, by pretending to be dead, and so giving his Wife her full swing, to see what she would do, and whom she really preferred. So he stretched himself out, full length, along a bench, held his breath, and remained quite motionless, as if dead.

Now, in this little trick Mr. Fox did not show himself half so wise as cunning old Foxes are in general, for he laid up for himself no end of grief. First of all, there was the sorrow of his poor Wife, who really loved him, and who wept very much; next, there was the listening to what his neighbours said about him, especially the Wolf, who suggested that it would be a great waste to bury such a fat old gentleman, and made a party, in the Fox's own hearing, to act as resurrection-man, and dig him up out of his grave the same night, and hold a jolly supper off his remains. That was not pleasant; but what was worse, was the hearing the different suitors who came courting his Wife, even before he had been measured for his coffin; and what was worse than all, to see how, as these different lovers came courting her, one after the other, his Widow appeared to take comfort gradually, as if things were not so bad that they could not be mended.

"Only let me get well up this time," said the Fox to himself, "and I will never die any more."

Mrs. Fox, as in duty bound, as soon as the first burst of her grief was over, went up-stairs to her bedroom, leaving her Servant-maid, young Miss Cat, to receive visitors; and the Cat knowing there would be sure to be a good deal of company on such a melancholy occasion, immediately began baking cakes on the hearth, and frying sausages in the pan.

The sad news soon spread about the neighbourhood, and several lovers speedily called to pay their respects

MR. WOLF COMES TO COURT THE WIDOW FOX, AND IS RECEIVED BY MISS CAT.

to his Widow, each seeking to be first, as it is gene-rally believed that you can't propose too soon to a Widow. When the first rat-a-tat came at the front door, the Maid went to the window, and putting out her head, inquired, in the well-known language of the poet, "Who's that knocking at the door?"

Whereupon, a genteel young Fox, with a very beau-tiful brush, and whiskers in the first style of fashion, replied—

> "Good afternoon, my Kitten dear.
>   Is your Mistress asleep or awake?
> Do you think it likely she will appear,
>   Or will you my message take?"

The young Cat replied—

> "I wish you were a young Mouse,
>   You'd soon find out who's a-sleeping;
> We are always awake in this house,
>   Just leave us alone to our weeping."

"Thank you for your politeness, Miss Kitten," said the young Fox. "But how is Mrs. Fox?"

> "Crying, sighing, dying,
>   And mourning full sore,
> Mrs. Fox sits in her bedroom—
>   Mr. Fox is no more!"

replied the young Cat.

No. 22.

"Poor dear lady!" said the young Fox, wiping a false tear with his brush; "but pray go and tell her that Young Brown Fox is here, and you can see he wishes to marry her; and hark'ye, you young Puss, here's a shilling for yourself."

Up-stairs went the Cat—slipping the shilling into the side-pocket of her apron, and not forgetting to spit upon it first for luck—pit-a-pat, gently to her mistress's door, at which she tapped softly, and whispered, "Are you there, Madam Fox?"

"Yes, my good little Cat," was the reply, in a low, trembling voice.

"There is one of them come already, Ma'am."

"What do you mean, Pussy?—surely not——"

"Yes, Madam Fox, as sure as you are there, a handsome young Fox—Brown Fox, Esq., that's his name—is now at the door, and he wants to marry you!"

The Widow Fox gave a gentle scream of alarm, and then said, "What does he look like?"

You should have seen the twinge in the Old Fox's left leg at this, as he lay on the bench, pretending to be dead!

"Has he got nine beautiful tails, like my dear old husband?" inquired Mrs. Fox.

"I can't say he has, Madam," replied the young Cat.

"Then tell him I won't have him," said the Widow, peremptorily.

So the young Cat went down, and sent "Brown Fox, Esq.," away. Presently, there came another knock at the door, and in came another Fox, rather a stout gentleman, with two tails—but he would not do, and fared no better; and then came six more Foxes, each with an extra tail beyond the other; but the Widow would have none of them, and, to the Old Fox's great joy, sent them all away, without seeing one of them.

They had hardly gone, when Mr. Wolf came to the door, and knocked. "Good day, Miss Cat; how charming you look this morning, and how very nicely your sausages smell! How are your master and mistress?"

"Master's dead, and mistress is fretting;
But come in, and give your lips a wetting,"

replied the Young Cat.

"Thanks, many thanks," answered the Wolf, as he walked in, and sat down to a large plateful of sausages, which he washed down with a quart of ale. "I am really very sorry for my poor old friend there; I suppose he will cut up pretty warmly—something heavy in the strong box, eh? Pray carry my compliments to your mistress (and there's a dollar for yourself, you little Puss!) and tell her, if she wishes for another husband, that I am her man, and that I am here."

So the Cat slipped the dollar into her other side-pocket, and ran up-stairs, her tail trailing behind her, to the chamber door, and knocked five times, and said, "If Madam Fox wishes for a nice husband, there's one down-stairs—a real gentleman, and a rich one—'Anastasius de Wolfe, Esq.,' that's the name on his card."

"Has the noble gentleman a painted mouth, and a scarlet tongue, and does he wear red stockings?"

"No, indeed, Madam!" replied Miss Cat.

"Then I will not have him; and you may tell him so," was the reply of the unrelenting Widow.

The Old Fox, as he lay on his pretended death-bed, was glad to hear this, and he would have liked to jump up and kick the Wolf out of the house, for the smell of the sausages, and the agitated state of his feelings, had made him uncommonly hungry; and he saw how the Wolf, all the while the Cat was up-stairs, was helping himself to the sausages out of the pan, smoking hot, platterful after platterful, and drawing off jug after jug out of his own (Mr. Fox's) favourite barrel of Allsopp's Pale Ale.

When the young Cat tripped down, and told the Wolf her mistress's mind, he heaved a deep sigh, drew a long breath, took another swig at the beer, lighted his cigar, chucked the Young Cat under the chin, and walked out of the house, smoking away his sorrows.

After him came a Dog (who finished up the sausages, and, in the intensity of his feelings, licked all the platters), a Stag, a Hare, a Bear, and a Lion,—but none answered to the Widow Fox's idea of what her lamented husband's successor should be; so they were all dismissed, and when outside, breakfasted together mutually, off each other, finishing with a fight after the Irish fashion, in honour of the deceased Mr. Fox.

At last, there drove up to the door, in a dashing curricle, a handsome Young Fox, who gave the Kitten-maid a guinea, and he proposed for Madam Fox; and when the Young Cat was asked whether this young gentleman—at whom the Widow Fox could not help taking a peep from behind her window-curtain—whether he had a painted mouth, and a scarlet tongue, and wore red stockings, and had nine tails? she replied, that he possessed every requisite that could make the Widow happy.

"Then throw the Old Fox's body out of the window, into the back yard, on to the dung-hill, and put a couple of fowls into the pot for our wedding supper, and ask the noble gentleman to walk up-stairs," said the Widow.

Up jumped the Old Fox, and giving a cruel snap at Young Fox, bit off six of his nine tails, and sent him howling off; then he rushed up-stairs, and gave his Widow a good drubbing; and, finally, kicking the Cat out of doors, he established himself, once more, as master of his own house, and resolved never to die again, as long as he could help it.

THE GRATEFUL RAT.

THERE was once an Old Woman, who had in her house a Dog, a Cat, and a Rat, that she had brought up together. They lived, all four of them, in a very good understanding with each other; slept in the same bedroom, took their meals at the same hours, often at the same table, and sometimes out of the same dish. The Cat never troubled herself about the Rat, who was always paying her little attentions. As for Master Lick-pot, the guardian of the house, he was the very happiest of dogs, never barking but twice a-day, once when they went to breakfast, and again at supper-time; passing the greatest part of his time stretched out at full length, asleep before the fire; during which period, Madame Moufflette, the Cat, curled herself up and purred between his legs, and the Rat trotted here and there along his body, as the Lilliputians did over that of Gulliver.

One day, the Old Woman summoned her family solemnly together. All the three sat in a circle on their hind legs, while she thus addressed them : " My friends, it is now fifteen years that we have lived together. I have brought you up, nourished and educated you. You, Lick-pot, have turned out a sad idle dog, but you have well guarded the house. As for you, Moufflette, if you had nothing to eat but the mice you catch, you would have died of hunger long ago; but you are an elegant Cat, and your gentle purring assists my slumbers. Rat, my lad, you have

never been of any use to me; but I have not, for all that, turned you out of doors. You ought, then, all of you, to be satisfied with what I have done for you."

Lick-pot took to barking, by way of saying " Yes;" Moufflette uttered certain mi-yows, in which might be recognized a heartfelt acknowledgment of her mistress's kindness; and Rat bowed his little head, in token of assent.

"Very well, my good friends," went on the Old Woman; "I see you are not ungrateful, and it pleases me. But times, look you, are about to change. My neighbour, the Miller, who is a bad fellow and covetous, is greedily anxious to get possession of my house and my garden. You are aware of his having brought an action against me, are you not?"

Her three auditors gently nodded their heads and wagged their tails, as implying that, in fact, they were all acquainted with the affair.

"Well, then, my friends," their mistress went on, "I can't say what stories the Miller may have told the Judge; but, after what I have heard, I fully believe that I shall lose the action, and that in eight days I shall be without hearth or land."

Lick-pot at once stretched out his snout, and began howling in the most pitiable style, as if his heart would break; Moufflette squealed like a child when it it cries; the Rat, alone, never stirred.

"Crying is not all that is to be done," said the Old Woman, interrupting these dolorous demonstrations; "we must consider how to defend ourselves. As for you, Lickpot, it is time to throw aside your idle habits, and go out hunting, as quickly as possible, to catch a hare, and carry it to the Judge, as a present. For you, Moufflette, as you have a pretty white furry skin, and know well how to present yourself and do the agreeable, you must go at once to the Judge, and tell him you come from me to free him from the mice

which gnaw his bands. And as for you, my poor Rat, since you are fit for nothing, why just stop in the corner until my fate is decided. If I gain, you shall always be well fed; but if I lose, so much the worse for you; you must then change your lodgings, and look out for a living as best you may."

At these words, Lick-pot and Moufflette started off, each on their several errands. As for the Rat, he retired to his corner, leant his head on one side, and caressed his moustache with his fore-paws—a sign, in rats, of very profound reflection.

Moufflette went direct to the Judge, made him a polite curtsey, and said to him : "I come, Sir Judge, on the part of my mistress, who has a trial pending before you, to offer my services in ridding you of the mice that nibble at your bands."

Now, it unluckily happened, that the Judge had on, at this very moment, a pair of bands most miserably torn, and he thought the Cat had come to mock at him. He was just about to drive her off with his cane, when he remarked her white and silky fur. "Stop!" said he; "I have not got any ermine for my gown; here is what will just suit me."

He immediately gave Moufflette in charge for an attempt to bribe him, called his people together, commanded them to kill the too lovely Cat, and with her fur made himself a new ermine.

An instant after this abominable murder, in came Lick-pot with a hare in his jaws. "See," said he, "here is a small present of game, that I bring you on the part of my mistress."

"Oh, oh!" said the Judge, "you sport, do you? Have you the right to do so? Let me look at your license."

Alas! poor Lick-pot had not got any license.

"There is no need," said the angry Judge, "for you to make me a present of this hare. I confiscate your hare, and I confiscate yourself."

In spite of all poor Lick-pot could say or do, he was seized and sent a long way off—a very long way off—to a farm belonging to the Judge, where he was sentenced to watch the sheep.

Such was the sad fate of Lick-pot and Moufflette, on whom the Old Woman had counted for winning her action.

Meanwhile, the Rat, whom she had thought good for nothing, was labouring hard to be of use to her; he had introduced himself into the house of the Miller, to find out what tricks he was after. Just as he reached the mill, a superb trout was brought in, which the Miller wrapped up in fresh grass, and ordered to be carried, next morning, as a present to the Judge. The Rat, when he overheard this, took care to mark down the shelf where they put the fish, and squatted down in a corner to watch it. During the night, he went and nibbled away at the trout. So when they carried it to the Judge, and he saw it all nibbled and spoilt, he flew in a rage with the Miller. "Does this man mean to mock me?" said he; "I will remember this insolence, at a proper time and place."

The Rat went back next day to his mistress, whom he found buried in sorrow for the loss of Moufflette and Lick-pot. In addition to this, she had another cause for disquietude.

"Ah! Master Rat," said she, when she saw him coming into the house, "my affairs are going badly, indeed; I am told that this horrible Miller has plotted with his Lawyer—a fellow no better than himself—to forge some papers, which will make me lose my cause. The Lawyer is about to send them in to the Judge; and they have taken their precautions so well, that I shall not be able to put in an answer. If the Judge see these papers, there will be no hope for me. I have lost Lick-pot; I have lost Moufflette. There only remains you, and you are not good for anything."

The Rat listened to what she said with great attention, stroked his moustache, and thought over it for half an hour. At the end of that time, he went out without saying a word.

All through the day he prowled about the mill. When night fell, he climbed along the wall, got into the granary by a dormer window, and thence came

down into the apartment of the Miller, where he sat at supper with his wife and son. In the centre of the table there was a large game pie.

"Remember, John," said the Miller to his son, "you are to carry that pie to our Lawyer in the morning; and don't forget to tell him to send on to the Judge the papers you know about. Without them, our cause will come off badly."

The Rat, snugly hidden in a chink in the wall, lost not a word of this important conversation. From time to time he pushed his nose out of the hole to see what was going to be done with the game pie. This was put away in a cupboard, which they locked with a key; whereupon, the Rat drew himself back into his hole, and waited.

When all the family had gone to bed, he sneaked gently out from his hiding-place, and turned towards the cupboard to search for some opening, but could find none but a little hole in the cornice, so small, that he could hardly get one of his paws into it. Then he set to work bravely, nibbling at the wood, which, luckily, was already worm-eaten; and at the end of half an hour's hard work, had made an opening sufficiently large for him to pass through, with a little squeezing. Once within the enemy's citadel, the Rat —neglecting the nuts, the bacon, and the cheese, which were there in profusion—ran straight to the game pie, adroitly raised the upper crust, and feasted on the contents. So much of this savoury delicacy did he devour, as well from appetite to please himself, as out of spite to the Miller and his Lawyer, that he made a hole in it bigger than himself; so that, when he had handsomely regaled, he squatted down in the place he had dug out, let down the crust over his head, as it had been before, and went comfortably to sleep.

He was awakened next morning by a motion from side to side, such as people feel when travelling by sea. It was the Miller's son carrying to the Lawyer the pie and his enemy. The Rat heard the thanks which the Lawyer addressed to the young man.

"You need not fear," he said to him; "the papers shall be sent to the Judge to-morrow. Your cause will then be as good as gained."

"You're reckoning without your host, my fine fellow," said the Rat, at the bottom of the pie.

The Lawyer having directed this dainty present to be set aside for a dinner he was to give next day to some friends, our Rat made his escape quickly from his prison of crust and fat, and followed the master of the house, with furtive steps, to make sure of the place where lay hid those famous papers which were certain to condemn his mistress's case. The Lawyer sat down to his desk, took up several papers, and attentively perused them; then, finally, to the great relief of the Rat, who was watching him anxiously from a corner of his office, read out aloud the papers in question, stopping at every line to see that all were properly drawn up, so as to ensure the defeat of the Old Woman.

"Good!" said he to himself, as he finished reading; "with this our cause is made sure."

He then placed the papers in a separate box; but

the Rat never lost sight of his movements, and being thus master of the secret he wanted to know, he withdrew into a hole, where he nibbled at some nuts, and waited the night.

As soon as all noise had ceased throughout the house, he went straight to the Lawyer's desk, climbed over the cases, rumpled and turned over the briefs, made a hole in the box where the papers were secreted, and then, not content with tearing them with his paws, nibbled them with his teeth, so much and so well, that he made terrible rags of them; in less than a quarter of an hour, not a single one remained whole.

Then, taking advantage of the night, and the silence that prevailed all round, our Rat ran again into the cupboard, and ensconced himself in the pie, which he found so good, that he thoroughly emptied it of its contents, so that nothing remained of it but the crust.

This last trick, it must be confessed, was nothing but an act of gluttony on the part of our friend Raton, as well as an act of impudence that had nearly cost him dear. In fact, he was still at the bottom of the pie, nibbling at the last savoury morsel, when he heard a soft step coming across the office; and resting his fore-paws and his snout on the top of the parapet of his castle of crust, as he looked out attentively, saw, from the end of the chamber, the flashing eyes of a Cat! He hid himself quickly in his retreat; but a brief reflection made him comprehend that there was little safety for him there, for its walls were not of a character to alarm or resist such an enemy. He slipped out, therefore, without further notice; and the Cat, who heard him leap down, pounced upon him at once. Master Rat felt the claw of his enemy on his back, but lost none of his presence of mind. Quick as light he turned round, gave the claw a bite, and escaped by slipping under the door by a narrow crack, through which the Cat could not pass. He was just in

time, for, in two bounds, Puss had come up with him, and, furious at the bite she had received, would have made a heavy reckoning with him. But on reaching the door, her efforts to find a passage through were all in vain.

Upon this, the Rat, who saw himself in safety, began to think of having a joke with his now powerless enemy; so, turning round, and putting his snout under the door, he set to squealing and imitating the plaintive mi-yowings of a cat,—a pleasantry which the Cat took in such ill part, that she went into a furious passion, scratching and tearing the door with her claws and teeth. Perceiving, however, at last, that her rage had no other result than to redouble her enemy's enjoyment, she sudddenly changed her tactics; and, as if her efforts had exhausted her, uttering a heart-rending cry, such as would mean, in the language of cats, "I am dying!" fell on her back, stretched at full length, and motionless.

This trick had often answered her purpose; but she had now to deal with an old stager, who had seen it, and played it off upon others. Master Rat at once descried the snare set for him, and let a little grunt escape him, which, in the language of rats, was as much as to say, "Oh, she's dead! bravo! I can now go in again!" at the same time pushing his nose under the door, as if about to repass the frontier. The Cat, who followed him from a corner of her eye, laughed in her sleeve—that is, she would have done so, if cats had sleeves for such purposes—and began to think what a fine supper he would make: when she experienced, all of a sudden, a sharp pain, that made her draw up her paws, and cry out; this was through the Rat, who bit her tail, and took himself off, crying, "Set a thief to catch a thief, Mistress Pussy!"

Next day, the Lawyer was astonished at finding his papers in the pitiable state they were left by the Rat.

173

But his vexation was still greater at dinner. Before opening the pie, he had vaunted highly of its excellence to his guests; when he lifted the crust, judge how he gazed with wonder at finding it empty!

Of course, all the guests, who had made up their mouths to enjoy this so much-vaunted dainty, were highly indignant with the Lawyer for disappointing them; while he, on his part, was so angry with the Miller, that he pleaded his case so crossly as to lose it completely.

At last, the Rat, who had spent two days in digesting the game pie, of which he had eaten too much, returned, all-exulting, to his home, where he found his mistress bathed in tears.

"I have gained my cause," she said; "but that wicked Miller is so enraged, that he swears he will burn me alive in my own house. He has been prowling about all day under my window. He will set fire to our house to-night; and I, who am a lone woman, aged and infirm, what can I do? Where can I go? What will become of me?"

The Rat sat himself up on his hind paws, and stroked his moustache.

At the end of an hour, he was still in this meditative position; and all the while, the Old Woman kept on bewailing her sad condition. At last, he got up and addressed his mistress: "When night comes, go quietly to bed, and rest in peace. Before the Miller has set your house on fire, I shall have given him something to look after at his own."

Master Rat started off on a journey. He trotted on for a long time—a very long time—until he arrived at a great lake, which he was obliged to swim across; then he climbed up a steep rock, which was pierced by a hole, and as dark as an oven at the bottom. The Rat entered within this dusky and narrow passage; and, at last, came out into a vast subterranean cavern, that might have served for the grave of an entire town.

It was the City of Ratopolis, the capital of the republic of Rats.

The houses of this city were scarcely higher than a hat. Some of them were built simply of earth—these were the dwellings of the common people; others were constructed of nutshells, the bark of trees, and small polished bones, some even of oyster-shells—these were the mansions of the grandees, the magistrates, and the nobility. In the middle of the town, the great trunk of an oak, pierced with a narrow passage, by which a kind of platform could be reached, served for a citadel. Above this platform hung a small bell, torn from a shepherd's dog which had died in the fields. Transplanted hither with unheard-of exertion, it was the great bell of Ratopolis, the alarm that sounded in the moments of greatest danger to their State.

Our traveller mounted the platform, and rang the alarm-bell. At this signal, all the inhabitants of Ratopolis swarmed hurriedly to their place of public assembly. Our hero mounted the tribune, and addressed them in the following terms:—

"Illustrious citizens of Ratopolis! A great peril ...... our Republic. In the centre of the country,

where I live, an enemy of our race is preparing to exterminate us. He has sworn our destruction; and he is training for this purpose, in his dwelling, thousands of cats, whom he is about to lead against us. This barbarous man is a cruel Miller, whose vast granaries are gorged with grain and every kind of provision.

"Let us hasten, while there is yet time, and the cats are yet too young,—let us hasten to prevent and avert this danger. I propose to take advantage of the darkness, and this very night to surprise our enemy while he is asleep.

"Thus shall we save our Republic. I will not speak to you of booty—of the heaps of corn, the sacks of nuts, or the sides of bacon which we shall find in the mill" (here his auditors licked their lips); "I know you are actuated by no other feelings than those of glory!"

The proposal was carried unanimously. The drums beat to arms, the ranks were formed, and they marched forth. On coming out of the cavern, which debouched upon the lake, they made an appeal to the Water-rats, who joined their army in great numbers. At this time the war standard was raised, which consisted of the tail of a Cat killed in battle; and then the whole army, regulating its movements by words of command from its generals, trotted off upon six hundred thousand little paws, across woods, mountains, and valleys.

This valiant little army was under the guidance of Master Rat, who, after three hour's march at a charging pace, brought it in view of the mill. There he cried, "Halt!" and all the army came to a stop.

It was arranged to dig away the foundation of the house, and to wait for its falling down, to pillage it. In an instant, two hundred thousand claws and four hundred thousand teeth were scratching and biting the earth; they sawed through the timbers, and nibbled away the very stones.

While the army of Rats were engaged at this work, Raton kept an eye on the Miller. He saw him come out of the mill, with his wife and son, who were as bad as himself. The three advanced together towards the house of the Old Woman, and each of them carried a faggot.

The Miller mounted a ladder placed against the window of the granary belonging to the poor Old Woman. On arriving at the top, he threw in first his own faggot, then those of his wife and son. His son handed him a small piece of burning tinder; the Miller took out a match to light it, and fire the faggot. Raton, who followed him with his eyes, saw with anxiety the blue flame of the sulphur, which the Miller was guarding from the wind with his hand. Happily, a puff of wind extinguished the match. He had to light another. The Miller then put this one under his hat, the better to shelter it : at last, the match caught, and the wretch was about to throw it amongst the faggots, when a dreadful crash resounded on all sides, and made him shudder with terror. His mill had fallen in! The match fell from his hands on to the ground.

The Rats, who had prudently retired to some distance at the moment of the mill's falling, rushed back to gorge themselves with the vast store of provisions buried amongst the ruins. At break of day they regained Ratopolis.

The Miller, as may well be supposed, thought no more of his wicked design. Tormented by conscience, and not knowing to what cause to attribute such an unforeseen accident, he regarded it as a punishment from Heaven. He saw himself, who had desired to usurp by fraud his neighbour's house, and had even sought her death, now, by a just retribution, plunged into the most abject misery.

The Miller, his wife, and son, seeing themselves nearly ruined, uttered cries of distress. The good Old Woman compassionated their sufferings, and offered to take them into her house until their mill was built up again. They were too happy to find shelter under a roof which they would have burnt down.

This event changed their hearts, and they became, thereafter, three honest persons.

THE FAIR ONE WITH GOLDEN LOCKS.

THERE was once a Princess, so exceeding fair, that nothing could be more beautiful in the world. Because she was so extremely amiable, she was called The Fair One with Locks of Gold, for her hair shone brighter than gold, and flowed in curls almost down to her feet. These beautiful ringlets were always encircled by a wreath of the sweetest flowers, and her garments were adorned with pearls and diamonds, so that it was impossible to behold her without admiration.

There was a young Prince, whose territories joined to hers, who was not married, and who was both rich and handsome. This Prince having heard what was reported concerning The Fair One with the Locks of Gold, though he had never seen her, fell so desperately in love with her, that he could neither eat nor drink; so that he resolved, by a magnificent embassy, to demand her in marriage. Accordingly, he ordered a sumptuous coach to be made for his Ambassador, allowed him a hundred horses and a hundred lackeys, and conjured him, if possible, to bring the Princess back with him.

When the Ambassador had taken his leave of the King, and was departing the kingdom, the whole discourse of the Court was of nothing but this match; and the King, who made no question but The Fair One with the Locks of Gold would consent, began to make great preparations of rich apparel and royal furniture. The Ambassador, in the meantime, arrived where he was sent, and having his audience with The Fair One with the Locks of Gold, he delivered the subject of his embassy to her. But whether it was that she was not that day in a good humour, or that she did not like the compliment, she thanked the Ambassador for the honour his master did her, and said she had no inclination to marry.

Hereupon, the Ambassador left the Princess's Court very sad and pensive, because she had refused to go with him; he also carried back all the presents which he had brought from the King; for she was prudent, and knew that virgins should never receive presents from young men, so that she would accept of none of his diamonds or curiosities; but that she might not seem to despise or affront the King, she took a thousand of English pins.

When the Ambassador arrived at the King's chief city, where he was expected with great impatience, the people were extremely afflicted to see him return without The Fair One with Locks of Gold; and the King wept like a child, nor could his courtiers give him any consolation.

There was a youth at Court, whose beauty outshone the sun, the gracefulness of whose person was not to be equalled, and for his gracefulness and wit he was called Avenant. The King loved him, and indeed everybody except the envious, who could not bear that the King should be kind to him, and entrust him, as he did, with all his affairs.

Avenant being one day in company with some persons, who, speaking of the Ambassador's return, said he had not been able to prevail with the lady, he inconsiderately said, "If the King had sent me to The Fair One with Locks of Gold, I dare say I could have prevailed on her to return with me."

These enviers of Avenant's prosperity immediately ran open-mouthed to the King, saying, "Sir! Sir! what does your Majesty think Avenant says? He boasts that if you had sent him to The Fair One with the Golden Hair, he could have brought her with him, which shows he is so vain as to think himself handsomer than your Majesty, and that her love for him would have made her follow him wherever he went." This put the King in a violent rage, and his passion was so great that he hardly knew what he did. "What!" said he, "does this youngster make a jest at my misfortune, and pretend to set himself above me? Go, and put him immediately in my great tower, and there let him starve to death."

The King's guards went and seized Avenant—who thought no more of what he had said—dragged him to prison, and used him in the most cruel manner. The poor unfortunate youth had only straw to lie upon, and must soon have died, but for a small stream that ran by the foot of the tower, of which he drank a little sometimes to moisten his mouth, which was almost dried up by hunger.

One day, when he was almost quite spent, he said to himself, fetching a deep sigh, "Wherein can I have offended the King? He has not a more faithful subject than myself; nor have I ever done anything to displease him." The King happened at that time to pass by the tower; and hearing the voice of the person he had once loved so well, he stopped to hear him, notwithstanding the persuasions of those that were with him, who, mortally hating Avenant, cried out, "Why stands your Majesty listening to that abandoned young rogue?"

"Hold your peace," replied the King, "and let me hear him out;" which having done, and being greatly moved by his sufferings, the tears trickled down his cheeks. He opened the door of the tower, and called him by his name; upon which Avenant came forth in a sad and pitiful condition, and, throwing himself at the King's feet, "What have I done, Sir," said he, "that your Majesty should use me thus severely?"

"Thou hast ridiculed me and my Ambassador," replied the King; "and hast said, that if I had sent thee to The Fair One with Locks of Gold, thou couldst have brought her with thee."

"It is true, Sir," replied Avenant, "for I would have so thoroughly convinced her of your Majesty's transcending qualities, that it should not have been in her power to have denied me; and in this, surely, I said nothing offensive to your Majesty."

The King found in reality he had done no injury; so, casting an angry look on those who had spoken ill of his favourite, he took him away with him, repenting heartily of the wrong he had done him.

After having given him an excellent supper, the King sent for him into his cabinet. "Avenant," says he, "I still love The Fair One with Locks of Gold, and her refusal has not discouraged me; but

I know not by what means I may gain her consent to marry me. I have a mind to send thee to her, to try whether thou canst succeed."

Avenant replied, he was ready to obey his Majesty in all things, and would depart the very next morning.

"Hold!" said the King, "I will provide thee first with a most sumptuous equipage."

"There is no necessity for that," answered Avenant; "I need only a good horse, and your letters of credence. Upon this, the King embraced him, being overjoyed to see him so soon ready.

It was upon a Monday morning that he took leave of the King and his friends, to proceed on his embassy all alone, without any pomp or noise; and thought of nothing as he went but how to engage The Fair One with Locks of Gold to marry the King. He had a table-book in his pocket, and when any good thought came into his head, fit to be made use of in his speech, he alighted from his horse, and sitting under the shade of some tree, wrote it down in his book, that he might forget nothing.

One morning, being upon his journey by break of day, and entering into a spacious meadow, a fine thought came into his head. He alighted immediately, and seated himself under some willows and poplars planted along the bank of a little stream that watered one side of the meadow. After he had done writing, he looked about him every way, being charmed with the beauties of the place, and suddenly perceived a large gilded Carp, which stirred a little, and that was all it could do; for having attempted to catch some little flies, it had leaped so far out of the water, as to throw itself upon the grass, where it was almost dead, not being able to recover its natural element. Avenant took pity on the poor creature, and though it was a fish-day, and he might have carried it away for his dinner, he took it up, and gently put it again into the river, where the Carp, feeling the refreshing coolness of the water, began to rejoice, and sunk to the bottom; but soon rising up again, brisk and gay, to the side of the river, "Avenant," said the Carp, "I thank you for the kindness you have done me; had it not been for you, I had died; but you have saved my life, and I will reward you." After this short compliment, the Carp darted itself to the bottom of the water, leaving Avenant not a little surprised at its wit and great civility.

Another day, as he was pursuing his journey, he saw a Crow in great distress, the poor bird being pursued by a huge Eagle, a great devourer of crows, which would have seized and swallowed it, as hogs do acorns, had not Avenant taken compassion on the unfortunate bird. "Thus," said he, "do the stronger oppress the weaker; for what right has the Eagle to devour the Crow?" Saying this, he took his bow, which he always carried abroad with him, and aiming at the Eagle, let fly an arrow, which pierced him through the body, so that he fell down dead, which the Crow seeing, came in an ecstacy of joy, and perched upon a tree. "Avenant," said the Crow, "you have been extremely generous, to succour me, who am but a poor wretched Crow; but I am not ungrateful, and will do you as good a turn."

AVENANT MEETS WITH THE GIANT GALIFRON.

Avenant admired the wit of the Crow, and continuing his journey, he entered into a wood so early one morning, that he could hardly see his way, where he heard an Owl crying out like an Owl in despair. "Surely," said he to himself, "this Owl, wherever it is, is in deep distress, and may perhaps be caught in some fowler's net." So looking about everywhere, he at length came to a place where certain fowlers had spread their nets in the night-time to catch little birds. "What pity 'tis," said he, "men are only made to torment one another, or else to persecute poor animals who never do them any harm!" So saying, he drew his knife, cut the cords, and set the Owl at liberty; who, before it took wing, said, "Avenant, it is not necessary I should say much to make you sensible how greatly I am indebted to you: the action speaks for itself. The fowlers are coming; I should have been taken, and must have died, without your assistance. I have a grateful heart, and will remember it."

These were the three most remarkable adventures that befel Avenant in his journey. He was in so much haste to get to the end of it, that he lost no time; and when he arrived, he went immediately to the Palace of The Fair One with Locks of Gold, where everything he viewed was surprising. Diamonds lay in heaps like common stones; and the treasury was so amazingly rich, and the wardrobe so wonderfully fine, that he thought, if the mistress of it should marry his master, he would be a happy man. He immediately washed himself, combed and powdered his hair, and put on a suit of cloth of gold; which having done, he put a rich embroidered scarf about his neck, with a small basket, wherein was a little Dog which he was very fond of. And Avenant was so amiable, and did everything with so good a grace, that when he presented himself at the gate of the Palace, all the guards paid him great respect, and everyone strove who should first give notice to The Fair One with Locks of Gold, that Avenant, the neighbouring King's Ambassador, demanded audience.

The Princess, hearing the name of Avenant, said, "It has a pleasing sound, and I dare say he is agreeable, and pleases everybody."

"Yes, indeed, Madam," said her Maids of Honour, "for we saw him out of the chamber window, where we prepare your Majesty's flax for the wheel; and while he was under the window we could not do anything."

"A pretty amusement, indeed," replied The Fair One with Locks of Gold, "to spend your time in staring upon handsome young men! Go, fetch me my rich embroidered gown of blue satin; dress my hair, and bring my wreaths of fresh flowers. Let me have my high shoes, and my fan; and let my audience chamber and throne be clean and richly adorned; for I would have him everywhere with truth say, that I am really The Fair One with Locks of Gold."

Thus all her women were employed to dress her as a Queen should be; but they were in such haste that they perplexed and hindered one another. At length, however, she went to her great gallery of looking-glasses, to see if anything was wanting; after which, she ascended her throne of gold, ivory, and ebony, the fragrant smell of which was superior to the choicest balm. She also commanded her Maids of Honour to take their instruments, and play to their own singing, so sweetly, that none should be disgusted.

Avenant was conducted into the chamber of audience, where he stood so transported with admiration, that, as he afterwards said, he had scarce power to open his lips. At length, however, he took courage, and made his speech wonderfully well, wherein he prayed the Princess not to let him be so unfortunate as to return without her.

"Gentle Avenant," said she, "all the reasons you have laid before me are very good, and I assure you I would rather favour you than any other; but you must know, about a month since I went to take the air by the side of the river, with my Maids of Honour; as I was pulling off my glove, I pulled off a Ring from my finger, which by accident fell into the river. This Ring I valued more than my whole kingdom, whence you may judge how much I am afflicted for the loss of it; and I have made a vow never to hearken to any proposals of marriage, unless the Ambassador who makes them shall also bring me my Ring. This is the present which you have to make me; otherwise you may talk your heart out, for months, and even years, shall never make me change my resolution."

Avenant stood astonished at this answer; but, however, at last he begged her to accept the little Dog, together with the basket and scarf. But she replied, she would have none of his presents, and bade him think on what she had said to him.

When he returned to his lodgings, he went to bed supperless; and his little dog, who was called Cabriole, made a fasting night of it, too, and went and lay down by his master, who did nothing all night but sigh and lament, saying, "How can I find a Ring that fell into a great river a month ago? It would be folly to attempt it. The Princess enjoined me this task merely because she knew it was impossible."

He continued to be greatly afflicted, which Cabriole observing, said, "My dear master, pray do not despair of your good fortune, for you are too good to be unhappy; therefore, when it is day, let us go to the river side."

Avenant made no answer, but gave his Dog two little cuffs with his hand, and being overwhelmed with grief, fell asleep.

But when Cabriole perceived it was broad day, he fell a-barking so loud that he waked his master. "Rise, Sir," said he, "put on your clothes, and let us go and try our fortune."

Avenant took his little Dog's advice, got up, and having dressed himself, went down into the garden, and out of the garden he walked insensibly to the river side, with his hat over his eyes, and his arms across, thinking of nothing but taking his leave; when all on a sudden he heard a voice call, "Avenant, Avenant!" upon which he looked around him, but seeing nothing, he concluded it was an illusion, and was proceeding in his walk; but he presently heard himself called again. "Who calls me?" said he.

Cabriole, who was very little, and looked closely into the water, cried out, "Never believe me, if it is not a gilded Carp!"

Immediately the Carp appeared, and with an audible voice said, "Avenant, you saved my life in the poplar meadow, where I must have died without your assistance; and now I am come to requite your kindness. Here, my dear Avenant, here is the Ring which The Fair One with Locks of Gold dropped into the river." Upon which he stooped and took it out of the Carp's mouth, to whom he returned a thousand thanks.

And now, instead of returning home, he went directly to the Palace with little Cabriole, who skipped about and wagged his tail for joy that he had persuaded his master to walk by the side of the river.

The Princess, being told that Avenant desired an audience, "Alas!" said she, "the poor youth is come to take his leave of me! He has considered what I enjoined him as impossible, and is returning to his master." But Avenant, being admitted, presented her the Ring, saying, "Madam, behold I have executed your command; and now, I hope you will receive my master for your Royal Consort."

When she saw her Ring, and that it was noways injured, she was so amazed that she could hardly believe her eyes. "Surely, courteous Avenant," said she, "you must be favoured by some Fairy, for, naturally, this is impossible."

"Madam," said he, "I am acquainted with no Fairy; but I was willing to obey your command."

"Well, then, seeing you have so good a will," continued she, "you must do me another piece of service, without which I will never marry. There is a certain Prince, who lives not far from hence, whose name is Galifron, and whom nothing would serve but that he must needs marry me. He declared his mind to me, with most terrible menaces, that if I denied him, he would enter my kingdom with fire and sword; but you shall judge whether I could accept his proposal. He is a Giant, as high as a steeple; he devours men as an ape eats chesnuts; when he goes into the country, he carries cannons in his pocket, to use instead of pistols; and when he speaks aloud, he deafens the ears of those that stand near him. I answered him, that I did not choose to marry, and desired him to excuse me. Nevertheless, he has not ceased to persecute me, and has put an infinite number of my subjects to the sword. Therefore, before all other things, you must fight him, and bring me his head."

Avenant was somewhat startled by this proposal; but having considered it awhile, "Well, Madam," said he, "I will fight this Galifron; I believe I shall be vanquished, but I will die like a man of courage."

The Princess was astonished at his intrepidity, and said a thousand things to dissuade him from it, but all in vain; and he retired to provide himself with proper weapons, and everything else that was necessary. When he had got what he wanted, he put Cabriole in his little basket, mounted his flower of coursers, and being arrived in Galifron's kingdom, he demanded of all he met, where he might meet with him; and everybody told him, he was such a Demon, that nobody durst come near him; and the more this was confirmed to him, the greater were his fears. But Cabriole encouraged him, saying, "My dear master, when you are fighting with him, I will bite him by the legs; and while he looks behind him, to drive me away, you may take that opportunity to kill him." Avenant admired the wit and ingenuity of his little Dog, but was sensible his assistance would not avail.

At length, he arrived at Galifron's Castle, the roads all the way being strewed with the bones and carcases of men, which the Giant had devoured or cut in pieces. And it was not long before he saw him come stalking through a wood, taller by the head than the highest trees, and with a dreadful voice singing—if it could be called singing—the following words:—

"Oh, for a meal of children's flesh,
Tender, young, new-killed, and fresh;
My teeth are sharp, and half a score
Would serve till I could get some more."

In answer to which, Avenant immediately sang the following:—

"Approach, and see your conqueror here,
Who from thy jaws thy teeth will tear;
Your barbarous deeds I will requite,
And send your soul to endless night."

These rhymes were none of the best; but considering they were made extempore, and Avenant, at the same time, in a most terrible fright, it is a wonder they were no worse. When the caitiff heard them, he looked about, and at last perceived Avenant with his sword drawn, who called him by two or three injurious names, on purpose to provoke him. But there was no occasion for this, for being in a most dreadful passion, he lifted up his iron mace, and had certainly beat out the gentle Avenant's brains at the first blow, had not a Crow at that instant perched upon the Giant's head, and with his bill pecked out both his eyes. The blood trickled down his face, whereat he grew desperate, and laid about him on every side; but Avenant took care to avoid his blows, and gave him many great wounds with his sword, which he pushed up to the very hilt, so that the Giant fainted and fell down with loss of blood. Avenant immediately cut off his head; and while he was in an ecstasy of joy for his good success, the Crow perched upon a tree, and said, "Avenant, I did not forget the kindness I received at your hands, when you killed the eagle that pursued me; I promised to make you amends, and now I have been as good as my word."

"I acknowledge your kindness, Mr. Crow," replied Avenant; "I am still your debtor and your servant." So saying, he mounted his courser, and rode away with the Giant's horrid head.

When he arrived at the city, everybody crowded after him, crying out, "Long live the valiant Avenant, who has slain the cruel Monster!" so that the Princess, who heard the noise, and trembled for fear she should have heard of Avenant's death, durst not inquire what was the matter. But presently after, she saw Avenant enter with the Giant's head, at the sight of which she trembled, though there was nothing to fear. "Madam," said he, "behold, your enemy is dead; and now, I hope, you will no longer refuse the King my master."

"Alas!" replied The Fair One with Locks of Gold, "I must still refuse him, unless you can find means to bring me some of the water of the Gloomy Cave. Not far from hence," continued she, "there is a very deep Cave, about six leagues in compass, the entrance into which is guarded by two Dragons. The Dragons dart fire from their mouths and eyes; and when you have got into this Cave, you will meet with a very deep hole, into which you must go down, and will find it full of toads, adders, and serpents. At the bottom of this hole there is a kind of cellar, through which runs the Fountain of Beauty and Youth. This is the water I must have; its virtues are wonderful, for the fair, by washing in it, preserve their beauty, and the deformed it renders beautiful; if they are young, it preserves them always youthful, and if old, it makes them young again. Now judge you, Avenant, whether

I will ever leave my kingdom, without carrying some of this water along with me."

"Madam," said he, "you are so amiable, that this water will be of no use to you; but I am an unfortunate Ambassador, whose death you seek. However, I will go in search of what you desire, though I am certain never to return."

The Fair One with Locks of Gold did not alter her resolution; so Avenant departed, with his little Dog, for the Gloomy Cave, in quest of the Water of Beauty and Youth; and everybody he met upon the road said it was a thousand pities so amiable a youth should go to meet his death with so much cheerfulness. "He goes alone," continued they, "but were a hundred to go with him, they would all share the same fate. Why will the Princess desire nothing but impossibilities?" But Avenant continued his journey, without speaking a word, though he was very sad and pensive.

At length, he arrived at the top of a mountain, where he sat down to rest himself, giving his horse liberty to feed, and Cabriole to run after the flies. He knew the Gloomy Cave was not far off, and looked about to see whether he could discover it; and at length he perceived a horrid rock, as black as ink, whence issued a thick smoke; and immediately after he spied one of the Dragons casting forth fire from his jaws and eyes, his skin all over yellow and green, with prodigious claws, and a long tail, rolled up in a hundred folds. Cabriole saw it also, and knew not where to hide himself for fear.

Avenant, with a resolution to die in the attempt, drew his sword, and with the phial which The Fair One with Locks of Gold had given him to fill with the Water of Beauty, went towards the Cave, saying to his little Dog, "Cabriole, here is an end of me; I never shall be able to get this water, it is so well guarded by the Dragons; therefore, when I am dead, fill this phial with my blood, and carry it to the Princess, that she may see what her severity has cost me. Then go to the King my master, and give him an account of my misfortunes."

While he was saying this, he heard a voice call, "Avenant, Avenant!"

"Who calls me?" said he; and presently he spied an Owl in the hole of an old hollow tree, who, calling to him again, said, "You rescued me out of the fowler's net, where I had been assuredly taken, had not you saved my life. I promised to make you amends, and now the time is come. Give me your phial. I am acquainted with all the secret inlets into the Gloomy Cave, and will go and fetch you the Water of Beauty."

Avenant most gladly gave the phial, and the Owl entering without any impediment into the Cave, filled it, and in less than a quarter of an hour returned with it well stopped. Avenant was overjoyed at his good fortune, gave the Owl a thousand thanks, and returned with a merry heart to the city. Being arrived at the Palace, he presented the phial to The Fair One with Locks of Gold, who then had nothing farther to say. She returned Avenant thanks, and gave orders for everything that was requisite for her departure, after which she set forward with him.

The Fair One with Locks of Gold thought Avenant very amiable, and said to him sometimes upon the road, "If you had been willing, I could have made you a King, and then we need not have left my kingdom." But Avenant replied, "I would not be guilty of such a piece of treachery to my master for all the kingdoms of the earth; though I must acknowledge your beauties are more resplendent than the sun."

At length, they arrived at the King's chief city, who, understanding that The Fair One with Locks of Gold was arrived, went forth to meet her, and made her the richest presents in the world. The nuptials were solemnized with such demonstrations of joy, that nothing else was discoursed of.

But The Fair One with Locks of Gold, who loved Avenant in her heart, was never pleased but when she was in his company, and would be always speaking in his praise. "I had never come hither," said she to the King, "had it not been for Avenant, who, to serve me, has conquered impossibilities. You are infinitely obliged to him; he procured me the Water of Beauty and Youth, by which I shall never grow old, and shall always preserve my health and beauty."

The enviers of Avenant's happiness, who heard the Queen's words, went to the King, saying, "Were your Majesty inclined to be jealous, you have reason enough to be so, for the Queen is so desperately in love with Avenant, that she can neither eat nor drink for thinking on him; she does nothing but talk of him, and how much you are obliged to him; as if, had you sent anybody else, they could not have done so much as he."

"Indeed," said the King, "I am sensible of the truth of what you tell me. Let him be put in the great tower, with fetters upon his feet and hands."

Avenant was immediately seized, and in recompense for having served the King so well, confined in the great tower, where he saw nobody but the gaoler, who at times brought him a little black bread and water, which he gave him through a lattice. However, his little dog Cabriole never forsook him, but cheered him the best he could, and brought him all the news of the Court.

When The Fair One with Locks of Gold was informed of his misfortune, she threw herself at the King's feet, and all in tears besought him to release Avenant out of prison. But the more she besought him, the more was he incensed, believing it was her affection that made her so zealous a suppliant in his behalf. Finding she could not prevail, she said no more to him, but grew very pensive and melancholy.

The King took it into his head that she did not think him handsome enough; so he resolved to wash his face with the Water of Beauty, in hopes the Queen would then conceive a greater affection for him than she had. This water stood in a phial upon a table in the Queen's chamber, where she had put it that it might not be out of her sight. But one of the chamber-maids, going to kill a spider with her besom, by accident threw down the phial and broke it, so that all the water was lost. She dried it up with all the speed she could, and not knowing what to do, she bethought herself that she had seen a phial of clear water in the

King's cabinet very like that which she had broken. Without any more ado, therefore, she went and fetched that phial, and set it upon the table in place of the other.

This water which was in the King's cabinet was a certain water which he made use of to poison the great lords and princes of his Court when they were convicted of any crime; to which purpose, instead of cutting off their heads or hanging them, he caused their faces to be rubbed with this water, which cast them into so profound a sleep that they never woke again. Now, the King one evening took this phial, and rubbed his face well with the water, after which, he fell asleep and died. Cabriole was one of the first that came to the knowledge of this accident, and immediately ran to inform Avenant of it, who bid him go to The Fair One with Locks of Gold, and remind her of the poor prisoner.

Cabriole slipped unperceived through the crowd, for there was a great noise and hurry at Court upon the King's death; and getting to the Queen, "Madam," said he, "remember poor Avenant." She presently called to mind the afflictions he had suffered for her sake, and his fidelity. Without speaking a word, she went directly to the great tower, and took off the fetters from Avenant's feet and hands herself, after which, putting the crown upon his head, and the royal mantle about his shoulders, "Amiable Avenant," said she, "I will make you a Sovereign Prince, and take you for my Consort." Avenant threw himself at her feet, and in terms the most passionate and respectful returned her thanks.

Everybody was overjoyed to have him for their King. The nuptials were the most splendid in the world; and The Fair One with Locks of Gold lived a long time with her beloved Avenant, both happy and contented in the enjoyment of each other.

THE YELLOW DWARF.

THE handsome Sir Ludolph, the youngest son of the Count of Tecklenburgh, though destined for the church, had a vocation for the army, which his father determined to indulge, though it was with some difficulty he could furnish him with the means. This was at last effected, and away started the gallant youth, resolved to carve out for himself a fortune with his sword, by fighting for the cause of the injured Princes of Thuringia. Now, the cause of the Princes was a just and honourable one. Their father, Albert the Depraved, had disinherited them and banished their mother, in favour of a worthless mistress and his illegitimate son, for whom he anxiously endeavoured to procure the investiture of his dominions after his decease. Not succeeding in this notable project, and bent upon the ruin of his own children, he sold his landgraviate of Misnia to the Emperor Adolphus, who dying before he could be benefited by his purchase, bequeathed this right, to which he had no right at all, to his brother Philip of Nassau, who, poor in character, and still poorer in purse, was now levying an army, aided by the Emperor Albert, to deprive the legitimate heir, Frederic with the Bite, and his brother Dictman, of their rights and possessions. To this project they were by no means disposed to consent, more especially as their mother, Margaret, daughter of Frederic the Redbeard, continually kept alive their resentment against their worthless father and his abandoned associates. This Princess, on being years before separated from her children by her husband, had requested permission to take leave of them ere their departure, which being granted, she, in the frenzy of rage and grief, left a singular memorial of her wrongs with her eldest son; she bit a piece out of his cheek, and the impression remaining upon his face for ever, inflamed his indignation against the original author of this disfigurement; so that, when capable of bearing arms, he deposed his father and assumed his place, to thrust him from which Philip of Nassau was now threatening, and to oppose whom half Germany was rising in arms to assist the cheek-bitten Frederic, and among many others, the handsome Knight of Tecklenburgh.

Margaret of Suabia, the mother of the Princes, during the early part of her life, had been confined by her husband in the castle of Wartzburg, in order that she might be removed the more readily into a still smaller abode, whenever the proper opportunity should occur, and which he piously determined not to neglect. She was at this period in a situation which might have interested any man but such a husband, for she promised to increase his illustrious family by an additional son or daughter; but as he cared for no children but the son of his mistress Cunegunda, this circumstance rather operated against the poor Princess, who was left to amuse herself as well as she could in superintending the infancy of her sons, and hunting in the haunted forest of Eisenac. One day, while thus diverting her attention from the many anxieties which oppressed her, she found herself suddenly separated from her attendants; but hearing a horn sound to the right, she spurred on her palfrey in that direction, till, after an hour's hard riding, she began to fear she was removing still farther from her people, for no sound could she hear but that of the eternal bugle, no hoof-tramp but that of her own steed. Still the horn sounded, and still the Princess galloped, till at length, wearied by her exercise, and finding herself in a large open plain, she dismounted to reconnoitre; at the same moment she remarked the silence of the horn, and the appearance of a gigantic Orange Tree, loaded with fine fruit, in the centre of the tranquil plain. Astonishment she certainly felt on beholding so extraordinary and beautiful an object; but hunger and fatigue had entirely banished all notions of fear; besides, Dame Margaret, having no small share of the curiosity of her grandmother Eve, could no more resist the temptation of tasting these oranges, than the first woman did the apple; so climbing up into the tree, she regaled herself to her heart's content with this fine fruit of the forest. By the time she had fairly dined, and was as weary of eating as she had previously been of riding, she bethought her of the boys at home, and with what glee they would have marched to the sack of the Orange Tree. But as that was not possible, she determined they should not be without share of the spoil, and therefore began to fill her huge pockets with the ripest and largest of the fruit. But this action displeased the hospitable master of the table at which she had been so plentifully regaled. "Eat, but take nothing away," had been one of his maxims, and he was mortally offended to see this honest rule set at nought in the person of a Princess—a lady who, he thought, ought to have understood better manners.

Before, therefore, she had laid up provisions for the march, a little shrill voice from the tree commanded her Highness "Not to steal his fruit," and, at the same instant, there issued from the trunk, which opened to give him a passage, a figure which effectually satisfied the Princess of Suabia. The animal which now quickly ascended the tree, and placed himself *vis à vis* with her Highness, was a little deformed Man, about three feet and a half high, with a face as yellow as the oranges upon which he lived, hair of the same hue hanging down to his heels, and a monstrous beard, of the same bilious complexion, gracefully descending to his feet; if you add to this, the gaiety of his yellow doublet, short cloak, and hose, you will not wonder that Margaret did not altogether relish the *tête à tête* in which she found herself so suddenly and singularly placed, independent of the awkwardness of paying a first visit in the boughs of a tree. "Princess," said the little Yellow Devil, after staring at her some time with his two huge goggling eyes, "what business have you here?"

"I have lost my way," she replied, "and being fatigued, was going to gather an orange to appease my hunger."

But he, without the least respect for his guest, or the rank of an Emperor's daughter, rudely answered, "Woman, you lie! you were stealing my property to carry away."

At this insolent reproach, Margaret, whose patience was never proverbial, felt a strong inclination to treat the Demon as she afterwards did her son; but fearing that the little gentleman might not endure it quite so temperately, prudently restrained this effort of her indignation, and only said, "I did not know the tree had any other owner than myself, or I would not have gathered any; what I have eaten I cannot restore, but here is the last I have taken." And she threw it rather roughly at the Dwarf, who, irritated excessively at this behaviour, told her, grinning hideously, and exhibiting for her admiration his monstrous overgrown yellow claws, that he had a strong temptation to tear her to pieces, which nothing but his wish to be allied to the blood of the Emperors should have prevented. "My oranges," said he, "which you have stolen, I estimate above all price, except that which I am going to demand. I am a powerful Demon, and rule with unbounded sway many thousand spirits; but I am unhappy in not having a wife with whom to share my power; as Adam was not delighted in Paradise, neither am I in my Orange Tree, without a companion. You are about to present an infant to your lord, who is utterly indifferent about the matter; it will be a girl, and I demand her in marriage on the day she

will be twenty years old. Consent to be my mother, and I will avenge your injuries upon your husband, and load you with honours and riches; refuse, and I will tear you in pieces this moment, and furnish my supper-table with your carcase."

Margaret, who had never been so terrified in all her life, and would not only have given her daughter, but her sons and husband into the bargain, to have got away, readily promised to agree with the Drawf's wishes, who now became exceedingly polite, embraced his dear mother, and assured her of his devotion. He then informed her he would give her notice some months before he should claim his wife, placed her carefully and tenderly upon her palfrey, and mounting behind, spurred on the animal, who flew like the wind to the entrance of the forest, where, again embracing his good mother, he dismounted and disappeared.

Margaret, freed from the odious company of the Yellow Dwarf, began to reflect with no very pleasant feelings upon her present adventure and future prospects. She was, indeed, safe out of the orange-coloured clutches of her dutiful and well-beloved son; and, vexed as she was by the horrible promise she had been obliged to make, she could not help congratulating herself with great sincerity upon this circumstance, and began, like all who have just escaped a present danger, to make light of the evils in the distance. The farther she cantered from the Orange Tree, the easier her mind became; and taking a few hints from "Time, the comforter," she reflected that many things might occur before the expiration of twenty years: it was a long period to look forward; the little Yellow Devil might die, (and, indeed, she could not but allow that he looked most miserably ill,) or he might forget his bargain, or he might be conquered and killed by some black, pea-green, or true blue Devil, who might be stronger or more powerful than himself; or, in case of the worst, she could secure her daughter in some strong castle or convent, or marry her, before the expiration of the term, to some Prince capable of protecting her. "At all events," thought Margaret, "sufficient to the day is the evil thereof;" and, delighted by these soothing reflections, and charmed to find herself in a whole skin, she trotted along with great complacency, and arrived quite comforted before the gates of Wartzburg.

Twenty years is indeed a long period to look forward, but a short one to look back; and so thought the now widowed Princess, when, nineteen years and some months after her adventure in the forest, she sat beside her lovely daughter in the Palace of Erfurt, listening with earnest and tender attention to the plans of her warlike sons for wresting their dominions from the iron grasp of Albert the One-eyed and Philip of Nassau. It was necessary that they should give battle to their enemies; and as the Margrave of Misnia intended to fight for his country in person, this would unavoidably deprive her beloved daughter of that powerful protection which hitherto had been her security against the threats of the Yellow Dwarf. It now wanted but six months of the period when he had determined to claim his bride; and as he had not hitherto given any indication, according to his word, of his appearance for this purpose, she trusted he might have forgotten it altogether, and, quietly resolving not to complain of this breach of promise, forbore to mention the subject to her children.

One day, during the bustle of preparation for the approaching warfare, a Knight, splendidly attired, arrived at the Palace, and demanded to be introduced to the Princess Margaret, who no sooner beheld him than she recognized in the colour of his arms the livery of her dear son-in-law, the Dwarf of the Orange Tree. He announced himself as the Knight of the King of the Oranges, and his embassy was to place abundance of gold at the feet of the Princess Margaret, and to carry away her daughter as the bride of his master. Concealment was no longer possible, so sending for her children, she informed them of her forest adventure, and its unfortunate result. Poor Brunilda fainted away; her brothers swore as lustily as ever Queen Elizabeth did, and fairly bullied the Knight Ambassador for his presumption in daring to think of their sister as a helpmate for the little dirty low-lived Sorcerer his master; and Margaret, who before their entrance had been absolutely terrified to death by his presence, now finding herself protected, suffered her tongue to wag at a most unconscionable rate against the poor Ambassador. She told him she had a great mind to cut off his ears for bringing such a message; that his master was a little conceited monster; that if, with all his gold and silver, he would buy a fine castle, cut off his beard, and live like a gentleman, he should not want her interest with one of the dairy-maids; but as it was, the thing was utterly impossible—he would not succeed even with the lowest scullion.

"Madam," replied the Knight, with a grim kind of gravity, which was not half relished by the Princess, "I would have you to understand I came not hither to bandy words with you, nor to listen to a catalogue of my master's perfections. I must, however, inform you, that he would not part from his Orange Tree, nor with his beard, for all the Princesses in the universe, the fair Brunilda included. If you do not think proper to keep your promise, he will find means to oblige you. Neither does he require human aid to obtain his betrothed Bride; but his gallantry and good-nature will not allow him to force the will of the fair Princess, if he can relinquish his determination with honour. He is fully aware of your present repugnance to his nuptials, and he is now whispering me to say, that if the Princess herself declines his vows (which he can hardly believe), he will release her, upon condition of her finding a Champion that shall conquer me, and afterwards my invincible master, before the six months have expired, in single combat on horseback or on foot, with lance or sword, according to his Highness's good pleasure at the time of meeting. Shall I say these terms are accepted?"

"You may," replied the Margrave, to whom these conditions did not appear very hard, and who thought it better to comply with than refuse them, as he was not aware of the strength of the enemy to whom his mother's promise had really been given; and he remembered he should probably be compelled to leave his lovely sister unprotected, while absent on his distant wars. The arrangements were, therefore, soon made, and the Yellow Champion was satisfied.

And now a splendid scene opened to view in the territories of Frederic with the Bitten Cheek. No sooner, each day, had the bells rung out the hour of prime, than the trumpet sounded to proclaim the challenge of the Yellow Knight, and the promise of the Margrave of Misnia, that the successful Champion of the fair Brunilda should obtain her hand for his reward. Day after day did some knight essay the adventure; and day after day did the noble Margaret enter the lists, attended by her lovely daughter, who looked, through her fan of peacock's feathers, as charming, and carried herself as "daintily," as whilom did the beauteous Esther, when she entered into the presence of the loving Ahasuerus. But not like that beautiful daughter of the scorners of pork did she obtain her petition, for day after day was she compelled to witness the ruin of her hopes, in the repeated triumphs of the yellow Haman over her own black, brown, or party-coloured champions. Knight after knight fell beneath his ponderous arm, and were obliged to resign their claims to the fair Brunilda, to her infinite regret, and their bitter mortification. Already had the Counts of Wartzburg, Oettingen, Henneberg, Hanau, and Conrad of Reida, been compelled to acknowledge the superiority of his powerful arm, when the arrival of the handsome Knight of Tecklenburgh, who just came in time to hear a week's rest proclaimed, in order to gain time for the approach of other knights from the more distant parts of Germany to the aid of the endangered Princess, revived the hopes of Brunilda. He came, he saw, he conquered—not the sword of the Yellow Champion, but the heart of the charming Princess, which was formed of too tender materials to hold out against so well-looking and redoubtable a warrior. She fell instantly in love with him to distraction, and he, on his part, was too well-bred to be behindhand. In the extravagance of her fondness, she thought all things possible to her lover, and made no doubt that he would be victorious in the combat. Ludolph was precisely of the same opinion, and, to manifest its justice, was most irritably impatient for the day of combat, which was still at the distance of several halting sun-risings and sun-settings, which that long-legged old ragamuffin, Time, did not carry off, in the opinion of the lovers, quite so rapidly as he ought to have done.

But it came at last, that day, that morning of miracles; it came, and brought nothing with it to daunt the brave spirit of the Knight of Tecklenburgh. Light as the plume in his casque, gay as the colours of his harness, he entered the lists, and gallantly opposed his person against the ponderous carcase of the Yellow-coloured Champion. Blow after blow was freely given, and as freely received, till the spectators began to doubt whether either of the men before them was really made of flesh and blood. Proof decisive, however, was soon given, for the sword of Ludolph cleft the helmet of his antagonist, and dashed his weapon from his hand, so that, defenceless and at the mercy of his conqueror, he yielded up his claim to victory,

183

and was content to beg his life. The acclamations of the people proved to Ludolph the difficulty of the conquest he had just achieved. The nobles were all anxious to testify their esteem and admiration, though some in their hearts were bursting with envy, and felt themselves almost choked by the fine things they thought it necessary to utter. Ludolph took them all in good faith, with perfect confidence in their sincerity, for he was too happy and too honest to suspect; and then turning to the poor Champion, whom he hardly allowed time to recover breath, recommended him to return to his little Lord, and bear his defiance, as he should quietly wait to fulfil the last condition, ere he received the hand of the beautiful Brunilda.

The Yellow Champion took the advice thus kindly offered him, and quitted the Palace of Erfurt, leaving his conqueror busy enough in accepting those disinterested professions of service which are seldom offered except to those who do not want them, or from whom an adequate return may not unreasonably be expected.

Ludolph waited with great impatience the Dwarf's reply to his challenge. His time was passed, meanwhile, in making love to the Princess (who, on her part, was tolerably well disposed to listen to him), and laying up a stock of devotion, by prayer and fasting, to serve as occasion should warrant, in the approaching combat with the Demon, of whose power he had formed other notions, since his residence in the Misnian Court, than either thinking him so harmless or so insignificant as he had formerly done. But the days rolled on, and no Dwarf appeared.

Margaret, who sincerely admired the valour of Ludolph, was anxious to end his suspense and Brunilda's terrors, by uniting him at once to her daughter, without waiting for the presence of the Lord of the Orange Tree, of whom she could not think without shuddering. But the Margrave, who, much as he loved his sister and her noble deliverer, was too much of a gentleman to break his word, even with a dwarf, determined they should stay the full time allotted by the Demon. The latter was too gallant, and too much in love with the Princess, to forget his engagement; and accordingly, one morning, as the trumpets were sounding the usual summons to the lists, the Dwarf himself entered them in his customary dress, mounted upon a yellow steed, and surrounded by a large troop of knights in his colours.

The nobles and ladies of the Margrave's Court, struck by the oddity of his appearance, entirely forgot their politeness, and burst into as hearty and unanimous a laugh as ever was heard in our Lower House at any Hon. Member's blunders. But it was no laughing matter to Brunilda; she saw, for the first time, her intended husband, and she felt that his ugliness even exceeded her mother's report, and heaven knows that had not been flattering. She cast a look of tender entreaty upon Ludolph, who, impatient to punish his rival and relieve her anxiety, couched his lance, and spurred forward to meet the Demon, who, not to be behindhand in courtesy, advanced to receive him. But the Knight suddenly sprang back, on observing the singular dress of his adversary, the extraordinary lightness of whose accoutrements struck

him with astonishment. "Sir Knight of the Orange Tree," said he, "except the lance in your hand and the sword in your belt, I see no sort of preparation for a combat; sheathe your person in harness, I pray you, that so, at least, the chances may be more equal between us."

"What is that to thee?" replied the Dwarf; "it is my pleasure to fight in these garments. Thief as thou art, conquer me in them, if thou canst. For thee, sweet lady, I am here, to prove my right to thy hand, to rescue it from this craven, and fear not but I shall deserve it. My Palace is ready, thy dowry is ready, and twice a thousand slaves wait to obey thy wishes."

Ludolph could not endure this insolence, so, rushing forward as the yellow knights retired from the person of their leader, he began a most furious attack upon the animal who pretended to rival him in the affections of his lady. Alas, poor Brunilda! if she had trembled before, during the combats with the Yellow Knight, what anxiety must not have filled her bosom now! The lances were soon shivered to pieces; the champions drew their swords, but seemed to make very little impression with them. Ludolph had not yet received a wound, and Yellow Jacket seemed determined to make good his boast, and hold the Knight of Tecklenburgh a tug. Vain was all the skill and strength of the latter; though he struck with all his might and main, and heart and soul, he could not cut through a single hair of the Dwarf's long beard, which seemed to wag at him in derision. Poor Brunilda sat as uneasily upon her canopied throne as if she had been upon a bed of nettles. She prayed to all the saints in heaven, and St. Henry the Limper in particular, to assist her dear knight in this terrible combat; but St. Henry the Limper was not in good humour, or was otherwise engaged, for he did not appear to pay the least attention to her request, and Ludolph was left to fight it out by himself as he could. In truth, he did not want inclination to put an end to the business. After pegging and poking at every inch of the Dwarf's invulnerable carcase, he espied a little unguarded spot on the left side of his throat, exactly open to his right hand. Delighted by the prospect of slicing off his ragamuffin head, he aimed a mighty blow with all his force, which the little Demon parried; he struck a second with no better success; but the third was triumphant, for it sent the yellow head flying from the shoulders, and bounding to another part of the area. The Knight leaped from his saddle, to seize the head and hold it up to the view of the people; but in this race, to his horror, he was outstripped by the Dwarf himself, who, likewise, darting from his horse, flew to the head, grasped it firmly, gave it a shake, clapped it upon his shoulders, and fixed it again as firmly and steadily as ever! Then, ere the spectators could recover from the stupor into which this unexpected *contretemps* had thrown them, he struck the staring Ludolph to the ground, seized the Princess by her flowing locks, swung her behind him, and bolted out of the area. His knights wheeled round to follow him; but the Misnian nobles, recovering from their confusion, surrounded them with drawn swords, and began a desperate battle, in which it

E. EVANS. S.

THE YELLOW DWARF SURPRISES BRUNILDA WITH A DECLARATION OF LOVE.

appeared they clearly had the worst, only hacking and hewing each other; for the knights, squires, pages, and horses of the enemy suddenly vanished from their sight, and in their places appeared a waggon-load of oranges, bowling and rolling about the area in the most amusing manner possible.

It was some time ere the nobles could direct their attention to the unfortunate Count of Tecklenburgh, who, stunned by the blow given to him as the parting blessing of the spiteful Dwarf, was lying insensible on the ground. The moment he recovered, he declared his intention of pursuing the enemy, in which he was seconded by all the knights present, who, headed by Margaret as guide and commander, resolved to storm the Orange Tree itself, and liberate the captive damsel. They set forward with great courage and in good order; but they might just as effectively have stayed at home, for, after wandering about the

No. 24.

forest for three days, they returned crestfallen enough, not only being unable to discover the Orange Tree, but even the plain in which it stood! Poor Ludolph, whom the Princes had vainly endeavoured to comfort with the assurance that he had fairly gained the victory, though he had lost the fruit of it, did not return with them. They lost him from their company the first day of their search, and they firmly and devoutly believed the Yellow Dwarf had hooked him also in his infernal claws. Margaret gave herself up to grief; and her sons, finding nothing else was to be done, endeavoured to forget theirs in the bustle of the approaching war.

In the meantime, Brunilda was jogging on at no easy rate behind the Yellow Dwarf, who, when arrived at the Orange Tree, opened the trunk by a sign, and, dismounting, bore his lovely burthen into it. She felt herself, immediately after, descending a flight of steps, which, from the duration of time, appeared to be endless. They did terminate, however, at last, and the Dwarf, placing her roughly upon her feet, retired swiftly from the place, closing the entrance at the bottom of the stairs carefully after him. It was some time after his departure ere Brunilda took courage to open her eyes and look around her; when she did, she found herself in a subterraneous apartment as large as the bedchamber of the Empress Constance (an open field, in which, to satisfy the doubts of the nobles, the Emperor Frederic II., her son, was born). Every article about it was of silver, and there was a magnificence about this underground Palace, which made her conclude it to be the castle and principal residence of her intended husband, the Yellow Dwarf, whose company she did not covet, and who, to do him justice, did not appear to torment her. Food was supplied, and every attention paid to her wishes by many attendants of both sexes, who, however, never exchanged one single word in her hearing. Wearied out by this continual taciturnity, she began to wish for the sound of the human voice, and, thinking she might probably learn something of the Dwarf's intentions from himself, she one day, instead of questioning her dumb attendants as usual about her lover, demanded some tidings of their master. "He cannot approach your presence, Madam," replied one of the mutes, breaking his hateful silence, "unless you request his appearance. A mighty Spirit, one of the enemies of my master's and your felicity, has contrived this misfortune by his spells; but, if you command it, he is permitted to attend you."

Brunilda, who, in giving this required permission, never dreamed of anything more than making inquiries after her family and lover, was confounded to hear the Dwarf, with the most rapturous impertinence, volubly thank her for this approval of his, and generous acknowledgment of her passion. Putting aside his long beard, lest it should throw him down, he knelt fantastically at her feet, seized her white hand, and declared himself the happiest of all demon-born beings. It was in vain that Brunilda reasoned, entreated, and scolded: he protested he was satisfied with the proofs she had given of her love, and, in order to spare her modesty the pain of appearing to

yield too soon, he should put a gentle restraint upon her liberty, and not suffer her to quit his Palace till she became his wife. At this avowal the poor Princess grew outrageous; she asked the little Monster how he had dared to select a Princess of her exalted rank to share his hole under ground, and burrow like rats in the earth? why he had not rather chosen some humble cast-away maiden, who, having nothing in the world to lose, might be contented out of it?

"Rank!" replied the irritated little Demon; "and what is this rank of which you are so vain? An imaginary splendour, bestowed upon some men by the cringing servility of others; the weak fancy that decks one with this supremacy, gives birth to the slavish fear that ensures to him its possession. Rank!" continued the atrabilious little viper, swelling into a respectable width by the overflowing of his angry venom,—"rank! it is power gained by force, won by the sword, by fraud, by oppression! The strongest is the noblest; and if so, I am more than your equal, beautiful Brunilda, for, Princess as you are, you are my captive, and I am your master."

Brunilda wept at this insolence, and, like all who know not how to controvert what they yet cannot bear to acknowledge, hated the Dwarf more than ever, and resolved to prove it to him by seizing every opportunity of annoying him. With this laudable intention, she renewed the attack by commenting with great severity upon his frightful little person; she sneered at his long beard, short legs, and large head. She demanded if he had ever looked in a mirror? and, if he had, how he could presume to imagine he could captivate any woman under such a detestable form? In no age have ugly people borne to be laughed at, for, however hideous they may happen to be, they seldom find it out themselves, and are, in consequence, very much surprised and offended when informed of it by others; and, as vanity is usually the reigning passion of the most disfigured, they seldom pardon an offence which is mortal.

The Dwarf, the ugliest animal the eyes of Brunilda had ever encountered, could hardly believe this possible, and saw no joke in her mirth at his expense; and, as he had his full share of that precious commodity, vanity, he raved, stormed, and became so insolent, that Brunilda was compelled to order him out of her presence. This command, which he was obliged to obey, irritated the little creature to madness, and he swore that, since he could not enter her presence without her permission, he would find a mode of making her give it whenever he should condescend to require it. This threat had more of truth in it than Brunilda imagined.

A few days after this animated conversation, the Dwarf sent to ask leave to be allowed to pay his visit to the Princess, which was immediately refused. This threw him into a rage, and he informed the Princess, by one of his mutes, that her lover, Ludolph of Tecklenburgh, was in his power, and that his head should pay for the scorn with which she thought proper to treat her lord and husband.

Poor Brunilda hastily gave the required permission, upon condition that Ludolph should accompany him;

and her "lord and husband," as he styled himself, entered a few moments after, followed by the Knight, whom his Demons had seized in the forest. "There, Madam," said he, grinning like Grimaldi, but not so merrily, "I found this stranger in the neighbourhood of my Orange Tree, and I have brought him hither to secure a welcome for myself. Did I not tell you I would make you glad to receive me? Here shall this valorous Knight remain, a hostage for your good behaviour; and never shall you receive him without admitting me at the same moment."

Brunilda, who would have been delighted, in her present condition, to have seen any human being whatever, was in raptures at the sight of Ludolph, who, on his part, was content with his captivity, since he shared it with her; and unrestrained by the presence of the Dwarf, they so often and so tenderly repeated their mutual delight to each other, that their grim gaoler could not endure the sight of their happiness, and, rather than witness it, withdrew himself and Ludolph from the company of Brunilda, which he did not again seek for some time. When, attended by Ludolph, he next entered her apartment, his jealous tortures were increased by the renewed endearments of the lovers; and, resolving in his own mind not to endure what he flattered himself he could easily remedy, he threw a spell over the unlucky Brunilda, which he generously hoped would destroy all the little tranquillity she enjoyed. The charm operated upon the sight of the Princess, who no longer beheld her lover, but a hideous Negro advancing towards her. Brunilda was terrified, but, reassured by the explanation of the Dwarf, who felicitated himself on her mortification, she resolved to punish him in kind; so, collecting all the woman in her soul, and conquering her dislike of the ugly shape he presented to her, she gave it a most affectionate welcome, and caressed it as her dear Ludolph. The Dwarf would willingly have annihilated him; but, obliged to keep him in existence to ensure himself admittance to Brunilda, he resolved to embitter that existence as much as lay in his power, and, having once more recourse to his spells, the handsome Ludolph, unchanged to himself, appeared to the eyes of the fascinated Princess a furious and monstrous Tiger, armed with tremendous fangs and claws. But love penetrates all disguises, and the Princess was now a match for the Sorcerer. She knew that the fangs and claws, however terrible to others, had no danger for her; and she suffered him to lie at her feet, kiss her snowy hand, and put his shaggy head upon her lap, without manifesting the slightest apprehension, to the great annoyance of the Dwarf, whose dull wit was sharpened by his jealousy; and he now contrived the masterpiece of spells, to the increased misery of poor Brunilda, over whose clouded senses the charm once more operating, presented her beloved Ludolph only under the form of the Yellow Dwarf himself. This transformation was horrible to both the sufferers, for each of the figures maintained that he was the Knight, and persisted in execrating the other as the impostor; while Brunilda, wearied with gazing on their hateful countenances, dared not afford the slightest notice of either, lest she should

bestow the tenderness designed for Ludolph upon his detestable rival. In vain did she weep, threaten, and supplicate the Dwarf to give her lover "any shape but that." She knew not even to which of the pair she ought to address her petition. But the Demon was inexorable, listened unmoved to her sorrows, for his heart was as hard as Pharaoh's, and even inwardly laughed at her agonies. In vain did she examine their features, in the hope of discovering some slight difference that might point out her lover: both grinned the same ghastly smile,—both exhibited the same unvarying ugliness of feature. Alas, poor Brunilda! Lavater himself could not have assisted thee, though, hadst thou lived in our days, or Dr. Spurzheim in thine, some professional examination of the cerebral organization of the two dwarfs might have set the question at rest. Doubtless, some bump extraordinary, some wonderful dilation of the organ of self-esteem in the skull of the true Dwarf, or amativeness or combativeness in that of the false one, might have aided thee to discover the unbrutified soul confined in the brutified body. But, as it was, they were both brutes to Brunilda, and, as she had no wish to charm the Yellow Dwarf, she wept her disappointment incessantly. Nor was Ludolph less busy than the Princess in employing threats and prayers by turns to mollify the Dwarf, though one was to as little purpose as the other, in the presence of the Princess. The cunning Demon reiterated the same whining petition, used the same arguments, and denounced the same vengeance as the unhappy Ludolph; and when retired from her apartment, laughed at his success, and replied to every threat with mingled hate and defiance. It was in vain that Ludolph accused him of having broken all laws of chivalry, held even by Demons so sacred. He told him he regarded no laws, except those which he had made himself. It was to no purpose he argued his right to be set at liberty at least. The Dwarf, who was a philosopher in his way, replied that men had no rights, and that *might*, which he possessed, was a much better argument, and a more effective weapon. All this was unluckily true, but it did not convince the Westphalian.

Some one has said, that we have two ears, and but one tongue, that we may hear much and say little. It is a wise observation, and happy are those that profit thereby. Our two captives might, if they had had the good luck ever to have heard it; but as they had not, they acted directly counter, for they so heartily used their two tongues, and so entirely spared their four ears, that their gaoler grew outrageous; and therefore, except when he went to torment Brunilda, he resolved to free himself from the society of the Count of Tecklenburgh, who paid for his garrulity by being condemned to talk to himself in one of the most dreary dungeons of the cavern. Here he had full leisure to think of his misfortunes, and execrate the contriver of them. He prayed night and morning, with all the strength of lungs he could command, to all the saints in the calendar, to give him a lift out of this purgatory. He was too good a Christian not to abhor all thought of magic; but,

187

finding how little notice was taken of his petition by the higher powers, he could not help thinking of the lower, and wishing and vowing, that if some Sorcerer, Witch, or even Demon, would but come to his assistance now, he would find time enough for repentance hereafter, and heal his conscience and propitiate Heaven by many good deeds to be done in perspective. "I would walk to Jerusalem, for a penance," said he; "or give the spoils I shall take in my next battle to the church; or I would, when I shall be able, endow an abbey. Either of these designs would be satisfactory," continued he, "and oh, that I had the good luck to be able to put them into execution! Oh, that some friendly spirit, some Gnome of these caverns, or Demon of this forest, would come to my assistance!"

No sooner said than done: the sinner trembled at the instant fulfilment of his wicked wish, and began with real alarm to suspect that he was a bit of a conjurer himself; for there arose in the moment, from the bosom of the earth, a gigantic dusky-looking Figure in the human shape, inquiring his commands. "I could not come to your assistance," said the Object, "till you summoned me, or you should not have suffered so long. I am the mortal foe of the Yellow Dwarf, and the legitimate Prince of these mines, into which he has intruded himself during my absence in a short journey I made to the centre. He has fixed himself pretty firmly in my Palace by his spells, but I shall contrive to dispossess him. I will begin by assisting you. Speak, Knight of Tecklenburgh; how can I serve you?"

Ludolph, who, recovered from his first fright, desired nothing better, immediately struck a bargain with the friendly Gnome; the first article of which was, that he should liberate himself and the Princess.

"I can free you instantly," replied the Gnome, "but the spells around the Princess are too powerful to be suddenly broken; nevertheless, with your help it may finally be done. We must possess ourselves of the charm in which lies the power of the Dwarf; this, unfortunately, is his beard, for it will be a work of difficulty to master it. Could you, in your combat, have cut off that, instead of his head, all would have been well; but, as long as that beard hangs to his chin, his body is invulnerable, for, cut him into fifty pieces, and he will unite together again. Notwithstanding all these difficulties, observe faithfully all my directions, and, ultimately, we may accomplish our wishes. Beneath those mountains of Bohemia which bound the marquisate of Misnia, there is a diamond mine, as yet unknown to the human race, whose sacrilegious hands have not there torn open the heart of their mother earth, and disturbed the spirits who sleep in her bosom. There, concealed many fathoms beneath the mountain, has been hidden for centuries the magic weapon which alone can conquer the Yellow Dwarf. It is that identical Pair of Scissors with which the Demon Fate cuts asunder your mortal destinies; these, and these only, can secure our enemy. It will be in vain to cut off his head, so long as he retains his beard; and that beard is unapproachable, except to the Magic Scissors of Fate. The chief difficulty will be in obtaining pos-

session of this wonderful instrument; since only a knight of unstained loyalty, pure, spotless, free from all taint of libertinism, drunkenness, and bloodshed, can take them from the hands of the statue which holds them, without incurring the severe penalty of instant death. When such a knight shall be found, the Scissors must be put into the hands of a woman who has never told a lie, for only such can use them in cutting off the formidable beard; should any other woman attempt it, the inevitable consequence would be also death from the Scissors themselves."

Poor Ludolph was as much depressed by the end of this discourse as he had been elevated by the beginning. Such a knight it was indeed next to impossible to find. He himself was as good and true as most; his loyalty was indeed unstained; he had not shed blood in a murderous or treacherous manner; but he had been too frequently engaged in his father's petty and often unjustifiable wars, to undertake an enterprize that demanded hands free from stain. Then, as for drunkenness,—alas for poor Ludolph!— though naturally a very sober man, he knew he had too often shared many a "t'other flask," and too frequently drowned his fears of the Abbot of Fulda in the big bowl of Tecklenburgh, to permit him any chance of success in the achievement. In his own person, therefore, he gave it directly up, satisfied of his incapacity from the fore-mentioned weaknesses, without carrying his self-examination any further, but at the same time almost despairing of finding a substitute. "For the truthful virgin, friendly Gnome," said the honest Westphalian, "there I have better hopes, since there are enough at Court, and I shall find this part of my task easy enough."

"Not quite so easy as you imagine, Knight," replied the Gnome, "since there is not an unmarried lady in all Thuringia who will not lay claim to that honour, and you may thus be the innocent cause of the death of many; but I can assist you here, and make this part of the undertaking much less difficult. Here is a Magic Girdle: obtain permission to try it, without speaking of its virtues, upon the ladies of the Margrave's Court. Should the dame who shall buckle it on be a deceiver, the Girdle, though now appearing of a large size, will shrink into the smallest compass, and will not even encircle her slender waist: should the lady be the object of your search, it will set closely and gracefully to her form."

"A thousand thanks," replied the honest Knight; "I have no fears for my success in this point, and perhaps I may be more fortunate than I expect in the other. Now then, generous friend, accomplish your kind intention, release me from this dungeon, and I will immediately hasten to Eisenac and seek a maiden who may assist to break these abominable enchantments."

"I will," replied the Spirit; "but do not forget that to other eyes as well as Brunilda's you still wear the form of the Yellow Dwarf; this is occasioned by three orange-coloured hairs from his formidable beard, tied round your right arm; unloose them, and you will appear to others as you do to yourself and me. Be under no alarm for the safety of the Princess, since I have already prevented your enemy's entering her presence without her permission, and will still continue to watch over her."

The Knight again thanked the Gnome for his friendly care, and shutting his eyes, by command of his companion, and opening them again the next instant, found himself, to his infinite joy, standing near the Orange Tree, round which his horse was quietly grazing. He soon sprang lightly into his saddle, and turned his head from the wood, determined to reach Eisenac ere daybreak. With this resolution he spurred on gaily, thinking on the joy he should feel upon liberating his beloved Brunilda, when, in a turn of the wood, he suddenly encountered a troop of knights in the livery of the Yellow Dwarf. A cold shivering seized him, for he expected to be dragged back again neck and heels to the Orange Tree; when, to his utter astonishment, they all lowly saluted, and respectfully made way for him to pass. He now remembered that he had not yet removed the orange-coloured hairs from his arm, and feeling himself indebted to this circumstance for his safety, resolved to let them remain till he should be quite out of the infernal forest. Dwelling fondly upon his hopes and brightening prospects, the young morning sun found him entering Eisenac, where he was greeted with a loud shout by a troop of boys, who seemed to recognize an old acquaintance. Soon the boy crowd was augmented by a multitude of citizens, who surrounded Ludolph, yelling like fiends, seized his bridle, pinioned his arms, and saluted him with a volley of dreadful curses. "Sorcerer, Robber, Demon!" rang in his ears in all directions, and, while the uproar raged in its greatest violence, he was dragged from his horse, and thrown on the ground. At this extraordinary treatment, the Count demanded to be conducted to the Margrave, to the Princess Margaret. He was told that the Court had quitted Eisenac, but they were resolved to burn him alive, in revenge for his treatment of their beloved Princess and the noble Count Ludolph, her destined husband.

Solomon said, that "Fear is nothing else than a betraying the succours which reason offereth;" and in this case it was most truly so, for the Knight's agitation in the first part of the attack, had made him forget to remove the orange-coloured hairs from his arm. Their last exclamation had shown him their mistake, and his own fatal imprudence. Now he found that he was in danger of being burnt alive for the sins of the execrable Dwarf, unless he could immediately free himself from the charm. "Hear me, dear friends," he cried, "I am truly the unhappy Ludolph, but your eyes are bewitched by the sorceries of that abominable Demon, and you see me only under his resemblance; release my arms for one moment, and I will convince you."

At this insult to their understandings, the wise men of Eisenac set up a most tremendous howl, and were still more anxious to collect faggots for his service. They kicked, buffeted, and reviled his person till he was almost delirious with rage, and the foamings of his indignation confirmed them in their belief that he really was, what he appeared, the Demon of

the Orange Tree During one of the pauses made by his guards to listen to his earnest entreaties for a moment's liberty, he found means to disengage his hands from their grasp, tore open his sleeve, and furiously rending away the slight bandage of hair, stood before them in his own proper person.

Astonishment for a moment tied up the tongues of the assembly, but quickly recovering themselves, before Ludolph could gain time to explain, they declared it a new piece of sorcery, and swore that the form of their gallant favourite should not shield the Wizard who, they firmly believed, was his murderer.

The magistrates and officers of Eisenac, aroused by the seizure of the Demon Dwarf, had assembled upon the spot, and, startled by the wonders they now heard, trembled to think of the consequences of the unbridled fury of the mob, should the story told by the equivocal Knight be really true. Anxious to avoid the spilling of innocent blood, they proposed conveying him to prison, and awaiting the decision of the Margrave; but the people anticipated a sight, and rather than lose so excellent a joke as that of roasting a Sorcerer, they would willingly have run the hazard of sacrificing even Ludolph himself. But the magistrates, much to their honour, continued firm, and, through their interference, poor Ludolph, who already felt the flames crackling under him, with much difficulty obtained permission to say a few words to them in his defence. "Noble magistrates and discerning judges," said the mob-hunted Count of Tecklenburgh, "I trust that you will believe that I really am myself, as I declare to you by my knighthood I am. As for the Yellow Dwarf—a curse on him!—I am his victim, not his ally; since it is from his infernal enchantments, and still more infernal malice, all my misfortunes have arisen. How you can for a moment imagine that I could be his friend, because I have been unlucky enough to appear under his odious form, I am at a loss to imagine; since nobody surely can possibly believe such a transformation to be a matter of choice."

The female part of the audience perfectly agreed with this last observation of Ludolph, and the magistrates, puzzled by the sincerity with which he had delivered his remonstrance, determined to save him, at least, from the fire and the faggots. But, as the people had expected a show, thought the wise men of Eisenac, "a show they must have," or the consequences, they knew, of their disappointment in an affair so essential to their well-being, might not be entirely insignificant to their betters. So, while acquitting him, in their consciences, of being the Yellow Dwarf, and forbidding the animating use of fire and faggots, they condemned him to be put to the ban, as a nobleman, for dabbling in a little private sorcery in conjunction with the Demon, in whose villanous shape he had just appeared. No sooner was this righteous sentence pronounced against the unlucky Ludolph, than he was seized by the soldiers and followed by all the crowd, who, anxious to join in the fun, exhibited many a practical witticism at his expense, and cracked all their superfluous jokes upon his unfortunate person; then stripping him of his armour and knightly accoutrements, and clothing him in raw and filthy goatskins, they set him upon a sorry mule, with his face towards the tail, and led him through the town, the herald proclaiming before him, "We declare thy wife, if thou hast one, a widow; thy children, if thou hast any, orphans; and we send thee, in the name of the Devil, to the four corners of the earth." Thus sent upon a long voyage, with such a friendly benediction, it would not have been wonderful if the heart of the Knight had sunk with his circumstances, which any heart would have done except a Westphalian one; but that was employed in swelling with indignation, and meditating the best mode of returning the compliments of the Eisenac mobility. While thus occupied, he heard a voice close to his ear, which whispered, "Attend to my orders, and you are safe." He looked earnestly in the direction of the sound, and saw, to his satisfaction, the dusky face of his friend the Gnome beneath the helmet of a soldier. "Let these people continue to believe you the Yellow Dwarf," continued the Spirit; "it is the only way to preserve you from suspicion in your real character; here are the hairs which, in your haste, you threw away. Resist not, while I tie them round your arm, and leave the rest to me."

Ludolph sat silent awhile, under the appearance of a new insult; his instructor twisted the light band round his arm, and the shrieks of the people a moment after announced that the charm had taken effect upon their senses. "It is the Sorcerer," they cried, "the horrible Dwarf! Seize him, tear him, burn him!"

But, for this time, their kind intentions were completely frustrated, for the Gnome, entering into the sorry mule which carried the prisoner, communicated to his worn-out frame such inconceivable vigour and rapidity, that a few minutes were sufficient to bear his rider far beyond the pursuit of his enemies, who remained in the market-place, staring after the beast and cursing the Yellow Dwarf.

The representative of that malignant little Demon was meanwhile receiving a few drops of a powerful cordial from the hands of his friend, the Gnome of the Mine, who politely apologized for not knowing earlier the mischiefs into which his dear crony had fallen, owing, however, entirely to his own excessive carelessness, which he should never have suspected. "And, in truth," continued the friendly Spirit, "I concluded you were safe at the Margrave's Court, which is at Weimar, and whither I had intended to follow you. Passing over Eisenac, I rested to know the meaning of the tumult I witnessed, and was just in time to rescue you from the rage of the mob, who would not have quitted their prey, even after the soldiers should have set you at liberty. Here," continued the Gnome, giving him a heavy bag of coin—a most welcome present to a half-naked knight-errant—"hasten to equip yourself according to your rank, and lose no time in joining the Court at Weimar, where you must select a damsel to conclude the adventure, ere Brunilda can recover her liberty, or you be freed from the malice of the Yellow Dwarf."

Ludolph heartily thanked his good friend, though he could not help thinking it would have been as well if his assistance had been tendered some few hours earlier. But still, "better late than never," thought the Knight; and, though he had received a few cuffs and many bitter curses, yet hard words break no bones, and the cuffs he hoped one day to repay with interest. In the interim, his honour was preserved by the contrivance of the Gnome, as no man in Eisenac, no, not even the sapient magistrates themselves, would ever believe the creature they had pounded and worried so unmercifully, was any other than the Yellow Dwarf himself. Receiving from his hands once more the Magic Girdle which he had lost in the confusion, he bade farewell to the Gnome, who promised to meet him in the forest, when he should have obtained the Magic Scissors, upon which their success depended; and, after accoutring himself as became his condition, not this time forgetting the three red hairs, he set forward once more for the Court of the Margrave; and, as he was by no means of a melancholy complexion, his past misfortunes had no other effect upon his spirits than elevating them to a joyous pitch for glee that he had so well escaped the dangers which he believed would have ended more tragically. And thus gay, and hoping much from the future, he arrived, without any farther adventure, at the Palace of Weimar.

The Princess Margaret was overjoyed once more to see her Brunilda's lover, and she welcomed him with the sincerest regard. She listened with burning indignation to the account of the Dwarf's treatment of his captives, and to such other parts of his history as he thought proper to relate; for he carefully suppressed, in the presence of the Court, his adventures at Eisenac and his release by the Gnome, lest the friendship of this good-natured Spirit should again subject him to the charge of sorcery; and as he had already smelt fire at Eisenac, he was particularly anxious to avoid so warm a reception elsewhere.

He informed the good Princess that the Girdle would only fit the damsel appointed by Destiny to break the enchantment; and, of consequence, all were anxious to try it. Three of the most beautiful ladies in Misnia attempted, but, strange to relate, in vain, to fix on the Magic Cestus. It shrank to nothing round their forms, and Ludolph began again to tremble for the fate of his poor Brunilda. In vain did the most prudish ladies of the Court present their slim forms to the Girdle,—it would not meet around them. Several of those who had been most rigid in their own conduct, and most bitterly virtuous in regard to that of others, took the Girdle with a devout air and a blushing modesty, that quite revived the hope of the Westphalian Knight. Alas! the Cestus not only refused to clasp the waists of these fair ones, but even flew outright out of their hands the moment they touched it; and this circumstance so disheartened Ludolph, that he foolishly enough, ere above twenty ladies had made the attempt, gossiped out the secret of its virtues in the delighted ear of the Princess Margaret. That good lady thought the joke too excellent to be confined to so few persons; and there being among the unlucky twenty some whose beauty rivalled that of her beloved Brunilda, she lost no time in publishing the secret, which had all the effect of making them abhor Ludolph, and defeating the plans he was so anxious to carry into effect; for now, not a single woman acquainted with the virtue of the Cestus would even try it on, and instead of laughing with the Princess and Ludolph at the unlucky discoveries made by the twenty, they made, much to their honour, common cause against them, and vowed to smother the mischievous Knight whenever they could conveniently catch hold of him. It required all the authority of the Margrave, who at this juncture arrived at Weimar from the camp, to protect the unfortunate Knight from their vengeance, who began to be as much afraid of these beautiful destroying angels as he had been of the fire-loving devils of Eisenac, or even the Yellow Dwarf himself. "Alas! I am surely the most unfortunate of men," said he to the Margrave; "I have been transformed to the detested shape of the Yellow Dwarf, for wishing to deliver your sister out of his hands. I have been very near roasted alive for killing myself; I have been put to the ban for suffering myself to be tormented by my powerful enemy; and now I am in danger of being torn to pieces by the loveliest women in the world, only for being anxious to find one truthteller in their company. Ah, my poor Brunilda! what will become of thee?"

The Margrave comforted the Knight with the assurance that he would certainly be successful, if he could but prevail upon the ladies only to try on the Girdle; and, in case of their obstinacy, he advised him to put the Magic Scissors into the hands of Brunilda herself, "For if she be not worthy to use them," said the proud Frederic with the Bitten Cheek, "she is not worthy of liberty, nor the tender love you bear her. For the other conditions, I fear we must despair, since I do not believe there is a knight in my Court, no, nor in all the courts of Germany, that will venture to accept the challenge; though, against mortal foes, they are the bravest men in the univesre."

The Margrave was right. Each knight knew his own secret weaknesses too well to accept the office, when the conditions were stated to them, no one being willing as they honestly avowed, to hazard an ignominious death, by disregarding the injunctions of the Gnome. There was not a man among them who had not, at some time or other, offended by drunkenness, licentiousness, or breaking heads in an unjust quarrel. Indeed, with regard to the latter peccadillo, it was scarcely possible, in the time of which I am treating, for it to be otherwise; since not only disputes of chivalry, and all injuries, whether public or private, were settled by the sword, but even cases of felony and suits of law were arranged by the same expeditious decision; so that he of the strongest arm and stoutest heart infallibly gained his cause, whether right or wrong, as his adversary could no longer contend, either for reputation or property, after the dagger of mercy had been struck into his heart, or drawn quietly across his throat.

But, to return to our good Westphalian and his difficulties. After many objections, disputings, hopings, and fearings, the Margrave at last found a salvo for Ludolph, and a stainless knight for the service of the King of the Oranges. This was his own son, a boy of ten years old, upon whom, finding all other hope fail, he conferred the honour of knighthood, and released him from his martial studies, in which the gallant child spent all his time, and sent him to handle the Shears of Atropus, and share in the glory of shaving the orange-coloured beard of the execrable Dwarf. The little Knight Herman of Misnia was highly delighted by his admittance to this post of honour, and attached himself fondly to his good cousin Ludolph, who now began making preparations for his march.

So great was the terror inspired among the people by the Yellow Dwarf, that it was with much difficulty he could collect troops sufficient to defend the son of the Margrave upon this voyage of discovery, as all the nobles, knights, and regulars of Thuringia, were gone to the camp, in daily expectation of an attack from the Emperor Albert, who, having been just overreached in his views upon Bohemia, by his good cousin Henry of Carinthia, was advancing in no very good humour upon the troops of the Margrave of Misnia. After a proclamation of some days, in which Ludolph puffed the vast riches of the diamond mine with almost as much skill as Day and Martin puff their blacking, a number of strays from all parts of the empire gathered themselves together under his standard; and though he could not boast of commanding many of the nobles of Misnia, yet, upon the whole, his troop was about as respectable as David's at the cave of Adullam, when only those who were in debt, or distress, or discontented, enrolled themselves in his service. But great endings spring from small beginnings. From a captain of half-starved ragamuffins David became a king; and Ludolph hoped that his regiment of blackguards would finally conduct him to the feet of a princess. With this notion he set forward, full of expectation, with the youthful Knight committed to his charge. On their road, fearful of any other delays, he inspirited his companions by dwelling, with affected rapture, upon the spoils of the diamonds, which were so soon to be at their service, in the sack of the mine. These observations acted like electricity upon his respectable warriors, and sent them galloping towards the confines so rapidly, that before he had either hoped or expected it, they had arrived at the foot of the mystic mountain, where the whole troop made a halt, to await the return of Ludolph, who, with his young companion, was to descend first into the caves, seize the Scissors, and then leave the coast clear for the plunderers to attack the mine. Matters were soon settled. The two Knights found the entrance with some difficulty, and boldly descended into these dismal abodes, the residence of the infernal Spirits who were in the pay of the Yellow Dwarf. After traversing many dreary caverns, they entered the last, where, elevated on a golden pedestal, stood the gigantic Statue which held the Scissors of Fate, and was the guardian of the life of the Yellow Dwarf. Forgetting, in his joy at the sight, the caution of the Gnome, he was advancing towards the Statue, when a tremendous box on the ear from the marble fist taught him to know his distance. He fell back accordingly, and young Herman of Misnia approaching, the Statue grinned as hide-

191

ously as his protegé, but made no attempt to injure the boy, as fearlessly he climbed the pedestal, and, without any regard to the rights of property, grasped the Magic Scissors, and brought them away in triumph. Ludolph received them from his hands with the wildest sensation of delight; but prudence conquering his emotions, he took his young preserver in his arms, and retraced his way to daylight. Here he was greeted with shouts of applause from the soldiers, who, in spite of the entreaties of Ludolph, persisted in ransacking the caves, pursuant to their original agreement. In vain did he assure them the Margrave's enemies would furnish more spoils for them than the vaults, and that his share should be divided among them. Vainly did he describe the threatening looks of the Statue, and assure them he still felt the tingling of the marble thump in his ear, with which it had complimented him. It was talking to the winds, or, as old Baker quaintly saith, "to as little purpose as if he had gone about to call back yesterday." Down they all dashed together, neck and heels, with tremendous outcries, into the diamond caverns. But their return was silent and orderly enough. The cave of Trophonius could not have effected a better or more expeditious change. They were all as grave as judges, and every man appeared with his mouth twisted exactly under his left ear. Ludolph could gain but little information as to what had befallen them; all he understood was, that they had seen the Statue, who had given the first man such a thundering slap of the face that its shock was felt by all the rest of his companions, and left the consequences which he now beheld, and which they had such good reasons to deplore. But, while the Knights of the Scissors and their wry-mouthed confederates are pursuing their road to Weimar, let us pop our heads underground, and see what has become of Brunilda.

The poor Princess, much disconcerted by the diabolical contrivance of the Yellow Dwarf, gave way, when alone, to that indulgence of grief which she resolutely suppressed in his presence. She had encouraged the visits of the two Dwarfs, in the tender hope that, though they afforded no consolation to herself, they might yield some satisfaction to the bosom of her tormented lover. This being the real state of her feelings, she was deeply distressed when, the day after Ludolph's release by the Gnome, they neglected to pay her the customary visit, and therefore sent to request the presence of her tyrant.

He came, and in no very good humour, for he had just failed in the effect of a spell, which he hoped would discover the runaway. He told her, even more brutally than usual, that Ludolph had escaped; that he was endeavouring to discover him; and that, in case he succeeded, of which he had no doubt, he would immediately hang him, unless the Princess would save his life by giving her hand to his rival.

Delighted by the escape of the Knight, Brunilda could not keep her joy to herself, but expressed it so imprudently, and with such heartfelt glee at the Dwarf's vexation, that it irritated all the bile in his little yellow body, and provoked him to have recourse to his most powerful spells to discover the abode of Ludolph. It was, luckily for the Knight, a work of time and difficulty, since the Gnome of the Mine was at hand to unravel all his charms as fast as the other wrought them; and he was, by this means, obliged to desist, in order to find the invisible enemy who thus thwarted his plans and protected his victim. The indefatigable Gnome was still at his elbow, and poor Yellow-Beard continued as much in the dark at the end of his spells, as he had been at the beginning. All this gave the Knight time, which was what the Gnome wanted; and the Dwarf remained in ignorance of his movements, till the Spirits, who were the guardians of his talisman in the mountain caves, informed him of his danger and the seizure of the Magic Scissors. Such a contrivance as that of knighting a child the Demon had never contemplated, but finding one half of the adventure accomplished, he determined, as far as in him lay, to prevent the achievement of the other. Learning by his Fiends that he was threatened with danger from Brunilda, he made it his principal care that the Magic Scissors should not be wielded by her, and accordingly penned her up more closely than ever, surrounding her by spells, not only inaccessible to mortals, but even to his own attendant Spirits, whom he would not trust too far, lest his tyranny should have inspired them with hatred to his person, and laxity in his service. Among his equals in the Demon world, he well knew and feared the indignation of the Gnome of the Silver Mines, whose territories he had invaded, and before whose power, if joined to that of other enemies, he would have good reasons to tremble. These considerations determined his conduct; and to prevent Brunilda from handling the Scissors, and the Scissors from approaching his Beard, he devised a spell so potent, that he fondly hoped and believed he was safe from the attacks of, and might bid defiance to, all sorts of enemies, natural and supernatural.

In the meantime, Ludolph and his companions had arrived at the Court of Weimar, to the great joy of the Margrave and his mother, who, looking upon the adventure as nearly finished, entreated Ludolph to lose no time in joining his friend the Gnome in the Enchanted Forest. He himself had no wish to delay the business; and, after making one more unsuccessful attempt to prevail upon the ladies of Misnia to try on the Girdle, he set off to present it to his lovely Brunilda; and, arriving near the Orange Tree, was met by the friendly Gnome. "It is not yet in my power to introduce you to the presence of the Princess," said he to the Count, "as I have not yet conquered the spells by which our enemy has surrounded her. The cavern is inaccessible at present to any human foot, but it is not in the power of the Demon to limit my steps in the territory of which I am the legitimate lord. His Spirits are as powerful as mine, and thus I am obliged to have recourse to artifice to conquer him, which I should not be able to effect, if he had not, by obtruding into my dominions, placed the secret of his spells in my power. Unlike the free Spirits who have existed from the beginning of the world, and who will probably survive its demolition, the Dwarf is mortal-born, though, by magic

192

BRUNILDA DISENCHANTS THE YELLOW DWARF, BY CUTTING OFF HIS BEARD.

spells, he has lengthened his life many hundred years; but his birth subjects him to death, which will be inevitable, should the infernal power by which he has accomplished his purposes be defeated. To prevent this catastrophe, he has placed his life on a talisman, which he believes unconquerable, but which, I trust, we shall overthrow. Caution is, however, necessary, for his spells are mighty, and the Spirits subjected to his command are many. In the interim, you shall rest here, and I will provide for your necessities till I shall be able to conduct you to Brunilda, to whom you must explain the virtues of the Scissors of Fate; for, by an immutable decree which no Spirit dares violate, I am restrained from appearing before her till she herself shall summon me." The Gnome then raised a comfortable tent for Ludolph, loaded it with provisions, drew a line of protection about it, and vanished.

Three days passed tranquilly enough with Ludolph, while patiently awaiting the reappearance of his friend the Gnome; but the fourth was beginning to hang very heavy, when the Spirit entered the tent in the middle of the night. "I triumph," said he; "I have unloosed the spell that kept you from the presence of Brunilda. The Dwarf, being mortal-born, is subject to mortal necessities, and at this hour he sleeps; rise, and throw yourself at the feet of the Princess; give me your hand, and close your eyes."

Ludolph obeyed, and the next moment found himself in the apartment of Brunilda. As I, the honest chronicler of the loves of the Westphalian Knight and Misnian Princess, am no great dealer in sentiment, I shall omit all the particulars of the meeting, and only say how truly happy Brunilda was to receive him, and how grateful she felt towards the obliging Gnome, whom she gladly summoned to her presence. To the great relief of Ludolph, who trembled and doubted grievously while making the proposal, she had not the slightest objection, even after she was made acquainted with its virtues, to try on the Enchanted Girdle, which fitted her graceful form as if it had been purposely made for her. Her lover could not help commending the taste of the Yellow Dwarf, and was as much overjoyed at this earnest of success, as if he already held the Demon's beard in his hand. The Gnome then gave Brunilda the fatal Scissors, and telling them that the Spirits of their enemy could not perceive them, from the powerful spells by which they were surrounded, desired them to follow his footsteps fearlessly to the inner caverns, where slept the Demon, and whom sleep would probably render defenceless. Stretching out their necks, and stepping on tiptoe, the lovers followed the Gnome to the private apartment of the Dwarf, whom Brunilda anxiously hoped to serve in quality of barber extraordinary. With beating hearts they beheld their guide throw open the door of his chamber, and desire the Princess to advance, at the same time approaching the couch of the Demon, and drawing back the curtains.

Brunilda obeyed; mustering all her courage, and collecting a little army of disagreeable remembrances to her aid, she found herself so strengthened, that, like Judith, she resolved to finish the business with a single snip. But the Holofernes of Germany had more wit than his drunken predecessor, and had taken much better care of his shaggy head; for the Judith of Misnia looked in vain for the yellow beard that was to fall beneath the fatal Scissors. That that had disappeared was not wonderful, since the face to which it formed such a remarkable appendage had entirely vanished from the body! There lay the carcase of the Dwarf, sleeping, it might be; but his head was dozing in some other place, for the body was very quietly reposing without it! Poor Brunilda shed tears of vexation, and the Gnome looked silly enough, to find himself thus completely outwitted; but knowing that he could find no remedy for the disappointment by standing gaping at the Demon's trunk, he drew the lovers from the chamber, conducted Ludolph back to his tent, and again had recourse to his spells, which told him that the Dwarf, fearful of surprise while disarmed by sleep, took off his head every night, and concealed it in some place of safety, but where he could not dis-

cover. This was a vexatious incident; but, "trick for trick," thought the Gnome, and to work he went, with a fresh resolution to outspell the Yellow Conjuror, and liberate the lovers.

In the meantime, the Demon awoke from his invigorating slumber, and hastened to replace his ugly head upon his shoulders; and then, head and tail once more united, sat down to consider the possibility of recapturing the Knight of Tecklenburgh, in whose hands, notwithstanding the success of his spells, he did not like to leave the Magic Scissors. Brunilda, it is true, was safe enough; but the Dwarf knew (though Ludolph could not discover them) that there were more truthful ladies than one in the Misnian Court; and that the Count wanted neither eloquence to persuade such to assist him, nor resolution to attack his enemy, when that difficulty should be conquered. In the midst of these cogitations, he was aroused by a summons from the Princess, who had not permitted him to approach her since the day after Ludolph's departure. The little coxcomb was enchanted by the message, and hastened to arrange his looks in the most becoming manner possible, ere he presented himself before the eyes of his lovely captive. Brunilda was in tears when he entered her apartment; and no sooner did she behold him, than she poured upon him such a torrent of reproach and abuse, that the Dwarf, though in general tolerably well skilled in the use of that cutting weapon the tongue, stood utterly confounded, and knew not what to reply. She accused him vehemently of the murder of her lover, her dear Ludolph; which secret, she said, had been revealed to her in a dream by her patron saint that very night, and she had therefore sent for him to accuse him to his guilty face. The Dwarf listened in surprise; but, this time, far from retorting with his usual bitterness upon Brunilda, he was hugging himself in the notion that the patron saint might have told the truth, and that Ludolph, whom all his arts had failed to discover, might really be no longer an inhabitant of the earth; in which case, he flattered himself he might possibly succeed him in the affections of the fair Brunilda, whose hand he coveted no less than her brother's lands, of which he resolved to dispossess him whenever he should become the husband of his sister. Full of these agreeable hopes and ideas, he soothed the weeping Princess as well as the ruggedness of his nature would permit, and assured her, that though her lover was dead (a circumstance of which, he averred, he was well aware, though compassion had hitherto prevented his informing her), yet he had no hand in his death, and would endeavour, by every mark of tenderness and attention, to reconcile her to this inevitable loss. Brunilda suffered herself to be comforted, and even allowed his yellow lips to press her fair hand, which so delighted the lover, that he released her from her severe confinement, and permitted her to roam at large through the caverns, and occupy her former apartment, where he continued to visit her daily, and daily quitted her with the flattering hope that he had at length discovered the mode of making himself agreeable.

Brunilda encouraged this delightful dream by her changed method of conduct; she ceased, after the first two interviews, entirely, to reproach the Dwarf, and permitted his attentions without any ill humour. From suffering his devotions, she gradually appeared to desire them, and even frequently condescended to rally him upon the oddity of his dress, and the old-fashioned cut of his hood; he immediately adopted another to gratify her taste, and was exceedingly vain of the notice she took of him. She admired his flowing hair, and even his long beard had ceased to be an object of disgust to her; everything became beautiful by custom, she said; and she now discovered, what her indignation before had prevented her from observing, that the colour of his beard was the same as that of her great grandfather the Emperor Frederic II., who was universally accounted a very handsome man.

The Dwarf smirked, bridled, and was equally delighted with Brunilda and himself, since he now hoped no farther opposition on her part would be offered to his proposals; he grew excessively fond of, and very indulgent to the Princess, suffering her to command in his caverns, and taking great delight in exhibiting to her the riches of which she was so soon to be the mistress.

In all ages, among all nations, flattery has ever been the shortest and the surest road to the human heart; and men, however they may affect to smile at this weakness in the gentler sex, are not themselves, whether giants, middle-sized men, or dwarfs, one whit less subject to this poor human frailty than the ladies themselves, in whom it is so pardonable. Let us see what effect this pleasant medicine, so gently administered, had upon the mind of the little Dwarf. He was, in truth, the happiest of all yellow men; for, deceived by the tranquillity of his life and the strength of his spells, he believed his enemy had given up the task of conquering him, and left him to wear his beard in quiet.

Brunilda still continued amiable, and heard him frequently, without any marks of indignation, express his hope that, when the time of her sorrowful mourning for the Count of Tecklenburg should be over, she would listen with compassion to the sufferings of a truer lover. She neither checked nor encouraged these expectations; and the happy Demon determined not to forfeit her affection by any precipitation on his part. All this amiable conduct, however, on the part of Brunilda, was, in fact, but a contrivance of the friendly Gnome, who thus hoped to extort by her means the secret of his nightly pillow from himself. According to the plan agreed upon by the allies, the Gnome, at this period of his enemy's courtship, began again to disturb and puzzle him by his enchantments; and he succeeded in discomposing the harmony of his feelings so much, that he was obliged to have recourse to Brunilda, and (secure of her attachment to his person) vent all his complaints and vexations in her compassionating bosom. She was all astonishment at the cruel designs projected against the Dwarf by his ungenerous enemies; she implored him pathetically to take care of his head, (a request with which he graciously promised to comply, more for her sake than his own,) and exhibited such anxiety to know if his precautions were sufficient, that the Dwarf almost betrayed his secret, overcome by the excessive vanity

her conduct was so well calculated to inspire. Relaxing from his habitual caution, he was about to inform her of some arrangements of his spells, when Brunilda, overacting the part assigned to her, entreated him, if he valued her happiness, to commit his precious head every night to her keeping, promising to guard it with the utmost tenderness and care. At this imprudent request, all his suspicions returned; he eyed Brunilda askance, and gravely told her that, even were she his bride, he could not grant her desire, as it had always been his opinion, that the less wives were trusted with the care of their husband's heads the better. He left her surlily; he had himself told her of his headless rest, but he did not expect such a request would follow his information; and Brunilda, alarmed by the consequences of her ill-timed petition, summoned the Gnome of the Mine to her presence. He chid her precipitation, but gave her a small phial, containing a delicious cordial, which should repair the mischief. "You may have observed," said he, "that the Dwarf neither eats nor drinks of your food; prevail upon him once to sup at your table, and pour a few drops of this cordial into his drink; he must take it willingly, or it will have no effect. In the sleep which follows the enchanted draught, he will be partly in my power, and compelled to answer any question you may propose to him. I need not direct you what to ask; but should he reply according to our wishes, summon me to your side, and the business is done."

The Gnome gave her the potion, and vanished; while Brunilda diligently applied herself to remove the suspicions of the Dwarf. In a few days she completely succeeded; and the flattered Demon, on hearing her frequently complain of the insipidity of supping alone, requested permission to attend her at table during her supper. This request was readily granted, and the visit constantly repeated by the Dwarf, who at length, at her earnest entreaty, consented to partake of her repast. This was continued till all suspicion was removed from the mind of the Dwarf; and in one of his happiest moods she insisted upon his pledging her in wine; he obeyed, and, with the contents of the bowl, swallowed the magic cordial. With what anxiety did Brunilda count the hours till she deemed the Dwarf had retired to rest! how she trembled as she quitted her chamber for that of her tyrant, whose beard, ere day-break, she hoped, would be the reward of her courage! With a beating heart she entered his apartment, and stepping up to him, demanded, in a trembling voice, "Dwarf of the Orange Tree, where hast thou hidden thy head?" The stubborn carcase made no reply to this straightforward question; and Brunilda shivered from head to foot as she considered the possibility of his not yet being asleep, and both hearing and understanding her question. "Should it be so, I am indeed utterly undone," said poor Brunilda; "for how shall I ever be able to deceive him again, since he must now be aware of my motives?" Another reflection brought more comfort; she recollected that, as the head only can hear, so the head only can answer questions; and she determined to walk quietly through all the caverns, and repeat the question in each.

195

She had but a short time allowed her for action, as the Dwarf was an early riser; and she lost none in putting her scheme in execution. Away she sallied, quick as anxiety would allow her; unwearied she pursued her task, but ranged through every apartment of the subterranean palace without obtaining an answer. She almost thought the Dwarf had removed his head farther off; when, passing through a dismal-looking hole, in which were two iron pillars, she paused to repeat the charm—"Dwarf of the Orange Tree, where hast thou hidden thy head?" "Here!" replied a well-known voice; "here, in the pillar on your left hand." Brunilda started at the sound, but quickly recovered her spirits, and turning to the east, summoned, as agreed upon, her coadjutors to her assistance:— "Gnome of this Mine, I call thee hither: bring with thee my lover, and the Magic Scissors of Fate." In the next instant, her friends were at her side, and the Scissors glittered in her hand. She explained in few words the happy result of her enterprise; the Gnome struck the pillar with his mace, the massy substance divided, and the ugly head of her detested gaoler rolled at the feet of the delighted Brunilda, who, without any apology, seized it, and began most nimbly to ply the Magic Scissors. At that moment, the Dwarf, awakened by the near approach of morning, flew to replace his head upon his shoulders, and discovered, with the utmost rage and alarm, the intruders upon his premises. The opened eyes of the head now directed the motions of the body, which rushed forward, and bounced upon them so suddenly, that Brunilda shrieked, and dropped the head, only retaining a grasp of the beard. The Dwarf as nimbly caught it, and endeavoured to wrest it from her; but the Princess, invigorated by despair and the exclamations of her friends, kept fast hold of it, and struggled stoutly with the Demon. The Gnome lent her his assistance, in holding the head for her Scissors; while Ludolph kept shoving, thrusting, and hacking with his sword at the invulnerable Demon, in the hope of obliging him to loosen his grasp of his head. The struggle continued some minutes, the Dwarf pulling, Ludolph shoving, and Brunilda, utterly regardless of the scratches he was liberally bestowing upon her lover, cutting away at the yellow beard with all her might and main. At length, she observed, that the longer she cut, the weaker grew the resistance of the Demon, and this gave new force to her delicate fingers; she snipped on, till the last hair was separated from the chin, and the yellow head and deformed body both fell senseless together upon the ground. Brunilda was quietly looking upon her fallen enemy, when the magic instrument of her success suddenly sprang from her hand, and she beheld the Scissors of Fate gliding away rapidly through the air, as if borne off by an invisible Spirit. The friendly Gnome then conducted the lovers to the Margrave's Court, (after demanding from Brunilda the Magic Belt, which, he said, would be too dangerous a weapon in the hand of a lady); and a few weeks after the battle of Luckow, in which the Margrave was successful, they were united, to the great joy of all parties, but more particularly of those who expected to be invited to the wedding dinner.

196

The day was happier than it was long, for all thought its felicity was too short-lived, except Ludolph and his Princess, who had many still brighter, as long years of happiness was the reward of their few months of suffering. The Gnome of the Mine returned to his recovered territories, and, as he had now no farther occasion for their services, never since that time interfered in the concerns of mortals. The Princess Margaret lived to a good old age, and died at last in the odour of sanctity, eschewing evil, Satan, sin, and the Yellow Demon of the Orange Tree.

JOHN'S THREE TRIALS.

SOMEWHERE about half-way towards the middle of that period of the age of the world which is known as "Once upon a time," men used to understand the language of animals, and could understand what they said to each other; but this knowledge has been unfortunately lost since the invention of reading and writing. But sometimes this knowledge has been preserved in some old families; and it happened that, a long time ago, there lived a King, who was famous beyond all the monarchs of his time for his superior knowledge and wisdom. It seemed as if nothing was too high or too deep for him; and even the birds of the air, it was thought, flew from all parts to convey to his ear the most hidden things and secrets.

Now, this Wise King had a strange custom. He always dined by himself, and every day, after the table was cleared, his body-servant John brought in a silver dish, covered up carefully, and placed it before him. This was done day after day; but even the trusty fellow that brought in the dish, and placed it before the King, never knew what was on it, for the King would never lift the cover until the attendant had backed out from his presence. When he was quite alone, then he would raise the cover, and partake of whatever it was.

At last, one day, John, the trusty Servant, was so worked up by his curiosity, and his fingers itched so to lift the cover, that he could not resist any longer, and rushed with the dish past the King's banqueting-room, and up-stairs to his own bedroom, determined, if he died for it, to see what the King had every day as a finish for his dinner. He locked the door behind him, and then lifted the cover off the silver dish, on which lay a White Snake! He did not admire the King's taste much, but thought he would taste a bit; but scarcely had his tongue touched it, than the voice of the Major-domo was heard loudly calling for the King's body-servant to bring in the King's dish; so John clapped on the cover again, and ran down stairs, just in time to avoid the King's notice.

After leaving the Royal presence as usual, he returned up to his room; but on passing the cage of the Queen's Parrot, was surprised to hear the bird say to itself distinctly, "What a fool our John seems to-day! Something's wrong with him. He has got the look of a thief about him."

This rather surprised John, for he had never heard the Parrot say so much before. But when he got back into his bedroom, and heard his favourite Canary talking through the bars of his cage to some Sparrows, that were hopping about on the window-sill, and found that he could understand every word that passed between them, he began to understand that the morsel of the White Snake that he had eaten off the King's dish had given him the power of understanding the language of birds—no very great accomplishment, as far as he could judge, for he thought there was quite enough time wasted already in listening to women's chattering. But John soon learnt that there is no branch of knowledge, however small, that, once acquired, may not some day turn out extremely valuable. Let us see how this was brought about.

It happened that, on that very day, the Queen had lost the most precious of her rich diamond rings; it could nowhere be found, and as John, being the King's confidential Servant, had the care of the jewels worn on the Royal person, suspicion fell on him regarding it, especially as the Queen's Parrot chattered a great deal to her Majesty, and the King, happening to come into the room, understood what the Parrot was so anxious to tell the Queen; this was, how John had skulked up into his room in a great hurry that very day, and how like a thief he looked when he came down.

"Oho!" said the King; "send for my John instantly."

John was brought in, and felt and looked very like a culprit, fearing to be asked about the White Snake. But when he understood what the matter was, and found that the King questioned him as if his Majesty thought that he, his faithful Servant, had taken the Queen's ring, John's courage increased, and he fired up with the indignation of an honest man. No! John was one of those that would lick a dish, or go out in his master's best hat while his own was being cleaned, or wear his master's gloves; but John would not steal a sixpence. However, as the King said, denials go for nothing. The Queen wanted her ring, and she must have it; and unless John found it for her by the next day, he and his character would be hung up together. It was in vain that he protested his innocence: the King ordered him out of his presence, and refused to alter his determination.

Poor John felt uncommonly downcast as he wandered forth into the courtyard of the stables of the Palace, and stood moodily looking into the pond where the horses were watered, and in which, at that time, there were a great many Ducks disporting themselves.

Two or three white Ducks, in particular, were pluming themselves, and holding a familiar quacking conversation as they smoothed their feathers. Presently they waddled close up to John, and he could hear what they were chatting about. It was the usual reminiscences of nothing of ordinary discourse, such as whereabouts they had waddled, and how their children were, and who was about to be married, and who ought to be, interspersed with remarks on the misconduct of certain Drakes, and their own illnesses and little ailments.

"What stuff!" thought John to himself, and was just about to turn away in disgust, when he heard one stout Duck say, "There is something very hard in my stomach."

"Try a little duckweed, my dear Mrs. Aylesbury," remarked another matronly Duck; "it assists digestion."

"No; that is not it," replied the Aylesbury Duck; "it is the ring I swallowed under the Queen's window this morning, in my haste to gobble the pieces of a Dutch herring her Majesty threw out to us at breakfast-time."

John did not stop to hear more, but he caught Mrs. Aylesbury up by the neck, and in spite of all her flapping and quacking, carried her into the kitchen, and said to the Cook, "Here is a capital fat Duck; just kill it."

"Yes, it is," said the Cook, weighing it in her hand; "why, this Duck must have been fit for table at least a week ago." Then she chopped off the Duck's head without farther delay; and when she came to draw it, in John's presence, what should come out of its stomach but the Queen's ring!

Great was the joy in the Royal kitchen and household on that occasion; for nothing makes servants in a family so miserable as the loss of any article of value, when every one can be suspected, and no one accused.

The King was very sorry for what he had said to John, and the Queen was much rejoiced at regaining her lost jewel. She determined to make some reparation to John, and offered him the next place of honour that fell vacant in her Court. But John's feelings had been wounded; and he requested permission to go away from the Court and the service in which he had been degraded.

But the King insisted on his accepting a horse and arms, wherewith to set out on his travels to see the world, to which the Queen added the present of a purse of money; and then he set forth to travel awhile, to get rid of his melancholy.

He had been out about three days, when, as he was journeying along, he came to a pond; and while looking at it, and thinking how lucky he had been about the Ducks, he remarked three Fishes, which had got entangled among some reeds, and lay gasping for water.

John found now that he could understand what fishes said, as well as birds; and he observed that although fishes are said to be dumb, yet they certainly do utter gentle sounds, perfectly intelligible to each other and all who understand their language. The poor things were complaining that they should have to die so miserably, unable to help each other, and with nobody to help them.

"Not so," said John, getting off his horse, with true compassion in his heart; and he put the three Fishes back again into the water.

Right merrily they splashed as they touched their native element again, and received fresh life and vigour. Then they put up their three little heads out of the water, as they saw John mounting his horse to go away, and wriggled their tails, and waved their fins, and opened their jaws, as they murmured as loudly as they could, "We shall be grateful—you will find us so."

197

"This is a strange adventure," thought John, as he rode along. "How many things there are in the world that one never knows anything about! Perhaps some day we shall know it all, and find that we have had even more to be thankful for than we now think we have."

While thus he bethought himself of his own ignorance, with that humility that is sure to accompany every fresh acquisition of knowledge, which teaches us how much more we have yet to learn, he fancied he heard a voice in the sand, right under his horse's feet. Then he listened, and heard the King of a busy colony of Ants complaining: "Here comes a great awkward clown, treading and crushing my poor industrious subjects, without care, or thought, or mercy. Oh! if these men did but know or think how many there are that have quite as good a right to this life and this world as themselves!"

The truth of this remark struck John very forcibly, although it was not for the first time such a consideration had been presented to his mind. So he turned his horse gently into a side path, and passed out of the course of the operations and travels of the little hardworking insects.

"Go your ways for a real gentleman," said the Ant-King. "We will be grateful to you, and your good feeling will not be without reward."

"Never mind that," said John to himself, as he rode on; "it is a comfort, anyhow, to have well-wishers, even amongst the poor and weak."

Then John's eyes were opened, and he saw, by this new light of kindness and sympathy with small things, how many beautiful things there are in Nature that are lost to the dull and besotted mind of ignorant and selfish, self-sufficient and self-satisfied people. In the beautiful flower of the carnation that he wore in his button-hole—a flower given him at parting by one of the Queen's bower-maidens—he could see sitting in the centre a little airy being, not bigger than one of its leaves, and as transparent as glass. It was an Elfin Sprite or Genius; for in every flower there dwells such a little Spirit, which lives and dies with it. His wings were of the same colour as the leaves of the carnation, but they were so fine that they looked as if the hue were but the red tint that fell from the flower in the moonlight; golden locks, finer than the seed-dust, glided down over his shoulders, and waved in the wind.

Then, as John looked at the open flowers by the wayside more closely and observant, he could see that such a little being rocked in every flower, with wings and airy dress of the same tinge as that of the flower in which it lived. Each rocked on its light leaf, in fragrance and in moonlight; each sang and laughed, but it was as when the wind passes gently over the attuned Æolian harp.

Then he saw hundreds and hundreds of Elves, in quite different habits and forms, coming forth from the dark pine-trees and heath-blossoms along the wayside. What a chattering there was, and such rocking and dancing! They often sprang right over his horse's head, even his very nose, and were not ashamed to perform a circular dance on the rim of his hat. These

Pine-Elves looked like real wild men, with lance and spear; and yet they were airy as the fine mist which, in the morning sun, exhales its fragrance from the bedewed rose.

Then, as John looked on to the great heath he was travelling over, and which, before, he had regarded as so dull, and ugly, and sandy, he could see how every grain of sand was a glittering rock; the long grass-straw, full of dust, that hung out on the road, was the prettiest macadamized way one can imagine for the little Elves. Such a little smiling face peeped forth from every leaf! The pines looked like Towers of Babel, all complete and finished, inhabited by myriads of Elves, from the lowest wood-branch to the very top. The whole air was filled with the strangest figures, and all as clear and quick as light. Four or five Flower-Genii rode on a white butterfly they had driven out of its sleep; whilst others built palaces of the strong fragrance and the finest moonbeams. Some of the Elves were dancing on the thistledown without moving it; others were standing on the round dew-drops; and when they rolled under their feet, and their light drapery fluttered in the air, they looked like the most charming picture of Fortune and her rolling ball. All regarded John with friendly looks, and nodded to him, and recognized him as a man of a kind and tender disposition, a sympathizer with Nature, equally regardful of her smallest as of her largest productions.

John slept well and happily that night; the Elves and Fairies tended him; and though his fare was humble, and his bed hard in the poor inn of the rude village on the heath, his dreams were such as monarchs might have envied. Oh! my little readers, there is no such nightcap, no such coverlet, and no such bed of down, as are furnished by acts of kindness, charity, and mercy, done in the previous evening.

John was up with the lark next morning, light-hearted and singing like that merry morning bird, and, like her, with thoughts soaring upwards in thankfulness. His way led him through a forest, where, looking up into a tree at an unexpected noise, he caught sight of a Male and Female Crow, standing on the edge of their nest, and earnestly engaged in kicking their grown-up children out of it, to make their own way in the world. The old birds dragged the young ones out without mercy, and shrieked, "Be off with you, you young rapscallions! we have fed you long enough; you are big enough to help yourselves, so be off!" The poor young creatures lay on the ground, deploring their hard fate, and vainly fluttering and beating the ground with their wings. "What shall we do?" they cried piteously; "oh! what shall we do? We can't fly yet; we shall have to lie here and die of starvation!"

Then John dismounted from his horse, and taking from his saddle a bag of corn that he carried for the journey, he opened it and spread it out before them. They hopped joyfully upon it, and began to peck away; and when they were satisfied, and saw that there was enough in store to last them until their wings were full grown, they cried out to John, "We will be grateful; you shall be rewarded for this."

"All right, and in good time," remarked John; "honest thanks break no man's bones." Then he went upon his journey, until he came to a great city, in the main street of which he met a great procession of heralds and trumpeters, headed by a Marshal on horseback, who proclaimed aloud: "Our Princess wants a husband, and he who seeks may have her for a wife, on condition that he perform a difficult task that will be set him; failing in which, he will lose both a Royal wife and his head."

"What is this?" asked John of a Tradesman, who was standing at his shop door; "this seems a capital chance."

"Don't heed him, Sir Traveller," said the honest Tradesman.

"Oh! I suppose the Princess is old and ugly?"

"Not at all," replied the Shopkeeper; "on the contrary, she is both young and handsome; but so difficult is the task allotted, that, although many, dazzled with her beauty and their own ambition, have tried to accomplish it and win her, they have miserably failed, and been cruelly put to death."

"At any rate, I won't buy a pig in a poke," said John to himself. So he went to the King's Palace, and having produced letters of introduction and recommendation from his own Sovereign, was graciously received. When he saw the Princess, he found her so beautiful, that he determined at once to risk his life to win her hand, and mentioned his intention to the King her father, without farther delay, in the somewhat unnecessary anxiety of a jealous lover, that some one might step in and carry off the prize he so ardently coveted.

The King and Queen, who liked his appearance and manners, endeavoured to dissuade him from the impossible task; but he would not be refused. So they led him down to the sea, where there was a deep whirlpool of raging waters, and the King threw down into this a golden ring, and told him he must fetch that golden ring back again from the bottom of the sea, with this pleasant conclusion to his Royal speech—"If you come up again without this ring, you will be thrown in again and again, every time, until you are drowned."

"Then it is very plain that drowned I shall be," thought John to himself. But he put a bold face on the matter, seeing there was no help out of it; and the pitying crowd, and the Court, and the King and Queen, and even the Princess, could not help sorrowing to see so handsome a young man in such peril of his life. Then they left him alone upon the sea-shore, somewhat disconsolate, and looking about him as one thinking what was best to be done.

Presently, he saw three Fishes swimming fast towards him, and as they came nearer, he recognized them as the very three Fishes whose lives he had saved by disentangling them out of the reeds in the pond. "Just the very fellows I want," said John; "now, if they only would——"

But his wishes had been already forstalled; for the middle one of the three grateful Fishes bore a mussel-shell in its mouth, and brought it up close to the shore, and laid it down in the shallow waters that the tiny waves flung rippling up to John's feet. The youth picked it up, and, to his great joy, saw within it, snugly ensconced, as if in a Royal jewel case, the golden ring which the King had thrown into the sea.

He hastened with it, full of joy, to the King's Palace, expecting to receive the promised reward of the hand of the beautiful Princess. But it was not so to be. That haughty young damsel, though her heart felt an inclination towards the handsome youth, resolved, nevertheless, that she would not be too easily won, and insisted on another trial.

This time she resolved to see to it herself; so she stepped forth into the Palace-garden, and strewed over the lawns ten bushels of millet-seed. Then she told John that he was to pick up and bring back to her every grain of that millet-seed before the sun rose next morning; and that if he failed in restoring it by so little as one single grain out of the whole ten bushels, his life would be the forfeit.

The young man looked at the hopeless task before him, and saw that it was impossible. However, he undertook with a good grace to accomplish it—said there was plenty of time, and no need for hurry, and that, after dinner and the ball at the Palace, he would begin. The Princess stared at his coolness, but could not help admiring his courage and perseverance; so they sat by each other at dinner in the afternoon, and danced at the ball in the evening; and so pleased was the beautiful Princess with Handsome John's attention and polite conversation, that she forgot his humble birth, the discovery of which had before so much annoyed her, and even offered to help him in picking up the ten bushels of millet-seed; and had he spoken but half a word, I really believe, from what I have seen of Princesses and other young ladies under similar circumstances, she would have let him entirely off that part of the bargain, and married him the next morning.

But Handsome John's spirit was up, and what he had undertaken he determined to go through with; so he bade the Princess good-night after the last dance, and when she went to bed, he went out into the Palace-garden.

But now the difficulty of the task came fully before him, and he sat and looked on the lawns in the moonlight disconsolately, until night faded into morning, when he watched the streaks of the early dawn, expecting the glorious coming of the sun, as bringing the message for his death.

But it was not so to be; for no sooner did the first rays of the sun shed their golden radiance over the garden, than he saw that the ten sacks, that had been spread out empty at his feet the previous evening, were now all filled and standing by him, while not a single grain of the millet-seed remained in the grass. The grateful Ant-King had visited the Palace-garden in the night with his thousands and thousands of troops, and the little busy insects had worked all night laboriously, until they had gathered up every grain of the ten bushels of millet, and garnered it in the sacks.

When the Princess came down, she saw with wonder how perfectly Handsome John had accomplished his task; but the proud heart of the Royal Fair had

199

grown stubborn again with her night's rest, and she said: "Although he may have done these two things, yet, for all that, he shall not be my husband until he has brought me an Apple from the Tree of Life."

"And I should like him to show us a little money," added her Royal Father; "there are so many ups and downs now-a-days, and so many revolutions and changes, that who knows what may happen to our Royal selves? and then who is to keep our daughter? No man ought to think of marrying any young woman until he can, at least, maintain her in equally as good a condition of life as that he takes her from."

"Oh!" said John to himself, drawing a long breath, as he saw all his visions of happiness fade before him. Where was he to find the Tree of Life, on which grew the Golden Apple? where was he to pick up a treasure sufficient to support a Princess in Royal dignity? All he could reply to the King was, "Why didn't you say so before?" and then he took his way out of the city, searching and searching after the Tree of Life, and wandering about, anywhere and everywhere, until he was leg-weary, and footsore, and almost heartbroken.

At last, in the evening, he came to a forest, and sat down under a tree, on a bank. While he was vainly endeavouring to snatch a few moments of repose for mind and body, he heard a rustling in the branches over his head, and saw three Crows. Presently, down came a Golden Apple plump into his hand, and then the three Crows flew down, and perched on his knees, and said to him, "Here we are! and you see we are grateful, as we told you we should be. We are the three young starveling, fledgeling Crows, whom your kindness preserved from dying of hunger, when our parents turned us out of the nest. We have been growing up all this while, and are right strong on the wing; so as soon as we heard that you were searching anxiously for the Tree of Life, to get a Golden Apple from it, we winged our rapid way over the far sea, even to the end of the world, where stands the Tree of Life, and we fetched an Apple for you. So now go back, and marry your proud and fair Princess, and we wish you every happiness in your wedded life; but think of us sometimes, and don't turn your children out in the world without a feather to fly with. Caw! Caw! Caw!"

Then John fell asleep, and rose up with the dawn, pleased that his errand was thus far accomplished. He travelled all day, until he came with the evening to a lonely Castle, where he asked for a night's lodging.

"Yes," said the Lord of the Castle, "you shall have a night's lodging, certainly; but you must do what is required of all travellers here on their first visit. You must sleep down below, in that tower; but I warn you that it is a very perilous undertaking, for it is full of Wild Dogs, that bay all night, and bark and howl at every one; and at certain hours a man must be thrown to them, whom they devour."

"I suppose your Lordship does not have many people call twice?" remarked John.

"No," replied the Lord of the Castle, drily.

True enough that was; for, on account of these Dogs, all the neighbouring country was in grief and terror, for no one could prevent their ravages, and almost every family in turn had lost a son, or some other male relative, through their ferocious propensities. But John, after what he had gone through, was afraid of nothing except a rival in the Princess's affections, in case he should not get back to her father's Palace in time to claim her; and he up and spoke boldly to the Lord of the Castle: "Only let me in among these barking curs, and give me something to throw to them; they won't hurt me, and I will teach them a lesson."

They acceded to his wish, though not very willingly, and gave him some meat, and let him down into the tower among the Wild Dogs. But he spoke to them at once in their own language, and as soon as he touched the ground, they ran up to him in the most friendly and familiar manner, wagging their tails, and only barking in their gentlest and most pleasurable manner. They ate the meat he brought for them, and, instead of devouring John, discoursed politely with him over their dinner.

John slept there that night, and the next morning, to everybody's astonishment, he came forth quite unharmed, and told the Lord of the Castle how the Wild Hounds had informed him, in their language, the reason of their bringing such waste and destruction on the land. They had been placed there by a Giant Sorcerer, long since dead and destroyed by a more powerful Magician, to watch over his treasures that lay buried in the vaults underneath that tower; and so powerful was the spell, that, although the Sorcerer was dead, they could not move from the spot until that treasure was raised up and carried away.

"Oh! pray take it up, and remove it where you please, if you can," exclaimed the Lord of the Castle; "I have got quite wealth and lands enough, and all I want is, to be rid of the nuisance and annoyance of these perpetually howling and cruelly devouring Dogs."

"Then I can manage that for your Lordship," said Handsome John; "the Wild Dogs told me how it was to be done."

Then there was a general rejoicing, and Handsome John succeeded in raising the treasure, a part of which he gave to the attendants, a part to the Lord of the Castle, and the rest—amounting to thirteen millions three hundred and forty-three thousand of golden ducats, besides jewels innumerable—he conveyed to the Palace of the Fair Princess, who, seeing the Golden Apple, gave him her hand willingly at last; and when he showed his treasure, the King her father gladly received him as a son-in-law. They were married, and lived happily; but how long, and whether they are, even yet, dead, I am not able to tell you.

OLD BARBEL FEELS HIMSELF SEIZED BY THE FOOT.

OLD BARBEL, THE FISHERMAN:
A WONDERFUL HAUL.

Once upon a time, there was an Old Fisherman, known in that part of the country where he lived as FATHER BARBEL. No one could tell much of where he came from; and, as for himself, why, he knew little more than the rest. All he could remember was, that, from the time he was ten or twelve years old, he had lived on the banks of the same river, passing his days in fishing, and sleeping sometimes in the open air, sometimes

No. 26.   201 in the barn of a neighbouring farm, and, at other and harder times, in a forge in the neighbourhood. In the course of time, he built himself, on a little islet hardly more than twenty feet long, a shed of wood, thatched with reeds; and this islet became to him his country and his kingdom, where he reigned, with despotic authority, over a dog, a cat, three fowls, and some dozen or so ducks, with whom he often promenaded the river bank. All his subjects were under implicit submission, with the exception, however, of certain inhabitants of his domain, who lived in a perpetual state of insurrection against his authority; these were the water-rats, a stubborn and independent race, who revolted against his dog, chased his cat off the field, and devoured his fowls' eggs. Father Barbel waged continual war with them, and stretched out nets for them, which they cut through like thread, and traps of osier, which they gnawed with their sharp teeth. However, by the aid of his dog and his iron-pronged staff, he managed to get enough of them together to make out of their skins a large cap, of frightful aspect, with which to cover his bald head triumphantly.

This strange head-gear, with his long grisly beard, gave him the look of one of those wild men that children are frightened at; although, as far as he was himself concerned, Father Barbel was rarely seen wandering out of his own domains. The river and banks seemed all to belong to him. During the day, he would be mending and setting his nets, sharpening his harpoon, casting lead weights for his net, or making small baskets, which he went about selling in the neighbourhood; sometimes, also, he slept; and very often he would lay himself down in the sun, and do nothing, except feel tired of doing nothing. But when evening came on, he woke to his real life, and the night was his best time. As soon as that dark, yet bright-eyed lady, had cast over the water her sombre and mysterious mantle, Father Barbel would take his nets, get into his little boat, and rummage the river in every sense; not a winding, not a hole, not a corner of the stream, but was known to him quite as well as to the fish.

One day—or, rather, one night—he had passed full three long hours on the water, without getting a single haul, and was beginning to grumble, and use some forcibly unkind expressions, both as regarded fishermen and fish in general, when, having cast his net for the last time, he felt the cord shake in his hand. This was always a delicious moment for Old Father Barbel. He felt, at such times, all the ardent emotion and eager anxiety of a miser who scents out a treasure. As soon as his net had touched the bottom, he "tasted" the cord—that was his own expression—as much as to say, he stretched it rigid, and gave it one or two shakes, to disturb the fish which might be there; if a trembling of the cord followed upon these shakings, it was a good sign—"She answers!" Thus, this was a moment of very agreeable emotion, since, after three hours' useless research, he felt it "answered." What was more, the answer was of a strong kind, and the shaking was rapid and violent, so much as to threaten to drag the cord out of his hands.

"Halloa!" said Father Barbel to himself; "there is a handsome prisoner down there."

He stopped an instant, to enjoy his feelings and have another "taste" of his cord. The shaking began again, and with still greater violence.

"Yes, yes," said he, "I hear you, my friend! Come now, not so much of that knocking about. You can waggle for a whole hour, when in my boat, if you like. Again! Ah! ah! He is a strong fellow, that; he ought to weigh about fifteen pounds, or I am mistaken; and it is a pike, I am sure. I should like it to be that very chap that escaped me the other night, by tearing my net. Ah! this time, my young pickle, you have got your work to do; but you won't get out."

Father Barbel kept on talking to himself after this fashion, for some time longer; for, though it was perfectly useless, there being no one to hear or understand him, it yet afforded him an opportunity for prolonging his delicious expectation. At last, he determined to take his net out of the river, and let it fall, all dripping, into his boat. Then, lifting up the lead and the meshes, he saw a great fish, with an enormous head, that regarded him with a sly look. The fact is, this inhabitant of the waters had a real face, with great green eyes, a narrow muzzle, a little gullet, that bore some resemblance to a mouth, and a lower jaw-bone that would have answered very well as a chin.

"I don't know this gentleman," said Father Barbel, as he ran his eyes over the fish with much anxiety; "he is neither a trout, nor a carp, and, certainly, not a pike; what can he be? Ah! there you are, my fine fellow!" added he, as he leant over his prisoner; "where do you come from? out of what river, or what lake? for you are none of our parts, I am quite certain. Perhaps you came from the sea; but the sea is a very long way from here. After all, what does it matter where you come from; here you are now, with me. But what a droll fellow! he does not look as if he were at all astonished."

The fish, in fact, kept his eye steadily upon the Fisherman, and, strange to say, had the appearance of laughing in his face.

"'Pon my word!" said the Fisherman to himself, with astonishment, "that fish there seems to me like a joker. I must have a look at him closer, to-morrow, in the broad daylight."

Hereupon, he threw the fish into a kind of box, which formed the stern of his boat, and was kept full of water. On his arrival at his hut, he drew the fish out of its prison, for fear it would kill itself by its summersaults against the sides, and threw it into a store-pond that he had dug by the side of his house, where he kept alive such fish as he was not going to sell for some time.

"It is curious!" he said to himself, as he went to bed; "it is rather hard to have lived fifty years on a river, and yet not know all its inhabitants."

II. THE WATER-SPRITE.

WITH the first glimmer of the dawning day, Father Barbel got up. All the while he was putting on his clothes (and that was not very long) he was thinking of the fish he had caught the night before. "What can it possibly be?" said he to himself. "I have taken some trouble to rummage my old memory, but I can't call to mind having ever seen a fish of this species. But, now it is daylight, I will go and examine him better, and see after what fashion he conducts himself in the water."

He went straight to his store-pond. What was his astonishment at seeing, right in the middle of the water, a Child, who swam like a fish, and was plunging, and turning over, and playing down there, like a bird in the air! He gazed on him for an instant without speaking a word, so great was his surprise.

"Faith!" said he, at last, "he is a grand swimmer! I know a few carp to whom this young lad there might give one or two points; and he dives—just look at him!—like a water-hen."

During this time, the Child continued playing about in the store-pond, disappearing and re-appearing by turns, plucking a flower, catching the butterflies as they flew over the surface of the water, and pursuing the fishes, who did not seem afraid of him. It was, to all appearance, a merry little creature; its hair was golden, like the leaves of autumn rushes; its eyes of a tender green, and with a slight grimace, which gave it a wicked look, that was pleasant to see.

"I have quite enough to do to stare at you," said the Old Fisherman, more and more surprised; "I never saw but one child. This is quite a child. Little one, who are you? Where do you come from? Tell me that, my boy, and then you shall teach me to swim like you do, for you have a famous stroke to boast of, and I don't think our first swimmers have one equal to yours."

The Child remained motionless, his head out of the water, as if he were hanging by the surface, and applied himself to gazing at Father Barbel; but still without speaking a word.

"Well, now, will you answer me?" said the latter.

The Child still kept silence, his large eyes fixed upon the Fisherman.

"Are you dumb? Give me some sign that means Yes or No."

The same immobility, and the same silence.

"How you do stare at me with your great green eyes! Answer me now."

The Child set-to laughing; but still without saying a word.

"Ah! that's it; I think you are making fun of me, my little droll. Wait awhile; we are now going to see who will laugh the last."

He went into his cabin, and came back with his casting-net, a portion of the meshes of which he took up in his right hand, and threw back the other point over his left shoulder, all ready to make his cast.

"You can see my casting-net plainly," said he to the Child, with a threatening gesture; "it runs all over the store-pond; I am going to throw you on your back, if you don't answer me. Once—twice—thrice. Ah! you mock me. Take care of yourself—look out, young pickle!"

And he threw the casting-net, and it struck the water with a rattling splash.

"Good!" said he, "I have caught you, my little duck; now we can have it out at once."

He drew out his casting-net instantly, and threw it on the grass; but found in it only a number of fishes, and among others, that one he had caught the night before, and which still regarded him with a sly look.

"Yes, my fine fellow," said he, "I recognize you as well. But that young rogue, I don't see him. How has he been able to escape me? I can't comprehend this at all."

He cast the net a second time; but again no Child!

"Faith!" said he, "this is getting droll. It can't be helped, I must keep a good heart about it."

And while speaking, he took off his boots, tucked up his trowsers, and went into the water. He searched a long time, and went over every corner of his store-pond, but found nothing. During this time, the great fish, which he had left on the bank, floundered about, and made great bounds on the grass. Fearing it was about to leap back into the river, he went to look after it; when, by a more violent exertion than heretofore, it sprang up into the air, and fell back again into the store-pond.

"Good!" said Father Barbel; "though you are down there, you are quite right now."

And he went on with his search. Suddenly, he felt himself sharply pricked in his feet, his calves, his legs, all at the same time.

"Faith!" said he, "I must have thrust myself into some nest of crabs. After all, I don't see him here. Ah! these are not crabs—this is a bite. Have my pikes revolted? Oh! they are all going at my legs, the shabby rascals! Oh! oh! oh!"

He hastened out of the water, to avoid their bites; but at the moment when, with one foot resting on the bank, he was just drawing up the other leg, he found himself caught by the foot.

"Halloa! what's that—what's that?" he exclaimed, in a fright.

He turned round, and saw the Child, who had caught hold of his foot, and was laughing with all his might.

"How, you little rogue!" said he, "was it you that held me so tight? Where do you come from, now? But, first, let me go; will you let me go, I tell you?"

The Child kept on laughing, still holding the good man in this critical position.

"He grips live a vice!" said the latter, in astonishment. "Who could think that, with little hands like those, this young pickle could hold back a river-wolf like me? Another pinch! you rascal, let me go, or I will ——. Oh! oh! you grasp me like an otter-trap."

"He will laugh best who laughs the last," said the Child, upon this, releasing his foot.

"Ah! you have recovered your speech!"

"Yes, Father Barbel."

"What! you know me?"

"A long while."

"Really! where have you seen me?"

"For fifty years past, every night, on the river."

"Fifty years! How old are you then?"

"Well, I shall be two hundred and sixty-five years old, come next Martinmas. That begins to reckon up, don't it?"

Father Barbel gazed attentively on the Child, whose rosy face did not bespeak more than ten years at the utmost.

"My poor little fellow," said he, "I am sorry to tell you, that I am afraid you are talking nonsense."

"No more than you are, Father Barbel—you, who did not recognize me, though you saw me only an instant ago."

"Is it only an instant ago?" said the Old Fisherman, fixing his eyes on the Child; "I have not been here longer than that. Yet—no, it is impossible. Yet you resemble my big fish, as much as a drop of the river water does a drop of the pond water. There—there it is! the nose—the little mouth—the green eyes—all are there. Is it possible that you are a Hobgoblin? Ah! my boy, tell me at once, for I don't want to have anything to do with any agents of the Evil One."

"Nay, re-assure yourself," said the Child; "I am a Good Genius, a Water-Sprite of your own river, and I came to protect you, since you have great need of it at this moment."

"Do you mean that I am menaced with any danger?"

"I am here to tell you of it; but, first, I must get out of this."

"Wait a moment, while I fetch you a blouse and boots."

"Pray don't trouble yourself in that matter; I will go and gather myself a complete suit."

And at one leap, the Child darted towards the river, into which he plunged; but soon reappeared with a vest of rushes artistically woven, trowsers of water-moss, and two large leaves of the water-lily for shoes, which were laced round his feet, and made excellent short shoes, and, lastly, on his head a crown of reed flowers.

III. THE KING OF THE PIKES.

"Well, now! this is what I call buying clothes at a good market," said Father Barbel, when he saw the Child come back thus accoutred; "you must teach me how to get myself dressed in this style, for it will be a rare saving to me. You must give me

204

some lessons, also, in your stroke in swimming. Ah! I hold you to teaching me that stroke; when a man can swim as you do, he need have no fear of the water. Faith! how you did flutter about down there! there is not a swimmer in all the country who has a chance with you, my little——what do they call you?"

"Water-Sprite; I told you so before."

"That's not a name."

"I have none other, however."

"Then we must be content with that, my boy. Well, now, my little Water-Sprite—— By-the-bye, what is a Water-Sprite?"

"An old fisherman like you ought not to be ignorant of that. The Water-Sprites are the Genii of the water, as the name points out. We live at the bottom of the springs, and our duty is to feed them, and to care for the freshness and the clearness of their water; we live, without growing old, so long as runs the spring which our King confides to our care; but if, by any negligence, we allow it to stop, we die along with it. This will explain to you how I appear young, in spite of my two hundred and sixty-five years."

"And have you, then, been the Water-Sprite of our river, all the while I have fished in it?"

"Yes; I generally live up at the source, and often take a walk over its waters."

"And I am menaced, you told me, with some great danger! What is it I have to fear?"

"Have you observed that for the last month business has gone badly with you?—that your fishing has not been prosperous?"

"That is true; I take nothing but the small fry—too glad, indeed, when I can catch them."

"And that, one time, in your store-pond, all the fish there sickened and died?"

"True again; but how did you know that?"

"I will tell you very soon. You remember, also, that about a month since, you caught in your casting-net, for an instant only, however, an enormous pike?"

"Yes; it must have weighed thirty pounds at least;

"I will go and gather myself a complete suit."

and it must have had famous teeth, for it tore my net, so that it was impossible for me to mend it. But I will be revenged of the scoundrel yet."

"Take good care what you do."

"Why so?"

"You are a lost man if you ever try to catch him again."

"Ah! that's it? Who, then, is this monster?"

"The King of the Pikes!"

"Faith! I never suspected I had caught a king in my casting-net. Only fancy, if I had kept him, and had sold His Majesty for twenty shillings!"

"From that moment," went on the Water-Sprite, "the King of the Pikes, greatly irritated against you, has sought to do you injury. He follows you about without your perceiving it; he plays the spy upon you, and seeks how to draw you into some snare. Listen well to what I recommend. If by any chance you see him, throw him a few small fish to appease his appetite. Above all, never go near the Great Lake. You must also refrain from catching pikes for one month; and, if you find them, throw them back into the water. Do not allow yourself to be carried away by the ardour of fishing, or the King of the Pikes may manage to lure you into his dominions, and then I don't know how I can get you out of them. In any case, whenever you may be in danger, give me notice of it by brandishing over the water a torch of burning resin, and shouting out 'Water-Sprites! Water-Sprites! Save the Old Fisherman!'"

"I thank you, my boy, for this warning and protection. I must confess, however, that it all seems to me exceedingly droll; and, besides, I shall never bring myself to confess that an old otter, like me, can be afraid of a pike."

"Be prudent, Father Barbel; the Water-Sprites protect you; but these are not all-powerful, and there are plenty of dangers at the bottom of the waters."

"Be easy, my pretty guardian; I know the river, just as well as my own house."

"Too much confidence leads to ruin. Adieu, Father Barbel; good luck to you, and may you never stand in need of my help."

At these words, the Water-Sprite darted out of the cabin with a bound, plunged into the river, and was lost from the wondering gaze of the Old Fisherman, as he said, "Beware of the Great Lake!"

IV. THE WITCH OF THE WATERS.

"THE Water-Sprite is right," said Father Barbel one day to himself, while emptying his nets, in which a multitude of fishes were leaping about. "Ever since I have followed his advice, the carps come, as if of their own accord, under my casting-net; the eels wriggle into my pots; and all this sort of thing makes a good market. Faith! I shall soon be able to take a holiday."

Then he took out of a huge tobacco-box of shell a quid, which he chewed with much deliberation, and next began to hum an old tune, that had, as he pretended, the power of charming and attracting the fishes, as he walked along the banks of the river, and, like all fishermen, having an eye for anything besides, although he knew every inch of it, he said, as if it were his own house. We cannot take upon ourselves to pronounce whether his monotonous song had really the effect of charming the inhabitants of the waters; but it is a fact, that Father Barbel could see them glide along, and play at the bottom of the river, as if there were no one witnessing their sports. The sight of this was one of the grand delights of the Old Fisherman. He amused himself, on such occasions, with noticing the different species of fish, studying their habits, and divining the

"He explored, with scrutinizing gaze, the bottom of the river."

direction they were about to take, and to what corner they were about to withdraw. He would speak to them as beings of his own species, without frightening them, well aware of the fisher's proverb, that "fishes can swim, though they can't talk."

"Oh, what a noble Trout!" said he; "see, how it hides itself under the grass! it is watching its prey. Look out, young gudgeon—you, there, playing in the middle of the river: this is not the time for childish gamboling, my lad. There you see her! how gently she glides along, the traitress! Save yourself!—be quick—save yourself, poor little one—or, by Jove!——Snap! there he goes—caught—vanished—

swallowed! So much the worse for you, little fool, after the warning I gave you. But, if it be any comfort to you, I will avenge you; this night yon ogress shall be in my stock-pond."

He kept on walking thus, for some time, following the fish with his eyes, and talking to them, all the while humming his old ditty. Then, after marking down the spots where the fish were most numerous, he went back to his hut, got ready his fishing implements, and awaited the coming of night. Towards ten o'clock he came forth, threw into the boat his casting-net, torch, and lantern, and sculled gently up the stream.

He caught, in no great time, a decent number of fish, but all of them of small size; and then pushed along to the spot where he had marked down the Trout. Here he made many a cast with his net, but without catching anything.

"I must find her, at any rate," said he; "she can't be very far from this spot." He went up the river for some time, then drew in his oars, and left the boat to glide silently, of itself, down the current, on the surface of the water. Meanwhile, lantern in hand, and leaning over the boat's head, he explored with scrutinizing gaze the bottom of the river—a trick of fishing he had cunningly taken to, from having learnt that by night fish are attracted, and, as it were, fascinated, by any bright light. Suddenly he saw a head peep out from under a mass of grass.

"That is my Trout," said he to himself; "we have got it all to our two selves, my dear, so let us make each other's acquaintance at once."

Then he stopped his boat, hung his lantern on the bow, spread out his casting-net, and threw it over the tuft of grass, which it completely enveloped.

"Caught!" he exclaimed, with glee.

Before taking up his net out of the water, he gave himself the pleasure of "tasting" the cord, as we have before described; but how great was his surprise at finding it motionless, and at receiving no reply.

"This is funny!—but it must be down there. Come along, old lady—don't pretend to be dead; come here, and show us your agility."

He drew up his casting-net into the boat, and lifted up the lead: there was nothing at the bottom!

"Faith!" said he, in disgust, "it's myself that's caught! But how could she have got away? However, I have caught enough for to-day, and will trap her some other time."

He was just turning back, when he heard the reeds rattle at his side, and, leaning over to the spot, saw the Trout, distinctly, threading its way among the rushes, as it went up the current; it seemed now even larger than before.

At this sight he felt his ardour redoubled.

"I will have her," he cried, "even though I must follow her to the depths of the sea!"

So he took up his sculls, and followed the direction taken by the Trout. Three or four hundred paces from there the river divided into two channels; the left branch was a kind of narrow canal, leading to the Great Lake.

"Hallon!" said he, stopping himself; "we don't go any farther—the Water-Sprite would not like it. Be-

206

sides, that abominable Mother Trout must be just here; it is wide and deep. There she is, right in the middle! I will make her show up."

He made some more casts with his net—all in vain! So he began to feel irritated at such fruitless exertions, while the pursuit after a victim that always eluded him, became a matter of pride, and almost of honour. In the persuasion that the Trout had taken the right arm of the river, he remained without moving, and kept his eye on that side, as if attracted by some invisible power. He was well aware that the Great Lake offered magnificent resources to an old fisherman, such as himself; and the warnings his young protector had given him began to be rubbed off his memory, while his eyes sparkled with such impatience as the war-horse shows, when it hears the trumpet call, and scents the battle from afar.

He was a prey to this kind of hesitation, when a sharp blow, struck on his lantern, caused him to turn his head round; and he saw, falling back into the river, a large fish, that by a violent leap had darted out of the water, so near to him as to strike his lantern.

"Halloa!" was all he could say. He leant over the water, and saw the Trout, which was going up the canal on the right. At sight of this, he could contain himself no longer; his passion was roused on the instant, in all its force, and his resolution was taken.

"This is going too far!" he exclaimed. "I do believe that Trout was mocking at me. Now, then, no more hesitating; forward's the word, and if all the Pikes in the world come against me, I am ready for them!"

So he seized his sculls, and rowed with a vigorous arm in the direction of the Great Lake, whither the Trout had preceded him. At the moment of his entering the canal on the left, a small voice sang, in a clear gentle voice, out of a clump of reeds:—

"Fisher! of the Witch beware!
Fisher! be quick, and say a prayer!
The fish to-night will be your match,
For the fish their fisher now will catch!"

But he did not pay much attention to this song. Leaning to his oars, he pulled and tugged away with a kind of rage, until, some moments after, he reached the entrance of the Great Lake.

V. THE GREAT LAKE.

This was an immense lake, shut in, along its whole length, between the sides of a deep gorge, where the winds sometimes were engulfed with such violence as to raise up the waters like waves of the sea. Reeds with their large leaves, enormous rushes, water-lilies with their long stems, rendered the navigation here both difficult and dangerous. The centre formed a vast whirlpool; such is the name given, in that neighbourhood, to a deep and narrow gully, where the waters rush in, tumbling over one another in turbulent waves, and, attracted by some hidden abyss, turn and whirl over each other, in the shape of a funnel.

It was a very dangerous spot; if any imprudent swimmer came too near it, he found himself drawn within the eddy of the whirlpool, where no human effort would avail to save him. He was carried round, for a time, with the water on the top of the gulf; then the abyss sucked him down quickly, whirling him fantastically round and round, like a top. There were but few fishermen who would venture on this lake, of which they told all sorts of stories. It was full, they said, of all kinds of monsters, such as the sea never saw. Crabs, old as the rocks, and as big as porpoises, wandered about in its depths; unknown fish floated in its waters; and the grasses and the weeds trembled continuously, as their branches were shaken by concealed beings. A herdsman, who, one night, had wandered that way, told of his having seen a tall white man walking on the water. It was in vain to laugh at him, and say, that what he had taken for a phantom could only be a mass of vapour, which the moon was shining upon, and the wind driving along. Stories like this, spread over the country, had rendered the gorge in which the Great Lake was encased almost deserted.

It was a superb night when Father Barbel arrived there. Not even a whisper ruffled the surface of the water, as it shone in the moonlight like an immense plate of silver. The sky, unspotted by a cloud, was reflected in the depths of the lake, with all its stars; while a thousand small, mysterious, and confused sounds that filled the air, formed a harmonious murmur, as they came upon the ear from afar. This glorious spectacle struck the Old Fisherman, and he pulled along more slowly. Soon the calm of this dark valley seemed to weigh heavy on him, and a vague feeling of terror came over his spirit. By degrees, all the murmurs were at rest, and there was silence, dead and immeasurable, over the waters. Father Barbel was almost afraid of the sound of his oars, which made the waters groan, and alone troubled the solemn calm. He stopped, and cast his eyes around; it seemed to him as if he could perceive, far, far down the valley, a form, uncertain and white, rising above the waters. They were the vapours of night, mounting into the air. Father Barbel knew this, and yet he could not help thinking of the phantom in the old man's story. Soon, a little blue flame was seen to rise along the banks of the lake, mount gently into the air, then descend, and vanish in the water. Another succeeded, then another yet; and, in an instant, the valley appeared to be filled with these fires, which rose, came down, crossed each other in every direction, and spread over the surface of the lake a pale and undecided light, that gave it the appearance of some naked and desolate plain, lighted by a winter sky.

Father Barbel was gazing with astonishment on all these blue flames dancing on the waters, when he saw a human form rapidly dart athwart the mass of them, and dash across the lake. It was a young girl, whose long fair hair, lighted up by these glimmers, fluttered about her as she went, her blue robe floating in waving folds upon the wind. She glided on the surface of the lake with a marvellous agility, and seemed to fly like a sea-gull, as it skims, on the wing, the summit of the waves. Others followed her quickly, and, like her, set-to running over the lake in pursuit of each other, with ringing bursts of laughter, that sounded like the liquid sounds given out by musical glasses. Children also were seen mingling with the merry group, and they wound themselves together into a choral dance, in cadence with the music of the distant harmony of sounds. Father Barbel gazed for a long while at their graceful gambolings with each other, as they glided over the water like light skaters over the ice, the Will-o'-the-wisps all the while casting over them a wandering and capricious light. Soon he saw them range themselves in a circle, and heard them singing to the accompaniment of unknown instruments:—

"It is night! The bird sleeps on the bough; the zephyr sings among the reeds; the green hills are exhaling their white cloud-robes of wreathing mist. Come forth, ye Spirits of the Waters! let us dance upon the streams.

"Night has spread her veil o'er the waters. To the bosom of the lake, where shines the reflected heaven, come, Spirits of the Waters! and let us gather the stars, the golden stars, which, down there, smile upon us!

"The wildfires are flying all over the deep valleys; the water is full of mysterious sounds. Come, ye Spirits of the Wave! Let us dance, fair Spirits! Let us weave the pale and silent chorus of the night!"

Father Barbel listened with delight to their liquid and melodious voices, sent back to him, softened and in dying tones, by the echoes of the valley. He quite forgot his fishing.

The song ceased. The young girls and the children seemed to be speaking together, and pointed with their fingers to the horizon. During this time, a thick cloud, like a blot, ascended, expanding as it rose upon the starry sky. The wind began to rise. Father Barbel, who, with his looks fixed on these beautiful apparitions, was all eyes and ears, felt his boat suddenly agitated by a tumult of little waves, that beat against the side of his frail bark. This circumstance brought back his attention to his fishing. He took his lantern, and leant over the waves; a multitude of fishes were taking their airing round his boat, and came together under his lantern. Quickly he unfolded his net, and made a cast. The net plunged in, and plunged in so much in advance, that Father Barbel felt the cord that held it, fastened to his arm, draw him down towards the water. He leant over as far as he could, to enable it to reach the bottom, but this was in vain; the drag-net remained suspended in the void of waters.

"Halloa!" said he, "this is a hole, indeed! I never before met with such deep water."

He drew up his casting-net, and took to his oars again, in search of a more favourable place. The fishes continued to follow his boat; and Father Barbel could distinctly see the Trout, as it swam at their head, and appeared to lead them. The sight of this irritated him; this Trout had become, in regard to him, an enemy, of whom he must, at any price, make a prisoner. He halted, and hung his lantern on the bow of the boat, to attract the adversary, who was always avoiding him.

Meantime, the small cloud had mounted up to the sky, and rapidly increased in size. One by one the stars disappeared under it; the moon was veiled; the darkness became still deeper; and the Will-o'-the-wisps could hardly be seen, as in the far-off distance they crossed to the right. The wind growled sullenly between the sharp sides of the valley, and raised the waves, which, every moment, mounted higher and higher.

At this instant, Father Barbel once more heard the fair Phantoms of the Lake, as they took up again their interrupted song. But this time their voices seemed trembling and uneasy, while the song, hurried and more hurried, by degrees sank into the distance:—

"Here comes the King! the King of the water deep,
   At sight of whom the lake shakes off its sleep,
   The storm's let loose, the monsters from below
   Rise to their Monarch's voice. We Water-Sprites must go!"

VI. A NIGHT-STORM.

THEY all vanished quickly. A profound darkness enveloped the valley that abutted on the lake. Thunder began to mutter in the distance, and, coming nearer by degrees, made the old rocks in the valley tremble. At the same moment, lightnings furrowed the sky, and multiplied with such rapidity, that the lake, whose rising waves shone with livid brightness, had the appearance of an immense furnace.

In the midst of this terrible tempest, the poor little boat of the Old Fisherman was tossed up like a nutshell to the tops of the waves, and quickly came tumbling down again, as if it was going to be swallowed up. Father Barbel, however, surprised at such a sudden discord of the elements, did not lose his presence of mind or his courage. He took to his oars again, and prepared to turn back. But the violence of the waves and the wind, which was against him, drove him, in spite of all his efforts, towards the centre of the lake. The lightnings ceased at intervals, and then the unfortunate man had to row at hazard, in the midst of such a fearful night, without knowing whither his efforts were taking him. Suddenly a terrific clap of thunder made the whole valley tremble; while an immense flash of lightning came down from the cloud like a torrent of fire, engulfing itself in the lake, the depths of which it all at once lit up. By the glimmer which this kind of blaze threw out, Father Barbel could see a crowd of fishes, pressed so close together, that they appeared to form a compact mass. In the middle of them, an enormous Pike, with a black back and powerful fins, was cleaving the waters, which raised up his large tail; a crown of blood was marked on his head; his eyes shone like lightning, and his long jaws, which opened and shut alternately, swallowed, each time, twenty fishes at once.

"Halloa!" exclaimed Father Barbel, "that's the gentleman! It is the King of the Pikes! Into what new hole have I thrust myself? Look at him, how he comes at me with all his court! Is it possible that he can wish to attack me? Very well, let him come! It shall never be said that a pike, however big, was able to make Father Barbel recoil."

Just as he had ended these bold words, he saw, at a few paces from him, the monster open his jaws, bristling with long and sharp teeth. He seized his harpoon; it was a solid trident of iron, fitted on to a long staff, which a cord held fastened to his arm. At

208

the moment when the Pike closed his jaw and swallowed his prey, Father Barbel raised his arm, and darted at him, with all his force, this iron harpoon.

"Take your death!" cried he.

On a sudden the water boiled up; the harpoon rebounded violently in the air, and fell back perpendicularly into his boat, which it transfixed like an arrow; at the same time, the head of the monster appeared above the waves, with his bloody crown and his flaming eyes.

The Old Fisherman, terrified, threw himself back. The boat danced and twisted at the mercy of the waves; the water began to come in by a leak which the harpoon had opened; a few instants more, and he would have sunk. He hastened to bale out the water, and resumed his oars.

The Pike had disappeared. A fearful darkness reigned on the lake. Father Barbel tried in vain, in the midst of such obscurity, to find out his position. Where was he? He had no power of knowing, and began to be discouraged at thinking that every pull he gave was probably carrying him still farther out of his right road. On a sudden, the lightnings began again with a terrible violence, and by their light the Old Fisherman saw, to his horror, that he was not more than a couple of hundred feet from the terrible whirlpool that formed the middle of the lake.

At this sight, he rose upon his oars, plunged them in the water with redoubled energy, and sticking his feet against the sides of his boat, pulled with all his strength against the waves. This effort advanced him a few paces; he raised his oars again, to give another tug, and gain a second stroke; but during these few seconds, the boat went back about three times as much as he had gained before. Then he perceived the eddy which the whirlpool formed at some distance on the top of the water, and his frail vessel began to twist round into the waters, being attracted towards the centre. Father Barbel now felt that all his efforts must be useless. He abandoned his oars, and had no farther care but how to have recourse to the signal agreed upon with the Water-Sprite. He took up his torch of resin, and tried to light it. But the moment he opened the little wicket of his lantern to introduce it there, it shook so with the blowing of the wind, as to be almost extinguished. He quickly withdrew the torch, and closed the door of his lantern.

Meanwhile, the circle in which the boat was turning began to diminish more and more. At last, the unfortunate man could hear the waters roaring close by his side. As he drew nearer and nearer, the gulf seemed ready to devour him; he tried a second time to open his lamp; his right hand trembled, while his left endeavoured to protect the quivering flame. Suddenly the torch caught fire. Speedily he brandished it aloft in the air; and just as his bark sank, and while still dancing round the sides of the whirlpool, he shouted out loudly, "Water-Sprites! Water-Sprites! Save——"

He had not time to complete the sentence, for the water covered his voice, and the boat and the Old Fisherman disappeared together in the dark, whirling abyss.

"WHERE AM I?" SAID OLD BARREL, RUBBING HIS EYES.

VII. THE MYSTERIES OF THE WHIRLPOOL.

FATHER BARREL, rendered giddy by the noise of the water, and the twisting round of his boat, had fallen to the bottom of a grotto, where reigned complete darkness; and, although he had gone right through all the depth of the lake, he was scarcely wet. When he had a little recovered from the fall, he tried, by touching, to reconnoitre the place in which he found himself. His feet and his knees met, every instant, some slippery surfaces, that rendered his walking difficult; his hands, too, placed themselves upon viscous objects, which he felt to move as if they were living beings. A dull and continuous sound groaned above his head, and he seemed to hear all round him murmurs and a kind of smacking of lips.

"Where am I?" cried he, stopping, and rubbing his eyes.

Laughter sounded through the grotto; and he felt a crowd of little bodies like rain about his head, the nature of which he could not divine, but which resembled animals leaping about him by millions. He halted, and tried to distinguish something across the darkness, for his eyes were beginning to accustom themselves to the obscurity. He seemed to see beings of strange shapes ranged in a half circle; and in the midst of them a living mass, that appeared to be throned on a rock. By degrees these objects became more distinct; and he was at last able to make out about twenty persons of extraordinary appearance, half men, half animals. The man in the middle was a kind of monster, whose legs were stuck together, his body covered with little spots, and his head narrow and flat. His mouth, or rather his throat, was elongated like a beak.

Father Barbel recognized his mortal enemy, the King of the Pikes. Soon, in fact, he could clearly distinguish the bleeding crown which he wore on his forehead, the insignia of his royalty. The others had all, like him, their legs joined together in one piece, in the shape of a tail; but each one could be distinguished by its head, which bore a semblance to the muzzle of a fish. By the side of the King was seated a woman, or something somewhat like one, whose royal garments were spotted with little red and blue stars, and whose head resembled the muzzle of a Trout. In her Father Barbel recognized the one he had pursued right up to the Great Lake. This was the Witch of the Waters, commissioned to draw within the snares of the King of the Pikes, such imprudent fishermen as that terrible monarch might have determined to make the victims of his vengeance.

"It's all over with me now," thought Father Barbel, at sight of his enemies. In fact, he saw the King make a sign to his subjects, as he pointed him out. These latter seized him with their fins; and, raising him in their arms, held him suspended over the head of the King, who, leaning back, shut his eyes with an air of beatitude, and opened his large gullet. Father Barbel threw a terrified glance down this abyss, bristling with teeth that formed in themselves a formidable saw, and he seemed to see, right at the bottom of the entry of the living sea-tub, the head of a man, a portion of the royal dinner!

At this horrible sight he shut his eyes, and endeavoured to struggle, so as to get rid of the restraint of his enemies. But these worthies held him firmly. They balanced him, for an instant, above the gullet of the King, and were just about to hurl him down it, when the Witch of the Waters rose suddenly, and stopped them.

"No," said she; "a death such as that would be too gentle a punishment for his delinquencies. He has yet to purchase, by torments proportionate with his crimes, the honour of being devoured by our King, and of being entombed in his sacred bowels."

At these words, they laid Father Barbel down on

210

the ground, while the King rose up from his chair with an air of displeasure and disappointment.

They all deliberated together, in a low voice, on the torments to which they were about to submit their victim. During this time, the unfortunate man took a survey of the grotto, through which a feeble light just shone. It was hung with mosses and stalactites, and from the vault above depended an immense lustre formed of icicles. The light which sparkled from the eyes of the King played in these crystals, and was the only method of lighting this lustre, and the only light that pierced the shade of the subterranean den. Around him was posted a cordon of oysters, that passed their time in opening and shutting their shells alternately—a range of lazy mouths, gaping and yawning with sleepiness. Frogs, eels, and leeches, strewed the ground in such profusion, that he could not walk a step without crushing some of them, and many other reptiles that Father Barbel had felt while walking in the grotto.

The deliberation was soon over. First, all the weapons used by Father Barbel in fishing were successively brought out of the boat, and laid in the middle of the cavern. A great Carp brought in the net; a young Pike the casting-net; a whole regiment of Crabs carried the eel-pot, and a little Gudgeon the line. These were the executioners of criminals. When all were arranged, the assistants took their seats again; and the Pike, taking the end of a line, bound Father Barbel with it. They then placed before him a morsel of bread. The unhappy wretch had not eaten for twenty-four hours; and they knew that his hunger being pressing, he would use every effort to disembarrass himself of his covering, and clutch this meagre breakfast. At first, Father Barbel took it all very easy, thinking he could soon break the light web of rushes. So he took his knife from his pocket, and cut those that were in front of him. Next, he stretched out his arm to seize the morsel of bread; but it was stopped by another of the lines.

"I thought, however, I had cut them all," said he to himself; "but one blow of the knife more." He passed his hand across the hole he had just made in the net. What was his astonishment to feel a new resistance, and to see new meshes filling up the void he had made. He remained motionless for a moment, as he asked himself if he was not the sport of some dream; then he took out his knife again, and went to work. This time, however, he saw clearly the meshes become reproduced again, just in proportion as he destroyed them, and even grew thicker as renewed. At sight of this useless labour, and this obstacle, so slight, but always renewed, despair seized upon him, and he awaited he knew not what. Meanwhile, his hunger became more pressing, and the sight of the morsel of bread still farther augmented his impatience and suffering. At last, not being able any longer to control himself, he got up, and behaved towards the net just as a water-rat in a trap; for, in a great rage, he tore with his hands and his teeth whatever was in his way. He saw he had made a large hole, but there were still obstacles remaining. A little calmed, however, by seeing this result, he continued his exertions, with somewhat more method, for he thought he remarked that the meshes broken by his teeth were the only ones that did not grow again. In fact, the fishes not having any but this means of breaking their nets, it was the only one they had not guarded against.

As soon as Father Barbel did as they did, he, in a few minutes, found himself at liberty. He quickly seized the morsel of bread, and devoured it rapidly, while his judges made wry faces at seeing their secret discovered.

But a morsel of bread is but a poor dinner for a hungry fisherman, who has not had any breakfast. So he searched all about with his eyes for some other victuals, until, out of a corner of the cave there came some Eels, who set a table before him laden with delicious viands. At sight of this feast, which, to a man in his situation, appeared even better than it was, Father Barbel remained quiet and uncertain, dreading some new snares on the part of his enemies.

"It is not from any goodness of heart," said he to himself, "that they offer me this jolly good dinner; there is some trap in it. However, there is nothing very suspicious about the table, that I can see. Would they poison the dishes? Faith! it is better to die of poison than of hunger."

All the while he was thus talking, he was sitting down to table, and beginning to eat, but timidly, at first, and still observing a certain mistrust.

"Capital style of poison this, at any rate," said he, as he tasted one of the dishes, which had a most savoury odour.

Then he went on eating with greater confidence, and his hunger almost made him forget that he was in the midst of enemies. However, he soon began to think he saw them all laughing as they looked at him, and remarked that their laughter increased every time the Trout pulled a cord that she held in her hand. He conceived the idea of watching where ended this cord, the least movement of which so delighted the assembly. Following the direction, his eye arrived at the summit of the vault, where he saw, with terror, his harpoon, suspended by a hair joined to the cord.

He jumped up, uttering a cry of terror, and leaving on one side the meal he had begun. As soon as he thought himself out of reach of the terrible weapon, he stopped, and turned his eyes towards the vault: the harpoon was no longer there.

"Faith!" said he, believing they were going to let it fall, "it was high time for me to be off."

He was about to sit down to table again, when, turning round, he saw the harpoon, which, guided by the cord held by the malicious Trout, was about to plunge itself into his back. He made a bound in advance, and sought refuge at the other end of the cavern; but the harpoon was there quite as soon as he was. Afraid, and almost out of his senses, he set to work running and crying, while the harpoon pursued him like an avenger. He knew not where to conceal himself to avoid this new danger. Guided by his inquiet and blind course towards a corner of the grotto, he saw himself suddenly brought to a stop by an eel-pot, which obstructed the entry of a kind

of passage, like those that are open for fish in canals. The harpoon was behind him, and left him no means of returning in the rear. The unfortunate man instinctively stooped, as he saw the trident of iron threatening his head, and found himself thus in the gullet of the creel. At the same moment, he felt the points of the trident touch his feet, made a desperate effort to avoid the contact, and caught his head in the narrow opening of the creel. The osier twigs closed and opened, but the harpoon still pressing on him from behind, he went forward in spite of himself, and ended by entering entirely within that osier prison, his hair in disorder, his face covered with scratches, and his body trussed up like that of a fowl.

Quickly the laugh resounded all round him; while a Carp, taking hold of the creel, shook it violently, as does a fisherman who wishes to make the fish fall out that are within it. These repeated shocks had the effect of making the unhappy prisoner descend towards the opposite opening, a narrow and long passage, where a child would be troubled to creep through. At last, his head came out, and the Carp, placing the creel on its end, allowed those present a fine view of this mass of basket-work, surmounted with a human head, all bristling, which gave to Father Barbel the air of a great cheese-maggot, without feet or arms. When the hilarity provoked by this spectacle had exhausted itself, they kept on shaking the poor fellow, until he came, at last, entirely out of his cage, and fell upon the earth, on which he rolled quite beaten and exhausted.

"Faith!" cried Father Barbel, as soon as he rose up, "I never thought myself capable of making such a tour as that. It is a happy thing I am not too fat; I should never have squeezed out of there. It's all the same; if they continue to squeeze me in that fashion, I shall end by becoming an eel, and shall pass through the neck of a bottle. Those gentlemen, there, have a style of amusement, that they can only have learnt from the imps below. After this, I shall not be surprised to find myself nearer than I like to a certain hot place! Two or three more jokes such as these, and it will be all over with you, my old friend Barbel. But what more can they do with me? Oh, the rascals!" he went on, on seeing the casting-net and the line; "I have two punishments yet to undergo."

In fact, it had been decreed to exhaust these different instruments of torture. The King of the Pikes gently opened the casting-net, then threw it with all his force over Father Barbel's head, who found himself caught and netted, nor more nor less than a fish. They then passed the cord of the casting-net through a hook fixed in the vaulted roof; and each taking hold of the rope, one after the other, drew it up, and relaxed it alternately, so making the net go up and down by turns. He came down to the earth with more or less violence, according to the strength of the one who pulled at the cord, his repeated falls causing shouts of laughter in the assembly. The game was, who could pull the rope strongest, and make him fall from the greatest height. The Trout imparted a shock so violent, that Father Barbel was almost stunned; but when it came to the Gudgeon's turn, the efforts he

211

made to raise such a mass were all in vain, and, in shaking it impatiently, he let go the cord, which rebounded suddenly, as of itself, to the top of the vault.

The executioners saw with sorrow the net rising from the ground, as if drawn up on high by some invisible hand. Two or three Frogs leaped up to catch it, and bring it down again; but it still continued going up, going up, and soon disappeared through the vaulted roof, that opened to give it passage.

VIII. DRY LAND AGAIN.

FATHER BARBEL was greatly astonished to find himself, on a sudden, stretched on the grass, on the border of the Great Lake. By his side was the Water-Sprite, holding a handful of odoriferous herbs, with which he was vigorously rubbing Old Barbel's body.

"Oh, it's you, my boy!" said the Old Fisherman, as he recognized him. "Do just tell me what all this means. It seems to me, as if, for the last two or three days, I had been asleep, and that I have passed the whole of that time in dreaming some very disagreeable dreams. I have certainly seen some strange things, such as you can have no idea about, my lad."

"Just so, Father Barbel; only I know perfectly well what they were."

"Explain to me, then, at once, what all this means, since you are so knowing."

"The meaning is, Father Barbel, that you are an imprudent fellow. That, instead of following my advice, you allowed yourself to be carried away by your passions; and that you have been punished for it, and rightly so."

"Halloa! how severe you are, my young master! If you had been in my

"The head of the monster appeared above the waves."—See page 208.

place, you would not say so."

"If I had been in your place, I should not have gone on to the Great Lake, and then I should not have had what you are pleased to call a bad dream."

"Come, don't be angry; but tell me a little of what it means, and how I must conduct myself for the future."

"So as to be safe, after not following my advice; is it not so, eh?"

"Decidedly; you are malicious, and will forgive me nothing. Let us see, whether it is because you preserve some rancour against me. Will you, also, range yourself on the side of my enemies? I suspect you of some interest down there; you wished to avenge yourself for not having been listened to."

"Yes; by taking you out of the jaws of the King of the Pikes; for you had a narrow escape, and without me you would have been, at this very moment——"

"Within the sacred bowels of his Majesty, as they said."

"Yes, most assuredly. You would have been already swallowed and digested."

"Faith, it makes me shudder! It seems, when I only think of it, as if I felt his teeth plunging into my body. What a throat the monster had!—a gulf, an abyss! But how did you manage, my friend, to get me out of it?"

"I was watching for you. While they were making you undergo your punishments, I was hidden in the roof of the cavern, awaiting a favourable moment to liberate you, for I had heard your voice in the midst of the tempest. At last, when I saw the cord slip out of the Gudgeon's

"Soon he saw them range themselves in a circle."—See page 207.

fingers, I secured it, and drew up the casting-net. That's the way you were saved. But take care of yourself."

"Is it possible these villanous creatures would attempt anything more against me?"

"Yes."

"In what manner, then?"

"All that they have made you suffer, and more yet. Moreover, their power over you has increased, while mine has diminished."

"You are frightening me, my boy."

"Attend well to what I say. All those weapons for fishing, which have served for your punishment, are for the future forbidden to you. If you use a net, you will find yourself caught within it, as you have been already. If you make use of your harpoon, your harpoon will leap back upon you; so will the other things. One only is permissible, that which they had not time to use against you—the line. You can fish with the line, then, but not otherwise. Moreover, it is forbidden you to catch a Pike; as soon as you see one come under your line, draw up the line. I give you notice that they will tempt you often. Their King will send his subjects round you, even at the risk of some of them perishing. It will always be easy for you to recognize them, even though you cannot see them. Every time a Pike nibbles at your bait, you will see the float of your line dance on the water, and make somersaults and plunges, just like a duck when it is fishing. Whereupon, be careful not to make a movement; let your line go quickly, and remain there until the next day. The Pike will have been caught on your hook, and will die—so much the worse for him; as for you, you have nothing to fear, for you will not have pulled him out of the water."

"Halloa!" said the Old Fisherman, "this is a bad look-out, indeed! How shall I make out my living in such a manner! What! not set an eel-creel? or throw one cast of my net?"

"It cannot be done."

"But that's no kind of life at all."

"It is your own fault."

"Faith! that piece of stupidity has cost me rather dear."

"It is always so. Our faults cost us much more than the effort we should make to avoid them."

"You speak golden words, my lad; but, nevertheless, it is very hard."

"Come, be comforted, Father Barbel. You are growing old. A casting-net is too heavy for your hand; fishing by line is what better suits your age; it is your retirement that you are now undertaking."

"I am much obliged to you, my good lad, for your advice; and I will profit by it. I will keep to the line, since it must be so."

"But look well after yourself; your enemies will take advantage of the least negligence."

"Be at ease; I won't allow them to get hold of me again."

"In any case, remember our signal."

"Very well. But this is not all; I have to get back to my cabin, if it still exist; for now-a-days I really don't know what to expect."

214

"Be at rest on that score; you will find your cottage in the same state as you left it. The only difficulty is, we must get there by swimming."

"Halloa! Why, it is more than three miles from here?"

"So much the worse."

"So much the worse! that's very easy to say; but I don't think I could ever swim as far as that. I am old, as you say, and, besides, those monsters there have tortured me until I can scarcely move my limbs. However, I can't remain here all my life."

"We will both swim in the same direction, and will start off on our voyage together."

"Let us try, then; but I have not much of a chance, if I don't get a rest on the road."

"Don't be afraid, I will help you; although I am so much older than you."

"You have always something to make me laugh. I like that; it makes me young again. Decidedly you are my Good Genius; with you, I fear nothing, not even in the middle of the water."

At these words, both of them plunged into the Great Lake, and directed themselves, as they swam, towards the canal that led to the river.

Father Barbel, at first, bore the fatigue of his maritime voyage tolerably well; but soon he complained of the cramp, which took him in the right foot.

"It's the one that suffered so much pain in going into that creel. Those rascals of fishes! they have jolly well paid me out for the war I have so long waged against them."

He kept on, however, although with difficulty. At last, feeling his strength becoming exhausted, he called to his companion, who was swimming in front with admirable ease.

"Dear Water-Sprite," said he, "if you do not come to help me, I must stop here. But I am thinking what you can do? You can't take me on your back."

"All right," replied the Water-Sprite, "I shall find a good plan for relieving you; I have got you out of a much worse scrape."

"That's true; come, I trust myself in your hands entirely. Do just what you like with me."

The Water-Sprite rapidly, with his body all the while suspended in the water, gathered a bundle of reeds, which he bound with the stem of a water-lily.

"Support yourself on the top of this," said he to his companion, "and remain without moving."

"It is time," said Father Barbel, seizing the bundle, which he placed under his arms, and which supported him on the top of the water.

The Water-Sprite tied round his own body the other end of the lily-stem fixed round the bundle of reeds, and set to work swimming, and dragging along with him the bundle of reeds and Father Barbel. The latter, without moving, and having nothing to do but lean on his bundle of reeds, had plenty of time to contemplate his young companion. The Child swam with wondrous agility, and his convoy did not hinder his sporting in the water, just like some bather, who is there only to enjoy himself. Sometimes he would halt, leave the bundle of reeds to float past him down the stream, then suddenly dive in, and Father Barbel would soon see him re-appear at ten yards from him. At other times, he would lightly shake his little green cable, and set the bundle of reeds rocking.

"Take care!" Father Barbel would say, "you will upset my flotilla; I have not got good sea-legs; and I don't feel myself at all too firmly seated."

"Don't be frightened," said the little Water-Sprite, laughing; "there's no cause for fear."

"You are always confident; but I have all the feeling, just now, of one who is learning to ride on a horse that has not been broken; if you set my horse a-rearing, I shall not be able to keep on him, that is certain."

This bye-play seemed to enliven the voyage, which otherwise would have been tolerably wearisome for the Old Fisherman. For the rest, he could not but admire the skill and address of his companion.

"How he swims!" he kept on saying; "what a swimmer he is! By-the-bye, you have forgotten to teach me your stroke; what a famous stroke!"

"Here's just the occasion; you have now the time for studying. Now then, watch me well."

Then the Water-Sprite, stooping his head a little under the surface of the water, stuck his left arm along his body, then striking out rapidly with his right, clove the waters like an arrow. He ran through, in this way, nearly half a mile, to the great astonishment of Father Barbel, who gazed on him with amazed eyes.

"It is not more difficult than the other way," said the Water-Sprite, suddenly raising his head.

"Not more difficult!" replied Father Barbel; "you are a funny fellow! How

"Two or three Frogs leaped up to catch it."—*See page 212.*

do you think I could stop a quarter of an hour under water, like you?"

"Perhaps that might trouble you, Father Barbel."

"That's a clever discovery of yours. Teach me to breathe under water, or else——"

"Ah! as regards that, it's another question; I can't teach you anything down there."

"Then I can't learn your stroke, and that's a pity."

"You'll never want it; you will always be a-head of me."

"When a man passes his life on the water, as I do, he always wants such knowledge."

"What! for fishing with a line?"

"Ah! you bring back my cares. To fish with a line! It's very well, from time to time, in fine spring days, under a bright sunshine; but at night, what can I do then?"

"You will sleep, Father Barbel; that will be all the better for you."

"Such is the fact. Perhaps you are in the right; but it's plain I begin to be tired of it at the very beginning. When I think—but here we are, arrived at home. I see my little islet. Oh, I feel my strength return! I must swim to it; it is no distance to speak of."

So he left his bundle of reeds, and started off for a swim, with a joyful ardour, that made him, for the instant, forgetful of his fatigue. In a few yards he touched the banks of his islet, though he had some trouble in getting on to it.

"Eh, eh!" said he, as soon as he was on shore; "I am before you, my lad; Father Barbel has some vigour in his old limbs yet. Well, here we are. But where can he be?" added he, as he looked in vain

215

over and on, and up and down the river, for the Water-Sprite.

He rubbed his eyes, and looked again, all round, and up and down : the Water-Sprite had vanished.

"What a funny young chap!" said Father Barbel, with his eye still fixed on the river. "What did I call him?—a young chap? He is much older than me; he might be my father, or my grandfather. What strange things I have seen within the last few days!"

IX. DANGER OF FISHING WITH A LINE.

FATHER BARBEL was as pleased as a child on re-entering his cabin, which he had thought, at one moment, he should never see again. He visited his store-pond, distributed crumbs of bread among his fish, as a father to his children; and called his ducks, who ran, flapping their wings, and sprang familiarly on his shoulders, while his fowls pecked from his hand the morsel, that he tried maliciously to snatch from their greediness.

"Yes, yes; it's me," he said to them; "it's your old master, it's your papa, come back to you! Ah, my children! you have had a narrow escape of not seeing me again. He has had a narrow escape, your poor Father Barbel; I will tell you all about this some other time. Meanwhile, feast away, my little ones. Well, now, why are you looking so hard at me, my big duck? Why don't you eat? Oh, very well, I understand you; you find the bread a little hard. What would you have? It is now three days that I have been absent, but that is not my fault. But attend, my children; I am going to give you a soaking in the water, and to make you some nice soup."

Half an hour passed in these recreations, and in this review of the guests of the island,—half an hour of happiness, that made Father Barbel a real king,

OLD BARBEL TUMBLES INTO THE RIVER.

returning in triumph to his capital, encircled by the love of his people. It is quite true, that this kind king waited on his own subjects like a servant, which is scarcely according to the habits of sovereigns. But, like a good prince, he had no haughtiness, nor even self-love, a circumstance that did not fail to add to his happiness.

After a few moments of thorough enjoyment, he re-entered within his cabin; but there his joy vanished at once. He saw there his nets, his casting-gear, his eel-creels, all his fishing instruments—tools for work and weapons of triumph, that had become to him indispensable articles of furniture, and almost as companions. For the first time, perhaps, in his life, the tears came into his eyes, as he thought he must renounce all these, quit his friends, and give up, so to say, his past life. He took them up, one after the other, examined them, and tried them carefully. Having remarked a fracture in his net, he could not

avoid mending it, although thenceforth it was of no more use to him. He finished, by hanging up all these tools on the walls of his cabin, like an old soldier, who, on returning home, arranges as a trophy on his walls arms now useless, and spoils won from the enemy.

"Come, rest thou there," said he, as he hung his trident on a nail; "moulder there, die there, my old companion; it must be done! And thou, my jolly eel-pot—thou, whom I have woven with so much care; thou, who hadst an air so coquettish, as you bobbed up and down in the clear and running water, with the grass and moss hanging about thee; thou, who sat'st enthroned like a queen in the middle of the river; here must thou now remain, dry, empty, weary!—for wearied thou soon must be—far from the freshness of the waters, the gold sand, and the humid rushes. No more wilt thou see the green reeds bending over thee their caressing heads; no longer hear the gurgling of

216

"THE HARPOON PURSUED HIM LIKE AN AVENGER."—*See page* 211.

the gentle streams, nor feel again the prisoned gudgeon leaping against thy sides. We must now renounce our pleasures, my friends; we have all of us grown old. It is you, especially, who are the cause of all this," said he, turning to his casting-net; "but go! I desire you no longer. You have given me many pleasures; you have made me happy nights, and I shall not forget them. I have a large heart," added he, as he wiped his eyes with the back of his hand; "it is right that I should have."

He took his line, and went and placed himself on the banks of the river, where he remained until evening, but brought home only a few fish. The next and following days passed in the same manner. His life became monotonous, and weariness consumed him by degrees. At night he slept not, but would often get up, and walk silently along the river, slowly following its winding banks. When the moon shone upon the waters, he stooped down to see the fishes playing together; but the sight of them only saddened him the more.

"How happy they are, down there!" he would say to himself, as he contemplated them, just as a miser does his treasure; "how tranquilly they play under my very eyes! They seem as if they know they have nothing more to fear from the poor Old Fisherman. Truly, they make me envy them; I should like to live and swim amongst them!"

During the whole year, he spent every day of his life seated on the banks of the river, line in hand, waiting for the fish, that would scarcely nibble at his bait. True it is, he did not seem to trouble himself much about that. In spring, he would cast his line carelessly in the water, and sleep, while the eager gudgeons ate the insects badly fastened on to his hook. The pikes would profit by this carelessness, to try and surprise him; and had it not been for the vigilance of the Water-Sprite, who hardly ever left his protegé, he would soon have become the victim of the Bleeding Crown.

"After all," he would sometimes say, "when the reckoning's made up, what does it matter if a man die one way or the other? It is not much of a life, this, always fishing with a line, always and always. Besides, I have grown old—I am tired of myself; I begin to wish I was at the bottom of the water."

One day, while he was asleep, according to his usual custom, with his line in his hand, a number of pikes were looking out for this moment. One of them darted suddenly upon the hook, swallowed it whole, and in struggling to get off, woke Father Barbel. This latter, feeling that a fish was caught, made an effort to draw the line out of the water; but the pike gave it such a violent shock, as to make him fall into the river. The Old Fisherman comprehended his danger at once, but he was too late. He tried to swim, but his rheumatic limbs moved with difficulty. Feeling he could not save himself, he called to his friend.

"Water-Sprite! Water-Sprite!" he cried, "save the Old Fisherman!"

The Water-Sprite ran up at his voice.

"I can no longer save you completely," said he;

218

"but I can mitigate your punishment. You shall live, but you are condemned to live here!"

Father Barbel was desirous of replying, but his mouth, already lengthened into a muzzle, could not articulate a word. His legs stuck together in one piece; and his feet, twisted back, formed the extremity of the tail of a fish. His arms grew thinner by degrees, and then becoming wider, formed fins. His long white beard separated itself on each side of his mouth, in two kinds of fleshy tresses; and, finally, all his body became that of a fish. This fish has preserved his name, and still bears on each side of his mouth two little beards, or *barbillons*, that recal the face of FATHER BARBEL.

THE DOG'S DUEL.

POOR Old Towser! He had been a faithful servant to his master, the Woodcutter, for many years. But Towser had grown old, and almost blind, and had lost his teeth, so that he could no longer bite, or even hold anything fast.

One bright morning, the Woodcutter was standing at his cottage door with his wife; and seeing Old Towser munching at a bone, and making many mouths at it, "I shall shoot Old Towser to-morrow," said he to his wife, "for he is no longer of any use."

"Oh! pray don't," replied his wife, who was a kind-hearted and compassionate woman; "only think how Tommy—our little boy—loves him; and surely we can afford to give food, for the rest of his days, to one who has served us so long and faithfully."

"Nonsense, my love," said the Woodcutter; "you women are always so feeling—out of your husband's pocket. He has had a good dinner every day for what he has done for us, and he can't work any longer; so no work, no wages—that's my rule."

And a very cruel rule it is, and a very wicked one, too, I think; and you will find no blessing rest upon those who are thus hardhearted. However, the poor old Dog, who was basking in the sun just under his master's feet, heard all that was said, and deeply grieved he was, you may suppose. To-morrow, then, was to be his last day, and he was to die by his masters' hand—the master he had served so long and so well—the master he so dearly loved! Poor Old Towser!

Now, the old Dog had one friend—a strange one, you will say, for he was a Wolf, an old Wolf, who lived in the forest hard by. So he slipped out to him in the evening, and told him all his sorrow, and the sad fate that awaited him in the morning.

"Take courage, Father Towser," said the Wolf, kindly, after a few minutes' reflection; "I will just go and consult my attorney, the Fox, who lives a few doors off, and I dare say we shall be able to help you out of your trouble."

In half an hour the Wolf came back, and said: "We have contrived it all nicely. Your master will go out to-morrow haymaking, and take his wife and little Tommy with him."

"I won't have little Tommy hurt," said Old Towser, getting up, and growling; "no, not if it were to save my own life."

"Don't be so stupidly fond and honest," said the Wolf; "that is always the way with you; but nobody means to harm Tommy. But when his mother lays him down under the hedge, while she goes to help his father——"

"Can't you leave Tommy out of the play-bill?" said Old Towser, anxiously.

"By no means," went on the Wolf; "but they will be sure to leave you to watch him. Then I will spring out of the hedge suddenly, and catch up the child."

"What! trust Tommy in your mouth?" exclaimed Old Towser.

"Don't be a fool!" went on the Wolf. "When I do this, you are to run after me in hot haste; and then I shall drop the child, and make the best of my way off, leaving you the victor on the field. Then you will carry back the child to his alarmed parents, and they will ever love you, and keep you as long as you live."

"Take care you don't hurt Tommy."

"Oh! upon my honour!" replied the Wolf.

"Then it will be a famous plan," said Old Towser, with the tears running from his eyes.

And so it all came off, just as the Fox and the Wolf had planned it. The alarm of the fond parents was excessive when they saw the Wolf running off with their child; but when Old Towser rose up, and rushed after the Wolf, and shook him, and rolled him over, and the Wolf dropped the child and ran away, and Tommy put his arms round Old Towser's neck, and the Dog licked his face, and then carried him back safe in his mouth, and laid him at his weeping mother's feet, the Woodcutter said, "Never again will I think of shooting my dear old Dog; not a hair of your head shall be touched; and victuals you shall have, as much as you can eat, to the end of your days."

Then he told his wife to go home and boil a mess of meal and broth for Old Towser—something that did not require biting; and also to take the cushion out of his own chair, and give it to the poor old Dog to lie upon. Good times these were for Old Towser, you may be sure; when both master and mistress make a favourite of the same Dog, a happy Dog indeed is he!

Some days after this, the Wolf visited his old friend, who received his congratulations, and thanked him heartily.

"Father Towser," said the Wolf, slily, "of course you will close your eyes if I steal a fat sheep now and then from your master."

"Don't reckon on that," replied Old Towser; "I must be faithful to my master. I dare not give you his sheep."

But the Wolf thought Towser did not mean it, and came slinking and sneaking into the farm-yard after the sheep. But the Woodcutter was made aware of his coming by the Dog, and stood there with his flail ready to give him welcome. The Wolf scampered off, with whole bones, but sorely bruised; and as he ran limping along, he roared out to the Dog, "Wait awhile, you old rascal! I will serve you out for this pleasant joke."

Next morning came the Bear, with a challenge to the Dog from the Wolf; and as the Bear refused to accept the explanations offered by Old Towser as satisfactory, it was arranged finally that they should meet in the forest to settle the affair. The Bear was to act as the Wolf's second; but Old Towser, who had few acquaintances, and most of whose friends had died out, found considerable difficulty in procuring a second. At last, he remembered a veteran friend, one Captain Cat, of the 14th Mewtineers, who, having served in the German war, had lost a leg, but was a brave old fellow still, for all that. Old Tom readily assented to act for Old Towser, and away they went together towards the forest, the poor old Cat limping along, and holding his tail high in the air, from pain. The Wolf and the Bear were already on the ground; but as they caught sight of Old Towser at a distance, with the Cat's tail waving before him, they imagined it to be a sabre that he was brandishing; and whenever the poor old Cat hopped up on his three legs, they fancied it a huge cannon-ball that Towser was bringing along with him, to discharge from his loaded pistol. These thoughts and sights made them very nervous, and their courage oozed out so fast from their tails, that the Bear found it necessary to hide himself in a bed of dried leaves, while the Wolf climbed up a tree. Thus, when Old Towser and Captain Cat arrived on the ground, there were no adversaries to be seen anywhere. But the Bear had not hid himself entirely; his ears were sticking up out of the leaves, and one of them shook a little, and the old Cat thought it was a mouse, and jumped at it, and scratched it so fiercely, and gave it such a sharp bite, that the Bear uttered a great howl, and ran away, shouting out as he went, "There's the real offender, up in the tree!"

The Dog and the Cat looked up and saw the Wolf, who was all of a tremble, and so piteously cowed, that he humbly begged the Dog's pardon, and promised to offend no more; and finally, being invited down, entered into a treaty of peace, and invited all the party to dinner at the nearest tavern, and paid all the expenses of a most liberal treat.

THE STORY OF MASTERFUL HARRY.

Once upon a time, there was a bold, bluff little Boy, who could not abide his parents' control; and thinking, as foolish children often do, that the best way to punish his father and mother was to do some injury to himself, he ran away, one fine morning, from home.

He ran along across the fields, until his father's cottage was out of sight, and then, being rather hot and tired, sat down by the first way-side he came to, on a heap of stones.

Now, it so happened, that seated at the other end of the heap of stones was an ugly Old Woman in a red cloak; it was plain that she had been out begging, and the fulness of the two bags she carried showed that she had not done a bad morning's work. There was bread and butter, and jam, and honey, and ham, and bacon, and hot rolls—the sight of all which set the naughty little fellow's mouth watering; for though he had left his home and his lessons behind, he had not failed to bring his appetite with him.

Seeing his eager look at the various broken bits, the ugly Old Woman invited him to partake of her scraps, which he did with great relish. She then inquired if he would like a job, and on his thankfully assenting, hired him on the spot to carry her bags home across the hill to her cottage on the heath.

They soon trudged off; but they had not gone above a couple of miles up the hill-side, when the boy kicked his foot against a Scarlet Garter.

He picked it up, and took it to the ugly Old Woman, who looked at it, examined it up and down, turned it over and over again, and then told Harry to put it in his pocket—he should have it for his day's wages.

"That's liberal," thought Harry to himself.

But instead of putting it into his pocket, he fastened it round his knee, and thought himself very much the smarter for it. More than this, he found himself immediately a great deal stronger, and felt as if he was master of the world and all that was in it.

"Now then—come along," said the Old Beggar-woman; "don't waste your time dawdling here; we have got to walk over the hill."

So on they went; but when they had mounted half-way up the steep path, the Old Woman declared she was too weary to go farther, and must sit down to rest.

But Masterful Harry had very little rest in him, and the spell of the Scarlet Garter was strong upon him; so he climbed up to the top of a high crag, and looked out for some sign of a house. It was not long before he saw something glimmering in the distance, which, from its steadiness, he imagined to be the fire showing through some cottage window not far off. "Come along, Old Lady," said he to the Old Beggar-woman; "here is a house and shelter."

"I can't move a step," replied the Old Beggar-woman; "we must stop here until daylight."

"Not so," replied Masterful Harry; "I should like to have some supper."

Then he took up the Old Woman's bags with one hand, and tucked the Old Woman herself under the other arm, and stepped out quickly in the direction of the light. It was not long before they came to a large house, like a brick castle.

"Don't go in there," cried the Old Woman, kicking with all her might, to escape from under Masterful Harry's right arm; "that great house belongs to an Ogre."

"Never mind," replied Masterful Harry, in a cheerful voice; for, thanks to his Scarlet Garter, he felt, at that moment, strong enough to fight a dozen Ogres, and hungry enough to eat them afterwards. "Never mind that, Dame; see how the lights shine, and how warm the fire looks, and I can smell supper just taken out of the pot."

So in he went, dragging the unwilling Old Woman and her bags along with him. But what met his gaze

220

at his opening the door certainly did surprise him, and so frightened the Old Woman, that she went right off into a swoon. This was a monstrous man, twenty-four feet high, with a head six feet round, sitting on a great wooden bench.

"A fine night, Daddy," said Masterful Harry, stepping boldly up to the Ogre, and shaking him by the hand.

"Well, you do grip hard!" said the Ogre, blowing his knuckles—for Master Harry had taken care to give them a tolerable squeeze, by way of making a proper impression at the commencement; "I have sat here now more than a thousand years, and I never had such a friendly greeting, or was called Daddy, before."

So Masterful Harry took a stool, and sat down side by side with the Ogre, and they had a pleasant gossip together.

Suddenly, the Ogre looked round, and observed the Old Beggar-woman lying on the floor.

"What's the matter with you, mother?" said he; "I think she has fainted away; had not you better look after her?"

Then the Boy went to her, and poured some water on her face, and pulled her along the floor, which set her kicking and screaming, for she thought the Ogre was going to eat her. But the voice of the Lad re-assured her; and at last she came to herself, and sat in the corner by the fireside, but did not venture to look up, for the sight of the terrible Ogre was too much for her.

"Can you give us a bed here to night?" said the bold Boy; "it is quite plain that the Old Dame can't go any farther before morning."

"Oh! certainly," replied the Ogre; "but you must have some supper besides."

Then he threw a couple of oak-trees on the fire, and when they had burnt nicely to hot embers, he went out, and brought in a whole fat bullock, which he killed with one blow of his huge fist, and then skinned, and spitted, and roasted, until it was brown. "That will do nicely," said the Ogre; and he went to a side cupboard, about as large as a cottage, and took out a huge silver dish, on which he laid the roasted ox. Then he spread a table-cloth as large as the mainsail of a man-of-war, and went down into his cellar, and brought up a hogshead of wine, out of which he knocked the head, and put the whole cask on the table as a drinking-cup. He did not bring out any forks, as they were not in fashion at the period, but there were quite enough of knives to make up for the want of them, for each of the two he laid on the cloth was six foot long.

"Now then, Old Lady," cried the Ogre, "come and sit down to supper!"

It was not easy for Masterful Harry to bring up the Old Woman to the table; but at last he whispered in her ear, that if she did not come, the Ogre would grow angry, and perhaps kill her. Then she let him drag her to a stool, but when she saw the enormous knives, she began whimpering again; but the bold Boy took one of them up, and cut her a fine rump-steak; and after she had eaten, he lifted the hogshead of wine off the

able on to the floor, and raised her up to it, so that
he could lean her head over, and drink as much as she
wanted. For his own part, he climbed up the side,
and did the same, hanging on like a cat while he did
so. Then, having finished his eating and drinking, he
put the cask back again on to the table, and thanked
the Ogre very politely for the excellent repast he had
provided for them.

"You have not very great appetites, either of you,"
observed the Ogre. "Now I shall have my supper."

"Oh dear!" thought the Old Woman; "now he is
going to eat us!"

"Be quiet, you stupid old thing," whispered Masterful Harry in her ears—for he suspected she was
about to scream out; "don't you think that good roast
beef is much better than a stringy Old Woman?"

This made the Old Beggar-woman very angry, and
she determined to be revenged on the Lad for such an
affront, but for the present wisely held her tongue.
Meantime, the Ogre had made a tolerable supper in
very short time, for he had eaten up the whole of
the ox, horns, head, hoofs, and all, and finished the
wine, every drop, out of the cask. Having done which,
and apparently feeling much comforted thereby, he
rubbed his stomach cheerily, after the well-known
fashion of Ogres, and then sat down by the fire.

"Where can I sleep?" inquired Masterful Harry,
after they had had a little more talking, in which the
Old Beggar-woman, by this time somewhat appeased,
managed to take a part.

"You can jump into the cradle," said the Ogre,
pointing to a huge affair as big as a four-post bedstead; "and the Mistress can take my bed."

So the Boy turned into the cradle, where he lay
snug among the blankets; but he did not think it wise
to go to sleep too soon, but laid awake to hear what
was passing between the Old Beggar-woman—whose
looks he did not half like—and the Ogre.

Presently, she began carneying the Ogre with her
palavering talk, until the Monster, who was as stupid
as he was big, began to think she was a very sensible
and comfortable sort of body, and just the woman to
make an Ogre's house comfortable. At last, he said,
"What is to hinder your stopping here always with
me?"

"Oh! I can't," replied the Old Woman.

"But I mean honourable," added the Ogre.

"If that's the case," said the Old Beggar-woman,
chuckling in her sleeve, at the thought of the great
gudgeon she had hooked,—"if that's the case, Sir;
but what's to be done with the Lad?"

"Oh! we'll soon dispose of him," said the Ogre,
yawning; "I'll tell him you are going to spend a few
days here, to recover from your sprained ankle—you
know you have sprained your ankle."

"Quite bad," said the Old Woman, rubbing a great
bony foot like a hoof.

"And then," went on the Ogre, "I will take him
out up the hill to the quarry, after breakfast; and
while he is hacking at the stones underneath, I will
go to the top and roll down a rock on him."

"All right until morning, at any rate," thought
Masterful Harry, and went off quietly to sleep.

Next morning, there was a great deal of civil conversation between the Ogre and the Old Woman at
breakfast-time; and, at last, he asked her very politely
to stop and spend a few days with him, to which she
assented, with all the pleasure in the world, as she
said, if Masterful Harry had no objection, and could
make it convenient to remain too.

Harry agreed; and in the afternoon, when the Ogre
took up a great iron crowbar, and said he was going
to quarry some stones, the Boy volunteered to accompany him, for he felt strong enough for anything,
while the Scarlet Garter was on his leg.

After they had split out a few stones, the Ogre went
up to the top of the hill, telling Harry to go below,
and square off the rock a little; and there he worked
away hard with his great iron crowbar, until he had
loosened a whole crag, which he toppled over right on
to the place where the Boy was busied. But Masterful Harry put up one hand, as he saw the stone come
rolling down upon him, and gave it a hoist out of his
way.

"That's your little game, is it?" said Masterful
Harry, calling up the hill to the Ogre, who was looking down, expecting to see the Boy crushed to atoms.
"Just come down here yourself, and see how you like
it, for I shall not risk my bones any longer with such
a careless workman."

The Ogre, who was astounded at the strength exhibited by such a puny urchin, did not dare to disobey
him; so he took the lower place in the quarry, and
Masterful Harry took the upper; and thus they worked
some time, until the Lad loosened such a large stone,
and sent it rolling down so quickly, that the Ogre, who
was rather dull and heavy, as many very big men are,
could not get out of the way in time; so it fell upon
him, and broke one of his legs.

There he lay under the great rock, and roaring, in a
sad plight, until Masterful Harry came down to his
assistance, and lifted the rock off him, and raised him
on his own shoulders, and carried him home. But in
doing this the Lad was not too merciful, for he trotted
along at such a pace, that the Ogre screamed and
shrieked with the shaking he got.

His new Old-Wife put him to bed; and when he got
a little easier in the evening, the wicked couple began
their old conversation again, of how they were to get
rid of the Boy, who, they could now see, was mischievously disposed towards them. The Old Woman
confessed herself as much puzzled as before; but the
Ogre declared he knew a plan that would make short
and sure work of the young rogue.

Then he told the Old Woman that in his garden he
had got twelve Lions, and if only they could get one
grip of Masterful Harry, they would tear him into a
dozen pieces, and leave not a limb of him behind.

Now, Masterful Harry heard all that was said, while
pretending to be asleep in his four-poster cradle; so
when the Old Beggar-woman shammed next morning
to be very sick, he was quite ready to pretend to pity
her; and when she said that she fancied she should
never get better until she had a pint and a half of
Lion's milk, he said, "I wish I knew where to run for
it, even if it were to the end of the world; but I really

don't know anywhere where we are likely to procure such a dainty, for love or money."

"Oh! if that's what's wanted," said the Ogre, "and you are man enough to fetch it, the Lion's milk can soon be got. There's my brother lives close by, and his garden runs up to our back-door. He has a great fancy for Lion's milk himself, and keeps a herd of twelve Lions to supply his family with milk. That's the way we bring up the young Ogres."

"Then I am the man to fetch it," said Masterful Harry. "Hand over the key of the garden gate."

So he took the great key and a milking-pail, and started off to milk the twelve Lions in the Ogre's brother's garden. True enough! when he had unlocked the gate, and gone into the garden, there were the twelve Lions, face to face with him, all sitting gravely on their haunches. But when they saw Masterful Harry and the pail, they rose up at once on their hind-paws, with their manes flowing back, and their fore-paws striking out in a fighting attitude—just that rampant posture in which you see the great Golden Lion, with his tail cocked up, on one side of the Queen's Arms. On they came at Masterful Harry, rolling their eyes, stretching out their tongues, gnashing their teeth, and lashing their tails. But the bold Boy was not at all frightened; he took the first one that came up by his fore-paws, and dragged him round the garden, and knocked him against the trees and walls until he had knocked him all to pieces, and there was nothing left of that raging, roaring, rampant Lion but the two paws in Masterful Harry's own hands.

When the rest of the twelve Lions—eleven in number—saw this, they became so frightened at such an outrageous show of strength and courage combined, that they cowered down, and became submissive, and licked the boy's feet like so many beaten dogs. He had no more trouble with them; so he milked one of the Lionesses, who licked his hand during the operation; and then bidding them follow him, he went back to the Ogre's house.

Here he bade the eleven Lions remain outside, which they did like patient hounds, with their paws resting on the door-sill.

"Here's the milk, Mother," said he, as he opened the door.

"I don't believe it," said the Ogre; "the young jackanapes could not possibly have escaped the Lions. Milk a Lioness, indeed! what next, young braggadocio?"

"This next!" said Masterful Harry, walking up to the Ogre's bedside, and lifting him out, and throwing him to the Lions, who entered in a body as soon as he opened the door.

But the Ogre roared so shockingly, and the Old Woman begged so earnestly, that the Boy's feelings got the better of him. So he snatched away the Ogre—who was greatly lacerated, as you may suppose—out of the very jaws of the Lions, and laid him back upon the bed again.

"Now don't you call names any more," said Masterful Harry.

That night, the Ogre, far from being grateful to

Masterful Harry for having thus saved his life, was even more malicious and spiteful than the Old Beggar-woman. "I wish," said he, as they laid in bed, "you would plan some method of getting rid of this audacious young rascal. Can't you hit upon some plan?"

"Not I," said the wicked Old Woman; "he quite overmasters me. If you don't find out the way, he must go home to-morrow. Have you not got some friends that can help you?"

"It seems so silly," replied the Ogre, "to ask the aid of grown-up Ogres, in flogging such a puny lad as that. However, I certainly have two brothers, who live in a castle some miles away from here. They were the oldest and the strongest, and so they drove me away."

"What use can they be to you, then?" asked the Old Woman, pettishly.

"I remember," the Ogre replied, "that when I was a boy, there used to be a garden round that castle, with an orchard, wherein grew some apple-trees, the fruit of which is very fine and beautiful to look at, but whoever eats one of them is sure to fall asleep for three days and three nights. I think, if the little rascal were only to see one of these nice apples, he could not refrain from a nibble at it, and then he would fall asleep, and then——"

"We could tear his eyes out, and pinch his nose off," joined in the malignant Old Beggar-woman.

"Just so," went on the Ogre, trying to rub his hands, which, however, he could not do, for the Lions had bitten them so grievously.

Then it was agreed between these two cruel and wicked people, that the Old Woman should pretend to be taken very badly once more, and should work upon Masterful Harry's feelings, so that he might agree to fetch her some of the apples.

But they little suspected that all this while the Lad had been lying awake, and was listening to what they were plotting against him, and chuckling over the new adventure they were preparing for him.

As soon as Masterful Harry was up, and had got breakfast ready—for the Ogre could not move about for his broken leg, and the Old Woman lay grunting and squeaking with a pretended colic—the wicked old wretch called him to her bedside, and told him, with many piteous tears and groans, that she felt she was dying, and that she hoped he would take care of her poor husband, the Ogre, after she was dead.

The Lad promised to do this, with a deal of affected sympathy; but the Ogre said that the Old Woman might soon be cured, if she could but procure some of the famous anti-cholera apples, that grew in the garden of a castle a few miles distant, which belonged to his two brothers; but, at the same time, he thought it his duty to Masterful Harry, to say that they were cruel Giants and bloodthirsty Ogres, and spared nobody that came within their reach.

"Never mind that," said Masterful Harry; "only let them keep out of my way; the Old Woman shall not die for the want of a beggarly pennyworth of apples."

So he started off that instant; but he took care to whistle to his eleven Lions to follow him. The castle came in sight, and the garden, and the orchard, which were growing fourteen glorious apple-trees, one of which he climbed, and picked some of the ious fruit that hung clustering in rosy and golden fusion on every bough.

"Truly, these are very pretty apples, indeed," said Lad to himself; "I wonder if they taste as nice as y look;" and then, like a Boy as he was, he took one bite—only one; then another; and they were very sweet, and fresh, and juicy, that he ate half a en. Feeling rather drowsy, he bethought himself what the Ogre had said, and came down hastily on the tree; but scarcely had he reached the ground, fore a drowsiness fell heavy on his eyes, and he lay etched slumbering under the tree in a heavy sleep. Luckily for him, the Lions lay all around him in a g, and watched him like shepherd's dogs do their sters; and so he slept on, tranquil and undisturbed, rough two whole days and two whole nights.

When the third day came, out came the Ogre's others into the garden; but they did not make their pearance in their natural forms as Giants, but as o tall bony Horses, such as, in the olden days, used devour men instead of oats and hay; and they me rushing and snorting forth, and soon smelt out r little Lad, where he was lying fast asleep under e apple-tree. "Who dares come here and steal our uit?" roared they. "We will tear him to pieces!" But no sooner had they approached, and turned und for a good kick first, and a bite afterwards, than o rose the eleven raging Lions from round their umbering master, and tore the Ogres themselves into ch small pieces, and so cracked up even their bones, at there was nothing left of them but their hoofs d skulls. All this while Masterful Harry slept on; d when he woke up at last, and rubbed his eyes, he ondered at the confusion and marks of the conflict ll about him. However, he could plainly see that mething had happened, and patted the heads of the ions very kindly, and said to them, "Good Lions, ood Lions!" at which they showed themselves highly elighted, and frolicked about him, and caressed his nds and knees, and wanted to lick his face, but at he would not permit; for a Lion's tongue, let me ll you, if you never felt one, is rather rough, and ey are not the pleasantest animals to play with.

"Well, there are eight hoofs," said Masterful Harry, and two skulls, which plainly proves there were two nimals; and as there were two Ogres, perhaps the ions have given them both such a lesson, that we hall hear no more of them. At any rate, however, t will only be civil to make a call at their castle, and hank them for their nice apples."

So he went up to the castle, and blew loud and hrill at the horn that hung by the gate; but no one ame to open it. At last, after a deal of rapping, and orn-blowing, and shouting on the Lad's part, a very retty young Maiden looked out of a window, and aid, "I have seen it all, and you ought to be very hankful that you were not awake while the Lions ought the man-eating Horses, or rather Ogres."

"No fear for my life," said Masterful Harry; "but re you sure the Ogres are dead?"

"Come in, and see for yourself," replied the sprightly Young Lady "I shall be glad to have some one to talk to, for I have not seen a human-looking creature ever since I was brought here."

So she came down, and opened the castle gate; but when she caught sight of the Lions, she was in a terrible fright, and screamed so loud, that Masterful Harry was too glad, at last, to order the docile beasts to remain outside, although he had many misgivings as to the prudence of entering the castle without his attendants. However, the Young Lady was so pretty, and, withal, had such a simple, innocent way with her, that it was impossible to doubt her assurance that all was secure. So they walked on through the castle together, and on the way she told him how the cruel Ogres had forced her away from home, and shut her up in that castle against her will. She was the King of Mesopotamia's daughter.

After a great deal of talking and walking, it became quite evident to both that they were just suited to make each other happy; for Masterful Harry admired her beauty and wit, and she admired his boldness and good sense. At last, he ventured to ask the fair Princess in what manner it would be her pleasure to act—whether she would go home to her parents at once, or would prefer to marry him. The Princess, without hesitation, replied, that she would rather be married to Masterful Harry. So, of course, he said he would espouse her without delay, and that she should not go home to her royal father's Palace in Mesopotamia, where it might be a long time before he could see her again.

This important question being settled, they resumed their walk over the castle, and came at last to a vast hall, on the walls of which were hanging the armour of the Ogres, and their two great swords.

"Look at those monstrous weapons," said the Princess of Mesopotamia. "What powerful men those Ogres must have been, to wield such tremendous weapons! I don't suppose you could so much as lift one."

"Indeed!" said Masterful Harry—who thought this a reflection on his manhood, and wished to show off as much as possible before the Princess—"Indeed! only look here."

So he piled two or three stools and benches one on the top of the other, and climbed up so as to be able to touch the end of one of the swords with the tip of his finger, and then he gave it a jerk that threw the sword up in the air, and caught it by the hilt as it came down, and flourished it over his head vauntingly, and struck such a blow with it on the floor of the hall, that the whole of the castle shook. After which, he tucked the sword under his arm, and carried it about with him as his familiar weapon.

They spent several pleasant days in the castle together, until, one morning, the Princess was seized with a fit of propriety, and began to think it was time to go home to her royal father in Mesopotamia, and inform him of their intended marriage. Masterful Harry heard this with much sorrow, for it seemed as if the brightness of his life was about to leave him; but, nevertheless, he had the good sense to see that

223

the Princess was in the right. So they freighted a ship with rich presents from the castle stores, and after many adieux and mutual promises of fond remembrance, the Princess sailed away from the castle to Mesopotamia.

A few days after her departure, when the lad began to feel rather more easy in his mind—for, somehow or other, these partings of young lovers seldom break any bones—the thought struck him, that he had come to the Ogre's castle on an errand, and that the Old Woman's health might be suffering from the want of the apples. At any rate, it was his duty to go and see how she was getting on, as they had both started on the journey together, and he had not yet fulfilled his part of the bargain in carrying her bags home. So down he went, with a bagful of apples, and his eleven Lions at his heels, to the Ogre's house, whistling as he went; and on arriving there, found the ugly couple both well and hearty.

Then he told them his story, and how he had become the sole possessor of that noble castle, handsomely furnished, stored with wine and beer, and filled with every comfort and luxury; and he invited them to leave that ugly red house in which they were living, and come and reside with him, to which they both cheerfully assented.

As they were walking along to the castle together over the fields, after dinner—at which the Ogre had brought out an extra hogshead of his best wine, in which he pretended to be rather choice—the Old Woman, who had kept on all dinner-time praising the Lad's bravery and his discretion, and asking questions about the Princess of Mesopotamia and her beauty, inquired of Masterful Harry, as if accidentally, how it happened that he had become so suddenly possessed of such great strength. His courage, she said, she knew was his own, but surely his wonderful power must be a special gift.

"Quite right, Old Lady," said Masterful Harry, whose vanity was tickled by the old wretch's artful compliments; "I am brave by nature; but the power I have comes from that Scarlet Garter you despised so, and gave me for my wages. There it is, on my leg, round my right knee."

"What, that old worsted thing?" said the Old Woman.

"It is a fine silk Garter," replied Masterful Harry; "just look at it." Whereupon, he incautiously took the Garter off, and placed it in the Old Woman's hands.

Then she gave him that very moment a smack on the head that sent him reeling. "And now," she cried, as he came rushing vainly at her—for he was now but a poor weak Lad—"I'll dash your brains out, if you come a step nearer."

And so she could have done, for she had got the Scarlet Garter round her arm.

"That's altogether too good for such an audacious young scaramouch," said the Ogre. "First let us burn out his eyes, and then send him adrift on the sea yonder."

Alas, poor Harry, no longer Masterful! They tore his eyes out, and then turned him adrift in a little boat

224

on the sea. But, luckily, the weather was mild; and as the boat drifted along, the Lions swam after and with their paws directed its course towards island, where they dragged it up on the shore, and laid the poor wounded and bleeding Lad under a plane tree. Then the eleven noble Lions held a consultation and they went out hunting, and caught a number birds, from which they plucked the feathers, and made him a bed of down, and fed him with the flesh, which however, he was obliged to eat raw. Poor fellow! suffered greatly from his blindness, and the thought how he was separated for ever from his charming Princess of Mesopotamia.

Now, it happened one day, as the noblest and cleverest of the Lions was out Hare-hunting, he noticed that the Hare was blind, and ran straight on without knowing where, until at last it ran right against the stump of a tree, and was knocked back with the blow and fell over into a brook just by. The Lion thought he had lost his game, and pitied the poor Hare; but greatly to his surprise, it not only jumped out of the brook, but had recovered its eyes, and so sped straight as well as nimbly on its way, and thus finally escaped the jaws of the pursuing Lion.

"So, so!" thought the King of the Lions, "this may be a happy discovery." Then he trotted briskly to the plane-tree, and pulled poor Harry gently by the sleeve, until he made him understand that he wished him to get on his back, and then carried the Lad to the brook-side, and toppled him in. Whereupon Harry, greatly to his own wonder and delight, found that he immediately recovered his sight.

After having knelt down and thanked Heaven for his blessed restoration, Harry hastened back to where his friends, the eleven noble Lions, were assembled and having thanked them for their kind and generous assistance, he motioned them all to come together, and form, as it were, a raft for him with their backs, on which he stood up while they swam with him to the main land, which the pretty creatures did, quite pleased with the adventure.

Having accomplished this feat successfully, he concealed himself until nightfall in a copse, the Lions couching quietly all that time; and then he crept up stealthily and unperceived to the Castle, where he got in by a back window, and peeping through a key-hole, saw the Ogre and his wife in bed and snoring. The Old Woman's clothes were lying at the foot of the bed—for she was an untidy creature—and round the bed-post was the Scarlet Garter!

Oh! happy Harry, if the Ogre would but keep on snoring!—which he did, and Harry snatched up the Scarlet Garter; and then didn't he stamp, and halloo and call out, enough to wake the dead!

Up jumped the Ogre, and out of bed sprang the Old Hag. "Oh! give me my Garter, my dear Boy!"

"I'll give you your Garter, you Old Hag," said Masterful Harry; "I'll give you what you wanted to give me!" and, with that, he gave her one cuff on the head, that knocked her brains out, for he was in a great rage at her treachery.

"Oh! oh! oh! oh! oh! oh! oh! oh! oh!" cried the Ogre; and he moaned so piteously, and whined so

MASTERFUL HARRY IS CARRIED TO THE MAIN-LAND ON THE BACKS OF HIS ELEVEN LIONS.

mournfully, and begged and prayed so hard to have his life spared, and his head not knocked off, that at last Masterful Harry said, "You shall live, and you shall keep your head, but I must have your eyes." So he blinded the wretched Ogre, and put him in a washing-tub, and turned him adrift in the sea; and you may rely upon it that the Lions, who followed him down to the shore, roaring with anger and delight, did not go after him into the water to pull him on shore to any island.

Then Harry went back again to his Castle, and refreshed and reposed himself after his fatigue, and gave his Lions a great treat of eleven fat bullocks, which they greatly enjoyed. But Harry could enjoy nothing; every place he saw reminded him of the lost and lovely Princess of Mesopotamia; and at last, unable any longer to endure the pangs of absence from the loved object, he made up his mind to go forth and search for her until he found her, and then to marry her off-hand—a course in which, now that he had repossessed

No. 29

himself of the Scarlet Garter, he saw very little difficulty.

Then he armed himself once more with the great sword, and took a heap of gold out of the treasury, with which he hired a brave crew and four ships to carry him to Mesopotamia. They sailed along merrily with a fair wind, that carried them swiftly in the right course for four days, when the wind fell, and a calm ensued just as they were under the high cliffs of a rocky island.

Tired of rolling about idly on the waves, they manned their boats and went ashore, where the sailors wandered about, hither and thither, looking about for anything that might be novel or strange. At last, they came upon an enormous egg—an egg as big as a house! They tried to crack the shell, to see what sort of fowl was likely to be inside; but though they threw stones at it, and kicked it, the shell was so hard that their blows were of no avail. At last, up came Masterful Harry, and in the pride of his heart, to show how much stronger he was than every one else, he struck it a blow with his sword, and the egg-shell split into a hundred pieces, and out stalked a monstrous cock-chicken, as large as an elephant!

Then Harry remembered what he had read in the "Voyages of Sinbad the Sailor," and understood how this was a roc's egg. "We had better get away from this place as quickly as possible," he said; "this egg may cost us our lives. Are any of you sailors bold enough to sail with me over to Mesopotamia in four-and-twenty hours? The breeze is strong, and we must hoist all sail."

Then out stepped forty nimble fellows, and said they could sail to Mesopotamia in twenty-four hours, if the breeze would but hold out; and so they hoisted all sail, and the breeze blew strong, and they reached the mouth of the great river in twenty-three hours and three-quarters.

No sooner had they cast anchor, than Masterful Harry ordered all the crew to hurry on shore, and bury themselves out of sight in the sand, while he and his Sea-captains mounted on the top of a high rock, where, sheltered and concealed by lofty and wide-spreading cedar-trees, they could watch what was about to happen. "For that darkness which you see coming on in the air," said Masterful Harry to his men, "is caused by the shadow of the great bird, the roc, that is pursuing us to revenge the breaking of her egg."

Nor was the lad in the wrong. In half an hour afterwards, an enormous bird came in sight, the whirring of whose wings as it flew was like the roaring of a whirlwind. It carried a vast island in its claws, with which it first hovered over the ships, and then let it drop right down upon them, so as to sink them, with all on board, as it supposed. This done, it flew on to the shore, and the very flapping of its wings raised a wind that nearly blew off the sailors' heads; and when it rose from the earth, and passed over the rock, so great was the force of the concussion in the air, that it turned Masterful Harry right round. But his sword was in his hand, and he made one cut at the monster bird, which brought it down fluttering to the earth in a death-agony.

226

Then he went on his journey into Mesopotamia, and soon heard the news, how the King's daughter had been spirited away by certain wicked Ogres, and how she had come back again, with great wealth, but so sad with love, that the King could not bear to see her, and had hidden her away in some unknown castle; and how His Majesty had made proclamation, that whoever could find out where she was, should have her to wife; but, to prevent impertinent curiosity, whosoever should undertake to find her, and did not succeed, should lose his head, as a punishment for his interference.

Then Masterful Harry sat down by the road-side, and thought for three hours. After which, he stopped a man that was passing with bear-skins, and bought from him the skin of a White Bear, with which he covered himself all over, so as to look exactly like a Bear, at the same time mimicking the antics of the beast, in such a manner as to render the disguise perfect. One of his Sea-captains held him by the chain and collar, and thus they went about the capital city of Mesopotamia, playing all kinds of pranks, to the immense diversion of the populace.

One day, as they were followed by a large crowd, laughing and shouting, as Masterful Harry pretended to dance and roar like a White Bear, the noise drew the King to the window of his Palace, and he ordered the Bear to be brought into the courtyard at once, and his tricks exhibited. No sooner had they entered, than Masterful Harry played off such a variety of capers, that all the Court thought the Bear must have gone mad, and they were much frightened, for they said they had never before seen a wild beast in such a savage state. The Sea-Captain, however, assured them that there was no danger so long as they kept from laughing at what the Bear did. If they laughed, the Bear became so mortified, that he would tear to pieces the first person he caught. So the King ordered them all not to laugh; and it doubled the fun to see them all keep such solemn faces, while the White Bear played off the funniest antics, taking care to keep his eye on any one that ventured to smile, and pretend to make a rush at him, tugging furiously at the chain with which the Sea-Captain pretended to hold him back.

It was late in the evening before the show was over; and the King, who had a design of his own, directed that the Bear should be brought into his ante-chamber to sleep, and got a whole waggon-load of pillows and cushions spread out for it, and some fine raw steaks for its supper, which Masterful Harry was not at all pleased with. However, he made the best of it for the time, resolving, in his own mind, to steal down into the pantry, as soon as he heard the King begin to snore.

The King, however, did not go to sleep at all; but as soon as the clock struck midnight, came into the room where the White Bear was sleeping, or pretending to sleep; and taking hold of the chain, led him through gallery after gallery, up one staircase and down another, until at last, passing by a secret door out of the Palace they came to a long pier, or landing-place, which ran some distance out into the sea.

"I don't think I shall let him drown me," said Masterful Harry to himself. "I wonder what His Venerable Majesty means to do."

When they had reached the extreme end of the pier—to walk along which sorely puzzled the pretended Bear's paws and claws, as every opening between the planks caught his feet, and went nigh to throwing him over—the King halted, and began to pull up first one post, and then another, pushing this one up, and that one down, until, at last, some machinery appeared to be set in motion, and a pretty little waterproof house rose up above the water's edge. The King knocked at the door, and—greatly to the delight of the White Bear—who should open it, but the Princess herself! In fact, this was the hidden place in which the King of Mesopotamia kept his daughter concealed. Then he told her all about the wonderful White Bear, and his amusing pranks, and his having brought the curious beast to show to her. The Princess, at first, was afraid to look at it; but the King persuaded her, and said there was no danger, if she did not laugh. So the Bear was brought in, and danced, and capered, and played the fool, and knocked over one of the maids that laughed at him. At last, it was settled, as the Bear growled a great deal, and seemed unwilling to quit the Princess's parlour, that it should be left there with the Princess. So the Bear rolled himself round, and laid himself down by the stove, as if going to sleep; but no sooner had the King gone away than he rose up, and asked the Princess, with much polite ess, to undo the collar round his neck.

Such a request from such a party alarmed the fair Princess to such a degree, that she almost fainted outright; but something in the Bear's manner re-assured her, and being a bold girl, and of a brave spirit, she felt about his neck until she got at the collar, and un-clasped it. Scarcely was this done, than the Bear politely took his head off, just as a gentleman would his hat, and she recognized her own darling boy, her betrothed, her preserver—Masterful Harry!

When she saw who it was, she was so overjoyed, that she wished at once to run after her father, and acquaint him with the happy tidings of her deliverer's arrival. But the Lad begged her to be patient, and said he would rather earn her once more, for he did not feel by any means sure that the King was a man of his word, or would relish having a mere nobody like himself for his royal son-in-law.

So they sat up all night together in the Princess's parlour, talking of old times, until morning came, and they could hear the King rattling at the posts above. Then Masterful Harry drew over him the bearskin once again, and stretched himself out on the hearth-rug.

To the King's inquiry, whether the Bear had lain still, the Princess replied that he had not even turned or stretched himself. So the King took the rope, and led the Bear back into the town, where, as soon as he could do so with safety, he took of his disguise, and ordered from a fashionable tailor a suit of clothes, such as would become a Prince. Then he went boldly to the King, and told him his wish to set out in search of the Princess.

"I am sorry for it, Sir," said the King; "for if you fail in twenty-four hours, you not only do not find my daughter, but you also lose your own life."

But Masterful Harry had made up his mind to do the deed, although, greatly to the King's surprise, he remained for twelve hours listening to the band playing, and dancing with some ladies of the Court, and he kept up the dancing until twenty-three hours had expired; and then, having only one hour left, he told the King he was ready to begin his search for the Princess.

The King asserted that the time was up; but Masterful Harry pulled out his watch, and showed him that there was still one hour, and so he insisted on the King lighting his lamp, and taking his bunch of keys, and following him to the pier which ran out into the sea.

The King was not best pleased at this, and pretended that such a journey would be useless, as the pier only led down into the sea, and kept on delaying in every possible manner.

"I have got just five minutes yet," said the Lad, as he pulled and pushed at the posts and pins until the house, in which the Princess lay hid, floated up to the top of the waves.

"Time's up!" shouted the King. "Headman, come hither, and take off this unlucky young gentleman's head."

"Not so," replied Masterful Harry; "there are three minutes good, yet. Give me the key, and let me go into the house."

But the King knew better than to do so; and, at last, he said he had not any key.

"Then, this will do it," said Masterful Harry; and he gave the door one kick, which burst it open, and the Princess came out, and threw herself into his arms, and told the King how Harry had been her deliverer, and was the only man she ever would marry.

And so she did; and that was the way the Beggar-woman's boy came to marry the daughter of the Great King of Mesopotamia.

THE FAIR MATILDA.

MANY years ago, a great Emperor had a lovely daughter. So beautiful, indeed, was the Fair Matilda, that it was impossible for any man to look upon her face and not to fall in love with her. Now, this was a great deal more inconvenient than you would suppose; for, though the charming Princess, when she came of age, would have been much pleased to have had one, or even two, young Princes, who visited her father's court, as admirers, it was not a comfortable thing to have every male creature—old or young, ugly or handsome, great or lowly, rich or poor—equally ardent in their attachment. Everything went wrong in the country, as well as the court, owing to the general inflammation occasioned by the Princess's beauty; so that, at last, when a whole regiment of her father's Horse Guards fell off their horses on to their knees, at a review in her presence, and declared their uncontrollable attachment, the Princess felt convinced that there must be some magic in her charms, and resolved on counteracting the spell.

So she applied to the great Sorcerer of the day, Trismejistus of the Hartz Mountains; who, however, was himself so struck by her excessive loveliness, that he would enter into no engagement to render her Imperial Highness an ugly woman, at any price, less than that she should belong to him afterwards.

The Fair Matilda chose what she thought was the least of the two evils; and reflecting, that when ugly, her chances of marriage would be materially lessened, to say the least of it, she consented to the terms of the Sorcerer Trismejistus, but not without annexing a condition, which, as she was as witty as she was pretty, she thought might enable her to obtain her wish without paying the penalty.

This condition was, that if Trismejistus did not find her sleeping the first three times he came to her, she should then be free from her part of the engagement.

Then the Fair Matilda took her needle and silk, and commenced embroidering a courtly robe, whilst her little dog Queddle sat by her side. Every time she fell asleep, and the Sorcerer came near her, the faithful Queddle barked, and the Princess was again awake and busy at her embroidery. This went on until the third time, when the Sorcerer found the Princess so sound asleep, that even the barking of the dog would not awake her, for she had become accustomed to the sound. The happy Sorcerer approached, and stooped down to take her hand, when the highly irritated Queddle jumped up and bit his nose. This set the Sorcerer roaring, which, with the still more vociferous barking of the greatly incensed Queddle, effectually aroused the Princess, and defeated the Sorcerer.

Trismejistus, seeing himself duped, and obliged to fulfil his promise, took care to perform the task as maliciously as possible. He passed his ugly claw over her lovely countenance, and gave it a squeeze, so that her beautiful arched brow was pressed down, and her imperial nose made broad and flat; her little mouth he extended, with a finger on each side, until it reached to her ears; and he breathed on her beautiful bright eyes, and dulled them, so that they appeared like lead and mist.

How soon all the love that had annoyed her so much was changed to aversion and disgust! The court, the camp, and the country, resumed their ordinary tranquillity. Not so, I am sorry to say, the Fair Matilda. She had not calculated on such a general desertion. She became disgusted and disappointed with life, and built for herself a great abbey, to which she retired, with her faithful dog Queddle, and of which she was the first abbess. You will see them both, carved in sandstone, if ever you go to Quedlingbourg, which is near Geslar, in the Hartz Mountains; and certainly, if the Fair Matilda was like the statue that represents her, it must be said that the Sorcerer Trismejistus honestly performed his half of the bargain.

THE INVISIBLE PRINCE.

THERE was a King and Queen, who had only one son, for whom they had a most passionate affection, though he was very ill-favoured, for he was as thick and gross as the most corpulent man, and as low as the smallest dwarf. But the ugliness of his countenance, and the deformity of his body, were nothing to the wickedness of his mind, for he was obstinate and self-willed, and sought to disturb the peace of everybody. The King was sensible, from his most early youth, of the vileness of his disposition; but the Queen doated on him, and contributed to the spoiling of him by her excessive fondness, which made him sensible of the power he had over her; and the only way to win her favour, was to praise her son for his wit and beauty. She determined to give him a name which should procure him both fear and respect; and after long consideration, she called him Furibon.

When he came to be of an age to have a tutor, the King made choice of a prince, who had an ancient title to the crown, which he would have maintained like a man of courage, had his affairs been in a better condition. But he had long laid aside all thoughts of this, and wholly applied himself to give his only son a noble and virtuous education.

Never had any youth a sweeter disposition, or more lively and penetrating wit, or a more docile and submissive temper. Whatever he spoke was with an agreeable manner and a peculiar grace; and his person was without the smallest blemish.

The King having made choice of this great lord to educate Furibon, he commanded him to be very obedient; but he was such an incorrigible dunce, that all the whipping in the world was to no purpose. His governor's son was called Leander, and was beloved by all that knew him.

He was almost always in Furibon's company, but that only rendered the deformed Prince more hideous. "You are very happy," said he, looking upon him with a malicious eye; "everybody are lavish in their praises of you; but not one of them has a good word for me."

"Sir," replied Leander, modestly, "the respect they have for you restrains them from being familiar."

"They do very well," said Furibon, "for otherwise I should knock their heads and the wall together, to teach them their duty."

One day, when a certain ambassador arrived from a remote country, Furibon, accompanied by Leander, stood in a gallery to see them pass by; but when the ambassadors beheld Leander, they approached him with profound reverence, testifying by signs their admiration. Afterwards, observing Furibon, they took him to be his dwarf; and taking him by the arm, they turned him about as it were to view him round, notwithstanding all he could do to prevent them.

Leander was vexed extremely; in vain he told them it was the King's son, for they understood him not; and the interpreter was gone to wait their appearance before the King. Leander, finding he could not make them understand him, redoubled his respects to Furibon; but the ambassadors, as well as those of their train, believing he was in jest, began to laugh at Furibon's angry impatience, and endeavoured to fillip him upon the nose, as they used to serve monkeys in their own country. Furibon at last drew his sword, which was not much longer than a lady's bodkin, and might have done some mischief, had not the King appeared to meet the ambassadors. He was greatly surprised to behold his son's behaviour, and begged their excuse, if any incivility had been offered them. They replied, the matter was of no consequence, for they perceived the little ugly dwarf was of a bad disposition. The King was greatly chagrined to find that his son's ill-favoured mien, and his extravagancies, had made his rank to be so widely mistaken.

When they were gone, Furibon took Leander by the hair, and plucked off two or three handfuls; nay, he would have throttled him if he could, and forbid him ever to appear again in his presence. Leander's father, offended with Furibon's behaviour toward his son, sent him to a castle of his in the country, where he always found himself employment; for he was a great lover of hunting, fishing, and walking: he understood painting, read much, and played upon several instruments; so that he looked upon himself happy in being freed from the fantastic humours of the Prince, nor was he tired in the least with the solitude of the place.

One day, as he was walking in the garden, finding the heat increase, he retired into a grove, whose lofty and thick-tufted shade afforded him a cool retreat. And here he began to play upon his flute for his diverson, when he felt something that wound itself several times about his leg, and grasped it very hard; he looked to see what it was, and was surprised to find it was a great adder; he took his handkerchief, and catching it by the head, was going to kill it. But the adder, winding the rest of his body about his arm, and looking stedfastly in his face, seemed to beg his pardon and compassion. At this instant, one of the gardeners happened to come to the place where Leander was, and spying the snake, cried out to his master, "Hold him fast, sir! it is but an hour ago since we ran after him to kill him; it is the most mischievous creature in the world; he spoils all our walks." Leander, casting his eyes a second time upon the snake, which was speckled with a thousand extraordinary colours, perceived the poor creature still looked upon him with an aspect that seemed to beg compassion, and never stirred in the least to defend itself. "Though thou hast such a mind to kill it," said he to the gardener, "yet, as it is come to me for refuge, I forbid thee to do it any harm, for I will keep it; and when it has cast its beautiful skin I will let it go." He then returned home, and carrying the snake with him, put it in a large chamber, the key of which he kept himself, and ordered bran, milk, and flowers, to be given to it for its delight and sustenance; so that never was snake so happy. Leander went sometimes to see it, and when it perceived him, made haste to meet him, showing him all the little marks of love and gratitude of which a poor snake was capable, which did not a little surprise him, though, however, he took no farther notice of it.

In the meantime, all the court ladies were extremely troubled at his absence, and he was the subject of all their discourse. "Alas!" cried they, "there is no pleasure at court since Leander is gone, of whose absence the wicked Furibon is the cause! Ought he to injure him, because he is more amiable and better beloved than him? Would he have him disfigure his shape and countenance to please him? Would he have him dislocate his bones, slit his mouth up to his ears, lessen his eyes, and shorten his nose? How ridiculous and unjust is such a desire! But he will never be pleased as long as he lives, for he will never find one who is not handsomer than himself."

But let a prince be never so ill-natured, never so wicked, he will have his flatterers, and many times the worst of princes have more than others. Thus, Furibon also had his parasites, for his power over the Queen made him feared; so that they told him what the ladies said, which enraged him to a degree of fury; and in his passion he flew to the Queen's chamber, and vowed he would kill himself before her face, if she did not find means to destroy Leander. The Queen, who also hated Leander, because he was handsomer than the monkey her son, replied, that she had long looked upon him as a traitor, and, therefore, would willingly consent to his death. To which purpose she advised him to go a-hunting with some of his confidants, and contrive it so that Leander should make one, and that then he might teach him to remember how he gained the love of everybody.

Accordingly, Furibon went a-hunting; and Leander, when he heard the horns and the hounds, mounted his horse, and rode to see who it was. But he was surprised to meet the Prince so unexpectedly; immediately he alighted, and saluted him with profound respect; and Furibon received him more graciously than he expected, and bid him follow him. All of a sudden, he turned his eyes, and rode another way, making a sign to his ruffians to take the first opportunity; but before he had got quite out of sight, a lion of a prodigious size, coming out of his den, leaped upon Furibon, and pulled him from his horse. All his followers betook themselves to flight, and only Leander remained to combat this furious animal. He attacked him sword in hand, at the hazard of being devoured, and by his valour and agility saved the life of his most cruel enemy, who was fallen in a swoon for fear, so that Leander was forced to lend him assistance of another kind; and when he came to himself, he presented him his horse to remount. Now, any other but such an ungrateful wretch would have highly and cordially acknowledged such signal obligations, and made suitable returns; but Furibon did no such thing; for he did not even look upon him, nor did he make use of his horse to any other purpose than to ride in quest of the ruffians, to whom he repeated his orders to kill him. They accordingly surrounded Leander, and, but for his courage, he had been certainly murdered. He got with his back to a tree, to prevent being attacked behind, and behaved with so much bravery, that he laid them all dead at his feet. Furibon, believing him by this time slain, made haste to satiate his eyes with the sight; but he came to a spectacle that he least expected, for all his ruffians were breathing their last. When Leander saw him, he advanced to meet him, and with a submissive reverence, "Sir," said he, "if it was by your order that these assassins came to kill me, I am sorry I made any defence."

"You are an insolent villain," replied Furibon, in a passion; "and if ever you come into my presence again, you shall surely die."

Leander made him no reply, but retired, sad and pensive, to his own home, where he spent the night in pondering what it was best for him to do; for there was no likelihood he should be able to defend himself against the King's son, and therefore he at length concluded to see the world. Being ready to depart, he recollected his snake, and calling for some milk and fruits, carried it to the poor creature, designing to take his leave and dismiss it; but, on opening the door, he perceived an extraordinary lustre in one corner of the room; and casting his eye on the place, he was surprised to see a lady, whose noble and majestic air made him immediately conclude she was a Princess of royal birth. Her habit was of purple satin, embroidered with pearls and diamonds; and advancing towards him, with a gracious smile, "Young Prince," said she, "you are no longer to seek here for the snake which you brought hither; it is not here, but you find me in its place, to requite your generosity; but to speak more intelligibly, know that I am the Fairy Gentilla, famous for the feats of mirth and dexterity which I can perform. We live a hundred years in flourishing youth, without diseases, without trouble or pain; and this term being expired, we become snakes for eight days, and this is the only time which may prove fatal to us, for then it is not in our power to prevent any misfortune that may befall us; and if we happen to be killed, we never revive again. But these eight days being expired, we resume our usual form, and recover our beauty, our power, and our riches. Now you know how much I am obliged to your goodness, and it is but just that I should repay my debt of gratitude; think how I can serve you, and depend upon me."

The young Prince, who had never conversed with a Fairy till now, was so surprised, that he was a long time before he could speak. But at length, making her a profound reverence, "Madam," said he, "since I have had the honour to serve you, I know not any other happiness that I can wish for."

"I should be sorry," replied she, "not to be of service to you in something; consider, it is in my power to make you a great king, prolong your life, make you more amiable, give you mines of diamonds, and houses full of gold; I can make you an excellent orator, poet, musician, and painter; I can make you beloved by the ladies, and increase your wit; I can make you a spirit of the air, the water, or the earth."

Here Leander interrupted her. "Permit me, Madam," said he, "to ask you what benefit it would be to me to be invisible, or a Spirit?"

"A thousand useful and delightful things might be done by it," replied the Fairy; "you would be invisible when you pleased, and might in an instant traverse the whole earth; you would be able to fly without wings, and descend into the abysses of the earth without dying, and walk at the bottom of the sea without being drowned; nor doors, nor windows, though fast shut and locked, could hinder you from entering any of the most secret retirements; and whenever you had a mind, you might resume your natural form."

"Oh, Madam!" cried Leander, "then let me be a Spirit; I am going to travel, and prefer it above all those other advantages you so generously offered me."

Gentilla thereupon stroking his visage three times, "Be a Spirit!" said she; and then embracing him, she gave him a little red cap, with a plume of feathers. "When you put on this cap, you shall be invisible; and when you take it off, you shall again become visible."

Leander, overjoyed, put his little red cap upon his head, and wished himself in the forest, that he might gather some wild roses which he had observed there; his body immediately became as light as thought; he flew through the window like a bird; but he was not without fear, when he was soaring in the air and flying over any river, lest he should fall into it, and the power of the Fairy not be able to save him. But he arrived in safety at the rose bushes, plucked three roses, and returned immediately to the chamber where the Fairy still was, and presented his roses to her, overjoyed that his first experiment had succeeded so well. But the Fairy bid him keep the roses, for that one of them would supply him with money whenever he wanted it; that if he put the other in his mistress's bosom, he would know whether she was faithful or not; and the third would prevent his being sick. Then, without staying to receive his thanks, she wished him successful in his travels, and disappeared.

Leander was infinitely pleased with the noble gifts he had obtained. "Could I have imagined," said he, "that such great and unusual advantages as these would have been my reward for rescuing a poor snake out of my gardener's hand? How happy I shall be! what delightful hours I shall have! how many things I shall know! I may be invisible whenever I please, and may inform myself of the most secret affairs." He thought he might now be agreeably revenged upon Furibon. So, having settled his affairs, he mounted the finest horse in the stable, called Gris-de-line, and was attended by some of his servants in livery, that his return to court might sooner be made known. Now, you must know that Furibon, who was a very great liar, had given out, that had it not been for his courage, Leander would have murdered him when they were a-hunting; and as he had killed all his followers, he demanded justice. The King, being importuned by the Queen, gave orders that he should be apprehended. But when he came, he showed such courage and resolution, that Furibon was too timid to seize him himself; and therefore, he ran to the Queen's chamber, and told her Leander was come, and prayed her to order him to be seized. The Queen, who was extremely diligent in everything that her son desired, went immediately to the King; and Furibon, being impatient to know what would be resolved, followed her without saying a word, but stopped at the door, and laid his ear to the key-hole, putting his hair aside, that he might the better hear what was said. At the same time, Leander entered the court-hall of the palace, with his red cap upon his head, so that he was not to be seen; and perceiving Furibon listening at the door of the King's chamber, he took a nail and a hammer, and nailed his ear to the door.

Furibon, in sharp pain, and all bloody, fell a-roaring like a madman. The Queen, hearing her son's voice, ran and opened the door, and pulling it hastily, tore her son's ear from his head, so that he bled like a pig. The Queen, half out of her wits, set him in her lap, and took up his ear, kissed it, and clapped it on again upon the place; but the invisible Leander, seizing upon a handful of twigs, with which they corrected the King's little dogs, gave the Queen several lashes upon the hands, and her son as many over the nose; upon which the Queen cried out, "Murder! murder!"— and upon her crying out, the King looked about, and the people came running in; but nothing was to be seen. Some cried, that the Queen was mad, and that her madness proceeded from her grief to see her son had lost one ear; and the King was as ready as any to believe it; so that when she came near him, he avoided her, which made a very ridiculous scene. Leander gave Furibon some more jerks; and then leaving the chamber, went into the garden, and there assuming his own shape, he boldly fell a-plucking the Queen's cherries, apricots, and strawberries, and cropped her flowers by handfuls, though he knew the Queen set such a high value on them, that it was as much as a man's life was worth to touch one. The gardeners, all amazed, came and told their majesties, that Prince Leander was making havoc of all the fruits and flowers in the Queen's garden.

"What insolence!" cried the Queen. Then turning to Furibon, "My pretty child," said she, "my dearest love, forget the pain of thy ear but for a moment, and fetch that vile wretch hither; take our guards, both horse and foot, seize him, and punish him as he deserves."

Furibon, encouraged by his mother, and attended by a great number of armed soldiers, entered the garden, and saw Leander under a tree, who threw a stone at him, which wounded his arm; and the rest of his followers he pelted with oranges. But when they came running with a full career towards him, thinking to have seized him, he was not to be seen; he had slipped behind Furibon, who was but in a bad condition already; but Leander played him one trick more, by hampering his legs in such a manner with a cord, that he fell upon his nose upon the gravel, and bruised his face so that they were forced to take him up, carry him away, and put him to bed.

Leander, satisfied with this revenge, returned to his servants, who waited for him, and giving them money, sent them back to his castle, that none might know the secret of his red cap and roses.

As yet, he had not determined whither to go; however, he mounted his fine horse Gris-de-line, and laying the reins upon his neck, let him take his own road; and thus he rode through woods and forests,

over hills and dales, resting sometimes for eating and sleeping's sake, without meeting anything remarkable; but at length he arrived in a forest, where he stopped to shelter himself from the extremity of the heat.

He had not been above a minute there before he heard a lamentable noise of sighing and sobbing; and looking about him, he beheld a man, that ran, made several stops, then ran again, sometimes crying, sometimes silent, then tearing his hair, then thumping his breast, as if he would have beaten his breath out of his body; so that he took him for some unfortunate madman. He seemed to be both handsome and young; his garments had been magnificent, but he had torn them all to tatters. The Prince, moved by compassion, made towards him, and mildly accosting him, "Sir," said he, "your condition appears so bad and deplorable, that I cannot forbear to ask the cause of your sorrow, assuring you of every assistance that lies in my power."

"Oh, Sir," answered the young man, "nothing can remedy my miseries; this day my dear mistress is to be sacrificed to an old jealous barbarian, who has a great estate, but who will make her the most miserable person in the world."

"Does she love you, then?" said Leander.

"I flatter myself so," answered the young man.

"Where is she?" continued Leander.

"In a castle at the end of this forest," answered the lover.

"Very well," said Leander; "stay you here till I come again, and in a little while I will bring you good news."

He then put on his little red cap, and wished himself in the castle. He was hardly got thither, before he heard the pleasing sound of soft music; but when he arrived, the whole castle resounded with all sorts of music. He entered into a great room, where the friends and kindred of the old man and the young lady were assembled. Nothing could be more amiable than she was; but the paleness of her complexion, the melancholy that appeared in her countenance, and the tears that now and then dropped as it were by stealth from her eyes, discovered the trouble of her mind.

Leander now became invisible, and placed himself in a corner of the room, that he might discover who the persons were; and he soon perceived the father and mother of the maid, by their private chiding her for not appearing with the sprightliness of a bride; which, after they had done, they returned to their seats. Leander, placing himself behind the mother's chair, and laying his lips to her ear, "Assure yourself," said he, "that if you compel your daughter to give her consent to marry that old dotard, before eight days are expired, you shall certainly be punished with death."

The woman, frightened to hear such a terrible sentence pronounced upon her, and yet not know from whence it came, gave a loud shriek, and fell upon the floor. Her husband asked her what she ailed. She cried, she was a dead woman if the marriage of her daughter went forward; and therefore, that she would not yield to it for all the world. Her husband laughed at her, and called her a fool. But the invisible Leander, accosting the man, "You old incredulous fool," said he, "believe your wife, or it will be the worse for you; break off this match, and bestow her upon the person she loves." These words produced a wonderful effect; for the old man was immediately dismissed, with an excuse, that all matches were made in heaven, and that they had received an immediate order from thence to break off this. He would fain have been at his whys and wherefores, and what the devil is the matter? and threatened them with the spiritual court; but Leander trod so hard upon his gouty toes, and rung such a larum in his ears, that not being able any longer to hear himself speak, away he limped, murmuring like a hackney coachman that would have more than his hire.

Now the distracted lover was sought for, when he the least expected it, and was brought to the castle, where Leander with impatience waited for his coming. The lover and his mistress were ready to die for joy, and the entertainment prepared for the nuptials of the old man, served for those of these happy lovers. Leander, assuming his own shape, appeared at the hall door, as a stranger drawn thither by the report of this extraordinary wedding.

As soon as the married lover perceived him, he ran and fell at his feet, thanking him in terms inspired by the warmest sense of gratitude. He stayed two days in the castle, and if he would have ruined them he might, for they offered him all that they were worth, and it was with regret that he quitted such generous and benevolent company.

From hence he travelled on, and came to a great city, where, upon his arrival, he understood there was a great and solemn procession, in order to the shutting up a young virgin, against her will, among the vestal nuns. The Prince was touched with compassion; and thinking the best use he could make of his cap was to redress public wrongs and relieve the oppressed, he flew to the temple, where he saw the young virgin crowned with flowers, clad in white, and with her dishevelled hair flowing about her shoulders. Two of her brothers led her by each hand, and her mother followed her with a great crowd of men and women. Leander being invisible, cried out, "Stop, stop, wicked brethren! stop, rash and inconsiderate mother! heaven forbids this unjust ceremony; if you proceed any farther, you shall be squeezed to death like so many frogs!" They looked about, but could not conceive from whence these terrible menaces came. The brothers said it was only their sister's sweetheart, who had hid himself in some hole, to counterfeit a voice from heaven. At which Leander, in wrath, took a long cudgel, and they had no reason to say the blows were not well laid on. The multitude fled, the vestals ran away, and Leander was left alone with the victim; immediately he pulled off his red cap, and asked the virgin wherein he might serve her. She answered him, with a confidence rarely to be expected from a virgin of her age, that there was a certain gentleman whom she would be glad to marry, but that he wanted an estate. Leander then shook his rose so

232

long, that he supplied them with ten millions; after which, they married, and lived happily together.

But his last adventure was the most agreeable: for entering into a wide forest, he heard the lamentable cries of a young person, as if some violence was offered to her. Looking about him every way, at length he spied four men, well armed, that were carrying away by force a young lady, thirteen or fourteen years of age; upon which, making up to them as fast as he could, "What harm has that virgin done," said he, "that you do her this violence?"

"Ha, ha! my little master," cried he who seemed to be the ringleader of the rest; "who made you an examiner?"

"I command ye," said Leander, "to let her alone, and go about your business."

"Oh, yes, to be sure!" said they, laughing; whereupon, the Prince alighted, put on his red cap, not thinking it otherwise prudent to attack four, who seemed strong enough to fight a dozen. They must have had good eyes, who could have seen him when his cap was on. One of them stayed to take care of the young lady, while the three others went after Gris-de-line, who gave them a good deal of exercise. The robbers thinking he was fled, "It is not worth while to pursue him," said they; "let us only catch his horse."

The young lady continued her cries and complaints: "Oh, my dear Princess," said she, "how happy was I in your palace! How is it possible for me to live without your company! Did you but know my sad misfortune, you would send your Amazons to rescue poor Abricotina."

Leander having listened to what she said, without delay seized the ruffian that held her, and bound him fast to a tree before he had time or strength to defend himself. At length, upon his hideous outcries and continual bawling, one of his comrades returned, puffing and blowing; and seeing him in that condition, asked him how he came bound. "Old Nick did it, I think," cried the fellow; "for whosoever I felt, I am sure I saw nobody."

"That is a lame excuse," said the other; "but I always took thee for a cowardly rascal, and now I find it true, to let a girl bind thee to a tree;" and with that he laid him over the shoulders with a good stirrup-leather, till he made him roar again.

Leander having diverted himself awhile with his cries, then went to the second, and taking him by both arms, bound him in the same manner to another tree just opposite, so that he stood facing his comrade, who could not forbear retorting upon him, "Who is the brave, the stout, the valiant Hector now?—art not thou a cowardly whelp, to suffer thyself to be tied to a tree by nobody at all?" The fellow said not a word, but hung down his head, ashamed and astonished to find himself bound by an invisible power.

In the meantime, Abricotina made the best of her good fortune, and betook herself to her heels, not knowing which way she went. But Leander missing her, called out to his Gris-de-line three times; who finding a force upon him to obey his master's call, by two kicks with his hoof rid himself of the two ruffians who had pursued him; one of them had his head

LEANDER APPEARS TO THE PRINCESS, IN THE CHARACTER OF APOLLO.

broke, and the other three of his ribs. And now Leander only wanted to overtake Abricotina; for he had thought her so handsome, that he wished to see her again, and presently overtook her. But he found her so weary, that she was forced to lean against a tree, not being able to support herself. When she saw Gris-de-line coming towards her, "How lucky am I!" cried she; "this pretty little horse will carry me to the Palace of Pleasure. Leander heard her, though she saw not him; he rode up to her, Gris-de-line

stopped, and Abricotina mounted him; Leander clasped her in his arms, and placed her gently before him. Oh! how great was Abricotina's fear, to feel herself fast embraced, and yet see nobody! She durst not stir, and shut her eyes for fear of seeing a spirit.

But Leander taking off his little cap, "How comes it, fair Abricotina," said he, "that you are afraid of me, who delivered you out of the hands of the ruffians?" With that she opened her eyes, and knowing him again, "Oh! sir," said she, "I am infinitely obliged to you; but I was afraid I had been with an invisible."

"I am not invisible," replied Leander; "but the danger you were in has disturbed you, and cast a mist before your eyes."

Abricotina would not seem to doubt him, though she were otherwise extremely witty; and after they had prattled for some time of indifferent things, Leander requested her to tell him her age, her country, and by what accident she fell into the hands of the ruffians.

"Sir," said she, "you have too highly obliged me, to deny you the satisfaction you desire; but pray let not your listening to my story slacken your pace. Know then, Sir, there was a certain Fairy, who for knowledge had not her equal; yet she fell so deeply in love with a certain Prince, that though she was the first Fairy that ever had the weakness to be over-ruled by that passion, she married him in despite of all the other Fairies, who continually represented to her the wrong she did her whole order; so that they excluded her out of their society, and all she could do was to build herself a great palace upon the borders of their kingdom. But the Prince she had espoused grew weary of her, and was quite angry, because he could do nothing but she presently knew it.

"The Prince, therefore, finding himself so tormented by the excess of her kindness, stole away one morning, and taking post horses, rode a long way, quite out of knowledge, on purpose to hide himself in a dark cave at the foot of a desert mountain, where she might not be able to find him out. But he was mistaken in his project; for she followed him, found him out, and told him she was with child, and therefore conjured him to return to his palace, where he should never want money, horses, hounds, nor arms; and that he should want no sports nor pastimes befitting a great Prince. But all this did not prevail upon him; for he was naturally obstinate, and one that would not be curbed of his liberty. He said a hundred harsh and uncivil things to her; called her Old Fairy and She-devil. 'Well,' said she, 'it is happy for thee that I have more wit than thou hast folly; for now, if I pleased, I could turn thee into a cat, to be always mewing on the tops of the houses; or into a nasty toad, croaking in the mud; or into the ugliest of owls —nay, I could transform thee into a flea, to torment the back of some puppy all thy life. But the greatest mischief I can do thee, is to leave thee to thy extravagancies; continue in thy den, in thy dark hole, among bats and owls; thou wilt find in time the difference between such company and the society of a Fairy, who can make herself as charming as she pleases.'

"Saying these words, she immediately got into her flying coach, and disappeared with the swiftness of a bird. And when she was returned to her palace, she turned off all her guards and officers, and took women of the race of the Amazons; and these she sent to keep strict guard upon all the avenues to her island, with strict orders not to let any man set his foot in it. This island she called the Island of Calm Delights, and would often say, there could be no real pleasure in keeping company with men; she educated her

234

daughter in these sentiments, than whom there is not a more lovely person in the world, and this is the Princess whom I serve; and as all pleasure accompanies her, we never grow old in her palace; what you see me now, I have been these two hundred years. When my mistress was grown up, her mother, the Fairy, left her the island, and gave her most excellent lessons to make her life happy. After this, the mother returned to the Fairy-land, and the Princess of Calm Delights governs her little territories with admirable good conduct.

"I do not remember, since I came into the world, that I ever saw any other men beside yourself and the ruffians that would have carried me away. Those people told me, that they were sent by a certain deformed, ill-shaped person, called Furibon, who pretends to love my mistress, though he has only seen her picture. Those fellows hovered about the island for several days, but never durst venture in, our Amazons being too vigilant to let any man enter into it. But, as I have the care of the Princess's birds, it was my misfortune to let her beloved parrot fly away; and fearing her anger, I imprudently ventured out of the island in search of it; and then it was that the ruffians seized me, and had certainly carried me away, but for your generous and timely rescue."

"Well, then," said Leander, "if you think this service merits any return, may I hope, fair Abricotina, to get admission into the Island of Calm Delights, and have a sight of this wonderful Princess?"

"Oh, sir," said she, "it is as much as both our lives are worth to make any such attempt. You ought not to be disturbed for want of happiness you never knew; you never was in this palace, and therefore you need only imagine there is no such thing in being."

"It is not so easy as you think," replied the Prince, "to forget things that are pleasing to the memory; nor can I agree to the sentiments of your Princess, that there is no way to enjoy tranquillity, but by excluding society with our sex."

"Sir," answered Abricotina, "it is not for me to decide this point; but I must acknowledge that if all men were like you, I would advise the Princess to make other laws; though, as I have seen no more than five, and have found four of them so wicked, I conclude that the number of the bad is much superior to that of the virtuous, and therefore it is the best way to banish them all."

While they were thus conversing, they came to the bank of a large river; Abricotina alighting with a nimble jump from the horse. "Farewell, Sir," said she to the Prince, making a profound reverence, "I wish you so much happiness, that all the world may be an island of pleasure to you wherever you come; make haste from hence, for fear of being discovered by our Amazons."

"And I," said Leander, "wish you a sensible heart, that I may have now and then a small share in your remembrance."

So saying, he galloped away, and soon entered into the thickest part of a wood, near a river; where he unbridled and unsaddled Gris-de-line, that he might feed at liberty; and putting on his little cap, wished himself in the Island of Calm Delights, and his wish was immediately accomplished; for, at the same instant, he found himself in the place of the world the most beautiful, and which had the least of what was common in it.

The palace was of pure gold, and stood upon pillars of crystal and precious stones, which represented the zodiac, and all the wonders of nature, all the arts and sciences; the sea, with all the variety of fish therein contained; the earth, with all the various creatures which it produces; the chases of Diana and her nymphs; the noble exercises of the Amazons; the amusements of a country life; flocks of sheep, with their shepherds and dogs; the toils of agriculture, harvests, gardening, flowers, bees. And among all this variety of representations, there was neither man nor boy to be seen, not so much as a little winged Cupid; so highly had the Princess been incensed against her inconstant husband, as not to show the least favour to his fickle sex.

"Abricotina did not deceive me," said Leander to himself; "they have banished from hence the very idea of men; now let us see what they have lost by it. With that he entered into the palace, and at every step he took, he met with objects so wonderful, that when he had once fixed his eyes upon them, he had much ado to take them off again. Gold and diamonds, transcended not so much by their own lustre, as their exquisite disposition. In every room attended youth and beauty, with looks of innocence and love. He viewed a vast number of these apartments, some full of china, no less fine than curious for the sportive fancy of their colouring; others of porcelain, so very fine, that the walls, which were built of those materials, were quite transparent. Coral, jasper, agates, and cornelians, beautified the rooms of state; and the Princess's presence-chamber was one entire mirror, with the panes so artificially closed together, that it was impossible to be discerned, and everywhere exposed the charming object.

The throne was one single pearl, hollowed like a shell, whereon she sat environed by her maids of honour, glittering with rubies and diamonds; but all this was nothing in comparison of the Princess's incomparable beauty. Her air had all the innocence and sweetness of the most youthful, joined with the superior dignity of riper years. Nothing could equal the vivacity of her eyes; it was impossible to find any defect in her; she smiled in the most gracious manner upon her maids of honour, who were that day dressed like nymphs, for her diversion.

Now, as she did not see Abricotina among the rest, she asked where she was. The nymphs replied, that they had sought for her, but in vain. Upon that, Leander being very desirous to speak, assumed the tone of a Parrot, for there were many in the room; and addressing himself invisibly to the Princess, "Most charming Princess," said he, "Abricotina will return immediately. She was in great danger of being carried away from this palace, but for a young Prince, who rescued her."

The Princess was surprised at the Parrot, his answer was so extremely pertinent. "You are very pert, little Parrot," said the Princess; "and Abricotina, when she comes, shall chastise you for it."

"I shall not be chastised," answered Leander, still counterfeiting the Parrot's voice; "moreover, she will let you know the great desire that stranger had to be admitted into this palace, that he might convince you of the falsehood of those ideas which you have conceived against his sex."

"In truth, pretty Parrot," cried the Princess, "it is a pity you are not every day so diverting; I should love you dearly."

"Ah! if prattling will please you, Madam," replied Leander, "I will prate from morning till night."

"But," continued the Princess, "how shall I be sure my Parrot is not a Sorcerer?"

"He is more in love than any Sorcerer can be," replied the Prince.

At this moment, Abricotina entered the room, and falling at her lovely mistress's feet, gave her a full account of what had befallen her, and described the Prince in the most lively and advantageous colours.

"I should have hated all men," added she, "had I not seen him! Oh, Madam, how charming he is! His air and all his behaviour has something in it so noble and divine; and though whatever he spoke was infinitely pleasing, yet I think I did well in not bringing him hither."

To this the Princess said nothing, but she asked Abricotina a hundred other questions concerning the Prince; whether she knew his name, his country, his birth, from whence he came, and whither he was going; and after this she fell into a profound thoughtfulness.

Leander observed everything, and continued to prattle as he had begun. "Abricotina is ungrateful, Madam," said he; "that poor stranger will die for grief, if he sees you not."

"Well, Parrot, let him die," answered the Princess with a sigh; "and since thou undertakest to reason like a person of wit, and not like a little bird, I forbid thee ever to talk to me any more of this unknown person."

Leander was overjoyed to find that Abricotina's and the Parrot's discourse had made such an impression on the Princess. He looked upon her with pleasure and delight. "Can it be," said he to himself, "that the masterpiece of nature, that the wonder of our age, should be confined eternally in an island, and no mortal dare to approach her? But," continued he, "wherefore am I concerned that all others are banished hence, since I have the happiness to be with her, to see her, to hear, and to admire her; nay, more, to love her above all the women in the universe?"

It was late, and the Princess retired into a large room of marble and porphyry, where several bubbling fountains refreshed the air with an agreeable coolness. As soon as she was entered, the music began, a sumptuous supper was served up, and the birds from several aviaries on each side of the room, of whom Abricotina had the chief care, opened their little throats in the most agreeable manner.

Leander had travelled a journey long enough to get him a good stomach, which made him draw near the table, where the very smell of such viands was agreeable and refreshing. The Princess had a curious tabby cat, for which she had a great kindness. This cat one of the maids of honour held in her arms, saying, "Madam, Bluet is hungry." With that a chair was presently brought for the cat, for he was a cat of quality, and had a necklace of pearl about his neck. He was served on a gold plate, with a laced napkin before him, and the plate being supplied with meat, Bluet sat with the solemn importance of an alderman. "Ho, ho!" cried Leander to himself, "an idle tabby malkin, that perhaps never caught a mouse in its life, and, I dare say, not descended from a better family than myself, has the honour to sit at table with my mistress! I would fain know whether he loves her so well as I do; and whether it be reasonable that I should only swallow the steam, while he has choice bits to feast upon." Saying this, he placed himself in the chair, with the cat upon his knee, for nobody saw him, because he had his little red cap on; and finding Bluet's gold plate so well supplied as it was, with partridge, quails, and pheasants, he made bold with them; so that whatever was set before Miss Puss disappeared in a trice. The whole court said, no cat ever eat with a better appetite. There were excellent ragouts, and the Prince made use of the cat's paw to taste them; but he sometimes pulled his paw too roughly, and Bluet, not understanding raillery, began to mew and be quite out of patience. The Princess observing this, "Bring that fricasse and that tart to poor Bluet," said she; "see how he cries to have them." Leander laughed to himself at the pleasantness of this adventure; but he was very dry, not being accustomed to make such large meals without drinking. By the help of the cat's paw he got a melon, with which he somewhat quenched his thirst; and when supper was quite over, he went to the beaufet, and took two bottles of delicious wine.

The Princess now retired into her chamber, ordering Abricotina to follow her, and make fast the door; but they could not keep out Leander, who was there as soon as they. However, the Princess, believing herself alone with her confidant, "Abricotina," said she, "tell me truly, did not you exaggerate in your description of the unknown Prince, for methinks it is impossible he should be so amiable?"

"Madam," replied the damsel, "if I failed in anything, it was in coming short of what was due to him."

The Princess sighed, and was silent for a time; then, resuming her speech, "I am glad," said she, "thou didst not bring him with thee."

"But, Madam," answered Abricotina, who was a cunning sly girl, and already penetrated her mistress's thoughts, "suppose he had come to admire the wonders of these beautiful mansions, what harm could he have done us? Will you live eternally unknown in a corner of the world, concealed from the rest of human kind? To what purpose serves all your grandeur, pomp, and magnificence, if nobody sees it?"

"Hold thy peace, prattler," replied the Princess, "and do not now disturb that happy repose which I have enjoyed these six hundred years. Thinkest thou that if I had led an unquiet and turbulent life, I could have lived so great a number of years? Only innocent and calm delights are able to produce such rare effects. Have we not read in the most famous histories the strange revolutions of great kingdoms; the unforeseen turns of inconstant fortune; the unheard-of disorders occasioned by love; the pains of absence and jealousy? And what is the cause of all this, but our converse with men? I am, thanks to my mother's care and good instructions, free from these evils; I am a stranger to the griefs of the soul, the vanity of desires, and the pangs of envy, love, and hatred. Oh! let us live, let us still live, and always live, in the same indifference!"

Abricotina durst make no reply; and the Princess, having waited her answer for some time, asked her whether she had anything to say. Abricotina then said, she thought it was to very little purpose, her having sent her picture to the courts of several Princes, where it only served to make those who saw it miserable; that every one would be desirous to have her, and being unable to satisfy their desire, it would make them desperate.

"Yet, for all that," said the Princess, "I could wish my picture were in the hands of this same stranger."

"Oh, Madam!" answered Abricotina, "is not his desire to see you violent enough already? would you augment it?"

"Yes," cried the Princess; "a certain impulse of vanity, which I was never sensible of till now, has bred this foolish desire in me."

Leander heard all this discourse, and lost not a tittle of what she said; and as there were some of her expressions that gave him hopes, so there were others which absolutely destroyed them.

But it now growing late, the Princess retired to her chamber to go to bed. Leander had a great mind to have followed her to her toilet; but, though he might, yet the respect he had for her would not let him. He thought it became him not to take any more liberty than what she might have lawfully granted him; and his passion was so delicate and ingenuous, that he was nice in the most minute circumstances.

He therefore entered into a cabinet adjoining to the Princess's chamber, where he might have the pleasure at least to hear her. The Princess presently asked Abricotina whether she had seen anything extraordinary during her short travels. "Madam," said she, "I passed through one forest, where I saw certain creatures that resembled little children; they skip and dance upon the trees like squirrels; they are very ugly, but have wonderful agility and address."

"I wish I had one of them," said the Princess; "but if they are so nimble, as you say they are, it is impossible to catch one."

Leander, who had passed through the same forest, knew what Abricotina meant; and presently, wishing himself in the place, he caught a dozen of little monkeys, some bigger, some less, and all of different colours, and with much ado put them into a large sack; then wishing himself at Paris, where he had heard that a man might have anything for money, he went and bought a little gold chariot, which he taught six green monkeys to draw, harnessed with fine traces of flame-coloured morocco leather, gilt. He went to another place, where he met with two monkeys of merit, the most pleasant of which was called Briscambril, the other Pierceforest, both very spruce and well educated. He dressed Briscambril like a king, and placed him in the coach; Pierceforest he made the coachman; the others were dressed like pages; all which he put into his sack, coach and all; and the Princess not being gone to bed, she heard a rumbling of a little coach in her long gallery; at the same time her nymphs came to tell her that the King of the Dwarfs was arrived, and the chariot immediately entered her chamber, with all the monkey train. The country monkeys began to show a thousand tricks, which far surpassed those of Briscambril and Pierceforest. To say the truth, Leander conducted the whole machine. He drew the chariot, where Briscambril sat arrayed like a king, and making him hold a box of diamonds in his hand, he presented it with a becoming grace to the Princess.

The Princess's surprise may be easily imagined. Moreover, Briscambril made a sign for Pierceforest to come and dance with him. The most celebrated dancers were not to be compared with them in activity. But the Princess, troubled that she could not divine from whence this curious present came, dismissed the dancers sooner than otherwise she would have done, though she was extremely pleased with them.

Leander, satisfied with having seen the delight the Princess had taken in beholding the monkeys, thought of nothing now but to get a little repose, which he greatly wanted. But fearing lest he should enter the apartment of some of the Princess's maids of honour, he stayed some time in the great gallery; afterwards, going down a pair of stairs, and finding a door open, he entered into an apartment the most beautiful and most delightful that ever was seen. There was in it a bed of cloth of gold, enriched with pearls, intermixed with rubies and emeralds; for, by this time, there appeared daylight sufficient for him to view and admire the magnificence of this sumptuous furniture. Having made fast the door, he composed himself to sleep.

He got up very early, and looking about on every side, he spied a painter's pallet, with colours ready prepared, and pencils; remembering what the Princess had said to Abricotina, touching her own portrait, he immediately (for he could paint as well as the most excellent masters) seated himself before a mirror, and drew his own picture first, and then in an oval that of the Princess; for he had all her features so strong in his imagination, that he had no occasion for her sitting. And as his desire to please her had set him to work, never did portrait bear a stronger resemblance. He had painted himself upon one knee, holding the Princess's picture in one hand, and in the other a label with this inscription:—

"She is better in my heart."

When the Princess went into her cabinet, she was amazed to see the portrait of a man; and she fixed her eyes upon it with so much the more surprise, because she also saw her own with it, and because the words which were written upon the label afforded her an ample subject to exercise her curiosity and deepest thoughts. She was alone at that time, and could only form conjectures on an accident so extraordinary. She persuaded herself that it was Abricotina's gallantry; and all that she desired to know more, was, whether the portrait were only an effect of her fancy, or from a real person. She rose in haste, and called Abricotina, while the invisible Leander, with his little red cap, slipped into the cabinet, impatient to know what passed.

The Princess bid Abricotina look upon the picture, and tell her what she thought of it. After she had viewed it, "I protest," cried she, "'tis the picture of that generous stranger, to whom I am obliged for my life. Yes, yes, I am sure it is he; his very features, shape, hair, and air."

"Thou pretendest surprise," said the Princess; "but I know it was thou thyself that put it there."

"Who? I, Madam!" replied Abricotina; "I vow and protest, Madam, I never saw the picture before in my life. Should I be so bold to conceal from your knowledge a thing that so nearly concerns you? And by what miracle could I come by it? I never could paint; nor did any man ever enter this place; yet, here he is, painted with you."

"Some spirit, then, must have brought it hither," cried the Princess.

"How I tremble for fear, Madam!" said Abricotina; "was it not rather some lover? And therefore, if you will take my advice, let us burn it immediately."

"'Twere a pity to burn it," cried the Princess, sighing; "a finer piece, methinks, cannot adorn my cabinet." And saying these words, she cast her eyes upon it.

But Abricotina continued obstinate in her opinion that it ought to be burnt, as a thing that could not come there but by the power of magic.

"And these words—

'She is better in my heart.'"

said the Princess; "must we burn them too?"

"No favour must be shown to anything," said Abricotina, "not even to your own portrait."

Abricotina ran away immediately for some fire, while the Princess went to look out at the window, no longer able to behold a picture that made such a deep impression in her heart. But Leander, being unwilling to let his performance be burnt, took this opportunity to convey it away without being perceived. And he was hardly got out of the cabinet, when the Princess turned about, to look once more upon that enchanting picture which so infinitely pleased her. But how strangely was she surprised to find it gone! She sought for it all the room over; and Abricotina returning, she asked her whether she knew what was become of it. But she was no less surprised than her mistress; so that this last adventure put them both into the most terrible fright.

As soon as Leander had hid the picture, he returned, for he took great delight in seeing and hearing his incomparable mistress. He ate every day at her table with the tabby cat, who fared never the worse for that. But Leander's satisfaction was far from being complete, seeing he durst neither speak nor show himself; and he knew it was not a common thing for ladies to fall in love with persons invisible.

The Princess had an universal taste for fine things; and in the present situation of her heart she wanted amusement. One day, when she was attended by all her nymphs, she was saying to them, it would give her great pleasure to know how the ladies were dressed in all the courts of the universe, that she might choose the most genteel. There needed no more words to send Leander all over the world. He wished himself in China, where he bought the richest stuffs he could lay his hands on, and got patterns of all the court fashions; from thence he flew to Siam, where he did the same; and in three days he travelled all the four parts of the world, and from time to time brought what he bought to the Palace of Calm Delights, and hid it all in a chamber which he kept locked to himself. When he had thus collected together all the rarities he could meet with—for he never wanted money, his rose always supplying him—he went and bought five or six dozen of dolls, which he caused to be dressed at Paris, which is the place in the world where most regard is paid to fashions. They were all dressed variously, and as magnificent as could be; and Leander placed them all in the Princess's closet.

When she entered it, she was never more agreeably surprised, to see such a company of little mutes, with every one a present of watches, bracelets, diamond buckles, or necklaces; and the most remarkable of them held a picture-box in its hand, which the Princess opening, found it contained Leander's, for her idea of the first made her easily know the second. She gave a loud shriek, and looking upon Abricotina, "Here has appeared of late," said she, "so many wonders in this place, that I know not what to think of them. My birds are all grown witty; I cannot so much as wish, but presently I have my desires; twice have I now seen the portrait of him who rescued thee from the ruffians; and here are silks of all sorts, diamonds, embroideries, laces, and an infinite number of other rarities. What Fairy, or what Demon, is it that takes such care to do me these agreeable services?"

Leander was overjoyed to hear and see her so much concerned about his picture, and calling to mind that there was in a grotto, which she often frequented, a certain pedestal, on which a Diana, not yet finished, was to be erected; on this pedestal he resolved to place himself, in an extraordinary habit, crowned with laurel, and holding a lyre in his hand, on which he played like another Apollo. He waited immediately the Princess's retiring to this grotto, which she did every day, since her thoughts had been taken up with this unknown person; for what Abricotina had said, joined to the sight of the picture, had almost quite destroyed her repose; her brisk lively humour changed into a pensive melancholy, and she grew a great lover of solitude.

When she entered the grotto, she made a sign that nobody should follow her; so that her young damsels dispersed themselves into the neighbouring walks. The Princess threw herself upon a bank of green turf,

sighed, wept, and even talked, but so softly, that Leander could not hear what she said. He had put his red cap on, that she might not see him at first; but soon after, having taken it off, she beheld him with an extraordinary surprise. At first, she took him for a real statue; for he observed exactly the attitude in which he had placed himself, without moving so much as a finger. She beheld it with a kind of pleasure, intermixed with fear; but pleasure soon dispelled her fear; and continuing to view the pleasing figure, which so exactly resembled the life, the Prince, having tuned his lyre, played on it most delightfully.

Though the Princess was so greatly surprised that she could not resist the fear that seized her, she grew pale of a sudden, and fell into a swoon. Leander being alarmed, leaped from the pedestal, and putting on his little red cap, that he might not be perceived, took the Princess by the arms, and gave her all the assistance that his zeal and ardour could inspire. At length she opened her charming eyes, and looked about her in search of him, but she could perceive nobody; yet she felt somebody who held her hands, kissed them, and bedewed them with his tears. It was a long time before she durst speak; and her spirits were in a confused agitation, between fear and hope. She was afraid of the spirit, but loved the figure of the unknown. At length, "Courtly Invisible," cried she, "why are you not the person that I desire you should be?"

At these words, Leander was going to declare himself, but durst not do it as yet; "For," said he, "if I affright the object I adore again, and make her fear me, she will not love me." This consideration made him keep silence, and determined him to retire into a corner of the grotto.

The Princess then, believing herself alone, called Abricotina, and told her all the wonders of the animated statue, that it had played divinely, and that the Invisible had greatly assisted her when she lay in a swoon. "What pity 'tis," said she, "that this Invisible should be so frightful, for nothing can be more amiable or acceptable than his behaviour!"

"Who told you, Madam," answered Abricotina, "that he is as frightful as you imagine? Psyche thought that Cupid had been a serpent; and your case and her's are much alike, neither are you less beautiful; and if Cupid loved you, would you not return his love?"

"If Cupid and the unknown person are the same," replied the Princess, blushing, "I could be content to love Cupid; but, alas! how far am I from such a happiness! I am attached to a chimera; and this fatal picture of the unknown, joined to what thou hast told me of him, have inspired with me inclinations so contrary to the precepts which I received from my mother, that I am afraid of being punished for them."

"Oh, Madam," said Abricotina, interrupting her, "have you not troubles enough already? why should you anticipate afflictions which may never come to pass?"

It is easy to imagine what pleasure Leander took in this conversation.

In the meantime, the little Furibon, still enamoured

of the Princess, whom he never saw, expected with impatience the return of the four men whom he had sent to the Island of Calm Delights. One of them at last came back, and after he had given the Prince a particular account of what had passed, told him that the island was defended by Amazons, and that unless he sent along with him a very powerful army, it would be impossible to get into it.

The King his father was dead, and he now lord of all. Disdaining, therefore, any repulse, he raised an army of four hundred thousand men, and put himself at the head of them, appearing like another Tom Thumb upon a war horse. Now, when the Amazons perceived his mighty host, they gave the Princess notice of it, who immediately despatched away her trusty Abricotina to the kingdom of the Fairies, to beg her mother's instructions what she should do to drive the little Furibon from her territories. But Abricotina found the Fairy in an angry humour.

"Nothing that my daughter does," said she, "escapes my knowledge; the Prince Leander is now in her palace; he loves her, and she has a tenderness for him. All my cares and precepts have not been able to guard her from the tyranny of Love, and she is now under his fatal dominion. Alas! that cruel deity is not satisfied with the mischiefs he has done to me, but exercises his dominion over that which I love more dearly than my life. But it is the decree of destiny, and I must submit. Therefore, Abricotina, begone; I'll not hear a word more of a daughter, whose behaviour has so much displeased me."

Abricotina returned with these bad tidings, whereat the Princess was almost distracted; and this was soon perceived by Leander, who was near her, though she did not see him, and beheld her grief with the greatest pain. However, he durst not then open his lips; but recollecting that Furibon was exceedingly covetous, he thought that by giving him a sum of money, he might perhaps prevail with him to retire.

Thereupon, he dressed himself like an Amazon, and wished himself in the forest to catch his horse. He had no sooner called him, than he came leaping, prancing, and neighing for joy, for he was grown quite weary of being so long absent from his dear master; but when he beheld him dressed like a woman, he hardly knew him, and at first thought himself deceived. But Leander mounted him, and soon arrived in the camp of Furibon, where everybody took him for a real Amazon, and gave notice to Furibon, that a lady was come to speak with him from the Princess of Calm Delights. Immediately the little King put on his royal robes, and having placed himself upon his throne, he looked like a great toad counterfeiting a king.

Leander harangued him, and told him, that the Princess, preferring a quiet and peaceable life to the fatigues of war, had sent him to offer his Majesty as much money as he pleased to demand, provided he would suffer her to continue in peace; but if he refused her proposal, she would omit no means that might serve for her defence. Furibon replied, that he took pity on her, and would grant her the honour of his protection; but that he demanded a hundred thousand thousand millions of pounds, and without that sum paid, he would not return to his kingdom. Leander answered, that such a vast sum would be too long in counting, and therefore, if he would say how many rooms full he desired to have, the Princess was generous and rich enough to satisfy him. Furibon was astonished to hear, that instead of demanding an abatement, she would rather offer an augmentation; and it came into his wicked mind to take all the money he could get, and then seize the Amazon and kill her, that she might not return to her mistress.

He told Leander, therefore, that he would have thirty chambers filled with pieces of gold, and that then, upon his royal word, he would return. Leander being conducted into the chambers that were to be filled, he took his rose, and shook it till every room was filled with all sorts of coin.

Furibon was in an ecstasy, and the more gold he saw, the greater was his desire to seize the Amazon, and get the Princess into his power; so that when all the rooms were full, he commanded his guards to seize her, alleging she had brought him counterfeit money. Accordingly, the guards were going to lay hold upon the Amazon, but Leander put on his little red cap, and disappeared; the guards, believing she had escaped, ran out, and left Furibon alone; when Leander, laying hold of the opportunity, took the tyrant by the hair, and twisted his head off with the same ease he would a pullet's; nor did the little wretch of a King see the hand that killed him.

Leander, having got his head, wished himself in the Palace of Calm Delights, where he found the Princess walking, and with grief considering the message which her mother had sent her, and on the means to repel Furibon, which she looked upon as difficult, she being alone with a small number of Amazons, who were unable to defend her; but on a sudden she beheld a head hanging in the air, without anybody that she could see to hold it. This prodigy astonished her so, that she could not tell what to think of it; but her amazement was increased when she saw the head laid at her feet, without seeing the hand who did it, and yet, at the same time, hearing a voice that uttered these words:—

"Charming Princess, cease your fear
Of Furibon; whose head see here!"

Abricotina, knowing Leander's voice, cried, "I protest, Madam, the invisible person who speaks is the very stranger that rescued me."

The Princess seemed astonished, but yet pleased. "Oh!" said she, "if it be true that the Invisible and the stranger are the same person, I confess I should be glad to make him my acknowledgments."

Leander, still invisible, replied, "I will yet do more to deserve them;" and so saying, he returned to Furibon's army, where the report of his death was already spread throughout the camp. As soon as he appeared there in his usual habit and countenance, everybody came about him; all the officers and soldiers surrounded him, uttering the loudest acclamations of joy. In short, they acknowledged him for their King, and that the crown of right belonged to him; for which he thanked them, and, as the first mark of his royal bounty, divided the thirty rooms of gold among the soldiers, so that this great army was enriched for ever. This done, he returned to his Princess, ordering the army to march back into his kingdom.

The Princess was gone to bed; and the profound respect he had for her, would not permit him to enter her chamber. He retired, therefore, into his own; but, by what accident I know not, he forgot to make fast the door, as he was wont to do.

The Princess could not sleep for the heat, and the disquiet of her mind; so that she arose before the sun, and in her morning dress went down into this lower apartment; but how strangely was she surprised to find Leander asleep upon the bed! However, she had then leisure enough to take a full view of him without being perceived, and to convince herself that he was the person whose picture she had in her diamond box. "It is impossible," said she, "that this should be a spirit, for can spirits sleep? Is this a body composed of air and fire, without substance, as Abricotina told me?" She softly touched his hair, and heard him breathe, and the sight of him raised alternate fear and pleasure in her breast. But while she was thus attentively surveying him, her mother the Fairy entered with such a dreadful noise, that Leander started out of his sleep. But how strangely was he surprised, how deeply afflicted, to behold his beloved Princess in the most deplorable condition! Her mother dragged her by the hair, and loaded her with a thousand bitter reproaches. In what grief and consternation were the two young lovers, who saw themselves now upon the point of being separated for ever! The Princess durst not open her lips to the incensed Fairy, but cast her eyes upon Leander, as it were to beg his assistance.

He judged rightly, that he ought not to deal by rugged means with a power superior to his, and therefore he sought by his eloquence and submission to move the incensed mother. He ran to her, threw himself at her feet, and besought her to have pity upon a young Prince, who would never change his affection for her daughter, but would make it his sovereign felicity to make her happy. The Princess, encouraged by his example, also embraced her mother's knees, and told her, that without the King she should never be happy, and that she was greatly obliged to him.

"You know not the misfortunes of love," cried the Fairy, "nor the treacheries of which lovers are capable; they bewitch us only to poison the happiness of our lives. I have known it by experience; and why will you suffer the same misfortunes?"

"Is there no exception, Madam?" replied the Princess; "the King's assurances, which I believe to be sincere, are they not sufficient to secure me from your fears?"

But neither tears nor entreaties could move the implacable Fairy; and it is very probable she would never have pardoned them, had not the lovely Fairy Gentilla appeared at that instant in the chamber, more brilliant than the sun. The Graces accompanied her, and she was attended by a train of little Cupids, that sung a thousand new and pleasing airs, and sported about her like so many little children.

Embracing the old Fairy, "Dear Sister," said she, "I am persuaded you cannot have forgotten the good office I did you when you besought a re-admittance into our kingdom; had it not been for me, you had never been admitted, and since that time I never desired any kindness at your hands; but now the time is come for you to do me a signal piece of service. Pardon, then, this lovely Princess; consent to her nuptials with this young Prince. I will engage he shall be ever constant to her; the thread of their days shall be spun of gold and silk; they shall live to complete your happiness, and I will never forget the obligations you lay upon me."

"Charming Gentilla," cried the Fairy, "I consent to whatever you desire; come, my dear children, come to my arms, and receive the assurance of my friendship." And so saying, she embraced both the Princess and her lover. The Fairy Gentilla was in an ecstasy of joy, and all her pretty train joined to form an hymeneal choir, which was so harmonious, that it awakened all the nymphs of the palace, who came to see what was the matter.

But what a pleasing surprise was this to Abricotina! She no sooner cast her eyes upon Leander than she knew him again; and seeing him hold the Princess by the hand, she made no question of their mutual felicity; which she was confirmed in, when the Fairy mother told them that she would remove the Island of Calm Delights, the castle, and all the wonders contained in it, into Leander's kingdom; that she would live with them, and do them still greater services.

"Whatever your generosity, Madam, may inspire you to do," said Leander, "it is impossible that you can honour me with any present comparable to that which I receive from your hands this day. You have rendered me the most happy of all men; and if I know myself, I shall never prove ungrateful."

This short compliment pleased the Fairy exceedingly; for she was of those ancient times, when they used to stand complimenting for a whole day upon one leg.

In the meantime, Gentilla had sent, by means of Brelic-Breloc, for all the generals and chief officers of Leander's army to attend and grace the nuptials; but it would require five or six volumes to describe the operas, plays, balls, music, tournaments, and the other magnificence of those charming nuptials. But what was most extraordinary was, that every nymph found amongst the gallants that Gentilla had sent for, as passionate lovers as if they had known each other ten years, though the most was four-and-twenty hours; but a Fairy's wand will produce effects much more extraordinary.

"SHE DROPS PEARLS AND DIAMONDS WHENEVER SHE SPEAKS."

TOADS AND DIAMONDS.

THERE was, once upon a time, a Widow, who had two daughters: the eldest was so extremely like her, both in temper and person, that whoever saw the one saw the other also; they were both so very proud and disagreeable, that nobody could live with them. The youngest, who was the exact picture of her father in good-nature and sweetness of manner, was also the most beautiful creature ever seen. As it is natural to love those who resemble us, the Mother doated upon the eldest, and no less hated the youngest. She made her eat in the kitchen, and work all the day with the servants.

Among other things, the poor child was obliged to go twice a day to draw water at a fountain more than a mile and a half distant from the house, and bring home a large pitcher filled with it, as well as she

No. 31.

241

could. One day, when she was at the fountain, a poor Woman came up to her, and asked her to let her drink. "That I will, Goody, most readily," said the sweet-tempered creature; and washing out the pitcher, she filled it at the clearest part of the fountain, and held it to the Old Woman's mouth, that she might drink the more easily.

The Old Woman, having drunk, said to her: "Since you are so pretty, so kind, and so obliging, my dear, I will bestow on you a gift," (for it was a Fairy in disguise who had asked her to drink, just to see how far the little girl's good-nature would go). "I give you," continued she, "that whenever you speak, there shall come out of your mouth either a rose or a diamond."

When the sweet girl got home, her Mother began to scold her for staying so long at the fountain.

"I ask your pardon, Mamma," said she, "for not being at home sooner;" and as she pronounced these words, there fell from her lips two roses, two pearls, and two large diamonds.

"What do I see?" cried the Mother, quite astonished; "as sure as anything, she drops diamonds and pearls from her mouth in speaking! My child, how happens this?" (This was the first time she had ever called her "My child.")

The poor girl told her Mother all that had befallen her at the fountain, dropping pearls and diamonds from her mouth all the time she was speaking.

"Upon my word," said her Mother, "this is very lucky, truly. I will send my darling thither directly. Fanny! Fanny! look! do you see what falls from the mouth of your sister when she speaks? Should not you like to have the same gift bestowed on you? Well, you have only to go to the fountain; and when a poor Woman asks you to let her drink, to grant her request in the most civil manner."

"Vastly pretty, truly, it would be, to see *me* go and draw water at the fountain! Not I, indeed!" replied the proud creature.

"But I insist upon your going, and this very moment, too," answered her Mother.

The pert hussy accordingly set out, taking with her the best silver tankard in the house, and grumbling all the way as she went.

She had no sooner reached the fountain, than a Lady, most magnificently dressed, came out of a wood just by, and asked her to let her drink. (This was the very Fairy who had bestowed the rich gift on the youngest sister, and had now taken the dress and manners of a Princess, to see how far the insolent airs of the haughty creature would go.)

"Am I come here," said the ill-bred minx, "to draw water for you? Oh, yes; the best silver tankard in the house was brought on purpose for your ladyship, I suppose! However, you may drink out of it, if you have a fancy."

"You are not very obliging," replied the Fairy, without putting herself in a passion; "but since you have behaved with so little civility, I give you for a gift, that at every word you speak, there shall come out of your mouth either a toad or a viper."

As soon as her Mother perceived her coming home, she called out, "Well, daughter!"

"Well, Mother," answered the pert hussy; and as she spoke, two toads and two vipers dropped from her mouth upon the ground.

"Oh, mercy!" cried the Mother, "what do I see? It is the jade thy sister who is the cause of all this! But she shall pay for it, I warrant her!" and she instantly went to look for her, that she might beat her.

The poor innocent ran away as fast as she could, and reached a neighbouring forest. The King's son, who had been hunting, happened to meet her, and, observing how very beautiful she was, asked what she was doing all alone in the forest, and why she cried.

"Alas!" said she, sobbing as if her heart would break, "my mother, Sir, has turned me out of doors."

The King's son, seeing pearls and diamonds falling from her mouth at every word she spoke, desired her to tell him the reason of such a wonder. The pretty creature accordingly related to him all that had befallen her at the fountain.

The Prince was so charmed with her beauty and innocence, that he fell violently in love with her; and recollecting, also, that the gift she possessed was worth much more than the largest marriage portion, conducted her to the palace of the King his father, and married her immediately.

As for her sister, she grew even more pert than before, and behaved, in all respects, so very ill, that her own mother was obliged to turn her out of doors; and the miserable creature, after wandering a great way, and vainly trying to prevail on some one to give her food and shelter, went into a wood, and there died of grief and hunger.

LUCK IN A BOTTLE.

ONCE upon a time, a Woodcutter, who was very industrious and very poor, by working from sun-rise to sun-set, managed to earn enough to provide for the immediate wants of his family, and to save a little money. One day, he said to his Son: "I have no other child than you, my beloved son, and the little money I have earned by the sweat of my brow, I intend spending upon your education. Do you, therefore, learn something whereby you may keep your poor old father when he can no longer work for himself; when his eyes have become dim, and his old limbs are stiffened with rheumatism, then shall you, my son, earn money, while he sits in his chimney-corner, and rests."

Thereupon, it was arranged that the Son should go to a great school, where, in a very little time, he gained much praise and notice by his close attention to his studies. He remained a long time there; but after he had gone through a long course of study, he found that he had not learnt half there was to learn; and as his father's stock of money was exhausted, he was obliged to return home again.

"Ah!" sighed the poor Old Man, "I can give you no more money, for in these dear times I can scarcely earn money to buy my daily bread."

"Make yourself easy on that point, my dear Father,"

answered the Son; "all that happens is for the best; I will suit myself to circumstances."

The next day, when the Father was about to go to the forest, to earn a little by chopping and clearing, his Son said to him cheerfully, "I will go with you, and I'll warrant we will make a good day of it between us, for I am strong, and can help you."

"Ah, my Son! but neither will nor strength can chop wood without an axe; and, alas! I have but one."

"Go, then," replied the Son, "and ask one of your neighbours to lend you an axe; I shall very soon have earned money enough to buy one for myself."

So the Father borrowed an axe, and the next morning, at sunrise, away they went to the forest together. The Son was very lively, and whistled and sang over his work; and when the sun was high in the heavens, the Father told his Son he must not work any more before he ate something, or his strength would be wasted, and he would not be able to work at all. So when he had eaten his bread, he said, "Father, rest here awhile, and take a nap, while I go and look after some birds' nests; you know I am not tired."

"Sit down, do, you silly fellow; for if you keep running about after birds' nests, you will be so tired, that you will not be able to lift an arm, let alone strike a blow."

But the Young Man could not rest, but went along, peeping into every bush, and peering up into each tree he came to, and looking for all the nests he could find. To and fro he walked a long time, and at last he came to an immense oak-tree, certainly many hundred years older than either you or I, and so big round, that five men could only just span it. He stood still to look at this tree, thinking that many a bird's nest must be up within it; when suddenly he heard, as he thought, a Voice. He listened, and wondered what it could be, when again came a half-smothered cry of "Let me out! let me out!" He looked eagerly around, but could see nothing; the Voice seemed to him to come from the ground. So he called out, "Where are you?" and the Voice answered, "Here I am, sticking among the roots of the oak-tree. Let me out! let me out!"

The Scholar eagerly sought at the foot of the tree, where the roots spread round and ran into the ground; and at last, in a small hollow, he saw a glass bottle. This he picked up, and turned it this way and that, and then, holding it to the light, perceived a creature, in shape like a frog, within. It kept hopping up and down. "Let me out! let me out!" squeaked this ugly thing again; and the Scholar, imagining no mischief, drew out the stopper of the bottle. In a trice, up flew a little Demon Spirit, which grew and grew so fast, that in a very few moments he stood before the Scholar like a frightful Giant, half the size of the tree.

"Do you know," roared the Giant, in a voice like thunder, "what your reward is to be for setting me free?"

"No," replied the Scholar, without fear; "that were a hard matter to guess."

"Well, then, I'll make you my confidant," said the Giant; "I must break your neck!"

"Why did not you say so before?" returned the Scholar, "and then you should have kept up your hop, skip, and a jump, in your pretty glass house until now; but rely upon it, my head was made to stop upon my shoulders, in spite of all you can do or say; for there are several people's opinions to be asked yet about that matter."

"That for your people!" said the Giant, disdainfully snapping his fingers; "you had better keep them out of my way. Do you suppose I have been shut up so long in this bottle out of mercy? No; it was as a punishment for my sins. I am the mighty Bimbo! and whoever lets me out, his neck I am bound to break."

"Softly, softly!" said the Student; "that is more quickly said than done. How can I make sure you really were in the bottle, and that you are in truth a Spirit? Now, if I were to see you go back again into the bottle, I could believe you, and then you might do as you liked with me."

Full of pride, the Spirit answered, "That is an easy matter;" and, drawing himself together, he became as small and thin as he had been at first, and soon crept, through the same opening, back again into the bottle. No sooner was he completely in, than the Scholar put the stopper back again into the neck, and threw the bottle down among the oak-tree's roots at the old place; so the Spirit was tricked.

Then the Scholar turned away to go back again to his Father; but the Spirit cried after him most piteously, "Oh, pray let me out! do let me out!"

"No, no, my fine fellow," cried the Scholar, "not a second time; you were ungrateful enough to threaten my life once. If I were to let you out now, you might take a fancy to serve me as you promised."

"If you will but set me free," pleaded the Spirit, "I will give you as much money as will last you your lifetime."

"Thank you, but I had rather not trust you; you have deceived me once, and 'once bitten, twice shy,'" answered the Student.

"You are keeping yourself poor when you might be rich. Let me out; I will not harm you, but will give you gifts worth the having, I can tell you," said the Giant.

"'Nothing venture, nothing have,'" thought the Student. "At all hazards, I will venture it; perhaps he will keep his word, as he has made a promise, and do me no injury."

So thinking, he took the stopper out of the bottle again, and the Spirit jumping quickly out, stretched himself out, and was a Giant again.

"Now then, for your promised reward," said the Giant; and, to the Scholar's great disgust, he handed him a little piece of rag, very like a plaster in shape. "Take this, and whatever you touch with one end of it, that has been wounded, it will make whole and sound again; while, if you touch with the other steel or iron, either will be changed into silver."

"That I must see for myself," replied the Scholar; and going to a tree, he tore off a bit of the bark with his axe, and then touched it with the one end of the rag; and in a moment the wounded tree was sound again, and looked as if nothing was the matter. "Now our bargain is at an end; it is all right," said the Student, "and we can separate." Then the Spirit politely expressed his gratitude for the kindness done him, while the Scholar returned many thanks for his present; and the Spirit went on his way, for good or evil, while the Scholar went back again to his Father.

"You are a pretty workman!" said the Old Man; "where have you been playing truant? I said rightly, when I told you woodcutting would never make your fortune."

"Be contented, Father; I will make up for lost time," said the Young Man.

"Yes, you're a brave hand to make it up, without even the tools to work with!" retorted the Father, angrily.

"Now only see, Father, what a stroke I will make; why, I'll cut down that tree with one blow!" and so saying, he took his rag, and rubbed the axe with it; then lifting up his arm, he made a vigorous stroke; but because the axe was changed into silver, the edge turned up.

"This is a nice sort of axe to give a man to work with!" said the Son; "see, it has no edge at all to it."

The Father was in a great fright, and said, "Ah! what have you done? Now, alas! I must find money to pay for the axe, for it is the one I borrowed, and I know not where it is to come from."

"Don't trouble yourself about the money, and pray don't be angry with me; I will very soon set it all to rights by paying for the axe," said the Son.

But the Father exclaimed, "Why, you simpleton! you talk as if you could make money; how can you pay, indeed, when you possess nothing but what I give you? This is a students' foolish fancy got into your head; it is very certain you know nothing at all about woodcutting."

After a little while, the Son said, "Father, I can't work any more; let us make a holiday now."

"Eh! What? do you think I can keep my hands in my pocket as you do? I must keep on; but as for you, you are as well at home as here, for the good you do; so get home with you."

The Son replied, that he did not know the way, as he had never been in the forest before; and at last, as his Father's anger had passed away, he persuaded him to accompany him home.

When they arrived at their home, the Father said to the Son, "Now you must go and sell the axe for whatever you can get for it; and then you must set to work and earn the rest, so that you may buy our neighbour a new axe for the one you have spoilt."

"All right," said the Son; and he took the axe to the Goldsmith in the city, who, after proving it to be real silver, laid it in his scales, and weighed it. "This," said the Goldsmith, "is worth four hundred dollars; but I have not so much money in the house. What is to be done?"

"Pay me what you have, and I will trust you the remainder," said the Scholar.

The Goldsmith gave him three hundred dollars, and left the other as a debt. Thereupon, the Scholar went home, and said to his Father, " Go, ask our neighbour what he will want for his axe, for I have money enough to pay him with."

"I know that already," answered the Father; "he would have one dollar and sixpence."

"Then give him two dollars and two sixpences; that is double, and enough, I am sure, in all conscience;" and he gave his Father the money, saying, "You shall never want money now; live at your ease."

"My goodness!" said the Old Man, "how could you have come by all this money honestly? Where did you get it from?"

The Son then related to his Father all that had happened to him, and what a good friend his luck had been to him. With the rest of the money he went to the University, and learnt as much as he possibly could; and afterwards he became the most celebrated surgeon in the world, because he could perform the most wonderful cures, and heal all wounds with his magic plaster.

DISOBEDIENCE PUNISHED.

A LITTLE Boy and his Sister were once playing upon the edge of a stream, where they had been told not to go, and they both fell in under the water; when a Water-Sprite caught hold of them, saying, "Now I have got you, I'll keep you, and make you work for me." She gave the Maiden some tangled dirty flax to wash and spin, while the Boy had to hew down a large tree with a rusty old axe; and they got nothing to eat and to drink but stale water and lumps of stony sand.

This treatment was so unendurable to children who had been used to a kind nurse, and a nice warm nursery, and sweet bread and milk to eat, that they determined to run away on Sunday. So they asked to go to church; and when it was over, they hastened out first, and ran away as fast as their legs would carry them.

The Water-Sprite soon fancied there was some game on foot; and all at once she looked out after the children, when she caught sight of them in the distance, and made some furious leaps after them.

The children, turning back, saw with dismay how fast she came after them, when the little Girl threw a large hairbrush, with hundreds of thousands of bristles in it, right in the pathway, so that it took the Sprite a long time to slip and glide through it; but with vast trouble and much pain to herself, at last she accomplished this, and again pursued them.

As soon as the children saw her, the Boy threw behind him a large comb, with hundreds of thousands of teeth; over this, also, the Sprite at last glided, as she knew how to save herself from the bristles.

Then the little Girl threw behind her a looking-glass, that the Sprite thought was a mountain of glass; it was so very slippery she could not get over it.

The Water-Sprite said, "Now I have you, and I will serve you out for the trouble you have given me all this time." So she turned home to get an axe to break this glass mountain in two; but when she got back, the children had got far enough away. So the Sprite went grumbling home, to do her own work; and the children ever after learnt to obey when they were spoken to.

THE THREE BILLY-GOATS GRUFF.

ONCE, when the weather was wild and rough,
Three Billy-Goats travelled, their name was Gruff;
Why they went to the hill-side is plainly seen,
To put fat on their bones, which were now very lean.

As they went to the hill they came to a bridge,
That crossed a chasm from ridge to ridge;
And just under the bridge there lived a Troll,
Who gobbled up all who could not pay toll.

His nose for a poker would very well serve,
And had an ugly, malevolent curve;
His eyes, like great tea-saucers full of red fire,
He flashed upon all with revengeful ire.

Then first the youngest of all the three
Came trotting along without company.
"Who goes there, trip-a-trap? Come, pay up your toll,"
In a voice like thunder roared out the old Troll.

"Just be good-natured, and let me pass free,
I'm the tiniest Goat of all the three."
"No, you must pay the toll, or to-night you won't sup,
For in two or three minutes I'll gobble you up."

"Oh! good Mr. Troll, now pray don't do that,
For my brother, who's coming, is nice and fat.
I think you've long fasted, and want a meal;
You had much better wait for him, I feel."

"Get you gone," he growled, "to the grass on the hill,
And when you are fat I'll have my fill."
Then up came the second, much bigger and fatter,
And asked, in a tremulous voice, "What's the matter?"

"What's the matter, indeed? Why it's this," said he,
"You'll not trip over this bridge scot-free;
And if this minute you do not pay toll,
The very next minute I'll gobble you whole."

"Stop," said the Goat, "I've the strongest objection
To being devoured without time for reflection;
But I've a fat and big brother coming this way."
Then be off," roared the Troll, "without farther delay."

Then up came the big Goat, so strong and so bluff,
And he spoke in a voice both angry and rough.
"Pay the toll, I tell you," the old Troll cried,
"Or I'll gobble you up, with your horns and your hide!"

"Come on," said the Goat, "for I've got a spear
That'll poke your eye-balls out at your ear;
And I have got two curling stones
That'll crush you to bits, both body and bones."

Then up flew the Troll in a terrible rage,
Thinking his hunger now to assuage;
But the Goat made a rush with his terrible spear,
And poked his eye-balls out at his ear.

Then he set to work with his curling stones,
And crushed him to bits, both body and bones;
Then he gave his dead body a dext'rous turn,
Right over the bridge to the depths of the burn.

Then across the bridge he went pit-a-pat,
To join his two brothers, who'd gone to get fat;
From the grass on the hill-side they ate their fill,
If they have not come back, why, they're feeding there still.

Now my story is done, so snip, snap, snout!
What I knew of the Goats I have fairly told out.

THE WITCH QUEEN AND HER DAUGHTER.

AGES ago, there lived an Old Enchantress, who was also a Queen, and her Daughter was the most fascinating and beautiful creature under the sun. But this wicked woman used her daughter's beauty as a trap to ensnare young men to her palace, that she might the more easily work their destruction, which was the greatest gratification to her in life. The way she managed this was, to impose the most puzzling tasks upon the suitors for her Daughter's hand, promising those who guessed them that they should have the lovely girl in marriage; and as all the gallants in those days behaved much in the same manner as they do now, when a pretty girl is in the case, there were no end of admirers of this dear little divine Princess, although they knew, if they did not solve the riddle put to them, they were obliged, by order of the wicked Queen, to kneel down, and submit to have their heads cut off!

Many and many a youth, lured by the tempting hope of possessing this rare and rich prize, had fallen a sacrifice; and yet another King's son, in the face of these facts, had willingly made up his mind to brave these cruel dangers, and begged of his father to let him go and win her.

"Never, while I live," said the King, "can I let you go forth to such a certain death. Your place is on my throne after me; let those go seek such adventures whose lives are of less consequence to the country."

When the Prince heard his father's decision, he fell very ill, and was nearly upon the point of death. So the doctors who were called in begged the King to alter his mind, for that nothing else could re-establish the Prince's health. When the King heard this, he grieved greatly for his son, but thought that perhaps he might be spared by some chance; and therefore the royal consent was reluctantly given to the Prince's starting upon his journey, as soon as he was strong enough to bear it; "For," said the King, "I know not how else to restore him."

No sooner had the King spoken, than the Prince's strength returned, and he jumped out of bed, feeling already quite strong enough to travel a thousand miles: such is the perverse nature of young people, when they want to have their own way.

He soon started off, and had not travelled long, before, as he was riding across a common, he saw, a long distance ahead, something lying on the ground like a hay-rick. As he approached this, he found it was a man, who had laid himself upon the earth, and was as big as a hill. The man waited until the Prince came up to him; and then rising, said, "I see, Sir Knight, that you ride unattended; if you need an esquire, I am at your service."

The Prince, although he was very well-bred, could not help laughing at this proposal; and the would-be esquire, feeling somewhat piqued, said, "You need not mind enlisting such an uncouth-looking fellow; for if I were a thousand times more clumsy-looking than I am, still I am capable of doing you good service."

"So be it," replied the Prince; "I may need the aid of faithful servants. Come, then, with me." So Fatty—for that was the esquire's name—accompanied the Prince.

Presently, they came to another man, who also was lying upon the ground, with his ear close down to the grass.

"What are you up to?" said the Prince.

"Hush! don't disturb me; I am listening," he replied.

"And what, in the name of wonder, are you listening to in the earth so attentively?" asked the Prince.

"Oh! I am listening to whatever is going on in the world around," said the man; "nothing in nature escapes my hearing; I can hear even the grass grow."

"That is good," answered the Prince; "perhaps, then, you will be kind enough to tell me what is going on at the court of the Witch Queen, who has a lovely Daughter?"

"I hear," replied the man, "the sharp whistling of a sword, which is about to cut off the head of an unsuccessful wooer."

"Follow me; I have work for you," said the Prince to the Listener. So away the three journeyed.

Presently, they came to where were lying two feet, and part of two legs, but they could not see the continuation of them until they had walked a good stretch, and then, what should they observe, but the body; and, at last, some distance farther off, the head!

"Halloa!" cried the Prince, "you're above the common run, I think."

"Oh! you have seen nothing," replied Long-Legs; "why, if I were to stretch my limbs out as far as I can, I am longer a thousand times, and taller than the highest mountain on the earth. I should like to be your servant, noble Sir. Will you take me?"

The Prince accepted his services, and on they all went together; when they soon came to a man who wore a broad bandage over his eyes.

"I suppose you have caught cold in your eyes, and are suffering from inflammation, that you bind them up in that way?" said the Prince.

"No," said the man; "but my eyesight is, unfortunately, so strong, and I am so sharp-sighted, that I dare not remove the bandage, for whatever I look upon with my naked eyes splits in two; nevertheless, if I can be of any service to you, I am your man, and ready to go with you."

The Prince willingly accepted his services; and so on they went, until they came to another man, who, although he was lying full length in the scorching heat of the mid-day sun, was, nevertheless, trembling and shivering so, that not one limb of his body would remain still for a moment.

"What ails you?" said the Prince.

"I am so cold, I am freezing," replied the man.

"Freezing in the bright sun! that is odd," said the Prince.

"Alas! my nature is different to everybody else," replied the man; "the hotter it is, the colder I feel. When it freezes everything else, then I am so hot,

that I cannot touch ice for the heat of my body, nor yet go near the fire, lest I should freeze it."

"You are one of the wonders of the world!" said the Prince. "Come along with me; perhaps I may find some use for your services."

So this fellow followed with the rest; and they soon came to a man, who was stretching out his neck to such a length, that he could see over all the hills, far away to a neighbouring country.

"What are you craning your neck after so eagerly?" asked the Prince.

"I have such a long, clear sight, that I can see to the depths of the sea, the tops of the mountains, into every field, forest, and hill, and round every corner of the world."

"You are just the man for my money!" said the Prince. "Come with me; I shall find work for you, I'll warrant."

The Prince now pursued his way on towards the city where dwelt the Old Witch Queen. When he arrived, he would not tell his name, but said he wanted the Queen's pretty Daughter, and he did not much mind what they set him to do for her.

"A bold man!" said the Old Enchantress, "and handsome, too; just the kind of gallant I like to get into my clutches." So she eyed him awhile, and then said, "I will set you three tasks to perform, and when you have executed them to my liking, I shall be happy to call you my son."

"Just as it should be," answered the Prince. "Tell me the first?"

"You must fetch for me a pale-pink coral basket, full of precious pearls, which I have let fall to the bottom of the Red Sea," said the Queen.

The Prince thought this not so easy to do; but he went to his Six Servants, and told them the conditions imposed upon him by the Witch Queen, and they consulted together.

"I will soon see where it lies," said he of the far, clear sight; and looking down into the water, exclaimed, "Why, there it is, hanging on a pointed jutting rock!"

"If I could but catch sight of where it is!" said Long-Limbs.

"Is that all?" said Fatty; and lying down upon the bank, he held his mouth down open to the water, and the stream ran into it as if into a pit, until, at length, the whole sea was as dry as a high road. Long-Limbs, thereupon, bent slightly over, and brought up the basket, without spilling any of the pearls, to the infinite delight of the Prince, who immediately carried it in triumph to the Old Witch Queen.

She was vastly astonished to see this request so soon complied with, but confessed it was the right basket, and complimented the young suitor upon the happy manner in which he had performed this service. But now comes the second: "Do you see those three hundred fat oxen grazing in my meadows before my palace? Well, all these you must consume —flesh, bones, skin, and horns; then, in my cellar you will find three hundred casks of wine of the finest vintage—all of these you must drink out; but, mark me, if you leave behind you one single hair

246

of the oxen or one drop of the wine, you will lose your life."

"I suppose I am not to dine so sumptuously alone?" said the Prince; "I like company at table."

"Well, you are welcome to one guest, but that is all," said the Queen.

Then the Prince went again to his Servants, and it was arranged that Fatty should be the invited guest; he willingly, of course, accepted the invitation; and setting to work with a good appetite, soon made an end of the three hundred oxen, skin and bones, horns and hide, while he felt satisfied at having made so good a meal. Next he began upon the wine, and emptied the casks without even the aid of a single glass, drained them dry to the last drop, and then took a nap for the sake of his digestion. Meanwhile, the Prince went before the Queen, and told her he had performed his task.

She grinned a savage grin, saying, "No one before has ever got so far as that;" but in her own mind she had determined that the Prince should lose his head this third time. "This evening," said she, "I will bring my Daughter into your room, and you must hold her round the waist with one arm; but beware of sleep while you sit there, for at twelve o'clock I shall come into the room, and if I do not find my Daughter there, you are a lost man—your life is forfeited."

"Neither an unpleasant or difficult task," thought the Prince; "there will not be much fear of my going to sleep, while I am with a pretty woman." Nevertheless, he did not altogether like to trust the Old Queen, lest she should play him some shabby trick; so he said to his Servants, "There must be watch kept to-night, so that no one passes out at the chamber door during that time."

As soon as night came, the Queen brought her lovely Daughter to the Prince, and then Long-Limbs drew himself out as thin as a wire, and wound himself round the waist of the pair in a coil; and Fatty placed himself at the doorway, so that no living being should pass out.

So there these two sat, without speaking a word; the moon shone through the window full upon the face of the maiden, and the Prince was well satisfied to gaze upon her beauty. He did nothing but look at her, with a heart full of love and happiness, and never felt a moment's weariness. Thus all went on well, until eleven o'clock, when the Old Witch threw a charm over them all, so that they fell fast asleep, and the very next moment she carried the Princess off. On they slept, never dreaming of their misfortune, until a quarter to twelve, when the charm had ended; then they all woke up again at the same time.

"Unhappy man!" exclaimed the Prince; "I am lost! Oh, my beloved Princess! could I but clasp you in these arms once again!"

The faithful Servants grieved for their master's misfortune; but the Listener said, "Keep quiet, and let me hear where she is." He listened a moment, and then said, "The Princess is sitting inside a cave three hundred miles from hence, deploring her unhappy fate."

"You alone can manage this task," said the Prince to Long-Limbs; "if you set to the work with good heart, you will be there in a couple of strides."

"Certainly," said Long-Limbs; "but Sharp-Eyes must go with me to pierce the rock."

Then he hoisted Sharp-Eyes upon his back, and in a moment, while one could scarcely turn his head round, there they stood, in front of the Enchanted Rock. Immediately Sharp-Eyes undid the bandage, and the rock was split into a thousand pieces; then Long-Limbs quickly seized the Princess out of the ruins, and carried her, in a twinkling, to the Prince, and then fetched Fatty. No sooner were they seated, rejoicing over their good fortune, than the clock struck the hour of twelve.

As soon as it had struck, the Old Enchantress slipped, with a horrid smile, into the room, for she made sure her Daughter was in the rocky cave, and the Prince her victim.

When she saw her Daughter in the arms of the Prince, she was terrified, and exclaimed, "I am outwitted at last: here is one who can do more than I can!"

She dared not, however, deny her promise, and so the maiden was betrothed to the Prince. But as the Prince had not betrayed his rank, and appeared only with the retinue of an ordinary gentleman, the Old Queen nagged at her Daughter, and said, "You shameless hussy, to listen to common folks; why not choose a husband of your own rank?"

These words pierced the Princess's heart, and she thought of revenge: and accordingly, the very next day, she had three hundred bundles of dry faggots collected together in a heap, and then she said, "My dear Prince, you performed your three tasks very easily and well, but still I will not marry you, until some one can be found who can sit upon the fire of those lighted faggots, and endure it."

"I have him, sure enough, now," she thought; "for who would like to be roasted alive for anybody's happiness? No; I am sure none of his Servants will do that for him; and so, out of love for me, he will be obliged to burn himself, and I shall get freed from him, and so quiet my mother's angry tongue."

But the Servants said Frosty had done nothing as yet, so they sat him down upon the top of the pile of wood. The fire was lighted, and burnt and crackled away for three whole days and nights, until every stick of wood was consumed; but when the fire was all burnt out, there stood Frosty, shaking as if he had an ague fit upon him, and declaring that the frost was so severe, that he should have perished if there had not come some change.

After this, no farther excuse could be made, and the Princess was obliged to take the unknown stranger for her husband.

But just as they came to the church, the Old Queen was nearly biting her fingers off with vexation; and at last declared that, come what might, she could not bear the shame of this marriage; so she sent her guards after the wedding party, with strict orders, at all risks, to bring them all back. "If you return without my Daughter, you shall all be put to death."

The Listener, however, had kept his ears open, and knew the secret designs of the Old Witch.

247

"What shall we do?" asked he of Fatty.

"Leave them to me," said he; so, spitting behind him once or twice a drop of the sea-water he had formerly drank, there appeared a great lake, into which fell the guards of the Queen, who were all of them drowned.

When the Queen saw this, she despatched her mounted soldiers; but the Listener heard the rattle of their trappings, and unbound the eyes of their fellow-servant, whose look, as soon as he directed it upon the enemy, shivered them all to pieces like glass.

The bridal party now passed on undisturbed; and as soon as the ceremony was over, the Six Servants took their leave, saying to their master, "You will no longer require us, therefore we will seek our fortunes elsewhere."

About half a mile from the Queen's palace was a small village, before which a Swineherd was keeping his pigs; and as the Prince and Princess passed by, the former said, "Do you really know who you have got for your husband? I am only a poor Swineherd, and no rich Prince. You see this man with the pigs: he is my father; so it will be but proper that we two should get out and assist him."

"What! a Princess attend pigs?" said she. "No, indeed! that I never will do." But her husband persisted in getting out of his carriage, and handed her out, and he took her into a wayside inn. He here ordered the host to carry away secretly, in the night, his wife's rich clothes; so that, when the morning came, the poor Princess had nothing to wear, and was obliged to dress herself in an old gown and slippers which the hostess lent her, saying, "If your husband had not begged so earnestly for them, you would not have got them, I can tell you."

The Princess now began to bemoan her sad fate, and to think her husband was really a Swineherd; and so she helped him to tend the drove, looking upon it as a just punishment for her haughtiness and pride. This lasted for some days, until she was so foot-sore and wounded, that she could no longer bear it. Just at this moment, two persons came up to her, and said, "Do you know who you have married, and where your husband is?"

"Ah me!" she replied, "he is a Swineherd; but is just now gone into some neighbouring village, to drive a little trade in ribbons and laces, that he may buy me some shoes, to keep me from the thorns and brambles."

"Come along with us, and we will show you who he is, and what he is after." So the Princess followed them until they got to the palace, where her husband stood, most gorgeously arrayed in his royal robes, in the great hall.

She did not, however, recognize him, until he caught her in his arms, and most affectionately embraced her, saying to her, "I have suffered much for you, and perhaps what little you have suffered for me will be a lesson to you for the rest of your life."

Soon after, their wedding was celebrated in due form; indeed, it was so grand, that I very much wish you and I had been there to have seen it.

248

THE KNAPSACK, THE HAT, AND THE HORN.

ONCE upon a time, there were three Brothers, who were very poor; but Fortune, not content with this, sank them deeper and deeper every day in misery and poverty, until, at last, they were well nigh starved to death, so great were their necessities.

At last, they said one to the other, "This way of living will never do; we cannot go on in this manner; we shall not have strength left us to stand, let alone to seek bread; while we can, we had better go forth into the world, and seek our fortunes."

With these words, they got up, and set out, and travelled many a long and weary mile, over green fields and meadows, without meeting with any luck. One day, however, they arrived in a large forest, and in the middle of it they came to a high hill, which they discovered, to their pleasure and delight, to be all of silver. At first sight, the eldest Brother said, "Now I have met with my expected good fortune, I am well content, and desire nothing better." So saying, he took as much silver as he could carry, and turned to go back again to his house.

The others, however, said, "Silver is good to possess, but we desire something better;" and they left the silver, without so much as touching it, and went on their way. After they had travelled a couple of days farther, they came to another hill, which was all of gold. There the second Brother stopped, and soon became quite dazzled at the sight. "What shall I do?" said he to himself; "shall I take as much gold as I can, that I may have enough to live upon, or shall I go farther still?" At last, he made up his mind to put as much in his pockets as he possibly could carry; and then, having said good-bye to his Brother, he made the best of his way to his own home again.

The third Brother, however, would not touch the gold. "I will travel," said he; "for silver and gold I care not; perhaps something better may turn up, who knows? Some good luck will happen to me, I have no doubt."

So he took courage, and travelled on for three days all alone, and at the end of that time he came to a great forest, which was very much more extensive than the one they came to before; indeed, it was so large, that he thought he should never find the end; and, besides being very weary, he was almost starved to death with hunger and thirst. He clambered up a tall tree, to try if by chance he could discover any outlet to the forest, but nothing but tree-tops met his gaze wherever he turned his eyes. His stomach now was pinched with hunger, and he was very troubled to know how he should satisfy its demands. He thought to himself, "Could I now have but a good meal for this once, I might be able to get on again."

Scarcely were the words out of his mouth, than, to his great astonishment, a napkin was spread out under the tree, covered with all sorts of food, most grateful to his senses.

"Ah!" said he, "this time my wish is fulfilled in the very nick;" and without giving a thought as to

"HE SAID, 'CLOTH, COVER THYSELF,' AND DINNER WAS INSTANTLY READY."

whose dinner it was, or who brought it, or who cooked it—that was quite out of consideration—down he sat himself, and began to eat to his heart's great content. When he was quite satisfied, he thought, "What a pity it would be to leave such a fine Napkin in the wood!" so he packed it up as small as he could, and carried it away in his pocket.

After this, on he journeyed again, and towards evening, as his appetite returned, he spread out his Napkin, to cheat himself into the belief that supper was coming; no sooner was it spread, than he said aloud, "I should like nothing better than to see you spread with good cheer again." No sooner were the words spoken, than, lo! the Napkin was covered with as many savoury and tempting dishes as it would hold. "Capital, capital!" he exclaimed, not being able to repress his delight; "now you are dearer to me, by far, than silver or gold, for I perceive you are a Wishing-cloth." Delighted as he was, however, he was not yet satisfied, but would go further and seek his fortune.

The next evening, he came up with a Charcoal-burner, who was busy with his coals, and who was roasting some potatoes at his fire for his supper. "Good evening, my fine black fellow," said our hero; "how do you find yourself in your solitude?"

"One day is like another," replied he, "and every night potatoes. Would you like to have some? if so, come, sit down, be my guest."

"Many thanks," replied the Traveller, "but I will not deprive you of your meal; you did not reckon on having a guest; but, if you have no objection, you shall have an invitation to supper."

"I should like to know who will invite me?" asked the Charcoal-burner; "I do not see that you have got anything with you, and there is no one in the circuit of two hours' walk who could give you anything."

"And yet you shall have a meal, and a good one," returned the other, "better than you have ever seen."

Then he took out his Napkin, and spreading it on the ground, said, "Cloth, cover thyself!" and immediately meats, baked and boiled, as hot as if they were just out of the kitchen, were spread about it. The Charcoal-burner opened his eyes in amazement; but he did not stare long, for he soon began to eat away, cramming his black mouth as full as it would hold. When they had finished, the man said, smacking his lips with a relish, "Come, yours is something like a Cloth; it pleases me much, and would be very convenient for me here in the woods, where I have no one to cook. I should like to strike a bargain with you. There hangs a Soldier's Knapsack, which is certainly both old and shabby, but then it possesses a wonderful virtue; and as I have no more use for it, I will give it you in exchange for your Cloth."

"You must tell me first in what this wonderful virtue consists," said the Traveller.

"I will tell you," replied the other. "If you tap thrice with your fingers upon it, out will come a corporal and six men, armed from head to foot, who will do whatever you command them."

"In faith," cried our hero, "I do not think I can do better; suppose we agree to change." So he gave the man the Wishing-cloth, and he took the Knapsack from off the hook in the wall, and he buckled it upon his back, and strode away with it.

He had not gone very far before he thought he might as well try the virtue of his bargain; so he tapped upon it, and immediately the seven Warriors stepped before him, and the leader saluted him and asked his commands:—

"What does my lord and master desire?"

"March quickly back, and demand my Wishing-cloth again from the Charcoal-burner," said our hero.

The Soldiers quickly wheeled round to the left, and before very long they brought him what he desired, having taken it from the Charcoal-burner without as much as asking or thanking him for it.

This done, he told them he had no present need for their farther services, and travelled on again, hoping his luck might shine brighter even yet. At sunset he came to another Charcoal-burner, who was likewise getting his supper at the fire, and he asked, "Will

you sup with me? Potatoes and salt is all I have, and that without butter; but you are welcome, if you will sit down and eat with me."

"No," replied the Traveller, "this time you shall be my guest." And he unfolded his Cloth, which was at once spread with the most delicious viands. They ate and they drank together, and soon got very merry; and when their meal was done, the Charcoal-burner said, "Up above there lies an old worn-out Hat, which possesses the wonderful property, if one puts it on and presses it down upon his head, of causing, as it were, twelve field-pieces to go off one after the other, and shoot down all that comes in their way. Now, the Hat is of no use to me up there, and therefore I should like very much to exchange it for your Cloth."

"Oh!" replied the Traveller, "I have no objection to that;" and taking the Hat, he left the Wishing-cloth behind him; but he had not gone very far before he tapped again upon his Knapsack, and ordered his Soldiers to fetch it back again from his guest.

"Ah!" thought he to himself, "one thing happens so soon upon another, that it seems as if my luck would have no end." And his thoughts did not deceive him; for he had scarcely gone another day's journey when he met with a third Charcoal-burner, who invited him, as the others had, to a potatoe supper. However, he spread out his Wishing-cloth once again, and the feast so pleased the Charcoal-burner, that he offered him in exchange a Horn, which had properties better worth possessing than either the Knapsack or the Hat; for, when any one blew it, every wall and fortification fell down before its blast, and even whole towns and villages were overthrown. For this Horn he very gladly gave his Cloth, but he soon sent his Soldiers back for it; and now he had not only that, but also the Knapsack, the Hat, and the Horn.

"Now," said he, "I am a made man, and it is high time that I should return home, and see how my Brothers get on."

When he arrived at the old place, he found his Brothers had built a splendid palace with their gold and silver, and were living on the fat of the land.

He entered the house; but because he came in with a coat torn to rags, the shabby Hat upon his head, and the old Knapsack on his back, his Brothers would not own him. They mocked him, saying, "You pretend to be our Brother, indeed! why, he despised even gold and silver, and sought better luck for himself. A likely matter he should come dressed as a beggar! no, we look for him accompanied like a mighty king." And so they hunted him out of the house in quick time.

Our tired Traveller was in a great rage at such unbrotherly treatment, and in his anger he knocked so many times upon his Knapsack, that a hundred and fifty men stood before him in rank and file. He commanded them to surround his Brothers' house, and two of them to take hazel-sticks, and thrash them until they remembered who he was.

They set up a tremendous howling when they found themselves so assailed, and the people ran to the house to assist the two Brothers; but their efforts were useless before so many Soldiers.

By-and-bye the King himself heard of the noise, and

he ordered out a captain and troop to drive the disturber of the peace out of the city; but the man with his Knapsack soon gathered together a much greater company, who beat back the captain and his men, and sent them home with their noses bleeding. At this sight the King was very much enraged, saying, "A pretty vagabond fellow, this, to dare to attack the King's troops! he shall be driven away;" and the next morning he sent a larger troop against him, but they returned at night in a worse condition than the first. The Beggar, as they called him, very soon ranged more men in opposition; and, in order to do the work quicker, he pressed his Hat down upon his head a couple of times, and immediately the heavy guns began to play upon the people, and all the King's men soon took to flight. "Now," said our hero, "since they have driven me to do so much, I will never make peace until they have given me the King's daughter to wife, and he places me upon his throne to rule over his whole dominions." This vow which he had taken he caused to be communicated to the King, who said to his daughter, "'Must' is a very hard nut to crack; what is there left for me, I should like to know, but to do just as this man desires? If I wish for peace, and to keep the crown upon my head, I needs must yield."

So the wooing was got over, and the wedding was celebrated; but the Princess was terribly vexed that she had only got a common man for her husband, and that he wore not only a very bad Hat, but also carried about with him a shabby old Knapsack. As these teased her so, she determined to get rid of them; and day and night she was always plotting how she should manage it. Suddenly it struck her that his wonderful power lay in his Knapsack; so she flattered and caressed him, saying, "I wish you would put aside that dirty old Knapsack; it becomes you so badly that I am quite ashamed to see you with it."

"Dear one," he replied, "this Knapsack is my greatest treasure; so long as I possess it, I do not fear the greatest power on earth;" and then he told her all its wonderful properties and powers. When he had done speaking, the Princess fell on his neck, as if she would kiss him; but she craftily untied the Knapsack, and, loosening it from his shoulders, ran away with it. As soon as she was alone, she tapped upon it, and ordered the Warriors who appeared to bind fast her husband, and lead him out of the royal palace. They obeyed; and the worthless, false wife, caused other Soldiers to march behind, who were instructed to hunt the poor man out of the kingdom. His reign would have been short, had he not possessed the Hat, which he pressed down upon his head as soon as his hands were free; and immediately the cannons began to go off, and demolished all before them. The Princess at last was obliged to go and beg pardon of her husband. As he loved his wife, he was moved by her supplications and promises to behave better in future; and she for some time acted so lovingly and behaved so well, that he told her his secret, that although he had been treacherously deprived of his Knapsack, yet so long as he possessed the Hat, no one could overcome him. No sooner did she know this, than she waited

until he slept, and then stole away the Hat, and caused her husband to be thrown into a ditch. The Horn, however, was still left to him, and in a great passion he blew a strong blast upon it; in a minute down came tumbling the walls, forts, houses, and palaces, and the King and his daughter were buried in the ruins. Luckily, he had no more breath to blow with, for had he kept it up any longer, all the houses would have been overturned, and not one stone left upon another. After this feat no one dared to oppose him, and he set himself up as King over the whole country.

SWEET-TOOTH AND SPRAT-PRATTLE.

A GOOD Dame was at work in her cottage, getting her batch of bread for the week ready for the oven, while her husband was out in the wood cutting faggots, when she heard her husband's favourite little dog— a rare sharp terrier he was—barking furiously.

"What can Sweet-Tooth be so angry about?" said she. "Here, Sprat-Prattle!"—calling to her son, who was so named because he was so very small for his age, and so very talkative—"Here, Sprat-Prattle! go out and see what Sweet-Tooth is barking at."

Out ran little Sprat-Prattle, and came in again with, "The dog don't like the look of an Old Woman that is coming up the path to the door; and I don't wonder at it, for she looks like a great, big, ugly Witch, with her bag under her back, and her head under her arm."

"Don't stop to chatter, there's a dear boy," said his Mother, in some alarm; "but just jump under the kneading-trough, out of sight; and mind you keep quiet until I have got rid of her."

So he did, and in quick time, too, before the Old Hag could step over the threshold.

"Good day!" said she; and funny it was to hear her voice speaking from under her arm.

"Heaven bless you!" replied the good Dame, not to be outdone in politeness.

"Isn't your Sprat-Prattle at home?" asked the ugly Old Hag, as civil and as mealy-mouthed as you please.

"No, Ma'am; he has gone out with his father into the wood, to carry his bill-hook."

"Deary me—how unlucky!" remarked the Old Hag. "I had got such a pretty little peg-top I wanted to give him."

"Hip! hep! here I am!" said the voice of little Sprat-Prattle, from under the kneading-tub; and out he came, shaking the flour from his ears and eyes. "Where is the knife?"

"Oh! you clever little fellow," said the head under the Old Hag's shoulder; "but I am so bad with the rheumatism, and so very stiff in the back, that I can't stoop; just creep into this bag, and fetch it out for yourself."

Sprat-Prattle, eager after the promised peg-top with a silver nail at the top, crept into the bag; whereupon, the Old Hag threw it over her back, and trudged off.

It was of no use for the good Dame to endeavour to resist her, or stop her going out; for as soon as she moved to do so, there was a general revolt in the cottage kitchen. The Broom ran and put himself in her way; the Spit made a point viciously; the very Loaves she had just made with her own hands jumped off the dough-board, and began to hit her in the face and eyes.

In the general confusion, the Old Hag took her bag, and made the best of her way out of sight of the cottage.

Sprat-Prattle, as you may well suppose, did not at all relish his novel position, shut up in a bag, in the dark, on the shoulders of an ugly Old Hag that carried her head under her arm. He tried several times to get his knife (who ever knew a boy without a knife?) out of his breeches-pocket, but the Old Witch jogged along at such a rattling pace, that he could not get a chance. All he could do, was to kick and jump about, and make the bag as troublesome and heavy as possible to the Old Hag's shoulders.

At last, when they had travelled, oh! so many miles, the ugly Old Witch grew tired, and inquired of Jack, from under her arm, "How far is it to Snoozing?"

Jack had never heard of the place, but he answered, rather than say nothing, which she might have thought rude, "Just half a mile."

"Oh! then I can take a rest," said the Old Hag.

So she swung the bag off her shoulders, and laid it down by the wayside, and composed herself to sleep on a bank. Then Sprat-Prattle saw his opportunity; and he slipped out his knife, and cut a hole in the sack, and crept out; and after putting a root of a fir-tree into the bag, to fill his place, betook himself, as quietly and as quickly as possible, homewards.

When the Hag woke, she threw the bag over her shoulder without looking into it, and trudged to her hut; and, oh! what a rage she was in, when she found little Sprat-Prattle had escaped out of her clutches!

Next day, the good Dame, Sprat-Prattle's mother, was still making her batch of bread, when she heard little Sweet-Tooth barking again, very loudly and angrily.

"Go and see what is the matter with the dog," said she to Sprat-Prattle.

"Oh, Mother! only think," said the boy, running in, greatly terrified; "there is that ugly Old Witch again, with her head under her arm, and another great sack on her back."

"Get under the kneading-trough, and hide, quick!" cried the Mother.

"Good morning, Ma'am," said the Old Hag, entering the cottage with all the impudence imaginable; "I hope your little boy came safe home last night. Is he in just now?"

"Quite safe, I thank you, Ma'am," replied the good Dame, as civil as may be, for she was too frightened to say much—"Quite safe; but he is not at home now; he did not think you were coming."

"That he certainly did not," said Sprat-Prattle to himself.

"And so he has gone out to take his father's dinner to him in the wood."

"Deary me," said the Old Hag, as sweet and as mild as boiled honey. "I am so sorry; I had brought with me such a pretty little silver fruit-knife, which I intended to give him."

"Hip! hep! hop! here I am!" exclaimed little Sprat-Prattle, coming from under the kneading-trough.

"Ah! my clever child, I thought I should find you; but I have got the rheumatism so bad, I can't stoop; do just fetch the knife out of the bag yourself."

Then little Sprat-Prattle stooped down to dip the silver fruit-knife out of the lucky-bag, as he thought, but he soon lost his balance; so she toppled him over, swung the bag round on to her shoulder, and, with a nod from her head under her arm to the good Dame, who was too astounded to cry out or move, set off to her hut, as fast as her Witch's legs would carry her.

But it would appear she was not a very good walker, or else must have been short of breath, from the awkward position of her head under her arm; for she soon knocked up, and halted in the wood.

"How far is it to Snoozing, I wonder?" said she.

"A full mile and a half," said Sprat-Prattle.

Over came the sack, and the Old Hag went into the wood to have a sleep in the shade. Out Sprat-Prattle whips his knife, cuts a hole in the sack, and comes forth.

"Well done Snicker-snacker!" said he, as he closed his knife; "you shall help me eat some bread and cheese to-night. Now for home."

Then he put a great stone in the sack, to satisfy the Old Hag's shoulders that they had got just weight, and then he hastened to the cottage to comfort his poor Mother.

As for the Old Hag, as soon as she got home, she ordered her Daughter to light a large fire on the kitchen hearth, and put the biggest pot on, with some fine herbs; and when the pot came to the simmer, she first flung in a handful of salt, and then lifted up the sack to pop Sprat-Prattle into it to boil. But out rolled a great stone, and plumped into the scalding water, and splashed it into her eyes. Then she was so angry, that in her blind rage, she gave her lanky red-haired Daughter a hearty cuff on the side of the head, which made her husband, the Ogre of the Red Eye, so angry, that he kicked the pot over into the fire, scalded the Old Hag's favourite cat, and then went out to spend the evening "in more pleasant company," as he said.

This set the Old Witch in a horrible passion. She blamed all her misfortunes to little Sprat-Prattle's impudence; and swore he should never take her in again, however heavy he might try to make himself.

Next day, at the good Dame's cottage, all went just as it had gone on the two previous days. Sweet-Tooth, who was a capital house-dog, and did not at all like seeing Sprat-Prattle make such a fool of himself, barked louder than ever.

"Go out and see what is the matter with Sweet-Tooth to-day again," said the good Dame.

Out went little Sprat-Prattle, but he soon ran in again, crying out, in terror and surprise, "Mother! Mother! here she is again! that ugly Old Woman, with her head under her arm, and her sack on her back."

"Jump under the trough once more," said his Mother; "and do be quiet and hide yourself this time."

"A fine morning, Ma'am," said the Old Hag, as bold as brass, and looking as if she had as much business there as the King's Taxgatherer. "How is Sprat-Prattle? is the dear little fellow at home this morning?"

"You are very obliging in your inquiries," replied the good Dame; "but you are generally unfortunate. Poor little fellow! he came home tired last night; I am afraid you treat him too well, and give him too much broth."

Here the Old Hag winced, for she thought of her kettle-broth over the hearth-stone on the previous night, and her lanky, red-haired Daughter, and her husband the Ogre of the Red Eye; and how he had beaten her, when he came home from the "Lively Tinder Box," at half-past two that morning.

"He has only just had his breakfast, and gone down to his father in the wood, who told me to tell you how glad he should be to see you."

"Much obliged to him for his goodness," said the Hag (she knew the Old Woodman would have chopped her head off); "but I am quite sorry about Sprat-Prattle; I have brought the dear boy a new suit of clothes, a jacket with silver-bell buttons, and trowsers with pockets."

"Hip! hep! hop!" cried little Sprat-Prattle, ready to jump out of his skin, and leaping from under the kneading-trough. "Oh! do let me try them on at once!"

"Go and take them out of the sack yourself, my dear little chap," said the carneying Old Crone; but when Sprat-Prattle got to the bag's mouth, she bundled him in, neck and crop, and shaking her fist at the good Dame, rushed out of the cottage door and on to her hut.

There was no sleeping or loitering this time. She got to her house just at church time, for it happened to be Sunday, and the bells were already ringing, and her lanky, red-haired Daughter was just coming out, in her French satin hat and hoops, with her red-heeled boots, and yellow silk stockings showing from under her new sky-blue damask silk petticoat.

"Oh! you were off, were you? while I, your poor mother, was toiling, and moiling, and slaving for your dinner!—off in your silks and satins! No, young lady; just turn back again, and see to the boiling of this young gentleman in the sack. Kill him first, nicely, skin him, and boil him slowly till I come back. I must go to church, and invite a few friends to the feast. Where's your father?"

"Oh, he is in such a dreadful temper, Mother! He has gone down to the 'Lively Tinder Box,' to look after some money he lost there last night."

"Just like him. Give me my hat and cloak."

So the Old Witch walked off, and left Sprat-Prattle alone with her lanky Daughter, who stood looking at him with her finger in her mouth, quite silly. The fact was, she knew she had to kill him, and she wanted to do so, but she did not know how. That was an awkward situation for a young lady, certainly; but you can easily fancy for yourself, how very probable it is that your own mother and father would have to dine off mint-sauce on Easter Sunday, if you were left at home, all alone, to kill any lamb, before its fore-quarter could be put down to roast.

That was precisely the position of the lanky, red-haired Daughter of the ugly Old Hag and the Ogre of the Red Eyes; and there she stood, in her red-heeled boots and yellow silk stockings, her sky-blue damask silk petticoat, and French white satin hat with a green cock's feather, looking at little Sprat-Prattle, and not knowing how to begin to kill him.

"Why don't you do it?" said Sprat-Prattle, in an impudent tone, and looking up at the red-haired girl with a saucy leer, for he began to see his way out of the scrape. It does not matter how little a man is, he is more than a match for the biggest of girls, any-how.

"I don't know how," said the lanky fair one, in a half-whimpering tone.

"Oh, then," said Jack, as polite as an Irish pedlar, "permit me, my dear young lady, to show you how to do it. Just lay your lanky head, in that charming white French satin hat and green cock's feather, with those beautiful carrots—beg pardon, red tresses—on the block, and you'll soon see!"

Quite flustered at such a many fine words from such a polite personage as little Sprat-Prattle, the poor silly lanky young lady laid down her red hair, and white satin hat, with her head in it, on the chopping-block; and Sprat-Prattle took up the axe, and chopped it off, cock's feather and all, just as if it had been a chicken's.

He folded up the body, neck and heels, and squeezed it nicely into the pot, and then set it on, to boil gently; but the head he laid down on the pillow, and pulled the bed-clothes up to it. Then, having put the soup-plates, and spoons, and table-cloth all in order on the table, ready for dinner, he climbed up into the rafters on the roof, taking the precaution to carry up with him the log of wood and the great stone that he had put in the Witch's bag on the two previous days.

When the Ogre of the Red Eyes and his wife, the ugly Old Hag, came back from church, they were highly pleased at seeing the dinner-table so nicely laid out, and the pot on the fire, and all smelling so nice. When they saw the head on the pillow, they thought their dear Daughter, having done her work, and made all ready for their return, was resting herself with a snooze, so they determined not to wake her.

While the Old Hag went into her bed-room, to take off her bonnet and change her gown, her husband, the Ogre with the Red Eye, began to feel lickerish at the toothsome smell of the soup in the kettle, and he thought he would have a taste; so he dipped the soup-ladle, and brought out a half-basinful of the rich broth. Smacking his lips as he tasted the savoury relish, he said—

> "Sprat-Prattle broth is dainty food;
> It is rich and fat, and does one good."

"Glad you like it," said Sprat-Prattle from his nest among the rafters above—

> "It's Daughter broth that's such dainty food,
> And her carrots that make it so rich and good."

But the Ogre with the Red Eye had just stooped his head into the pot for another lick, so he did not hear what Sprat-Prattle said.

The Old Hag now came in, and saw her husband helping himself so greedily, and she gave him a cuff on the head that knocked his face into the pot and scalded him; then she took out a ladleful for herself to taste, and said—

> "Sprat-Prattle broth is dainty food;
> It's very nice, and it does one good."

Whereupon, Sprat-Prattle laughed loudly, and cried out—

> "It's your Daughter broth that's such dainty food;
> Your Daughter meat will be twice as good."

"What's that you say, Miss?" said the Old Hag, running up to her Daughter's head, and pulling its nose; whereupon, the head rolled off the pillow, and they saw directly how their child had been so basely murdered! and they both screamed out, and ran forth raging to avenge her death; but just as they came outside the door, Sprat-Prattle rolled down on them the log of wood and the great stone, which fell on their heads, and broke them all to pieces. So they died; and then he came down, and collected all the gold and silver plate in the house, not forgetting the soup-ladle; and went home to his Mother's cottage, where he became a rich man, and lived happily all his life afterwards.

TOO CLEVER BY HALF.

It is of the utmost importance that a man who professes to be a Surgeon should understand his profession perfectly, or sad indeed might be the consequences of ignorance displayed by the operator. Now, there once lived three Army Surgeons; each one thought himself the most clever in the world, and so they determined to travel, in order that the world might be benefited by their skill and ability; and having travelled some distance they arrived at an inn, where they thought they would pass the night.

The Landlord was very curious to learn who they were, and all about them, and asked a great many more questions than landlords generally do upon a customer's arrival; and he particularly wished to know where they came from, and where they were going; and one of them said, "They were searching in the hope of finding employment for their talents."

"What are you so clever in," said the Landlord, "that you should travel so far a-field to display your talents?"

The first said, "He could cut off a hand over night, and put it on again in the morning, without difficulty."

The second said, "He could take out any one's eyes, and put them back the next day, without injury to them." And the third said, "He could remove a heart from the body, and replace it all right the next morning."

"If you do these things well," said the Landlord, "you deserve patronage, and must be well taught; but I should like to see you, first of all, practise your skill upon your own persons."

"All right," said they.

So the first cut off his hand, the second took out his eyes, and the third cut out his heart, just as they had said; then they asked for a plate, and having put all these upon it, they handed it to the Landlord, who delivered it to a Servant, with strict orders that it might be put safely by in a cupboard until the morning.

Now, they had a salve which healed whatever it touched, and they always carried it about with them.

The Servant to whom the plate was given, unfortunately for the Surgeons, had a Sweetheart on the sly, who was a soldier; and he coming in very hungry, coaxed her to give him something to eat. As soon as the Landlord had gone to bed, the Maid stole to the cupboard to fetch something to eat, and, like a bad and careless servant as she was, she left the cupboard door open. While she sat thus, apprehending no misfortune, but only intent upon making merry, the sly old cat came slipping in stealthily, and seeing the people too busy to watch her, she jumped into the cupboard, and seizing upon the hand, heart, and eyes of the three Army Surgeons, she ran away with them. As soon as the Sweetheart had eaten as much as he would, the Girl hastened to put the rest away in the cupboard, and then found to her dismay that the contents of the plate which her Master had given into her care were all gone. She was terribly frightened, and exclaimed, "Ah, me! whatever will become of me? for the heart is gone, and the hand is gone, and the eyes have gone too! What can I say? How shall I manage in the morning?"

"Be quiet, and cease that terrible noise, or you will be heard. Listen to me, and I will tell you how you can get over this difficulty. On the gallows outside hangs a thief, whose hand I can cut off. Which was it?"

"The right," said she; and she handed him a sharp knife from the dresser drawer, with which he went and cut off the hand of the thief, and brought it in. Then he caught the old cat, and took out her eyes; but what was to be done for the heart now became a question.

"I think you killed a pig to-day," said the Soldier, "where is its carcase?"

"Oh," replied the Servant, "that's in the cellar."

"Go quickly, then, and fetch the heart from it; that is the very thing we want."

The Servant did so, and they put them all upon a plate together; and having put them safely in the cupboard, the Soldier went on his road, and the Servant went to bed.

The next morning, no sooner were the three Army Surgeons up, than they asked for the hand, the heart, and the eyes. She brought the plate from the cupboard, and the first man spread the hand with salve, and immediately it joined on as if it had always grown there; the second took up the cat's eyes and placed them in his head; while the third put the pig's heart where his own came from. The Landlord meanwhile stood by, wondering at their cleverness and learning, saying he would never have believed them, if he had not seen what they did. They then asked for their bill, which, when it was given, they immediately paid and went away, much to the comfort of the Servant-girl.

They had not travelled very far, before the one with a pig's heart began to hunt and snuff about after the manner of swine. The others thought he was running mad, and tried to hold him back by his coat, but he broke violently from them, and would persist in hunting about in the neighbourhood. The second Surgeon all this while kept wiping and rubbing his eyes, and could not imagine what was amiss. "What have I done?" said he to his comrades; "these are not my eyes, I am sure; you must lead me, or I shall fall—I cannot see."

In this way they managed to travel on till evening, when they came to another inn. They stepped into the parlour, and there sat a very rich man, counting out his great hoard of riches. The Surgeon with the thief's hand went up and peeped and pried about him, and no sooner did the old gentleman turn his back a little, than the Surgeon pounced upon the money, and grasped a whole handful.

"For shame, comrade," said his companions; "who ever heard of a gentleman turning thief? You must not steal. What are you doing?"

"Oh, I cannot help myself," answered he; "my hand is drawn towards it, and I must take it whether I will or not!"

Soon after, they all went to bed, and it was so dark that one could not see another. All at once, the Surgeon with the cat's eyes woke up, and disturbing the others, cried out, "See, see how the white mice are running about the room!" The other two then looked about, but could see nothing. "It is very evident now," said they, "that we have been deceived by the Landlord, and have not got our own; we must go back to him again."

The following morning they rode back to the first inn, and demanded, in no measured terms, their own things again; for that one had got a thief's hand, the second a pig's heart, and the third a cat's eyes, and of course they were neither of use or value to them.

Then the Landlord called to the Servant-maid, but she had slipped out at the back door, and so made her escape, as soon as she saw the three Army Surgeons coming in at the front door; and she never returned again.

The three now threatened to set fire to the house if the Landlord did not give them a large sum of money to compensate them for their loss.

So the poor man was obliged to give them all he could possibly scrape together, with which they went away. But although each of them had money enough to last him his lifetime, each would gladly have relinquished it for his human eyes, hand, or heart, with which nature had endowed him.

NOURJAHAD.
AN EASTERN TALE.

SCHEMZEDDIN was in his twenty-second year when he ascended the throne of Persia. His wisdom and extraordinary endowments rendered him the delight of his people, and filled them with expectations of a happy and glorious reign.

Of all the persons who surrounded the monarch's throne, none appeared to possess the Sultan's favour and confidence like Nourjahad, the son of Namarand. Nourjahad was about the same age with Schemzeddin, and had been bred up with him from his infancy. To a very engaging countenance and person, Nourjahad added a liveliness of temper, and an agreeable manner of address, that won the affections of every one who approached him. The Sultan loved him affectionately, and the people expected to see him elevated to the highest pinnacle of honour.

Schemzeddin was indeed desirous of promoting his favourite; but, notwithstanding his attachment to him, the monarch would not appoint Nourjahad to the rank of minister of state, till he had consulted some old lords about the court, who had been the constant friends and able counsellors of the late Sultan his father. Accordingly, having called them into his closet one morning, he proposed the matter to them, and desired their opinion; but he perceived that these grave and prudent men disapproved the choice he had made of Nourjahad, to fill an office so important in its management to the welfare of the state. They accused him of avarice, and a boundless love of pleasure; and the Sultan dismissed them with evident marks of displeasure; but he said to himself:—

"It is the interest of Nourjahad to conceal his faults from me, and my attachment may blind me to his defects. I will probe Nourjahad's soul. From himself I will judge of himself, and if he passes through the trial unsullied, he shall be second only to myself in the empire."

Shortly after, the Sultan invited Nourjahad to walk with him one evening by moonlight, in the garden of the seraglio. Schemzeddin leaned on the shoulder of his favourite, as they rambled from one delicious scene to another, rendered still more enchanting by the silence of the night, the mild lustre of the moon, and the fragrance which arose from a thousand odoriferous shrubs. "Tell me, Nourjahad," said the Sultan, carelessly throwing himself upon a bank of violets, and inviting his favourite to sit near, "tell me truly what would satisfy thy wishes, if thou wert certain of possessing all thou couldst desire?"

Nourjahad remained some time silent, till the Sultan, with an affected smile of levity, repeated the question.

"My wishes," answered the favourite, "are boundless. I should desire to be possessed of inexhaustible riches, and I should also desire to have my life prolonged to eternity."

"Wouldst thou, then," said Schemzeddin, "forego thy hopes of Paradise?"

"I would," answered the favourite, "make a paradise of this earthly globe, by the variety of my pleasures, and take my chance for the other afterwards."

255

"Begone !" said the Sultan, starting from his seat, "thou art no longer worthy of my love. I thought to have promoted thee to the highest honours, but such a sordid wretch does not deserve to live. Ambition, though a vice, is the vice of great minds; but avarice, and an insatiable thirst for pleasure, degrades a man below the brute."

Thus saying, he was about to depart, but Nourjahad falling on his knees, and holding the Sultan's robe, said :—"Let not my lord's indignation be kindled against his slave, for a few light words which fell from him only in sport. I swear to thee, my Prince, by our holy prophet Mahomet, that my real desire for wealth extends no farther than to be enabled to procure the sober enjoyments of life; and as for length of years, let not mine be prolonged a day beyond that in which I can be serviceable to my sovereign and my country."

"It is not," replied the Sultan mildly, "for mortal eyes to penetrate into the secret recesses of thy heart. Thou hast called our great Prophet to witness thy oath; remember, God thou canst not deceive, though me thou mayest."

Schemzeddin then left him, without waiting his reply, and Nourjahad retired to his own house, which joined to the Sultan's palace.

He passed the rest of the night in traversing his chamber, regretting his imprudence, and tormenting himself with apprehensions of his disgrace. The next day he was unable to quit his apartment, and at night, wearied with anxieties, he threw himself on his couch, and fell into a deep sleep, from which he was roused by a voice that said—"Nourjahad! Nourjahad! awake, and possess the secret wishes of thy soul."

He started from his couch, and beheld a Maiden of more than mortal beauty, whose shining hair was encircled with a wreath of flowers, that shed around her the most fragrant perfumes.

"Fear not !" said the Maiden, "I am thy guardian Genius. I have power to grant thy wishes, be they what they may. Wouldst thou be restored to the favour and confidence of the Sultan, thy master ? or wouldst thou rather see the wish accomplished, which thou breathed last night to Schemzeddin in the gardens of the royal palace ?"

Nourjahad bowed his head, and answered: "Disguise to thee, O daughter of Paradise, were vain and fruitless. If I dissembled to Schemzeddin, it was to reinstate myself in his good opinion, by whose favour alone I have been able to exist; but my heart pants to possess that which I declared to the Sultan, and that alone."

"Rash mortal !" replied the Maiden, "reflect once more, before you receive the fatal boon; for once granted, you will wish in vain to have it recalled."

"What can I have to fear," demanded Nourjahad, "when I am possessed of endless riches and immortality ?"

"Your own passions," replied the Maiden.

"I will submit to all the evils they may inflict," said he, "give me but the means of gratifying them, in their full extent."

"Take thy wish !" cried the Genius, with a look of

256

disdain and discontent. "The contents of this phial bestows immortality upon thee, and to-morrow's sun beholds thee richer than all the kings of the east."

Nourjahad eagerly stretched his hand to receive a vessel of gold, enriched with precious stones. "Hold !" cried the Maiden, "there is one condition annexed to this dangerous gift. You will live to eternity, but you will be subject to fits of deep sleep, which will last for months, for years, nay, perhaps, for a whole century."

"Horrible !" cried Nourjahad.

"It is worth considering," said the Genius; "decide not too hastily; for if thou pervertest the power thou wilt possess, and inclinest thy heart to vice, thou wilt be punished with this suspension of thy faculties, which will last in proportion to the error thou hast committed."

"I accept the condition," cried Nourjahad, "for though I mean to enjoy all the pleasures of life, I will never commit any crimes; and after all, what is twenty, thirty, or even fifty years of sleep, for a man who is to live to all eternity ?"

"Here then," said the Genius, "swallow this liquid, and possess thy wish !"

Nourjahad applied the vessel to his lips, and drank a liquid so potent in its effect, that he fell back in a temporary trance, and when he again opened his eyes, the apparition had vanished, and his chamber was in total darkness.

He would have considered all that had passed as a dream, had he not still held the empty golden vessel in his hand, which he now placed under his pillow, and, filled with delightful expectations, he again composed himself to sleep.

The sun was in its meridian when he awoke the next day; but how great was his surprise, how high his transport, to see that his chamber was filled with large urns, containing gold and silver coin, diamonds, and all kinds of precious stones; on one of them was placed a scroll of paper, containing these words: "Thy days are without number, thy riches inexhaustible; thy prudence be thy guard! In thy garden is a subterranean cavern, where thou mayest conceal thy treasure. I have marked the spot. Farewell!"

Nourjahad having examined with increasing delight his treasures, hastened to the garden. In a remote corner, near the ruins of an ancient temple, he perceived a key of polished steel, hanging to a scarf of white taffety, and suspended at the branch of a tree. He was not long before he discovered a door behind the ruin, and opening it with the key, he descended by a few steps into a spacious cavern.

Nourjahad, glad to have so convenient a place in which to deposit his treasure, returned to the house, and ordered that no visitors should be admitted to him. This one day he resolved to pass in laying down plans of various pleasures to be enjoyed for ages to come.

Before the visit of the Genius, Nourjahad imagined, that if he had these boundless riches, he should employ them to notable and generous purposes; but he had deceived himself. There exists a wide difference between the fancied and actual possession of wealth, for Nourjahad, now absorbed in selfishness, thought only of the indulgence of his own appetites.

THE FAIR GENIUS GIVES NOURJAHAD THE GIFT OF POWER.

"My temper," said he, as he lay stretched at his ease upon a sofa, "does not incline me to take much trouble. I shall not aspire to high employments about the court, but I will have the finest palaces and gardens, the most splendid equipages, the most beautiful slaves in my seraglio, and the temperance of the Sultan Scheinzeddin shall be no pattern for me. Every corner of the earth shall be searched for dainties to supply my table, and bands of the choicest musicians shall entertain me while I enjoy my sumptuous banquets. Then no fear of surfeits—I will eat and drink to excess, and bid defiance to death."

Here Nourjahad started, for he remembered the Genius had not promised to secure him against the attacks of pain and sickness.

"Perhaps," said he, after a pause, "that advantage may be included. Besides, a little temporary pain now and then will be nothing; I shall the more enjoy my returning health. But I recollect that Schemzeddin used to talk of wisdom, and intellectual pleasures, as being the greatest enjoyment. Well, I can purchase those too; I will have half a score wise and learned men always at my command to entertain me with their conversation; and when I am weary of living in this country, I will make a tour of the earth, and see every curiosity the habitable world contains."

For three whole days Nourjahad was taken up with considering what scheme of pleasure he should begin with; and having entirely forgot to pay his court to Schemzeddin, the monarch, on the fourth day, was so offended at his absence, that he sent one of his officers to forbid him his presence for ever. "Tell him, however," said the Sultan, "that in remembrance of my former favour, I will allow him one thousand crowns a year for his support, and grant him the house he now lives in."

Nourjahad received this message with great indifference; not daring, however, to show any mark of disrespect, he answered, "Tell my Lord the Sultan, that I would not have been thus long without throwing myself at his feet, but I was hastily sent for to visit a dying friend at some leagues' distance, who has made me his heir. The thousand crowns, therefore, my royal master will be pleased to bestow on some one who wants them more than I do; but the house I will thankfully accept, and it will daily remind me, that Schemzeddin does not utterly detest his slave."

Nourjahad gave this turn to his acceptance of the house, which it would have been very inconvenient to have retired from, as he had already deposited his treasures in the subterraneous cavern of the garden. Thus he had already, in two instances, departed from the truth, in consequence of his ill-judged indulgence of unreasonable wishes.

He now bent his thoughts wholly on pleasure. He employed one Hasem, the principal of his domestics, to regulate his household, and furnish him with every gratification of costly furniture, magnificent habits, and a princely retinue. His slaves were all perfectly beautiful, and his table was daily furnished with the most expensive and rarest products of every country. A few men of science and learning were invited to his house, for the instruction and entertainment of his leisure hours; but leisure hours he had none, for he was either gratifying his appetites, or surfeited with excess.

Among the beauties of his seraglio he had selected a young maid, so perfect in loveliness, and so highly accomplished, that he gave her his entire affections, and made her his bride. By Mandana he was equally beloved; and longing to unbosom himself to some one on whose fidelity he could rely, he disclosed to her the marvellous story of his destiny. His mind thus relieved of its secret, he had not one anxious thought behind, and plunged at once into a sea of luxurious enjoyments. He forgot his duty towards God, and neglected all the laws of the prophet Mahomet. The cries of distress, or the sufferings of poverty, no longer melted his heart. Becoming daily more sensual and avaricious, his boundless wealth seemed scarcely sufficient to gratify his wishes. He soon grew idle and effeminate, and the pride he took in displaying the pomp of his retinue to the wondering eyes of the

people, was the only motive that incited him to action.

He thus continued to wallow in voluptuousness for three months uninterruptedly, when one day, as he was preparing to set out for a beautiful villa he had purchased for a rural retirement, the officer who had forbade his appearance at court arrived from the Sultan. "I am sorry, my lord," said he, "to be a second time a messenger of ill tidings; but the Sultan, hearing of the extraordinary splendour and magnificence in which you live, would needs know whence you derive your wealth, and has commanded me to conduct you to his presence."

Nourjahad was exceedingly startled at this unexpected summons, but he dared not dispute the Sultan's orders; and he followed the officer to the palace of Schemzeddin. He entered trembling, and prostrated himself at the foot of the throne.

"Whence is it, Nourjahad," said Schemzeddin, "that I am compelled, by the murmurs of my people, to inquire into the source of the extraordinary wealth that thou hast displayed? Who was the friend that bequeathed thy riches to thee, and what is their amount?"

Nourjahad, terrified at the dangers that threatened him, fell at the feet of the Sultan, and related the visit of the Genius, and its miraculous consequences. But the Sultan sternly commanded him from his presence, and likewise ordered that he should be conducted back to his own house, from whence he was not to stir, without permission from the Sultan, on pain of death.

Nourjahad, filled with grief and vexation, was led like a prisoner back to his own palace, and had the mortification to find the gates of his dwelling surrounded by the Sultan's guards.

He retired to his closet, repenting that he had made so imprudent a choice. "If," said he, "I had asked the Genius to restore me to Schemzeddin's favour, he would have advanced me to the highest offices of the state; I should have enjoyed my liberty, and have been respected, but now I am only envied and hated; and of what use is my wealth, since I am confined to one house? Unfortunate Nourjahad! where are all thy schemes of felicity?"

In two or three days he was more reconciled to his lot, and ordered a sumptuous banquet to be prepared; his musicians were commanded to exercise their utmost art to soothe his mind with all the enchanting powers of harmony; his apartments were illuminated with thousands of torches, composed of fragrant spices, and shedding delightful odours, and his slaves decked in the most costly jewels; himself attired in robes, such as the kings of Persia used to wear, was seated under a canopy of silver tissue. With all these splendid preparations, Nourjahad sat down to his banquet unsatisfied and dispirited, but resolved to elevate himself in some way; he forgot the laws of the religion he professed, which enjoin sobriety, for the historian who relates his life, affirms that Nourjahad that night, for the first time in his life, got drunk.

In this state he was carried insensible to bed; and when he next awoke from a slumber, he missed his beloved Mandana, and called aloud for his slaves, but no one answered. Being very passionate, he jumped out of bed, and ran into the antechamber, yet found none of his slaves in waiting. Enraged at this, he was about to descend the stairs, when a female slave appeared, who no sooner perceived him, than she gave a shriek, and was going to run away; but Nourjahad, seizing her roughly by the arm, commanded her to go and tell Mandana that he desired to see her.

"Alas! my Lord," said the slave, "I wish she were in a condition to come to you."

"What do you mean?" cried he; "I hope she is not sick; I am sure she went to bed in perfect health last night."

"Last night, my Lord! alas, alas!"

"Wretch!" exclaimed Nourjahad; "what do you mean?"

"My Lord, Mandana has been dead more than three years."

"Infamous creature! I'll teach you to trifle thus with your master;" and he shook her so violently, that her screams brought several other domestics, and, among the rest, Hasem, to her rescue.

"My Lord," said Hasem, "pardon your slave, and suffer us to rejoice in your recovery, when we had despaired of your ever unclosing your eyes, having slept four years and twenty days!"

At this instant, Nourjahad, with some confusion, recollected the condition the Genius had affixed to his gift. He ordered every one but Hasem to withdraw; and when they were alone, he said, "Tell me, then, Hasem, is Mandana really dead?"

"She is, my Lord; and when she was dying she called me to her, and ordered me to take charge of the household, assuring me that you would one day revive again. Here, my Lord, are the keys of the coffers she delivered to me, and I have endeavoured to preserve order and decorum in the management of your affairs; and your condition has been kept a profound secret from every one but your own family."

Nourjahad shed torrents of tears to the memory of Mandana, and for a long time he felt disgusted with everything around him; but as time passed away, his grief diminished, and he began to feel some inclination to return to his former excesses. He had the prudence to relate to Hasem the mystery of his destiny, to prevent the likelihood of being buried alive, should another deep sleep fall upon him.

Having taken this precaution, he selected from his seraglio a beauty, named Cadiga, and married her. And now he once more delivered himself up to intemperance of every kind. He forgot that there were wants and distresses among his fellow-creatures. He lived only for himself, and his heart became as hard as the coffers which held his misapplied treasures. The poets and sages whom he entertained in his house began to grow irksome to him; and at length, thinking their company tedious, he turned them out of his palace.

One day, the most extravagant project came into his head that ever filled the imagination of man; because his gardens were very beautiful, he fancied they must resemble the gardens of Paradise, and he ordered the women of the seraglio to personate the *Houries*, those angelic beings who are said to be the companions of true believers in the Mahometan Paradise. He called himself the prophet Mahomet, and gave orders to Hasem to prepare for the celestial masquerade. Neither art nor expense were spared on this extraordinary occasion. The fountains were ordered to run with milk and wine, instead of water; and fruits, blossoms, and flowers were gathered together to embellish this terrestrial paradise.

On the day the festivities were to commence, the weather being extremely hot, Nourjahad, who had been viewing the preparations with childish impatience, laid down on a couch to take a short repose, leaving orders to be awakened before sunset.

Nourjahad, however, opened his eyes without any one's having disturbed his slumbers; and finding the day already closed, he sprang up in a violent passion, and stamping on the floor, ordered the slave who appeared, to bid his women, one and all, to hasten into his apartment.

While he was resolving to punish the neglect with the greatest severity, they appeared, throwing up their veils as they entered his apartment. But, O heavens! what was Nourjahad's anger and astonishment, when, instead of the beautiful Houries he expected to see, he beheld only a train of withered and deformed old women!

Surprise and indignation deprived him of the power of speech, till the foremost stepped forward and offered to embrace him. He pushed her from him, crying, "Avaunt; fiend! where are my slaves? where is Hasem? Where are the women of my seraglio?"

"Alas, my Lord! have you entirely forgot me—forgot your beloved Cadiga?"

"Thou Cadiga? detested wretch, thou liest! This very day my Cadiga was as beautiful as an angel; and thou resemblest nothing but a fury."

"Alas! my Lord, you have not seen your Cadiga these forty years and eleven months, till this moment."

"What!" cried Nourjahad, "have I slept so long as forty years and eleven months?"

"Yes, my Lord; and we, your faithful wives, have, in the meantime, undergone the natural transformation from youth to age."

"By the temple of Mecca!" exclaimed Nourjahad, "this Genius of mine is no better than an evil spirit, or he could not take such delight in persecuting me."

"Ah, my Lord!" cried Cadiga, "I am not ignorant of the strange fate by which your life is governed; Hasem, your faithful Hasem, communicated to me with his dying breath——"

"Is Hasem dead?"

"Yes, my Lord; he died some months since, bequeathing to me your secret, and the care of your person and household."

Nourjahad now ordering them all to withdraw, threw himself again on his couch. "I see," said he, "the folly of my expectations. Mandana and Hasem are dead, and Cadiga is grown old and ugly, and already totters on the brink of the grave. I lose all whom I love, and my immortality does not secure me from affliction, nor can I purchase happiness with all my

259

wealth. Fool that I was to desire a step beyond the bounds of prudence and moderation. A friend shall no sooner become endeared to me, than death will deprive me of him; and if I marry again, how many bright eyes am I doomed to see for ever closed. Ah! it is a comfortless life that I have chosen. I find, too late, that my boundless riches cannot purchase happiness."

Nourjahad now grew peevish, morose, and tyrannical. Cruelty took possession of his breast; he abused his women, beat his slaves, and seemed to enjoy no satisfaction but that of tormenting others. Cadiga ventured to expostulate with him.

"To whom am I accountable," said he, "for my actions?"

"To God and our Prophet."

"Thou liest," he replied; "as I am exempt from death, I can never be brought to judgment."

"But hast thou no regard for the laws of society, nor pity for the sufferings of thy fellow-creatures?"

"Foolish woman! dost thou then talk to me of laws, who think myself bound by none?"

"Thou art a monster, and not fit to live!" said the undaunted Cadiga.

"Go tell thy Prophet so!" exclaimed Nourjahad, plucking a poniard from his side, and plunging it into her bosom. She fell at his feet, weltering in her blood; and he left the chamber, without showing the least concern for the deed he had committed.

That night he went to rest as usual, and when he awoke again, he beheld a man sitting near the foot of his couch, weeping. "What is the matter?" asked Nourjahad.

"Schemzeddin is dead, my Lord—the good Sultan is no more!"

"I am glad of it," cried Nourjahad; "I shall now have my liberty. Who is next to reign in Ormuz?"

"Doubtless, my Lord, the Prince Schemerzad, the eldest son of Schemzeddin."

"Slave! Schemzeddin had no son."

"Pardon me, my Lord; the Prince was born the very hour Cadiga died by your hand; and he is esteemed the wisest and most accomplished Prince of his age."

"Thou art very insolent, methinks, to mention Cadiga before me; and a Sultan of four-and-twenty hours old must needs be very wise and accomplished!"

"Nay, my Lord," replied the man; "the Prince this very day is twenty years old."

Nourjahad, on hearing this, looked in the face of the man, and perceived him to be a stranger. "Twenty years old!" said he, starting up, "it should seem, then, that I have slept twenty years; and who art thou, for I do not remember ever to have seen thy face before? and how camest thou hither?"

"My name," answered the stranger, "is Cozro. I am the brother of Cadiga, who sent for me when she was dying, and made me swear by our holy Prophet to her, that I would watch and attend on you carefully. I did not know till afterwards that you had murdered my sister; and when I did learn it, I could scarce refrain from inflicting vengeance on thee?"

"And pray what restrained thee?"

260

"Reverence for my oath, and the fear of offending the Almighty."

Nourjahad was struck with awe at this answer; but he continued silent, while Cozro proceeded to inform him that his slaves, even those he had most trusted, had plundered his coffers and absconded.

"Alas!" cried Nourjahad, "my treacherous joys have deceived me. I am bereft of hope; I am like a savage beast in the desert, whose paths are shunned by all mankind."

"Nourjahad," said Cozro, "I have heard thy story from Cadiga; and know, O mistaken man! that thy misfortunes are the consequences of thy crimes. Thou hast abused the power vested in thy hands; and by the immutable laws of Heaven, either in this world or the next, vice will receive its punishment, and virtue its reward."

"Alas!" replied Nourjahad, "thou hast awakened in me a remorse, of which I was never sensible before. I look back with shame and horror on my past life. What shall I do, O Cozro, to expiate my offences?"

"If thy repentance is sincere," replied Cozro, "the means are amply in thy power. Thy riches will enable thee to diffuse blessings among mankind."

"It shall be so!" exclaimed Nourjahad, with rapture. "My treasures shall be open to thee, thou good old man. Inquire out every family in Ormuz, whom calamity hath overtaken, and restore them to prosperity. Seek the helpless and the innocent, and by a timely supply of their wants, secure them against the attacks of poverty, or temptations of vice. Find out merit wherever it lies concealed, clogged by adversity, or obscured by malice; lift it up from the dust, and let it shine conspicuous to the world."

"Blessed be the purpose of thy heart!" said Cozro, "and prosperous be the days of thy life!"

Nourjahad now sent Cozro forth on his benevolent errand, and only waited to have himself released from the prohibition Schemzeddin had laid upon him, to join Cozro in his mission. No notice had yet been taken of a petition he had sent to the new Sultan, for the restoration of his liberty; but Nourjahad bore that with patience, and spent his days in his closet, laying plans for the benefit of his fellow-creatures. He was now temperate in all his appetites, and returned to the strict exercise of all the sacred duties of his religion.

One day, he was surprised to find that Cozro did not return at his usual time; but was still more amazed to see an officer, attended by a guard, enter his apartment, and accuse him of employing an agent to distribute large sums of money in the city, to bring about a revolt among the people. It was in vain that Nourjahad attempted to refute the charge. He was called a traitor, was dragged from his house, and lodged in one of the dungeons of the state prison.

At midnight, the gaoler entered with some bread and water; and from him he learned that his accomplice, as they called Cozro, refusing to confess the particulars of the treason in which he was concerned, was already condemned to death, and that the bell now tolling was the signal for his execution.

Nourjahad prostrated himself on the ground. "Alas!" cried he, "am I then to cause the death of the most virtuous man I know? Ah! why was I not content with the common lot of mortals? O holy Prophet!" he exclaimed, "take back the gift which I, in the ignorance and presumption of my heart, so vainly desired; and which, too late, I find a punishment instead of a blessing."

He had scarce pronounced these words, when the door of his dungeon flew open, and his guardian Genius, all radiant with light, stood before him. "Nourjahad," she said, "thy prayers are heard; yet examine thy heart once more. Art thou willing to become poor again, and subject to death, the common lot of mortals?"

"Most willingly," replied Nourjahad.

"Then joyfully do I resume the dangerous gift I bestowed on thy erring wishes. Prostrate thyself with thy face to the earth, and await what shall befall thee."

The door of the dungeon then closed, and Nourjahad continued in prayer and meditation, till the dawn of the following morning, when the keeper of the prison appeared, to lead him to the presence of the Sultan.

He was now carried out of the dungeon, and placed in an open carriage, between two officers, with drawn sabres in their hands. The chariot was surrounded by soldiers, and in this manner he was conducted to the hall of audience, where the Sultan was seated on his throne, with his emirs, his nobles, and all the great officers of his court standing round him.

Nourjahad stood before the Sultan with his eyes bent upon the ground; his deportment was modest and respectful, but, supported by conscious innocence, he discovered no symptoms of fear.

Schemerzad made a sign for every one to withdraw, except the Grand Vizier, who stood on the steps of the throne.

"Art thou prepared," demanded the Sultan, "to make a full confession of thy treasonable designs? Say, audacious wretch! to what end was thy profusion employed?"

"To obtain a blessing from Heaven," answered Nourjahad; "and, by relieving the wants and afflictions of others, to make some atonement for my own intemperate abuse of wealth, which ought to have been employed to better purposes."

"Wouldst thou persuade me that charity was thy only motive?"

"It was, illustrious Sultan. I have spoken the truth; and to convince your Majesty that I never harboured any treasonable design against your person or government, I am ready at this moment to deliver into your hands that immense treasure, which, had I been vile enough so to have employed it, would have bought the fidelity of half your subjects."

"Do, then," said the Sultan, "as thou hast spoken, and I will believe thee."

"If your Majesty will permit any one to go with me to my house, I will deliver into his hands all my wealth; and if my Lord permits me to live, I will henceforth labour to support myself."

"No," replied the Sultan; "I will not trust thee from my sight; instruct my Vizier where to find thy treasures."

Nourjahad then delivered up the key of the subterraneous cavern which contained the urns full of gold and precious stones, and directed the Vizier in what part of the garden he was to find the entrance of the cavern.

As the gardens of Nourjahad joined those of the royal palace, the Vizier was not long in going and returning, but he brought word that there was not a single urn, nor any vestige of treasure concealed in the cavern. Nourjahad instantly recollected that his guardian Spirit had probably reclaimed this, as well as the other gift, and said, "A Genius, who watches over my motions, has doubtless carried away my wealth."

"Wretch!" cried the Sultan, "darest thou suppose that affecting to be mad can save thy forfeit life?"

"My Lord," replied Nourjahad, prostrating himself at the foot of the throne, "I call Heaven to witness I have spoken nothing but the truth. The severest tortures you can inflict will extort no more. I was willing to sacrifice the wealth I believed myself to possess, and I am now as ready to yield up my life."

"Art thou not afraid to die?" said Schemerzad.

"No, mighty Sultan; I look upon death, to a virtuous man, to be the forerunner of everlasting happiness."

On this the Sultan arose and clapped his hands, which Nourjahad supposed was the signal for his execution; but, instead of slaves to seize him, he beheld his guardian Genius standing close to the throne of Schemerzad. Awed and amazed, he started back, and gazed on the vision, when the angelic Maiden, casting off the circlet that bound her forehead, and throwing off a head of artificial flaxen hair that flowed upon her shoulders, a fall of brown hair dropped in light curls upon her blushing cheeks; and Nourjahad beheld in the person of his seraphic guide, his beloved and beautiful Mandana.

At the same moment, the Sultan exclaimed, "Look up, Nourjahad! raise thy eyes to thy master's face—no longer the angry Schemerzad, but Schemzeddin, thy friend and protector."

"And for whom wouldst thou take me?" said the Vizier, throwing aside his turban.

"By Mahomet," cried Nourjahad, "if I do not dream, I behold the royal Schemzeddin; and in thee, Vizier, my faithful slave, Hasem!"

"It is even so," said the Sultan. "I loved you, Nourjahad, too well not to endeavour to work your reformation. I employed the beautiful Mandana to personate your guardian Angel. I introduced her into your chamber, through a secret door, unknown to you, which communicates with a gallery in the royal palace. You fell into the snare. The liquid you drank was an opiate, and while you slept, we conveyed the urns into your chamber, filled from the royal treasury. When you were settled in your imaginary felicity, Hasem offered himself to your service, and I had Mandana, who already loved you passionately, presented to you. No wonder her charms captivated your heart. As I

261

foresaw, you yielded to all manner of excess, and I. to awaken your remorse, had an opiate administered, and withdrew Mandana from your arms. The confinement I laid you under, was to prevent your having any communication beyond your own household, and you were served only by my slaves, who were bound by solemn oaths to keep my secret. You did not suspect that you had slept only a night instead of four years; but you were not reformed, and we imposed on you that you had a second sleep, of longer duration. Your beautiful slaves were conveyed away in the night, and old women introduced, instructed to personate them, which they did admirably; and Hasem, whom you supposed to be dead, remained secretly in your house, to govern the mechanism of our plot. Still you continued to rebel against the laws of God and man, and at length stained your hand with blood. Happily, you did not take the life you aimed at; she who personated Cadiga, still lives. I now determined myself to be an eye-witness of your conduct, and to try if any spark of virtue remained in your soul, which could be rekindled. When you awoke the next morning, I presented myself as Cozro; and I had soon the satisfaction to find you a new man.

"Fourteen months only have elapsed since we began our trial. The greatest part of the sums expended have returned to my coffers; and that which has been otherwise disposed of, I do not regret, since I find Nourjahad become worthy to be the friend of Schemzeddin. Take back thy amiable wife, Mandana, and receive the fixed confidence and love of thy Sultan."

History says, that Nourjahad was raised to the highest offices of state; that his wisdom and virtue proved an ornament and support to the Persian throne during the course of a long and prosperous life; and that his name became famous throughout the Eastern world.

HOW DISCONTENT GOT PUNISHED.

ONCE upon a time, a young Mouse, a little Bird, and a fat Sausage, felt very tired of remaining at home any longer with their parents, and thinking they knew as much as them, determined upon keeping house on their own account. They agreed very well at first; and so, as they worked in unison, they soon got rich, and put by quite a store of wealth. The Bird had to fetch the wood; the Mouse to draw water, light the fire, and sweep the room; and the Sausage had to cook whatever they wanted to eat, and considered she knew how to make spicy dishes.

Those who have riches seldom think they have enough, but are constantly wishing for more; and so it happened that the Bird, one day, met another Bird on her way home, and told her of her condition, in a very boastful manner. The other Bird blamed her very much, saying, "What a simpleton you are to work so hard, while your companions rest at their ease whenever they please. There is Miss Mouse, now, fancies herself a lady; and when she has drawn the water, and lighted the fire, and just swept up the

house, she can go and lie upon the sofa until she is wanted to lay the cloth for dinner; and then the Sausage, who is as fat and full as she will hold, sits upon her chair, resting her feet on the fender, until dinner-time comes, and then she has only to see it cooked well, and dress up the gravy and vegetables, and flavour it with pepper, and salt, and butter; and no wonder she is so fat, for many a rich lick she gets from the frying-pan that you know nothing of, while you are toiling all day to get wood, to make them warm and comfortable at home."

When the Bird arrived at home, she put down her burden, and finding all was nice and ready, she sat down to supper, and enjoyed it; and then they all went to bed, and slept soundly.

The next morning, the Bird got up in a very discontented mood, and began to dictate to her companions, and complain of the manner in which she was used. "One of you must fetch wood to-day," said she, "for I will not be your slave any longer; I have toiled long enough; so, for once, we must change about, and try some other plan."

The Mouse and the Sausage protested against this; but the Bird was still unconvinced, and got in a violent passion, and behaved herself in a very unladylike manner; she insisted upon some change taking place. They could not agree upon any plan, and so they tossed up to see how the work should be divided; and so it chanced that the fat Sausage had to fetch the wood, the Mouse to cook, and the Bird to draw the water, make the beds, and sweep the place clean.

And what do you think came of all this quarrelling? Why, the Sausage went into the forest to get wood, the Bird made the fire, the Mouse put on the pot, and waited at home until the Sausage should come in laden with wood for the next day. But it got very late, and no Sausage came home, and they got very anxious about her, fearing some mischance had happened; so the Bird flew round a little way, and saw a Dog, who, having met the Sausage, had seized upon it, and devoured it. The Bird lodged a complaint against the Dog, for being a public robber, before the proper authorities; but it availed nothing, for the Dog declared he found forged bank-notes upon the Sausage, for which her life deserved to be forfeited.

The Bird, full of grief, took the wood upon her back, and with a sorrowful heart made the best of her way home again, to relate the sad disaster that had befallen. Both she and the Mouse were very low-spirited, but they made up their minds to do the best they could. So the Bird laid the table, and the Mouse got the dinner ready; and in order to stir up the vegetables well, and mix all nicely together, she got into the pot, as the Sausage had been in the habit of doing; but, alas! before she had scarcely got in, her skin shrivelled up with the hot soup, and her hair came off, and she died in great torments.

When the Bird came in, and wished to sit down to table, she found no dinner ready, and shouted in a loud voice to know the reason why. She called the Cook, but no Cook answered; then she flew in a great passion, tossing the wood to the other end of the room. She ran all over the place, but no Cook could she see.

Unfortunately, she flung the wood too near the fire, and it caught light, and set their house on fire; so the poor Bird caught up the pail, to go to the brook for water to put it out; but she was in such a nervous tremble, that she let the pail slip, and in reaching after it, fell herself to the bottom of the brook, and was drowned.

THE LOST SON.

MANY years gone by, a beautiful young Queen sat listlessly in her garden, with her ladies of honour around, who all sought to divert her attention by some pretty act of kindness or other; one sang to her, another played, while others danced in sportive gaiety around her, but all to no use; the heart of the young Queen, amidst all this, was desolate, for she was childless; and her constant longing to become a mother, and be solaced by the sweet joys of maternity, overcame every other feeling.

One day, however, when she was more than usually depressed, a Fairy appeared to her, saying, "Be of good cheer, the desire of your life shall be accomplished; because you wished for natural and good gifts, you shall have a son, gifted with the power of having granted whatever he may desire."

Then the Queen went directly to the King her husband, and told him the joyful news, at which he rejoiced exceedingly; and in due time she bore him a son, when the King ordered all the bells to ring in the kingdom, and gave bounteous gifts to every poor person in his dominions.

As the child grew, the Queen took him every morning early into the park, that he might get the fresh, pure air; and she washed him in a clear spring that flowed there. One day, the Queen fell asleep with the boy in her lap, and the old Cook passing at the time, and knowing the child possessed extraordinary wishing powers, took it, and carried it away with him. Then he killed a fowl, and came and sprinkled the blood upon the Queen's apron and clothes. Then he carried the little tender thing away to a secret place, and gave it to a Nurse, to bring it up and take care of it. This black-hearted and cruel Cook then ran to the King, and said, that the Queen had suffered the wild beasts to come from the forests and seize her child, and devour it.

The King was greatly moved, and cried aloud with grief, but he still hoped to find the child in its mother's arms; but when he came to the brook, and found the Queen sleeping, with her apron covered with blood, and the child gone, his rage knew no bounds; he ordered her from his sight, and commanded that the poor bewildered Queen, who did not yet fully comprehend her loss, should be enclosed within the four walls of a high castle tower, where neither sun, moon, or stars shone; and that there she should be shut up for seven long years, without meat or drink, and so miserably perish.

The Fairy, however, as the Queen had committed no wicked action, but only been unfortunate, sent two beautiful doves to her twice a day, who carried her every dainty fit for a Queen, and waited until she had finished her repast, when they fluttered their little white wings over the table, to brush away the fragments, and then they flew away with the gold and silver dishes, to get them ready for the next meal.

At this time the wicked Cook was in great repute at the palace, on account of the good dishes he could prepare; so he thought to himself, "I may as well stay here until the Prince gets old enough to wish;" but he suddenly recollected that, as the child had the power of wishing, he might bring him into misfortune; so, as soon as the child could speak, he left the palace, and went to live with it.

The child had become a fine boy, and could now prattle away; so he said to the child, "You must wish for a noble house, and a fine garden, and servants, and, in short, everything a nobleman ought to have;" and scarcely was the wish out of the young Prince's mouth, than it all appeared just as he had wished for it.

The child grew towards manhood; and, one day, the Cook said to him, "It is not wise of you to live alone; you ought to have some lady to pass your time with; therefore, you must wish for a beautiful maiden, to love you, and keep you company." This the youth also did; and in one minute there stood before him a lady, more beautiful than poet could imagine, or painter depict.

The young people passed the days in pleasant dalliance, and grew to love each other with a rare and innocent affection; while the Cook went every day to hunt in the forest, like any other gentleman. One day, however, it occurred to him that it might so chance, that nature should assert her sway, and that the young Prince should follow her dictates, and wish to see his father, and so bring trouble in his path. To prevent this, he took the Maiden aside one day, and said to her, "To-night, when the youth sleeps, bury this poniard deep in his heart, and cut out his tongue; if you do not do as I desire, your own life shall pay the forfeit."

When he had gone out, the Maiden sat down to grieve over the wicked cruelty that had entered the old Cook's head. How could she sacrifice the life of one she so gently and fondly loved? So she determined, rather than hurt him, that she would take the life of a young calf. So she had one killed, and his heart and tongue taken out, and laid upon a plate; and when she saw the Cook return, she begged the youth to lie close in the bed, while she put the covering smooth over him.

Presently, this wicked, hateful Cook came in, and asked, "Where are the heart and tongue of the boy?" The Maiden reached him the plate; but the Prince, throwing off the covering, cried, "You old sinner! why should you seek to kill me? Now listen to your own doom: you shall become a fierce black Dog, with a gold chain round your neck, all your life; you shall swallow live coals, so that you shall breathe out fire, and no water shall come near you to quench your thirst."

No sooner were these words spoken, than the Cook became a large, fierce, black Dog, with a gold chain
263

round his neck; and when his dinner of live coals was served to him, a roaring flame burst from his mouth.

The King's son remained in the palace a short time, until, one day, he sat wondering where his mother was, and if she were still alive. At last, he said to the Maiden, "I must depart from hence, and visit my father; come, therefore, with me, and I will take care of you."

"Alas!" replied the Maiden, "the distance is great, and what can I do in a strange country, where I am entirely unknown?"

The young Prince, when he found she feared to depart with him, could in no way do violence to his affections by leaving her behind; so he wished her into a most delicate and lovely Pink, and carried her away in his bosom in that form. The black Dog had to run behind, and so they travelled to their native land. Then he went to the tower, where he was told his mother had dwelt; and as it was very lofty, he got a very tall ladder to reach to the top. Then he went up it, and called out, "Dearest mother, lady Queen, are you still alive, or am I bereft of you entirely?"

The Queen answered, "I have but just eaten, and am satisfied;" for she thought it was the doves who spoke.

But the Prince answered, "I am your dear son, whom the wild beasts were said to have stolen from your lap; but I am yet alive, and will soon rescue you."

So saying, he went down, and came to his father's palace, and caused himself to be announced as a Huntsman, who desired to enter the King's service. The King answered, that he might do so, if he could find any venison; but that, of late, no venison had been found upon any part of his territories.

Then the Huntsman promised to procure him as many deer as he could use for the royal table, and caused all the other huntsmen to be summoned to accompany him. So they went out, and the young Prince bade them enclose a large circle, open at one end, in the middle of which he placed himself, and began to wish. Soon, two hundred and odd head of game came running into the circle, at which the huntsmen began to shoot. All these were driven home upon sixty carts, heaped high up; and the King, to his great gratification, was enabled once more to have as much venison upon his table as his heart could desire.

The King, knowing how great a treat venison would now be to his court, invited them all to dine with him the next day at a grand festival. When they were all assembled, the King said to the Huntsman, "You are so clever, that you must sit by me to-day;" but he replied, "I am but a poor Huntsman; I therefore beg your Majesty to excuse me."

The King, however, insisted upon doing him honour, and therefore the Prince was obliged to comply. As he sat at table, his thoughts wandered to his dear mother; and he wished that one of the King's courtiers might inquire if the Queen were still alive, or had perished in the tower. Scarcely had he wished, than the Marshal began to speak, saying, "May it please your Majesty, here we are living in great happiness; but how fares it with our Sovereign Lady the Queen in the tower? is she still alive, or dead?"

The King answered, "Speak not of her; she slept when she should have been tending my darling son, and allowed him to perish by a cruel death; I will hear nothing of her."

The Huntsman could not withstand these words; he rose, and said, "My dear and gracious father, my mother is still alive, and I am her son, for the wild beasts neither sought me, nor took me; but that wretch, the Cook, took me from her lap while she slept, and then sprinkled the blood of a hen over her dress and apron."

Thereupon, he took up the black Dog with the golden chain, and said, "This is the wretch!" and he ordered live coals to be brought, and he was forced to eat in the presence of all, so that great flames burst out of his mouth. Then he changed him back again, and there was the Cook, with his white apron on, and a large knife by his side.

The King was terribly angry, and ordered him to be cast into a horrible dungeon, the deepest in the castle.

Then the young Prince asked the King if he would see the Maiden who had treated him so gently and lovingly, and had saved his life at the peril of her own; and the King replied, "Yes, most willingly."

"I will show you her, first, in the form of a flower," said the Prince; and gently placing his hand in his bosom, he took out his beautiful Pink, and placed it upon the royal table; and all confessed they had never seen so lovely a flower. "Now," said the Prince, "I will show you the real Maiden;" and wishing again, the lovely Girl stood before them in such rare beauty, that every head bowed before its magic power.

The King then despatched two heralds and two attendants to the tower, to bring the Queen into his royal presence.

The poor Queen, grieved at heart at the recollection of the great unkindness shown her by the King, could not eat even of the dainties that were set before her; and she trusted she might soon be relieved from the sight of her oppressor.

For three days she lingered on, and then, her conscience being free from guile, she died happily; and when she was buried, two white doves followed her, and hovered around her grave; these were the good Fairies who had fed and nourished her so long.

The old King grieved at heart for her some time, and at length died. Then the young King married his beautiful Flower Maiden, whom he had cherished in his bosom with fond affection; but whether they yet live is not known to me.

"THE CALIPH AND HIS VIZIER WERE CHANGED INTO STORKS."

THE CALIPH-STORK.

ONE fine summer's evening, a Caliph of Bagdad, Chasid by name, lay idly lolling on his divan. He dozed a little, but the heat was too great even for sleeping, and he woke up, in a remarkably good temper. Then he took up a pipe, to comfort and soothe his royal mind; and as he gently sucked down the aromatic breath of his imperial Cavendish through a long cherry-tree tube, and drank, at intervals, a cup of coffee handed to him by an ebony-coloured slave, he stroked his handsome beard, with a satisfied air. In a word, it was plain to see that his Highness the Caliph was in a state of perfect blessedness.

In moments like these, his Highness would not unfrequently forget his greatness, and show himself gentle and benevolent to the mere mortals whose duties brought them into his august presence : and, consequently, that was the time that his Grand Vizier Mansour selected to pay his daily visit. The Grand Vizier, then, came to the palace this day, according to his usual habit; but—what was very rare, indeed, in his case—with an absorbed and thoughtful air.

THE SLAVE BRINGS IN THE COFFEE.

"Eh! what is this? Where have you come from, with that dismal physiognomy, my Grand Vizier?" exclaimed the Caliph, in astonishment, as he took, for an instant, the amber mouth-piece of his pipe out of his lips.

"My Lord," said the Vizier, crossing his arms over his breast, and bowing low, "I know not whether my countenance betrays, in spite of myself, the secrets of my soul; but the fact is, that as I was entering the palace I met a Jew, who had so many fine things to sell, that I confess I felt quite vexed inwardly, at not having more superfluous cash to deal with him."

The Caliph, who had been some time on the look-out for some way of doing a kind turn to his Vizier, for whom he felt a real esteem, made a sign to one of his slaves to go and bring the Merchant into his presence.

The order was scarcely given before it was obeyed, and the Jew was brought before the Caliph. He was a little man, with a dark visage, and a small hooked nose, and lips drawn up on either side by two ugly yellow teeth, the sole relics of a former mouthful. His small green eyes, like those of an asp, sparkled and flamed from beneath his red eyebrows. As soon as he was within eyeshot of the Caliph, he struck the pavement with his forehead, and came forward in a creeping posture, with his features pursed up, by a vain endeavour to concoct a smile, into the most wonderful grimace that ever was impressed on a human visage. He carried before him, by a leather strap across his arched shoulders, a chest of sandal wood, in which were arranged all kinds of precious articles; these his dark and wrinkled hand contrived to make glitter in the eyes of the bystanders, with that commercial astuteness peculiar to the sons of Judah.

There were pearls of Ophir, set in ear-rings, rings of enamelled gold, covered with brilliants that the

eye could scarce look upon, such was their dazzling lustre; pistols richly damascened, cups of onyx, vessels of ivory incrusted with gold, and a hundred other knicknacks, no less rare and tempting. After passing the whole in review, the Caliph purchased for Mansour and himself some magnificent pistols, besides, for the Vizier's wife, a cup of chased silver, encircled with a garland of fine pearls, that rendered it at once the most costly and elegant present in the world.

Just as the Merchant was on the point of shutting up his box, the Caliph, who had not been able to take his eyes off it, caught sight of a small drawer—the only one that had not been opened—and asked if he had not in that some jewels yet to show. The Pedlar opened the compartment which the Caliph pointed out, and took out from it a kind of snuff-box of minute dimensions, containing a black powder, enclosed in a paper marked with strange characters, of which neither Mansour nor the Caliph could make out a single word.

"This box came into my possession," said the Pedlar, "from a merchant who found it on his road, as he was going to Mecca. I know not what it is, but it is also at your service, if you wish for it; as for me, I know not what to do with it."

Now the Caliph, though an exceedingly ignorant man himself, was a great connoisseur, and stored up in his bookcases all kinds of curiosities in the way of parchments. So he bought the snuff-box and the manuscript, and dismissed the Merchant, who backed out of his presence, bowing no less deeply to the ground than before.

THE JEW PEDLAR SELLS THE SNUFF-BOX.

Chasid eyed his new purchase with delighted eyes, but not without thinking that he should like to know what was the meaning of the words written upon it, as he mechanically turned and turned it over in his hands.

"Don't you know any person who could read this for me?" said he, at last, to his Vizier.

"Most gracious Lord," replied that excellent Minister, "I know a man in the Great Mosque, whom people call Selim the Sage. They say he understands all languages. Order him to be brought here; he, perhaps, can explain those mysterious characters."

The slaves were sent off, at once, to find Selim the Sage, and bring him to the Palace within an hour.

"Selim," said the Caliph, as soon as he entered, "they say you are well up in the knowledge of languages. Examine this writing for awhile, and see if you can read it. I'll give you a new pelisse of honour if you can explain its meaning to us. If not, you shall receive a dozen buffets on the face, and twenty-five blows on the soles of your feet, for having falsely usurped the title of 'the Sage.'"

SELIM THE SAGE INTERPRETS THE WRITING.

Selim bowed, and replied, "May your will be done, O Master!" Then he applied himself to a careful inspection of the manuscript submitted to him. All of a sudden, he exclaimed, "It is Latin, my Lord, or I will be hung!"

"Eh! Latin or Greek, tell us what is written there," said the Caliph, impatiently.

Selim applied himself to the translation, and this was what he read out:—

"Whoever you may be that shall find this, render thanks to Allah for the favour he has deigned to accord to you. Whoever shall sniff up a pinch of the powder enclosed within this box into his nostrils, and say, at the same time, 'Mutabor' (I will be changed), will be able to change himself at pleasure into any animal he may choose, and to understand, at the same time, the ideas of animals, and their method of exchanging them. When he wishes to return into his former shape, he must bow three times towards

the East, and utter the same word, when the spell will be broken. Only, let whoever he may be that tries this experiment, beware of laughing when he is in the changed shape, otherwise the magic word will entirely slip out of his memory, and he will be compelled to remain for ever one of the family of beasts."

In proportion as Selim the Sage advanced in his translation of the cabalistic paper, the Caliph felt a delight, such as he had never enjoyed before, developing itself within him. He could hardly contain himself; and after binding the Sage not to reveal to any one the secret he possessed, he hastened him away, but not before he had caused him to be invested with a magnificent silk pelisse, that added greatly to Selim's estimation in the eyes of all the people of Bagdad.

Scarcely had he gone, when the Caliph gave himself up to the full enjoyment of the situation. "This is what I call a famous bargain! How delightful, my dear Mansour, to be able to change oneself at any time into a beast! Come and see me to-morrow morning; we will go out into the country together, and, with the aid of my invaluable snuff-box, we shall be able to make out what all the singing, and whistling, and cooing, and twittering, and roaring, and barking means, that we hear so perpetually about us, and regard as mere idle sound, signifying nothing. The sea, the air, the sky, the earth, trees, forests, rivers, are now our own!"

II.—THE TRANSFORMATION.

THE night seemed as if it would never end to the Caliph, impatient of the morning, which at last broke, as it usually does; and with it, also, to the great astonishment of his attendant slaves, rose the Caliph. Nay, if historians do not deceive us, Chasid positively jumped out of bed, or rather off it; for Caliphs, like all other men in the East, sleep in their breeches, under a horse-rug or a shawl, gold embroidered, woollen, or hair-cloth, according to their rank and pockets. Breakfast and the putting on his waistcoat and turban were quickly despatched; and the Vizier, who was in waiting, according to orders, presented himself, to accompany his Highness in his promenade.

Without farther waiting, the Caliph slipped his magic snuff-box into his girdle, seized the arm of his Minister, gave orders to his attendants to remain behind, and commenced at once, in the company of his faithful Mansour, his expedition in search of adventures. They walked all round and across the vast gardens of the palace, but in vain, and without being able to meet with a single living being on which they could test their magic power. At last, the Vizier proposed to push farther on, until they should reach a lake, where, as he said, he had often seen a number of animals of all kinds, and particularly some Storks, whose grave looks and singular beaks had often attracted his attention.

The Caliph agreed to the proposition of his Vizier with all haste, and they set off briskly in the direction indicated. Scarcely had they reached the border of the lake, than our two friends caught sight of an old Stork walking along, with a serious air, backwards and forwards, hunting up frogs, and mumbling something or other in her long beak; almost at the same instant they discovered, high up in the air, another of these birds, whose flight seemed tending towards the same spot.

"I will wager my beard, your gracious Majesty," said the Vizier, "that these birds will, before very long, have a nice little conversation. What do you say? shall we change ourselves into Storks?"

"So be it," replied the Caliph; "but, before taking the final step, let us just go over once or twice, and fix well in our memories, how to become ourselves again."

"Nothing more easy," said the Vizier, in a careless tone; "we bow ourselves three times to the East, and say, 'We will be changed.'"

"And then I am once more Caliph, and you my Grand Vizier; all right. But, in the name of Allah, don't laugh, or we shall that instant be done for."

While the Caliph was saying this, he perceived distinctly, floating on the wing over their heads, and gradually descending towards the earth, the Stork that they had before seen over their heads, scarcely larger than a black spot, almost lost in space. Unable any longer to withstand his eager curiosity, he drew the snuff-box out of his girdle, took a large pinch of the powder from it, handed it to his Vizier, who did the same, and they both together cried, "We will be changed!"

THE CALIPH BECOMES A STORK.

Scarcely was the magic word pronounced, than their legs began to shrink until they were as thin as

walking-sticks, and spotted and brown. At the same instant, the beautiful yellow slippers of the Caliph and his companion were stuck upon the ugly pats of storks; their arms changed into wings, their backbones elongated themselves into tails. Lastly, and to complete the transformation, their beards disappeared, and the whole of their bodies was covered with soft down.

"You have a charming beak there, my Grand Vizier," cried the Caliph, as soon as, after a long time, he had roused himself from his first astonishment. "By the beard of the Prophet, I never saw anything like it before!"

"I thank your Highness very humbly," replied the Grand Vizier, wagging his long tail; "but if I dared venture the liberty, I could affirm to your Highness, that you seem to me to have even a more charming air as a Stork than as a Caliph."

"You are a flatterer," said the Caliph; "the change of form has not altered your mind."

"No; on my conscience," protested the Vizier, "I have said nothing but the simple truth. But let us go on a little, if such be your pleasure, to the side of our comrades, and see if, after all, we really know how to speak the Stork language."

While they were thus planning, the flying Stork had reached the earth. After she had coquettishly pecked her legs, and plumed her feathers with her beak, she advanced to the other lady Stork, who was looking after the frogs, and who continued still attentive to her housekeeping.

The Caliph and his Vizier hastened to join their party; and I leave you to guess what was their surprise, at hearing the following dialogue:—

"Good-day to you, Mrs. Longlegs; what makes you so early in the meadows?"

"A thousand compliments, my dear Pretty-beak; I was just fishing for a little luncheon, and shall feel much honoured by your taking a share of it. A quarter of lizard and a saddle of frog are, if I remember right, your favourite dishes."

"I am much obliged to you, but I am out of appetite this morning. To tell you the truth, I came out to the meadow for quite a different purpose. I have got to dance to-night at a ball given by my father, and I am anxious to practise some of the steps in my grand *pas*."

And even while thus talking, the young lady Stork began to leap up, and jump, and figure about on the meadow in the most comical manner. The Caliph and the Grand Vizier stared at her with amazed eyes and their beaks open, perfectly astounded. But when the young lady, after the fashion of the final *pas* of a ballet-dancer, stood on one claw, in the attitude usually represented as that of a dancing Sylphide, her body bent, and her wings gently fluttering, neither of them could hold out any longer. A burst of loud laughter broke from either long beak, so strong and so irresistible, that it was impossible to restrain it.

The Caliph, with whom gravity had become a habit, as a portion of his dignity, was the first to moderate himself.

"Truly," he exclaimed, "that was a fine bit of

buffoonery—there was no withstanding it. It is a pity, however, these creatures are affronted with us for laughing, otherwise we might soon hear some singing as well."

But just at this moment it came into the Vizier's mind, that to laugh was forbidden during the continuance of the transformation, on penalty of remaining ever afterwards in animal shape. Upon this, with a sudden pull up in his hilarity, and an air of great suffering, he imparted to the Caliph what was troubling him.

"By Allah!" cried the Caliph, "and by Mecca and Medina! this will turn out a bad joke for us! But try and think a little, if you can perchance remember the word that was to make us men again. I have no longer got the least idea of it."

"We must bow our heads three times to the East," his Vizier hastened to say, and to pronounce at the same time, "We will be ——" But not a word more could he get out. "Let us try, nevertheless; perhaps it will recur to us."

So the two Storks set themselves to bowing and saluting the sun until they were tired, but not a word of the magic sentence could they get out. In vain the Caliph bowed and bowed again; in vain Mansour exhausted himself in shouting out, "We—we—we!" Both one and the other had totally lost all recollection of the latter syllables.

So now, you see, the unlucky Chasid and his unfortunate Vizier were changed into Storks, and had to remain in their borrowed plumes some time longer than they desired.

III.—THE OWL PRINCESS.

OUR two poor enchanted friends wandered about, in dolorous plight, over the country, their brains perfectly addled by their efforts to break the charm that held them captive, and not knowing what to make up their minds to do in such a miserable condition. It was no use any longer hoping to get out of their Stork feathers. They thought, for a moment, of returning to the city, and endeavouring to make themselves known. But how could they get any one to believe that this miserable Stork was the brilliant Caliph Chasid? And then, supposing any one were inclined to believe this, would the inhabitants of Bagdad consent to be governed by a Prince in such a strange shape?

They wandered hither and thither for many days, nourishing themselves on a mean and stony kind of fare of wild fruit, which they found considerable difficulty in getting down, owing to the length of their beaks. As for the lizards and frogs, such as their new companions regarded as delicious, they had no particular stomach for such a regale, having some dread of the consequences to their digestion. The only pleasure that resulted from their dismal situation, was the power of flying—and this they had bought sufficiently dear! So they often flew on to the elevated roofs of Bagdad, to see what was going on in that city. The first time they visited it, they observed the people out in the streets, wearing the appearance of great disquietude, intermingled with true grief. This cut the poor Vizier to the heart. But towards the fourth day after their transformation, just as our two birds were about to perch on a pinnacle of the Caliph's palace, they all of a sudden caught sight of a magnificent procession passing through the streets of the town, to the joyous sounds of trumpets, fifes and drums. Mounted on a horse splendidly caparisoned, and which, under its velvet housings, Selim recognised as his own favourite steed, a man, arrayed in a robe of scarlet and gold, advanced with a triumphant air, surrounded by a band of guards in glittering costume, while the half of Bagdad was running after him, with shouts of "Long live Mirza! long live the Lord of Bagdad!"

At this moment, the two Storks, who had perched on the palace roof, looked at each other, and Chasid first spoke: "Now do you understand how our transformation has been brought about, my Grand Vizier? This Mirza is the son of my mortal enemy, the powerful Enchanter Kaschnur, who has sworn, in some fatal hour, an undying hatred to me. But I have not yet lost all hope. Follow me; we will go and visit the Tomb of the Prophet, and, it may be, the influence of the Holy Place may avail to break the charm."

The two Storks quitted the roof of the palace, and directed their flight towards Medina.

The poor creatures did their best to regulate their flight the one with the other; but this was no easy thing for them, inasmuch as they had had but little practice as yet. "My Lord," gasped the Grand Vizier, after a couple of hours' hard flying, "pardon me, but I cannot keep up any longer; you fly so much faster than I do. More than this, it is already late, and it would be prudent, I think, to seek out some nest for the night."

Chasid was a good-natured Prince; so he listened with compassionate ear to the prayer of his Grand Vizier, and immediately directed his flight to a kind of ruin, which he had just discovered at the bottom of a valley.

The spot where our Storks alighted appeared to have been occupied, in years long past, by some vast castle. The lofty and beautiful columns which rose out of the heaps of ruins, and numerous apartments still in some kind of preservation, attested the ancient magnificence of the building. Chasid and his companion, after wandering over a labyrinth of immense corridors, sought out some small place for shelter; when, on a sudden, Mansour stopped as if turned to stone: "Master," murmured the Vizier, in a smothered tone, "if it was not too foolish for a Prime Minister, and even more so for a Stork, to be afraid of ghosts, I would confess that I feel very much alarmed. There was a sigh and a groan just now, close here!"

The Caliph came to a halt, that he might the better listen, and heard something like a gentle sigh, that appeared to come rather from a human being than an animal. Full of anxiety, with the bold spirit of his nature, he would at once have marched up to the corner whence issued those plaintive sounds; but his prudent Vizier, catching him respectfully by the end of his tail, conjured him earnestly not to rush into strange and unknown dangers. Useless precaution!

The Caliph, who carried the heart of a brave man under the feathers of a Stork, tore himself violently from the beak of his Vizier, and, without hesitating, rushed headlong into the dark passage.

He was not long before he met with a door, which seemed merely pushed to, and on the other side of which the signs and groans, frequently repeated, became more distinct. Chasid continued resolutely advancing, but had scarcely passed within the door, when surprise nailed him, as it were, to the threshold.

In a chamber all in ruins, and dimly lighted by a narrow window barred with iron, he could just catch sight of an enormous Owl, retired in the darkest corner. Tears in abundance followed each other in quick succession from her great yellow eyes, while sighs and smothered sobs escaped from her crooked beak. Nevertheless, and in spite of the sorrow that seemed to weigh her down, she could not repress a cry of joy at the sight of the Caliph and his companion, who had just rejoined him. She wiped away, not without some sort of grace, with her brown-spotted wings, the tears that filled her eyes; and, to the profound amazement of the two adventurers, exclaimed, in excellent Arabic, "Welcome, dear birds! you are a sweet omen of my approaching deliverance; for it has been predicted to me that, one day, a pair of Storks would bring to me great good fortune."

As soon as the Caliph had recovered the surprise this strange apparition at first caused him, he bowed gallantly to the full extent his back would allow him, and steadying himself on his long legs as well, in the handsomest manner he could, replied: "My Lady Owl, after what you have said, I believe I am not mistaken in supposing I behold in you a person whose misfortune bears too great a resemblance to our own. But, alas! the hope you nourish, of obtaining your deliverance through us, appears to me very vain, and you will be better able to judge for yourself the extent of our utter want of resources and power, if you will deign to listen to the story of our misfortunes."

The Owl having politely requested him to relate it, the Caliph, who piqued himself on being able to tell a story extremely well, went through a recital of his misfortunes, just as we have told them to you already.

IV.—THE OWL'S STORY.

WHEN the Caliph had brought the story of his woes to an end, the Owl politely thanked him, as she said, "Now listen to my tale, my Lord, and see if my sorrows have been in any degree less than yours.

"My father is one of the most powerful kings in the Indies, and I, his only and most unfortunate daughter, was once called the Princess Lusa. This same Enchanter Kaschnun, who brought about your transformation, is also the wretch who has precipitated me to this same grief. Reckoning upon the terror which his diabolical knowledge of magic everywhere inspires, he had the audacity, one day, to present himself at my father's court, and demand my hand in marriage for his son Mirza. Indignant at such impudence on the part of a vile juggler, my father ordered the insolent wretch to be kicked down the

palace stairs. Kaschnun made the best of his way off, vowing to be revenged.

"A short time afterwards, this wretch, who can change his shape at will, managed to slip unperceived among the persons who were about me; and, as I can testify, one summer's evening, while I was walking in my garden, with the intention of taking the fresh air, he presented to me, in the disguise of a slave, a beverage of some kind, that brought about in me this terrible transformation.

"I fainted. On coming to myself I was in this masquerade, and heard the horrible voice of the Enchanter cry in my ears:—

"'You will remain in this shape to the end of your days, disfigured, hideous, the horror of even animals themselves, until some creature shall, of his own free will, and in spite of your repulsive aspect, come to meet you, and consent to take you as his spouse. Thus do I revenge myself on you and your proud father!'

"Since that time, many months have rolled by, and I, the sad victim of an infamous Magician, have mourned my lost life and hopes in these solitary ruins, an object of aversion and disgust to everything that breathes. You, at any rate, can enjoy the bright spectacle of nature spread before you; but I am blind during the day, and it is only when the moon pours out her wan light over the earth, that my eyes throw off the dismal veil that covers them."

The Owl finished speaking, and was again obliged to wipe her eyes with the tips of her wings, for the recital of her misfortunes had re-opened the well-spring of her tears.

While the Princess was speaking, the Caliph had fallen into a deep reverie.

"If I am not mistaken," said he, "there exists some common link between our two misfortunes; but how to find the key to this enigma?"

"My Lord," replied the Owl, "I have the same idea. I have already told you that a sort of magician predicted to me, in my youth, that some day a Stork would bring me some great good fortune. Well, then, I think I have now the clue that will help us out of this infernal labyrinth."

"Explain yourself," exclaimed the Caliph, full of anxiety.

"The Enchanter who has caused our fall," replied she, "comes once every month to these ruins. Not far from this spot is a vast hall, where he and his companions meet for their nightly orgies: often have I watched them there. They recount then, one after another, all the wicked tricks they have played off. It is not impossible that, in some one of these moments, Kaschnun may let drop the word you have forgotten."

"Oh, my dear Princess!" cried the Caliph; "tell me, quick, when will he come?—where is that hall?"

The Owl was silent for an instant, and then went on:—

"Do not take it in bad part, my Lord; but before aiding you in the work of your deliverance, I am forced to impose a condition."

"Speak on! speak quickly!" exclaimed the Caliph,

impatiently; "order what you like—I am ready for everything!"

"I could, as far as I am concerned, be set free this moment," sighed the Owl, casting down her eyes; "but this cannot be done," added she, looking as if she would blush, if she could, through her feathers, "unless one of you offers me his hand."

This proposition was one of a character to raise discussion between the two Storks; and the Caliph, nudging his Grand Vizier with his wing, brought him gradually a little to the front.

"Grand Vizier," said he to him, "here is rather an awkward bargain; but I reckon on your devotion to carry us through this affair."

"Yes, surely," replied Mansour; "but there is the thought of my wife coming before my eyes, when I shall go back to my home; and then, I am only an old fellow. But you, my Lord, who are still young and quite a lad, could get on much better with a young and beautiful Princess."

"Ah! there's the rub," murmured the Caliph, leading him up by the wing; "how do you know that she is young and handsome? We should be buying 'a cat in a bag,' as the proverb says."

They debated on the matter some time; at last, and not until the Caliph saw plainly that his Vizier would rather remain a Stork for the rest of his days than marry the Owl, he decided on himself fulfilling the condition she exacted.

Transported with joy at this assurance, the Owl declared that they could not have arrived there more *apropos*, for the Enchanter and his friends would, most probably, come that very night to their rendezvous. So, quitting their retreat, she guided the two Storks towards the hall where their fate would be decided.

After they had followed her for some minutes along a dark passage, a brilliant light appeared to them through a broken wall. The Owl urged upon the two friends the necessity of preserving the strictest silence, and they advanced together cautiously to the opening through which the light penetrated, and which was just large enough to permit of their observing at their leisure what was passing on the other side.

In the middle of a vast hall, a little less dilapidated than the rest of the castle, and which was lighted up with an immense chandelier, was a large table, groaning under the weight of dishes and wines of every kind. Eight men, in strange dresses, sat round this table, on rich sofas; and the hearts of the two Storks beat high, when they recognised among them the pretended Merchant, who had sold to them the magic powder.

The feast was kept up for a long time yet; the night was almost at an end, and our poor enchanted friends had not yet heard what it most concerned them to know. They began to despair. Half of the guests were asleep; the other half, fatigued with eating and drinking, seemed ready to do so likewise, when the next one to the false Pedlar, slapping him on the shoulder, said :—

"Ha! Kaschnun, tell us your last exploits—that will amuse us."

That worthy, without farther pressing, detailed a numerous string of infamous rogueries, amongst which he recounted the history of the Caliph and his Vizier.

"And what, in the name of Sheitan, was the word you gave them?" asked the questioner of the Magician.

"An ugly word in a foreign language," replied the other, with a roar of laughter, "and not at all easy to remember—'WE WILL BE CHANGED!'"

V.—ALL RIGHT AGAIN.

INTOXICATED with joy at again getting hold of the lucky word, the Storks hurried out to the outside of the ruins with such rapidity, that the Owl had great trouble in following them. The Caliph, however, turning towards her as soon as she had rejoined them, said to her, in a voice of emotion, "O thou who hast delivered us—O generous Owl! receive my hand, as an evidence of my eternal gratitude for the service you have rendered us."

Then, at the same time, they turned themselves, the one and the other, the Caliph and his Vizier, towards the East. Three times the long backs of the Storks inclined towards the sun, whose rays were just beginning to redden the summits of the mountains. At last, the famous "We will be changed!" escaped from their beaks, and the Storks became men once more. Quite beside themselves, and incapable of speech, so great was the joy that possessed them, the master and servant gazed on each other with a kind of ecstacy, and at last ended by falling into each other's arms, laughing and crying at the same moment.

But who can describe their surprise, when, on looking round, they saw by their side a young lady magnificently dressed! She held out her hand, with a smile, to the Caliph.

"Do you no longer recognise your poor Owl?" said she, so splendid in beauty, that the Caliph, all marvelling at her grace and charms, could not help exclaiming, as he fell on his knees before her, that he regarded it as the happiest event of his life that he had been a Stork, since to that transformation he owed the good fortune of a meeting with her.

The Caliph's return to Bagdad, in company with his good Mansour, was hailed by his people with unanimous acclamations of delight. But all the testimonies of affection that surrounded him only the more inflamed the hatred of Chasid and his Vizier towards Mirza, who had been foisted in his throne. They hurried to the palace, where they made prisoners of the Magician and his son. By order of the Caliph, the father was conveyed to the same den to which he had exiled the Owl, and there hung, out and out, from the top of the highest tower. As for the son, who knew none of his father's wicked tricks and magic arts, the Caliph permitted him the option of death or taking a pinch of the powder.

"Will you take a pinch?" said the Vizier, with the funniest look in the world, as he handed him the snuffbox; while, on the other side, stood a slave with a naked sabre, and ready to strike off his head at the least sign.

Mirza lost no time in plunging his fingers into the magic box. A large pinch, accompanied with the magic words, "We will be changed," firmly pronounced, changed him, in the twinkling of an eye, into a superb Stork. Then the poor creature was placed in a capacious cage, in which he served a long while as an amusement for the idlers of Bagdad.

Chasid and the lovely Princess his wife lived together many long and happy years; but the gayest moments of the Caliph's life were those when his Grand Vizier came to see him, about mid-day.

It often happened that they would talk over their strange adventure; and when the Caliph was in a merry mood, he amused himself with teasing his Vizier, and imitating his look as a Stork. With head stretched, and stiffened legs, he would walk gravely across the chamber, squeaking and frisking; then he would imitate the pantomime of the poor Vizier, when he was vainly bowing towards the East, and wearing himself out with crying, "We—we—we——"

This joke was, every time, a rare amusement to the Caliph's wife and children. But if Chasid squeaked, hopped, and cried out "We—we" too long, the Grand Vizier at last got out of temper at the silly portrait his master drew of him—he threatened to reveal to the Princess, his wife, the discussion that had been raised, at first, between them, about who should marry the poor Owl.

The Caliph was shut up directly; but he could not help beginning again the next day, in spite of the threats of his good Vizier, which, however, he good-naturedly never carried into execution.

FORTUNIO.

THERE was once a King named Alfourite, who was both amiable and powerful; but his neighbour, the Emperor Matapa, was still more powerful, and in the last battle they fought against each other, had gained a complete victory, leaving the King despoiled of all his treasures; these the Emperor conveyed to his own

palace, where he was received, on his return, by the Empress with great rejoicings.

In the meantime, King Alfourite was in the greatest affliction for the injury he had sustained, and began to think of making some endeavours to regain what he had lost. He accordingly assembled the small remains of his army, and, to increase its numbers, published a decree, that every gentleman and nobleman in his kingdom must come in person to assist him in his enterprise, or, in case of failure, pay a large sum of money.

On the frontiers of his kingdom there lived a Nobleman, who was eighty years of age; he had once been extremely rich, but, through misfortunes, was now reduced to a scanty provision for himself and three daughters, who lived with him in a happy and contented retirement. When this Old Nobleman heard of the King's decree, he called his daughters to him, telling them he knew not what to do; "For," says he, "I am too old to engage in the King's army, and to pay the tax would ruin us at once."

"Do not thus afflict yourself, my father," said his daughters; "some remedy may surely be thought of." "I," said the eldest, "am young and robust, and well accustomed to fatigue; why should not I dress myself like a Cavalier, and offer my services to King Alfourite?"

The Old Lord embraced her tenderly, and, seeing her earnestly bent on the experiment, gave his consent; and as soon as the necessary preparations could be made, she set out.

The Princess had not proceeded far, before she observed an Old Shepherdess, all in tears, endeavouring to draw one of her sheep out of the ditch, into which it had fallen. "What are you doing, Goody?" said the Cavalier.

"Alas!" replied she, "I am trying to save my sheep, which is almost drowned; but I am too weak to get it out."

"You are very unfortunate, truly," said she, at the same time spurring her horse to ride away.

"Adieu, disguised lady!" said the Old Shepherdess.

No astonishment could exceed that of the Earl's daughter, on finding herself discovered. "If this is the case," says she, "I had better return at once, since a single glance at me is sufficient to convince every one that I am not a man."

She accordingly returned, and related the whole to her father and sisters. The second daughter then said: "It would not have been thus if I had gone instead of you, for I am both taller and more robust; and I would lay any wager I should have succeeded."

The Old Lord, on her entreaty, was prevailed on to let his second daughter go on the same errand, who immediately procured a suit of clothes and another horse, and took the road her sister had done before. The Old Shepherdess was on the same spot, and still engaged in the occupation of drawing out a sheep that was drowning. Our young traveller asked what was the matter.

"Unfortunate that I am!" replied the Old Woman, "half my flock have I lost in this manner, for want of help."

THE AMIABLE CAVALIER OFFERS TO ASSIST THE OLD SHEPHERDESS.

"Some one will soon come by, no doubt," said the Cavalier; and was turning his horse to go, when the Old Woman cried out, "Adieu, disguised lady!"

In utter amazement, she stopped her horse, saying to herself, "I should only be laughed at, should I proceed, since even a poor Old Shepherdess, almost blind, discovers me without the smallest difficulty." She therefore followed her sister's example, and returned to her father, full of sorrow and disappointment.

When she had related her adventure, the youngest sister, who, on account of her amiable disposition, was her father's favourite, entreated she might not be denied the privilege of trying her fortune, as well as her sisters; which, at last, after much persuasion, the Old Lord agreed to; but as he had expended a good deal of money in equipping his two eldest daughters, he could provide the youngest only with a poor old cart-horse, and the meanest apparel imaginable. When these were ready, the old gentleman embraced her tenderly, and she bade both him and her sisters farewell.

Passing through the same field, the Old Shepherdess again presented herself, employed as before. "What are you about, my good woman?" said this amiable Cavalier; "can I be of any service to you?" and perceiving, as he advanced, the sheep struggling in the water, immediately jumped off his horse, and pulled it out.

Upon this, the Old Shepherdess turned to him, and said, "Charming stranger, you shall find me grateful for the kindness you have done me. I am a Fairy, and know well enough who you are, and I will be your friend." Accordingly, she touched the ground with her wand, and the most beautiful horse, superbly harnessed, stood before them, and seemed to invite the Cavalier to get upon his back. "The beauty of this horse," continued the Fairy, "is his least perfection; for he possesses the rare quality of eating only once a week, and the still rarer, of knowing the past, the present, and the future. If you wish at any time to know what you ought to do for the best, you have only to consult him; you should therefore regard him as your best friend." The Fairy added, that if he stood in need of clothes, money, or jewels, he must stamp with his foot upon the ground, when a morocco trunk, containing the article he desired, would instantly make its appearance. "We must next," said she, "supply you with a proper name; and none, I think, can be better than that of Fortunio, since you have had the good fortune to deserve my favour."

Fortunio assured the Fairy of his eternal gratitude; he stamped with his foot, that he might procure himself a magnificent suit of clothes; he dressed himself, embraced his bountiful friend, and pursued his way to the palace of the King.

At the end of his first day's journey, he thought of sending a sum of money to his father, and some jewels to his sisters; he therefore shut himself in his chamber, and stamped loudly with his foot; a trunk immediately appeared, but it was locked, and without a key.

Fortunio was at a loss how to remedy this new perplexity; when, suddenly recollecting that Comrade (so the horse was called) could most probably afford him some assistance, he paid him a visit in his stable. "Comrade," said he, "where can I find the key of the trunk filled with money and jewels?"

"In my ear," says Comrade.

Fortunio looked in his ear, and there was the key, tied to a piece of green ribbon. He then joyfully opened the trunk, and despatched the presents.

The next morning, he mounted his faithful Comrade, and proceeded on his journey. They had not gone far, when, passing through a thick forest, they saw a man cutting down trees. Comrade stopped, and told his master he had better engage this man, whose name was Strongback, in his service, as a Fairy had bestowed on him the gift of carrying what weight he chose upon his back at once. Fortunio approached, and found him extremely willing to accept his offer.

When they had proceeded a little farther, they saw another man, who was tying his legs together. Comrade again stopped, saying, "Master, you cannot do better than to hire this man also, for he has the gift of running ten times faster than a deer; for which reason

274

it is, that he is now tying his legs, that he may not run so fast as to leave all the game he is going in pursuit of behind him." Fortunio engaged Lightfoot also, without the least hesitation.

On the following day, they perceived a man, who was tying a bandage over his eyes. "He, too," said Comrade, "is gifted, for he can see at the distance of a thousand miles; on which account, as he is going to kill game, he wishes to make his sight less perfect, that he may not kill so many at a time, as to leave none for the following day; he cannot fail of being useful to us." Fortunio accordingly engaged him without difficulty, and found his name was Marksman.

At a short distance farther, they saw a man lying on his side, and putting his ear to the ground. Fortunio asked Comrade if he, too, was gifted, and if he thought he could be useful to him. "Nothing is more certain," answered Comrade. "This man has the gift of hearing in such perfection, as none before him ever possessed; his name is Fine-ear, and he is this moment employed in listening, to hear if some herbs he stands in need of are now coming up from the earth." Fortunio thought the gift of Fine-ear more curious than even the rest, and, accordingly, made him such proposals for entering his service as he thought proper to accept.

When they were on their last day's journey, they had the good fortune to meet with another man, who, as well as the rest, was gifted in the most extraordinary manner; for Comrade assured him that he could work windmills with a single breath. "Shall I engage him, too?" cried Fortunio.

"You will have reason to be satisfied, if you do so," answered Comrade. So Boisterer was instantly engaged.

Just as they were in sight of the city in which the palace stood, they observed two men sitting near each other on the ground. "Ah!" cried Comrade, "no one was ever so fortunate as you, my master: both these men are also gifted; if we had been one minute later, no doubt we should have missed them. He who sits nearest to us is called Gourmand, because he can eat a thousand loaves at a mouthful. The other drinks up whole rivers without once stopping to breathe; his name is Tippler. Get them both into your service, and your good fortune will be complete." Fortunio did not hesitate a moment in doing as he was desired; so he proceeded to the palace, attended by Strongback, Lightfoot, Marksman, Fine-ear, Boisterer, Gourmand, and Tippler, who all promised to use their extraordinary talents as he should be pleased to command.

Fortunio then stamped with his foot, and a trunk made its appearance, filled with the richest liveries to fit each of them; which they accordingly put on, and proceeded in great pomp to the King's palace, where Fortunio was most graciously received, and provided with the best apartments it afforded, the King having desired he would rest from his fatigue before he entered into conversation with him.

The next day, his Majesty requested to speak with Fortunio, who instantly obeyed the summons; he presented him to the Princess, his sister; who, having been married when young to a neighbouring Prince, was now a widow, and was living with her brother, to console him in his misfortunes. She received Fortunio very kindly, thinking he was the handsomest Prince she had ever beheld. The King asked Fortunio his name and family; and upon hearing he was the son of an Earl, who had formerly served in defence of his crown, loaded him with new distinctions, and assured him of his regard.

While preparations were making for the attack that was meditated against the Emperor, our young lady remained in the palace; and, being constantly in company with the King, perceived in him so many amiable qualities, that she would willingly have offered herself to be his page, if she had not feared that such a proposal might look like want of courage to fight in his army.

But while she was thus thinking she should like to spend her life with the King, the Princess, his sister, was thinking she should like to spend hers with Fortunio; for she had fallen exceedingly in love with his uncommon beauty. She loaded him with presents, always spoke to him in the softest manner imaginable, and was in hopes he would discover how much she wished he should feel for her the same affection.

Fortunio, however, appeared perfectly indifferent; and as the King's company was so very dear to him, he constantly left the Princess to obtain it; so that, at length, she said to her favourite companion, Florida, "He is so young and inexperienced, that he will never understand how much I love him, if he is not told of it. Go," continued she, "and ask him if he should not like to marry such a Princess as I am."

Florida left the Princess; but being herself no less in love with Fortunio, "whose condition and age," says she, "are surely more suitable to mine than to the Princess," she used the opportunity to tell him how very peevish the Princess was, and how disagreeable she found her situation. Then, returning to her mistress, she told her, that all she said made no impression on Fortunio, who, she did not doubt, was in love with some lady of his own country.

The Princess sent Florida from time to time upon the same expedition, without the least success. At length, she determined to see him herself in private; accordingly, she ordered Florida to watch when he should be walking alone near a small arbour in the garden. She did not wait long for the opportunity she desired; seeing Fortunio near the arbour, she waited till he had entered it, and then proceeded thither. Fortunio, on seeing her, would have retired; but she desired him to stay and assist her with his arm in walking. The Princess at first talked of the fineness of the weather, and the beauty of the gardens and the fountains. At length, she said, "You cannot, Fortunio, but be sensible of the great affection I bear you; I am, therefore, surprised that you do not take advantage of your good fortune, by asking me in marriage of the King my brother."

Fortunio was thrown into the greatest confusion, which the Princess interpreted as a proof that he did not dislike what she had proposed; but what was her surprise and indignation, when, a moment after, he said: "I feel for you, Madam, all the respect due to

the sister of so amiable a King; but I am not free to marry you." She was red and pale by turns; and after telling him he should repent his coldness, she left him suddenly.

The Earl's daughter was now in the greatest perplexity imaginable, and would have found some pretence for absenting herself from the palace till the army should be ready, if she could have left the King without the greatest pain. Her uneasiness every day increased, and she carefully avoided meeting the Princess alone.

One day, as the King, the Princess, and Fortunio were sitting at their dessert, the King looked very melancholy; and his sister asking him the reason: "You know," said he, "what an affliction has happened in my kingdom. A great Dragon has devoured several of my subjects, and many flocks of sheep; his breath poisons the waters of the fountains he approaches, and destroys all the fields of corn through which he passes. Can you, therefore, wonder at my sorrow?"

The Princess thought she could not have a better opportunity of revenging herself for the indifference of the young Cavalier. "Brother," said she, "here is the brave Fortunio, who would esteem it, no doubt, the highest honour to be permitted to kill this monster, and thus reward the kindness your Majesty has been pleased to show him."

Fortunio could not but accept the proffered honour; which the Princess was in hopes would be the means of revenging the affront he had offered her, by being the cause of his death. He had no sooner left the room, than he went to his faithful Comrade, to know in what manner he should set about the enterprise. "You should go," replied Comrade, "in pursuit of the Dragon, as the King requires, and take with you the seven gifted attendants you lately engaged."

Fortunio, the next morning, waited accordingly on the King and Princess, to take a formal leave. The King gave him the kindest assurances imaginable, and bade him adieu with the sincerest sorrow for the danger to which he would soon be exposed. The Princess tried to seem extremely sorry also, and expressed her wishes to see him return in safety. After this, Fortunio, mounted on Comrade, and attended by Strongback, Lightfoot, Marksman, Fine-ear, Boisterer, Gourmand, and Tippler, set out to find the Dragon. They were, indeed, of immediate use to him in this undertaking; for Tippler drank up all the rivers, so that they could easily cross from field to field, and catch the rarest kinds of fish for their master's dinner. Lightfoot ran after hares and rabbits; Marksman shot at partridges and pheasants; Strongback carried them all upon his back; and Fine-ear, by putting his ear to the ground, found out the places where the mushrooms and kitchen herbs were coming out of the earth.

They had not proceeded more than a day's journey, when they heard the cries of some peasants that the Dragon was eating up as fast as he could. Fortunio immediately asked Comrade what he should do. "Let Fine-ear find out in what place he is," answered Comrade. Fine-ear immediately put his ear to the ground, and informed his master the Dragon was seven leagues off. "Then," continued Comrade, "let Tippler drink up all the rivers that are between us, and let Strongback carry wine enough to fill them, and next strew some of the hares and partridges along them." Fortunio then entered a house that stood near, to watch the event. In less than an hour the Dragon was in sight, and, smelling the hares and partridges, began to eat voraciously; and finding himself at length thirsty, he drank no less eagerly of the wine; so that in a short time, being quite drunk, he threw himself on the ground, and fell fast asleep. "Now is your time, my good master," said the faithful Comrade. Fortunio immediately approached the Dragon, and with a single blow cut off his head, and then commanded Strongback to take him up, and carry him to the palace.

The King received Fortunio with the liveliest joy and affection; and the Princess, too, disguising as well as she could her disappointment, returned him thanks for the service he had done the whole kingdom. "At the same time," thinks she to herself, "it shall not be long before I find some better means of being revenged."

Soon after, the King being again extremely sorrowful, the Princess inquired the cause as before. "Alas!" said he, "how can I be otherwise, since the Emperor has not left me money enough to prepare the army I intended to send out against him?"

"Brother," answered she, "can you suppose that Fortunio, who was able to do what twenty armies could not have done, in killing the Dragon, is not also able to oblige the Emperor to restore your treasures? I am certain you are most unjust, if you believe the contrary."

Fortunio, though he fully understood the malice of the Princess, could not but assure his Majesty of his earnest desire to make the experiment; upon which, the King, after tenderly embracing him, and protesting that, should any accident befall him in the undertaking, he should never again be happy, gave him the necessary instructions for his departure.

Fortunio lost no time in consulting Comrade, saying, he feared his destruction was now certain. "Do not, my dear master, thus afflict yourself," said Comrade. "I have long foreseen that this would happen, and I have no doubt you will return from your undertaking as victorious as before. You should give to each of your attendants," continued he, "a new and splendid livery; let them be mounted on handsome horses, and we will set out without delay."

They arrived in a few hours in the city of the Emperor, when, after taking some refreshment, they proceeded to the palace, where Fortunio demanded of him an interview, in which he made a formal claim to all the treasures of King Alfourite. The Emperor, at this, could not restrain a smile. "Do you really think," said he, "that I should so easily resign what I took such pains to obtain? If you had brought an army with you, we might, to be sure, have contended for the victory; but as it is, I would advise you, young Cavalier, not to force me to use harsh means in sending you out of my kingdom." Fortunio replied, that

he meant no incivility, but begged the Emperor to consider of his request.

"This is really very extraordinary," said the Emperor; "however, as your demand is ridiculous enough, I will offer you a condition no less ridiculous. If you can find a man that will eat all the bread that has been provided for the inhabitants of this city, for his breakfast, I will grant your request."

Fortunio could scarce contain himself for joy. He replied, that he accepted the condition, and sent instantly for Gourmand; when, telling him what had passed, he inquired if he was quite sure he could eat the whole.

"Never fear, my good master," answers Gourmand; "you will see that they will be sooner sorry than I."

When the Emperor, the Empress, the Princess his daughter, and the whole court, had seated themselves to witness this extraordinary undertaking, Fortunio advanced, with Gourmand by his side; and seeing six great mountains of loaves, that almost reached the skies, he began to fear; but looking at Gourmand, and seeing how eager he was to begin, he again took courage. When the proper signal was given, Gourmand attacked the first mountain, and in less than a minute had swallowed the whole; he did the same with the second, and so on to the sixth; which having completely devoured, he told the Emperor he must take the liberty to say, he had had but a scanty breakfast, considering he was in the dominions of so rich a monarch.

Never was any astonishment so great as that of the spectators; and the inhabitants of the city, who had all assembled to see so singular a sight, now fell to crying, and said, "We shall have no bread to give our children for many days."

But the Emperor's disappointment was still greater; so, commanding Fortunio to approach, he said: "Young Cavalier, you cannot possibly expect that I should give you the treasures of King Alfourite, because you happen to have a servant who is a great eater. However, to show you that I hold you in some consideration, find a man who shall drink up all the rivers, aqueducts, and reservoirs, together with all the wine that is in the cellars of all my subjects, in the space of a minute, and I promise to grant your request."

Fortunio thought his Majesty acted very dishonourably, yet he did not hesitate to accept his new proposal; accordingly, Tippler was immediately sent for, and performed his task with equal ease, to the astonishment of the surrounding multitude.

The Emperor now looked extremely grave, telling Fortunio, that what he had seen, though extremely singular, was not enough to deserve the costly recompense he claimed: "Therefore," continued he, "if you would obtain it, you must find a person who is as swift in running as my daughter."

Fortunio, though extremely dissatisfied, was obliged to consent; and, sending for Lightfoot, bade him prepare for running a race with a Princess whom no one had ever yet been able to overtake. In the meantime, the Princess retired to put on the dress and shoes which had been made on purpose for her to run in; and on her return, finding Lightfoot ready for the contest, they prepared to set off at the appointed signal. The Princess now called for some of the cordial she was accustomed to drink when she was going to run; upon which Lightfoot observed, it would be but just that he should have some too. To this the Princess readily consented; and stepping aside, she dexterously threw into his glass a few drops of a liquid that had the power to throw him into a profound sleep.

The signal being given, the Princess set off full speed; while Lightfoot, instead of doing the same, threw himself on the ground, and fell fast asleep. The race was several miles long; and the Princess had proceeded more than half way, when Fortunio, seeing her approach the goal without Lightfoot, turned as pale as death, and cried out, "Comrade, I am undone! I see nothing of Lightfoot."

"My Lord," answered Comrade, "Fine-ear shall tell you in a moment how far he is off."

Fine-ear listened, and informed Fortunio that Lightfoot was snoring in the place from which the Princess began her race. Then Comrade directed Marksman to shoot an arrow into his ear, which he did so completely, that Lightfoot started up, and, seeing the Princess nearly arrived at the goal, set off with such rapidity, that he seemed carried by the winds, and, passing the Princess, reached it before her.

The Emperor was now almost frantic with rage; and, recollecting that he had some years ago displeased a Fairy, he concluded that the wonders he had seen performed were contrived by her, to punish him: he therefore thought it would be useless to propose farther experiments; and calling for Fortunio, he said to him, "It cannot be denied that you have accomplished my conditions; take, therefore, away with you as much of the treasures of King Alfourite as one of your attendants can carry on his back."

Fortunio desired nothing better; and being instantly admitted to the store-rooms which contained them, he commanded Strongback to begin to load himself. Strongback, accordingly, laid hold at first of five hundred statues of gold, taller than giants; next of ten thousand bags of money, and afterwards of as many filled with precious stones; he then took the chariots and horses; in short, he left not a single article that had formerly belonged to King Alfourite.

They then hastened from the palace, and proceeded to King Alfourite's dominions. No sooner were they on the road, than the seven gifted attendants began to ask what recompense they were to have for their services. "The recompense belongs to me," said Lightfoot; "for, if I had not outrun the Princess, we might have returned as we came."

"And, pray," says Fine-ear, "what would you have done, if I had not heard you snore?"

"I think you must both acknowledge," says Marksman, "that our success was owing to my shooting the arrow exactly into Lightfoot's ear."

"I cannot help wondering at your arrogance," says Strongback; "pray who brought away the treasures? To whom can you be indebted, but to me?"

Thus they were going on, when Fortunio interrupted them, with saying: "It is true, my friends, you

have all performed wonders; but you should leave to the King the care of rewarding you. He sent us to regain his treasures, and not to steal them. But," continued he, "should his Majesty fail to reward you, yet you shall have no reason to complain, for I will take upon myself to gratify your largest expectations."

Fortunio arrived in safety with the treasures at the palace of King Alfourite, who beheld him with amazement, and embraced him in the utmost transport; and his bravery so increased the attachment the Princess had conceived for him, that she, that very day, desired to speak with him in private, intending once more to question him as to his thoughts concerning her; "For," says she to herself, "when I remind him of the honours I have been the means of his obtaining, how can he do otherwise than return my affection?"

Fortunio received her summons, but sent her for answer, that he could not have the pleasure of waiting on her. The Princess, enraged by his disdain, ran to the King all in tears, in the middle of the night, and declared that Fortunio had sent Strongback to her chamber to carry her away by force, that he might marry her; that, previous to his late enterprise, he had himself engaged in a similar attempt. "In short, dear brother," said the artful creature, "nothing but the death of this presumptuous wretch can satisfy my vengeance, or ensure my safety."

The King's affliction at hearing this was greater than can be described; and having passed the night in lamenting the cruel necessity to which he was reduced of punishing him, he the next morning ordered him to be taken into custody, and to be tried for the offence.

When the time of trial came, it was in vain that Fortunio pleaded his innocence; no one believed it possible for a great Princess to invent so wicked a falsehood. So the judges declared him guilty, and condemned him to receive three darts shot into his heart that very day.

The King left the court shedding many tears; but the cruel Princess stayed to see the sentence executed. The officer, approaching Fortunio, unbuttoned his waistcoat, and then opened his shirt, that his heart might be bare to receive the darts; but no sooner was this done, than the snowy whiteness of the bosom that appeared, convinced all the beholders that the sufferer was a woman.

Every eye was immediately turned upon the Princess, to reproach her with the baseness of her conduct, in bringing so false an accusation against an innocent creature, and one, besides, who had shown such unexampled courage, and done the state such signal services; while she, unable to bear the shame that awaited her, took out of her pocket a sharp knife, and plunged it into her heart, saying, "Fortunio is revenged of my injustice."

Fortunio was led in triumph to the palace; and the King, when he had spent some weeks in bewailing the unfortunate end of the Princess his sister, made an offer of his hand and crown to Fortunio. Their marriage was celebrated with the greatest pomp. The old Earl and his two daughters were sent for on the occasion, and ever after remained at court. The first care of the new Queen was to provide a magnificent stable for Comrade, whom she visited daily, and consulted upon all affairs of importance, so that the King never after lost a battle. She settled a handsome pension on Strongback, Lightfoot, Marksman, Fine-ear, Boisterer, Gourmand, and Tippler, who all lived together in a splendid castle a few miles in the country; it being agreed between the Queen and them, that when her Majesty should have occasion for their service, she should say so to some one in the palace, so that Fine-ear might catch the sound, and send the person she desired.

The Queen sent an express to invite the Old Shepherdess to court; but she refused, saying, all she wished was the Queen's happiness, and that she should now leave the world with satisfaction.

RIQUET WITH THE TUFT.

THERE was, once upon a time, a Queen, who had a little son; but he had a hunch upon his back; and was, besides, so hideously ugly, that it was for some time doubted if he had the form of a human creature.

A Fairy, who happened to be present at the Prince's birth, assured his parents that, notwithstanding his excessive ugliness, he would make himself agreeable to every one, on account of his great wit and talents; she added, that this was not all, for that she had also bestowed upon him the power of endowing the person he should love best in the world with the very same qualities.

All this was some consolation to the poor Queen, who was dreadfully afflicted at the thought of having brought such a frightful little creature into the world. It is true, no sooner did he begin to talk, than he said the most charming things imaginable; and whatever he did was in so clever and agreeable a manner, that everybody loved and admired him.

Seven years after, the Queen of a neighbouring kingdom was brought to bed of twin daughters; the one that was born first was more beautiful than the day, which caused the Queen so very much joy, that it was thought by those about her that it would endanger her life.

The same Fairy who was present at the birth of little Riquet with the Tuft, was with this Queen in her confinement; and to remedy the inconvenience her too great joy had occasioned, she assured her that the new-born Princess should have no understanding at all, but that she should be as silly and stupid as she was handsome.

This assurance grieved the Queen very much: but in a few minutes she received a still greater disappointment; for the second Princess, when born, was the ugliest little marmot ever beheld.

The Fairy, seeing the Queen's distress, said to her: "I entreat your Majesty, do not thus afflict yourself. Your daughter shall be endowed with so much wit, that nobody will perceive her want of beauty."

"This would be a great comfort to me, indeed," replied the Queen; "but would it not be possible to bestow a small portion of the same charming advantage on the Princess who is so beautiful?"

"That is not in my power," answered the Fairy; "I cannot meddle with her understanding, but I can do all I please with respect to her beauty; and therefore, as there is nothing I would not do for your satisfaction, I will bestow on her, for a gift, that she shall be able to make the person she loves as handsome as she pleases."

As the two Princesses grew up, their perfections grew also, and nothing was talked of but the beauty of the eldest, and the wit and talents of the youngest. It is true, their defects increased in the same degree; for the youngest became every day more ugly, and the eldest more ignorant and stupid; she either did not reply at all to the questions that were asked of her, or spoke in the silliest manner possible. She was, too, so extremely awkward, that if she had to place half a dozen tea-cups on the chimney-piece, she was sure to break one of them; or if she attempted to drink a glass of water, she let half of it fall upon her clothes.

Though beauty is a great advantage to a young lady, yet the youngest of the Princesses was by every one preferred to the eldest. It must be confessed, that people first approached the eldest, to see and admire her; but they soon left her, to hear the clever and agreeable conversation of her sister; so that in less than a quarter of an hour the eldest always found herself alone, while all strangers got as near as they could to the youngest.

The eldest, though very stupid, observed all this, and would willingly have parted with her beauty to gain but half the wit of her sister. The Queen, notwithstanding her good-nature, could not refrain from reproving her now and then for her stupidity; so that the poor Princess was ready to die of grief.

One day, having retired to a neighbouring wood, where, without being seen, she might sit down and cry at her ease for the hard fate she was obliged to endure, she perceived a young man of small stature, and very ugly, coming near to her; he was at the same time magnificently dressed. This was the young Prince Riquet with the Tuft, who, having fallen violently in love with this Princess, from the portraits he had everywhere seen of her, had left his father's kingdom to have the pleasure of seeing and conversing with her.

Delighted at so unexpected an opportunity of meeting her alone, he addressed her with all imaginable respect. Observing, after the first compliments were over, that she appeared very melancholy, he said: "I cannot imagine, Madam, how it is possible for a lady, possessed of such beauty as yours, to be so unhappy as you appear; for though I can boast of having seen a great number of handsome ladies, I can assure you, none of them could, in the smallest degree, be compared to you."

"You are pleased to flatter me," replied the Princess, without adding another word.

"Beauty," continued Riquet with the Tuft, "is so great an advantage, that it supplies the place of every-thing else; and she who is endowed with so great a

278

blessing ought be insensible to every kind of misfortune."

"I had much rather," said the Princess, "be as ugly as you are, and possessed of wit, than have the beauty you praise, and be such a fool as I am."

"Nothing, madam," replied the Prince, "is a surer mark of good sense than to believe ourselves in want of it; indeed, the more sensible we really are, the plainer we see how much we fall short of perfection."

"I know nothing of what you are talking of," answered the Princess; "but I do know that I am very, very foolish, and that is the cause of the grief in which you see me."

"If this is all that makes you unhappy, Madam," said the Prince, "I can very easily put an end to your affliction."

"By what means?" replied the Princess.

"I have the power," said Riquet with the Tuft, "to bestow as much wit as I please on the person I am to love best in the world; and as that person can be no other, Madam, than yourself, it depends only on your own will to be the wittiest lady upon the earth. I shall ask of you in return but one condition, which is, that you shall consent to marry me."

The Princess looked at him with astonishment, but did not speak a word.

"I see," continued Riquet, "that my proposal makes you uneasy, and I am not surprised at it; I will therefore give you a whole year to consider of your answer."

The Princess was so very stupid and silly, and at the same time so much desired to be witty, that she resolved on accepting the offer made her by Prince Riquet with the Tuft; she even thought a whole year a very long time, and would gladly have made it shorter if she could. She accordingly told the Prince she would marry him on that day twelvemonth; and no sooner had she pronounced the words, than she found herself quite another creature : she said everything she wished, not only with the greatest ease imaginable, but in the most natural and graceful manner. She immediately took her part in a lively and agreeable conversation with the Prince, in which she showed herself so extremely witty, that Riquet began to fear he had bestowed upon her more of the charming quality she so much longed for than he had kept to himself.

When the Princess returned to the palace, the whole court was thrown into the utmost astonishment at the sudden and wonderful change they observed in her; for everything she now uttered they found to be as clever and entertaining as it had before been stupid and ridiculous.

The joy at this event was the greatest ever known throughout the court: the youngest Princess was the only person who did not partake of it; for as she had no longer the advantage of wit over the beauty of her sister, she could not but appear to every one the most ugly and disagreeable creature in the world.

The King now consulted his eldest daughter in the affairs of his government, and was even guided by her advice in matters of the greatest importance. And the news of this great change being everywhere talked of, it soon reached the ears of the neighbouring Princes, who all hastened to present themselves at her father's palace, to gain, if possible, her favour, and demand her in marriage of the King. But the Princess listened with equal coldness and indifference to all they had to say : not one of them had wit enough to make her think for a moment of accepting his offer.

At length, there came a Prince, so powerful, so rich, so witty, and so handsome, that she could not help feeling a great affection for him. The King, perceiving this, told her that she had only to choose for a husband whom she liked best, and that she might be sure of his consenting to her marriage with him. But as the most sensible persons are always the most careful in determining on such serious matters, the Princess, after thanking her father, begged him to allow her time to consider of what she should do.

Soon after, the Princess chanced, in her walk, to wander towards the very wood in which she had met with Riquet with the Tuft; and wishing to be free from interruption while thinking of her new lover, she proceeded a good way into it.

When she had walked about for some time, she heard a great noise under ground, like that of many persons running backwards and forwards, and busily employed on some affair of importance. After listening for a moment, she distinguished different voices : one said, "Bring me that kettle;" another, "Fetch the great boiler;" another, "Put some coals on the fire." At the same moment the ground opened, and a spacious kitchen, filled with vast numbers of cooks, assistants, and scullions, together with all sorts of utensils fit for preparing a splendid dinner, appeared to the view of the astonished Princess. Some had rolling-pins, and were making the most delicate sorts of pastry; others were beating the syllabubs and turning the custards; and at one end of the kitchen she saw at least twenty men-cooks, all busily employed in trussing different sorts of the finest game and poultry imaginable, and singing all the time as merrily as could be.

The Princess, in the utmost surprise at what she beheld, inquired of them to whom they belonged.

"To Prince Riquet of the Tuft, Madam," replied the head cook, "whose wedding dinner we are preparing."

The Princess, still more surprised than before, and instantly recollecting that this was exactly the day twelvemonth on which she had promised to marry Prince Riquet, was ready to sink on the ground. The reason of her not recollecting this before was, that when she made the promise she was quite silly, and that the wit the Prince had endowed her with, had made her forget everthing that had happened to her before.

She tried to walk away from the place, but had not gone twenty steps when Riquet with the Tuft presented himself before her, dressed magnificently in the gayest wedding-suit that ever was seen.

"You perceive, Madam," said he, "that I have kept my promise faithfully; and no doubt you have come hither for the same purpose, and, by bestowing on me your hand, to make me the happiest of men."

"I must frankly confess," replied the Princess,

"that I am not yet come to a resolution on that subject, and also, that I fear it will never be in my power to consent to what you desire."

"You quite astonish me, Madam!" answered Prince Riquet.

"That I can easily imagine," continued the Princess; "and certainly I should be greatly perplexed what to say to you, if I did not know that you possess the best understanding in the world. Were you a silly Prince, you would no doubt say to me: 'The promise of a Princess should not be broken, and therefore you must marry me.' But you, Prince Riquet, who have so much more sense than any other, will, I trust, excuse me for what I have declared. You cannot have forgotten that, when I was but a silly, stupid Princess, I could not be prevailed on to consent to marry you; how, therefore, now that I am endowed with understanding, and for that reason must naturally be the more difficult to be pleased, can you expect me to choose the Prince I then rejected? If you really wished to marry me, you did very wrong to change me from the most silly creature in the world to the most witty, so as to make me see more plainly the faults of others."

"If, Madam," replied Riquet with the Tuft, "you would think it but reasonable in a Prince without sense to reproach you for what you have declared, why should you think proper to deny to me the same advantage, in an affair in which the happiness of my whole life is concerned? Is it just that persons of sense should be worse treated than those who have none? You, my Princess, who are now so very clever, and so much wished to be so, can you really determine to treat me in this manner? But let us consider a little. Is there anything in me, besides my ugliness, that you dislike? Are you dissatisfied with my birth, my understanding, my temper, manners, or condition?"

"With none of these," replied the Princess; "I dislike in you only the ugliness of your person."

"If that is the case," answered Riquet, "I shall soon be the happiest man alive, since you, Princess, have the power to make me as handsome as you please."

"How can that be possible?" resumed the Princess.

"Nothing more is necessary," said Riquet, "than that you should love me well enough to wish me very handsome; in short, my charming Princess, I must inform you that the same Fairy who at my birth bestowed upon me the gift of making the lady I love best as witty as I pleased, was present also at yours, and gave to you the power of making him you should love the best as handsome as you pleased."

"Since this is the case," said the Princess, "I wish you, with all my heart, to be the handsomest Prince in all the world; and, as much as depends on me, I bestow upon you the gift of beauty."

The Princess had no sooner finished speaking, than Riquet with the Tuft appeared to her eyes the handsomest, best-shaped, and most agreeable person she had ever beheld.

Some people were of opinion that this surprising change in the Prince was not occasioned by the gift of the Fairy, but that the love the Princess conceived for him was the only cause; and they also added, that the Princess thought so much of the perseverance of her lover, of his discretion, and the many excellent qualities of heart and mind he possessed, that she no longer perceived either the ugliness of his face, or the deformity of his person.

The hunch on his back now seemed to her to be nothing more than the easy carriage in which men of quality indulge themselves, and his lameness a careless freedom in his gait, which appeared extremely graceful; the squinting of his eyes, in those of the Princess, did but make them seem more brilliant and more tender; as also, his thick red nose, in her opinion, gave a warlike and heroic air to his whole face.

However this may be, the Princess promised to marry Prince Riquet with the Tuft immediately, provided he could obtain the consent of the King her father.

The King, being informed that his daughter entertained a great esteem for Prince Riquet with the Tuft, and having heard of the extraordinary qualities of both his heart and mind, received him with pleasure for a son-in-law; so that the following day, as the Prince had long expected, proved to be that of his union with the beautiful and no less witty Princess.

THE FLOWER BRIDE.

On a hedge-side, close by a field of hay,
Three flowers blossomed, in the month of May;
These lovely flowers three gentle girls had been,
But now were changed to flowers by some Witch Queen.

They filled the air all day with rich perfume;
At night, two only remained there to bloom:
The fact was this, one was but lately married,
And would get lectured if she out had tarried.

But when the night had passed, and daylight came,
She stood beside them, as before, the same,
Opening her brilliant leaflets to the sun,
Until he through his daily course had run.

But now she pined, and much deplored the fate,
That took her daily from her loved helpmate.
"To-morrow morning, dear," with voice so bland,
She cried, "oh! come and pluck me, as I stand;

"Then I from duties loved no more shall roam,
But live a gay, contented wife at home."
"Oh! pleasure much to be desired," said he;
"How shall I know you, love, from all the three?"

"The flowers," she said, "that don't belong to you,
Will have their leaves impearlèd with the dew;
Whilst I, who nestling in your arms have lain,
Have neither felt the falling dew or rain."

When morning came, quick to the field he hied,
And gathered there his fragrant blooming bride;
But since that hour, I've ever heard it said,
The perfumed lily droops her modest head.

LITTLE MOUCK'S RACE WITH THE ROYAL COURIER.

LITTLE MOUCK.

MULEY, a lively young merchant, when travelling with a caravan of merchants from Damascus to Jerusalem, on being called upon for a story, during a halt in the evening, told the following:—

There dwelt at Nicea, when I was a child, a strange personage, whom people used to call Little Mouck. I can now see him before my eyes, with his grotesque look, and a physiognomy the queerest you ever met; but I had a reason beyond this for remembering him, as it was on his account that I received, one day, a severe hiding from my father.

Little Mouck was already an old boy when I made his acquaintance, and yet he was scarcely three feet and a half high; and all over he was something remarkable, for while his body was small and thin, his head had developed itself to an enormous size, and rested on his shoulders like a gigantic dome on a light colonnade, that it threatened to crush with its superincumbent weight; or rather—to use a less ambitious comparison, and one more in keeping with the hero of my tale—his head had the look of a pumpkin, stuck on the top of a walking-stick; while Mr. Mouck himself, as a whole, head and body, reminded one forcibly, in figure, of a cup and ball

He lived all alone in his house, and got all his meals himself; and thus no one in the place knew whether he was dead or alive, as he only came out once a month, about mid-day, when everybody else was in-doors from the heat. Besides this, at times, though rarely, we caught a glimpse of him, as he took a walk on the terraced roof of his house, the balustrade of which almost covered up all his form, in such a way that, from the street, all that could be seen was a head walking along the roof.

My playfellows and myself, who were ever on the look-out for fun, and ready to make it out of any object, especially one so queer-looking as little Mouck, reckoned it as good as a holiday every time the little gentleman came out into the street. On one of those days when he was sure to make his appearance, we assembled before his house, and waited his coming forth. The door opened, and the great head, with a great turban upon it, shaped like an enormous

LITTLE MOUCK COMES OUT.

pumpkin, appeared in front, and cast a look of exploration to the right and left, on either side; after which, the rest of the little body ventured itself over the threshold. Mouck now exhibited himself before us in all his glory: his shoulders covered with a short mantle rather the worse for wear; his legs lost in vast sacks of trowsers; and his waist girded with a tight

282

belt, which held a poniard of large size. At last, he set out on his way, amidst shouts of joy from us boys, as we threw up our caps in the air, and danced and frisked like mad, round and about the little fellow. He bowed to us on the right and left, with a grand, serious air, as he advanced down the street with slow steps, forced, as he was, to drag his feet after him in walking, that he might not lose his slippers, too big by half. As we followed him, we sang a merry song, with a rattling chorus, about his pumpkin hat, and his pumpkin head, and his little cloak, and large slippers; and we did this so often, and made such game of him, that at last, I am sorry to say, I went on, as is too often the case, from fun to rudeness. I called to him that he would lose his large breeches; I pulled him by the cloak; I pelted his turban with pellets of paper; and there was no sort of mischief to which I did not have recourse to tease him. At last, I took my measures so well, as to succeed in treading on the heel of one of his large shuffling slippers, and the poor little fellow was thrown on his nose to the ground. This only made us laugh the more; but the joke lost much of its pleasantry, as far as I was concerned, when I saw Little Mouck, after just stopping to brush the dust off his knees, start on his way once more, but, this time, directing his footsteps to my father's house. I well knew the severity of the paternal discipline, and could foresee what would be the end of the incident. However, I slipped behind the door, from whence I saw Little Mouck come forth again, conducted out by my father, who held him respectfully by the hand, and made numerous bows and excuses in taking leave of him.

All this salaaming boded no good to me; and I began to feel very qualmish as to how the agreeable morning I had spent would end. So I kept out as long as I could, until, at last, driven home by hunger, which came upon me, in actual suffering, more dreadful than the beating I had every reason to expect, I sneaked into the house, with my head down, and stood before my judge.

"You have committed an outrage on the good Mouck, you wicked boy," said he to me, in a severe tone. "Come here, and let me tell you the story of that poor little man, and I feel assured that, when you know his marvellous adventures, you will never think of mocking at him again."

I was just rejoicing inwardly at the turn affairs had taken—a nice story of wonderful adventures, instead of a sound flogging with a thick cane—when my father added: "But, by way of fixing such grave recollections the better on your memory, you will receive, before and after the story, the *usual* dose!"

This "usual" allowance signified the twenty blows which my father was in the habit of laying on my shoulders, when I was in fault, counting them scrupulously all the while. This time, he was more particular than ever in keeping the reckoning, and harder in the whacking than I had ever felt him before. When the twentieth blow resounded on my wincing shoulders, my father ordered me to give him my closest attention, as he commenced the STORY OF LITTLE MOUCK, in the following terms:—

The Father of Little Mouck was a man of letters, who, although little indebted to Fortune for any favours, enjoyed great consideration in Nicea. He lived, generally, almost solitary, just as his son does now. Unfortunately, he took a dislike to his child, from a feeling of shame and ridicule at his dwarfish size. When Little Mouck had reached the age of six, he was still babbling and playing like an infant child; and his father, a man to whom all trifling was abhorrent, reproached him time after time with his foolishness, without, however, thinking it necessary to take any pains himself to educate or awaken the dormant mind of his child, whose intelligence seemed just as short and backward as his size.

At last, it happened that the Old Mouckrah fell down and broke his leg. Fever came on; he dragged on some time, and then died, leaving behind him Little Mouck, in poverty, and, what is worse, in ignorance—that is to say, in every respect incompetent to provide for his own necessities. Mouckrah, perpetually buried in scientific abstractions, had hardly ever thought of his own very moderate means, and, beyond all doubt, was on the very verge of ruin just at the moment of his death. Some of his hardhearted relatives, who had already obliged Mouckrah with money at heavy interest, now made their appearance, and turned Little Mouck out of his father's house, but not without first giving him some good advice.

"Be off, boy," they said, "take a run over the world; keep stirring, and you will end by lighting upon a fortune."

Mouck had never received any instruction, and his innocence was beyond all bounds, except those of his ignorance. He happened, however, to possess natural good sense, and saw at once that entreaties would avail him nothing: under the cousin's skin he saw the creditor.

"That will do," he replied; "but you might, at least, let me carry away my father's clothes."

Now, this was not by any means a sumptuous wardrobe, you may be sure; so they gave it him readily, after a few protestations of the great value of the gift.

Old Mouckrah was a large and robust man: I need not say how his coat and the rest of his garments fitted on the small figure of our poor Little Mouck. But he cut them short where they were too long, and then put them on his back, without imagining for a moment that it was necessary to reduce their breadth as well. Hence originated that strange costume, that he wears even to this day, and that he seems to have made a vow always to wear, for you never see him in any other accoutrements.

With a low bow to his excellent relations, Little Mouck stuck his father's old sword in his girdle, took his staff in his hand, and went his way. He walked along merrily during the first half of the day; for, since he had set forth to seek his fortune, he thought himself sure, no doubt, of meeting with it. So reasoned our innocent Mouck, whose dreams were, as yet, unbroken by the rude touch of experience. Life, to him, was all illusion; if he saw a bit of glass sparkling in the road, he picked it up as a precious treasure, and thought it must be a diamond; when he caught sight, in the distance, of the cupolas and minarets of some town sparkling in the sunlight, or of some lake, smooth as glass, and shining like silver in the horizon, he sprang forward with joy to what he regarded as the entrance of some Fairy Land. But, alas! the nearer he advanced to them, the more the deceitful images lost their enchantment; and soon there came over poor Little Mouck a weariness that took all power out of his small legs, and, what was worse, a grumbling of the stomach, that told him that he had not quite reached the Paradise of his dreams.

And so he kept running, walking, lounging, limping, crawling, for two days; wearied, hungered, saddened, feeding upon some wild and bitter fruit, very hard nuts, even for young teeth to crack, and berries whose juice would have been physic to a full-meated stomach. His only bed was the hard, cold ground, that scratched his ears as he lay down upon it for a pillow. Hence he was beginning to have dark thoughts as to his coming fortune, when, one morning, from the top of an eminence, he caught sight of the walls of a large city. The rising sun shone clear and gay on its gilded domes; and the flaunting flags, as

they floated in the breath of morning, seemed to Little Mouck as if they were making signals for him to enter. A moment's halt, and he took time to think; then, slapping his breast with a magnanimous air, tightening his girdle, loosening his great sabre in its sheath, and pressing his turban on his brow—"Yes," said he to himself, as he advanced a step forward—"yes! it is here that Little Mouck will find his fortune." In spite of his weariness, he gave a joyful bound, and shouted, with as much voice as he had, and as loud as he could, "Now, then, Little Mouck!—a name, here or nowhere!"

Then he gathered up his strength, and directed his steps towards the town; but, however near he was to it, he was not able to reach it before mid-day, for his little limbs entirely refused to do any more work. At last, he reached the goal; and having arranged the folds of his cloak, set his turban straight on his head, tightened his girdle once again round his little waist, and given his poniard a more martial inclination, he made his entrance into the city with every possible bravery.

He went through numbers of streets, crossed many squares, trod many courts; still no door stood open to welcome him: there was no one waiting for him—no one to say, "Little Mouck! Little Mouck! are you hungry? Come in here, Little Mouck, and eat and drink, and rest your weary limbs."

He halted, at last, before a large and handsome house, and was looking at it with the melancholy feeling arising from an empty stomach, when an Old Woman appeared at one of the windows, and began singing the following queer song :—

"Pussy, Pussy, Pussy,
    Come to a treat;
The soup is just ready,
    So come here and eat.
Look, look!
Here's a capital cook!
A famous good dinner,
For every young sinner.
Come with a whoop, and come with a call;
Come with a good will, or don't come at all.'

"Just the thing," thought Little Mouck; "now is my time; that is just the invitation I wanted to hear."

Suddenly, the door opened, and innumerable dogs and cats ran up from every side, and went into the house.

THE OLD LADY INVITING THE CATS AND DOGS TO DINNER.

Little Mouck was greatly astonished at this, and stood gaping with his mouth wide open. He stood puzzling over what he saw for a little while; but, at last, the voice of his stomach gave a new turn to his thoughts; and with some little hesitation at first, but growing bolder at every step, he approached the haggard and strange-looking female, the very sight of whom inspired him with a vague terror. At last, summoning up courage, for his stomach would not keep quiet, now that the soup mentioned began to smell more savoury at a nearer approach, he stepped over the threshold of the mansion, a pair of young pussies

trotting up before him. These he determined to stick close to, sagaciously conjecturing that they would make straight towards the victuals.

When he got to the top of the staircase, he was stopped by the Old Lady whom he had seen at the window, who demanded of him, in a fierce tone, what he wanted there.

"I heard you invite everybody to your table," replied Mouck; "and as I have been horribly famished for three days past, I followed those I saw entering your doors."

The Old Woman grinned and nodded her head. "But, my funny little friend," said she, "have you not observed the kind of guests for whom I issued my invitations? Dogs and cats—these are my friends; none of you men!"

"I am hungry, very hungry," said Little Mouck; "and then, Madam, I am so little, so very little, that I shall scarcely eat more than a cat."

Softened by the entreaties and evident distress of the poor little fellow, the Old Woman consented to receive Mouck at her table, and seated him down by the side of a couple of old tabbies, who regarded him as an intruder, a matter about which our young friend cared very little at the moment, so occupied was he in cleaning out his spoon and bowl of broth.

"Little Mouck," said the Old Lady to him, after he had made what he called "a good feed," "would you like to be a servant in my house, where there is little trouble and good eating? Will that suit you?"

Mouck, whose soul was in the soup, joyfully gave in his assent to this proposal, and engaged himself, on the spot, in the service of Mrs. Towsy-Mowsy—for that was the odd name of this very queer old lady.

What he had to do was light enough, to be sure, but his duties were somewhat peculiar. Besides the animals of the neighbourhood, for whom Mrs. Towsy-Mowsy kept an open table at certain hours, she possessed two cats and four dogs of her own, and to these she devoted a special attention. Little Mouck's duty it was to attend particularly to these blessed animals. Every morning he had to wash, comb, and oil with fine scented mixtures, their several coats. Whenever their mistress went out, Little Mouck sat at the head of their table, and carved for them; and every night he put them to bed snugly on soft silk cushions, wrapping them up, besides, in velvet counterpanes.

There were several little dogs besides, young and old, pretty and ugly, in the house, under Little Mouck's excellent care; but for these so much attention was not required as for the cats, the objects of Mrs. Towsy-Mowsy's special affection, and beloved by her as if her children. For the rest, Little Mouck's life was just as lonely and hermit-like as it had been in his father's house; for, with the exception of his mistress, he saw nobody all day but the dogs and cats.

This kind of life failed not to suit him pretty well for some time. He ate what he liked, had little to do, and his old mistress appeared quite satisfied with him. But this quiet state of things was not to last long; the cats grew difficult to manage, and brought all sorts of disagreeables on poor Little Mouck. No sooner had the Old Lady gone out, than they began leaping and bounding about the room as if they were possessed, playing, frisking, running after one another, and knocking over, in their gambols, whatever came in their way. In this manner it happened, that they broke several vases of great value. The moment they heard their mistress's foot on the stairs, they ran to roll themselves on their cushions, purring with so calm an air, that Mrs. Towsy-Mowsy could have no hesitation in regarding the unlucky Little Mouck as the only cause of the confusion that pervaded all the furniture of the apartment. Vainly did the poor fellow protest his innocence, and tell how it really happened; the Old Lady gave more credit to the gentle looks of her cats than all the words of her serving-man, and went so far, one day, as to threaten him with a good hiding, if he did not keep a better watch over her pensioners.

Tired and vexed with her perpetual grumbling, from which it was not in his power to escape, Mouck determined on quitting the service of Mrs. Towsy-Mowsy. But, as he had had an experience in his first voyage, of how hard it was to live without any money, he looked out, beforehand, for some means whereby he might obtain the wages his mistress had promised him, but of which he had never yet been able to bring her to the payment.

There was, in the mansion, a certain mysterious chamber, that Mrs. Towsy-Mowsy took great care always to keep shut close, and in which Little Mouck had often heard a loud knocking. When thinking about his wages, it occurred to him, that probably it was there that the Old Lady kept her money; so he set about cogitating how he could get into that apartment.

One morning, that Mrs. Towsy-Mowsy had gone out, one of the little dogs, which she treated very badly, but the favour of which Mouck, on the contrary, had won, by all sorts of good offices, pulled him gently by his full-bagged pantaloons, as if inviting him to follow. Mouck, who was partial to playing with this animal, and understood its mute language quite well, allowed it do as it pleased, and in this manner reached the bedchamber of his old mistress. The dog went round the room, sniffing and snuffling, until he stopped before a panel of cedar-wood, against which he placed himself on his hind legs, with a look back at Little Mouck, who lost no time in tapping on the panel, which sent forth a hollow sound, as high as he could reach. This, then, must be a door; but how was it to be opened? There was not the slightest sign of a keyhole or a bolt. But the dog kept sturdily leaning against it with his fore-paws, and seemed excited at the sight of a kind of figure of a dragon let into the panel with steel nails. Mouck ran his hand over the figure, the outline of which he examined curiously, until, suddenly, one of the nails yielded to the unintentional pressure of his finger, and the panel, turning round of itself, disclosed to the wondering eyes of Little Mouck that chamber, an entry into which he had so much coveted.

The aspect of this interior was strange and striking. It was a veritable old curiosity shop, wherein lay, in confused disorder, hundreds of things of all kinds: costumes of every country and every period, horns, beds, balloons, stuffed birds, snakes twisting round pillars or writhing upon the floor, skeletons of men and animals, magic mirrors, bird-cages, tablets with cabalistic characters, masks, telescopes, and things innumerable, unmentionable, and indescribable—all the apparatus and appliances of sorcery!

Mouck stood aghast; then he went from one object to another, examining all with the curiosity of a child, and, just like a child, touching everything. A magnificent vase of Bohemian glass attracted his attention above all, by its beautifully shining and varied colours. He turned it over on all sides, and could never sufficiently admire its beauty; when, suddenly, there was a sound! Mouck jumped back, and the vase, slipping out of his hands, broke into a thousand pieces on the floor, with a noise like the explosion of a bombshell.

It had been only a false alarm, but the misfortune it had occasioned was all too real. After such an end to his explorations, there was nothing left for the poor little fellow but to decamp as quickly as possible, unless he wished to settle accounts with his old mistress.

His resolution was taken at once; but, not forgetting the object for which he had come, he set to work rummaging on all sides, in the hope of finding, if not money, some garment or utensil that would fetch enough to pay him his wages. Whilst looking about with this intent, his eye fell upon an old pair of *papooshes*, or slippers, of a superannuated style and shape, but of a size that seemed to him the very thing; for our Mouck had the folly of all little men, and liked to have everything very big about him: little men always marry large women. These slippers had evidently been made, at first, to fit the feet of some giant, and would have found lodging and every accommodation for two such feet as those of Little Mouck. That was exactly the reason why he was so taken with them; with such shoes he would look quite a man, and no one could then attempt to treat him like a child.

A pretty little cane, surmounted with a bear's head, sculptured, as its top, struck him, at the same moment, as being an article quite unsuitable for Mrs. Towsy-Mowsy, while it might be very serviceable to him during his travels. So he took possession of that,

MOUCK RUNS AWAY WITH THE MAGIC SLIPPERS, AND THE MAGIC SLIPPERS RUN AWAY WITH MOUCK.

and without pushing his researches farther, went out of the chamber, and also out of the house, and then ran, without casting one look behind, right to the gates of the city. Even when there, he hardly thought himself safe, but continued to run, until his breath failed him for another step. Never in his life before had our little Mouck made so long and so rapid a run; yet, in spite of the fatigue that weighed him down, he felt an inward desire to keep on running—anything to go on, and get along. It was as if some supernatural impulse drove him onward, even in spite of himself. Now, our Mouck had a clever, sharp, and subtle wit, as we have already remarked; so he conjectured he must be under the influence of some charm or other, which must be in connection with his new shoeing; so he set to crying out, as one does to a horse one wishes to stop, when he has sprung off in a gallop, "Woa, woa! Stop! Soho, there—soho! Softly, lad, softly!"

The papooshes came to a halt at once, and Mouck fell to the ground, spent and exhausted. There he lay, and slept off his fatigue.

While he was soundly sleeping, the little dog of Mrs. Towsy-Mowsy's appeared in a dream, and yapped and barked at him, and wagged his tail, after the following meaning, when expressed in language:—

"My dear Mouck, as you know only imperfectly the use of your fine papooshes, learn, then, that when you have put them on your feet, and turned thrice round on your great toe, you will fly up into the air, and have it in your power to direct your course in any direction you please. Learn, also, that your little cane conceals the real staff of Jacob, and that by means of it you may discover all treasures that are hidden in the earth; since, wherever there is gold underneath it, the stick is obliged to rap three times on the ground, and twice to show where silver is to be found."

Such was the dream that Little Mouck dreamed: but he did not despise it, as some people would; for no sooner were his eyes open, than a desire to test the truth of the dream-revelation, led him to put on his slippers, before essaying an experiment with his walking-stick. So, slipping on his shoes again quickly, he lifted one foot up in the air,, and began to turn round on the other, balancing himself on his great toe.

Now, if any one will try to execute this little step three times, in slippers too large for him, he will very soon find out that it is not the most easy of manoeuvres to accomplish. So he will not be astonished that Little Mouck, the heaviness of whose great head overbalanced his small body to one side or the other, was not by any means successful the first time. On the contrary, he fell down, heavily, on his nose. But he was not to be discouraged by failure, and recommenced his experiments so well, that, at last, he succeeded. Like a well-turned top, he started off with three good spins, wishing, at the same time, to be carried to the great city just within sight. His slippers carried him up into the air, and ran along the clouds, as if over a smooth pavement; and thus, before Mouck had time to look about him, he found himself right in the middle of a great square, from which rose a magnificent palace, that he entertained no doubt must be the royal residence.

Now Mouck was in possession of two very valu-

able talismans; but while waiting to make use of them, it was necessary that Mouck should have something to eat; but Mouck had not got a sixpence in his pocket, wherewithal to buy even a loaf. A stick that could point out where treasures were hid was a very fine thing, certainly; but he had not yet come to a place where the cane began to dance, and might not do so for some days. These flying slippers were a superb thing, also; but running without object does not fill a man's belly. So have I seen a man of infinite wit, without victuals, and one who could draw bills on immortality, without credit for a shilling. Poor Little Mouck! Just at this moment, there passed close by him one of the King's messengers, on his way to the palace, all over dust, breathless and exhausted.

MOUCK HAS AN INTERVIEW WITH THE STEWARD OF THE HOUSEHOLD.

"Halloa!" exclaimed Mouck, "that's just the office for me! These gentlemen are well paid and cared for. I will go and enter my name in their list, and shall soon, thanks to my papooshes, be at the head of them all."

Then he pursued his way into the palace, and persisted in his importunity, until he obtained an audience of the Steward of the Household, to whom he offered his services as a Courier.

The Steward of the Household burst out in a loud laugh, when he cast his eyes down upon the little abortion that made such a grand offer.

"You! a Courier!" said he to the bold Dwarf.

"Yes, I—Mouck, the son of Mouckrah, surnamed Little Mouck—a man who is ready to undertake to run any given distance more alertly than any of his Majesty's present couriers."

The self-possession of the Dwarf made an impression on the Steward; although he could not believe one word Mouck had spoken, the swaggering pretence of such a squab of a mannikin venturing to contest the prize of swiftness with couriers as long-legged and as lean as a pair of compasses, was in itself a joke. Besides, how his Majesty would laugh, when the race was run between Little Mouck and his champion runner.

"Be it so," said he, "I engage you at once. Go down to the kitchen, and tell them to give you something to eat; but, at the same time, get ready to give a taste of your quality immediately to his Majesty himself."

Mouck did not trouble him to repeat his invitation to dinner twice over, but went down the stairs four at a time, the way to the kitchen being shown him by a slave, who directed the Chief Cook to give him all he wanted.

An hour afterwards, Mouck, thoroughly refreshed, was conducted to a piece of well-turfed lawn, that stretched far out under the palace windows, where the contest spoken of by the Steward of the Household was appointed to take place.

There happened to be, at this moment, a great dearth of amusement at the Court. Chincilla, the King's favourite monkey, was just dead of indigestion; and his best falcon was moulting, and as featherless as a fowl on the spit. The royal gold fish still remained; but, after some time, his Majesty found the constant looking at them rather monotonous. The proposition of the Steward of the Household was therefore welcomed with applause, and their Majesties came down with delight to witness a race, in which a Dwarf, as they were told, had promised to outrun all their fleetest couriers.

When Mouck appeared in the meadow, all the Court was at the windows; and there was a universal burst of laughter when he was seen advancing, giving himself all the airs of a first-rate pacer, his little body topped by a huge beard, which he inclined from right to left in saluting the assemblage. But the shouts of laughter did not put our little friend at all out of countenance; and taking his place proudly by the side of his opponent—a fellow leaner and more long-sided than a leveret—he awaited, without moving a muscle, the appointed signal.

The Princess Amarza waved her fan, and, at the moment, like two lines drawn to the same point, the two runners darted off into the plain. At first, Mouck's opponent made great play, and shot ahead: but soon the Little One, carried along by his magic slippers, caught him up, passed him, and reached the goal a long time before the other, who, when he came in, was exhausted and out of breath, while Mouck breathed as calmly and as easily as if he had only taken a gentle stroll.

The spectators were at first silent with astonishment and admiration; but as soon as they saw that the King thought it worth while to applaud Mouck, they shouted loudly, "Long live Mouck, the king of all runners!"

From that moment, Mouck was attached to the person of the King as ordinary and extraordinary Courier, and every day brought him more into the good graces of his master, he was so rapid, and displayed so much intelligence and fidelity in delivering the messages entrusted to him. The favour he enjoyed was not long before it brought upon him, as generally happens, the jealousy of his fellow-servants, who lost no opportunity of showing Mouck what their feelings were towards him. This state of things afflicted him much; and, disposed as he was in himself to sympathise with all the world, he could not endure to be hated by his fellow-men, or even coldly looked upon. "Perhaps," thought he, "if I were to do them some great service, it might operate to change them." And then he called to mind his little stick, which the prosperity of his present position had quite driven out of his memory. "I don't care to hunt after treasures for myself," thought he, "for the King is so liberal that he leaves me nothing to desire; but if I could just light upon some hidden store, I might share it with my companions, and that would doubtless dispose them to look more favourably upon me." From that time, he never went out anywhere, whether for a walk or a message, without carrying his stick with him, in the hope that, some day, a lucky chance would lead him to a cavern in which treasures were buried.

One evening, while wandering alone in a very secluded part of the royal gardens, he felt the cane jump up three times in his hand. Joyfully he drew his poniard, and cut several branches of the trees thereabout, so as to know the place again, and then made the best of his way back to the palace. When night approached, he armed himself with a spade and a dark lantern, and returned to search for the treasure, that was about to cost him more trouble than he could have expected; for it is one thing to find a mine of gold, and another to dig it. Now, poor Little Mouck's arms were of the feeblest, and his spade heavy. and he had to dig three whole hours before he had excavated hardly two feet of earth. At last, his spade struck something hard, and the sound was the ring of metal. On he went, shovelling out and delving more eagerly than ever, to dig out and clear entirely some object, one of the sides of which he could now see. It was a coffer of great size, which, when he had succeeded in getting off the cover, he saw was full of gold-pieces of the previous King's reign.

The coffer was too much of a dead weight, besides being too large, for Mouck to think of carrying it away; so he contented himself with filling his pockets, breeches and breast, as well as the girdle round his waist, as full as they would all hold; then he poured a quantity into his mantle, and thus loaded, got back to his chamber; not, however, without taking care to fill up the hole he had made, with turf, moss, and branches of trees.

When Little Mouck saw himself in possession of such a large sum, he thought matters would put on a new face, and that he would gain, by this fine stroke, not only the affection of his friends, but the aid of warm partisans, whom, up to this time, he had been obliged to reckon as his enemies. Good Little Mouck! Such fancies as he then indulged in, showed how very little knowledge he had of life; otherwise, how could he have imagined that gold ever makes friends for any man? Alas! better had it been for him to have donned his slippers, and, while his pockets were full of money, to be off as quickly as possible!

Up to this time, men had been jealous of him, but they kept their jealousy to themselves, for fear of the King. But now that he lavished gold, in a never-failing stream from both hands, on all sides about him, they hated him, they abused him, they cursed him, and they scandalised him!

Ayoti, the Head Cook, said, "He is a coiner of false money."

"He has robbed somebody," said Achmet, the Chief Eunuch.

But Archaz, the Lord High Treasurer, the most open of his enemies—a fellow who himself dipped his fingers from time to time in the King's coffers—the traitor Archaz added, "Assuredly he is robbing the King."

True or false, accusations like these rarely fail to ruin the man against whom they are levelled, and if he escape death, it is only to expiate, by a long life of suffering, the favour he once enjoyed. The conspiracy of envious wretches soon concocted a plan. The Chief Cupbearer, Kirchuz, presented himself one day before the King, sad and dejected. At first, his Majesty took no notice of this, suspecting Kirchuz had been smoking too much the night before; but when the rogue kept up the appearance of great distress for a long time, and sighed and groaned full often, the King grew impatient, and at last insisted on knowing by what fatality it occurred, that tears were thus mingled with his wine.

"Alas!" replied the impostor, "I am wretched at having lost the good graces of my master."

"What's put that in your head, sirrah?" cried the King, good-naturedly pinching his ear; "since when, pray, has the sun of my favour ceased to shine upon you?"

The Chief Cupbearer prostrated himself, and then,

288

in an harangue full of all kinds of misrepresentations, and in every phrase of which the expression of his own devotion recurred with a disgusting repetition, he found means to slip in, that Mouck had been making such an utter waste of money for some time past, that the King must have placed his coffers at his disposal; "Unless," added the treacherous rascal, "the unlucky Dwarf is a coiner, or has helped himself to other people's money. Such was the state of things, how-ever, that he, and other faithful servants of his Majesty, thought it high time to bring to his ears what was passing under his eyes."

In fact, Mouck's recklessly giving away his money right and left, had already attracted the royal atten-tion, and when represented in this insidious light, assumed a graver aspect. So the King ordered the doings and the goings in and out of the Dwarf to be scrupulously watched, in secret, and an endeavour to be made to catch him, if possible, in the act of robbing the royal treasury.

When the Lord Treasurer, who was fond of fishing in troubled waters, heard this, he was in a perfect jubilee of joy at the turn matters had taken, and en-tertained the hope that this suspected default of Little Mouck would help to square his own accounts, which were by no means in a clear state.

On the evening of this day, Mouck saw, in turning out his pockets, that his prodigality had drawn them dry; and as he had not heard a breath of what had taken place about his matters, he resolved to go back that same night, and pay a visit to his treasure. He was a hundred miles off from suspecting that a spy was set upon his every action, and that the very men amongst whom he had determined to share the fruits of his discoveries, were sworn to work out his ruin. At the very moment when, having cleared out the hole, he was about to lift the top off the coffer, and plunge his arm into the golden shower up to the elbows, a hand of iron seized it, and he heard—"Ah! I have got you now! This is where you lock up your pickings and stealings, is it?" The voice was that of Archaz, and he was followed by Ayoti, Achmet, and Kirchuz, while all the company joined in the cry. Little Mouck, with such a chorus deafening his ears, had not the power to utter a word. So he was tightly bound, almost strangled, and then carried before the King.

His Majesty, whom this interruption of his sleep did not put into the sweetest of tempers, received his unfortunate private messenger with a great deal of irritation, and ordered him to be put on his trial with all despatch. The coffer, still half full of coins, was placed before the King, and with it the spade and the cloak of the unlucky Mouck; and at last, to complete these evidences of guilt, the Lord Treasurer came forward to bear testimony that he had seized Mouck in the very act of burying the coffer-full of gold in an out-of-the-way corner of the royal gardens.

"No, no! not at all!—not so! not at all!" cried Little Mouck, bursting with the knowledge of his innocence, and imagining that one word from him would suffice to set the matter as clear as daylight to all eyes. "So far from hiding this gold in the earth,

THE INGENIOUS SURGEON CURES THE PRINCESS'S NOSE, BY CUTTING IT OFF.

I was doing just the contrary—I was digging it out, after finding it by chance."

Murmurs of incredulity and ironical sneers followed this explanation of the Dwarf's, and added fuel to the fire of the King's indignation, who shouted, in a terrible voice, "How, wretch! do you trump up such a gross falsehood to cheat your Sovereign, after having so impudently robbed him? What does it signify, whether you dug up this gold, or whether you were burying it? In either case, you had no right to dis-

pose of it. But here is what shall confound you: my Lord High Treasurer, Archaz, have you not remarked that, for some time past, enormous sums have been taken away from our exchequer? Have you not, of late, had your suspicions directed towards several persons?"

Archaz shivered in his slippers at the peril he had so narrowly escaped, for he certainly had remarked these defalcations, and knew too well whom to suspect —namely, himself; so he hastened to reply—"Yes;

No. 37.

yes! your Gracious Majesty has solved the riddle that puzzled all your Lords of the Treasury and Clerks of the Exchequer. This gold has been taken out of the royal coffers, and that queer young rascal, there, is the thief!"

After such an impudent declaration from his Treasurer, the King could not be otherwise than satisfied with his own judgment. So he made a sign to remove the unhappy Mouck from his presence, and ordered a high gallows to be erected, on which the poor little fellow was to be strung up on the next morning.

Mouck had felt no inclination, before this, to acquaint his royal patron with the secret of his gold-finding staff, lest his Majesty should despoil him of so valuable a talisman; but when he heard his sentence of death pronounced, and reckoned up the impossibility, while he was so tied with cords, of availing himself of the aid of his slippers to escape, he decided on sacrificing one half his fortune, to save the other half, with his life into the bargain. So, having asked the King to grant him a private interview, as he had something to disclose, when he had obtained it, he threw himself at his Majesty's feet, weeping, as he said: "Great King, appearances are weighing me down; it is true they are against me, but yet they are not true!"

"It is very clever of you to say so, Little Mouck; but though your tongue should run faster than your feet used to do, you can never outstep the evidence brought against you."

"I seek not to do so, Gracious Highness; what has been said to you, you have heard, and what you have heard you have said, and when you have said it, it becomes truth; and so I am guilty, even though I think I am innocent."

"That confession becomes you, my little man. Go on," said the King, "for that, of course, is not what you wanted to say to me, for that would be of no use."

Mouck shuddered at the cold-blooded manner in which his Sovereign spoke of a man's life. "Deign, Sire," said he, "to listen to me for a moment, and you will learn directly who are those that have betrayed you, and whether your faithful Little Mouck is of their number."

"I don't want to hear any more, Little Mouck," said the King, yawning; "I can't pardon you, and I don't wish to be troubled with punishing them. Be satisfied with setting them an example."

Mouck thought to himself, that he would rather change places, and give his foes the benefit of teaching lessons of practical wisdom by their own martyrdom; for Mouck, though a good man, was not a great one—a shrewd person, but not a philosopher—knowing, not wise; he thought of himself, and not of the world in general. "Oh!" said he, "great King! good Sovereign! royal Patron! grant me but your royal word that my life shall be safe——"

"Away with him!" roared the King, throwing open the door of his cabinet, and summoning the Chief of his Black Eunuchs.

"And I will make you the richest——"

His Majesty closed the door carefully with one hand, as he extended the other graciously to Little Mouck.

"Go on, my lad," said he.

"——The richest Sovereign in all the world!"

"Let us hear more of that," said the King; "what do you mean? how can you do it?"

"By the beard of the Prophet——"

"Nay, blaspheme not!" said the King, devoutly bowing towards the East.

"By the beard of the Prophet, I swear to you, that I will teach you a secret that shall make you more wealthy than ever was the superb Caliph Haroun Alraschid, or Sindbad, the famous Voyager!"

His Majesty, whose finances had been for some time in a sadly dilapidated condition, lent a willing ear to this proposition, and pledged himself, on the word of a King, to pardon Little Mouck, if he would actually put him in possession of such a fine secret.

Mouck immediately presented the little staff to his master, and, having explained to him all the mystery connected with it, added: "And now, O gracious Sovereign, permit your faithful and most unfortunate slave to make one simple request. The experience I have had of life in a Court, has disgusted me with it for ever; suffer me, then, to retire from a world which so little agrees with my habits, and into which the chance of accidental circumstances alone has thrust me."

But, all the while our friend was expressing this request in proper terms, the King was thinking in his own mind, that Little Mouck, who could discover treasures with his staff, must have yet some other magic powers in his wallet. He thought over, especially, the swiftness of the Dwarf in running, though his legs were scarcely as long as a hand; and he reckoned that this remarkable velocity must be occasioned by engines of sorcery. No sooner had this idea entered his royal brain, than he determined to wring the secret, somehow or other, from Little Mouck. His royal word was rather in his way; but an ingenious expedient, suggested to him, some years since, by a wise Mufti, when consulted in a similar case of conscience, occurred to his memory; and turning, with a paternal air, towards his Courier, he thus addressed him:—

"I have promised, friend Mouck, that your life shall be safe, and I swear still that not a hair of your head shall be touched; but the crime of which you have rendered yourself guilty, is too great an offence against the laws of the realm for me to accord you an absolute pardon; justice would murmur, and the example might be dangerous. You shall live, then; only you must pass the rest of your days in prison."

The Dwarf shuddered. After a short silence, during which the Monarch watched an expression of terror pass over the visage of the Dwarf, he, blandly, went on:—

"——That is to say, unless you consent to avow to me the means by which you are enabled to run so rapidly; in which case, you shall be immediately set at liberty."

Little Mouck had, as yet, spent only one night in the dungeons of the palace, but that had been enough to give him no wish to return to them, and especially with the prospect of remaining there for ever. He yielded, therefore, and confessed that all his skill lay in his slippers. He had the good sense, however, to keep one half of the secret to himself, and not to acquaint the King with the manner of flying off, by turning round three times on his great toe.

"All right!" said the King, after he had put on the slippers, the power of which he wished to test without delay; "all right! You are free, Mr. Mouck—free to quit my states immediately, without exchanging a word with any person, or casting a look behind you. One hour's delay, one indiscreet word to any one whatever, and I will have you roasted alive! Away with you! Begone!"

Having passed this fine sentence, the King hastened to lock up, under triple lock and key, the slippers and the staff—precious records of the royal rascality, and in which His Majesty gloried, as likely to afford him excellent sport and uncountable money as long as he lived.

While the King thus gloated greedily over his two talismans, Mouck made his way to the frontier, with empty belly, and weary, dragging feet. Once more he had become as poor as when he had left his father's house; but then he could, at any rate, throw the blame of his miserable condition on Fortune, while, at present, he had no one to accuse but his own simpleness, his stupidity, and doltishness! Such were the thoughts of poor Mouck, now utterly forlorn and out of spirits; many, too, were his regrets, as he thought over, in his heart, the fine part he might have played, with a little more address and knowledge of the ways of the world. By good luck, as it happened, the kingdom from which he was banished was not of very large extent; and about eight hours' hard walking brought him to the outside of its inhospitable confines, although many times, during that distance, the absence of his wonderful slippers made him pause to recover his breath.

Up to this time, Mouck had gone straight on end; but, as soon as he had passed the frontier, and was no longer urged on by the fear of being pursued and clapped in prison again, he struck out of the high road, and plunged into a wood that bordered the way, with the intention of settling down thenceforward, and living, solitary, in that place; for all his latter adventures had inspired him with an extreme hatred and horror of his fellow-men.

As he wandered about among the trees, he came upon a pretty spot that was clear; a cool spring, trickling along, noiseless, among the water-cresses, traversed the little valley, which was skirted on all sides by fig-trees, with knotty trunks and large leaves, and on which grew abundant fruits, full, juicy, ripe, and beautifully coloured, seemingly inviting the hand of the hungry, hot, wearied traveller to pluck and be refreshed. Figs such as these were enough to make the mouth of a well-fed man water; how much more then, did they excite the appetite of our poor Little Mouck, whose stomach had been crying out for food ever since the morning!

In the twinkling of an eye, he had plucked and devoured a dozen of the finest within his reach. They were delicious; Mouck thought he had never before tasted fruit so exquisite in flavour.

When he had made about half a meal, he felt as if he should like something to drink, and lay down on his stomach at the brink of the brook, to have a drink; but quickly he threw himself back with a violent spring, just as a man would do, under the same circumstances, when a snake had bitten his nose—ready to drop, with haggard eyes fixed on the water, as if he there saw some hideous reptile.

He stood motionless for an instant, as if petrified; then, with reflection, came back his natural courage. "No, no!" said he to himself, "it is impossible; I am the sport of some deluding fancy!" Then he approached the brook again, and slowly craned his neck over the water, until his enormous head was visible, reflected on its surface distinctly—too much so—adorned with two immense ass's ears, while his nose projected, in advance of his face, just like the snout of a tapir!

"My eyes deceive me!" exclaimed the astounded Mouck; and he seized his head with both hands: his ears had grown more than half an ell! and his nose, still growing larger and larger, made him squint horribly. "It is rightly done, and I deserve it," he exclaimed, with much bitterness; "I have conducted myself like a stupid donkey, and I deserve to wear the ears of an ass!" Then, worn out with the fatigue of his journey, not less than despair at such a hideous metamorphosis, he threw himself upon the grass, and ended by falling asleep through exhaustion and lassitude.

It was about an hour before he woke up again, urged by the murmurs of his still hungry stomach, and set to looking after something more substantial for his teeth than these figs. But, although he wandered hither and thither, turned and returned, went and came, and beat the wood from one side to the other, it was impossible for him to discover anything but figs—always figs! True it is, that they were of different kinds—some green, others yellow, some red, others purple; but still they were all figs, nevertheless. For want of something better, Mouck was obliged to content himself with this variety in his dining; so, as he had already tasted the purple figs, he picked a good dozen of green figs, which he found no less savoury than those he had first tasted.

He had turned his steps towards the brook, to moisten his frugal repast with a drink of water, when, on a sudden, he came to a halt, held back by the idea of finding himself once more face to face with the ignoble portraiture of his new ears and nose. He thought he would try to push up under the folds of his turban the monstrous ears that decorated each side of his enormous head, rising to the right and left of it, like two minarets flanking the great dome of a mosque; but his hands kept exploring all round his head-dress, without feeling any trace of those so much-dreaded ears. Trembling all over with joy, he ran to the brook, and convinced himself, to his infinite satisfaction, that his head had recovered its usual appearance.

But our Little Mouck was not one of those careless spirits, that see some phenomenon accomplished under their eyes, and profit by its consequences, without caring to know how it has been brought about. Carefully running over the circumstances that had preceded and followed the curious changes he had undergone, he became convinced that they were owing to the figs he had eaten—that the one excited the horrific development of nose and ears of which he had been the terrified victim, and the others acted as an antidote to the first. Continuing his meditations on this adventure, Mouck recognised how his Good Genius had a second time placed in his hands the means of making a fortune, or, at any rate, of getting back again all that he had suffered to escape him, if not, even, something more.

Then he gathered as many of the figs, both green and purple, as he could hold in his cloak, of which he made a kind of bag, and slung over his shoulders. Loaded in this way, he retook his way back to the country he had just quitted. At the first town he came to, he dressed himself in disguise, so as not to be annoyed in his dealings, and pursued his road, without farther stopping, until he reached the capital where the King resided.

It was precisely that season of the year when fresh fruit is still rare; and Mouck, who knew the ways of the palace, had no doubt that his figs would attract the attention of his Majesty's purveyors, always on the look-out for the earliest delicacies of every kind. And so it turned out; he had scarcely installed himself in the great square, amongst the other vendors, when he spied out, at some distance, the approach of the Chief Cook and Majordomo, on their way to make their accustomed round of the market. They had already passed by most of the stalls, apparently without having seen anything that pleased them, when they cast their eyes, at last, on the basket of figs belonging to little Mouck.

"Capital! very lucky! just in time!" exclaimed the Majordomo; "here is something fit for the table of the King! How much do you want for this basket? I will take the whole," inquired he of the pretended merchant.

That worthy asked only a moderate price, which was given to him without abatement; and the Major-

domo, having given the basket into the hands of a slave to carry to the palace, went on his way, to push his researches farther.

Meanwhile, Mouck, his marketing concluded, thought it best to be off as soon as possible, and make his preparations for the new character he had yet to play, before bringing his present performance to its right conclusion.

On the evening of the same day, there was a grand gala at the palace, in honour of the twentieth anniversary of his Majesty's coming to the throne. The Chief Cook had surpassed himself, and the Maître d'Hotel had already received several benignant smiles from his Sovereign, as one dish after the other afforded his royal nose or appetite fresh gratification; when there appeared in the midst of the dessert, high elevated on a rich basket of golden filagree, and surrounded with brilliant lights, green leaves, and bright flowers, the superb figs purchased from Little Mouck, built up in a pyramidal form. At sight of them there was a universal cry of admiration; and the King, who had already exhausted all the forms of praise, in expressing his satisfaction at the dishes that had preceded this, detached from his own cap of state the Grand Order of the Silver Fork, and deigned with his own hand to fix the decoration on the breast of his Maître d'Hotel, who received the precious distinction on his knees.

His Majesty then gallantly ordered the fruit to be handed to his Queen, and to the Princesses his daughters, as well; and, after having been served himself, gave over what was left to the other guests at the banquet, among whom were present all the Princes of his family, together with the Great Officers of State.

One of these last, the Grand Mufti, who prided himself on his eloquence, had reserved for this moment a speech, which he was in the habit of addressing to the King on such occasions—a speech always couched in the same terms, and which the King always listened to with the same serious air; but, on this occasion, scarcely had the Grand Mufti unrolled his manuscript, and pronounced his customary beginning of "Great King!" than he heard shouts of laughter, vainly attempted to be smothered, but bursting through all control, ringing all round and about him.

The orator, though slightly taken aback, did not allow himself to be more than a moment interrupted by such an unusual and uncourteous reception of his rhetorical display, but kept spouting along, until, in a more than usually animated passage, he happened to cast his eyes around the table, and then he began to sniff, and snort, and giggle, and puff out like his neighbours; while all round the room there broke forth an almost frightful shout of merriment.

But, it must be confessed, that if the laughter was strong, it was not for long. Each of the guests, on seeing his neighbour's ears, felt an inclination to make sure of the state of his own, and all soon perceived that they had nothing to envy one another in the way of cartilage. As for the ears of the King, they were so majestically elongated, that the Grand Mufti himself seemed but a young donkey-foal by the side of him, although he had a good foot's length of ear beyond his cap.

Great was the despair of the whole Court, on seeing themselves accoutred in such a fashion. They called in, on the instant, Doctors of all sorts—Physicians, Surgeons, Apothecaries, and General Practitioners—who each of them, altogether and individually, consulted on this extraordinary case. It ended, of course, in their not being able to hit upon any method of curing it, although they did not forget to write and gabble a waggon-load of learned nonsense about symptoms and nosology; but that was all.

An ingenious surgeon came forward, however, on the occasion, and proposed, without farther delay, the simple method of cutting off of the offending length of ears and nose; offering to produce presentable noses and ears on the heads and faces of all who honoured him with their confidence, and submitted to the operation. But every one thought the remedy worse than the disease, with the distinguished exception of the Princess Amarza, who could not be comforted for the loss of her pretty little rosy nose, and her delicate and exquisitely curled ears. But, alas!—O hideous disappointment!—it was no use that she faced the horrible operation. Poor child! Scarcely had the cruel steel quitted her delicate visage, than a finer pair of ears, and a nose longer than ever, budded forth upon it!

While all this was going on, the news reached the King, that an old Dervish requested a few words with him, and that he strongly asseverated that it was in his power to remedy the dreadful accident which had thrown the Court into despair.

"Bring him in, this instant," said the King.

A little Old Man, all bent double with years, enveloped in a black robe of ample dimensions, wearing on his head a turban as high as a pyramid, and with a long white beard descending to his feet, was introduced by the slaves, with numerous salaams.

"The disease that has stricken thee and thine," said he to the King, "is not a natural one, such as the ordinary remedies of the physician can touch. It must be the punishment for some great crime committed by you long ago, the necessary expiation for which you have neglected to make. With the blessing of Allah, I can cure you, however—I can cure you all; and, as a proof of my ability—behold!"

While speaking, the Dervish had drawn near to the Princess Amarza, who kept in a corner from mere shame, and endeavoured to hide her ugliness by burying her face in her two little hands. "Take this, my child, and eat it," said he to her, as he handed her a small box, containing something like preserved fruit, of a green colour.

The Princess would have swallowed live snakes, if needs must, to regain her beauty; she therefore required no pressing to swallow the Dervish's medicine. Suddenly, an exclamation of admiration rose throughout the aparment; the Princess had become again as handsome as ever, and more so, as she was able to assure herself, when, with a charming impetuosity, she knelt before the mirror that had afforded her such a gratifying testimony.

Hereupon, the Dervish, turning towards the King,

who gazed on his daughter with jealous eyes, "What will you give me," said he to him, "if, by the power of my art, I do for you—and for all—what I have done for the Princess Amarza?"

"Speak, good Dervish! tell me what you wish, and I promise to accord it to you!"

The Dervish was silent, as if hesitating what to ask, or, perhaps, in doubt of the royal assent to his demand.

"Come," said the King to him, "come!"—and leading him into his treasury, he displayed before his eyes all the riches that were laid up there, begging him to choose whatever he pleased, or even to take all he was worth, if so it seemed good to him, the Dervish, so long as he restored to him, the King, his human visage.

From the moment of his entering the treasury, the Dervish, or rather Mouck—for it was our little friend, as you have doubtless recognised before this—had fixed his eyes on his cherished slippers and walking-stick in a corner; and all the while he was pretending to admire and examine attentively the marvellous objects that decorated the apartment, kept advancing, little by little, in that direction. When he had got within three paces of the slippers, he jumped right into them at a bound, seized his little stick with one hand, as with the other he tore off his false beard, and showed himself to the eyes of the astonished King, in the well-known guise of the exiled Mouck.

"Perfidious King!" he exclaimed, "imbecile Monarch! who payest with ingratitude the faithful services of thy true friends, while your stupidity allows yourself to be deceived by audacious rascals!—the deformity you have come to is the just punishment of your knavery and your stupidity. You shall keep your ass's ears—you shall wear them as long as you live, that they may recall to your mind, unceasingly, the unworthy treatment you made poor Mouck undergo."

"Scoundrel!" said the King, coming out of his first amazement, "you shall die under the bastinado!" Then, with all the power of his lungs, he shouted to his servants to come to his aid.

But Mouck turned rapidly round on his own axis, wishing, at the same time, to be transported a hundred leagues from the spot; and darting through the window like a bird, pulled the King's long nose, and pinched his ass's ears as he passed, and was out of sight before any one of the slaves could arrive.

After running about all over the world for some time, and securing, by the aid of his two talismans, a sufficiently easy maintenance for the rest of his days, Little Mouck came back, to fix his residence here in his native town, where he has continued to reside ever since, but always by himself; for he has still preserved—not a hatred, for of that his gentle soul is incapable—but a profound contempt and disgust for mankind in general, from experience of his own dealings with them. He has, moreover, acquired in his travels a rare experience and wisdom; and, in spite of his strange exterior, Little Mouck—"remember this well," said my father, as he finished his story—"the good Little Mouck is entitled, by his sufferings and his virtues, to the respect and admiration of all, rather than mockery."

Throughout the whole of this narration, I had given an unflagging attention to it; and when it was finished, I protested, with an abundance of regrets, that I felt I had been guilty of unworthy conduct towards the little man. My father congratulated me very much on my return to proper feelings, and pledged me to persevere in them; but, as he never failed to keep his word, he took up his rattan once more, and scrupulously administered the second half of the correction he had been good enough to promise me.

I took care to recount to my comrades Little Mouck's adventures; his childish goodness, as well as the secret powers of which he was the possessor, inspired us all with such a veneration for him, that none of us, from that day, endeavoured to play off the least trick upon him; on the contrary, as long as he lived, we paid him every respectful attention, and whenever he happened to pass by us, on the days that he came out, we made our best bow to his great slippers, with as much respect as we could have done to the Cadi himself, or the Mufti of the Grand Mosque.

THE WHITE CAT.

A KING had three sons, all remarkably handsome in their persons, and in their tempers generous and noble. Some wicked Courtiers made the King believe that the Princes were impatient to wear his crown, and that they were contriving a plot to deprive him of his sceptre and authority.

The King felt that he was growing old, but, as he found himself as capable of governing as ever, he had no inclination to resign his power; and therefore, that he might pass the rest of his days peaceably, he determined to employ the Princes in such a manner, as at once to give each of them the hope of succeeding to the crown, and fill up the time they might otherwise spend in so undutiful a manner.

He sent for them to his cabinet, and after conversing with them kindly, he added: "You must be sensible, my dear children, that my great age prevents me from attending so closely as I have hitherto done to state affairs. I fear this may be injurious to my sub-

294

jects; I therefore desire to place my crown on the head of one of you; but it is no more than just that, in return for such a present, you should procure me some amusement in my retirement, for I shall leave the capital for ever. I cannot help thinking, that a little dog, that should be handsome, faithful, and engaging, would be the very thing to make me happy; so that, without bestowing a preference on either of you, I declare that he who brings me the most perfect little dog shall be my successor."

The Princes were much surprised at the fancy of their father to have a little dog, yet they accepted the proposition with pleasure; and accordingly, after taking leave of the King, who presented them with abundance of money and jewels, and appointed that day twelvemonth for their return, they set off on their travels. Before taking leave of each other, however, they took some refreshment together, in an old palace about three miles out of town; where they mutually agreed to meet in the same place on that day twelvemonth, and go altogether, with their presents, to Court. They also agreed to change their names, that they might be unknown to every one.

Each took a different road; but we intend to relate the adventures of only the youngest, who was the handsomest, most amiable, and accomplished Prince that could be imagined.

No day passed, as he travelled from town to town, that he did not buy all the handsome dogs that fell in his way; and as soon as he saw one that was handsomer than those he had before, he made a present to some one of the last; for twenty servants would have been scarce sufficient to take care of all the dogs he was continually buying, and the Prince was quite alone.

At length, wandering he knew not whither, he found himself in a forest; night suddenly came on, and with it a violent storm of thunder, lightning, and rain; to add to his perplexity, he lost his path, and could find no way out of the forest. When he had groped about for a long time, he perceived a light, which made him suppose he was not far from some house; he accordingly pursued his way towards it, and in a short time found himself at the gates of the most magnificent palace ever beheld. The door that opened into it was made of gold, covered with sapphire stones, which cast so resplendent a brightness over everything around, that scarcely could the strongest eye-sight bear to look at it: this was the light the Prince had seen from the forest. The walls of the building were of transparent porcelain, variously coloured, and represented the history of all the Fairies that had existed from the beginning of the world. The Prince, coming back to the golden door, observed a deer's foot fastened to a chain of diamonds; he could not help wondering at the magnificence he beheld, and the security in which the inhabitants of the earth seemed to live: "For," said he to himself, "nothing would be easier than for thieves to steal this chain, and as many of the sapphire stones as would make their fortune."

He pulled the chain, and heard a bell, the sound of which was so sweet, that he concluded it must be made either of silver or gold. In a few moments the door was opened; but he perceived nothing but twelve hands in the air, each holding a torch. The Prince was so astonished that he durst not move a step; when he felt himself pushed gently on by some other hands from behind him. He walked on in great perplexity; and, to be secure from danger, he put his hand upon his sword. He entered a vestibule inlaid with porphyry and lapis-stone, when the most melodious voice he had ever heard chanted the following words:—

"Welcome, Prince! no danger fear,
Mirth and love attend you here;
You shall break the magic spell,
That on a beauteous maiden fell.
Welcome, Prince! no danger fear,
Mirth and love attend you here."

The Prince now advanced with confidence, wondering what these words could mean; the hands moved him forward toward a large door of coral, which opened of itself to give him admittance into a splendid apartment built of mother-of-pearl, through which he passed into others so richly adorned with paintings and jewels, and so resplendently lighted with thousands of lamps, girandoles, and lustres, that the Prince imagined he must be in an enchanted palace.

When he had passed through sixty apartments, all equally splendid, he was stopped by the hands, and a large easy chair advanced of itself towards the chimney; the fire immediately lighted of itself; and the hands, which he observed were extremely white and delicate, took off his wet clothes, and supplied their place with the finest linen imaginable, and then added a commodious wrapping-gown, embroidered with the brightest gold, and all over enriched with pearls. The hands next brought him an elegant dressing-table, and combed his hair so very gently, that he scarcely felt their touch. They held before him a beautiful basin, filled with perfumes, for him to wash his face and hands, and afterwards took off the wrapping-gown, and dressed him in a suit of clothes of still greater splendour.

When his dress was complete, they conducted him to an apartment he had not yet seen, and which, also, was magnificently furnished. There was in it a table spread for a repast, and everything upon it was of the purest gold, adorned with jewels. The Prince observed there were two covers set, and was wondering who was to be his companion, when a great number of cats marched, by two and two, into the room, and placed themselves in an orchestra at one end of it; some had books, which contained the strangest-looking notes he had ever seen; others guitars; and one of them held a roll of paper, with which he began to beat the time, while the rest played a concert of music.

As he was reflecting on the wonderful things he had seen in this palace, his attention was suddenly caught by a small figure, not a foot in height, which just then entered the room, and advanced towards him. It had on a long black veil, and was supported by two cats dressed in mourning, and with swords by their sides; they were followed by a numerous retinue of cats, some carrying cages full of rats, and others mouse-traps full of mice.

The Prince was at a loss what to think. The little figure now approached, and throwing aside her veil, he beheld a most beautiful White Cat. She seemed young and melancholy, and addressing herself to the Prince, she said: "Young Prince, you are welcome; your presence affords me the greatest pleasure."

"Madam," replied the Prince, "I would fain thank you for your generosity, nor can I help observing that you must be a most extraordinary creature, to possess, with your present form, the gift of speech, and the magnificent palace I have seen."

"All this is very true," answered the beautiful Cat; "but, Prince, I am not fond of talking, and least of all do I like compliments; let us, therefore, sit down to supper."

The trunkless hands then placed the dishes on the table, and the Prince and the White Cat seated themselves. The first dish was a pie made of young pigeons, and the next was a fricassee of the fattest mice imaginable. The view of the one made the Prince almost afraid to taste the other, till the White Cat, who guessed his thoughts, assured him that there were certain dishes at table in which there was not a single morsel of either rat or mouse, and that these had been dressed on purpose for him; accordingly, he ate heartily of such as she recommended.

When supper was over, the Prince perceived that the White Cat had a portrait set in gold hanging to one of her feet. He begged her permission to look at it; when what was his astonishment to see the portrait of a handsome young man, that exactly resembled himself! He said to himself, there was something very extraordinary in all this; yet, as the White Cat sighed, and looked very sorrowful, he did not venture to ask any questions. He conversed with her on different subjects, and found her extremely well versed in everything that was passing in the world.

When night was far advanced, the White Cat wished him a good night, and he was conducted by the hands to his bed-chamber, which was different still from anything he had seen in the palace, being hung with the wings of butterflies, mixed with the most curious feathers. His bed was of gauze, festooned with bunches of the gayest ribbons, and the looking-glasses reached from the floor to the ceiling.

The Prince was undressed and put into bed by the hands, without speaking a word; they then left him to repose. He, however, slept but little, and in the morning was awakened by a confused noise. The hands took him out of bed, and put on him a handsome hunting-jacket. He looked into the courtyard, and perceived more that five hundred cats, all busily employed in preparing for the field, for this was a day of festival. Presently, the White Cat came to his apartment; and having politely inquired after his health, and how he had passed the night, she invited him to partake of their amusement. The Prince willingly accepted, and mounted a wooden horse, richly caparisoned, which had been prepared for him, and which, he was assured, would gallop to admiration. The beautiful White Cat, at the same time, mounted a monkey, dressed in a dragoon's helmet, which made her look so fierce, that all the rats and mice ran away in the utmost terror.

Everything being ready, the horns sounded, and away they went. No hunting was ever more agreeable; the cats ran faster than the hares and rabbits; and when they caught any, they were hunted in the presence of the White Cat, and a thousand cunning tricks were played. Nor were the birds in safety; for the monkey made nothing of climbing up the trees, with the White Cat on his back, to the nests of the young eagles.

When the hunting was over, the whole retinue returned to the palace; when the White Cat immediately exchanged her dragoon's cap for her veil, and sat down to supper with the Prince, who, being extremely hungry, ate heartily, and afterwards partook with her of the most delicious liquors, which, being often repeated, made him forget that he was to procure a little dog for the old King. He thought no longer of anything but of pleasing the sweet little creature who received him so courteously; and, accordingly, every day was spent in new amusements.

The Prince had almost forgotten his country and relations, and sometimes even regretted that he was not a cat, so great was his affection for his mewing companions. "Alas!" said he to the White Cat, "how will it afflict me to leave you whom I love so much! Either make yourself a lady, or make me a cat."

She smiled at the Prince's wish, but made him scarcely any reply.

At length, the twelvemonth was nearly expired; the White Cat, who knew the very day when the Prince was to reach his father's palace, reminded him that he had but three days longer to look for a perfect little dog. The Prince, astonished at his own forgetfulness, began to afflict himself; when the Cat told him not to be so sorrowful, since she would not only provide him with a little dog, but also with a wooden horse, which should convey him safely in less than twelve hours. "Look here," said she, showing him an acorn, "this contains what you desire." The Prince put the acorn to his ear, and heard the barking of a little dog. Transported with joy, he thanked the Cat a thousand times; and the next day, bidding her tenderly adieu, he set out on his return.

The Prince arrived first at the place of rendezvous, and was soon joined by his brothers; they mutually embraced, and began to give an account of their success; when the youngest showed them only a little mongrel cur, telling them, he thought it could not fail to please the King, from its extraordinary beauty. The brothers stepped upon each other's toes under the table, as much as to say, "We have not much to fear from this sorry-looking animal."

The next day, they went together to the palace. The dogs of the two elder Princes were laying on cushions, and so curiously wrapped round with embroidered quilts, that scarcely would one venture to touch them. The youngest produced his cur, dirty all over, and every one wondered how the Prince could hope to receive a crown for such a present. The King examined the two little dogs of the elder Princes, and

declared he thought them so equally beautiful, that he knew not to which, with justice, he could give the preference. They accordingly began to dispute; when the youngest Prince, taking the acorn from his pocket, soon ended their contention; for a little dog appeared, which could with ease go through the smallest ring, and was, besides, a miracle of beauty.

The King could not possibly hesitate in declaring his satisfaction; yet, as he was not more inclined than the year before to part with his crown, he could think of nothing more to his purpose than telling his sons, that he was extremely obliged to them for the pains they had taken; and that, since they had succeeded so well, he could not but wish they would make a second attempt; he therefore begged they would take another year for procuring him a piece of cambric, so fine as to be drawn through the eye of a small needle.

The three Princes thought this very hard; yet they set out, in obedience to the King's command. The two eldest took different roads, and the youngest remounted his wooden horse, and in a short time arrived at the palace of his beloved White Cat, who received him with the greatest joy, while the trunkless hands helped him, as before, to dismount, and provided him with immediate refreshment; after which, the Prince gave the White Cat an account of the admiration which had been bestowed on the beautiful little dog, and informed her of his father's further injunction.

"Make yourself perfectly easy, dear Prince," said she; "I have in my palace some cats that are particularly expert in making such cambric as the King requires; so you have nothing to do but to give me the pleasure of your company while it is making, and I will take care to procure you all the amusement possible."

She accordingly ordered the most curious fireworks to be immediately played off in sight of the window of the apartment in which they were sitting; and nothing but festivity and rejoicing was heard throughout the palace for the Prince's return.

As the White Cat continually gave proofs of an excellent understanding, the Prince was by no means tired of her company. She talked with him of state affairs, of theatres, of fashions; in short, she was at a loss on no subject whatever, so that, when the Prince was alone, he had plenty of amusement in thinking how it could possibly be, that a small White Cat could be endowed with all the powers of a human creature.

The twelvemonth in this manner again passed insensibly away; but the Cat took care to remind the Prince of his duty in proper time. "For once, my Prince," said she, "I will have the pleasure of equipping you as suits your high rank;" when, looking into the courtyard, he saw a superb car, ornamented all over with gold, silver, pearl, and diamonds, drawn by twelve horses as white as snow, and harnessed in the most sumptuous trappings; and behind the car a thousand guards, richly apparelled, were waiting to attend the Prince's person.

She then presented him with a nut. "You will find in it," said she, "the piece of cambric I promised you: do not break the shell till you are in the presence of

THE PRINCE AND THE WHITE CAT GO OUT HUNTING.

the King your father;" then, to prevent the acknow-ledgments he was about to offer, she hastily bid him adieu.

Nothing could exceed the speed with which the snow-white horses conveyed this fortunate Prince to his father's palace, where his brothers had just arrived before him. They embraced each other, and demanded an immediate audience of the King, who received them with the greatest kindness. The Princes hastened to lay at the feet of his Majesty the curious present he

had required them to procure. The eldest unwrapped a piece of cambric that was indeed extremely fine, so that his friends had no doubt of its passing through the eye of the needle, which was now delivered to the King, having been kept locked up in the custody of his Majesty's treasurer all the time. Not one of them but supposed he would certainly obtain the crown. But when the King tried to draw it through the eye of the needle, it would not pass, though it failed by the smallest difference imaginable. Then came the

No. 38.

second Prince. who made as sure of obtaining the crown. as his brother had done, but, alas! with no better success; for though, to all appearance, his piece of cambric was exquisitely fine, yet it could not be drawn through the eye of the needle. It was now the youngest Prince's turn, who accordingly advanced, and opening a magnificent little box, inlaid with jewels, he took out a walnut, and cracked the shell, imagining he should immediately perceive his piece of cambric; but what was his astonishment to see nothing but a filbert! He did not, however. lose his hopes; he cracked the filbert, and it presented him with a cherry-stone. The Lords of the Court, who had assembled to witness this very extraordinary trial, could not, any more than the Princes his brothers, refrain from laughing, to think he should be so silly as to claim with them the crown, on no better pretensions. The Prince, however. cracked the cherry-stone, which was filled with a kernel; he divided it, and found in the middle a grain of wheat, and in that a grain of millet-seed. He was now absolutely confounded, and could not help muttering between his teeth, "Oh! White Cat, White Cat! thou hast deceived me!" At this instant. he felt his hand severely scratched by the claw of a cat; upon which, he again took courage, and. opening the grain of millet-seed, to the astonishment of all present, he drew from it a piece of cambric four hundred yards in length, and fine enough to be drawn, with perfect ease. through the eye of the needle.

When the King found he had no pretext left for refusing the crown to his youngest son, he sighed deeply, and it was plain to be seen that he was sorry for the Prince's success. "My sons," said he, "it is so gratifying to the heart of a father to receive proofs of his children's love and obedience, that I cannot refuse myself the satisfaction of requiring of you one thing more. You must undertake another expedition; and whichever, by the end of a year, shall bring me the most beautiful lady, shall marry her, and obtain my crown."

The two eldest Princes took care enough not to murmur, for they had now another chance of success; and the youngest was too dutiful to complain of the great injustice he had suffered. So they again took leave of the King, and of each other, and set out without delay; and in less than twelve hours our young Prince again arrived, in his splendid car, at the palace of his dear White Cat, who received him as before. He gave her an account of all that had passed, and the new request of the King his father. "Never mind it, my Prince," said she: "I engage to provide you with what you want; and, in the meantime, let us be as merry as we can, for it is only when I have the pleasure of your company that I am the least inclined to entertainments or rejoicings of any kind." Accordingly, everything went on as before, till the end of another year; only that the Prince felt great uneasiness at being unable to discover by what means it could be that his companion had at once the sense of a creature like himself, and the form of a cat.

At length, only one day remained of the year; when the White Cat thus addressed him: "To-morrow, my

Prince, you must present yourself at the palace of your father, and give him a proof of your obedience. It depends only on yourself to conduct thither the most beautiful Princess ever yet beheld; for the time is come when the enchantment by which I am bound may be ended. You must cut off my head and tail," continued she, "and throw them into the fire."

"I!" answered the Prince, hastily, "I cut off your head and tail! You surely mean to try my affection, which, believe me, beautiful Cat, is truly yours."

"You mistake me, generous Prince," said she; "I do not doubt your regard; but if you wish to see me in any other form than that of a Cat, you must consent to do as I desire, when you will have done me a service I shall never be able sufficiently to repay you."

The Prince's eyes filled with tears as she spoke, yet he considered himself obliged to undertake the dreadful task; and the Cat continuing to press him with the greatest eagerness, with a trembling hand he drew his sword, cut off her head and tail, and threw them into the fire. No sooner was this done, than the most beautiful lady his eyes had ever seen stood before him; and before he had sufficiently recovered from his surprise to speak to her, a long train of attendants, who, at the same moment as their mistress, were changed to their natural shapes, came to offer their congratulations to the Queen, and inquire her commands. She received them with great kindness; and then, ordering them to withdraw, she thus addressed the astonished Prince :—

"Do not imagine. dear Prince, that I have been always a Cat, or that I am of obscure birth. My father was the monarch of six kingdoms; he tenderly loved my mother, leaving her always at liberty to follow her own inclinations. Her prevailing passion was, to travel; and, a short time before my birth, having heard of some Fairies, who were in possession of the largest gardens, filled with the most delicious fruits imaginable, she had so strong a desire to eat some of them, that she set out for the country in which they lived. She arrived at their abode, which she found to be a magnificent palace, on all sides glittering with gold and precious stones. She knocked for a long time at the gates; but no one came, nor could she perceive the least sign that it had any inhabitant. This difficulty, however, did but increase the violence of my mother's longing; for she saw the tops of the trees above the garden walls, loaded with the most luscious fruits. The Queen, in despair, ordered her attendants to place tents close to the door of the palace, as she was determined to watch for an opportunity of speaking to the persons who should go in and out, and remained in them for six weeks with her whole court. But in all this time not a single creature had passed the door of the palace; so that the Queen fell sick of vexation, and her life was despaired of.

"One night, as she lay half asleep, she turned herself about, and opening her eyes, perceived a little Old Woman, extremely ugly and deformed, seated in the easy-chair by her bed-side. 'I, and my sister Fairies,' said she, 'take it extremely ill that your Majesty should so obstinately persist in getting some of our fruit; but since so precious a life is at stake, we consent to give you as much as you can carry away with you, provided you will give us in return what we shall ask.' 'Ah! kind Fairy,' cried the Queen, 'I will give you anything I possess, even my very kingdoms, on condition that I eat of your fruit.' The Old Fairy then informed the Queen, that what they required was, that she would give them the child she would shortly have, as soon as she should be born; adding, that every possible care should be taken of her, and that she should become the most accomplished Princess. The Queen replied, that, however cruel the condition, she must accept it, since nothing but the fruit could save her life.

"The Fairy immediately touched her with a small gold wand, telling her she would now be able to see the door open when she should knock, and to hear the voice that answered her: 'For,' added the Fairy, 'our palace is well filled with inhabitants, and they pass in and out continually, though your Majesty had not the gift of seeing them.'

"In short, my Prince," continued the Cat, "my mother instantly got out of bed, was dressed by her attendants, entered the palace, and satisfied her longing. When the Queen had eaten her fill, she ordered four thousand mules to be procured, and loaded with the fruit, which had the virtue of continuing all the year round in a state of perfection. Thus provided, she returned to the King my father, who, with the whole Court, received her with rejoicings, as it was before imagined she would die of disappointment. All this time, the Queen said nothing to my father of the promise she had made, to give her daughter to the Fairies; so that, when the time was come that she expected my birth, she grew extremely melancholy; till at length, being pressed by the King, she declared to him the truth.

"Nothing could exceed his affliction, when he heard that his only child, when born, was to be given to the Fairies; he bore it, however, as well as he could, for fear of adding to my mother's grief, and also believing he should find some means of keeping me in a place of safety, which the Fairies would not be able to approach. As soon, therefore, as I was born, he had me conveyed to a tower in the palace, to which there were twenty flights of stairs, and a door to each, of which my father kept the key; so that no one came near me without his permission.

"When the Fairies heard of what had been done, they sent first to demand me; and on my father's refusal, to be revenged, they let loose a monstrous Dragon, who devoured men, women, and children, and the breath of whose nostrils destroyed everything it came near, so that the trees and plants began to die in great abundance.

"The grief of the King at seeing this could scarcely be equalled; and finding that his whole kingdom would in a short time be reduced to famine, he determined to give me into their hands. I was accordingly laid in a cradle of mother-of-pearl, magnificently ornamented with gold and jewels, and carried to their palace; and the Dragon immediately disappeared.

"The Fairies placed me in a tower of their palace, magnificently furnished, but to which there was no door; so that whoever approached me was obliged to come by the windows, which were a prodigious height from the ground. From these I had the liberty of getting out into a delightful garden, in which were baths, and every sort of cooling fruit. In this place was I educated by the Fairies, who behaved to me with the greatest kindness; my clothes were extremely splendid, and I was instructed in every kind of accomplishment: in short, my Prince, if I had never seen any one but themselves, I should have remained perfectly happy.

"When they visited me, it was always seated on the back of the Dragon I have already mentioned. They never spoke of my parents; and as they called me their child, I believed myself really so. My only companions in the tower were a Parrot and a little Dog, and both were endowed with the gift of speech.

"One of the windows of my tower overlooked a long avenue shaded with trees, so that I had never seen in it a human creature. One day, however, as I was talking at this window with my Parrot, I perceived a young gentleman, who was listening to our conversation. As I had never seen a man, but in pictures, I was not sorry for the opportunity of gratifying my curiosity. I thought him a very pleasing object, and he at length bowed in the most respectful manner, without daring to speak, for he knew that I was in the palace of the Fairies. When it began to grow dark, he went away, but I vainly endeavoured to see which road he took.

"The next morning, as soon as it was light, I again placed myself at the window, and had the pleasure of seeing that the gentleman had returned to the same place. He now spoke to me through a speaking-trumpet, and informed me he thought me a most charming lady, and that he should be very unhappy if he did not pass his life in my company. I dared not reply; but I threw him some flowers, which he seemed to consider as a mark of my being pleased with what he said. He next begged my permission to come every day at the same hour to speak with me, desiring me, if I consented, to throw down something by way of token. I accordingly threw down a ring, at the same time making a sign for him to withdraw hastily, as I heard the approach of the Fairy Violent, on her Dragon, who brought me my breakfast.

"The first words she uttered, after getting in at the window, were, 'I smell the voice of a man.' You may imagine my terror. Finding no one, she appeared satisfied, and said no more. At length she left me, leaving me a new distaff, and recommending me to employ myself more in spinning: 'For,' said she, 'you have done scarcely anything these two days.' No sooner was she gone, than I flung away the distaff, and again placed myself at the window; and having a spying-glass in my tower, I discovered my new acquaintance at some distance, richly dressed, and surrounded by a number of attendants. I concluded from this that he was the son of some king in the neighbourhood: and fearing he might think of paying me another visit that day, I sent my Parrot to him with a message, requesting him to avoid the danger I feared of meeting the Dragon.

"The Prince, for such he was, sent back my Parrot, having first delivered to her a ring and a picture, of which he begged my acceptance. The picture was of himself, and my joy was inexpressible at thus being able to see the features of the Prince so near.

"Just at this time, the Fairies took it into their heads to think of choosing me a husband from their own race, and accordingly appointed a day for his paying me a visit, desiring me to look as engagingly as I could. When I was alone with my Parrot, she began to tell me how much she should pity me if the Fairies obliged me to marry Migonnet, the Prince they had thought of; 'For,' said she, 'he is a dwarf not two feet high; he has a hunch upon his back, his head is larger than his whole body, his nose is so long that twenty birds may roost upon it; he has the feet of an eagle, and walks on stilts.' I was ready to die with horror, when I thought of this creature as my husband; and from that moment I resolved to find some means of escaping from my tower with the engaging Prince I had seen. I was not long in devising a means for the execution of my project; I begged the Fairies to bring me a netting-needle, a mesh, and some cord, saying, I wished to make some nets, to amuse myself with catching birds at my windows. This they readily complied with, and in a short time I completed a ladder long enough to reach the ground.

"I now sent my Parrot to the Prince, to beg he would come to the usual place, as I wished to speak with him. He did not fail; and, finding the ladder, mounted it, and precipitately entered my tower. I was at first somewhat alarmed, but the charms of his conversation had restored me to perfect tranquillity; when all at once the window opened, and the Fairy Violent, seated on the Dragon's back, rushed into the tower, followed by the hideous Migonnet in a chariot of fire, and a troop of guards, each upon the back of an ostrich.

"My beloved Prince thought of nothing but how to defend me from their fury, for I had had time to relate to him my story, previous to this cruel interruption. But their numbers overpowered him, and the Fairy Violent had the barbarity to command the Dragon to devour my Prince before my eyes. In my despair, I would have thrown myself into the mouth of the horrible monster; but this they took care to prevent, saying, my life should be preserved for greater punishment. The Fairy then touched me with a wand, and I instantly became a White Cat. She next conducted me to this palace, which belonged to my father, and gave me a train of cats for my attendants, together with the twelve hands which waited on you, my Prince. She then informed me of my birth, and the death of both my parents, and pronounced upon me what she imagined would be the greatest of maledictions—that I should not be restored to my natural figure, till a young Prince, the perfect resemblance of him I had lost, should cut off my head and tail. You, my Prince, are that perfect resemblance; and, accordingly, you have ended the enchantment.

"I need not add, that I already love you more than my life; let us therefore hasten to the palace of the

300

King your father, and obtain his approbation to our marriage."

The Prince and Princess accordingly set out, side by side, in a car of still greater splendour than before, and reached the palace just as the two brothers had arrived with two beautiful Princesses. The King, hearing that each of his sons had succeeded in finding what he had required, again began to think of some new expedient to delay the time of resigning his crown; but when the whole Court were with the King assembled to pass judgment, the Princess who accompanied the youngest, perceiving his thoughts by his countenance, stepped majestically forward, and thus addressed him:—

"What pity that your Majesty, who is so capable of governing, should think of resigning the crown! I am fortunate enough to have six kingdoms in my possession; permit to bestow one on each of the elder Princes, and to enjoy the remaining four in the society of the youngest. And may it please your Majesty to keep your own kingdom, and to make no decision concerning the beauty of the three Princesses, who, without such a proof of your Majesty's preference, will no doubt live happily together!"

The air resounded with the applauses of the assembly; the young Prince and Princess embraced the King, and next their brothers and sisters; the three weddings immediately took place, and the kingdoms were divided as the Princess had proposed, in each of which nothing for a long time prevailed but rejoicings.

THE TAILOR-PRINCE.

THERE have been many Princes who ought to have been tailors—indeed, most Princes, of late years, have shown their fitness for such a trade by nature, as they seem never to be happy but when regulating the cut of their soldiers' clothes—but we do not often see a Tailor who has been a Prince.

Selim Baruch, a merchant of Bagdad, while travelling across the Desert with the caravan to Damascus, at the resting-place from the mid-day heat, told the following story:—

Once upon a time, there was a fine young Tailor, whose name was Labakan, or, "the Soul of a Goose" —a goose being an implement used by tailors in their trade, and, as being both flat and hot-tempered, singularly happy to give the character of our Labakan. He worked for one of the cleverest master-tailors in Alexandria. No one could say that Labakan was not expert with his needle, or idle, or inattentive; on the contrary, he was a right good workman, very handy at fitting and cutting out in every fashion, and generally assiduous when at the shop: but the odd character of this chap rendered it difficult to depend upon him. Sometimes, he would sew away for hours together, with such wonderful ardour, that the very needle grew hot in his fingers, and the thread smoked again. But sometimes, on the other hand—and this sometimes, unluckily, occurred very often—he fell into a kind of ecstacy, during which, he would remain motionless, his head erect, his eyes fixed, with something altogether, in his air and manner, that his master and the rest of his shopmates could not understand, and which only caused them to shrug their shoulders, and say, "Here is Labakan, with the airs of a Prince on him again!"

On a certain Friday, at the hour when the other workmen were returning quietly into the house to resume their labours, after the hour of prayer, Labakan came out of the mosque, arrayed in a magnificent suit of clothes, that he had procured at a great expense, and walked about in it for a long time, with grave step and haughty mien, up and down the streets and public places of the town. Whenever any of his shopmates, who met him, said, "How d'ye do?" or, "Peace be with you!" or, "How is friend Labakan?" our Tailor-lad answered him with a slight condescending wave of the hand, as if assuring him of his protection, and then kept on his way. When his master said to him, in a jesting manner, "You look like a Prince out of luck, Labakan!" the expression seemed to delight him very much, and he replied briskly, "You have noticed that, too, have you?" and then said to himself, in a low tone, "I have long since thought so."

From that moment, the madness of the poor Tailor-lad went on increasing; and if he had not been a good fellow in other things, and a clever workman to boot, his master would assuredly have given him notice to quit.

While all this was going on, Selim, the Sultan's brother, in passing by Alexandria, sent to the master-tailor a court-dress, to have some of the embroidery upon it altered, and the master confided the task to Labakan, who usually had charge of the finest work. When evening came, all the workmen withdrew, to rest from the fatigues of the day; but an irresistible attraction retained Labakan in the workshop, where the dress of the Emperor's brother was hung up on a peg.

Plunged in his usual reverie, he eyed the garment with a fascinated gaze, admiring now the brilliancy of the embroidery, now the glowing colours, the light and shade of the velvet and silk. "Suppose I were to try it on, and see how it becomes me." No sooner said than done; and, strange to say, the dress fitted his figure exactly, as well as if it had been made for him.

Labakan strutted up and down before the glas, gesticulating, speaking loud, and doing his best to give himself great airs.

"And what, after all, is a Prince?" said he, as he contemplated himself in a mirror; "one man dressed more richly than the rest, and there's the whole of it! If the Sultan wore the rags of a common fellah" (peasant)—"if the Archbishop, or the Lord Mayor, were despoiled of the adornments of their dignity—who would look at them, as they passed by, and say, 'There goes the Sultan! there the head of our clergy; and that other noble-looking person, the head of our civic magistracy, or, it may be, the Commander-in-Chief of our armies? The Emirs, too, the relations of our Prophet—who would know them, if it were not for their green turbans? Yes! dress is the grand

thing; if I could only procure a frock-coat like this, who, then, would doubt my quality as a Prince? and I might so, at last, find out my noble parents! But, to do that, I must first take myself off, out of Alexandria, where the people are so vulgar and dull, that they can't form any idea of my having an illustrious origin."

At that moment, there passed through the heated brain of the princely Labakan, how it would be his right course to impale half-a-dozen of his compatriots, as an example to the survivors; but he called to mind, at the same time, that, Prince though he was—and who could doubt it? had not his master already said that he had the air of a banished Prince?—yet that he was not yet sufficiently firm in his dignity, to allow himself that trifling satisfaction; so he brought his noble mind back to the original position of stealing the coat before him. as the first step towards seeking the throne of his ancestors. That charming coat of the Sultan's brother, with its embroidered button-holes, seemed the very thing, sent by some good Genius, expressly to point out the course he ought to follow. Should he reject such an opportunity. such excellent advice, and such protection? No! He would greatly dare, and do, at once. So he slipped his arms into the golden coat, sneaked out of the shop, and, thanks to the darkness, gained the gates of Alexandria, without being seen by anybody.

As the morning broke, and found him on his onward way—whither he knew not exactly—our new Prince could not help feeling somewhat abashed at the looks of curiosity with which he was regarded by the passers-by. The more he threw out his chest, and sniffed the air with elevated nostrils, the more people

wondered, that a personage so grandly dressed should travel on foot like a common fellah. When occasionally questioned on this subject, Labakan replied, with an air of mystery, that he had his private reasons for doing so; but, observing that his explanations were generally received with sneers and ridicule, he made up his mind to complete his equipment by purchasing a horse. So, going to market with a moderate sum, he managed to procure an old roan mare, of a quiet temper, and as gentle as a lamb; for our Labakan had no pretensions to being an accomplished cavalier, seeing that he had never had even a stable in his establishment.

One day, as he was slowly ambling along upon his Murva (for so he named his mare), he was joined by a horseman, who asked permission to accompany him, as conversation shortened the tedium of a long journey. The new-comer was a young and merry lad, handsome, well made, of a distinguished appearance, with sharp black eyes; and Labakan would willingly have received him as an equal, if he had only been better dressed. However, by degrees they fell into conversation, as they jogged along the road; and before the day was out, Omar—for such was the name of our Labakan's fellow-traveller—had told the whole story of his life to his fellow-traveller. Labakan, on his part, was not so entirely confidential; here and there he left out an episode; and sometimes he plastered over the brickwork of his true ancestry with the fine cement of some noble line; he said nothing, moreover, of needles and thread, but gave Omar occasion to understand that he was a personage of high birth, and travelling only for his pleasure.

Master Labakan was on his guard against entering into too many details, after hearing Omar's story; especially when it turned out, that the young fellow, whose dress appeared to him so shabby, was no less a personage than the son of a King.

This was, in fact, what Omar told him:—

"From my earliest infancy, I had been brought up in the Court of Elfi Bey" (Bey means "General"), "the Pasha of Cairo, whom I believed to be my uncle. Lately, he called me into his presence, and when we were alone, announced to me that I was not his nephew, but the son of a powerful King in Arabia, who had felt himself constrained to part with me soon after I was born, for the purpose of averting some fatal influence, which, according to the dictum of the astrologers, threatened my life up to the age of twenty-two years.

"Elfi Bey did not impart to me the name of my family—for he was forbidden to mention it; but these are the marks and directions I received from him, and by aid of which I am to find my father:—

"On the fourth day of the month of Ramadam—of which this is the first—I shall have completed my twenty-second year. On that day I am to be at the foot of the column El-Serujah, which is four days' journey from Alexandria, eastward. Certain persons will meet me there, to whom I am to show a dagger given me by Elfi Bey, pronouncing, as I do so, the words, 'I am he whom you seek.' If they say, in answer, 'Glory be to the Prophet, who has preserved you!' my orders are to follow them, and these men will lead me to my father."

The Tailor had listened to the whole of this history with ever-increasing wonder. In his mooning moments, it had often happened to him to make himself the hero of similar adventures; and now, on a sudden, under his very eyes, his dreams had taken upon them substantial flesh, and were actually being realized—but to the profit of another. Surely another man's profit is an injury to ourselves! (That is the way that selfish persons too often argue; and for want of knowing the possibility of such wicked reasoning, we are often puzzled to make out the meaning of some people's actions.) Labakan was actually quarrelling with Providence, because some one else than himself was fortunate. What was wanting to make him a Prince? Why, the being the son of a King—that was all! And was not he, Labakan, quite as worthy to be the son of a King as his fellow-traveller, Omar?

So our Labakan regarded Prince Omar with jealous eyes. What irritated him more than all was, that Omar, who from his childhood had already enjoyed the position of a Pasha's nephew, should have farther thrust upon him the dignity of a King's son; while he, poor Labakan, had got nothing but obscure birth and a miserable education.

All through the day the Tailor-lad chewed the bitter cud of such stupid notions. They seized his imagination through the night, and hindered his enjoying a wink of sleep; but when he woke in the morning, and saw young Omar sleeping tranquilly by his side, dreaming, perhaps, of the honours and royal welcome that awaited him, Labakan felt an odious thought creeping within his heart, like some poisonous reptile:—"If it should happen by any chance—if the Prince were to die—what would there be to hinder him, Labakan, from taking his place, assuming his name, and presenting himself as the son of the King?"

Omar still slept. The dagger that Elfi Bey had given him, as the means of recognition by his royal father, stuck up half out of his girdle—a magnificent weapon, with a handle studded with rubies—a perfect jewel! Labakan drew closer to admire it, put his hand towards it, drew it from its sheath, and read, on the blade, these words—which seemed to him to have the force of an oracle—"If God pleases."

"Yes," repeated he, in a low voice, looking with glaring eyes upon the slumbering Prince; "yes, 'if it please God,' this fellow will never wake again, and I shall be—I, myself—Prince Omar!" His grasp closed convulsively on the hilt of the dagger, and he was about to strike—when, at the thought of blood, the cries of his victim, or perhaps a struggle, his heart failed him.

But if the horror of murder was revolting to the timid nature of the young Tailor, he had no such scruples in regard to theft; and I can assure you that on this occasion, and under the circumstances, he looked upon himself as conferring an obligation on young Omar, in leaving him his life, though he took from him his name. "By acting thus," said he, "I shall attain my point quite as well; and if the other comes to reclaim it from me—why then he will arrive too late, and it will be he who will be taken for an impostor."

Whereupon, having thus made up his Princely mind, the noble Labakan stuck the dagger into his own belt, jumped on the Prince's fast horse; and when Omar awoke, his perfidious fellow-traveller was already many miles ahead of him.

It was on the first day of the month of Ramadam that all this happened, and, consequently, there were still three days left for Labakan to reach the spot indicated. There was plenty of time, therefore, to perform the distance; but, goaded on by fear, lest the true Prince might catch him again, and vindicate his own, he spurred on, as if his very life depended on his haste.

Towards the close of the second day, Labakan saw the column El Serujah on the horizon. It stood on the summit of a gentle eminence, in the centre of a vast plain, and thus could be seen two or three hours before reaching it. The heart of Labakan beat strongly on beholding it. There were two days yet remaining, for him to think over the part he was about to play, and prepare himself accordingly; but his evil conscience perpetually tormented him, by placing before his eyes the chastisement he was sure to receive, if his tricks were found out; he ran the risk, in fact, of being impaled, there and then, or, at the least, of being beaten and branded as a vile thief.

Every time he thought of this, Labakan felt as if cold water were pouring down his back; yet the greedy desire he had of being a Prince quickly got the better of his shame and fear, and he determined to go through with the adventure.

While thus conning over his situation, he stepped with his horse into the shelter of a clump of palm-trees, under whose shade he could the better arrange his reflections, and await the hour marked by his destiny.

At last it came; and when Labakan, on the morning of the fourth day, cast his eyes over the plain, he beheld, with a ravishing joy, a group of magnificent tents, spread out at the foot of the gentle hill from which rose the pillar.

Labakan made haste to smarten up his appearance, and plume his gayest feathers—a labour of love which it was not in his character to neglect; the growlings and grumblings of his conscience he soon managed to quell, then jumped on his horse, summoning, at the same time, all his bravery, as well as his little store of skill as an equestrian, to get up a decent gallop; and then urged his steed straight towards the hillock.

At the foot of the column was seated an old man, surrounded by slaves, guards in rich uniform, and a respectful circle of attendants; all of whom, the master included, seemed to be awaiting with anxiety some one's arrival.

The whole party rose up when they saw Labakan approaching; and that worthy, on his part, concealing his anxiety and emotion with the best face he could put on—or rather, hiding it as much as possible, by making a low bow—prostrated himself at the feet of the old man, presenting to him, at the same time, the dagger of Elfi Bey, and murmuring, in a voice trembling with emotion, "I am he whom you seek."

"All praise to Allah, who has preserved you!" replied the old man, with tears of joy. "Come to my arms—come! that I may kiss your forehead, and bless you, my thrice-dear son, my Omar!"

These solemn words in some degree touched the soul of the Tailor-youth; but he had gone too far to recede, so he threw himself, sobbing, into the arms of the Old Prince.

He was not left long to enjoy in quiet the delights of his new condition: even while disengaging himself from the old man's embrace, he saw a horseman pushing his way over the plain towards the hill, as fast as the wretched and jaded hack he bestrode could lay legs to the ground. One gaze was sufficient; Labakan recognized the real Prince and his own shabby mare, Murva. How get out of this? There was only one method—he must face it out, and audaciously keep up the character he had assumed.

"Stop! stop!" shouted the Prince, as, breathless and exhausted, he reached the summit of the hillock. "Do not allow yourself to be abused by an infamous impostor; I—I alone—am the true Omar!"

At this wonderful concatenation of circumstances, a profound astonishment became observable on the countenances of all the attendants; while the looks of the old man, wandering first to one face then the other, with a still-increasing anxiety, seemed anxiously to require the explanation, which was indispensable.

Prince Omar, with an emotion that forbade him speech, placed both hands upon his heart, in the effort to repress its impetuous beating. Labakan took advantage of this moment of respite, and with a forehead of iron, and a voice of hypocritical calmness, said: "Gracious lord and father, do not permit yourself to be imposed upon by that fellow there: he is a poor wretch of a tailor—a sort of insane fool—whose madness has taken the turn of his fancying himself a Prince, and who really deserves less anger than pity."

These impudent words raised the anger of the Prince to the highest pitch of fury; foaming with rage, he wanted to rush on Labakan; but the guards of the Old Prince darted between them, and, by their master's order, seized upon poor Omar, and bound him hand and foot.

For an instant, when he found himself subjected to such indignities, the young Prince thought that he must be really out of his senses. His eyes, staring with rage, saw nothing but red mist floating before them; there was a confused buzzing in his ears; the veins of his temples beat as if they would burst; and he would have actually expired on the spot, if the very excess of his affliction had not brought about an instantaneous reaction, which relaxed his over-excited system, and suffused his eyes with tears.

Omar remained in a kind of prostration of all faculties for a long time; but when the Old Prince happened to approach him, he could not avoid saying to him, with much emotion and many tears, "Yes! yes! my heart assures me that you are my father! Oh, listen to me! I conjure you, by my mother's memory, listen to me!"

"Allah protect us!" said the old man, getting as far out of his way as possible; "here is this fellow gone mad again! What strange fancies get into people's heads sometimes!"

Once more taking the arm of Labakan, he went down the hill-side, leaning upon the one he thought to be his son. They both of them mounted noble steeds, magnificently caparisoned, while the unfortunate Prince followed, on the back of one of the camels of the escort, fast bound and tied, so as to prevent any farther movement on his part.

The Old Prince, whose paternal love was thus made the subject of a shameless fraud, was Saad, the Sultan of the Mechabites. After a life of many years without children, his ardent prayers were rewarded by the birth of a son; but the astrologers, whom he consulted on the future destinies of the young Prince, told him, when they had drawn out his horoscope, that up to his twenty-second year, Prince Omar would be in danger of being supplanted by a rival. For this reason it had happened, that the old Saad had resolved to confide his son to the care of his faithful friend, Elfi Bey, in the hope of averting the fulfilment of the fatal oracle. When his twenty-second year had passed, all was to go on favourably for the young Prince, and the stars promised him a long and prosperous reign.

While the Sultan was telling this story to his pretended son, as he rode beside him, Labakan was accustoming himself, more and more, to the part that he was playing, of a Prince; and although his natural empty-headedness remained the same as before, yet he managed to put on a kind of dignified stolidity, which served him so well, that on entering his states, not one of his subjects but declared him to be as fine a Prince as ever eyes had looked upon.

Triumphal arches, fireworks, reviews, banquets, rejoicings, serenades, and addresses, awaited them in every halting-place. Green boughs and fresh flowers were strewn along their path; carpets of gay colours hung from every balcony; and the people, unanimously, went into a delirium of joy, shouting, singing, and chorusing prayers and thanks to Allah and the Prophet, for the return of such a noble Prince.

Such a glorious reception, such popular enthusiasm, such luxurious living, and such splendid apparel, filled the soul of the vain young Tailor with exquisite delight. Not so the poor Omar, who, cuffed and kicked from one to another, among the crowd of royal domestics, was compelled to assist in the lying triumph of his unworthy rival. But it did Omar good; he was now able to judge how much of this popular esteem was false—how much belonged to the coat and jewelled turban, and how little to the man himself. It made Omar a philosopher, but then—it left him a turnspit! No one troubled themselves about him, in the midst of such universal joy—triumphs of which he was the real subject. "Omar" was in every mouth; but Omar, all the while, had

304

scarcely a bit of meat within his lips. He was still tied on a camel's back; and sometimes, when some good soul took the trouble to inquire who the poor fellow was, and why he was bound so tightly, the answer fell like a lump of lead on the ears of the miserable Prince: "Oh, that's a poor young Tailor, that's out of his mind!"

At the end of the eighth day's march, the royal party arrived at the capital of the Sultan's states, where every preparation had been made to welcome the return of their Sovereign and his royal son, in a grander style than any of the minor cities they had already gone through were able to exhibit.

The Sultana Valedie, a lady of venerable age, watched the arrival of her husband and son, surrounded by the whole of her Court, in the most sumptuous saloon of the palace. It was evening, and thousands of lamps, in crystal globes, were hung in the palace halls and gardens; the galleries and staircases shone resplendent with lights of every colour; and the whole palace bore the aspect of some fairy vision.

The Sultana, like her husband, had never set eyes upon her son since the day of his birth; but his image had appeared to her so often in her dreams, and the features of the vision—always the same—were so strongly impressed upon her mind, that she would have recognized the child of her bosom among a thousand.

When Saad, therefore, leading Labakan by the hand, approached the Sultana's throne, and said:—

"Here, my dear, I bring back to you the child for whom you have sighed so long."

The Sultana interrupted him suddenly, with a repulsive air:—

"That my son?" she exclaimed. "No! no! those are not the features which the Prophet has revealed to me."

Saad was beginning to reproach the Sultana for her silly superstition, when the doors of the saloon were thrown open with a loud crash, as Omar forced his way through them, and rushed into the middle of the assembled courtiers, despite all the efforts of his guards, whom he dragged in after him. Exhausted with the struggle he had just gone through, he fell at the foot of the throne, exclaiming, as he did so, "Let me die here! Order my death, oh! cruel father! I can no longer endure this ignominy!"

A violent agitation followed this unexpected scene. They fell upon the unhappy Prince from all sides; and his guards would have bound him hand and foot once more, but for the Sultana, who, with the deepest emotion and anxiety, hurried down from her throne, and ordered the guards to stand aloof from the young man. They would have obeyed her, had not the Sultan shouted, in an imperious and angry voice, "Remove this madman from our presence! I alone have the right to command here. Let all the world hear, tremble and obey!" Then, turning to his Sheiks, Beys, Captains, and other officers, he placed his hand on Labakan's shoulder: "Are a woman's dreams to avail against irrefragable testimony? This young Prince, here—I again repeat, and assure you—is my son. He it is who brought to me the sign agreed between us—the dagger of Elfi Bey."

THE FAIRY GULGUL GIVES THE TWO CASKETS TO SULTAN SAAD.

"He stole it from me," roared the young Prince. "I met this swindler on the road, was induced to tell him my story, and the traitor has supplanted me. My silly confidence, alas! has been my ruin."

These cries from a desparate man had no effect upon the Sultan. It was difficult for any idea to enter his royal head; but once there, it was impossible to dislodge it. So he ordered Omar to be dragged out of the hall by main force; while he himself, with Labakan, entered the interior of the Palace.

But the Sultana was not so easily appeased or silenced. She was not so satisfied with the clearness of her husband's perception in the way of fatherhood, and brooded over the thought of the unfortunate so-called madman being her own boy, and actually in the full enjoyment of his senses, with feelin s outraged at the ignominy he was enduring. What were proofs to her? Had not she a mother's instinct? What other reason was necessary than a woman's reason? She believed it to be so, and it must be so. She

No. 39.

305

did not fancy the looks of Labakan; he had a low brutish way with him, and a down look; rode like a sack, and walked like a porter. It was plain to her that he was an impostor; but how make that clear to her husband? The Sultan was not a man to be contradicted indiscreetly; you might scold him in a private room, but before his Court and his generals, he was a trout that required tickling. However, she must convince him of his error by some means or other—but how to begin? She made herself acquainted with all the details of the expedition, the meeting at the pillar, the sign agreed upon, the challenge of the true Prince. All this she learnt by examining the guards and attendants who had accompanied the Sultan. This done, she took counsel of her faithful slaves. Numerous were the plans proposed and rejected; at last, a wily old Circassian woman, Melecsalah by name, put in her word: "If what I have heard be true, thrice-honoured mistress, the one that brought the dagger to the Sultan, would pretend that he, whom you yourself think to be your son, is a poor mad Tailor-youth, named Labakan?"

"Yes," said the Sultana; "but what are you driving at?"

"What would you think, madam," Melecsalah went on, "if the impostor who robbed your son of his birthright, should also have had the impudence to give him his own name? One would hardly believe this possible; but, if it be so, I know of a plan to make the false one show himself in his true colours and real person."

Here Melecsalah whispered in her mistress's ear, and said some words in a low voice. The royal lady seemed to enter into the spirit of the plan, whatever it was, for she rose up directly, and took her way to the Sultan's apartments.

She was a clever woman, this Sultana; but what is the use of saying that?—are they not all clever, when they have a point to carry? She thoroughly understood her husband's obstinacy, but she also knew his weak points, and how to turn them to account. "Sire," said she, "forgive me the first impulse, that led me to act contrary to your wishes. For many long years the whole of my thoughts have been occupied with my absent son, and I had formed for myself an ideal image, with which the son you brought me did not correspond. Be not angry, my lord, with a woman's weakness—it has past. I believe what you tell me, and I am ready to acknowledge as my son the young man who presented you with the dagger of Elfi Bey."

"Just the right thing!" said the Sultan, much softened.

"But on one condition," the Sultana hastened to add, in a calm tone. "I should like," said she—"it is a folly, a bit of childishness, a whim, yet what, after all, does it matter?—I should like—now promise to grant it to me."

"So be it—but what is it?" asked the Sultan, impatiently.

"You swear, then, to grant my request?"

"I swear! Speak—say on!"

"I wish the Prince of Omar and—the other one—should give me some proof of their cleverness. I don't

ask them to mount on horseback, to throw the lance, to try their sword-play, or any other such feats of martial prowess: no! such jousts are oftentimes dangerous, and may have fatal results. I am a woman, and wish for gentler tests. I want them to make, each of them, a coat, and then we shall see who has worked best to please me."

The Sultan laughed, and shrugged his shoulders. "By the beard of the Prophet," he exclaimed, "here is a clever idea, indeed! So, my son is to put himself in rivalry with this idiot of a Tailor, in a trial as to who can make the best coat? No, assuredly; that shall not be."

"You have given your word, great Sire."

"I have sworn it—I have sworn it, beyond all doubt," growled the Sultan; "but I swear to you, that I never expected any such extravagant whim."

"But you have sworn it, Sire."

Now, the Sultan was the slave of his word, and he felt himself bound to act in accordance with it; but not without a distinct protest, that, whatever might be the result of the experiment, it should not in the slightest degree modify the resolve he had arrived at.

The Sultan, having done this official act, proceeded to call upon him whom he called his son, and entreated him to lend an ear to this fantastical wish of his mother, who had a desire, for once, to have a pelisse made by his hands, and had promised, at that price, to receive him into favour.

LABAKAN MAKES A COAT, AND HANDS IT TO THE SULTAN.

At these tidings, the heart of the simpleton Labakan leapt with joy. "If I could once set myself right with the Sultana," said he to himself, "all would go well afterwards, and I could do as I please with the others."

So the Sultana's whim was carried out, and two chambers prepared, one for the Prince, the other for the Tailor, each of whom was supplied with a piece of silk, scissors, needle and thread, but nothing else.

The Sultan was greatly desirous to know what his son would do in the way of coat-making; but the Sultana's heart beat fast with anxiety as to the success of her stratagem.

The time allowed for the accomplishment of the task was forty-eight hours, and both were locked up. On the third day, Labakan strutted forth, with a triumphant air, and spreading out his coat before the astonished eyes of the Sultan, "Look here, dear father," said he; "see, my noble mother, if this coat is not a masterpiece. I will wager that the cleverest tailor about the court is not able to make one equal to it!"

The Sultana smiled, and, turning to Omar, said, "And you—what have you brought us?"

The young Prince threw to the other end of the chamber the silk and the scissors, and, in accents of indignation, exclaimed, "I have been taught to master a horse, to wield a sabre, and my arrow flies straight to its mark; but to dishonour my fingers with a needle —no, never! That would indeed be unworthy a pupil of Elfi Bey, the valiant ruler of Cairo!"

"Oh! thou art indeed the true son of my husband and master!" exclaimed the Sultana, in an ecstacy of joy; "thee only do I name my son! Pardon me, Sire," said she, turning towards the Sultan, "forgive the trick I have employed: but do you not now see which is the Prince and which the Tailor?"

The Sultan made no reply; rage and vexation disputed the possession of his soul; but his dignity as a master of wives enforced the necessity of self-command. "This trial is insufficient," he finally said; "but if I have been abused"—and here he cast a terrible glance on the miserable Labakan, who made a sufficiently foolish countenance—"if I have been abused, there remains—thanks be to Allah!—a sure means of knowing and penetrating the mystery. Let the swiftest of my horses be brought hither. I shall not be long before I return; but, in the meanwhile, let no person leave the palace."

At no great distance from the town, an ancient forest existed, in the depth of which, tradition placed the dwelling of a Good Fairy, named Gulgul, who, as report run, had, on more than one occasion, assisted the Sultan of the nation with her advice in time of need.

It was to Gulgul that the Sultan now betook himself. When he had reached the centre of a vast opening, surrounded by giant cedars—the place where the Fairy was supposed to dwell—the Sultan alighted, and in a loud voice said: "If it be true that you have heretofore aided my ancestors with good advice in the hour of need, refuse not, O Gulgul, to bestow your protection on their descendant also, and deign to come to my aid on the present occasion."

Scarcely had the Sultan concluded this speech, than one of the great cedar-trees opened out from within, and afforded passage for a pretty little woman of very minute proportions, veiled in folds of long white drapery.

"I know for what reason you come to me, Sultan Saad," said the Fairy, in a voice as soft, clear, and musical as the note of a musical glass; "your intentions are straightforward and pure, and I will willingly afford you my aid. Take these two small caskets, and let each of the two young gentlemen, who pretend to the honour of your name, freely make choice of them. I know that the Prince Omar—and you will soon have proof under your own eyes—will find in the one that he may choose that which will confirm his high rank, while the contents of the second will declare the impostor. Go! and may the Prophet deign to shower upon your whitened hairs the dew of his consolation."

Thus spoke the Veiled Fairy; and after placing in the Sultan's hands two coffers of ivory enriched with gold and pearls, she vanished in the air like a mist.

The Sultan, now alone, felt a lively curiosity within his breast as to the contents of the coffers. He looked at the lids, but could not see any hinges or keyhole, and he could not go to the extent of breaking them open. They were both exactly alike in size and appearance, and could not be distinguished from each other but by the difference of the inscriptions upon them, which were marked out in diamonds. The legend upon the one was, "Honour and Glory;" on the other, "Happiness and Riches."

As soon as the Sultana heard from her husband's lips the account of his visit to Gulgul, and what the Good Fairy had promised, her heart leapt with joy. Confident in the Protectress of the Sultans, she no longer doubted that he, towards whom she was attracted by a secret instinct, must inevitably be the real Prince, and her own son, and would be sure to make choice of the right casket, and, so, afford proof of his royal extraction. Orders were given, in all haste, for the trial to be made upon the spot, in presence of the whole Court, and in a solemn manner.

On a table of porphyry, in front of the Sultan's throne, were placed the two coffers. The Emirs and Pashas formed a semicircle behind their sovereign. When all had taken their places, Labakan was brought into the presence. The silly fellow had, in the interim, enjoyed sufficient leisure to gain breathing-time and recover himself; and as he had not been driven out ignominiously at once, he said to himself, that his part of the play was not yet quite played out. He advanced up the saloon with a haughty step, bowed to the throne, and said, "What are the orders of my lord and father?"

After the Sultan had explained to him what he had to do, Labakan stepped towards the table, and applied himself to a careful consideration of the two caskets. He hesitated a long time, not knowing on which to fix. "Thrice-honoured father," he exclaimed at last, "there cannot, in my eyes, any greater good fortune exist than that of being your son; and that man possesses all riches who enjoys your love. Mine, therefore, be the casket which bears the legend, 'Happiness and Riches.'"

"We shall soon know if you have made the right choice," said the Sultan; and turning towards a slave, he added, "Bring in the other."

Omar came forward slowly, with depressed look and

307

saddened glance; his whole being seemed crushed by the violent emotion he had been forced to endure during some days. His aspect excited a general interest in those present, as he prostrated himself before the Sultan's throne, and requested him to make known his will.

The nature and object of the proof to which he was to be submitted having been revealed to him, Omar arose, and walked towards the caskets pointed out to him. He read the two inscriptions carefully, seemed to ruminate upon them attentively, and then, in a gentle and firm voice, said: "Brought up on the steps of a throne, I have believed, up to this day, in the excellence of Fortune, and the permanence of her gifts. Alas! these last few days have taught me how frail is good fortune—how riches pass away! But what I also know, is," he went on, with head exalted, and flashing eye, "that the heart of the brave conceals within it an imperishable good—*Honour*; and that the brilliant star of *Glory* does not go out with that of happiness. Yes! though I lose a throne, the lot is cast: *Honour* and *Glory*, I have made choice of ye!"

Then he would have stretched forth his hand towards the casket, the noble device on which had attracted his soul; but the Sultan checked him with a gesture, and at the same time commanded Labakan to approach the table and await his orders.

While the two rivals thus stood side by side—the impostor with difficulty concealing the unquietness of his inward feelings under an affectation of audacity; the other abiding the decision of Fate with modest assurance—the Sultan ordered a silver basin to be brought, filled with clear water drawn from the sacred fountain at Mecca, which believers call *Zemzem*. In this he made the sacred ablutions, turned his face three times towards the East, and prostrated himself three times, saying, at the same time, "O Allah! who for ages past hast preserved our race pure and unmixed, suffer not an ignoble being to pollute the blood of the Abassides; and through your aid let my son—my true son—be revealed to me by this last proof!"

308

At a sign from the Sultan, the two young men placed their hands each on the coffer they had chosen; whereupon, the lids, which no effort had been able to raise up previous to this, opened suddenly of themselves.

In the casket of Omar lay, upon a cushion of crimson velvet, a small crown and a golden sceptre in miniature. At the bottom of that of Labakan, was a long tailor's needle and a skein of thread!

At sight of this, the film of deception fell from the Sultan's eyes, and his understanding recognised what a mother's heart had felt at the first stroke. But, as if to show that the hand of Destiny, and not a blind chance, determined the choice of the caskets, scarcely had the Sultan touched the little crown, than it grew, and grew, until at last it attained the dimensions of a real crown. The old Saad placed it, with trembling hands, on the head of his son Omar, who knelt before him; and raising him, kissed his forehead, and made him take a seat at his side.

Then, turning towards Labakan, who knew not how to look, and trembled in his skin, while awaiting the chastisement he deserved: "As for you, dog of a Tailor," exclaimed the Sultan, "you shall die under the stick!"

"Pardon for him!" said the Prince Omar; "refuse me not, Sire, the first request I have ever made to you, nor suffer the joy of my return to be saddened by exhibitions of punishments."

"Let the wretch be spared, then," replied the Sultan, "since such is my son's wish; but let not the rising sun catch you in my territory, Master Labakan, unless you wish to furnish a supper for the crows when he sets!"

Confused and stunned, as it were, the poor Tailor-youth had no power to speak a word. He fell on his face before the Prince, and with a face bathed in tears, muttered, indistinctly, some expressions of unintelligible gratitude. Meanwhile, the Emirs and Grandees of the State came thronging round Prince Omar to congratulate him; and Labakan, who was now no more noticed than the meanest scullion or slave, sneaked out of the palace, and with the threat of the Sultan ringing in his ears, made the best of his way, in all haste, along the road to Alexandria.

Had he known the reception that awaited him there, he would not have been in so great a hurry to reach it quite so soon. But it was his doom to receive yet another lesson, to disgust him altogether with grandeur, and cure him, once for all, and radically, of his madness after princedom.

When Labakan presented himself in the shop of his late master, that person, not recognising him at first, made him a low bow, asking, at the same time, "what he could have the honour of doing to serve his Highness?" But when the silly fellow drew closer, and the master saw the face of this stealer of coats, he summoned his men and boys, who all fell together upon Labakan, like so many furies, and heaped blows and abuse upon him. They reproached him with the theft he had committed; they laughed at his extravagant pretensions; they threatened him with the Cadi; and the poor wretch was pinched, bitten, scratched, martyrised on all sides and everywhere, by the sharp points of their needles and scissors. He succeeded, at last, in getting out of the hands of his companions, with his clothes torn to rags, his face scored, and half dead; but their hootings pursued him along the street, until he found shelter in a caravanserai, to lay down his weary head.

Crushed, harassed, broken in spirit, and with aches in every bone, the unfortunate Labakan remained, during forty-eight hours, on his bed, unable to stir hand or foot. But the time thus devoted to rest was not entirely lost to him, for he employed it in reflection on his past faults, and the conduct he ought to hold on to for the future. "The proverb which says, 'Every man to his trade,' is quite in the right, and should be ever in our ears. In my desire to ensure the being a Prince, I have gone near to sullying my soul with an abominable crime, and been nearly killed by my fellow-shopmen with needle-points. Come, then—enough of greatness! and if I can only find some shop where they will give me work sufficient for a modest subsistence, I ask no more from the Prophet!"

Upon this excellent resolve, Labakan fell into a deep sleep. On first awaking—as always happens after a succession of extraordinary adventures, and great disturbance of the usual operations of the brain—he remembered nothing at all of what had happened; and, as he saw through his window the tall minarets of the mosque of Alexandria—of which it seemed as if he had never lost sight—the events of the last few days appeared to him nothing more than a strange dream, ending with a horrible nightmare.

Suddenly his eyes fell upon an object that recalled him to their reality—it was the casket of Gulgul! Labakan had no recollection whatsoever of how he had carried it off in his sudden flight; but, after a diligent consideration of the worth of the material, he said to himself, in a low voice, "All this fine work would not be good-for-nothing, and it would be better for me to sell it to some Jew, who might give me a round sum for it, which I could use to good purpose." He therefore directed his steps towards the nearest bazaar of shops, with his coffer under his arm, and offered it for sale to an honest son of Israel, who proffered twenty times less than its real value. Even that, however, was a tolerably round sum; and Labakan, with his money in his girdle, was going his way in great glee, when he heard himself called back by a nasal voice—"Ho, young man! Ho! halloa!" It was his customer, who held out to him, in a jeering fashion, the little skein of thread and the needle he had just found in the casket. "Catch hold of these, my young friend; these are of no use to me, and coffers of this character are not made to keep odds and ends of this sort in. However," said he, surveying the poor fellow from head to foot, "they may be of use to you in sewing your coat up together again, while you are counting the money out to buy another."

Labakan put out his hand, and took, mechanically, the things the Jew held out to him; and then, as he looked down at his clothes, saw that the hands of his companions had, in fact, reduced his portable wardrobe to a mere hanging fringe of tatters. While looking about for a ready-made clothes shop, where he might rig himself out in a more becoming style, he observed one, on which there was a notice, "To be Let." This he entered, and, while trying on a new suit, saw that the shop and fixtures were just what he wanted, and likely to suit him, if not too dear. A brief bargain with the landlord, who agreed to reasonable terms, on payment of a quarter in advance, concluded the affair; and in less than an hour Labakan was installed, with his legs crossed on his own shopboard.

His first job, pending the coming of other customers, was the mending his own breeches, and the repairing and taking up the torn parts of the coat that his fellow-shopmen had so grievously ruined: in doing this, he made use of the needle and thread which the old Jew had returned to him. The damage done was great, and required a good deal of time in repairing it. Before he had got to the end of his work, Labakan was obliged to leave off, and to go out and look for some provisions, to satisfy the imperious cravings of his hungry stomach. He remained absent about half an hour; but on his return, what a marvellous spectacle met his gaze! The needle was sewing away of itself, without any hand to direct it; and it made its stitches with a nicety and elegance, that Labakan himself—capital workman though he was—could not have attained without difficulty. Another prodigy! the skein of thread was inexhaustible; and with all the moving of the needle hither and thither, through seam after seam, the skein of thread never became less by the thickness of a hair!

The poor Tailor-youth, who, on the first opening of the casket, had regarded its contents—needle and thread—with rage first and disgust afterwards, as accusing witnesses, brought forward to heap shame on his head, now understood how the smallest gift of a Good Fairy may be of priceless value. He saw, at a glance, the use such wonder-working tools would be to him in his business: all he had to do was, to buy the cloth, cut it out, and make the first few stitches—the needle would do the rest of itself, and finish the job. Need we say, that as Labakan did his work cheaply, quickly, and well, he soon had as much custom as he wanted? His fellow-tailors kept wondering how Master Labakan was able to get through so much work without either workmen or apprentices, and why he always did his work with the shutters closed. Labakan let them talk, and took no heed: he kept his own secret, and they soon ceased talking, and began to oppose. This led to a general reduction in the price of clothes throughout the city of Alexandria; and "emporiums" and "establishments" became the rage throughout all the great cities of Egypt; but long before this, Labakan had made his fortune.

Thus was fulfilled the promise held forth by the legend on the casket, of "Riches and Good-Fortune" to its possessor. Good-fortune and riches, in fact, accompanied, in a modest but sufficient degree, everything the lucky Tailor undertook; so that when he heard people speaking of the glory of the young Sultan Omar, whose name was on every lip—when they vaunted him as the hero of the age, the pride of his

309

people, and the terror of his enemies—when they reported the valiant acts of this Prince, his exploits as a warrior, the dangers he ran in combat, and how his bravery and skill had brought him through all—the timid Labakan felt, with an involuntary shudder running all over his body, that the trade of a Prince and a hero was not made for him, and that he should have played but a sorry part on a battle-field. Thus he came, at last, to rejoice rather than grieve, at the manner in which his adventure had ended; and while doing his tailoring, sewing, stitching. and cutting out, became the more and more confirmed in the belief of all good Mussulmen, "that no man can alter his destiny."

THE PROUD DARNING-NEEDLE.

ONCE upon a time, a certain Darning-Needle was seized with a fit of pride. We are all of us, now and then, inclined to be proud, as you know; and so this proud Darning-Needle fancied herself a Sewing-Needle, a real drilled-eyed "Kirby and Beard's."

"Now, pray take care, and hold me tight," said this proud Darning-Needle to the Fingers, when they took her up. "Remember, I am a person of quality. Don't drop me, for I am so fine, you will never be able to find me again."

"What nonsense is this?" said the Fingers, giving her a hard tug.

"Don't you see what a train I have behind me?" said the Darning-Needle, drawing out a long thread after her.

Then the Fingers picked up the Cookmaid's slippers. The upper-leather was torn, and required a strong needle to sew them together.

"Oh dear!" exclaimed the Darning-Needle, who thought such nervousness a proof of her fineness. "What a low kind of work! pray call in the cobbler's awl."

Here the Fingers stuck her into the upper-leather.

"Ah! pah!" said the proud Darning-Needle, wriggling and writhing with vexation. "I never shall get through this. Oh, I shall break! and I will break, and I must break; I break—I am breaking!" And so she did break, with her airs, and shams, and twistings. "Did not I say so?" she went on; "I am much too fine for such vulgar tough work."

"You are good for nothing now," said the Fingers; but the Cookmaid—who wanted to fasten her neckerchief, and had stuck the last pin from her gown into the paper over a breast of lamb, to keep it from burning—picked up the two pieces, and dropping a bit of

sealing-wax upon them, fastened them together, and stuck the Darning-Needle into her bosom.

"Only to think!" said the Darning-Needle, now prouder than ever, "I am now a Breast-Pin! I knew I should get up in the world. When one is something, one can always come to something." So she sat proudly in the Cookmaid's neckerchief, looking about and smiling, as if she were riding in her carriage.

Presently, the Cookmaid picked up a Pin, and stuck it in beside the Darning-Needle.

"Permit me to ask if you are a Gold Pin?" inquired the Darning-Needle of her neighbour. "I used to know several of that family in my early days." (This was a downright fib, for her early days had been spent in Whitechapel.) "Indeed, I can see you are one of the family; you have such an elegant slimness, and such a peculiar head—rather small, though, for your position. You must be careful not to fall through, for it is not every one of us that has sealing-wax dropped upon them." And here the proud Darning-Needle drew herself up in so stately a manner, that she fell out of the Cookmaid's neckerchief into the sink, and went rattling down with the dirty water.

"Now for our travels!" said the Darning-Needle. "Travelling gives one an extra polish; but I don't want to go too far." But, for all that, she did go very, very far.

"Oh dear! oh dear!" said she, when she stopped at last, stuck in the mud at the bottom of a street gutter. "I feel I am too fine for this world. However, I know myself and my position, and that is something." So she held herself erect, and was in as good humour with herself as ever, in spite of all the dirt and disagreeables she had gone through.

All kinds of scraps, in a strange medley, came swimming past her—fragments of wood, straw, scraps of old newspapers.

"There they go," said the Darning-Needle, "sailing along, little thinking what is sticking up underneath them—myself, a fine, exquisite, elegant Needle! But what avails beauty to those who cannot feel it? A National Gallery is worth nothing to the blind, and a book of noble thoughts only waste paper to those who can't read. So here I sit, and here I may stick. There goes a shaving! He is only thinking of himself; his thoughts don't rise above shavings. Don't be so vain, Mr. Shaving; a splinter is of a better family, and more genteel. There swims a straw. See how he turns round and round! You think too much of yourself, Sir, and fancy the world is watching your vagaries! Pass on, straw! You will be carried against some stone soon, and there will be an end to your career then. Here comes a newspaper, puffing out, and swelling down the stream! It has been read, and all it has to say has been forgotten; yet see how it spreads itself out! So much for the folly of people in false positions! I sit still, and say nothing, and bide my time—that comes of being of the real quality. I know what I am, and that I shall always be the same; come what may, poor or rich, I shall always be a lady."

While she was thus talking to herself, her eye was attracted by something that glittered and sparkled brightly in the stream. "Oh, charming!" thought she to herself, "here is a Diamond! At last I have found some one that I can speak to." In good truth, what the proud Darning-Needle saw was only a Bit-of-Glass; but, pleased with its pretty light, she addressed it, first taking care to introduce herself as a Breast-Pin. "Surely you must be a Diamond? Who would have thought of our meeting in such a place!"

"Oh, yes," said the Bit-of-Glass, with equal modesty and truthfulness, "I am something of that kind." And so each thought the other to be some precious trinket, and each felt the grander for being in the other's company, and both kept up their false looks, to their mutual great delight; and then they began to complain of the pride of people in general.

"I remember," said the proud Darning-Needle, "when I used to live in a box belonging to a young lady" (that was the Cookmaid), "she had five Fingers on each hand, and anything so stuck up and so meddlesome as those Fingers, I never saw. After all, what had they to do?—only to wait on me. What were they good for? Nothing, but to take me out of the box, and put me back again in the box."

"But were they all bright? Did they shine?" inquired Bit-of-Glass.

"Shine, indeed!" said the proud Darning-Needle. "There was no polish about them. But they thought quite enough of themselves, for all that, I can tell you. They were five brothers, all of one family, Finger being their family name. They were not all of the same height, but they stood erect, side by side. The first was Captain Thumbkin, a little, dumpy, short, thick fellow, who stood out of the rank before the others. He had only one bend in his back, so that he could only bow once; but he was proud of his military rank: 'Because, if Captain Thumbkin,' as he said, 'were cut off, no man could be a soldier.' Next came Professor Fore-finger. He used to press the pen in writing, and was always putting himself forward everywhere, and tasting everything, sweet or sour, and pointing out the way. Then came a tall fellow, named Middle-finger, who could look over all the others' heads; then Ring-finger, who wore a gold belt round his waist, by way of distinction; and then a young rogue named Little-finger, who seemed to be of no use and never did anything, and was very proud of that. Indeed, they were so proud and gave themselves such airs, that I took myself off into the gutter."

"And now we sit in our crystal bower together, and shine," said Bit-of-Glass, becoming quite tender.

"Oh, for shame!" said the proud Darning-Needle, her heart of steel softening a little. What might have happened, it would hardly be fair to think, for just at that moment the Cookmaid threw down a pailful of slush, and the gutter overflowing, the rush of dirty water carried the Bit-of-Glass rolling along with it.

"'Twas ever thus!" sighed the proud Darning-Needle. "But why regret our parting? It has led to his advancement. He has gone, but I remain. Perhaps it is for the better. A single lady is always the more respectable."

So, still she stuck where she was, thinking over the old thoughts, and enjoying them because they were her own.

"How fine I am—how very fine!—almost too fine; I can hardly be seen. I wonder if I were made from the end of a sunbeam—all point and light! Yet the sunbeams do not come here to look for me. I am alone—alone! Some heart is wandering about and looking for me; but I am too fine, even my brother could not find me. Alas! I could weep at the thought! and yet how can I? I have lost my eye—it broke. If I had it, too, I must not cry; it is not elegant to shed tears."

One day, some little boys came early out of school; their master had the toothache. They did not go home, of course; and as it was raining, and they could not enjoy themselves in the fields, they took to raking out the gutter, and hunting after old nails, rusty halfpence, buttons, and such-like treasures. It was not a very clean employment, certainly; but what better could a school-boy find for himself in a holiday on a rainy day? Oh, those boys!

"Halloa!" cried one of the boys, as he pricked his fingers with the proud Darning-Needle. "Here's a fine fellow!"

THE DARNING-NEEDLE FOUND.

"Better language to young ladies," exclaimed the proud Darning-Needle, in a passion; but it was all of no use, for no one heard her. The sealing-wax top had rubbed off, and she was now quite black; but black, she knew, was becoming to the figure, and so she thought herself the more genteel.

"Pick up that egg-shell," said another boy, "and let us make a ship."

So they stuck the proud Darning-Needle into the shell for a mast.

"White walls and a lady in black!" said the proud Darning-Needle; "that is a striking contrast, and has a very pretty effect. Now every one can see me! Oh dear! I hope I shall not be sea-sick, for then, I feel sure, I shall be doubled up with those dreadful feelings, and break. Oh dear! I will never go yachting any more." But she did not break, and she was not sea-sick. "Ah!" thought she, "your true breed—the finer one is, the more one can bear."

Crash went the egg-shell; a waggon-wheel rolled over it.

"Oh, oh!" cried the proud Darning-Needle, "how it squeezes! I shall break—I shall break!" But she did not break, although the hind-wheel went over her as well. She only went the deeper into the mud; and long did she lie there—and there let her lie!

BLANCH AND ROSALINDA.

In a pleasant village, some miles from the metropolis, there lived a very good sort of woman, who was much beloved by all her neighbours, because she was always ready to assist every one who was in need. She had received, in her youth, a better education than the inhabitants of the little village in which she dwelt, and for this reason the poor people looked up to her with a degree of respect.

She was the widow of a very good man, who, when he died, left her with two children. They were very pretty girls: the eldest, on account of the fairness of her complexion, was named Blanch, and the other Rosalinda, because her cheeks were like roses, and her lips like coral.

One day, while Goody Hearty sat spinning at the door, she saw a poor old woman going by, leaning on a stick, who had much ado to hobble along. "You seem very much tired, dame," said she to the old woman; "sit down here and rest yourself a little;" at the same time she bid her daughters fetch a chair: they both went, but Rosalinda ran fastest, and brought one. "Will you please to drink?" said Goody Hearty. "Thank you," answered the old woman, "I don't care if I do, and methinks if you had anything *nice* that I liked, I could eat a bit." "You are welcome to the best I have in my house," said Goody Hearty, "but as I am poor, it is homely fare."

She then ordered her daughters to spread a clean cloth on the table, while she went to the cupboard, from whence she took some brown bread and cheese, to which she added a mug of cider. As soon as the old woman was seated at the table, Goody Hearty desired her eldest daughter to go and gather some plums off her own plum-tree, which she had planted herself, and took great delight in. Blanch, instead of obeying her mother readily, grumbled and muttered as she went. "Surely," said she to herself, "I did not take all this care and pains with my plum-tree for that old greedy creature." However, she durst not refuse gathering a few plums, but she gave them with a very-ill will, and very ungraciously. "As for you, Rosalinda," said her mother, "you have no fruit to offer this good dame, for your grapes are not ripe." "That's true," replied Rosalinda, "but my hen has just laid, for I hear her cackle; and if the gentlewoman likes a new-laid egg, 'tis very much at her service;" and, without staying for an answer, she ran to the hen-roost, and brought the egg: but just as she was presenting it to the old woman, she turned into a fine beautiful lady!

"Good woman," said she to Goody Hearty, "I have long seen your industry, perseverance, and pious resignation, and I will reward your daughters according to their merits: the eldest shall be a great Queen, the other shall have a country farm." With this, she struck the house with her stick, which immediately disappeared, and in its room up came a pretty little snug farm. "This, Rosalinda," said she, "is your lot! I know I have given each of you what you like best."

312

Having said this, the Fairy went away, leaving both mother and daughters greatly astonished. They went into the farm-house, and were quite charmed with the neatness of the furniture; the chairs were only wood, but so bright you might see your face in them. The beds were of linen-cloth, as white as snow. There were forty sheep in the sheep-pen; four oxen and four cows, in their stalls; and in the yard all sorts of poultry, hens, ducks, pigeons, &c. There was also a pretty garden, well stocked with flowers, fruit, and vegetables. Blanch saw the Fairy's gift to her sister without being jealous, and was wholly taken up with the thoughts of being a Queen; when, all of a sudden, she heard some hunters riding by, and going to the gate to see them, she appeared so charming in the King's eyes, who was there, that he resolved to marry her.

When Blanch was a Queen, she said to her sister Rosalinda, "I do not care that you should be a farmer; come with me, sister, and I will match you to some great lord." "I am very much obliged to you, sister," replied Rosalinda," but I am used to a country life, and I choose to stay where I am."

Queen Blanch arrived at her palace, and was so delighted with her new dignity, that she could not sleep for several nights. The first three months, her thoughts were wholly engrossed by dress, balls, and plays, so that she thought of nothing else. She was soon accustomed to all this, and nothing now diverted her; on the contrary, she found a great deal of trouble. The ladies of the Court were all very respectful in her presence; but she knew very well that they did not love her, and when out of her sight, would often say to one another, "See what airs this little country girl gives herself! sure his Majesty must have a very mean fancy, to make choice of such a consort." These discourses soon reached the King's ears, and made him reflect on what he had done; he began to think he was wrong, and repented his marriage. The courtiers saw this, and accordingly paid her little or no respect; she was very unhappy, for she had not a single friend to whom she could declare her griefs; she saw it was the fashion at Court to betray the dearest friend for interest, to caress and smile upon those they most hated, and to lie every instant; she was obliged to be always serious, because they told her a Queen ought to look grave and majestic. She had several children, and all the time there was a physician to inspect whatever she ate or drank, and to order everything she liked off the table: not a grain of salt was allowed to be put in her soup, nor was she permitted to take a walk, though she had ever so much a mind to it. Governesses were appointed to her children, who brought them up contrary to her wishes; yet she had not the liberty to find fault. Poor Queen Blanch was dying with grief, and grew so thin, that it was a pity to see her. She had not seen her sister for three years, because she imagined it would disgrace a person of her rank and dignity to pay a visit to a farmer's wife. Her extreme melancholy made her very ill, and her physicians ordered change of air. She therefore resolved to spend a few days in the country, to divert her uneasiness, and improve her health.

THE FAIRY PUNISHES BLANCH BY MAKING HER A QUEEN.

Accordingly, she asked the King's leave to go, who very readily granted it, because he thought he should be rid of her for some time. She set out, and soon arrived at the village. As she drew near Rosalinda's house, she beheld, at a little distance from the door, a company of shepherds and shepherdesses, who were dancing and making merry. "Alas!" said the Queen, sighing, "there once was a time when I used to divert myself like these poor people, and no one found fault with me." The moment Rosalinda perceived her sister, she ran to embrace her. The Queen ordered her carriage to stop, and alighting, rushed into her sister's arms; but Rosalinda was grown so plump, and had such an air of content, that the Queen, as she looked on her, could not forbear bursting into tears.

Rosalinda was married to a farmer's son, who had no fortune of his own; but then, he ever remembered that he was indebted to his wife for everything he had, and he strove to show his gratitude by his obliging behaviour. Rosalinda had not many servants, but those she had, loved her as though she had been their mother, because she used them kindly; she was beloved by all her neighbours, and they all endeavoured to show it. She neither had, nor wanted, much money; corn, wine, and oil, were the growth of her farm; her cows supplied her with milk, butter, and cheese. The wool of her sheep was spun to clothe herself, her husband, and their two children. They enjoyed perfect health, and when the work of the day was over, they spent the evening in all sorts of pastimes. "Alas!" cried the Queen, "the Fairy made me a sad present in giving me a crown. Content is not found in magnificent palaces, but in an innocent country life."

Scarce had she done speaking, before the Fairy appeared. "In making you a Queen," said the Fairy, "I did not intend to reward, but punish you, for giving me your plums with an ill-will. To be contented and happy, you must, like your sister, possess only what is necessary, and wish for nothing else."

"Ah! Madam," cried Blanch, "you are sufficiently revenged; pray put an end to my distress."

"It is at an end," said the Fairy; "the King, who loves you no longer, has just married another wife, and to-morrow his officers will come to forbid you returning any more to the palace."

It happened just as the Fairy had foretold; and Blanch passed the remainder of her days with her sister Rosalinda, in all manner of happiness and content, and never thought again of Court, unless it was to thank the Fairy for having brought her back to her native village.

THE WITCHES' DANCE ON THE FIRST OF MAY.

In the olden time, there lived in Switzerland a scythe-founder, whose name was Christoph; he was in wealthy circumstances, and had a pleasant abode, with workshops and farm-buildings, on the borders of a forest, where the heavy machinery required for his art, was driven by the thundering and rapid currents of a neighbouring river. He had an only son, named Rudolf, whom he wished to make a parson, thinking he would one day grow to be of much importance, and, perhaps, be invested with a gold chain and cross.

Rudolf, however, did not like the life his father had chosen for him, but thought it would be very grand to be a soldier. From his earliest youth, his inmost heart had beat with indescribable emotions, when bands of soldiers happened to stop on their march, and obtain refreshments at the farm-house. Then, if they talked of their services under the great Wallenstein, his eyes gleamed, and his blood circulated with new fervour through every vein. Rudolf was, nevertheless, established at the Benedictine Convent for his education; and on a very grand procession on Corpus Christi day, he was chosen to play a principal part. He was among the handsomest and the oldest of the scholars, so that he was chosen to carry the largest banner, and stand at the rustic altar, reared, Swiss fashion, on the banks of the Lake Constance. Maidens in white carried baskets of flowers in their hands, and wore garlands of the brightest flowers they could procure in their hair. One of these girls, by far the handsomest of the party, happened to steal a glance at Rudolf from her innocent blue eyes, that shone under her coronet of Narcissus' flowers; when, as if struck by a magician's wand, he was lost to all around him, and very nearly let the banner drop from his hands. She, also, appeared very confused, and after stretching out her hand, drew it back again, and remained like a statue, with her eyes on the ground, until a companion whispered, "Alice, your gifts!" when she hastily threw them on the altar, and took her place again in the procession.

From that moment, Rudolf's every thought was of Alice—her image never faded from his remembrance, and he very soon contrived to find out her name and place of residence. Her father was very poor, and lived in a remote cottage in the mountains, where he maintained his family by the profits from a small field. To this cottage Rudolf managed to find his way, though at the risk of his neck, by way of the rocks behind this humble dwelling; and Alice's looks, the first time they met, betrayed she had not forgotten the tall standard-bearer of the Corpus Christi procession. From that day, Rudolf and Alice often met; and he made up his mind he would never become a priest, and lost no opportunity of declaring his determination to his father, but took very good care to say nothing of the reason, which chance, however, very soon discovered. His father flew into a violent rage with him, and declared, if he dared to cherish a single thought for the contemptible goatherd's daughter, he should punish him with his lasting malediction; and vowed that now he should live in the convent altogether, and be treated like a younger member of the brotherhood. The consequence, as might be expected, of all this imperious temper on the part of Master Christoph, was, that Rudolf disappeared; and the only consolation his father had, was, that he would return when he wanted money. Rudolf was heard no more of, until it was known he had joined the army of the Archduke Leopold Wilhelm. Master Christoph spoke with a travelling artisan, who had seen the lost youth, mounted on a fine horse, among the Pappenheim Cuirassiers.

Three years had passed, and, during this time, Alice and his father had received many letters and tokens from Rudolf; and the father, hearing he had greatly distinguished himself, became comforted with the hope, that he might some day gain high promotion in the army. Just about this time the old man fell dangerously ill, and his son was sent for to hasten to his sick bed, but arrived only in time to receive his father's blessing. Master Christoph left his son all his property, which was considerable; and therefore Rudolf obtained his discharge from the army, and determined to live upon the paternal estate.

On the Sunday following his father's funeral, this handsome, rich, and gallant soldier excited no small attention at the church, in his showy hussar uniform, with his red sash, large boots, stately helmet with waving feather, and honorary medal; every woman, old or young, of course turned towards this dazzling visitor; and every unmarried girl, from this moment, had an eye to Rudolf's handsome person and substantial business and estates.

The Baron's Land-steward had a daughter, upon whom Rudolf's appearance made a lasting impression.

"I," she said, "am the richest and genteelest girl in the village; surely Rudolf will be mine." And her father comforted her, saying, "Calm yourself, my dear **Gertrude**; I shall make proposals for your marriage, which are sure not to be refused." A few days after, however, Gertrude sought her father sorrowing, saying, "Can you believe it? Rudolf, insensible to my love, has declared the most ardent affection for the daughter of a miserable goatherd on the mountains!" Enraged at this, Gertrude was not utterly discouraged; and set to work, in a most contemptible manner, to darken the fame of the gentle and innocent Alice.

"How hard," said Alice, one day, "is it to hear these cruel calumnies; from whence can they arise?"

"Heed them not," replied Rudolf; "rest happy in my love, and the assurance that I know your conscience to be free from these wicked imputations."

One night, the lovers sat under a thicket of elders, covered with the fresh verdure of spring, talking as lovers only talk; and time, as it does in such cases, had passed unheeded, until twilight gave place to the fast-gathering night. The glow-worms twinkled amid the darkness, and from the shadow of the fir-trees gleamed the slender solitary crescent of the new moon; the night-hawks burst, flapping their wings, from the covert, and the owls began to shriek.

Alice suddenly exclaimed, "Let us return home; I don't like these noises;" and she trembled when a frog or green lizard rustled in the grass.

"Ho!" he laughed, "surely you are no coward?"

"No," she replied, "but, I must own, a supernatural dread hangs over me at this moment, and I am unable to conquer my inward agitation."

Even the young man's attention was at this moment raised, he fancied he heard light footsteps through the darkness, as of some one approaching them. He lifted the almost fainting girl in his arms, and walking forward a step or two, said, "Who is there? who wanders here at such an hour?" The moonlight, though very faint, was yet strong enough to allow him to distinguish a female form, wrapped in a mantle, glide along the steep winding path from the mountain, and which now, uttering a painful hollow cry, passed the lovers, and went on rapidly towards the village.

"Oh!" exclaimed Alice, in a paroxysm of fright, "that is some Witch returning from her incantations and abominable orgies on the hill-top, where there stands a circle of large stones, and the ground is blighted by the unhallowed feet that dance at midnight, so that the grass cannot grow there. You, dear Rudolf, have disturbed this Sorceress, and so have raised her malice against yourself, and must suffer for it all your life."

"Nonsense," replied Rudolf; "did you not see it was Gertrude, the rich Steward's daughter?"

"Nay, nay," said Alice, "why should she, so proud, forsooth, and so finely dressed always, trust herself alone in these woods? Do you not know that witches can take any form they please? and therefore this affords no proof to my mind that we are safe."

By this time, Rudolf had brought his trembling bride to her father's cottage, and determined to think no more of this event for the present, at any rate. On Alice the impression was too strong to be easily effaced.

Rudolf was in the right when he thought he recognized Gertrude, for it was not the first time the rising of the crescent moon had lured her forth, in disguise, along the lonely road towards the mountains—unhappy girl! vainly, like the wounded hart, flying restlessly through the fields to escape the torment of the hunter's forked arrow.

Gertrude, pause! little do you know how much you must suffer in your unholy plan of gaining Rudolf's affections. Alice and Rudolf's love is too pure for your wicked incantations to part them; leave your detestable schemes, for they must fail. The lovers always wear their rosary, and are in heart so pious, you cannot work Alice's downfall.

Gertrude's unhappy passion remained unconquerable, and at last Alice and Rudolf were betrothed in church. Through that fatal Sunday her grief knew no bounds, and at the sinking of the sun she hastened forth, in this direful emergency, to seek counsel from her wicked confidante.

When Gertrude arrived at the Witch's cottage, she came out grinning with the greatest composure, and recommended her to have patience, saying: "I am just at this moment employed on certain incantations which will enable me to meet your wishes. The stars have been, of late, very propitious, and all I now want is, to pluck seven hairs from your beautiful tresses?"

With these words, the Witch stretched out her bony shrivelled arms, like those of a fiend, and forced Gertrude down on a low root of a tree, that served as a chair.

"Oh!" screamed Gertrude aloud, as the hag with violence plucked the seven hairs from her head, which caused her so much pain that she was stunned and senseless; and when she revived, she found she had been thrust outside the cottage with resistless force, and then the old hag screamed out through the keyhole, "Come when the now crescent moon is at the full. Peril not your life by crossing the path before."

Gertrude was quite unable to move for a long time from the door, and then a nameless horror possessed her; every moment she seemed to behold some horrible apparition. In returning, as she neared the thicket of elders, she actually heard whispering voices, and saw the outlines of a human form. She went on, she knew not how; then she recognized Rudolf—the man she so devotedly loved—with Alice in his arms; and uttering the hollow cry that had surprised them, she rushed towards the village. How she counted the day and hour for the coming of the full moon, that only promised her new and desperate encounters.

At last the night arrived, when the full moon shone forth in all her resplendent glory; and wrapping herself in her mantle, Gertrude hastened to the Witch's cottage. There was no light but the moon, and Gertrude looked upon the Witch with extreme horror and apprehension, for every feature in that horrible countenance seemed, to-night, distorted with unutterable meaning. Perhaps the old hag knew the effect her presence produced upon the unhappy girl, for she grinned as if in scorn and mockery.

In the interior of the cave there was a large fire, on which a kettle stood boiling. The Sorceress brought a pair of bellows, and poker and tongs, to rouse the flames well up, in which task Gertrude advanced to help her. "Fool!" cried the old hag, "if thou shouldest now dare to cross the threshold, thy life would be forfeit. Remain where thou art. unless I summon thee!"

Gertrude shook and trembled at the entrance. The kettle boiled more fiercely. and now a thick stupifying vapour mounted in wreaths to the ceiling, while the wrinkled visage of the old woman became more and more intolerable, until Gertrude could no longer gaze upon her. At length. the words, "Now, now! Look yonder!" were shrieked forth through the thick smoke which had collected in a distant corner of the cave, and she beheld a luminous spot, that increased in size and brightness, till it assumed the form of a large mirror; then there arose upon her sight a well-furnished room, where a man was sitting at a table, busily engaged in cleaning a musket and other military accoutrements. This man was Rudolf—not his picture, but himself—as unmistakably and vividly before her as she had seen him a few days ago. Two lovely children were also there; one of them played in innocent childish sport upon the carpeted floor, and the other lay asleep in a cradle near the fire-place. At last the door opened, and a woman entered the room, and Gertrude beheld herself as plainly as she had ever seen herself mirrored. This woman went up to Rudolf, and was embraced by him with the greatest confidence and affection. Then she saw her take her seat by the fire, when she lifted the baby from the cradle, and nurtured it from her bosom, while the father looked on with delight

At this scene. Gertrude's heart beat high, and her eyes gleamed. It was she herself—the wife of Rudolf—and her children were his! A cry of joy and exultation escaped from her lips; but, at that moment, with a frightful crash, the whole illusion vanished from her sight. The old woman seized her by the arm, and forced her from the gateway, which was violently closed. She then broke forth in a torrent of reproaches, on account of the cry the poor girl had uttered, at a time when she should have been as silent as the grave. Gertrude, however, let the old lady scold on, without making any remonstrance, only asking now and then, "Will it ever be so? Shall I ever be his wife?"

"Thou hast already seen it," said the Witch; "for the present this must suffice you; trouble me with no farther questions." Then she forced the unhappy girl from the cottage, as she had done before, saying, "Your folly this night has been inexcusable; come not here again until I send for you."

This interdiction was not so unbearable to Gertrude now; for had she not seen the veil lifted from futurity, and herself established as Rudolf's wife? What more could she ask? She walked home as in a dream; her happiness was great, although she could not yet see by what stratagem Alice's marriage could be hindered or delayed. All the interval she watched, with miserable and wasting anxiety, for every word of news that could be gathered from the neighbours; and so great was her anxiety, that, notwithstanding the Old Witch's injunction, she had been twice up the mountain, but had, to her mortification, found the door firmly closed against her, and prayers and entreaties were alike useless.

Two days before the marriage was to take place, Gertrude heard that the Witch's hovel was found empty, and the door open, so that she could no longer hope to

see her return. Gertrude now felt convinced that, to her other misfortunes, she had been basely deceived; the old hag only mocked at her vain credulity, and in her wicked malice rejoiced at the pangs she suffered.

Not being able to remain and witness the rejoicings this wedding would call forth, Gertrude determined to visit a town at a considerable distance, where there resided a sister of her mother. Once at her aunt's house, she would at least be freed from the humiliation of being present at Alice's wedding festival.

The next day she started on her journey; and when she had crossed to the other side of the lake, she could not help turning to look at Rudolf's dwelling, where she could see the smoke rising over the flourishing little farm, where her detested rival. in another day, would be secure in the affection of the handsomest husband in the Canton. Once more, in her heart, she denounced the Witch who had so cruelly deceived her; and in a state of the deepest melancholy she arrived at her aunt's. Even here, in due time, a dazzling description of the marriage festival reached her ears, and tormented her; and little else was talked of than, "How handsome Rudolf looked in his hussar dress at the church!" and, "How meekly and modestly the bride had conducted herself, in her dress of white silk, embroidered with pearls!"

Then came an account of the grand banquet which followed the wedding, and of the many presents received by the aged and poor, of money and articles of dress. There was no escape from the poisoned arrows that were aimed against her. Her pride was wounded, her heart was crushed; but her unhappy passion was unabated.

Her attention, however, was after a time somewhat diverted from its object, by the frequent visits to the house of a retired Ironmaster, who was a man of very large independent fortune; and as she was the daughter of the Baron's Land-steward, and would have a large dowry, he thought he could not do better than entreat her aunt to speak in his behalf. Gertrude took the matter into consideration: the man was advanced in years; his person was neither handsome nor agreeable; moreover, his residence was on the Alps—a long way from her native village. These were all great objections; but then, he was very wealthy, and she felt anxious to show the world she could do better than marry Rudolf, who had deserted her for a goatherd's daughter. She determined to accept this offer, upon the condition that he must give up the farm upon the mountains, and come to reside at her birth-place. She excused this whim, by saying she should like to be near her parents; but, as to the real motive, she did not even dare to confess them to herself. She panted to outshine her hated rival, by means of her large fortune, and to humble the man by whom she had been rejected.

Judge the surprise of the villagers, when, after a few weeks. Gertrude returned among them as the wife of the far-famed Ironmaster, who was known to be one of the richest freemen in the Canton. Every one talked of it; but the two whose fate it was to influence —Rudolf and Alice—were so entirely occupied with their own domestic happiness, and so much engaged with forming plans for a new farming establishment, that they were entirely ignorant of all that was going forward; so that it was not until a whole fortnight had elapsed, that Alice heard, on a Sunday at church, of Gertrude's marriage.

With the wife of the Ironmaster, matters went very differently; she never could forget Rudolf. According to all outward appearances, her circumstances were brilliant and prosperous. Their house was the best in the village; their domestic economy was richly provided; and from every fair her husband brought her home costly jewels, embroidered gown-stuffs, and new furniture. But her concealed love for Rudolf gnawed at her heart; and whenever she saw him, at church, or at any holiday festival, she was dreadfully agitated, and at such moments felt a burning pain in her head, where the old hag had, now nearly a twelvemonth ago, plucked the seven hairs, when she visited her cottage. In health and temper, a great change came over her, and her discontent became visible to everybody. At last, when the birth of a fine boy seemed to complete the happiness of Rudolf, her torments increased so as to be quite insupportable.

Now it was rumoured that the Old Witch had been seen again at her cottage. Huntsmen and foresters were the first to bring this intelligence, and they declared they had found traces of her wonted nightly orgies within the Druid's Circle on the hill-top. Gertrude garnered all this in her heart; and there arose within her a violent longing to visit the frightful old hag, if it were only to reproach her for the vile delusions she had been guilty of. At last, this wish prevailed over all other considerations, and Gertrude again went up the mountain to the old woman's; the door was no longer closed against her, but she was invited to visit there as often as she could, and her whole future appeared in a new and promising aspect.

Gertrude's endless caprices and uncertain temper, which had often made her intolerable to her husband, now entirely disappeared. At holiday meetings she was very gay and happy—she seemed filled by a kind of inward confidence; she entered into the amusements of her friends, and looked kindly upon Alice, whom she often invited to share her seat in church. Alice, of course, was incapable of repressing any advances she saw on the part of Gertrude, to atone for the past, and entered freely into conversation with her.

At last, this intercourse was carried so far, that one fine Sunday, Gertrude, who had frequently praised the beautiful situation of Rudolf's farm, accompanied his wife on her walk all the way home; her visit was short, but it was followed by others that were longer. Alice thought herself obliged to return these visits, but went as seldom as possible, for to leave her husband and child, if only for half an hour, was to her like giving up all the world. Besides, he had from the first warned her against making too intimate an acquaintance with one who had betrayed such evil intentions; and this alone would have deterred Alice from making any farther advances. Rudolf was at last, however, obliged to give up all suspicion; the Ironmaster's wife seemed so polite and kind, that he could not suppose she had any selfish views. He was willing to believe the most perverted mind might become changed, and seek to retrieve past errors; so he gradually conquered his dislike, and no longer offered any objection when he saw the two friends together.

One circumstance, however, almost roused his former suspicions: he heard that Gertrude's intimacy with the hag was renewed, and that she was often seen at the cottage, and it was well known and believed that this woman was a notable Sorceress. This rumour, however, he gave very little credence to, so that he did not venture to draw any fixed conclusion. Besides, Gertrude always visited Alice when he was from home, so that no jealousy could exist, or this, in itself, might have put an end to the friendship of the young women.

Towards the spring, Rudolf was obliged to make a long journey from home, and they both thought with great pain on the separation that awaited them. Gertrude cherished her hopes and plans more firmly than ever upon this change; but her outward conduct remained very cautious and guarded. The day came, at last, when Rudolf was obliged to depart; and as his return could not be expected before the month of May, Alice had a long and uneasy time before her. Gertrude, however, made her visits as frequent as possible, in order, as she said, to divert her friend's attention.

Men and women were now almost always in the fields; the labours of the spinning-wheel were nearly at an end; and Gertrude, in the lonely evenings, gained a complete ascendancy over Alice, by relating to her most wonderful stories, of which she had an inexhaustible stock. She spoke of extraordinary dreams, forebodings, and apparitions, in which Alice was a firm believer; and when such legends had been discussed, went on to speak of other mysteries, which seemed to open a new world to Alice. Gertrude told her, how certain persons could make themselves invisible, and also appear in two places at the same time; that they were able to pass over a vast extent of country in a single minute; that the dead could even be raised from their graves, and be made to reveal all secrets, past, present, and to come. Pretending great caution, and under promise of secrecy, she made Alice acquainted with some adventures that had happened to herself, while she was staying with her aunt, who, she led Alice to believe, was initiated in these occult arts.

Now Alice, like most mountaineers, had from her youth been very fond of such marvellous stories. Every word that Gertrude said only added fuel to the flame of her own heated imagination. At length, her deceitful friend ventured to hint that she herself had been more than an idle spectator at these ceremonies, and, moreover, was acquainted with many spells by which natural means might be used for supernatural effects. Alice evidently drew back and shuddered, but became reconciled, when she reflected that Gertrude's conduct had been irreproachable for a long time; her husband's farming establishment was so successful, that it seemed as if a blessing rested on their house; and, whatever had been her designs against Rudolf twelve months ago, yet no one could deny that she was now a regular attendant at church. After this conversation, she not only kept up her intercourse with Gertrude, but was drawn more deeply into the snare.

March, and the best part of April, had passed away, and Rudolf was expected home, at the farthest, in ten or twelve days; and Alice's heart heaved with delight, to think that she would so soon behold her husband—the father of her darling child. Gertrude, too, was on the alert; and it so happened, that, on a mild pleasant evening at the end of April, the two friends were sitting together at the door of the farm-house, and for some time Rudolf's return was the only theme of their conversation. Now, however, the colours began to fade in the landscape, and distant objects were lost in confused masses; till, at length, the stars had one by one shone out, and were reflected in the Giessbach, which after thundering like a cataract over the mill-wheels, passed by them in its quieter course to join the waters of the lake. In the dense thickets on the shore, and on the slope of the mountains, it was already dark night, and fire-beetles hovered round them with their silent green light. Gertrude, all this time, seemed to watch these winged lamps with breathless earnestness, while now and then an exclamation of surprise or anxiety betrayed how much she was excited; when, suddenly, a clear ball of fire rose from the elder-tree thickets on the hill-side, came straight towards Gertrude, hovered for some time before her, then moved rapidly away, and fell into the mill-race, where it was extinguished, with a hissing noise, in the water. "Aye, indeed," said Gertrude, "I expected no less! I shall not fail to come."

Poor Alice started up with affright, and stared at her companion. "What means this?" she said, crossing herself, and keeping at a distance.

"Foolish girl!" said the other; "why should you be alarmed? It means only that I am invited to the grand festival on the First of May!"

"On Walpurgis' Night!" said Alice, with increasing fear; "and would you venture to go then?"

"I cannot well act otherwise," answered Gertrude, "to neglect the invitation would be seriously resented; to accept it, may be attended with much amusement."

"Great powers defend me, Gertrude! you surely would not go to the Blocksberg mountain, where the demons and their imps hold their court!"

"Alice," said Gertrude, "don't speak so foolishly, I beg of you; you talk just like the ignorant common people. Yet why should I vex myself, or wish to explain the matter to you? for that you will not travel with me I am certain."

"Of that, indeed, rest assured," replied Alice; "but, I should like to see you set out on your journey."

"Nothing can be more easy," rejoined the other; "but it is better to say no more on the subject. You, by nature, are too timid; and, to confess the truth, such adventures are safe only for the stout-hearted and resolute."

Alice remained silent; what she had seen and heard this night was far too wonderful to be forgotten. She could not, however, help referring to the subject, and gained so much confidence, that she wished to hear what really happened at the Blocksberg mountain; whereupon Gertrude gave such a magnificent account of a fairy banquet, at which all the guests appeared in glittering dresses, and were enlivened by the most ravishing music, that the picture remained impressed in the most glowing colours on Alice's recollection.

Some days had yet to pass away before Walpurgis' Night; and Gertrude's visits were less frequent, being, as she declared, busy in preparing for her journey. But, meanwhile, whatever she said at their short

318

meetings, was artfully contrived to heighten her friend's curiosity. All this, however, deeply and slily as it had been planned, failed to obtain the wished-for object; for Alice was really too pious to engage in any such enterprise, and, above all, without her husband's consent. Only, she thought she might safely allow herself to see her friend set out in her travelling carriage; or, if neither traveller or carriage were to be seen, to hold conversation with one who remained invisible. So it was agreed that Gertrude should knock at Alice's window, where she would look out for a minute, and convince herself that the account she had received was not a mere fable.

The night of the First of May had at length arrived; the moon shone with enchanting radiance. Alice had retired as usual, but lay sleepless upon her lonely bed, while alternate thoughts of her husband and Gertrude's wonderful stories conflicted in her mind. Then a small clock in her room slowly struck eleven. Alice felt an ice-cold shuddering, as at some undefined danger, in every limb; and just as the clock ceased to strike, she heard a slight knocking at the window, "That must be Gertrude," she said; but now it seemed, also, as if she heard a voice—the tones, perhaps, of some guardian spirit—that said to her, "Hush, hush! Make no answer!" The knocking was repeated, and the clear moonlight threw into the room the shadow of some one that stood at the window. "She is not invisible, at all events," said Alice; "and it would be rather unkind, after she has taken all this trouble, not to answer her signal." She rose, therefore, put on most of her usual attire, and opened the lattice, at which Gertrude stood, magnificently dressed, but in glaring, unusual colours. "You see I have kept my promise," said she, with a strange unnatural smile; "I am here, and my carriage, too, is in waiting."

"Nay, I see no carriage," answered Alice; "you are on foot."

"What nonsense!" said the other; "of course I have alighted; but if you will come to the threshold of the front door, you will see our equipage at the corner of your field."

"You promise me there is no danger?" said Alice.

"What a needless question!" answered Gertrude; "how can it make any difference, whether you stand at the door or the window?"

Again Alice heard the same voice admonishing her, "Do not go—do not go!" She went, however; but feeling determined not to cross the threshold, stretched out her neck at the half-open door, and descried some dim object, to which she could attach no distinct form. She saw, however, that instead of horses there were two enormous monsters, shaped like bats, that waved their black wings, as if with impatience at the chill night air. Gertrude had, in the meanwhile, clasped her arms round Alice's waist, as if to put her in a position to see this detestable conveyance; when, all of a sudden, the poor girl felt herself seized, as by the grasp of an irresistible giant or demon. In vain did she shriek aloud, and implore her friend to have compassion; she was forced from her house towards the field. The carriage advanced to meet them; and in an instant she found herself seated in it by Gertrude's side, when they directly mounted up into the air!

louder and louder she now screamed for mercy, but in vain. Her senses forsook her for a space, and when she revived, she could only descry the moonlight gleaming on the lakes, at an immeasurable distance beneath. Now she began to feel for her cross and rosary, which she had unfortunately left on the bed; Gertrude, aware of what was passing in her mind, laid her hand anxiously on her lips: "Remember your lesson!" said she; not a word, not a name must be pronounced, that would bring us into danger. Be silent, for you are in my power, and any attempt to escape will only end in your destruction!"

Alice obeyed; she was too well convinced of the horrible truth. As she looked downwards on the awful realm of space, and beheld from afar, towns, seas, and mountains, as in a map, every nerve of her frame vibrated with terror. With bitter self-reproach she thought of her husband's repeated warnings, which, had she heeded them, would have saved her from the powers of this wicked Sorceress. She thought of his despair, should he return home and not find her there; above all, when she remembered her forsaken helpless child, her inmost heart was agonized, so that she had not strength even to weep.

How long they had travelled, Alice could not tell, but suddenly she became aware of a detestable noise in the air, a whizzing of wings, and screaming of many voices. It seemed as if, at once, the before empty space was filled with monstrous owls and bats with human faces, besides a thousand nameless forms, all so hideous, that she was obliged to shut her eyes for protection. "Now, then, we are at our journey's end," cried Gertrude; and at these words, our heroine felt the violent motion of the carriage decrease, and they sunk gradually downwards. Alice opened her eyes, and by a red glaring light, as from a furnace, she beheld the summit of a woody mountain, which seemed to be in flames, and yet nothing was consumed; the tall fir-trees stood unscathed amid the lurid radiance, not a blade of grass seemed to be injured.

Meanwhile, on a fiery platform, surrounded by a circle of moss-grown stones, were visible a multitude of hideous shapes, whirling vehemently in the dance; others were chasing each other through the air, accompanied, instead of music, by a noise of hissing, howling, and whistling, so intolerable, that Alice lost both sight and hearing, Forgetting all the instructions that had been forced upon her, she exclaimed, in a loud voice, "Merciful Powers protect me!" At that moment, with a noise like thunder, the whole spectacle vanished away. She was enveloped in thick darkness, and felt herself sinking through the air. She thought death was now inevitable, and lost all self-possession.

The morning of the Second of May had arisen in all its luxuriance and beauty; when, behold, under the shelter of a tree, lay a hapless female wanderer—our poor deluded Alice. She awoke as from a dream, to look over a wide level country, all strange to her, without one object she could recognize. She was stupified, and could not have explained to any one how she had come hither. It was a long time before she was sufficiently collected to observe that, although there were hamlets and houses, none seemed nearer than half a German mile. She was so exhausted, she thought she

could not possibly reach one of these; but as it was absolutely necessary to take some measures, she rose, and tottered for awhile along a narrow footpath. Here, it chanced, a good-tempered peasant-lad met her, and she asked him the name of the nearest hamlet. His accent was so strange, that she could hardly recognise it as German, and she remembered hearing her husband speak of the place as being a long way off. She tried once more to rouse her spirits, and walked on towards the village. It was all in vain, however—her strength failed her; and, in her desolation and helplessness, she fell upon the grass, and wept bitterly.

Soon after, a man advanced in years approached her, dressed in black, with a dignified calm countenance, who inquired if he could help her. She begged to know how far it was from hence to her native village? The old man could give her no information. "How far, then, is it," she said, "to Linz, on the Danube?" "Oh! my child," said he, "that must be two hundred leagues from here." Poor Alice became deadly pale, and a moan of despair broke from her inmost heart. She could answer nothing to his many inquiries, and could not refrain from tears.

"I am Schoolmaster of this parish," said he," and if I knew that you were deserving, I might be able to interest some one in your behalf." Alice felt she must tell him some story, and this grieved her; she dared not trust herself to speak without reflection. "Have patience with me, kind Sir, and I will tell you all," said she. Then she told him how she had been engaged by an English family at Linz, who were travelling towards the north of Germany; and not being able to bear the fatigue of travelling, she had fallen sick, and they could not wait for her recovery. She was better now, and wished to make her way homewards, but found this impossible without money. Her innocent looks and gentle voice won the old man's confidence. "I would help you to the money, if I could, but I am too poor," said the Schoolmaster.

"But," she replied, "if any one would take me as a servant, I might at least earn enough to support life. I am but a poor farmer's daughter, and should not be afraid of any task imposed upon me."

"In truth," said the old man, "we have just lost a faithful servant, who had been with us seventeen years; and my wife, who is frail and old, is inconsolable at this event. Let us therefore make a trial together; even if you do not suit, I trust we shall not quarrel."

Alice gladly followed the old man to his house; and although the wife objected at first to her youth and great beauty, she soon found her a patient and industrious servant. Two years passed, and still no news reached Alice from Switzerland; but now her old mistress died, and soon afterwards the old Schoolmaster followed her to the grave. She found they had left her money enough, besides her stipulated wages, to enable her to make the long-cherished journey to her native land. She learnt the route she was to take. After some laborious weeks of travelling, sometimes in waggons, sometimes on foot, the snow-clad tops of the Alps once more rose on her view; she was so overpowered at the sight, that she burst into tears. The last station to her birth-place she determined to go on foot, wishing to enter her native place unrecognized. She passed through a narrow ravine, which alone lay between her and the sight of the wide-gleaming lake, and her former beloved habitation. With every step her agitation increased, till, behold! the beautiful expanse of water, the wooded cliffs, the smiling village were unrolled to her, as if by magic. Feeling her strength exhausted, she stopped at the door of an old woman, who sat with her spinning-wheel; here Alice begged some refreshment, and a jar of milk and some brown bread were set before her, and Alice was invited to rest herself. On inquiring who lived at the farm, whence the smoke was rising, and hearing Rudolf's name, Alice ventured to ask many questions regarding him, pretending that she had known him when he was a soldier. The old woman kindly answered all her questions, and as to Rudolf, she said that he was living in his usual way, with his wife and two children.

"His wife!" exclaimed Alice, turning deadly pale, "to whom, then, is he married now?"

"She was a poor goatherd's daughter, of this neighbourhood," answered the woman, "and they have been man and wife now some years."

Poor Alice was petrified with astonishment. "Does he," she inquired, "live happily with his wife?"

"On the contrary," answered the old woman; "she is said to be so ill-natured and whimsical, that the good young man's life will end in absolute martyrdom."

A strange feeling crept over Alice; she began to ask about Gertrude, the wife of the rich Ironmaster.

"As to this Gertrude of whom you speak," replied the other, "she was always a very strange woman, and people said she was devoted to wicked witch practices. This I know, she went to the lake to bathe, before sunrise, as she was accustomed to do, it was thought, to preserve her beauty, and that the water was enchanted by her spells. But she never appeared again; the servants became alarmed, and ran to look for her: her clothes were lying on the shore, but she herself was never again discovered. It is not unlikely, as the lake has many deep places, that the unhappy woman had fallen into one of these, and been drawn down by a whirlpool. However it may be, she never has been seen among us from that day."

Alice thanked the good dame for her kindness, and summoned all her strength for a final effort to reach the home she felt she must once more visit, if only to behold her dear husband and child again, and then quit a scene for ever dear to her. At length, she saw her own beloved dwelling-place—the rivulet on whose banks she had so often sat with Rudolf, the farm-yard, the garden—all as she had left them; and drawing near, she heard from within the plaintive accents of a child's voice—perhaps her own child! On entering the court, she perceived some female figure at the fountain, but Alice could not see her features; she glided on to the half-open door, and there sat Rudolf, leaning his head upon his hand, and looking pale and disconsolate. She flew into his arms; but he angrily repulsed her. "What means this?" said he; "why these foolish pretences? and why have you dressed yourself out so absurdly?"

Alice was confounded at this reception; he appeared to know to whom he was speaking, and yet was so heart-lessly cold to her. "Alas! dear Rudolf," said she, "is it thus you greet me after two long years of separation?"

"Two years of separation, forsooth!" answered he, "half an hour ago you went out to the fountain, and now you come back in a strange dress?"

"Oh Rudolf, dear Rudolf! under what gross deception are you labouring? It is now two long years and three months since I had the happiness of seeing you." With these words, she stretched out her arms towards him. Her tears, her voice, and the whole expression of her countenance, moved him to the very heart. "Great Powers!" he exclaimed, "can this be true? It seems as if old times were indeed revived. Alice, is it possible! and do you indeed love me?"

At that moment, the door opened, and behold another Alice, in person the same, only different in dress, stepped into the room. "Can it be?" cried Rudolf, "have I, then, two wives?" But Alice, who had cherished her own suspicions, ran to a large tub of water, and, having made the sign of the cross, sprinkled some drops on the mysterious stranger; whereupon, the latter rushed with a horrid scream through the door, and in her flight revealed the form and features of Gertrude. Rudolf now began to understand the vile illusions by which his life had been rendered so wretched. With rapture he embraced his wife. "Can this be true?" said he; "am I so blest as once more to fold in my arms my own good and beautiful Alice?"

She was now weeping for joy, so that she could not answer. At length, she revealed to Rudolf all her unfortunate intercourse with Gertrude, her abduction at midnight, the Witches' dance, her violent descent, and her abode in the Schoolmaster's house. Rudolf then narrated how, when he had returned home that fearful Walpurgis' Night, he found his wife engaged in her household occupations, and his house in the best order, so that no suspicion arose in his mind. Soon after, the supposed Alice seemed completely changed, and from daybreak to nightfall the scolding and quarreling were incessant: he could in no way account for her mysterious conduct, until a talkative woman-servant related how her mistress had gone out on Walpurgis' Night with the wife of the rich Ironmaster, and did not return till morning, when she stole quietly into her chamber. Rudolf was horror-struck when he heard this; suspicions crowded on his mind. Alice seemed to live only to torment her husband by her unceasing jealousy, and her conduct towards her children was equally unaccountable. The elder——

"Have you another child, then?" cried Alice.

"Yes," answered Rudolf; "yonder it lies, in the cradle;" and Alice ran to it, but the cradle was empty, the child was an elfin child, and had vanished at the same moment with its mother. Alice clasped her own dear child in her arms, with a thankful heart at being restored to all she held dear in this world.

A few days after Alice's return, some fishermen found the long-sought-for remains of the Ironmaster's wife in the lake, and brought them to her husband. It is said, the body seemed as fresh and unchanged as if her death had only happened yesterday. The widower had it buried with much expense, and, it was said, was rather rejoiced to find, by this unquestionable proof, that she could never return to his house again.

SAID ATTACKED BY ARAB ROBBERS.

THE MAGIC WHISTLE.

In the time of Haroun Alraschid, the famous Caliph of Bagdad, there dwelt at Balsora a fine fellow, whose name was Ben Ezar, and of whom every one spoke as a model of wisdom and well-doing. He had just enough to live upon at his ease and in peace, without troubling himself with trade or occupation; and when an only son was born to him, when he was already a good age, Ben Ezar did not look upon it as his duty to alter his habitual course of living on that account. "Why should I go into business, or traffic and speculate in my old age?" he would say to his neighbours, "only to leave to my little Said a few hundreds more, or perhaps less, according as things might go well or ill with me? Why should I tempt fortune? 'Enough for two will keep three,' says the proverb. All that is necessary is, that my Said should turn out a good and a brave young fellow; and as for fortune, there is always enough of that about!" So said Ben Ezar of Balsora, and regulated his conduct accordingly. But if he took no care to give his son a trade or a profession of any kind, he did not fail to make him study carefully the book of wisdom, the divine Koran! More than this; having taught him wisdom, learning, and respect for age, the three greatest ornaments of youth, he now proceeded to add a brave arm and a bold heart, by exercising the lad in the rougher use of arms. Thanks to this bad style of bringing up, the young fellow soon acquired amongst the youth of Balsora the renown of being their most valiant champion; for, certainly, no youth of his own age could surpass Said in the arts of swimming, riding, and wrestling.

When he had reached his eighteenth year, his father thought proper to send him to Mecca, to perform his religious duties at the tomb of the Prophet, according to law and custom.

Said had brought his preparations to a close, and was just on the point of starting, when his father called him into his presence for the last time, and said to him: "To your past conduct, my child, I have already accorded the praise it deserves from a well-satisfied parent. I have given, for your future conduct, the best advice that my experience suggests, and I have furnished you with the money requisite for your travels. There remains, however, still a communication for me to make to you, not in my own name this time, but on the part of your venerated mother—dead, alas! twelve years ago, and of whose dear form your eyes can have preserved but little memory." Pausing to dry the tears which this reminiscence brought from his heart into his eyes, Ben Ezar went on as follows: "I do not share, as far as my own feelings are concerned, any of the notions that some people entertain about magic, nor do I believe at all, as do so many, in the existence of Genii, Fairies, Enchanters, Magicians, or whatever they may be called, whose conjurations can exercise any influence on the life or destiny of men. Your mother, on the contrary, believed in all these things as firmly as in the Koran itself; and, at the moment of her death, after making me swear that I would tell the secret to no one but to the son that was about to be born to her, revealed to me that in her own childhood she had been acquainted with a certain Fairy. Judging it useless to attempt to disabuse her mind, I contented myself with laughing at her innocent credulity. Yet, after all, I must confess, my dear child, that your birth was attended by some prodigies which caused some astonishment even to myself.

"All day long it rained and thundered, while the sky was so dark that we could not see to read without a candle. About four hours after mid-day, they came to tell me that a son was born unto me. I ran quickly to your mother's apartment; but her women prevented my entering, saying that no person could come in at that moment—'their mistress had given orders that she wished to be left entirely alone, and that no person whatsoever should be allowed to come in to her.' Taking no heed of their words, I threw them aside, called out, mentioned my name—but all to no purpose; the door remained closed.

"During the time I was thus biting my thumbs in the passage, among the servant-maids, the sky became clear suddenly, with a rapidity such as I had never seen before. But what surprised me more than anything was, that while a heaven of the purest azure surrounded our city of Balsora, all around it there still continued dark clouds, and grumbling thunders, and flashing lightnings. I was still absorbed in the contemplation of this strange spectacle, when your mother's chamber-door opened. Eager to behold and bless my first-born, I rushed into the chamber; but no sooner had I crossed the threshold than I was struck with such a strong odour of roses, that I stopped for some moments, as if stupified. Without seeming in the least inconvenienced by this intoxicating atmosphere, your mother hastened to raise you in her arms, and place you in mine; making me notice, at the same time, a little Silver Whistle that you wore round your neck by a long golden chain as fine as silk.

"'The Good Fairy, of whom I one day spoke, has been here,' said your mother; 'and it is she who has made your little son this present.'

"'And is it the Fairy, also, who has cleared up our sky so suddenly, and diffused this odour of roses? But if she is so powerful, she had better, I think,' said I, in raillery, 'have given our Said a better present than this trumpery Whistle.'

"Your mother put her hand on my mouth, as she conjured me not to jest any more in such a fashion. 'Be silent,' said she to me; 'the Fairies are very touchy bodies; they take offence in a moment, and may, in the twinkling of an eye, change their favours into misfortunes!'"

"I did not persist, for fear of contradicting her, and we did not even speak of the adventure to each other until six years afterwards, when my poor Zemira, although still young, became conscious that her end was approaching; she confided to me, therefore, at this moment the little Silver Whistle, with a charge to replace it round your neck when you should have attained your twentieth birthday, as she wished me not to part with you before that period. She died a short time afterwards; and here, my son, as the time has arrived, is the present that was made to you." Ben Ezar went on, as he took the trinket out of a casket:—"From whomsoever it may have come, I restore it to you just as it was entrusted to me; and if I do so previous to the time allotted, it is because you are going a long journey, and before you return—I am old, my child—it may be that I may have gone to rejoin my ancestors. Besides, I see no good reason why you should wait here the two years which your mother's anxiety induced her to fix as the proper term. You are a good and prudent young man; you handle your arms with all the vigour of a man of five-and-twenty; and so I can set you free to act for yourself two years beforehand, just as satisfactorily as I could do at twenty years of age. Go, then, my child; may my blessing accompany you! and whether in good or evil fortune—from which may Heaven preserve you!—sometimes give a thought to your old father."

Such were the words of Ben Ezar of Balsora in taking leave of his son, who, after kissing his father's grey hairs, went off in great emotion. He put the gold chain around his neck, and slipped the Whistle into his girdle. His horse was ready, and he leapt lightly on its back, and directed its course to the place appointed for the gathering of the caravan, where, in a short time, about fifty camels and more than a hundred horsemen assembled together. The signal for departure was given, and in less than an hour afterwards Said left behind him the gates of Balsora, which he was not to see again until many years afterwards.

The charm and novelty of such a journey, the incidents on the way, and the thousand objects, hitherto unknown, that for the first time met the gaze of our hero, entirely absorbed his attention during the first few days. But when they drew nigh to the desert, where the country became always bare, and the horizon more vast, Said, retiring within himself, began to think over much of the past, and, among other things, the strange communication made to him by his father at their parting.

He drew the little Whistle from his girdle, and began examining it curiously on all sides; then, at last, applied it to his lips; but no sound came from it. Said worked hard at it, puffing out his cheeks, drawing in his breath, and blowing with all his force; but still the Whistle remained silent.

"Here's a useless bauble, at any rate," said he, in a low voice, as he replaced it in his girdle, and began to think of something else.

Nevertheless, the mysterious words of his mother took a hold upon his mind.

Oftentimes, in fact, during his childhood, had Said heard tell of Fairies or Enchanters, and their doings; but never having learnt that such or such an one of his neighbours in Balsora were in communication with any of these supernatural beings, and, on the contrary, always hearing the recitals of this character as having reference only to places at a long distance, or periods far remote, our hero naturally came to the conclusion that the time for apparitions of that character was past, and that the Fairies had left off visiting mankind, or taking any interest in their adventures. But, while slowly pacing the solitary regions of the vast desert, in reflecting over matters, what was he to think, after the strange story his father had told him? By dint of passing and repassing through his mind the mysterious circumstances by which his birth had been surrounded, and endeavouring to come at some natural solution of them, Said became absorbed in a kind of reverie, so deep, that he sat his horse through the day like one in a dream, without exchanging a word with his fellow-travellers, or even hearing their songs and jests.

Said was a very handsome young man; his eyes sparkled with spirit and boldness, his lips were full and handsome, and, although scarcely eighteen years old, his form possessed a certain dignity rarely met with at his age. His noble look, further enhanced by his warlike costume, and the elegant manner and firmness with which he managed his fiery steed, drew upon him, as was natural, the attention of all his fellow-travellers.

A man already advanced in years, who rode by his side, and who appeared to take pleasure in his society, endeavoured by various questions to test his qualities. Said, profoundly imbued with the respect due to grey hairs, was discreet in his replies, but yet witty and to the purpose. This made his questioner much pleased with him, and rendered him even still more desirous to associate himself with his young companion. They chatted, therefore, as they went along, on all kinds of subjects; but Said's mind having been occupied by one subject only, it happened at last that the conversation, by degrees, took a turn in the direction of his thoughts, and at last fell upon the mysterious power of Fairies. The young man was thus led to inquire, in positive terms, if his companion believed that there were Fairies, Genii, or good and bad Spirits, and that men were protected or persecuted by them.

The old man stroked his long beard with his hand, shook his head, and said: "As far as regards myself, I have never seen either Giants or Dwarfs, Sylphs or Gnomes, Fairies or Enchanters; yet, nevertheless, I must confess that there are a number of stories, that cannot be doubted, in which one cannot do otherwise than acknowledge the intervention of superhuman powers." Then the old man went on to recount to Said so many marvellous adventures, one after the other, that Said felt as if everything was going round, his brain was all in a whirl, his eyes became dizzy; and, at last, he came to the conclusion that everything that had happened at his birth—the storm so suddenly dissipated, the balsamic odours diffused through his mother's chamber—were all presages, doubtless, that he was himself placed under the protection of a Good Fairy, the same who had presented him with the Magic Whistle, and whom he might be sure of being ultimately able to summon to his aid in case of need.

All through that night, Said's dreams were of strong castles, enchanted palaces, flying steeds, dragons, Genii, and the like; he lived, in fact, in the very midst of fairyland.

Alas! he had bitter experience next day, how vain were all the cherished visions of his night's slumbers. The caravan had plodded on its way peaceably during a great part of the day, and Said kept the same place by the side of his elderly friend, when suddenly there appeared at the extreme limit of the desert-horizon a kind of thick and ill-defined shadow. Some declared it to be a ridge of sand-hillocks; others, a mere cloud; some, again, recognized it as a new caravan; but the elderly man, who had crossed the desert many times, exclaimed, in a loud voice, that they must put themselves on their guard, for that this unknown object was neither more nor less than a troop of Arab robbers, who were coming down upon them. In an instant the men flew to their arms, the women and baggage were enclosed in the centre, and everything got ready to make head against the anticipated attack. The suspicious mass kept on unrolling itself slowly over the plain, and resembled at this moment an immense troop of cranes on their emigration to far-distant lands. By degrees, however, its progress grew quicker; and hardly could horsemen with lances be clearly distinguished, before the whole band rushed headlong on the caravan with the rapidity of a storm-wind, and enveloped it like a whirlpool. The travellers defended themselves bravely, but their assailants, being more than four hundred men, completely outnumbered them. After raining a shower of arrows on the caravan, which caused serious damage in its ranks, they prepared to charge it with their lances. In this critical moment, our hero, who had never ceased fighting in the front ranks, and signalizing himself among the bravest—Said suddenly called to mind his little Whistle: he seized it, put it to his lips, blew through it with all his strength, and—let it fall, with a sigh of sadness, for it uttered no responsive sound. Furious at such a cruel deception, and desirous, at any rate, to sell his life dearly, the valiant young fellow drew his bow with great force, and perceiving one of the robber-band as remarkable beyond the rest for the magnificence of his apparel, he pierced him through and through. The wounded man reeled for a moment in his saddle, like a drunken man, and then fell heavily from his horse.

"O Allah! what have you done, young man?" exclaimed the elder traveller; "we are lost, indeed, now!" Nor was it long before the event bore out his words; for scarcely had the robbers seen Said's victim fall, than they uttered a terrible cry, and rushed on the caravan with such rage, that the few men who had been able to bear up so far against them were hurled over

and dashed down in the twinkling of an eye. Said, on his part, was surrounded by five or six fierce Arabs; but he handled his lance with such rapidity, dexterity, and vigour, as to make head against them all. Already had he made two of them bite the dust, when a sudden shock threw him on his horse's crupper, one of the thieves having succeeded in throwing over his head the noose of a lasso, or long rope with a running knot, in such a manner that all our hero's efforts could not break it—the more he pulled against it, the tighter grew the cord round his shoulders and neck. And thus, in spite of his valour and desperate struggles, Said fell into the hands of his enemies, a prisoner and alive, contrary to his intention.

The whole caravan was now entirely defeated; some were killed, others prisoners: so the Arabs, who were not all of the same tribe, set to work to divide their booty and share their captives. This done, part of them went off in a southerly direction, the others to the east. Said marched along in the midst of four horsemen armed to the teeth, who darted glances full of rage upon him, all the while addressing him in terms of the vilest reproach. This gave him reason to suppose that the man whom he had killed must be doubtless some personage of distinction, perhaps even a prince; but such questions as he hazarded on this subject only excited greater rage in the band, and redoubled their apparent ferociousness against him, without drawing a single word in reply.

After a fatiguing march of three days, during which they only halted to breathe their horses, they caught sight, at last, of trees and tents in the distance. This was the principal village of the tribe. When the troop was within a short distance of the encampment, a crowd of women and children rushed forth to meet them; but scarcely had these new-comers exchanged a few words with the robbers, than a terrible cry burst forth from every bosom; every eye was turned upon Said, and curses were showered on his head from every lip. "That is he," they cried; "that is the miserable dog who struck the great Almanzor, the bravest of the brave! Let him die, and let his flesh be given as meat to the jackals of the desert."

The troop advanced through these cries of death, and halted when they had reached a smooth space in the centre of the camp. The prisoners were bound in pairs, and distributed among the tents, as was also the booty. Said, meanwhile, with the rope still round his neck, but by himself, was dragged within a tent much larger than the others; in this was seated an elderly man, richly dressed, and with a proud and grave air, that denoted his high rank. The fellows who had brought in Said became silent as they entered the tent, and bowed their heads.

"The wailings of the women give me some presage of coming evil," said the old man, running his eye anxiously over the ranks of the soldiers; "yes, your attitude confirms it—my son——"

"Thy son is no more," said the soldiers, with mournful voice; "but here is his murderer. Give orders, O Selim, what death he is to suffer. Shall we pierce him with our arrows, or drive him before us with our lances, like some beast of prey? Is it your will that he be hanged, or shall we drag him to pieces by tying him to the tails of four horses?"

"Who art thou, wretch?" demanded Selim, throwing a sombre glance on the prisoner, whose death was in preparation, but who, nevertheless, preserved a firm and becoming countenance.

Said replied to the question.

"Murderer of my son! thou hast slain him, I am sure, like some vile assassin. You dared not fight him face to face; it was in the back—a felon blow—that thy lance pierced him."

"Not so, my lord," replied Said; "I struck him in the front, in good, honest, fair fight, in the attack on our caravan, and after I had seen eight of our fellows fall beneath his blows."

"Dost thou say truly?" demanded Selim.

"He speaks the truth," replied the soldiers.

"Then," said Selim, in continuance, and commanding his great sorrow by an effort of heroism,—"Then he has only done as we would have done to him ourselves. He has fought and struck an enemy who wished to take from him life and liberty. Undo his bonds at once."

The soldiers regarded their sovereign with stupid astonishment, and seemed in no hurry to obey him. "Is this the way," said one of them, "that the murderer of thy son, the assassin of the brave Almanzor, is to escape punishment? We had better have cut his throat on the scene of combat, in the presence of the corpse of his victim."

"No! It is my will that he shall not die," cried Selim; "and I even intend to keep him in my own tent. I claim him as my rightful share of the booty; he shall be my attendant."

Said, in too great emotion to give utterance to his thanks, could do no more than kneel before his magnanimous preserver, and place his hand on his own forehead, in acknowledgment of submission. The soldiers, meanwhile, left the tent murmuring; and when the tidings of the aged Selim's singular resolve reached their women and children, mournful howlings were heard, and cries that, if his own father renounced his right of punishment, the blood of Almanzor should not want revenging in that of his murderer.

The rest of the prisoners had been divided among the different families of the tribe. Some were ransomed at an easy rate, others sent to various tasks, either to watch the herds of cattle, or cultivate the land, or such-like employments; and more than one, who had a dozen slaves at home to gratify his every wish, found himself now doomed to perform the lowest and vilest offices.

Things went otherwise with Said. Whether it was his good looks, his heroic countenance, or some secret charm, with which he had been gifted by his Fairy protectress, that turned the head of the old Selim in his favour, we know not; but he lived in the Chief's tent more like a son than a slave. The hatred which the tribe had vowed against him was not yet, however, appeased; and whenever he roved about in the camp, curses and threats reached his ears from all parts, and not seldom an arrow, evidently intended for him, would come whistling close by his

ear. When he troubled himself to report these matters to Selim, inquiries were made, and punishments threatened, but to no purpose; for the whole band was in league against the old man's favourite. So, one day, Selim said to Said: "I had reckoned that you would have filled in my family the place of the son whom you took from me; but I must give up this hope. All here are animated with the same hatred towards you, and I feel, alas! that the protection of the aged Selim is powerless to shield you. I have come, therefore, to a determination to send you back to your own country, under convoy of some faithful fellows, who will guide you across the desert."

"But," exclaimed Said, "is there one single man here, except yourself, noble Selim, in whom I can place trust? Once out of your sight, will they not cut my throat while crossing the desert?"

"Thy life will be guarded by their oath," replied Selim, with the greatest calmness, "and you may be void of fear. The word of an Arab is sacred."

A few days after this, a new attack, of which Said just escaped being the victim, reminded the old man too forcibly of the promise made to his adopted son. So, presenting our hero with arms, robes, and a horse, he chose five of the bravest men in the tribe as Said's escort; and having made them swear, by one of the most fearful oaths of their race, to respect the young man's life, he bade him adieu with many tears.

The five Arabs rode, darkly frowning, and in silence, by the side of Said, as they went forward into the desert. Their unwillingness to execute such a mission, so guarded, could not escape the observation of such a keen young gentleman; and what made matters much worse, was, that two out of the five had figured in the fight in which Almanzor fell. On the third day's march, he noticed that the countenances of his guides wore a still more sombre appearance, and heard them exchange a few words in a low voice. He listened attentively, to catch something of their discourse, which they carried on in a particular dialect, known only to their tribe, and never used except in matters where success depended on the most impenetrable secrecy. It happened, however, that during the period while Selim had hopes of keeping the young man with him, he had devoted many hours at night to instructing him in this mysterious language, and so it fell out that Selim was able to comprehend what these men said, to an extent by no means calculated to allay his fears.

"Here is the spot," said one of the fellows, "where we attacked the caravan. Here it was, that the most valiant of our warriors fell by the hand of this jackanapes."

"The wind has swept away the trace of his horse's feet," said another; "but I preserve in my heart the memory of the hero."

"And, to our eternal shame," said another, in a hoarse voice, "he who struck the blow still lives, and is free! Lives there a father who will not avenge the death of his only son? But Selim has grown old, and is in his second childhood."

"When a father fails," said a fourth, "it is the duty of a friend to avenge a friend. It is here, on this very spot, that the murderer ought to die. Such was the rule and custom of our ancestors."

"But we have sworn between the hands of the old man," replied the first; "we may not kill him—our oath is binding."

"True," said the others; "we have sworn. The murderer escapes us."

"No, not yet," said one of the robbers, the greatest scoundrel of the lot; "old Selim is prudent and keen, but not quite so much as he imagines, for all that. Have we sworn to him to conduct this lad to this place or that? No. We have pledged ourselves to respect his life—that is all. Let him, then, be spared from our weapons; but the sun, and the desert, and the sharp teeth of the jackals, will do the business of our vengeance for us. All we have to do, is to leave him here, well tied with a rope."

So spoke the robber; but Said already, for some minutes past, had been quite ready for whatever was to happen. The moment these last words were uttered, he drew his horse sharply to one side, and making him plunge with the spur, flew over the desert like a bird. The five brigands were for an instant taken quite aback with amazement, at the young man's having understood what they had been plotting against him; but their hesitation was not for long. Well broken in to hunts of this character, they divided into two groups, and darted off in pursuit of the fugitive.

Aware, much better than the unfortunate Said, of the difficulties of the desert, and how to avoid them, two of them soon got beyond him, and barred his farther passage; Said wished to try to get on one side once more, but the two other horsemen were then opposite to him, and the fifth was just behind him. The oath they had sworn prevented them using their weapons against him; so the brigands had recourse to their terrible lasso, and with it dragged poor Said off his horse; this done, they all gave him a good beating with the staves of their lances, bound him strongly hand and foot, and then threw him on the bare sand, an inert mass.

Said invoked their pity, their oath, their feelings, all in the most affecting language, but all to no purpose.

It was in vain that he promised them an enormous ransom—his whole fortune. To all his promises and his lamentable cries, the avengers of Almanzor replied only with shouts of ferocious laughter, and then remounting their steeds, without waiting to hear more, set off at a gallop. For some minutes, the unhappy, abandoned wretch could still hear the hoofs of their horses resounding, but soon lost them in the distance, and the desert fell back into its customary silence.

Now, then, poor Said gave himself up as utterly lost. He thought of his father—of the regret of the old man at not seeing his son return; then, coming back to himself, he reflected on his melancholy destiny, to die so young!—for there was no room to doubt that, at this moment, he was doomed to perish of starvation on the fiery sands of the desert, or—a still more horrible martyrdom—to see himself torn to pieces, while still living, by the teeth of some filthy jackal.

Higher and higher went up the sun into the heavens, darting its implacable rays on the head of the unfortunate. After innumerable struggles, he managed to turn over, by rolling himself along the sand. In this movement, the little Whistle, that he always carried about his neck, fell from his girdle. It was just a glimmer of hope, and the unfortunate fellow, tied up as he was, exhausted himself in efforts to bring it to his mouth. At last he succeeded in placing it just on his lips—in catching it between them—in blowing into it; but alas! even in this piteous situation, the Whistle gave no sound, the talisman remained still without power! Desperate, and now powerless for farther effort, with soul and body bruised, Said let his head fall back, and his mental powers becoming less and less under the rapidly increasing rays of the sun, he at last fell into a deep faint, or rather, it might be said, into absolute unconsciousness.

And so hour after hour rolled away, until, at last, Said was aroused by a loud noise at his side. At the same moment he felt himself violently shaken by the shoulder, and uttered a cry of terror, for he fancied himself already surrounded by a troop of jackals ready to eat him up. But human voices resounded in his ear, and soon gave him to understand that he had not to deal with the claws and teeth of wild beasts, but the hands of a man, who was anxiously occupied in untying his bonds, and saying to two or three other individuals, "He still breathes, but his head seems bewildered, and he mistakes us for enemies."

Said, at last, opened his eyes quite wide, and saw before him the figure of a man, short and stout, with ruddy face, little sharp eyes, and a long beard. This personage addressed him in a friendly tone, assisted him on his feet, and gave him something to drink and something to eat, the want of which poor Said had sorely felt. While he was recovering his strength by degrees, his preserver took pains to inform him, in compendious terms, that he was a merchant of Bagdad, named Kaloum Bek, that he dealt in shawls, veils, and other fine articles of female dress; adding, that he was crossing the desert, on his return to his native country, when he saw Said extended on the sand, fainting and half dead. Such a spectacle moved his pity; he halted, and had recourse to every possible expedient to resuscitate the dying man, and his cares had, at last, been successful in recalling him to life.

When the story of the merchant was ended, Said thanked him with much feeling, assuring him, at the same time, of his eternal gratitude; for it was evident to him that, but for the fortunate intervention of this worthy man, it could not have been long before he must have expired miserably. Kaloum Bek made numbers of excuses at not being able to set Said on his way—that he was himself pressed for time, and they expected his return at Bagdad, where his affairs called for his presence, etc., etc., etc. In a word, he invited the young man, on the contrary, to accompany him. Except that this would protract the termination of his own voyage, Said had scarcely any other part that he could play, and he resigned himself to it so much the more willingly, that the merchant assured him that he would be sure to find at Bagdad an immediate opportunity of getting back to Balsora.

While on their way, Kaloum Bek, who was a great braggart, did not fail to make Said acquainted with the travels of the magnificent Caliph Haroun Alraschid, Commander of the Faithful. He boasted of his love of justice, his sagacity, the simple and truly admirable manner in which he disentangled the knotty points of the most entangled cases; and, among other instances, told him the story of Abou-Hassan, the Cordwainer, and others known to every child now-a-days, but which, at that time, set the astounded Said really wondering. "Our Caliph," the merchant went on, "is a prodigy of a man! You think that he passes his nights like other men, in sleeping? Undeceive yourself: two or three hours of sleep, towards morning time, are all that he requires. I know what he does. Mesrour, his First Chamberlain, is my cousin. In place, then, of sleeping, like the rest of the world, the Caliph walks about during the greater part of the night, up and down the lanes and streets of Bagdad; and rarely does an evening pass without his meeting with some strange adventure. He does not go his rounds on horseback, in a brilliant costume, or surrounded by guards and torch-bearers, as he might assuredly do, if it so pleased him; but it does not. It is under the guise of a merchant, a soldier, a boatman, or a mufti, that he wanders here and there, and assures himself with his own eyes that all goes well and regularly. Hence it comes, that there is no city in the world wherein people are so polite to strangers they may meet at night as they are in Bagdad. In fact, there is no knowing but that some individual who has the look of a miserable Arab of the desert, may perhaps be the Caliph himself; and any untoward mistake may draw upon you the sure stroke of a bastinado."

Thus spoke the merchant; and for all that Said felt tormented with an anxious desire to see his father, he nevertheless rejoiced at the opportunity that offered itself, for his visiting the famous city over which reigned the celebrated Caliph Haroun Alraschid.

After ten days on the road, the travellers reached Bagdad; and in spite of all the descriptions that had been given to him, Said could not help being astonished, and exclaiming at the magnificence of that city, which at that time was precisely at the very highest point of its splendour. The merchant graciously urged the young man not to seek for any other lodging than his house. "I accept your offer," replied Said, "which adds another to the numerous obligations you have already heaped upon me, my dear Kaloum; for, all the while I was passing through this succession of wonders in wealth and architecture, I could not help recalling the thoroughly bare state in which those brigands left me, both as to pocket and person; and said to myself, that, except the fine air, and the water of the Tigris, and the steps of some mosque for my pillow, this town, in spite of all its riches, was not likely to offer me anything for nothing. You are a second time my saviour, my dear Kaloum." The merchant grinned a kind of modest smile, as if he did not wish to be praised for so simple an action, and led the young man towards his house.

The next morning after his arrival, our hero was dressing himself to take a walk through Bagdad, and, like every young man, was already rejoicing beforehand at the looks which his brilliant costume would be sure to attract upon him; when his host entered the chamber. After looking Said up and down, from head to foot, he said to him, with a slightly ironical sneer, "All these accoutrements are decidedly very handsome, young gentleman; but what the deuce are you thinking about? You are, it seems to me, rather of a light-headed turn, and have little care for the morrow. Have you, now, enough money to live in a manner suitable to the dress you wear?"

"My very dear sir," said the young man, in confusion, and blushing up to the eyes, "I have no money at this moment, it is true; the rogues who abandoned me in the desert despoiled me, then and there, of all I had about me, as I have already told you; but, as I have reason to believe, from the manner in which you have treated me up to the present time—if—I say—you will advance me a small sum wherewith to regain my native country; you may be certain that my father will largely repay any outlay and charges of every kind that I may occasion you."

"Your father, your father!" exclaimed the merchant, suddenly changing his tone, and breaking into an insolent laugh; "really, my lad, I think the sun has scorched up your brains, as they say. Do you, then, imagine that I have allowed myself to swallow all the stories you told me in the desert? Let us come to the point at once—let us understand each other. From the very first moment, I found out all your barefaced lies, and your impudence disgusted me. More than this: I know all the wealthy merchants of Balsora—indeed, I have business relations with all of them—and should certainly have heard the name of Ben Ezar mentioned, if your father had even so little as a few hundreds a year. It is, therefore, clear as the day to me, either that you are not from Balsora, or that your father is some poor fellow, to whose son I would not lend a farthing. That is the first fiction! And then, this attack in the desert! Ever since the wise Haroun Alraschid has purged the highways of commerce from the robber bands that infested them, when has it happened that thieves have dared to pillage a caravan, and still more, to carry off men into slavery? But, even

327

admitting that your story be true, the fact must have been known; and on the whole of my journey, and even here at Bagdad, whither flow in travellers from all the countries in the world, never, no, never at all, has there been any talk of any circumstance like it. See, now, down goes your second invention! Oh, you impudent young rogue!"

Pale with anger and wounded pride, Said would have cut short the speech of the saucy little man, but that he went on still louder than Said could talk:—

"And your third lie, O barefaced swindler!—your sojourn in the camp of Selim. Assuredly, the name of Selim is well known to every one acquainted with any Arab of the desert; but Selim is reckoned the most terrible as well as the most merciless bandit in existence. Yet you dare to tell us a story, about your having slain his son, and his not taking any vengeance on you, when he ought, in accordance with his well-known character, to have cut you in pieces! Your audacity in lying carries you farther yet, even so far as to want us to believe in inventions still more absurd. Selim must defend you against the fury of his own tribe!—he must coddle you up in his own tent, forsooth! and, at last, he must send you off home again, without ransom, instead of hanging you up on the nearest tree!—Selim, who has often acted thus to travellers against whom he had no cause of hatred, and only to enjoy the grimaces they made during the operation! Oh! you must confess it, you are an abominable liar!"

"No," replied the young man, ready to choke with constrained emotion—"No! I have not lied in the smallest degree! All, everything I have told you, is true—all—I swear by my soul!"

"By your soul! Verily," exclaimed the merchant, "a very scampish and fiction-loving soul! A pretty warranty, certainly!"

"I am not able, it is true, to furnish you with positive proofs of the truth of what I say," went on Said, compelling himself to repress his indignation; "but did you not yourself find me tied with cords, and dying in the midst of the desert?"

"That proves nothing," the merchant answered. "You are dressed from top to toe in the guise of some rich robber, and I am inclined to think that you are nothing else. Perhaps—how can I tell?—you had rashly attacked some traveller stronger than yourself, and he had got the better of you, and bound you just as I saw you."

In the face of such stupid and gross obstinacy, Said judged it useless to persist any longer. "You have saved my life," said he, "and, despite your injurious suspicions, I will still be grateful to you. But, to come to the point, what is it you wish to arrive at? If you refuse to come to my assistance, must I go begging? Assuredly, I will never hold out a hand for charity to one of my equals; I will go straight to the Caliph, and I will say to him——"

"Truly," said the merchant, in a sneering tone, "you will not address any person other than our gracious sovereign! This is what we call begging in an uncommon fashion. Ha! ha! ha! Reflect, however, my young adventurer, that the road that leads to the

328

Caliph passes by my cousin Mesrour, and that a word from me will be enough to warn the High Chamberlain of the prodigious skill with which you know how to lie. But, wait—let us talk seriously: I feel pity for your youth, Said; you may amend, and grow better; it is yet possible, I fancy, to make something of you. I should like to extricate you from your vagabond style of living; and for this purpose, it is my intention to place you in my shop at the bazaar. You can serve me there as clerk for one year; after that time, if it does not please you to remain longer with me, I will pay you your wages, and let you go where you please—to Aleppo, Medina, Constantinople, or Balsora, among your fellow-miscreants again, if that suit you—I shall be then no hindrance. I give you until noon to turn over my proposal in your mind. If you accept it, all right; if you refuse, I shall then reckon up, and charge you, as is right, with the expenses I have been put to on your account, and shall repay myself, right or wrong, with the fine clothes of which you seem to be so vain, and throw you out naked into the street. You can then, my lad, go and beg, as suits you, of the Caliph or the Mufti, and send me word what kind of reception they will give you." Having said this, the odious shopkeeper went forth from the chamber, leaving the young man to his reflections. Said saw him go out, with eyes full of contempt. The baseness of this wretch, who had succoured him, cherished him, and drawn him to his house—where he could have him in his power—only for the ignoble interest of gain, and to make him his slave, inspired him with disgust rather than anger. He tried, first, if it were possible to escape; but found the windows of the room barred, and the doors strongly fastened. Finally, after a long debate in his own mind, he resolved to accept, for the present moment, at least, what the merchant proposed; for he could see that, in his then situation, it was far the best course to be pursued. How, otherwise, desolate as he was, and altogether without friends or resources, would it be possible for him to regain Balsora? But he promised himself, aside, to claim for himself, at the earliest possible moment, the protection of the Caliph.

On the following morning, Kaloum Bek installed his new clerk in his shop at the bazaar. He displayed before him his shawls, his veils, and his rich silk stuffs, and pointed out to him the particular duties he had to perform. Dressed as a shopman, and no longer as an elegant cavalier, a shawl in one hand, and a gold-embroidered veil in the other, it was Said's duty to stand at the shop-door, address the passers-by, flourish his wares before their eyes, call out their price, and persuade all he could to enter and make purchases. In confiding this employment to the young man, the shrewd merchant well understood his own interests. Kaloum Bek, as we have already told you, was a little elderly man, extremely ugly; and, when he was his own shopman, and displaying and puffing off his goods, it not seldom happened that some neighbour or promenader cast in his teeth a joke or so about his looks. Sometimes, it was children whose sauciness he provoked; sometimes women, whose smothered laughter he could hear under their long

SAID DINES PLEASANTLY ON THE DOLPHIN'S BACK.

veils, as they went off, saying, "Oh! the ugly wretch!" But now, it was just the reverse; the young and handsome Said attracted all eyes, and every one was ready to stop, as he knew how to invite a passenger's notice politely, and direct their attention to his elegant silks with a captivating address.

When Kaloum Bek perceived that his shop at the bazaar was every day getting a larger number of customers, so long as Said managed it, he showed himself more friendly to the young man, and took

care that his repasts should be better than before, as well as furnishing him with more suitable and even elegant apparel. But Said took little pleasure in such evidences of an interested attachment; his regret after home was not to be alleviated, and his nights and days were passed in dreaming of some means of returning to his native land.

One day, when the sales had been very numerous, and the shopmen, whose business it was to carry the goods to the residences of the purchasers, were all out on business, a woman of middle age came into the shop, and made several small purchases. While engaged, apparently, in paying the master, Kaloum Bek, she asked him if he had not there a lad, who could go with her to carry her purchases home. " In half an hour," replied Kaloum Bek, " I will send them to you; at present it is impossible for me to do as you wish, unless you will consent to entrust your purchases to a strange porter."

" No, indeed, Master Kaloum Bek," exclaimed the lady; " really, for a tradesman of repute, you do things but in a poor chandler's-shop fashion. No! I tell you, I will take no street porter. Your duty, according to the usages and rules of business, binds you to have my parcel carried home, and I require it to be done."

" Only be kind enough to wait one half hour, noble lady," said the merchant, with a piteous air, twisting about in the most comic contortions of distress; " all my lads are out at this moment."

" Here's a precious shop, indeed, where there is not even an errand boy!" said the impatient customer. " But what is that big idle fellow doing now?" added she, turning to where Said stood; " come, let you and I be off together, on this job, my funny gentleman. Take up my parcel, and follow me."

" Stop there, stop there!" exclaimed Kaloum Bek, in a great hurry; " that is my shop-walker, my living standard, my best friend! He must not go beyond the threshold of my door."

" What is that he says?" replied the lady, disdainfully, as she flung the parcels into Said's arms, without taking any notice of the cries of the little old man. " Here's a fine tradesman, surely, and fine goods, certainly, that can't recommend themselves, but must have a puffer of this kind to set them off! Come, let us go our ways, young man; you shall not lose your time, and I promise you a good recompense."

" Go your ways, then, in the name of Satan and all his servants!" growled Kaloum Bek, in the ear of his clerk. " Be quick, and come back as fast as possible; this old witch will rouse the whole bazaar against me, if I longer refuse to let her have her own way."

Said followed the exacting old lady, who walked across several streets, and glided amongst the crowd of passengers with a step much lighter than belonged to her age. At last, she stopped opposite a magnificent mansion, situated in a retired quarter of the city, gave one knock, at which the gates opened, and exposed to view a rich flight of marble stairs, which the old lady slowly mounted, making a sign to Selim that he was to follow her. In this manner, they reached a saloon of vast proportions and lofty height, decorated with a luxury and elegance such as Said had never seen before. The old lady, as if fatigued, allowed herself to sink upon a soft divan at the end of the saloon, and signed to the young man to put down the parcel; then, after giving him a piece of silver as a gratuity, she directed him to depart.

He had already reached the gate, when a gentle and harmonious voice exclaimed, " Said!" Astonished at hearing his name pronounced in a place where there was not a single person he knew, the young clerk

turned suddenly round. A lady of marvellous beauty, surrounded by a crowd of pretty young girls, was seated on a divan, in the place just occupied by the old lady customer of the bazaar. Stupified with wonder, and mute with admiration, all Said could do was to cross his arms over his breast, and bend low before this ravishing apparition.

" Said, my dear child," said the lady, or rather Enchantress, " I much deplore the sad accidents that have brought you to Bagdad, which, nevertheless, was the only town marked by fate for the fulfilment of your destiny, if it so happened that you should quit your native town before your twentieth year was accomplished. Have you still your little Whistle, Said?"

" Have I got it? Certainly," exclaimed the young man, as he took from his breast the golden chain on which hung the trinket. " But, you yourself, noble lady "—and his voice trembled with emotion— " are you not the Good Fairy who made me this present on the day of my birth?"

" Yes; I was your mother's friend," replied the Fairy," and I will be yours also, so long as you preserve, as you have till now, a good and noble disposition. Ah! would that your father (but these clever people are so unlike the rest of mankind) would that your father had listened to the advice of his wife! you would have altogether avoided these trials."

" Never mind; it was to be so," replied Said, gaily, " so we will not complain of what is past; but, thrice-gracious Fairy, deign but to harness a north-east wind to your chariot of clouds, take me by your side, and in two minutes we shall be at Balsora, by the side of my good old father. I will stay there patiently, I promise you, until the six months that yet remain to complete my twentieth year have rolled away."

The Fairy smiled gently. " It is very well said, my poor Said," she replied, with a sigh, " but, alas! it is not possible to be done. Under present circumstances, when you have quitted your country, I am not able to work any prodigy in your behalf. So long as you are in the hands of Kaloum Bek, it is not in my power to deliver you; he is, himself, under the protection of a powerful Fairy, your most terrible enemy."

" How is this?" inquired Said; " have I not only got a Good Fairy, but also a bad one? Never mind; what does it matter after all? Since I have found you again, oh, my noble Protectress! I fear no more the malign influence of the other, and, if you are not able to take me out of his claws, it is permitted you— I hope so, at any rate—to aid me with your advice. Shall I do right, tell me, to seek the Caliph, recount my adventure, and implore his succour? He is a wise and just man, and will defend me against the evil practices of Kaloum Bek."

" Yes, it is true that Haroun is a sage, but he is a man for all that," said the Fairy, with a sigh; " he confides in Mesrour, his Chamberlain, as in himself; and he is right, for he has often tried Mesrour, and always found him faithful. Unhappily, the Chamberlain, in his turn, accords a similar confidence to his friend Kaloum Bek, and in that he is deceived, for the merchant is a very villanous fellow, although the relative of Mesrour. Kaloum Bek is a man full of craft. Immediately on his return here, foreseeing what might happen, he has built up against you some story or other, which he has intrusted to his cousin, and from him it has travelled to the Caliph, who desires to be informed, every hour, of what is going on in the town. Now, you can easily imagine that the portrait given of yourself, under such circumstances, is anything but flattering. Thus, then, my poor Said, in case you should ever obtain admission to Haroun's palace—a matter much to be doubted—you will meet there with a very sorry reception, as both the Prince and his minister are prejudiced against you, and will not give credence to a single word of your true his-

"But this is abominable," said Said, in great affliction; "here am I compelled to remain six months as the shop-walker of that odious Kaloum Bek! Could not you anyhow, Good Fairy, obtain me some grace? I have been brought up to the use of arms, and the greatest pleasure I know of is a good tourney, where men contend vigorously with lances, javelins, and blunt swords. The most distinguished young gentlemen of this city meet every week at jousts of this character; but one must have a rich dress, and, above all, not be of a servile condition, to enter into the lists. A lad of our bazaar would be driven out ignominiously. If, then, you would only condescend, my beautiful Protectress, that I should every week find here a horse, and dress, and arms, and that my countenance should not be recognised——"

"Quite right," interrupted the Fairy; "your desire is that of a noble young man. Your mother's father was the bravest warrior in all Syria, and his spirit seems to live again in you. Take good note of this house, then; every week you will find here a horse and two grooms fully equipped, a suitable costume, arms, and finally, a liquid, a few drops of which, on your face, will suffice to render you unrecognisable by all eyes. And now, Said, my gentle protected one, adieu! Be patient; may prudence and virtue always be with you! Above all, whatever trial you may yet have to endure, never despair; however great the miseries of mankind, the bounty of Allah is still greater."

The young man took leave of the Fairy with many protestations of devotion and respect, and after a careful examination of the house and the street wherein it stood, retook his way to the bazaar.

He arrived there just in time to see his patron in a tolerably critical position. A tumultuous assemblage was collected before the merchant's shop, and he seemed to be engaged in a very lively discussion with two individuals. A troop of saucy children, attracted by the noise, were leaping round the good man, uttering shouts and making faces at him, while the boldest came close to his legs and pulled at his garments—a scene which those outside appeared greatly to relish. This is the way this grotesque farce came to be acted:—

During the absence of Said, Kaloum Bek had taken the place of his young clerk outside the shop-door; but no person would stop, or pay the slightest attention to the invitations of such an old ape. While this was going on, two men entered the bazaar, and went over it a great many times, turning their eyes every-

where, as if in search of some one. At last, their looks fell on Kaloum Bek. Now this fellow, who had been watching them since their first coming in, and had observed their embarrassment, wished to try to make a profit of it. So he shouted to them, in his most insinuating manner, "Here, my handsome gentlemen—here! This is the place! What are you looking for? You will find in my shop everything you want: fine shawls, beautiful veils, exquisite tapestry, good——"

"Good man," said one of the two persons thus addressed, interrupting Kaloum Bek, "it is useless for you to trouble yourself with crying out so. Your goods may be quite as fine as you say they are, but our wives are of a capricious and whimsical temper, and it is the present fashion in Bagdad to buy no veils of any one but the handsome Said. That is the party we have been looking for, this hour past, without being able to find him. Point him out to us, then, if you can: we will make some purchases of you another day."

"Allah! Allah! Allah!" cried Kaloum Bek, joyously, "the Prophet has conducted you precisely to his door. You are seeking for the handsome clerk, to buy shawls of him? Enter, then, my lords; this is the shop."

At these words, one of the two men burst out laughing in Kaloum Bek's face; but the other, imagining that he had dared to pass a joke upon them, would not let the matter stop there, but heaped insult upon insult on the old shopkeeper. Almost beyond himself with spite and rage, Kaloum summoned his neighbours, and adjured them to bear witness that there was not in the whole bazaar another shop but his, known as the "Store of the Handsome Merchant;" but his neighbours, who bore him no good-will, and were jealous of his recent success, pretended to know nothing about him or his shop; and the two men, advancing upon the old boaster, as they called him, were preparing to administer to him a manual correction, as a warning against such rude jesting for the future. Kaloum, entangled as he was among his shawls and veils, which he dreaded every minute to see either torn or stolen in the affray, could defend himself but imperfectly. In the hope of attracting succour, he began to utter the most hideous howlings, which soon brought together an enormous crowd before the shop, but among these he found not one defender. A personage known as an arrant miser and a roguish master to more than half the town, was not likely to meet with much sympathy, and every one present rejoiced, on the contrary, in seeing him ill-treated. Already one of the two men had seized him by the beard, when, seized himself by a vigorous arm, he was lifted from the earth and thrown down with such violence that his turban rolled off on the ground, while his slipper flew far away in another direction.

The crowd, which, most likely, would have applauded the blow had it reached Kaloum Bek, uttered murmurs of dissatisfaction. The companion of the prostrate foe threw round him furious glances, seeking him who had dared to lift a hand against his friend; but, on finding himself face to face with a fine young fellow, well knit, with a glance of fire and a determined look, he thought it prudent not to make matters worse by too great a susceptibility, and stretching out a hand to his friend, to help him in getting up, they both left the shop as quickly as possible, even without buying shawls or veils of the handsome clerk, who had just made himself known to them in a fashion so little agreeable.

"Oh, you jewel of a clerk! Sunshine of the bazaar!" exclaimed Kaloum, as he drew the young man into his back shop. "By Allah! this is just what I call coming in time to put your finger in the pie. Ten minutes later, and, by my life, I should have wanted a barber to comb and perfume my beard! How shall I be able to recompense you?"

The heart and hand of Said, in this instance, had obeyed the impulse of an involuntary compassion. This first feeling over, he almost repented having spared the old rogue a just correction. "A dozen hairs in his beard less," thought he, "might have rendered him agreeable and tractable for twelve days or so." Nevertheless, he sought how to profit by the favourable disposition of the merchant, and demanded from him, in recompense of the service he had rendered him, to grant him every week one day of liberty. Kaloum consented at once. He knew right well that the young man was too sensible to run away, without money or resources of any kind.

Said thus obtained what he wanted. On the Thursday following—for that was the day on which the young men of noble family met in one of the public squares of the city for warlike exercises—he gave his patron notice that he wished to have liberty for that evening, and directed his steps in all haste towards the dwelling of his protectress. Scarcely had he touched the knocker, when the gates flew wide open. The servants seemed to be awaiting his arrival; for before he could express a wish, they invited him to ascend the marble staircase, and introduced him into a magnificent chamber, where they presented him, first, in a silver ewer, the water which was to render his features unrecognisable. Said bathed his face lightly with this, and then took a look at himself in a mirror of polished metal. He scarcely knew himself; his complexion was so thoroughly darkened, a beautiful black beard encased his visage, and he had the appearance of being ten years older, at least.

This done, the slaves conducted him into a second chamber, where there awaited him a complete costume of extreme richness. Besides a turban of the finest gauze, surmounted by an aigret of rare feathers, attached by a diamond clasp—besides an ample caftan, or pelisse, of red silk, embroidered and trimmed with gold—Said found there a coat of mail of such artistic workmanship, that, while it yielded to every motion of the body, it was at the same time proof against sword-cut or lance-thrust. A Damascus blade, in a handsome velvet sheath, completed our hero's warlike equipment. His toilet finished, he directed his steps to the door, where a black slave handed to him a fine handkerchief of silk on the part of the mistress of the house, with a message from her, that it was only necessary for him to wipe his face gently with that magic silk, to see all his brown complexion and black beard immediately disappear.

Three horses, superbly caparisoned, stood neighing in the court-yard of the mansion. Said leapt on the

finest and most fiery of the three, while his esquires mounted the two others, and together they took them towards the place of the tourney.

The meeting was composed of the noblest and most valiant young men in Bagdad; and even the brothers of the Caliph did not disdain to range themseves among their number.

When Said presented himself at the barrier, the son of the Grand Vizier galloped up to meet him with one of his friends, and, after courteously saluting the young man, invited him to join in their sports, requesting, at the same time, the favour of being made acquainted with his name and country. Not judging it wise, at this moment, to break through his incognito, Said replied merely, that his name was Almanzor, and that he came from Cairo; that he was on his way to Mecca, but that he had heard so much of the valour and skill in arms of the young gentlemen of Bagdad, that he had not hesitated, being himself a great lover of such exercises, to turn out of his road to come and take part in their sports, if they would be good enough so to permit him.

The ease and grace of Said-Almanzor, won him a ready welcome among the young gentlemen. Without seeking farther explanations, they handed him a lance and invited him to choose his side, as the whole party would divide themselves into two bands, which were to contend with each other, first in a body, and then one by one.

But if the attractive exterior of Said had, on his first appearance, drawn attention to him, it was quite a different style of thing when he came to exhibit his admirable skill in the use of arms. His horse was swifter than a bird, and his sword shone in his hand like a flash of lightning; he handled his lance as if it were a feather, and in spite of the curvetting of his courser, his arrow flew to the bull's-eye as direct as if his feet were steadily planted on the ground. After having gone through several brilliant charges in the *melée*, with his companions, Said made his appearance alone in the lists, and fought with, that is to say vanquished, successively, the most renowned champions of the opposing side, which won for him the honour of being proclaimed by the general voice the victor of the jousts.

Next morning, nothing was talked about in Bagdad but the young and handsome stranger. All who had seen him, not even excepting those he had conquered, were never tired of praising his noble manners, his elegance, and his bravery. For eight hours he formed the sole conversation among the loungers, and more than once the ear of Said, in Kaloum Bek's shop, was charmed by hearing his own praise. One thing only was a matter of general regret; no one knew where the noble Almanzor was dwelling; but the very mystery by which the young cavalier appeared to be surrounded, only still farther irritated curiosity, and increased the attraction that his presence had excited.

At the next tourney, our hero found at the Fairy's mansion a dress and armour even more magnificent still than those he had worn on the first day. This time, half Bagdad crowded early to the lists, and the Caliph himself deigned to witness the jousts from one of the balconies of his palace. Like the rest of the world, he admired the address of Said, and, at the conclusion of the games, deigned to place, with his royal hand, a massive chain of gold on the neck of the young victor, in testimony of his satisfaction.

During more than four months, Said astonished Bagdad with his deeds of prowess; until one evening, as he was going back to his lodgings after the jousts, he heard a voice, the accent of which struck him. Just in front of him four men were walking along with slow steps, apparently in consultation with each other. Said continued to advance, and all on a sudden recognised, not without some inward disturbance, that these men were conversing in the mysterious dialect appertaining to the horde of the Arab chief Selim. It came into his head immediately, knowing as he did their habits, that their only reason for coming within the city must be the commission of some robbery; and his first impulse was, to get as quickly as possible out of the way of such a set of thieves. But, on reflecting that he might possibly be able to get at the secret of their evil designs, he altered his notion, and, on the contrary, crept as close to them as possible, in the hope of counteracting what they were plotting.

"Bazaar Street," said one of the four, apparently repeating a direction to his pupils; "to-night, with the Vizier."

"Good!" said another one. "The Vizier does not alarm me; the good man is the same to me as a humble boatman. But the Caliph—that is another kind of thing: he is young, nimble, and must be well armed; without reckoning that he has doubtless about him, or, at any rate, at some very short distance, some ten or a dozen of his body-guards."

"As to that, no," rejoined a third; "every time he has been met and recognised at night, he was always alone with his Grand Vizier or High Chamberlain. There is, therefore, no necessity for fear, and we may easily, this night, carry off his person; but let it be well understood, that it is to be effected without doing him any injury."

"Assuredly," replied the first rascal; "his death would cost us too dear! It will be far better to hold him at our mercy; we can put on what ransom we choose. Now, this is the plan I propose, for my own part, so as to carry our point without incurring danger: to engage the Caliph's attention in front by a feigned attack, and in the meanwhile to throw over his head, from behind, a strong rope; that will leave him no power of defence. I say nothing of his companion; the old ape has caused too many of us to swing, to be surprised at our taking it into our heads to strangle a Vizier in our turn."

"Yes, that's the plan," said the three others, roaring with laughter at the brutal jest; "Selim himself will never have made such a glorious expedition all his life. Well! it is settled, then; ten o'clock, in Bazaar Street," they added, in a low voice. Then they separated instantly, and took themselves off in different directions.

Astounded at what he had just heard, Said could only think of one plan at first—to run to the Caliph's palace, and give him notice of the danger that threatened him. But, while on his way there, the words of the Fairy came into his mind, and he recalled what she had told him about the bad character that had been transmitted of himself to the Caliph; he reflected that they might possibly mock at what he told them, or regard it as the audacious attempt of an adventurer to insinuate himself into Haroun's good graces. Then, supposing that, to punish him for knowing something beyond the police, they were to arrest him—to clap him in prison! Said suspended his walk towards the palace, and, weighing all things well, thought that the better way was, to trust to his own good sword, and in his own person deliver the Caliph out of the hands of the thieves.

Instead of going back to Kaloum Bek's residence, therefore, our hero seated himself on the steps of a mosque, and waited there till the night was far set in. He then directed his steps towards the Street of the Bazaar, and having spied out, about its centre, a corner sufficiently deep, formed by the jutting out of a large house, he concealed himself to the best of his ability. At the end of an hour, or thereabouts, his eyes, directed towards the entrance of the street, perceived two shadows, which advanced on his side with a prudent and cautious step; when one of these night-walkers had lightly clapped his hands, two others ran up to him, at a slinking pace, out of a petty street which lay behind the bazaar. The four men—four thieves as they were—murmured a few slang words, and separated. Three came to take up a position in a dark place not far from Said, while the fourth, keeping watch, walked about up and down, so as to be able to give notice of the approach of the persons for whom they were waiting.

Half an hour had scarcely passed, when the sound of coming footsteps was heard in the direction of the bazaar. The watcher uttered the cry agreed upon, and the three brigands rushed suddenly from their hiding-place. But on the instant, Said, drawing his scimitar of fine Damascus steel, sprung out upon the robbers, with the force and swiftness of a thunderbolt, shouting out in a formidable voice, "Kill! Kill! the enemies of the great Haroun!" At the first stroke, one fell, stretched at his feet. Two more were busied in seizing and disarming the Caliph, over whose head they had succeeded in throwing their terrible noose. Said rained blows upon them, without giving them time to recognise him, and took his measures so well, that at one and the same stroke he succeeded in cutting through the noose and the hand of one of the thieves. At the shout which the mutilated man uttered as he sank down on his knees, that one of his companions who was engaged in a struggle with the Vizier hurried up to his side to succour or avenge him; but the Caliph, who, thanks to Said, had succeeded in extricating himself from the cord that was to strangle him— the brave Haroun could now take his share in the strife, and quickly drawing his dagger, drove it up to the hilt in the throat of this new assailant. The fourth robber had already taken to flight; the square was clear: the combat altogether had not lasted a minute.

"Now, by Allah! this is a strange adventure!" exclaimed the Caliph, as he advanced towards our hero; "and this audacious attack, and your sudden and fortunate coming to the rescue, are both equally surprising to me. But how did you know who I am? and how become aware of the criminal project of these wretches?"

"Commander of the Faithful," replied Said, "as I was going along El Malek Street this evening, these men were in front of me, and talking together in a foreign language, that circumstances have made me acquainted with; they plotted how to make you a prisoner, and murder your Grand Vizier. There was no time to give warning to any one; to be myself at the place where they were to lie in waiting, was all that I could do. I came there; and, by the help of Allah, have succeeded in spoiling the schemes of these scoundrels."

"Thanks, noble young man," said Haroun; "but the place is not suitable for long discourse. Take this ring, and come to-morrow morning to speak with me at the palace; we will there talk over this affair of mine and your own more at leisure, and see what we can do for you. Come, Vizier, let us be off! This place is not safe, and the joker who has escaped may bring back a fresh party of rascals to finish the dance with us. We have had quite enough for one night's pleasure; to-morrow we will see what it all means."

So spoke Haroun. But, before going off with his master, the Grand Vizier came up to Said, in his turn, and placing in his hands a heavy purse, "Take this," said he to him, "in the meanwhile, until other things come. To-morrow, I hope, we shall meet again; but to-day is our own, to-morrow belongs to Heaven."

Intoxicated with joy, Said made only one leap to his patron's house. As often happens when one comes home with a heart full of joy, he was received there with a shower of abuse by the greedy merchant, who believed that his clerk had run off, and was calculating, grumbling all the while he did so, the amount he should lose by his departure.

Meanwhile, the young man, who had cast a glance at the purse, and found it to be richly furnished, allowed Kaloum Bek to spit out his bile at his ease, feeling sure that he was now armed with the power to take the road to Balsora whenever he chose. At last the merchant stopped, out of sheer inability to go on any longer. Said then took the opportunity, without deigning to give him the least explanation of his long absence, to tell the surly old fellow, briefly and concisely, that he must look out for another clerk, as he was tired of such insolence and gross rudeness, and was determined to leave that very hour. "You may keep, too," added he, casting on the shopkeeper a look of sovereign disdain, "you may pocket the wages you promised me; I give you a receipt in full for them—adieu!"

He spoke, and was at the door instantly, before Kaloum Bek, mute with astonishment, could think of hindering him.

But when morning came, the merchant, who had reflected all night on this misadventure, had the whole city beaten up by his shopboys, but without discovering the runaway. For a long time their researches were in vain. At last, however, one of the couriers came back, and said that he had seen Said come out of a mosque, and enter a caravanserai, or inn; "Only," added he, "he is completely changed, and wears the rich costume of a cavalier."

334

On hearing this, Kaloum Bek vented his rage in curses, and exclaimed, "He must have robbed me, the wretch, to be so finely dressed!" So, without loss of time, he ran in the direction of the police-office. Being well known there as the relative of Mesrour, the High Chamberlain, he had no difficulty in procuring some officers with a warrant for the arrest of Said. Him they found seated in front of the caravanserai, and quietly talking over, with a shopkeeper he had just met, of the means and wants for his journey to Balsora. Suddenly, his comfort was brought to a close by a crowd of thief-takers, who surrounded him, and in spite of his protestations and inquiries, and struggles to resist them, bound his hands behind his back, and ordered him to reply to a series of questions which they put to him in the name of the law, and on the complaint of his lawful lord and master, Kaloum Bek. While these proceedings were being carried out in due course, greatly to the annoyance and indignation of the much-mortified Said, that little monster himself arrived, and, while jeering and rallying Said on his failure in running away, he rummaged the youth's pockets, from which he drew out, on a sudden, to the astonishment of all present, and especially his own, a long purse of silk, well stuffed and blown out with gold.

"See!" he shouted out; "look here! you see what he has taken away from my till, a master-thief as he is!" Upon this, the people whom this scene had brought together turned with horror from the young man, saying one to the other, "Who would have thought it, with such an open countenance? Here is your handsome clerk of the bazaar!—so young and so wicked! What a little serpent!" And then all began to shout together, "To the Cadi! to the Cadi! let him have a bastinadoing."

The Cadi gave the supposed thief a rough reception. Said wanted to explain, but was enjoined to hold his tongue, and let the Cadi first interrogate the complainant.

The judge, turning towards the merchant, presented the purse to him, with an inquiry if he recognised it as his own, and if the gold it contained was that of which he had been robbed?

Kaloum Bek swore that.

"It is false," exclaimed Said.

"Mere denial is no evidence," said the judge in a sharp tone; "all thieves can do that. Can you prove that this gold belongs legally to you?"

"I defy him, altogether, to do so," said Kaloum, putting in his word before the young man could speak in reply. "He had not a farthing in his pocket when I picked him up in the desert; for the last four months he has been in my service, and I have given him nothing. How, then, could he have got this cash?"

"It was given me," replied Said.

"For something to drink, perhaps," said Kaloum, ironically; "a pretty joke, certainly, and a likely piece of foolery! You were wont to be more clever in your lies. For my own part, I swear again——and my oath is worth more than thine, thou miserable adventurer—— that gold has been stolen from my cash-box, and you have abused the confidence I placed in you, and been cunning enough to elude my vigilance, so as to get away, little by little, such an enormous sum."

"It is enough," said the judge, "the cause has been heard. Take back your purse, Kaloum." Then turning to Said, he added, "According to the terms of a recent decree of his Highness, every theft committed within the bazaar, and exceeding a hundred pieces of gold in amount, entails a punishment of perpetual banishment to a desert island. You will be off to-morrow morning for your place of exile, my young joker, with twenty other honourable and innocent gentlemen like yourself."

Then, in all the pride of the excellent judgment which he had just pronounced in a breath, and without stammering, the Cadi descended from his judgment-seat and went away, without deigning to listen to the cries and supplications of Said, who demanded urgently to be taken before the Caliph: "His Highness only," he said, "could understand the explanations he had to give." But the only response his prayers could obtain, was a shrug of the shoulders on the part of the judge, accompanied by a grin from Kaloum Bek; and then the unfortunate young man was left in the hands of the stupid turnkeys, who dragged him along, with many blows of their staves from time to time applied, towards the felucca, which was to sail the next day on her voyage with a cargo of criminals.

Here, in a narrow space, so low that it was impossible to stand upright in it, twenty men were already lying all in a heap, stretched out upon some rotten stinking straw, like so many filthy beasts. The entry of our hero, whom they thought one of themselves, was welcomed with frenzied howlings, intermingled with abuse and the most disgusting imprecations against the judge and the Caliph; but on perceiving the noble physiognomy of the young man, and the silent tears that coursed each other down his disconsolate cheeks, they soon saw that he was no member of their gang, and thereafter turned their backs upon him, with contemptuous pity.

Such was the place, such the companions, in the midst of whom Said was now thrown. For the rest, the felucca, as the judge had said, lifted her anchor next morning, and proceeded to follow her course by the river Tigris, on her way to the Persian Gulf, and thence to the Indian Ocean.

Once every day, only, there came down into the hold, where they were confined, a bucket of bad rice and a tub of brackish water; this was all the food the prisoners had, and, disgusting as it was, Said was obliged to resign himself to taking his share, or else die of hunger.

After rather more than a week's sailing after this fashion, the unhappy captives, one morning, felt themselves rather more roughly shaken than was usual in their floating gaol. The waves beat furiously against the vessel's sides, and a confused trembling and a noise greater than common was heard on deck. Suddenly a terrible shock was felt by all; this was followed by an ominous crash—the ship had struck!

"By all the powers of darkness, the water is coming in upon us!" shouted one of the prisoners at this moment; and they all together struck the hatches

with repeated blows, in hope of having them opened; but no voice replied—no answer came—there was nothing stirring above them! They tried once more to stop the leak with their garments, but the breach in the side of the vessel was too large, and their means too small; the water still poured in, filled the hold, and rose up to within a few inches of their heads. A few minutes more, and all must have perished; but a last final effort, and the hatches rose up—the door of their tomb opened!

They rushed tumultuously up the ladder, but on reaching the deck they found it completely deserted—the whole of the crew had taken refuge in the boats. At sight of this, a roar, like that of wild beasts, burst forth from the convicts, and, troubled to madness at the notion of death, these degraded beings thought only of seeking in drunken orgies oblivion of their situation. Maddened, raging with drink, without consciousness of what was going on around them, they laughed, they sang, they danced or rolled about the deck, in the midst of barrels stoved in and emptied bottles, until the tempest, with renewed fury, tore away the vessel from the shoal on which it had struck, raised it like a feather on the foaming crest of a wave, and almost in a moment threw it down, in ruins, to the bottom of the deep.

Said, however, more wise than his companions, and knowing how to look death in the face without boasting or cowardly fear, had succeeded in fastening himself to a large spar; at the moment when the vessel broke up into a thousand pieces. The waves, still running high, threw him backwards and forwards, hither and thither, as chance directed, and at times washed over him entirely; but, thanks to his skill in swimming, and above all, to his indomitable energy, our hero always came up to the top again in the end. He swam about in this manner for half an hour, continually in danger of death, until, happening to press his hand against his chest, oppressed with fatigue, he felt under his finger his little Silver Whistle.

Often enough already, and very cruelly, had poor Said been deceived by his pretended talisman! He called to mind, however, the Fairy's words—"Never despair!" and summoning up the little breath he had left in his lungs, applied the Whistle to his lips. A clear and piercing sound issued from the Whistle, heard above even the tempest's roar; and suddenly, as if by a miracle, the waves were appeased, and the sea, up to this time troubled to its lowest depths, became, in the twinkling of an eye, as smooth as ice.

Said had scarcely time to get his breath again, and throw an inquiring look around, when the mast on which he was sitting spread itself out, and moved under him after a strange fashion; he could hardly help a kind of shuddering sensation on recognising that he was no longer sitting across a piece of inert wood, but riding with his legs across the back of an enormous fish of the dolphin species. He was not long, however, in recovering and settling himself well in his seat, especially as he saw that his aquatic courser swam, rapidly, it is true, but regularly, without shaking him, and always on the top of the water. Persuaded from this that such a marvellous transformation could only be attributed to his appeal, through the Whistle, to the influence of the Good Fairy, he addressed to her, on the winds, many fervent thanks.

The Dolphin threaded his way through the humid plain with such wonderful swiftness, that before the end of the day Said caught sight of land, and distinguished the mouth of a large river, up which the Dolphin quickly penetrated. But great dangers are by no means antagonistic to large appetites, and by this time our hero began to feel certain inward rumblings, that told him he had not breakfasted, lunched, dined, nooned, or supped within the last twenty-four hours. A Fairy that had appeased a tempest, might not impossibly cook a dinner. "Shall I try my Whistle again?" thought he. But to whistle for such a trifle! no—he resolved to bear it. Not so his stomach, which at last pinched him so hard that he was ready to faint; so, rather than die, he gave up his heroics, and blew a good sharp whistle. That very minute, his Dolphin came to a stop; and from under the water, on its tail, rounded into a support for a table, came up a tray loaded with dishes and wines of an exquisite flavour—none the worse for the sea, and as dry as if it had been eight hours in the sun. Our hero gave himself up to the hearty enjoyment of his dinner; we know on what short commons he had lately fared, and what need he had to recruit his strength. As soon as he had enough, he uttered his thanks to the Good Fairy, not doubting that somehow or other his words would reach her ears, as his Whistle had done. The tray sank down under the water, and the Dolphin, without any farther hint from Said, resumed his course.

Daylight was just in its decline, when a castle, at once elegant and grand in style, on the right bank of the river, greeted the eyes of the young man. He had scarcely time to express his wish to stop there, before he perceived that the Dolphin was directing himself exactly to the spot.

On the terrace of this grand mansion were visible two men in rich dresses; numerous slaves stood on the bank; all, both masters and servants, were following, with curious eyes, the movements of our hero, and clapping their hands in admiration. The Dolphin stopped at the foot of a staircase of white marble, that led from the river which bathed its lowest steps up to the castle, by an avenue of fine trees. Half a dozen slaves rushed forward to Said to assist him in landing, and invite him, on the part of their master, to visit his castle. The young man followed, and found on the terrace of the palace two men of noble mien, who gave him an affable and courteous reception.

"Who are you, wonderful stranger?" the youngest of the two inquired of him. "How are you named—you, who know how to tame and guide the sea monsters as the best groom does a war-horse? Are you an Enchanter, or a man like ourselves? Speak!"

"My lord," replied Said, "I am but a simple mortal, but one whom destiny has dragged through some strange and critical positions of late years; and if you are pleased to take any interest in what has happened to me, I will readily recite my story for your amusement."

"Speak; we are impatient to hear all about you."
336

Said then commenced reciting to his hosts the whole story of his life, and that prodigious succession of catastrophes which had been showered upon him from the moment he quitted his father's roof, up to the shipwreck from which he had escaped that very morning in a manner so miraculous. While he was speaking, he could observe, full often, in the faces of his listeners many signs of astonishment. The episode of the nocturnal ambuscade of the brigands directed against the Caliph—and from which the address and bravery of Said had succeeded in preserving him—this episode in particular seemed greatly to move the two men, and drew from them loud expressions of admiration; but when the young man had finished his story, the one who had already interrogated him, and who appeared to be the master of the house, took up the discourse again in his turn, and said with much vivacity: "However strange your adventures, Said, I believe them to be true from the first word to the last; there is in your look and air an accent of frankness that cannot deceive. But, in a word, if you were to meet with incredulous fellows who were to ask you for material proofs, could not you furnish them with one? You told us just now, that the Caliph gave you, one day, a chain of gold, at the close of a tourney, and that after the attack by the brigands he made you a present of a ring; could you not bring into presence these articles, at any rate?"

"Here they are!" replied Said, as he took from his bosom the chain and the ring.

"By the beard of the Prophet, it is quite right! This is my ring!" exclaimed the most noble of the two men; "Grand Vizier! our preserver is before us!"

But Said, prostrating himself, said, "Forgive me, Commander of the Faithful, that I have dared to speak to you as I have done; I knew not that I was in the presence of the noble Haroun Alraschid, the all-powerful Caliph of Bagdad."

"Yes, I am the Caliph, and your sincere and devoted friend," replied Haroun, as he embraced the young man. "Henceforth your troubles are over. I take you with me to Bagdad, and intend that hereafter you shall have no other dwelling than my own palace."

Said thanked the Caliph for his goodness, and promised to conform to his wishes, but only after he had gone home first to see his aged father, who must be under great uneasiness on his account. Haroun approved this resolution of the young man's, and applauded the feeling which dictated it. Shortly afterwards, they all mounted on horseback and took the road to Bagdad, which they entered just at nightfall.

Next morning, while Said was closeted with the Caliph and the Grand Vizier, Mesrour, the High Chamberlain, entered, and said: "Commander of the Faithful, deign to permit your servant to solicit a favour from your Highness."

"What is it about?" inquired Haroun.

"My good and dear cousin, Kaloum Bek, one of the most famous merchants of our bazaar, has just come to seek me," replied Mesrour; "he has a singular dispute with a man from Balsora, whose son has been clerk to my relative. This lad has run away from my cousin after robbing him, and no one knows where he is at this present time. His father, however, demands that Kaloum restore to him his son; and how can he do this, if he no longer has the fellow with him? My cousin, therefore, makes an appeal to the light of your justice, and invokes your Highness's intervention to deliver him from the annoying urgency of this man from Balsora."

"Yes, I will settle this difference," said the Caliph. "In half an hour let your cousin be here, and with him the man of whom he complains."

"By Allah! my dear Said," exclaimed the Caliph, when Mesrour had gone away, "your matters are arranging themselves, and here is an affair that could not happen more to the purpose. You were desirous of starting for Balsora, for the purpose of embracing your aged father—he is at Bagdad; I had a design to punish Kaloum Bek, and here is the traitor himself coming up full tilt to his chastisement! Certainly, it is impossible not to recognise in these events a direction from above. As for you, Said, conceal yourself behind the curtains of my throne, until I summon you; and as for you, Grand Vizier, issue a peremptory mandate immediately, summoning to our presence that too hasty and too partial Cadi; I should like to ask him a few questions myself."

The heart of Said beat full hard within his breast, when he saw Ben Ezar, with pale visage, and made still older by sorrow, enter, with tottering step, the hall of justice. He felt an almost irrepressible longing to run to him, and throw himself in his arms, and cry, "Here am I, my poor father! dry your tears, your Said is found again."

The entry of Kaloum Bek was calculated to give another turn to his ideas. That worthy, with an assured mien and a proud step, paraded himself by the side of his cousin the Chamberlain, chuckling and grinning, and winking his little dull eyes. The sight of this wretch threw Said into such a passion, that it cost him much trouble not to rush out of his hiding-place, seize him by the throat, and compel him to confess on the spot his infamous perfidy.

When the Caliph Haroun had taken his place on the throne, the Grand Vizier ordered silence, and demanded in a loud voice, if any one desired to appear as a complainant before his master.

Kaloum Bek, with a forehead all brazen with impudence, advanced and said: "Some days ago, I was at my shop door, when the crier, holding a purse in his hand, stopped before my door, and called out, 'A purse of gold to him who may be able to give any news of Said of Balsora!' This Said had been lately one of my clerks; I called to the crier, 'Come here, come here, comrade; I can gain the purse.' This man," (here he pointed with a disdainful gesture to Ben Ezar,) "this man, who wearies me constantly with his importunities, accompanied the crier. He came towards me at once, with a friendly air, and begged me to tell him what I knew about his son. I hastened to inform him under what circumstances I had first found him in the middle of the desert, how I had succoured, taken care of, and harboured him, and how, at last, I had brought him back with me to Bagdad. On hearing this, he handed over to me at once the

promised purse. But observe, noble Caliph, the folly of this man! When, to complete the information he sought for, I told him that his son had worked in my house, but had conducted himself badly there—that he had robbed me and run away—he refused to believe what I said; he abused me, and accused me of imposture, and for many days past has followed me up, and wearied me with his complaints, claiming back from me, at one and the same time, both his money and his son. Neither the one nor the other can I give back to him; for the money pertains to me of right for the tidings I told him, and as for his rascally son, where am I to meet with him?"

Ben Ezar here spoke in his turn. He represented his son to be a proud and noble youth, incapable of the unworthy action of which he was accused; and adjured the Caliph to institute, in regard to this, a minute inquiry among all the parties who knew him.

"That shall be done, if requisite," said the Caliph. Then turning to Kaloum Bek, "Did you not denounce the theft, as was your duty?"

"Yes, doubtless," exclaimed the merchant; "I handed over the man who robbed me to the Cadi."

"Let the Cadi be brought in," said Haroun.

To the astonishment of all, this judge was brought in at once, as if transported thither by some conjuration; and in reply to the Caliph's question, declared that he perfectly remembered the affair about which the inquiry was made.

"You interrogated this young man?" inquired the Caliph. "Has he confessed his guilt?"

"I interrogated him, my lord, but I could not obtain from him any precise and formal account. He pretended not to be able to explain unless in presence of your Highness."

"I do not remember having ever seen him," said the Caliph.

"For what reason should I have satisfied his wish?" replied the judge. "If one were to listen to fellows like this, they would have to be brought up every day in gangs to the foot of your Highness's throne."

"You know that my ear is open to all," objected the Caliph, with severity; "but, doubtless, the charge was so clearly proved, that there was no need for bringing the young man before my tribunal. And you, too, Kaloum Bek, you certainly did produce testimony that could not be refuted, that the theft of which you complained had been actually committed?"

"Witnesses?" replied the merchant, unable to conceal a slight degree of anxiety; "witnesses?—no. You know, my lord, the proverb runs, 'Nothing is so like one piece of gold as another piece of gold.' What witnesses could I produce to establish the fact that the gold stolen had been taken out of my cash-box?"

"But how, then, did you recognise that the sum belonged to you?" asked the Caliph.

"By the purse which held it," answered the merchant.

"You have this purse about you?" Haroun went on.

"Here it is," said Kaloum Bek, holding it out to the Vizier, for him to pass it up to the Caliph.

"But," said the Vizier, feigning astonishment, "what do I see! this purse belongs to you, you say, accursed dog? and I, for my part, affirm that it belonged to me, and that I gave it, with what it held—a hundred pieces of gold, more or less—to a brave young man who succoured me in a pressing danger!"

"Will you swear to this?" asked the Caliph, turning to his minister.

"Certainly! as I hope for a place in Paradise!" replied the Vizier: "I could not mistake it, moreover; my own daughter embroidered it."

"You have then judged wrong, Cadi?" said Haroun; "but, since there exist neither proofs nor witnesses of any kind, what is it that made you believe that the purse belonged to the merchant?"

"He swore it," said the judge, beginning to feel alarmed at the turn things were taking.

"Thus, you have taken a false oath!" exclaimed the Caliph, in a voice of thunder, addressing the merchant, who stood before him trembling and pale.

"Allah! Allah!" groaned the fellow. "I should not wish to give the lie to my lord the Grand Vizier; assuredly his word is worthy of all belief: but, nevertheless—it may be—such things have been seen— one is sometimes deceived. Oh, traitor Said! I would give a thousand pounds if he were here! he could not help confessing his guilt!"

"What sentence did you pass on this Said?" the Caliph asked of the judge; "where can he be found?"

"According to the law," stammered the judge, "I was bound to condemn him to perpetual banishment in a desert isle."

"O Said, my child, my poor child!" groaned the unhappy father, breaking out into loud sobs and cries.

But Kaloum, shouting out louder than all the rest, repeated with gestures of extravagant despair, "Yes, a thousand pounds—ten thousand pounds—would I give for Said to be here!"

"Appear then, Said!" exclaimed the Caliph: "come, and confound your accusers!"

At this cry—at sight of the young man—the merchant and the Cadi stood petrified, as if in presence of a ghost; they rolled their eyes hither and thither, with a haggard air; they endeavoured to speak, and could utter only inarticulate sounds. At last, they fell on their knees, and struck the pavement with their foreheads. But the Caliph, pursuing the inquiry with inflexible rigour, said: "Kaloum! Said is before you; has he robbed you?"

"No! no! Pardon!" howled the wretch.

"Cadi, you spoke of the law just now. The law ordains that the accused shall be heard, whoever he may be, and of whatever he may be accused; it ordains also that the guilty only shall be condemned. What proof had you of Said's culpability?"

"I was content with the testimony of Kaloum Bek, because he was a well-known and respectable person."

"Ha! have I then appointed you a judge, and placed you above all, only to listen to respectable people?" exclaimed the Caliph, with an impulse of generous anger. "I banish you for ten years to a desert isle. You will reflect there on the essence of justice, and on the obligations it imposes on those who are charged with its exercise."

"As for you, wretch!" said he, to the merchant, "vile and cowardly scoundrel, who revive and succour the dying, not from commiseration, but to make them your slaves: you offered just now to give ten thousand pounds if Said could reappear and give his testimony; you must give that sum on the spot."

Kaloum congratulated himself on getting out of this ugly business at such a cheap rate, and was on the point of prostrating himself to thank the Caliph for his indulgence, when that noble sovereign added, "Beyond that, and as a punishment for y   false oath about the hundred pieces of gold, you will receive, before you leave the palace, a hundred strokes of the stick on the soles of your feet. An indescribable grimace passed over Kaloum's face. "This is not all, yet," the Caliph went on; "I leave Said the choice either of taking your shop, with all its contents, and yourself a a makeweight, or to receive twenty pounds a-day for every day he passed in your shop."

"Let him go, oh! let him go, noble Caliph!" exclaimed the young man. "I will have nothing that belongs to him."

"No, by Allah!" replied Haroun. "I wish you to be   nified for all the annoyances that the avarice   this wretch has caused you. But, since you will no   etermine, I choose for you the twenty pounds a-day;   u have only to reckon the days you have been in the claws of this vampire. It is the love of gold that has pushe him on to evil; let the loss of his gold be his punishment." Then, at a gesture from the Caliph, the perplexed merchant and the unworthy judge w   removed from he presence by the guards, followed by the hootings and hisses of the assembled crowd.

Har   conducted Ben Ezar and Said into a retired saloon of his palace, and there insisted on himself relating o the old man the strange adventure through which   h d come to know the valour, the address, and the noble evotion of Said. Ben Ezar wept with joy at hearing this recital, which was only interrupted here and there by a loud cadence of sticks, mixed with nasal howlings and snortings, proceeding from Kaloum Bek, who was receiving just then, in the court-yard underneath the window, the blows on the soles of his feet, which that scoundrel had so well earned.

Invited   fix his residence at Bagdad, near his son, Ben Eza.   eived the proposal with joy, and vowed he would   er again part from the comfort of his age, the prese e of his only child—the pride and joy of his grey hairs.

Said lived like a prince in the palace conferred upon him by the gratitude of Haroun, beloved by his sovereign,   noured by all, and reckoning among his dearest friends the brothers of the Caliph and the sons of the Grand Vizier. The sweetness of his disposition, his noble spirit and generosity, had at last disarmed all envy, and he had learned how to secure to himself (a rare success indeed!) the love and the admiration of his fellow-citizens: so that, for many years, it was a proverbial expression in Bagdad, to wish any one the good-fortune and the bravery of Said, the son of Ben Ezar.

THE END.